# Party of Assassins

For Kathryne my daughter

Who learned from me everything
I never knew

STEVEN MAURER

**Chapter 1**

Xanthe stared at the girl, eyes filled with contempt.

What a sight. She was fifteen. Poor, obviously. Or at least not rich. Her hair a pedestrian pale blonde, done into long maiden's pigtails, well braided, but greasy for lack of unaffordable soaps. Dressed in a threadbare hand-me-down student's frock, she was clearly no rival for anyone's attention. Unlike well-fed daughters of high families, there was not even the slightest plumpness to her, except in her chest. But even that was flawed, as there was an ugly freckle nestled right in the cleavage which would make anyone wish to cover it up. And other than that? She eyed the rest and scoffed. Skinny. Tall. Common. Unstylish in body type. Her rear had no heft to it. Nor had she pleasingly plump legs. She had no haunches.

"You're just... ugly, Zan-thee," she sneered apologetically at the gawky, bookish, thing before her.

The mirror stood steadfastly silent.

The fluttering of the wild kestrel she'd rescued the day before interrupted her morose inspection. Sighing, and a bit grateful for the distraction, she picked her way through the clutter of the dusty frozen attic that was her bedroom, to the globe cage which held the purple-brown creature.

"Feeling better?" Xanthe slipped her hand in through the convex bars, grabbed it, and reached out with her touch to feel the inside each of the little animal's four wings. With it, came a deep sense of craftsman's satisfaction. Where yesterday there were broken veins and cracked bones, today there was mere inflammation. It was obvious in its manner too. Panic had replaced shock. It was flapping so hard, she worried that it might hurt itself almost as badly as it had yesterday on her window.

"Shh..." She whispered gently, lifted the cage from underneath, and with her other hand, pulled open the piecemeal glass door to her balcony. The bright light of a new morning streamed into the low A-frame of her attic, illuminating the dust in the air. The cage globe's latch was stuck but gave way after a few tugs.

With no thanks at all the kestrel fluttered free. It briefly headed the wrong direction into her room, but then back out into the clear fresh sky, over the jagged frosty roofs of Jagerfeld, and out of sight.

She stood posed next to the view. One of the few benefits of being poor was that you had a good one: snowcapped mountains, a fleck of distant sea, the sweeping arc of the Witchwood mountains, and closer in, yet still outside the defensive walls, farmer's fields and the husk of a steeltower, a torn ruin of the ancients. Below, chimneys on chain-draped Tudor houses were smoking, while high above in a thick swathe, the multiple bands of Haven's blue-gray rings arched across the sky. Fading from view, was her namesake, the little moon Xanthe, a pretty yellow in the orange-tinted light of the strengthening late winter sun. No one who could afford it would live more than one floor above street level. Yet for her, it was fifteen flights of stairs to trudge up every day just to go to bed.

By now she hardly felt it. Between this and her Hood Guild package delivery job, she'd have to slow down not to outrun most boys in town. Her thoughts turned dark again. That is, if she could get any to try. Already, below, there were a few decorations being put up for the Festival of Favors, and she hadn't even got started looking for hers, much less finding someone acceptable who might take it up.

A broomstick rapped sharply on her trapdoor behind her, and her father's muffled voice echoed up. "Rise and shine, angel. Time to start the day."

Misery heaped on misery. Common girls had chores but no school. Rich girls had school but no chores. Only she had both. Father was in the Scholar's Guild, so schooling was free. His colleagues were all so proud of her, they put her in every single class. It left her constantly late.

"We don't know why the War of the Ancients started," Mr. Griswold lectured. "Our ancestors had a thing called 'power', which was somehow lost. Without it, we only know a fraction of what we should. We just have legends and rare manuscripts of ancient hardcopy. But what we do know is absolutely *fascinating*."

In truth, he was the only one fascinated. Xanthe twirled a braid in her finger while she glanced around the homeroom at her squirming classmates. Sure, you could marvel at all the broken junk people called "artifacts", but it didn't get you a date. Besides, it was 992. Nearly a thousand years had passed since the Great Fall. Everything useful from nearby ruins had been scavenged hundreds of years ago. So, there was no point to it, unless you wanted to be a treasure hunter and risk getting killed in the deep wilds for some working technology and selling it for a mayor's ransom. The stuff of boy dreams.

A slight smile stole on her face. Mm... boys.... What would it be like if she were plump and had her pick of them? What would she want? Handsome, like Ginna's brother Royroy? Or strong, like one of the farm kids? Gurty was like an ox, for example. No. That didn't matter. He just had to be educated. She didn't want dumb as an ox. A go getter. But sensitive. While not clingy. Rich was almost a must. That came with the educated part; only rich families could afford to send boys to Scholars' school. Except he couldn't put on airs. Highcouncil was just filled with stuck ups. She couldn't stand any of them. Oh, that was asking too much. Maybe just the son of a bookseller. But the most important thing, more than anything else, was that all her tormentors had to be jealous. Just ragingly helpless. She saw herself walking arm in arm with some boy. She couldn't see his face, but he was clearly with her, and she did see Priscia staring jealously as they paraded by, her ribbon wrapped around his arm.

"Xanthe!"

She blinked. Mr. Griswold was staring straight at her.

She was vaguely aware that he'd said something before. "I... uh... didn't catch that last, sir?"

"Obviously," he remarked, unamused. "My question, again, is why was the Great Fall permanent? Is there perhaps a simpler explanation than divine retribution, why the Ancients might not have been able to reconstitute the great power they once had?"

"The accepted theory is that they didn't know how. The few survivors were nearly all children."

"Children can be taught by just one adult," he noted. Then added dryly, "At least one hopes."

"It is thought that they were too busy doing other things."

"For example?"

"Trying not to starve, mostly. When you're hungry, food is absolutely..." she mimicked his sonorous tone "...*fascinating.*"

The class laughed. Mr. Griswold said nothing. Xanthe's eyebrow rose while she smirked. She was right of course. That's why she was picked when no one else could answer. Same as all her classes.

He let her impertinence pass and turned instead. "The Years of Hunger were aptly named. Our ancestors had to relearn everything: to hunt, fish, farm, make clothing. Even today, plumpness is seen as a sign of wealth, success, beauty. The peoples of that era had been so dependent on things just working, that when it stopped, they didn't know what to do. Which is why, in this class at least, we merely study our ancestors. We don't worship them."

This last bit was a jibe at the Curate. Mr. Griswold didn't think the ancestors were holy, or that power was a gift from the Creator, rescinded due to humanity's sins. He also wasn't silent about his opinion that you couldn't get old artifacts to work just by praying over them. His refusal to adhere to dogma was why, despite otherwise impeccable credentials, the proctors has relegated him to the girls' wing.

The school triangle pealed out from the Early Years room. Some kindergartener had been allowed to bang it, and she wasn't being dainty. At the sound, everyone in Xanthe's class bolted for the door. Tari gave a wave as she walked out. Xanthe smiled back. They were going out together after class, shopping.

Mr. Griswold stopped her. "A word, if you please?" He asked soberly.

She had a sinking feeling in the pit of her stomach. "I..it was just a joke, Mr. Griswold! Please. Don't make me stay. Not today."

He stared down his hooked nose and ran a hand through his thin graying hair. Xanthe thought he could have been just like the kestrel she'd rescued. Well, if he were fifty years younger and a demibird. "This will only take a moment. It has nothing to do with school at all. Well, not directly. There's just bad news."

She squinted. "You're feeling guilty about all the special assignments you give me?"

"Xanthe," he scolded softly. "This is serious. We just received word that King Seraphus has suffered a stroke. I'm sure this doesn't mean much to you at your age, but it is bad news indeed."

She considered. Seraphus. King and President of the Nutearean Empire, the seat of the pre-fall government. They still pretended they ruled the entire planet. "Okay... but so? We're free of them."

"Doesn't matter. His death will make things dangerous for us."

"The presidential army is going to attack the Free Cities?"

He scoffed. "No. We're too distant. Too scattered and ornery. Too poor. Worth less than we'd cost. Most people think we're crazy living beyond the Nightmare Line as it is. It's just that Nutearean successions are notoriously bloody. In power vacuums, a lot of unsavory actors shake loose." His voice became intent. "Including the Sect of Penance. They always strike during times of political instability."

Xanthe's eyes grew wide. Witchkillers.

The ancients had been like gods, with the ability to shape life itself: plants, animals, and even humanity, giving their own children unnatural gifts that they themselves did not enjoy. These abilities were now collectively called the *touch*. Wandering bards told fanciful tales that they now were a shadow of their ancient power. Once upon a time, people were supposed to have commanded overwhelming magics by thought. Though most believed it mere storytelling, it was awe inspiring to dream about.

The touch now only seemed to come in girls, and those who had it were called witches. Yet few could make it useful. Some could make lights, cause shocks, or notice lodestone seeds at a distance. Xanthe had figured out how to do something else. She could feel insides of living things and heal them.

Not all were pleased. The Curate believed the touch to be abomination, the result of ancient usurpation of the Creator's sole authority to shape life. The Sect of Penance took it further. To them, mankind could only earn forgiveness for consorting with demons, if all those who enjoyed the unholy fruits of such iniquity were eliminated. Every witch girl slaughtered. The faithless killed. Their views were not official Curate doctrine, but far too many quietly agreed.

"Just for throwing sparks? But everybody can do that!" Right now, most every girl Xanthe knew was trying to figure out how to make her favor glow. Attitudes in the north were considerably laxer.

"Does seem out of the way, doesn't it?" Mr. Griswold stared off, working his jaw in anger. "Come all this way to murder our daughters when they could more easily kill their own? Their women have talents too, even if they won't admit it."

"But that's the point," he continued bitterly. "They *don't* admit it. They absolutely can't abide our recognition that the touch is part of humanity now. Because the people of Thule only pay lip-service to Prayerhome's views on the subject, we must be made an example of." His eyes turned back to her. "Which means that if they come, they'll pick a girl whose abilities are not trivial."

There was something about his expression that made her think he knew. "You mean... me? I don't think anyone would ever think I was important enough...."

"Don't kid yourself Xanthe" he uttered intently. "Please. Just lay low until this is over."

Xanthe swallowed. A chill ran down her back. "H..how did... Did father...?"

"At your age, I was convinced there wasn't a grownup with a clue," he declared with a grim, cynical smile. "And from watching politics, be it our greedy plutocrats or idiot theocrats, I don't think I was that far off. But every so often you run into an old man who actually pays attention."

A voice came from behind. "Howard!? Are ya keepin' this poor girl after class again?" Mrs. Fullbarn approached. Wearing a long blue dress and a paint-splattered white apron, the art teacher was deep into her middle age. She was from the countryside, possessing a sort of heavy matronly beauty that Xanthe envied. "Don't you know what th' date is? It's almost Festival!"

Mr. Griswold scoffed. "Almost? The blasted thing is still a dozen days away!"

"Come here, dear," Mrs. Fullbarn called soothingly. "What's he blatherin' on about, then?"

"That most grownups are clueless, but he isn't."

"Ha!" She barked a genial laugh. "Isn't myth makin' off topic for science class? No dear, I'll be rescuin' her now." Smiling, she put her hands on Xanthe's shoulders and steered her towards the door.

"Never understood the fuss," Mr. Griswold grumbled querulously as Mrs. Fullbarn pulled her away, guiding her through the crowded desks. "Girls dance along with trinkets tied with slick ribbons until they lose grip. Then some random boy picks it up. He returns it in exchange for a spring walk and a kiss. What sort of planning do you need for a silly thing like that?"

Mrs. Fullbarn led her out into the poorly lit hallway plastered with ancient slate boards and student projects. "I'm tellin' ya, he's a good man. But he don't got a romantic bone in his body."

Still nervous from the warning, Xanthe said nothing. But she agreed. At least as far as the Festival was concerned, it was anything but simple. You didn't just accidentally drop your favor. You dropped it on purpose in front of the boy you wanted. But you had to do it in a way that made it kind of seem like an accident, and him feel like picking it up was his idea, even though both of you knew it wasn't. That meant he had to want you enough to pick it up, which meant that he had to know who you were before the whole Festival got started. Well, unless your looks were amazing and you had incredible haunches, but then every boy knew who you were anyway. Those kinds of girls sometimes had a hard time getting their favor into the hands of the boy they really wanted before some other boy snatched it up.

But an actual prior agreement wasn't done either. Not unless you were practically engaged. In boy world, "Led around by her ribbon," was a cruel insult, because extremely cute or rich boys had all sorts of favors dropped in front of them. So even a whiff that a guy was doing things to try to get a girl to drop her favor, lowered him way down their social hierarchy of arm punching and snowballs-down-the-pantsing, even though everybody knew they all did exactly that.

It had to be seemingly by surprise. The boy you wanted needed to see you drop it, where you were already apart, had to like both it and you. You needed yours to stand out from all the rest. Colors, gems, special cloths, whatever worked. Just so he knew it was yours and it was attractive. That was almost impossible for a poor girl.

But worst of all was timing. No one wanted to seem too eager, but as the Festival wore on and all the most wanted got taken, everyone else began to get desperate. People would go down their list of second, third, and fourth choices, until eventually the dregs were forced to settle for the dregs. Or worse yet, not have your ribbon picked up at all. If that happened, you couldn't even walk through market without hearing laughter behind your back, and enduring feigned sympathy all summer long.

Xanthe knew she was the dregs. She had no clothes, no money, no makeup, a tallish wiry body, and worst of all, was educated. A Scholar's daughter no less. It was a kiss of death because so many boys didn't want to be shown up by a girl who knew letters when they didn't. She could count on the fingers of one hand the boys who were literate yet weren't so wealthy that they didn't already have two or three girls each plotting to drop their favors in front of them. Pretty girls. Plump in lace and satin. With nice fat thighs.

This had all seemed so funny last Festival when she was too young to be allowed out. But now she realized it was just terrible. The ancients, in their wisdom, would never have allowed their teenagers to be tortured like this. Or maybe that's what *really* caused the fall. Everyone had been too busy worrying about their favor to get the power back.

"Frettin' over th' Festival, dear?" Mrs. Fullbarn asked kindly as they finally reached the outside of the school, a tall but ramshackle old institution. Like most Jagerfeld buildings, it was a reconstructed stonework built over a superstructure of an ancients' tower, adorned with clockwork chains, and slivers of reclaimed glasssteel cemented in as windows.

"No, of course not!" Xanthe declared with sudden broad smile.

Mrs. Fullbarn appraised her, clearly dubious. "Well, just in case you are, dear, don't be. If you're anythin' like I were at your age, you're takin' this all way too seriously."

Xanthe's smile remained frozen. The first kiss in her life. Don't take it seriously?

Mrs. Fullbarn continued as if she'd read her mind. "There's no way you're escaping life without someone kissin' ya. So ya needn't be in such a hurry ta grow up. An' don't think the boy who returns your favor and claims his kiss will be the one ya end up with forever and ever. Even if ya like him! Youthful passion's the strongest stuff in the world, but it rarely lasts. You think it will, but it just don't."

"I wish it would for me." She just wanted the whole thing over. Decided.

The teacher laughed. "Oh, now don't sin like that! And I wouldn't want that for anyone. Now off with ya!" She shooed. "You've spent enough time inside as is. You need to go window shopping for favors, and boys." She pointed over. "See? You got friends waitin'." She smiled in the direction of Tari and Celeste. "Say hello ta your father for me when he comes back."

"Thank you, Mrs. Fullbarn," Xanthe curtsied hastily. But as she turned away, she felt nothing but doom crushing down on her. This Festival was going to be the worst. She just knew it. She was going to have the most awful time in her life. It almost made no sense to even try.

She wondered if it might be better to just meet a witchkiller.

## Chapter 2

"My life is... aaarrrghhhhh!"

Behind Tari, Xanthe scowled. The last thing you needed while trying to feel sorry for yourself was someone else doing the exact same thing.

"Feeling too pampered?" Celeste jibed Tari with her usual light mockery as the three trudged up the ice-covered cobblestones towards Founder's Square. "Too many favors to choose from? Too many boys who want it?" The little tomboy redhead was half a year younger, and greatly amused. Right now, she was even more annoying than Tari, because this was exactly how Xanthe had been like last Festival.

Lavender-haired Tari was dressed in the same schoolgirl uniform as everyone else, dark-purple skants and frock, but hers was adorned with an extra coat of fluffy firesnake feather, which made it both warm and outrageously expensive. This befitted the eldest daughter of the Outlets, a mercantile clan whose origins stretched back nearly to the ancients, and the building after which they'd named themselves. Her house was filthy rich and powerful and didn't mind if everyone knew it.

Tari never seemed happy though. She scowled. "I never get to choose anything."

"What do you mean?" Xanthe asked.

"Mo-ther has my date all picked out for me." Her scowl deepened. "Wormwood. Horace Wormwood."

"Ew," Celeste gave a crooked sideways smile. "If anyone's archangel material, he's it."

Celeste had a theory about boys and morality. The cuter they were, the eviler. She'd graphed a whole chart out on expensive vellum, listing what she claimed was every available boy in Jagerfeld by his "heat" on one axis, versus "jerk" on the other. According to her, it formed a straight line, proving not only that she was completely right, but that all the math they'd learned was actually good for something. Xanthe doubted most of the numbers she'd put down but didn't write the theory off completely. Celeste had this bizarre ability to just talk to boys, mostly because she had four older brothers.

"I don't think Horace fits your table," Tari grumbled. "His house is the only one in all Jagerfeld richer than mine, so everybody is going to drop their favor in front of him."

"Coin doesn't count," Celeste intoned authoritatively. "Heat alone determines evil."

Tari sighed. "Yeah, well, he's no sweetheart either. You know, all I just want someone nice. Sensitive. Well groomed. Likes the things I do. I don't even care about money. Why's it so hard to find a boy like that?"

"Easy!" Celeste grinned. "Guys like that already have *boyfriends*!"

"Celeste!" Tari gasped, scandalized. This only turned the younger girl's grin into a laugh.

The rasping sounds of a kranth slithering at a fast trot came up behind them. They all hopped out of the way. A three-ton herbivore resembling a gigantic furry brown iguana, the beasts were not anywhere near as fearsome as they looked, but could still kill you by running you over, and their eyesight wasn't the best. The sled-wagon it was pulling was unusual, being both overloaded and marked by fire. It had heraldry on it that Xanthe didn't recognize, a kairn-dragon and crown. It shot past about as fast as the kranth could move, disappearing up over the bend towards the plaza.

"What that all about?" Tari wondered, as the sled sped off uphill, urged by its frantic driver.

"Let's not be nosy nannies," Xanthe agreed. Yet as one, their pace quickened. Kranths weren't cheap, and it was still too early in spring for foreign dignitaries to come. Visitors from the neighboring Free Cities didn't usually start trickling in until nearer the Festival. But these flags were different. Whatever message they were bringing to Highcouncil was sure to be the talk of the town.

They didn't make it all the way. The sled had stopped at the corner of Temple Street, where it joined four other streets, making an informal plaza surrounded by three story apartments. Men in unfamiliar livery were out yelling for clergy bandagers in front of the gear-festooned Church of the Holy Ancestors where a mass was in service. Yet Xanthe was fixated on the horror of the coach. The cab door had opened, and blood poured from its floor onto the frozen ground, coming from dozens of men packed inside, both the wounded and dead. More noise came from down the street. She turned and saw three more sleds of the same type come racing up, these attended by some of Jagerfeld's gate guards.

In a matter of minutes, the square was pandemonium. The able bodied were busy trying to drag people out of the cold and into the church's atrium, while the clergy, unprepared for the onslaught, herded their parishioners out the back past the altar. Bystanders were mostly staring at the blood drenched foreigners not knowing what to do. Bandagers were nowhere to be found, and even if they'd been there, there were no medical supplies anywhere near the need.

"I'm gonna go," Celeste said. "I'll grab the stuff from the apothecary in back of the Tailor's Guild."

"The woven dressings...? How are you going to persuade anyone to give them to you?" Tari asked.

"Curse that depowered dung," Celeste smirked. "I'll just steal 'em. I'll get in trouble later." She ran off.

"Come on, let's go." Xanthe pushed in past the gawkers and up the steps through the double doors of the imposing stone and glasssteel church. Tari followed, pausing only to make a quick bow before the Holy Crossed Pliers and Wand. Inside, the wounded were laid out side by side, but the tall room was cold, and the thin carpet was little better than the stone floor underneath.

"Allow us into the hospitarium!" One of the able-bodied foreigners yelled angrily to the priest who stood quivering at the inner door, barring entrance to the church proper. The foreigner had epaulets on his shoulders, indicating that he had some sort of rank.

"It's too small," the little priest replied, not budging from his spot. "You have too many."

"We traveled near a league packed in sleds. We'll fit."

"I'm sorry. Not without the archdeacon's approval."

The foreign soldier might have pulled his sword, except that just then more wounded arrived, carried by some of the Jagerfeld guard. One saw him putting his hand on the hilt of his blade and they started an argument.

Xanthe slid unnoticed to the side and examined the injured men. This was no nightmare attack. That was certain. Much less grims. No one survived them striking in numbers, and there was no look of horror on any of the victim's faces. It had to be bandits. Lots. The men had slicing cuts, spear wounds, and far too many Talathian atlatl bolts, many still embedded in flesh. The nearest man had one sticking all the way through his shoulder.

*Lay low. Lay low.* Mr. Griswold's warning rang in her ears. The worry that she'd be exposed gripped her, intensified by the fear of being stalked by some foreign zealot. Yet she also knew she couldn't just walk away and let people die. Pointing to Tari's necklace she whispered, "Tari, give me your pincers." The best thing about the Mechanix Sect was that they always had a functional tool hanging around their necks as emblems of faith.

"What are you doing?!" Tari whispered in protest but sighed and pulled the gold necklace off anyway.

Xanthe grabbed the pincers and turned to tend the man's shoulder. Gripping the bolt tightly with her right hand to keep it from moving, she wedged its craw completely around the feathered end of the shaft and squeezed hard with her left. There was an audible snap as the bolt broke. "This may sting," she told him quietly, but he nodded stoically, seeming more relieved at the care than anything else. He didn't even scream when she grabbed the barbed head sticking out of his back, and quickly yanked. With a gush of fresh deep red and little streaks of black, the entire shaft came free.

"Tari, this need pressure. Hold both sides with your hands and squeeze as hard as you can until someone relieves you."

"But the blood!" Tari glanced squeamishly down, then back up. Her eyes widened. "Okay! Okay! I'll do it. Stop staring at me like that!"

Xanthe gave a fierce smile of thanks and turned away to see what more help she could give. At the sight, her heart sank. There were at least forty. Blood had soaked into the carpet and was spreading out onto the stone floor. Strident speeches came from everywhere except the wounded men. While others were noisily arguing, they were quietly dying.

"Creator's dodgy power," she swore to herself, moving past the first, a cold body with a badly cracked skull and brain clearly visible. The next had a broken ankle. He was moaning in pain but would survive no matter what. Then the third. Another bolt. This one in the gut. Savable. She stopped.

He wasn't old, no more than eighteen. He clung to the bolt with a death grip, but the feathered shaft was embedded just below his rib cage and would not come out. His face was a mask of pain and terror.

"Let me see it," she told him, putting her hands around his, gently trying to pry his fingers loose.

He refused to release his grip. "Neam akarok meag'alni," he told her, sobbing.

"You don't speak common, huh? Well don't worry. You are lucky." she stared deep into his eyes as she felt the *touch* come upon her. "For today," she whispered as the power took her, "You are a kestrel."

It had taken Xanthe almost a year to figure out why demibirds kept attacking her door in the attic of the Scholar's Tower. It was the reclaimed glass itself. The ancients had somehow enchanted it so that when the light fell just right, it seemed as if there was a mouseweevil on the other side. Her father called this a "hologram" and explained that the glasssteel had once been a piece of artwork. But now it was just a kestrel death trap. Every morning, the little predators would dive hungrily in, smack against the nearly invisible glass, and die on her balcony. Until one day she decided to save them.

Yet just because they were injured, did not mean they cooperated. When kestrels were strongest and best able to recover, they would spend their energy flopping around in terror and agony. So, she'd learned to reach out with her *touch*, to subdue them before they went into shock. And as with them, she did here, stretching her palm around the side of the young soldier's head, reaching out. To **see**.

*A body is an enormous city, countless tiny bubbles and lines of light. They form a constantly moving sculpture of living bones providing shape, hard-working organs, and muscle. Roads of blood, lymph, bile, nerves, the mysterious spiderwebs that only humans have, all crisscross through the body. Wires of energy, shifting, pulsing, constantly working in exquisite harmony to mysterious purpose. Even with injury, there is beauty. Streaks of little energies zoom impossibly fast through the tendrils into the bony spine, and spiderwebs, up into the temple, the unfathomably complex brain, an ocean of light, a galactic maelstrom of such profound complexity that you could stare at it hypnotized forever.*

*Somewhere in that storm is a mystery called consciousness. Somewhere unwillingness to release a grip. But nothing could ever tease that out. Nor would it be right. Instead, just a touch tells the tiny muscles around the arteries to squeeze. The blood slows, and the lights dim ever so slightly.*

Xanthe held the boy's head as he fainted and let him down gently. She loosened his fingers over the bolt, but, still connected to him, sensed the pain when his grip relaxed. Deeper in, she understood why. The bolt's barbed head was inside his abdominal cavity, and its wicked backward spikes were caught in the visceral lining of his abdomen, pressing its point into his liver. A vein was also cut and bleeding inside, though nothing much showed externally.

Fortunately, when focusing like this, Xanthe found she could simply *push* flesh. Though the pressure was not strong, perhaps no more than what she could do with her pinky finger, it did wonders when applied to the right place. Numbing his nerves, she levered the shaft around so that the head wasn't quite so much in danger of causing more internal damage. Then with a combination of causing muscle spasms, pulling with her hand, and using the touch to untangle when the bolt-head caught on flesh, she worked the whole thing free. The nicked vein came next. She *pulled* the flaps into the same place and *pinched* them with the touch so that they stuck together. Blood came rushing out of the wound. But it was dead. Better out than in. When most was out, she pinched his skin shut. Now healed, the boy looked worse than when she'd begun, lying unconscious in a pool of streaked red. But he would live.

In the background, she was dimly aware of screaming. The priest was refusing to allow a fire to be built to warm up the atrium, and from the anger of the voices, it sounded as if a fight might break out. Yet she was focused now and didn't care to worry about it. That Celeste had returned and was giving out bandages to Tari and others less seriously wounded, barely registered.

There were another two, one with a spear stab that had punctured his gut, and another with a bolt stuck halfway through the side of his neck which had miraculously missed all his major arteries. For the latter, working the barbed head back out was just too dangerous, so she numbed the man's nerves, gripped the shaft and shoved the bolt forward out through the other side of his skin. Then it was a simple matter to clip the head and pull it out cleanly. The other was a mess of pulling and pinching intestines shut. For that one, she was glad of the blood. It washed dung and alien life that had escaped his intestines, completely out of his body. Then came one with a cut artery that she patched up instantly, because he was bleeding out. Another with a cracked skull, but savable. Then an older brown haired one covered in blood not his own. His back was pierced and the nerves inside his spine, the little lines of light, had gone dark below the spot of the injury. With practice born of hundreds of kestrels, she pushed blood to them, washing away the wound-poisons and bringing them back to life; a few minutes of intense pressure, some impossibly delicate knitting with the touch that even she didn't understand how she did, and it was done. Then an unconscious man with a severed arm. She undid his tourniquet, aligned the bone, and pinched together everything: arteries, veins, nerves, muscles, tendons, even skin. Then more. Many more. She didn't even recognize them. She forgot as soon as she'd moved on to the next.

Sometimes in the throes of the touch, she felt as if she had no control. As if something greater was moving through her, using her hands, her power, for unknowable purpose. This was one such time. She just became lost in it.

She was working on one with a sword wound to the chest, tricky because blood had collapsed one of his lungs, and too much movement would reopen the artery she'd barely managed to seal, when she felt an interruption.

"What you do here?" a mountainous foreign soldier asked in a thick Lukomoryen accent, breaking her concentration.

"I'm bandaging," Xanthe replied, not shifting her eyes to him. She was focused on causing little spasms in the lungs to force blood out without blocking any airways.

"You hurt!" He told her and moved to turn her patient on his back.

She put her arm up to block him. "Stop."

"Get off, little gurl!" He pushed her back. Or tried to. When he grabbed her arm, there was a sharp electrical crackle. He jerked his hand back and stared in shock.

"You move him like that?" she warned in a dark feral voice, "he will die."

The man pulled his dagger. Xanthe felt a thrill of fear go through her. But just then, another foreigner came up from behind the first. He too was staring, wide eyed, as if she were a wild animal. He put a hand on the other's shoulder. "Do as she says, Yuri," he whispered in a Gaulic accent. He gazed superstitiously around the church and then back at her. "We are in zhe Nightmare Lands, and zhese are not called zhe Witchwilds for nothing."

But it was too late. She'd lost her concentration. All she felt was exhaustion.

With the breaking of her focus, she became aware of other things. Other people were entering. Half a dozen bandagers carried in supplies: blankets, dressings, poultices, and a huge pot of heated honey-water. Council adjudicators had arrived too and had brokered some sort of compromise.

No one seemed to be yelling any more. The room was even warming due to the crowd.

Finally, the High Deacon appeared, his holiness Darhan Jameson. Xanthe didn't attend services much, certainly never at The Grand Steeple, Jagerfeld's ruling church. Yet she still recognized him. Adorned in ornate vestments befitting his station, he was elderly, gray haired, and pudgy, but otherwise well preserved; his continence a continuous mask of absolute certitude. He didn't seem too shocked by the scene until he spotted her. His eyes then widened.

"By the Creator! They attacked little girls too?"

Xanthe was confused. Then she followed his eyes down. Her clothes were drenched in blood. Even her sandskin boots were leaving tracks.

Tari came up with marks of red on her clothes, but nothing like Xanthe's. "We were just bandaging, your Holiness," she explained, doing a quick apologetic courtesy. "No one else was around, and they needed help right away."

The archdeacon didn't appear pleased. "Girls, no one doubts your intent. But from appearances, it might have been better had you simply waited until those who knew what they were doing could come. And..." his voice trailed off in astonishment as Celeste stood up from behind the large hoard of stolen bandages she'd been distributing.

"Yeah, um," Celeste half smiled and waved tentatively. "Hi daddy."

"By the Creator!"

## Chapter 3

It was a crystal-eve. Some days in Jagerfeld when the sun dipped just behind the mountains, the light still striking haphazard cuts of glass embedded in the tower tops reflected a kaleidoscope of rainbow-colored spots down to the streets below. It was exceptionally pretty when they fell on the melting icicles of early spring.

Yet all this did was make Xanthe feel worse. She'd been stuck inside for two whole bells because it was improper for her to go outside covered in blood, but her requests to just borrow a quick change of clothes kept being delayed. Highcouncil grownups milled about complimenting Tari and Celeste, whose parents they knew, and squinting at her, trying to remember to whose family she belonged. Otherwise they ignored her, gossiping about where they'd been when they heard the news of the day. As the Archdeacon kept repeating the story about how his angelic daughter had quickly got supplies for the bandagers, Xanthe felt her clothes and hair grow progressively colder and stickier with drying blood. Their obliviousness had been so great, she'd even been able to sneak back to check on the wounded and satisfy herself on their progress. Her fickle touch had returned, and she secretly managed to fix a few things.

Eventually a priest she didn't know took her into the private clerical chambers where she was given, in order, a bucket of icy water, old baggy nun robes, cast off shoes better than the ones she'd ruined, and a scolding as if she were a Highcouncil daughter. No matter how notable her family, girls should know their place and not try to assume competence they did not have. Blah, blah, blah. Now she was out on the street, carrying her bundle bloodstained clothes, with the chore of washing her soiled outfit – the only one she had.

This left her with about a bell worth of time to shop, and no one to do it with. It was, as she thought about it, likely for the best. Such a pittance she had. Embarrassing. Three copper pennies. Tari probably spent more than that just getting her shoes waxed. She wondered what she'd been thinking, going shopping with her.

The little bell on the door jingled as Xanthe stepped in. Madam Saud's was pretty store, clean and well-ordered. While the plaza contained half a hundred open air stalls, most occupied by farmers peddling the last of their winter roots, this had something more. There were two wood stoves, always lit. The owner had a soft spot for youth, not shooing them away like other shops did, which turned it into a hangout. Perfect for Xanthe's purposes. Shopping was just a pretense.

Inside, boys were all huddled around their stove. With a brief glance, before averting her eyes, Xanthe examined them. There were eight in all. Two she knew by name, Liam and Horge, four she knew the faces of, and two she'd never seen before. All farm sons, in leathers with thick muscular hands. Not good. Guild boys were most forgiving of a girl with brains, and besides, they were way too old. In their twenties. They'd be advanced graduates if they went to school. They wouldn't be interested in her.

The girl's stove was even worse. Priscia was there. Beautifully coiffed and painted, with thick thighs made to seem thicker by expensive slats that were hidden in her hose, she was entertaining her clique of Nadeen, Sepia, and Candice, by gossiping about some girl, all punctuated by brief peals of high, mocking laughter. With tiny peeks at the boys, she showed off the sparks she could make with her touch. Metal glitter dropped from her plump manicured hands and fell as burning motes to the floor. She waved them around making colored patterns. It was all just showing off, as these farmers weren't in her league and she knew it. The sparkles were the most beautiful thing about her. She was vicious as a snow viper.

Xanthe groaned inwardly. Any thought of retreating there evaporated. She couldn't hang out with Priscia cutting on her constantly. That left only one thing. Really try to shop. She strode to the wood counter as if this had always been her plan, set down her clothes basket, and peered into the open cubbyhole lining the back wall.

She searched. Each space held something different. Madam Saud had good selection but not always reliable sources. You never found the same thing twice. Sometimes this meant a bargain if she was getting impatient to sell. But right now? Nothing. Not a favor. Nor even ribbons to make one. Everything was picked clean. The cheapest premade favor Xanthe saw was twelve pennies. It was braided pink-dyed dog hair and looked hideous.

"Can I help you?" Trina Saud appeared out of the back entryway. A matronly woman in her mid-forties, she was the owner's younger sister.

"I... uh..." Xanthe stammered. Her last hope fizzled. The older Saud had a soft spot for her delivery girl, or at least Xanthe hoped. Maybe enough for a freebie. Trina didn't know her at all.

The merchant sized her up instantly. "Can I show you what we have in the castaway bin?"

Xanthe winced, hoping that wasn't overheard. "No, no, I have copper," she lied, but then realized that was worse. If she bothered the shopkeeper to show her something, she'd be pressured to buy, and then have to admit she had no coin. "I... I just don't know what to get." She pointed randomly at a small jar in a bright red label, directly in front of her. She hoped it was cosmetics. That was something everyone could give back without losing face. You'd just say it wasn't your color.

"Ah! Excellent choice," the younger Saud told her, pleased. "You have a good eye. We just got this in. Dr. Varsuvious', certified and proven..." she paused dramatically, "Haunch Cream. Made of twenty-one secret ingredients, this little miracle in a jar is absolutely guaranteed to add pounds to troublesome spots on the female figure. Especially..." she winked salaciously, "your broad cheeks."

Xanthe was fascinated. "It fills you out?"

"Without fail... when used in conjunction with the recommended triple-butter diet and at least ten bells of strict chair-rest a day. Do those things, apply this miracle cure, and you'll be round and plump all over, especially down there!"

"That long sitting in a chair? How could anyone..." her voice trailed off. Xanthe already knew her dad couldn't afford butter. The Scholars' Guild wasn't rich at all.

"Well, I think you're supposed to sew while you're doing it or something. I don't precisely know, dear. But I'm sure it'll have at least some effect even if you don't do that part. It *does* say that it's certified."

Xanthe stared. Something twisted in her gut. Everything she wanted was in that jar. She could just imagine herself now, as if her dress was stuffed, thicker than Priscia's, except it was all real.

"Tis pricey, but the best things always are," the merchant-woman continued smoothly. "It normally sells for one twenty-five. But just for you, I can make it ninety-nine."

Xanthe stared silently and swallowed. There was nothing she could do.

"My goodness, Ma'am! That's still just too expensive!" Priscia's chirpy voice came from just behind. "You really should take off more than that."

Xanthe turned to see Priscia, confused as to why she was helping bargain. Priscia gave her a smarmy smile and continued. "I mean, at least consider giving her a bulk discount on the beauty cream." She smiled mockingly. "She *so* needs it."

In the background, Sepia and Candice giggled. But the shopkeeper wasn't happy. "One customer at a time, please."

"Oh, but she's not really a customer," Priscia declared, enjoying herself immensely. "She can't afford that jar. She probably only has enough coin to scrape broken buttons and used thread out of your castaway bin just to sew herself the ugliest favor in the Festival. While I..." she pulled out a leather pouch and tossed it casually on the counter, "can buy."

Xanthe felt as if she'd been slapped. Her stomach twisted into a knot. Everything Priscia had said was the absolute truth.

Madame Saud focused on the bag. It had landed with a substantial crunch. "That's a lot of copper."

"Silver," Priscia corrected. "If I wanted to, I could buy half your store."

Xanthe was surprised. Even Madame Saud raised an eyebrow. Priscia's family was rich. But that rich? Silver for a daughter's purse? It didn't matter though. Xanthe knew her time here was done. She was determined not to give Priscia the satisfaction of seeing her cry. She turned around.

Priscia put a hand on her shoulder. "Aren't you going to ask me why?"

Xanthe stared at the hand, then up at her. "No."

"Well I'll tell you anyway. Father's weapon business is doing amazing. He has a new partner. Prince Sol, the heir to Nutearea." She thrust her chin forward arrogantly.

Xanthe was shocked. "You met a southern prince?"

Priscia was triumphant. "Met? Far more than that. He likes me. A lot. And princes are generous with people they like when they become king." She sneered with condescension. "I'm so happy, that I was even thinking of buying you one of those jars of beauty cream you so completely need. After all, as they say, queens should show their station in both word and deed."

Xanthe froze. Leave it to Priscia to find new ways to get under her skin. The jar sat there on the counter, mocking her. But a deep sense of disquiet helped her keep control. She wasn't so much worried that Priscia was lying. More that she was telling the truth.

"Thanks, but no. I like myself just the way I am," Xanthe declared proudly, an utter fabrication. Yet despite her best efforts, her hands were shaking. When she bent down to grab her clothes basket, she managed to knock it over instead. Her blood-stained clothes spilled out.

"Ew," Priscia squealed, stepping quickly away. "What kind of chores has that loser father of yours have you doing now? Being a butcher?"

*Great. Just great.* Xanthe wondered if the day could get any worse. She knelt to gather them up. "Please just leave my father out of this."

"Why? The dung-master? How's he even in the Scholars' Guild, anyway? He fixes toilets! Makes so little, you support him skinning skrags and plucking chickens for pennies to bring home instead? No wonder you're so pathetic."

*At least I'm able to read.* The thought nearly slipped out Xanthe's lips when she saw thick pairs of leather covered legs approaching. Two farm boys, clipped blondes. They both towered over her.

"Wow, like..." Liam said. "They really do got blood in 'em." He looked on while scratching the back of his neck, as Xanthe stuffed the sticky clothes back into the basket and put the lid on.

"Yeah," said the other one, whose name she didn't know, but was missing a top tooth.

Priscia sniggered. "Oh, so precious. Now you've got even boys feeling sorry for you."

"Feelin' sorry?" Liam questioned in confused disagreement. "Naw. It's cool! Hayellspace, my pa still don't let me do the butcherin' yet, and I'm nearly a man now. He says killin's hard."

"And she's a girl!" The other boy nodded eagerly, sounding quite impressed. He gave Xanthe a frank stare, eyeing her up and down. It made her feel as if she were prize livestock being judged. "Ya know, yer kine-na not all filled out yet, but don't got a bad lookin' face at all," he concluded. "I mean. At all!" Suddenly he hesitated. "So... cen ya cook pie?"

Still kneeling, Xanthe stared open mouthed. "Cook... pie...?"

"That's way too straight, Hank," Liam chuckled, elbowing his friend sharply in the ribs. "See? Ya scared her. Gotta be more smooth 'an that when ya talk ta girls. Ya know, roun'about." He made a broad sweeping gesture with this palm.

"No I don't!" Hank replied hotly. "She likes straight up! She kills chickens!"

Xanthe tried to say something but couldn't. Her mind had gone completely blank except for knowing that if Celeste were here, she'd be howling with laughter.

"Excuse me," Madam Saud interrupted crossly. "Are any of you kids going to buy something? Or am I just wasting my time?"

Xanthe felt incredibly embarrassed but couldn't figure out why. Her face was pink as redfruit. She stood. "Talk to the rich girl," and thumbed towards Priscia, who was as equally as perplexed. "I... I have to go." Without another word, she walked out of the store.

It was only a few steps outside when Xanthe realized that she hadn't thanked Liam for rescuing her from Priscia, or Hank for pretending that her face was pretty. Not that she really *liked* them that much, and they were way too old. But she should have been polite. She thought of going back in, but that would be too forward. Now she cursed herself. The Hank boy had almost seemed like he might pick up her favor, except that for no reason other than being nervous and embarrassed, she'd walked out on him instead of smiling. He probably wasn't terribly stupid, at least not just as an escort for the Festival, though his missing tooth and country slang did give that impression.

*I'm the one who's stupid,* she thought. Hellspace, she could have been Priscia's friend, if she'd only been slightly more of a suck-up. But no. Always too proud. Although to be fair, she didn't think she could ever just stand by and laugh while a friend-Priscia picked on other girls. It was just all in all that... well, that her life was dung, and like dung, blood didn't come out of cloth without soap, of which she had none, so her clothes might be permanently stained as well.

She stopped in a dark alleyway and leaned against the cold stone brick. Sometimes when she was alone like this she would start going over and over every dumb thing she'd ever done in her life, helpless to change any of it, and just being miserable at all her foolishness. The night was cold though and feeling sorry for herself wasn't doing anything. Worse, it dawned on her that she was famished. She'd missed the night's meal and would likely have to beg for porridge from Miss Weatherpenny in the Guild larder, assuming she could even catch her before she went home. That would have to come before using the machines to beat the stains out of her clothes in the Guild's wash room. Another problem with being poor was that you were always so busy trying to survive, you couldn't even cry.

"Xanthe?" A voice spoke from almost right next to her.

She jumped and nearly screamed. The alley was black. When the sun dipped behind the mountains, night fell fast.

"It's just me." Celeste approached, casually assure. A silhouette of black on black, Xanthe could barely see her. "You left church so fast, Tari and I didn't even notice you were gone."

"Went shopping," Xanthe explained. "Didn't go so well. Priscia was there."

Celeste brightened. "Lemme guess! She bullied you, so you punched her lights out? Gave her a big fat lip? And then you pulled the ponytail of every girl in her doggy pack? Tied their braids together? Grownups had to pull you off, but you escaped? So, you're a truant now? Have to leave town to join the circus?"

"No." Xanthe glowered sullenly.

"Shoot!" Celeste snapped her fingers. "I was hoping. That would be cool!"

Celeste never showed any real sympathy, but somehow always seemed to make things better. Xanthe's stomach was still rumbling though. "So yeah, maybe I'll tell you what really happened tomorrow."

"Not a chance. You're coming with me. Tari's dad is hosting a dinner party. We got our parents to invite you along as a favor. That's why I'm here."

"What?! You're inviting *me*?"

"Inviting? Oh hellspace no. Way beyond that. Forcing. I used a daddy-favor for this, which I refuse to waste. I put up with days of reaming sermons for them."

Xanthe started breathing deeply. Now she really felt like she was going to cry. "I'd *love* to. I mean," she swallowed hard, "Look, I... I might have to eat and run. I need to get to the Guild washroom to beat as much of the bloodstains out of my clothes as I can."

"Creator's holy balls, Xanth! Just drop that off with one of Tari's servants at her house. Mrs. Driver will probably have it all cleaned and fire-dried before dessert." Celeste grabbed her hand. "Now come on! We'll be late."

Xanthe allowed herself to be pulled through the dark alleyways, hardly believing her good fortune. Dessert. Probably something sweet. Something she was lucky to taste on Landfall Day. Her clothes cleaned by a servant who probably made more than her dad did. This latter thought was disquieting as once again it sunk in who Tari and Celeste were.

The question burned, and after a minute of walking she had to ask. "Celeste? Why do you and Tari let me run with you?"

"Duh! You let us cheat off your tests!"

Eyes still wet, Xanthe laughed despite herself. "No! I mean for real!"

Celeste threw up her hands. "I *am* being real! Hellspace, half the time I joke, I'm not trying to. I just say what's true, and people start laughing. But come on, why wouldn't I?"

"Well, you know. Because I'm poor."

"So?"

At the fast pace Celeste had set, Xanthe nearly slipped on some ice, even in her sandskin boots. "Well... doesn't that matter?"

"Am I Priscia?" Celeste asked reproachfully.

"Um. No."

"Okay then. Besides, when I grow up, I going to be poor too."

"Oh, come on!"

"Sure. You see, just for you I'm going to punch her out. Then I'll have no choice but to run off and be a circus pretender, scamming the marks for copper."

Xanthe shook her head with a half-smile as they reached the Highcouncil walls, the gated and guarded inner district which glistened in the light of hundreds of expensive crystal oil-light and naphtha lamps. Celeste also seemed happy that she'd been able to get Xanthe out of her funk.

Celeste continued. "Yeah, I want to see the world. A circus is about the only way I'll ever be able to. You think I'm gonna spend the rest of my life being some nun or priest-wife, listening to sermons and counting the marks' donations?" She gave Xanthe a kidding smile.

But Xanthe saw the glint in her eye. She was dead serious.

## Chapter 4

The Lolita-dress was gorgeous. Purple with shiny midnight-blue ruffles and white cross-laces, Xanthe was amazed that Tari had insisted she wear it, even though it was just one of dozens in her second closet. It didn't fit and itched like mad but was so pretty that Xanthe didn't care. It also was short for her, which exposed her decidedly non-plump legs. So, she'd sat down alone at the long table in the ornate dining room while others still socialized out at the reception next door.

No loss. She didn't know anyone anyway, except her friends who were still being dressed. Just being here was amazing, high atop Manse Outlet, set amongst elegant gardens, within the guarded Highcouncil walls that protected it from the common riffraff.

Abruptly, two men entered. "There are three," Tari's father, Councilor Abriam Outlet remarked as he walked in with casual command. "From what's carried by the kestrels, Princes Flordeman, Zan, and Chadwick, all have the strongest positions." Behind him, Celeste's father followed meekly, merely listening. "Not that it matters at this point. Rarely do early leading princes end up being crowned. The others usually gang up on him, or they're downed by some clever assassin."

"Assassins! I only pray to the Creator that doesn't happen," the archdeacon muttered as the Councilor strode to the cordials table. Neither of them took any notice of her at all. It was as if she wasn't there.

Tari's father rattled icicles from a serving bucket into a crystal cup. "At least then they'd only be after each other." He splashed in a green liquor and swirled the ice. "Yet I hold little hope. King Seraphus isn't dead. His body is as hale as ever. Only his brain is gone. Not that he spent most of his rule thinking with it. You practically can't visit a southern port without tripping over some princeling he got bedding a local highborn back in his prime. Every one of them pretending to the throne with a blood drenched plan." He stared at the glass for a moment, then took a sip. "It's a recipe for disaster."

The churchman shook his head. "Half-brothers killing each other for rule. By the all-loving Creator! Yet still, why is this different from what happened in our fathers' time?"

The councilor sighed. "When a Nutearean king dies, all the princes rush to the royal conclave, lest a rival be crowned there. It's a convenient place, far from us, where they pretend to negotiate while poisoning each other's wine and sticking daggers in each other's backs. But since he's still alive, there's no conclave. And since he's incapacitated, there's no one to keep the mayoral houses from mustering armies to wage outright war upon their rivals. The Presidential Army is in complete disarray."

A chill ran up Xanthe's spine. If the two men hadn't been here, she would have been marveling at the décor. The place settings were antique plastic, an utterly priceless material no one could make anymore. Yet now, all she could think was how fragile it all was. In the lessons about the world outside Jagerfeld, everything had seemed so abstract. But now it wasn't. She wanted to believe that this was all just storytelling, the nightmares of powerful men, but a curious sense of dread hung over her. She was seized by a feeling that if anything, it would be much worse.

"And that's just the cities," Councilor Outlet continued. "Two different fleets in the Shimmering Isles each have their own pirate prince. A few more in the guilds. Several playing politics with factions within the Curate. Many more I'm sure that even I'm not aware of, and a few I'd prefer I weren't."

"Prince Sol." The words came out quietly. It was a moment before Xanthe realized they were her own. That was who Priscia had mentioned.

At her utterance, Abriam twisted his head sharply. His gaze fell straight upon her. "Who are you?"

She was suddenly terrified. She wanted to disappear but couldn't. "Xanthe, Sir."

"She's a spy?" the archdeacon asked, mimicking the councilor's gaze, his tone indicating that he'd more than half convinced himself of the accusation just by voicing it.

The councilor blinked, giving the archdeacon a brief stare of incredulity. "No, Darhan," he answered flatly. "She's just a friend of the girls. They begged us to invite her. Don't you remember?"

The archdeacon huffed. "Celeste is simply too innocent to understand the dangers."

"Well, either this is the youngest and most feminine spy on record, or I can conclude that Prince Sol has been making overtures to more than just me." The councilor gestured towards her with his drink. "Greetings young miss. I'm pleased to finally put a face to your name."

"So... who is Prince Sol?" Xanthe asked. "Speaking of names, I've only heard his recently."

"Not surprising. He came out of hiding only recently in Northfjord. He's trying to unite the Free Cities. He says Thule will give rise to an unstoppable army that will sweep down and conquer all of Nutearea under his banner."

"In other words, a complete idiot."

Behind his glass, Tari's father chuckled at her comment. "Basically, yes. Though for the moment, a dangerous one. There's no reason for Jagerfeld to get involved in this stupid foreign war."

"Sol's an enemy then?"

He paused, reflecting on the query. "Merely not a friend. I must admit he did us the favor of offing this *other* prince we didn't even know was in our lands." At Xanthe's questioning face, he explained: "Prince Christian. It was his defeated retinue that you girls bandaged today."

"Infidels!" Jameson exclaimed, shocked at the news. "Curse the Five and Eight! I had no idea Christian influence had spread so far north!" He then turned to Xanthe to give an unnecessary explanation of Curate doctrine. "You see my child, the Holy Pilot, a seraph of the Creator, piloted our ancestors to our planet named Haven. We were commanded to turn from our past. For humanity's cradle had become so polluted with waste, unholiness, and arrogance, that demons arose there. Alas, Christians cling to a faith of that defiled world, and so defy the Creator in preserving that evil. It is evident in their every action."

Xanthe couldn't help herself. "Oh? What evil have they done?" She asked innocently.

The archdeacon was taken aback at being questioned. "Well, um. They're evil, of course," he nodded as if this were self-evident, "because they're Christian."

"I see faith fills you," Xanthe agreed. "So, are they worse than witches? I mean, if a proctor knew of a Christian in one town, and a witch girl throwing sparks in another, who should they kill first?"

His eyes fell. "I... honestly don't know," he confessed. "I'm not privy to the inner councils of the Word of the Faith. Prayerhome is far away." He swallowed. "Also, well, the Sect of Penance's standing is quite disputed. Most believe minor witchery to be a mere venal sin. Even greatwitchery is not so terrible that it deserves death without tribunal and the opportunity to recant."

"Truly your Holiness?" Xanthe continued, wide eyed. "But then, how else can the Curate keep away evil, if it doesn't constantly kill?" Then her stomach growled, and she decided not to add anything more. She wasn't about to disinvite herself from dinner.

Abriam burst out laughing and grinned at the archdeacon.

"I don't understand," the churchman muttered in unhappy confusion.

"Razorthorns. So sharp, sometimes you don't even know you've been pricked." The councilor clapped his companion on the back. "Never mind, my friend." He turned to Xanthe. "You're the researcher's daughter. Has your father empowered any new technology recently?"

"He keeps Jagerfeld's septic pumps running," she replied quietly. "He helps other Free Cities and many hamlets as well."

Jameson snorted. "Other cities' researchers learn the use of artifacts. Ours mucks in dung."

"Yes," the councilman drawled. "That makes measuring his worth difficult. Still, perhaps the Convocation of Miracles could spare him... oh, I don't know... just a little? I rather do enjoy our fair city's lack of smell."

"Never! The Holy Creator would reward him with more worthwhile miracles of technological awakenings if only he were more devout. Why, does he even come to mass?"

Xanthe clenched her jaw. Her mind raced with stories about disease in hamlets where fly-ridden feces gathered in private cesspits that were then dumped into creeks upstream of where drinking water was collected. Her dad had saved hundreds, if not thousands, of lives. But she knew it was useless.

"Well, speaking of mass, that retinue of Prince Christian is coming to yours," Abriam stated. "They aren't Christian themselves. Just innocent mercenaries. Experienced too. I'm quite thinking of hiring them."

Jameson's mumbled reply was drowned out as the night-meal bell sounded from the kitchens. Servants outside the large sliding wall that separated the dining and reception rooms promptly drew it away. The guests were all suddenly together. Many Xanthe recognized from the church, except they'd changed into expensive consumes. The room filled with their chatter.

"Darnam! Nythiea! And of course, Tyan! Councilor Wormwood! You're just in time!" a woman exclaimed happily at some late arrivals. It was Mrs. Outlet, bedecked in a gown of brightly colored ancient plastic tarps. Tari followed sullenly in an identical getup, while behind her Celeste had on a white Virgin's Habit and her bland "I'm dunging you" smirk. She waggled her eyebrows at Xanthe.

"I took the liberty of placing my daughter and your Horace together," the elder Outlet continued in her conversation with Mrs. Wormwood, while maintaining a discrete hold on Tari's upper arm. "It's not strictly proper, but Tari just can't stop talking about him. Or the Festival of Favors. Ah, young love!"

Tari stared wide eyed in utter desperation. That, or she was plotting murder. It was hard to tell. But the two older women were so intent in their mutual mercenary cordiality that neither noticed.

*Proper. Proper.* Hiding her skinny legs behind the table, Xanthe stood. "We should all thank our host as is proper!" she announced, cupping her hands together in traditional manner. "Thank you, Councilor Outlet."

"Oh yes!" Celeste chimed in, picking up on the gambit. "The Creator and Host, all doth thank!"

Called to the formality, the assembly did as bidden, bowing slightly towards Mr. Outlet. Tari perfectly anticipated her mother's hesitation and wrenched free of her grip exactly at the right moment. She quickly fled around the table and appropriated the chair next to Xanthe, with a grateful smile. Tari's father also raised his glass in her direction, touched by her graciousness. It was too embarrassing, so Xanthe sat down.

"Have I ever told you how much I hate my mother?" Tari muttered in a low voice as the dinner party hubbub resumed. Her hair and makeup had been fussed over until it was perfect.

"At least you have one…" Xanthe peered past Mrs. Outlet's silent fuming to see a handsome boy dressed in livery, bearing a curiously grim expression. "Wait! What's Royroy doing here?" Ginna wasn't nice, but her brother was insanely cute.

"He showed up, said he really needed a job – but don't get ideas. He's with Aneece. Didn't you know?"

"I did." Xanthe sighed wistfully. "She's so pretty."

"Pretty dumb. Failed letters, so was pulled from school. Which is what mother has threatened me with if I don't play along. She doesn't like me in girls' school anyway. Says class is putting ideas in my head."

"Um…" Xanthe furrowed her brows. "Isn't that kind of the point?"

"You'd think!" Tari exclaimed, distraught. "What am I going to do?"

Everything is always so clear when it's not you. "Well, how bad is it to just play along? It's only a Festival, not marriage. I mean, do you even have anybody else in mind?" She searched in vain for the object of Tari's scorn, but the only one she recognized was Celeste pretending to be saintly in front of her father. "Seems pretty dumb making your mom so mad just to see your favor snatched by someone *else* you don't like."

Tari pouted. "Yeah? Well, I wonder just how you'd feel about it."

Xanthe had had enough. "Know what?" she whispered tartly, "I don't even *have* a favor. I can't afford one." Instantly hating herself for making such a confession, she dropped her eyes. "I mean," she swallowed. "I know I'm just your side-kick. But other people have problems too."

"Well…" Tari was about to say something, when for no reason, her eyes widened, and she grimaced. Just as Xanthe was about to ask what was wrong, Tari glowered behind her.

"Lovely ladies!" a boy called from too close in the cloying tones of an overly practiced introduction. Xanthe craned her neck around to see who it was. He was maybe twenty, but seemed younger, given his doughy face and heavy body. His eyes were set far too wide, but he was tall and covered in finery, plastics and lace, and had on a bracelet that he was clearly trying to show off. It was some ancient artifact.

"Oh. Horace." Tari's voice filled with midwinter chill. "I wondered when you would show up."

"And who is this?" He asked, shifting his eyes.

"Xanthe. You wouldn't know her. She goes to school."

He held out his hand to shake hers and turned his wrist, showing off his prize. Xanthe took his hand, and the hint. "So, what do you have there?"

"Oh, you noticed?" He pretended to be surprised. "It's a light-powered number adder. See?" He pointed at the display and the worn little plastic buttons that it still had, but she was more interested in the ancient script around the edges. As best as she could make out, the small wrist band read: 'Super Fun-Meal – Free Toy!' It had to be worth a fortune.

"See?" He brightened at her interest. "Let's say I put in two numbers like a one, two, three, four. That makes a big number. Then multiply. Then a nine. Press equals, it figures it out for you. Ancient magic."

*12340 less 1234; six on bottom and all but the top borrows to zeros.* "Ten thousand and six?"

This time Horace truly was surprised. He pressed the button and '10006' appeared on the display. "Um. Yeah. You're smart. Xanthe, eh? I'll remember that." Fazed, he gave a little nod and moved off.

"Idiot." Tari growled.

"Okay. He can't be *that* bad," Xanthe whispered, watching the young scion make his way around the table to a gaggle of cooing women twice his age. She thought of Hank. "At least he has all his teeth."

"It's not just that. He's had a string of girlfriends and it never ends well. I saw Clarissa of Axe crying for no reason. She wouldn't say why." Tari stared distantly. "I'm just glad I'm here. Not next to him."

Tari spoke too soon. As dinner started, her mother sat Horace directly across from her, and Xanthe didn't even risk a side-glance to see her reaction. Instead, she focused on the food. It was incredible. Meats, cheeses, dried fruits, sweet nuts, sauces, edible florets, and mashed fungal roots were all being served on ancient plastic. With butter. Loads of it. She wondered if she might even be able to get some nice appealing thigh fat if she ate enough, even without Dr. Varsuvious' Haunch Cream. Likely not, she morosely concluded. Fat just seemed to melt off her no matter how hard she tried to put it on. Still, it was impossible to be unhappy before such a feast, and with Councilor Outlet's traditional toast, "we shall not go hungry this eve," all the guests began to eat. A good end to a bad day.

Yet in the midst of chewing a roll of thinly sliced sweetmeat slathered with butter and jam, Xanthe felt a foot touching hers. She shifted slightly away, thinking she'd just accidentally bumped into someone, but it returned, this time sliding up her calf and sending tingles up her thigh. Cheeks overly full, she stared up in shock. Sitting across the table, resplendent in his stylish restitched plastic raincoat, Horace gave her a satisfied smile.

"Don't move, girl," he commanded from across the table as he touched her with his bare foot.

Xanthe was too surprised to try. She tried to swallow, but something stuck and briefly she couldn't breathe. There was a horrible choking moment when she thought she was going to cough everything out all over the table, but Tari perspicaciously put her napkin to her face, and hit the back of her chest, dislodging the obstruction. She still coughed, but managed to be more controlled about it, not making a scene. Horace kept rubbing her leg under the table like an overenthusiastic puppy.

"Whose family are you from?" he pressed.

"You wouldn't be interested, Horace," Tari interjected as Xanthe managed to finally clear her throat. "They're not Highcouncil."

"She's low?" he grinned. "I don't mind. I mean, even better. Cause let's be straight. I bet she fills out her dress as much as you do. But is more grateful. Innat that right, girl?" He smiled at her.

If he'd been trying to make Tari jealous, he failed miserably. She went from confused, to shocked, and finally settling on an emotion that never seemed to cross her face: sheer elation. "Yeah. I'm totally not appreciative like Xanthe is! Mother always says so."

Xanthe wasn't sure she agreed, but silently nodded along anyway.

"Make sure you're at the Festival," Horace told Xanthe. "I'd hate for you to miss it. I have this carriage. I just got back from Northfjord in it. Took the trip in dark winter under guard," he bragged.

Was he implying he might pick up her favor? She could hardly believe it. In truth, she wasn't even sure she liked it. It was seriously creepy to be approached so suddenly, right in the middle of a dinner party like this. But then she remembered what she'd daydreamed about. Priscia had told her that she'd never be able to attract anyone, much less a highborn. It stung especially bitterly, because Xanthe knew she was right.

But what if she wasn't? What if the richest boy in Jagerfeld picked her favor? To parade with him through the streets, with everyone admiring her for having caught him? That would prove Priscia wrong.

It would prove her own self-doubt wrong as well.

That settled it. Xanthe smiled and nodded.

## Chapter 5

Rumors spread the next day. An injured mercenary had risen, bleary and barely conscious. He'd walked outside to pee on the street, been yelled at to use the privy like civilized folk instead of a damned dirty bandit, grumbled a bit, and while finally relieving himself, massaged a place in his back that was killing him. Then he'd fallen down sobbing, because he remembered that he'd been speared there and lost all feeling in his legs. He'd spent the ride from the battle on the sled's floor begging for someone to kill him.

Men who'd taken gut wounds that were impossible to survive, did. Cracked skulls, broken jaws, severed tendons, were now little more than scars and bruises. Another whose sword arm had been cut clean off woke seeing his hand pink, weak but moving. When the tourniquet fell away, his whole arm was found reunited, swollen and angry-red, but otherwise whole. A disquiet fell upon the city. People spoke of it in whispers.

All during her delivery runs in the chill early morning, Xanthe felt a terrible mixture of pride and fear. Figuring out how she felt about Horace? Forget it. The Festival itself was now off limits. The local Curate tolerated much, rarely giving out more than sermons on sin and hellspace for spark throwing, but no one could shelter her from this, not even the Scholars' Guild. She'd be caught and branded a dreadwitch. She'd lose her freedom, her friends, even her classes. She'd no idea how she was going to break the news to father. Hopping down cold stone steps with her packages, she already felt as if she were being chased by heavily armed Curate proctors, come to drag her away to a tribunal. It made her run even faster.

When she got to school, Tari gave her a present. Xanthe was so distracted, she didn't even manage a smile of thanks. She just accepted and opened it by rote. Inside the expensive paper gift-wrap was an exquisitely crafted rose of multicolored glass, green leaves and colored petals, anchoring a long golden ribbon. "It's my Festival favor," Tari explained in a conspiratorial whisper. "I told mother I accidentally sat on it. We had a big fight!" She added with considerable satisfaction.

Xanthe was shocked. "You're staying in?"

"Oh, don't be silly! She's already out having a new one made. I don't even get to pick it out. Not that it matters!" Tari was entirely relieved, her typical gloom abated. "Horace likes you! Thank the Creator! It's perfect!"

"But your mom will be so mad. What will she do about your school?"

"That's the best part! If he chose some other Highcouncil girl, she'd blame me for not dropping my favor. But if he picks someone low like you? Then it'll be obvious it was him, not me!"

Xanthe deflated, and Tari looked contrite. "Oh dear! I'm sorry. That didn't come out right. You're not *really* low. I'm just... Look, this has to do with station. What I'm expected to do. You may not believe this, but you have it way better than I do."

Xanthe nodded morosely, knowing just how entirely Tari was mistaken, how little she understood what it meant to be poor. Yet also, Tari wasn't really a stuck-up. That wasn't what she was thinking about anyway. "Sorry I'm not happier. I just didn't know everyone was going to make it such a big deal." She stared down and away, her heart tight with worry.

Tari knew what Xanthe meant. Her voice dropped to an awed whisper. "I know! By the Creator! I mean, I've always known there's something incredible about you, but... wow!"

Xanthe stared. The nape of her neck chilled with sheer terror. "You haven't told, have you?"

"It wasn't obvious," Tari reassured. "I don't think anyone realized. Do you?"

"Maybe no," Xanthe whispered, but then realized that wasn't right.

Tari began to be concerned. "You're turning pale. What's wrong?"

"There were two soldiers. They know its me." There was a hollow feeling of panic inside her chest. What she'd heard it was like to be stalked by a grim. Except no one else was feeling it.

Tari scoffed. "Don't worry. We're a big city! Thirty thousand. And we're getting more visitors in every day! They won't see you again."

*Easy enough for her to say.* She wasn't the one being hunted.

"Even if they do, they won't know it's you. Not after the makeup I'm giving you!" Tari expressed in pure gratitude. And in her warmth, Xanthe's worry began to melt. If even Tari was in a good mood, maybe it wasn't so bad. Could foreigners really tell one pig-tailed schoolgirl from another? For the first time in her life, she didn't envy Celeste's unkempt ginger or Tari's lavender, as pretty as they were. Too identifiable. Blonde was much more common, though hers was depressingly golden white.

Yet when Celeste didn't show for class, the fear crept back. Her friend never missed school when she could help it, preferring the Guild entirely to her own home. So as Madame Coldroot lectured about Charon, Haven's larger black moon, supposedly with a city of the ancients on it, Xanthe wondered what had happened. Maybe some sermon of her dads she couldn't get out of? Something else inconsequential? Or...? Xanthe shuddered at the alternatives.

Consequently, Xanthe hiked to The Steeple after school. A late winter squall had dusted the city in white, leaving the cobblestone switchbacks that led to the landmark perched atop the Ancestor's Cliffs atypically deserted. The quiet hike left her alone to brood about life and freedom. As she strode between the turquoise Ancient's Metal pipes fronting Ancestor's Road, her feet crunching through the snow, a wild kestrel appeared above. They sometimes did that around her, almost seeming to be giving thanks for the lives she'd saved. This one was curiously black. It fluttered as if it were some sort of avian chaperone. At least it didn't hate her for what she was.

Past the great gear, and beneath the enormous emblem of the crossed piers and wand, Xanthe entered the church proper. The rebuilt ancestor ruin was huge, ornate, and had an overt engineering theme. Unidentified artifacts were everywhere, illuminated by dusty light slanting down from the high ceiling windows. Gadgets, gears, machinery, and a huge broken-down vehicle jacked up on the dais, all served as idols of prayer. The pews were empty, as it was neither the time nor day for mass. Her footsteps echoed in the silent halls. Only a lone kneeling acolyte took note of her presence. Yet as he was already fervently praying, which was custom not to interrupt, he did not rise to greet her. A mutual relief for both.

In the inner sanctum, at the end of a long corridor, were the clergy chambers. Here Xanthe arrived at Celeste's gear-and-stud-adorned door and knocked. Celeste opened it, took one look, then slammed it in her face.

"Celeste?" Xanthe rapped on the thick studded wood again.

"Go away," came a muffled response. She sounded furious.

"Celeste?! Did you tell...? About... you know? Me?"

That did it. Celeste opened the door, grabbed her by her school uniform, and pulled Xanthe in so fast that she tumbled to the floor. Celeste then slammed the door shut.

"Shut. Up." Celeste spoke each word by itself.

Prone, Xanthe looked up. Celeste seemed to tower over her in anger, which felt odd since she really was shorter. The habit she was wearing looked pristine, but everything else in the small room was a disaster. Papers, tools, clothing, and dried foods were scattered everywhere. She was packing. There was a stuffed backpack next to her bed. Only the walls were untouched. It was clear she didn't care for any of the holy equipment mounted on them.

"W-what's going on?" Xanthe asked. "Did they threaten to rack you if you didn't tell?"

In response, Celeste balled her fist. "I said. Shut. Up." She hissed. "I just decided. You're going to help me. Since you owe me and all."

"Help? How? What?"

"Run away, of course. I can't trust Geral." Celeste spoke of her eldest brother who was both least fooled by her act and most humored by it. "He might try to rescue me instead."

Xanthe was completely confused. "Just tell me what happened. If they're hurting you, I'll go confess." She could hardly believe what she was saying, but she meant it. Giving up. Turning herself in for whatever the punishment was. Maybe being sent to the Praetorians. But it was better than this.

Seeing her earnestness made Celeste throw up her hands in frustration. "It's not you, dung head! He thinks it's me!" Her eyes turned fully black.

"What?! He thinks..." Xanthe suddenly realized those eyes weren't natural. It was clearly a witch power.

"Dear daddy," Celeste explained, brimming with rage, "thinks I'm some new reaming saintess! Blessed by the Creator directly!"

If she hadn't been so shocked, Xanthe would have burst out laughing. A saintess? Celeste? That would be like giving a King of Nutearea an award for celibacy.

Celeste caught her look of amusement. "I'm not joking," she told her angrily through gritted teeth.

"Well, but still. So what? I mean, sure, your dad is..."

"He's a splooging idiot!" Celeste exploded in exasperation. "He actually believes all the dung he spews! He's got a whole prayer group around that jacked up carriage every Freeday trying to pray it into flying again, when any idiot could see that all it ever did was roll!"

"He doesn't think you're a witch?"

Celeste's voice dropped low, even though they both knew no one was around. "I wasn't near half of the ones you cured. I just told him I prayed over the bandages, begging the Creator for a miracle. You know – standard dung. How was I supposed to know you were actually healing them?!"

"Look," Xanthe found herself at a loss for words. "Okay, so why is this bad?"

"Because, Xanth, I'm going to end up in some reaming nunnery. He's already upstairs writing missives. Proclaiming the news of my miracle to every fool who wants to believe!" She pointed off, agitated.

"And you can't just deny it?"

Celeste glared with rending accusation. "Not without inviting more witch-like explanations."

Xanthe nodded, finally understanding. Celeste was protecting her. It still seemed humorous, but considerably less so. She sat up, cross-legged on the musty carpeted floor. "What do you plan to do instead? Become an amazon? Run away to a circus for real?"

She asked this largely facetiously, but Celeste nodded. "Circus. I got talents. A lot you don't know about."

That had to be the stupidest idea. Worse than any of Celeste's father's. While Celeste often teased others, she wasn't any more prone to wisdom when she lost her own cool. "The Syber Circus is closest. But they're wintering in Warmwell. Plus, the nights are still too long. Getting there on the roads alone, you risk running into a nightmare. A vask. Maybe even grims. Or more likely, run into bandits and wind up a slavewife."

Celeste set her jaw. "I'll chance it."

"No, Celeste. You won't." Xanthe told her flatly. "There's no need. Your dad isn't going cloister you tomorrow. He likely won't at all. He thinks you're a saintess. Can't you, of all people, think of the possibilities?"

"I have to keep saying things I don't believe. Except now, everyone will be watching. They'll know."

Xanthe raised an eyebrow. "Your dad's parishioners are less credulous than he is?"

"I..." Celeste trailed off, uncertain. The answer was clearly no. They believed even more. The blackness in her eyes faded, and she gazed at Xanthe pleadingly. "I can't spend my whole life pretending."

"Not your whole life. Just now," Xanthe counseled. "This isn't the time. You're barely fifteen."

"They'll make me a saint. Put me on a pedestal." Celeste protested. "I don't want that." A thought struck her, and she added as an aside, "I mean, you know. Unless some cute boy is trying to look up my skirt."

This time Xanthe did laugh.

Celeste stomped. "I'm not trying to be funny!"

"I know," Xanthe smiled knowingly. "But think. Only the evilest, hottest, of the bad boys will try to smooch you, you being so holy and all. You might even get your dad to let out early for the Festival, if the spirit of the Creator, for whom you speak, so wills."

That set Celeste to thinking. She bit her lip, squinting in thought. It was obvious she didn't really want to chance her life on frozen roads, in the season when monsters were especially hungry. She wasn't stupid. Just desperate. At last she looked up sharply. "If this goes bad, you promise to help me?"

"I do," Xanthe promised earnestly, though she decided to leave off an oath's traditional ending, '*I vow by the Creator*'. It didn't seem right.

At this, Celeste collapsed onto her huge feather bed in relief. While she stared at the ceiling, Xanthe picked up her room. It was the least she could do. For all Tari's generosity, she was also helping herself, while Celeste had decided to help her just because it was the right thing to do. She really was saintly under it all, though Xanthe didn't voice that for fear of being on the receiving end of a long string of profanities.

When they left, the acolyte was still there. Seeing Celeste though, he rose and quickly walked in their direction. The circular bald spot of his tonsure haircut gleamed in the window light where he intercepted them. His devotion was so intense that his eyes were wet from crying in his prayers. Now though, they held pure adoration. "Greetings, sacred one," he addressed Celeste almost as a personal savior.

Xanthe glanced over and saw her friend gritting her teeth beneath her smile. "Brother Axeman. I hope you've been settling in. We're not as well appointed as Prayerhome."

"I'd rather be here. The news of your miracle spreads like wildfire. Sacred redemption in an evil world."

"It is not *my* miracle," she rebuked crossly. "If you're going to give thanks, you should give thanks to the one who truly healed them, not me." Her eyes made a small flicker in Xanthe's direction.

The acolyte rocked back on his heels, squeezing his Holy Manual in a death grip. "Of course! I am truly corrected." His voice cracked with emotion. "I see now why you were so blessed, child. Anyone else would accept such praise, yet instantly you guide it back to the Creator where it belongs."

Celeste balled her fists but managed to control herself. "You're still doing it. I said, treat me normal. Because I am. I'm going outside into the real world." She moved to leave.

"Yes," the acolyte nodded, again, as another revelation struck him. "Of course! The word of the Holy Creator belongs out among the people, not locked up in the Curate to be visited but once a week."

"Exactly." She brushed on past him without any departing courtesy, clearly furious.

After her own courtesy, Xanthe rushed to Celeste's side as she stalked away, and almost tripped struggling to catch up. "Where are we going?" she whispered when they got out of earshot.

"I need," Celeste replied, striding with dark purpose, "to sin."

## Chapter 6

When Xanthe was younger, her father would take her out into the witchwilds, wandering the many-colored forests of giant violet fronds and fungi. Safe in his shadow, she'd play a game of watching leaves floating down tumbling mountain streams, and for each one, try to guess where they'd end up. Some sank early. Others caught against brambles. Still others swirled in endless eddies or fled at breakneck pace over rocks until they disappeared, maybe all the way to the ocean. Now though, she felt like a leaf. Her whole life had been swirling in an enormous eddy, round and round: sleeping, chores, study, school. Until suddenly, she'd slipped through a whirlpool. Something about the world had changed. She was now rushing down a frothy current of war, witch touch, and stumbling trying to keep up with Celeste's torrid pace. Where was she bound? Glory? Destruction? She couldn't imagine. Did she have any influence in it at all? Her only seeming choice was to abandon Celeste when she most needed a friend, and that was something she would never do.

"Where are we going?" Xanthe asked for the fifth time.

"We're almost there." Celeste's temper had mercifully cooled.

"That's not what I..." her voice broke off. She looked around.

They were in unfamiliar territory. The Storage District. Lumber and coal were packed high on either side of the roadway, and it was lightly trafficked as well. Many people stayed away from here due to persistent rumors that nightmares could fade through the city's walls. Only a handful of free roaming chickens were around, fixing her with suspicious stares. It seemed the ideal place to wind up murdered or raped.

"Here." At the end of an alley, Celeste pulled up in front of a blank wall of peeling stucco with a few abandoned crates lined up against it.

"We're climbing?" Xanthe peered up at the high walls. They seemed insurmountable.

Celeste look a quick look down the alley, and seeing no one, pulled open the side of a large abandoned crate. "In here," she whispered urgently.

Xanthe peered into the inside of the empty box, then back out. Celeste was looking at her impatiently. "You getting in or not?"

"Um, yeah." Xanthe wondered if the box was some sort of secret clubhouse, as if they were nine again. But it didn't look like much fun. It was way too dark inside.

When Celeste got in, she closed the panel behind her, turning the cramped box utterly black. "I've got a lantern in here, though I usually don't use it," Celeste whispered in the utter blackness, as she elbowed her way past. There came a sound of stone scraping, ruffling clothes, and a sudden smell of wet brick and musty air.

A few strikes of flint and a lantern lit. With light, Xanthe suddenly saw that the back board against the wall had not actually been part of the crate, but just laid up against it. Behind was a ragged hole in the stone, barely large enough to squeeze through. It led into a room in which Celeste stood, hovering over an oil-lamp in her underclothes. "Take off your dress. They'll dirty badly."

It was shocking. "How did you find this hole?" Xanthe asked.

"Made it myself," Celeste told her with a note of pride. "With a chisel. Hid the entrance and everything. I've never shown this to anyone else. You're the first. As to where we are, we're between the walls."

Xanthe stared in disbelief. This had to be a place of the ancients, buried right inside Jagerfeld. Stuff in these places could be worth a fortune. Like Horace's wristband. A dozen questions formed in her mind. She almost didn't know where to start.

"You found this? Well... but... Why didn't you tell anyone?"

"So I can be even more famous?" Celeste lifted the lantern. "Nah, I like keeping secrets."

That brought vague concern. Xanthe pulled off her school dress as Celeste suggested and crawled inside. There was a dusty table with a large sink and ancient faucet on which Celeste had put her habit, so she folded her clothes and did the same. While she did so, Celeste pulled the board covering her secret entrance closed. It seemed to be a lab, reeking with ancient technology. "Yeah, but places like this can have blackdust in them." That was an ancient poison of insanity that nothing could cure that sometimes grew on things of the ancients. "You have to be careful."

"I was. First time in, I was nervous too. But don't worry. I looked. By now this place is almost like a second home. My secret hideout."

"Really? Then why run off to join the circus? You could stay here."

In response, Celeste just turned the tap. "No water. No working toilets either, by the way. Besides, I want to see the world. Not be holed up." She then led to the other side of the room where they had to squeeze through some collapsed beams into a ragged carpeted corridor with darkened light fixtures visible through glass. In the lantern light, motes of dust glowed in the air.

"How far does this go?" Xanthe looked through wedged doorways into half-collapsed rooms.

"Quite a way. There's actually this place with a broken ladder that I haven't gone down yet because I don't know if I could get back up."

"Did you find anything? I mean ancient ruins always have something."

Celeste shrugged. "Didn't look. If I did, I'd have to explain where I found it. And the Steeple is already full of broken junk. It hardly needs more." Celeste reached an open panel with wires jutting from it and used it as a ladder to climb the wall up into a false ceiling. This was necessary because the passage through the hall was blocked by dozens of enormous pipes, all collapsed and dusty. "So, no collecting please."

Xanthe followed, wondering even more what she was getting into. It was hard keeping the lantern upright while crawling carefully across musty ceiling boards. When she wriggled through a tight opening to another ceiling space, a small wire sticking out of the crawl-space duct work scraped painfully along her side.

"Creator's dodgy power!" Xanthe cursed, rubbing the scratch.

Celeste turned and sat on one of the small slats that suspended the tiles. "Show me your healing jinx!" she commanded with happy anticipation.

"I can't," Xanthe explained crossly.

"Really?"

"I just can't. It's weird. I lose focus. It's like. I dunno. It's like trying to look behind your eyeballs. Best not to get scratches in the first place." Xanthe scowled, as the ridiculousness of the whole situation struck her. "Why are we here anyway... wherever in hellspace we are? We're not amazons! Boys do this kind of stuff. Not girls."

At this, Celeste feigned shock. "I was pretty sure." She looked down, checking her breast sling. "I mean it sure seems like..." She peeked in her panties. "Nope. Nope. Definitely a girl."

Xanthe pouted. "You're just making fun. Hey wait!" Celeste had already turned away and was heading on, making Xanthe scramble after. "Can you at least tell me where we're going?"

"A place." There was a gap in the tiles with an exposed piece of horizontal pipe. Celeste grabbed it and did a slow-motion somersault over, letting herself down into the corridor below. Xanthe tried to follow, but as she was also handling the lamp, she nearly fell. Celeste caught her shoulder, steadying her.

They were in a larger industrial room, filled with metal. Xanthe didn't even want to think about how much it was worth. Along the sides were ancient dust covered control panels, and in the center, surrounded by catwalks, was a huge rounded cylinder. It looked like a gigantic metallic seed-pod.

"Don't go near that thing," Celeste pointed. "It glows."

Xanthe squinted. The tank was dull gray metal, covered in dust. No light came from it at all. "You sure?"

Celeste added nothing else, but instead moved along the room's edge. She exited through a thick door, on which was a yellow triangle sign hung. It was etched with ancient runes and Xanthe paused to read them. "Celeste? Do you know what radio means?"

"You're asking me? You're the smart one, remember?" She was talking more quietly. The sounds of people were seeping through the walls. "Why?"

"That ancient script. It said 'Danger' and 'Active'. Except it has 'Radio' in front of it. What's that mean?"

"It means stay out of that room. Because it glows. Not nicely either. Kind of like the Creator's Eye. Blue-blue is a scary color."

Blue-blue? That wasn't a color. At least not to normal people. It must have been a phrase Celeste invented for herself to describe things that only she could see. Xanthe knew then that she was confiding her power. Showing off her witch touch. They'd always been friends, but this was a sign of serious trust. Xanthe felt honored by it. It felt good to have someone else to talk to about these kinds of things.

With footsteps crunching on scattered detritus, they reached a dead-end room, one of dozens. It should have been pitch black, but light was leaking through thin horizontal slits in the cold gray walls. The sounds of people were loud here, and Celeste held her finger up to her lips to signal to be quiet. She then padded quietly across to where one was waist high, enough to peer through.

"Where are we?" Xanthe whispered.

Celeste grinned mischievously. "You know the gate where the wall curves in? Where the steam pools are?"

Xanthe thought hard, furrowing her brows. Jagerfeld wasn't like Warmwell, with its volcanic streams everywhere, but it did sport one place near the outer walls. The steam baths were largely used by weary travelers. She remembered the ancients-metal over there in the walls. Impenetrable. Now she was behind them.

Celeste squatted and looked through the waist high slit. "There we go," she declared satisfied. "Look."

Xanthe peered. She blinked, adjusting her eyes to the light, and saw glazed walls. Steam wafted through the air, coming from a large warm pool. Two figures were there. Skin...

...and pulled back rapidly. "Celeste! That's..." she gasped in shock.

"...the men's baths," Celeste finished for her. "In another bell, the farm boys will be coming in to swim. The ground is thawing and they're out there hoeing with pick-axes. They come in all dirty and sweaty."

Xanthe was at once scandalized and embarrassed. Celeste had no compunctions. Growing up with boys nearly made her act like one sometimes. "Spying?!" Xanthe whispered urgently. "How can you do this?"

"I'm naturally curious!" Celeste smiled smugly. "That's what Geral always explained to his girlfriends whenever I caught them." She put her eye against the crack and went back to looking.

"Well, but..." Xanthe sputtered, her voice trailing off. She was first going to argue that ladies didn't do this sort of thing, but as they were here sneaking around in their underclothes, she doubted that tack would work. Or asking if she'd like some boy peeking on her in turnabout, except she had a terrible suspicion what the answer would be. Worse, she felt a terrible curiosity. "Do you see them naked?"

At this, Celeste pouted. "Not directly. They wear loin wear bath-suits. Even in the pool."

"You'd *like* to?!"

"Aren't you curious?"

Xanthe blushed furiously. The way Celeste was just so open about everything, it brought up all sorts of odd feelings she wasn't comfortable with. She whispered tartly. "Of all the things you could be doing with this amazing discovery, and you're just using it to perv."

Celeste was stung but unwavering. "If I told about this place like you want, some fool would end up trying to break open the glowing thing, which I couldn't tell anybody else was glowing unless I showed I was a witch. That would be... hmm... what's the word? Ah yes. Bad. Really bad. And even the ancients agree. Check close and you'll find that everything is lined in ancient metal except that one place I found which was bricked over. They didn't want this found."

Xanthe couldn't think of anything to say.

"So. Sit down. Enjoy the view. We're sinning." Celeste patted the spot next to her as shouts echoed strangely through the walls. Xanthe meekly kneeled. Inside dozens of young men far more scantily clad than was ever considered decent on Jagerfeld's streets, took jumps into the pool and splashed each other. Some roughhoused and wrestled, their chests, legs, and backs showing their thick muscles. Xanthe swallowed, trying not to imagine that in a few years, some boy would be wrestling with her. Except it was true. She wasn't naïve.

Yet at the same time, she didn't see a single boy she liked. Or at least not by just looking at their bodies. This was Celeste's thing. Not hers. And she didn't know what was. In fact, that was the whole problem with the Festival of Favors. She didn't truly *like* anyone. What did she want in a boy? Did she even like boys? She dreamt of them, but they were always faceless – and it was mostly about doing things she didn't want, and she woke just when something was about to happen anyway. It suddenly dawned that on Festival night, she'd be happier just cuddled up with a nice big hardcopy from school, learning something new. Blow off the whole evening. Except then, she'd be taunted over it. And now Tari was depending on her to be Horace's date.

After several minutes Xanthe had seen enough. "Thanks for showing me this," she whispered to Celeste, pulling back. "I'm going to look around."

There must have been something in her voice, for she didn't get any protest. Celeste merely nodded and told her quietly. "Come back if you need me."

Xanthe set off to explore the darkness, wishing that she could have an adventure, instead of her normal boring life. She trod as lightly as she could through half-blockaded portals, over ancient oddments and refuse covered in dust. Ancient materials stood up better than anything, yet time had not been kind here. It was all in poor condition, and obvious that the blockading had been intentional. In the narrow beam of flickering lamplight, she saw decaying beds propped up against doors and huge raking claw-like gouges were sometimes visible in their aged and brittle plastics.

Xanthe paused to examine. Grim marks. Echoes of ancient terror. Even the ancestors had been plagued by them, apparently. A shiver of undeserved fear ran up her back. They weren't here of course. Jagerfeld was always wary. Still, every winter outside the walls, people were caught out by nightmares or monsters, usually farmer boys braving the night when they shouldn't. Nobody talked about it much. There wasn't anyone could do. Grims didn't die. All anyone could do was make them dissipate for a while. It was better to run if you couldn't attack in overwhelming numbers. And even if you could, it was still better to run.

More sunlight. It glared a blinding white through a tiny metal crack at the dead end of a corridor. Curious, Xanthe peeked through, and knew where she was. This was Horse Court. A giant statue of the mythical beast stood as a landmark just inside the main gate. She was behind a recess in the wall, out from which the entrance plaza was clearly visible.

The glare suddenly dimmed. Someone was outside. "...when I do, I'll gut them like fish." A youthful foreign voice penetrated the wall, dark, murderous, and filled with rage. On the other side of the wall, he could not have been more than a foot away.

"Take care," an older man growled in council. "Your blade is thirsty, Damien, as it should be. But discretion and secrecy are still our best weapons."

"No. I tire of hiding. We wait, but then they will die. All of them. The gutters of this innocent little city will choke with their blood."

"That's what we're here for, isn't it?" the older voice chuckled in a genially cruel tone. "Just make sure in your haste, that none of that blood is your own."

Xanthe listened in shock. She almost laughed it seemed so absurd. What was this, some sort of joke? Maybe there was a puppet play on set up on the other side of the wall to entertain children with scary stories, the villain controlled by sticks and wires issuing a melodramatic threat? She looked again through the tiny crease but saw only cloth. It took her a second to understand why. It was a travel cloak. Then it was gone. There were no footsteps. The men walked silently by habit.

Xanthe backed away and tripped on a slightly open drawer sticking out from the ancient remains of a cabinet. She half-toppled over, making a terrible noise. A sudden panic filled her, but she steadied herself. Even if the men heard, they'd have to think the noise came from elsewhere. From outside it would seem like they were in a dark corner against a wall where no one else could hear. Still, she ran back to Celeste as quickly as she could.

"This better be good," Celeste announced upon returning to the spot, annoyed that she was giving up prime viewing time.

"It was right here. Two men. Maybe more. Witchkillers. I'm sure of it. I backed up and bumped into this."

Celeste stared at the wall. Then the cabinet. "Oh! You're right. There *is* something here." She leaned down to the furniture, becoming suddenly interested.

"Not that! The men!"

"And what are we supposed to do, exactly?" Celeste asked as she peered intently at a lower drawer. "You heard two foreigners plotting, didn't even see their faces. And now they're gone."

"We can tell the guard. I know one of their names. It's Damien."

Celeste pulled out a small piece of metal she had hidden in her breast sling and started levering at the ancient furniture's underside. While she did so, she asked conversationally, "And where would you say you were when you overheard them? Here?"

"Um." Xanthe hadn't thought that far. "I guess I could lie."

"You!?" Celeste scoffed. "You're a terrible liar. You know? I'm pretty sure everyone just pretends to believe you out of pity."

Xanthe scowled. "Well, we've got to do something. They're going to kill someone!"

"Of course we do!" On her back now, Celeste poked at the underside. "Catching assassins is gonna be way cool. Hey! How about this? We can chat up lots of Festival boys until you hear their voices again. That'll work. Since they don't know who you are, you're safe. Then you go get the guard and lie that you heard them say what they just said just now."

"You know, that's not a bad idea," Xanthe considered thoughtfully.

"Naturally." Celeste grinned smugly. "Since it's mine."

Xanthe rolled her eyes at her friend. "Oh sure, little miss I'm going to get myself killed running off in winter to join the circus."

Celeste stared up, sourly amused by the jibe. "You didn't used to be such a scaredy."

"There's a difference between scared and stupid," Xanthe told her. "I'm still the girl you used to run with. I'm just wiser now, that's all. No more jumping from towers into rivers."

"Nah," Celeste shook her head on the floor. "You really are different. Know why? You make ugly faces at mirrors, and then don't like the ugly faces you're making. The whole boy-thing is driving you crazy."

"Me, boy crazy? Me?!" Xanthe sputtered. "It's you!" She pointed back in the general direction of the peep hole. "You're the one sneaking around to see them all in their skivvies!" She still couldn't get over her amazement that Celeste was doing that.

"I'm not boy-crazy, I'll have you know." Celeste sniffed with mock offense. She put a hand to her chest. "*I*, my dear, am a boy *connoisseur*."

Xanthe laughed. 'Connoisseur' was one of Mr. Griswold's words of the day. He gave homework assignments to use fancy vocabulary in sentences outside school and report back on how you did. Celeste was going to break up the class tomorrow with that one. "Well miss connoisseur," she grinned, "let's make sure they're in the mood to pick up favors come Festival night by catching these assassins before they strike."

"Now that's the Xanthe I remember," Celeste smiled. There was a small snap where she was fiddling. "There we go. Try opening it now, okay?"

Xanthe pulled, and the drawer rolled open. Inside was pristine. No dust. There was also a box, an ancient design of printed lace and velvet. It had a bright ribbon as well, of pure, almost glowing, red. Yet that was not the strangest thing. Strange geometric patterns of light reminiscent of bismuth pulsed across its surface. It was still active. Almost alive. The patterns seemed to move more quickly now that it was disturbed.

"Creator's holy balls," Celeste exhaled in awe when she stood up. "You *did* find something."

Xanthe mused. She was still the leaf in the mountain stream, tumbling past random events at breakneck speed. First boys. Then killers. Now this. Mystery. The box was mesmerizing. Even reaching out made the patterns change. They flickered near her hands, casting eerie reflections off the walls.

She licked her lips. "So, is your no collecting rule still in effect?"

"I'm thinking," Celeste replied, staring at the box. "First ancient thing I've ever seen that isn't junk. But that's the problem. There's just no way we could show this off without questions."

Xanthe nodded. "We could open it here. Maybe what's inside isn't as obvious."

"Not sure I want to." Celeste stared at it nervously.

"Really?" Xanthe couldn't believe it. "Running away into the wilds doesn't spook you, but some ancient Landing-day present does?"

Celeste stared hard. "This isn't any normal present," she concluded. "It has power. Some flecks in it are blue-blue. Meant to last a long time. No way that was done accidentally."

"This was meant to survive the fall? Come on! How would they even know it was coming?"

Celeste's eyes were an eerie black, yet she was the one discomfited. "I don't know," she whispered.

Xanthe set her jaw. "Well I'm opening it." If she was going to be the old stupid-Xanthe, might as well profit from it. This was a serious find. Just the ribbon alone was treasure. A favor to keep in case Tari wasn't as generous next Festival. Yet when she reached out, she felt hesitant. The patterns on the box flickered near her hands. Celeste was spooking her. But after a moment, she just went ahead.

Music came out of nowhere. *Haaapeee Urrthh Daeee Tooo Ewwwwwww*. Xanthe pulled her hand back in shock, and Celeste squeaked, flinching and retreating.

*Haaapeee Urrthh Daeee Tooo Ewwwwwww*.

"What the ream?" Celeste asked from behind the doorway where she'd jumped.

*Haaapeee Urrthh Daeee. Haaapeee Urrthh Daeee.*

"It's some sort of ancient song." Xanthe explained needlessly, mostly out of nervousness.

"The box is singing?!" Celeste was perplexed. "Balls! It almost sounds like your dad."

That much was true. Although all Scholars cultivated an ancient tongue accent, Xanthe's father was widely known as an absolute expert. Some even joked that he could no longer pronounce some modern words the way they normally were. Due to this, she understood almost all of it. "It's singing happy Earth day, whatever that is."

As she spoke, the box lid slowly opened itself. In the center, there was a sheaf of black cloth, glistening in the dim light. On top was a large card upon which ancient runes glowed.

"What's it say?" Celeste asked from behind the doorway.

Xanthe read the card out loud.

# Childe of Light

*My gift for your 16th Earthday. It is part of me and returns what is due. – Aunt Adrasteia*

*Riftstring is for your friend.*

"Okay. Now we know," Celeste declared. "Ancients weren't just amazing. They were weird."

"I wonder who this was really for?"

"Meh. Who cares? But dibs on Riftstring. Whatever in hellspace that is."

"Hey, no fair! You wouldn't even know about it if I hadn't read this."

"Don't care. Called it. You can keep the cloth for wiping yourself," Celeste claimed smugly.

"Erg. Right. Fine." Xanthe reached out. The fabric was silky smooth yet oddly warm. There was almost a welcoming feeling when she touched it, as if it was reaching for her as much as she for it. Her response was instinctual. A deep chill crawled up her spine. She almost dropped it but decided not to. She rarely got gifts. This would serve well for her birthday, which was coming up. She was summer born. *Then* she would be properly sixteen. Old enough to wed.

"Aha!" Celeste snuck around and grabbed something at the bottom of the box. Triumphantly she held up the small tool in her closed fist.

There was a gleam in Celeste's eye. "Riftstring, eh? This is beautiful."

It was. Strange too. Xanthe couldn't discern its purpose. The pommel was made of a translucent material that gleamed black like polished obsidian, with flickering streaks that shifted and weaved under its surface as Celeste moved it in the dim light. When she held it up to sunlight piercing through a small hole in the wall, a nearly imperceptible break could be seen sticking out from one end. The thread of nothingness made the whole world behind it look as if it had a crack in it.

"Do you see that on the end?" Xanthe exclaimed.

"Of course," Celeste replied. "But don't touch it. It glows blue-blue. Way more than the box and ribbon."

"What do you think it's for?"

Celeste scrutinized. "I dunno. It's insanely heavy. Or seems to be. Except it's not. It's light as a feather twisting it this way. But this other way, it just doesn't move. Maybe it's for the big container?"

Xanthe felt a small pang of jealousy. She quickly suppressed it as she realized that by long settled venturing law, Celeste had rights to everything discovered here. Jumping someone else's claim was not only illegal, but unethical. Still, she was struck by a terrible sense of unease. For no good reason, she just wanted to grab the thing. Not for herself. She just had inexplicable anxiety. As Celeste admired her prize, pulling it about, the under-lighting about the room gave her face an uncharacteristic air of coldness.

Xanthe's own hand unexpectedly slipped. As the fabric fell, she clutched at it and managed to keep it off the floor. This partially opened it, enough so Xanthe could recognize what it really was: a full-length dress, sheer, and of course, black. The color of death.

"That's beautiful too," Celeste admired softly. "You should try it on."

"Not here. It's too dirty. In fact, if I do, everyone's going to know we were somewhere." She quickly gathered it back into its box.

"I've got spongi back where we came in," Celeste told her, referring to the common wet fungi found locally. You couldn't drink their juice, but they were a handy for a hand bath. "I use them to dust off, so nobody knows I've visited."

Xanthe nodded, feeling a bit better. No matter her misgivings about Celeste's find, her friend only pretended to be reckless. She had a strong practical streak that usually kept her out of serious trouble. "Let's go back then. And keep these things. They're small enough to keep concealed."

"Yeah," Celeste agreed. "Then we'll start doing your thing. We'll get these witchkillers in no time."

## Chapter 7

Every day over the next two weeks, Xanthe and Celeste searched dutifully. Up and down they paced Jagerfeld asking strange men their names, a pastime that delighted Celeste nearly as much as it embarrassed Xanthe. Yet aside from Celeste receiving several inquiries about whether she'd be carrying a favor, nothing happened. They found no one, nor was Xanthe exposed herself. People flooding into the city assured that. Everywhere, there were hawkers and entertainers, natives of Thule and true foreigners, wildsmen and highborn. Too big a crowd to pick anyone out in.

People dusted off Festival decorations and Jagerfeld turned into a riot of color. Xanthe's Hood Guild job of delivering packages and mail outside the clockwork pulley system got busy. She even got a few tips. Her dad came home and left so fast she barely had time to say hello. He just gave her a quick peck on the forehead, mumbled apologetically about being busy with repairs, and was gone again. Not that he could have helped anyway. She needed a Festival dress, and dad was hapless with those sorts of things. As she saw how well other girls prepared for the Festival, all the regular fears returned worse than ever. She'd be so ugly dressed in her school project attire that Horace wouldn't even consider picking up her favor.

At least Tari had mostly thrown off her usual melancholy. That helped. She'd never been so generous and was now constantly giving Xanthe small presents and hints on how to appeal to Horace. All seemed to boil down to "act as if you're Praetorian; compliment everything he says and pretend you don't have an opinion on anything". Xanthe now had all sorts of makeups, colored creams, unguents, things Tari's mother had pushed on her, but she didn't care for. The hoard now sat in a big pile in Xanthe's room to apply liberally on the big night. Having no mother or her own to love or hate, she didn't have much experience in makeup. But really, how hard could it be? More had to be better.

Everything was so normal, that she'd dared to hope that the witchkillers had fled, so news of the murder came as an unpleasant surprise. Nadeen, of all people, revealed it. "Ginna didn't elope," she whispered in the looming workshop when they were alone together on Festival-eve. Xanthe was there desperately trying to finish her ensemble, stitching patterned green cloth like mad. "Not even carried off as a bandit bride. She's dead. Got killed somehow. I heard from Dain that Royroy's been asking around about people who saw her last and let slip what happened. He's really broke up and angry."

Xanthe nodded unhappily. Her constant guilt made her try to take responsibility, but she knew it just wasn't logical. She'd done all she could. The odds of finding Damien before he found some random witch girl to murder had always been stacked against them. That was expected. What was surprising was Nadeen. Xanthe could never figure her out. She was in Priscia's clique, but never seemed nasty herself. She just passively followed people around. Ginna was worse. She actively mimicked what she saw, good or bad. She was almost friendly alone but could be a real bitch when around Priscia. Then it hit her. Not could be. *Had been.*

"And this happened when, exactly?" Xanthe inquired heavily.

"Half a season ago," Nadeen explained, surprised at how unsurprised Xanthe was at the news. "Just don't say anything! Royroy told Dain, because he's Dain's best friend. Dain told me because he kind of likes me, but I swore to him that I'd tell no one else, like he swore to Royroy. It's supposed to be a complete secret. Even only a few guards know."

Xanthe resisted the urge to roll her eyes at all the broken promises. "So why are you telling me?"

Nadeen got a pained expression. She put down her casually exquisite needlework and confessed. "Okay, I know Ginna wasn't always nice to you. Maybe Priscia isn't either. But everyone knows you're extra smart. I thought maybe you might figure out who did this and why, you know? It could be us next."

Xanthe heaved a disgusted sigh. "It's harder than it looks. I've been trying to catch them for the past two weeks. It's just that the city's so full, finding anyone is a real pain."

Nadeen's eyes widened in shock. "You already knew?"

"Only the killer's voices. Just not who, when, or where they'd strike." She didn't even bother to tell Nadeen not to tell anyone. It seemed pointless. Ginna was an ideal target too. She'd always gushed about her flashy witch power. She could make her sparks float. Did it all the time.

"How?"

"You're not the only one with secrets," Xanthe declared, but then shut up. It was Festival-eve. These Witchkillers weren't going to be found tonight, and she had other things to do. Her dress still wasn't done. She returned to her spindle, clumsily trying to make thread for the last piece of her ensemble. She'd put off making it until nobody else was around, because it was embarrassing.

While she still didn't have money for slats, she'd found a large sack of grain in the school larder. Taking it wasn't stealing, exactly. She planned to put it all back. She just needed it in a pouch to wrap around her thighs, so they would at least look thick. Then she'd finally have a bun worthy of a highborn. Her own substitute Haunch-cream. Well, okay. Totally fake. But you did what you had to.

Yet Nadeen kept staring. Xanthe felt her eyes on her, waiting, as if looking at her long enough would make her spill. Eventually she gave up.

"You know Xanthe, everybody knows you're weird, but sometimes you're almost cool too. Just find out what happened, okay?"

Then she left, leaving Xanthe not sure what to think. Was that a compliment? There wasn't time to care. It was late. She madly filled and sealed bags, stitching as fast as she could, and raced all the flights of stairs to her room. She applied all of Tari's unguents, perfumes, and makeup as best she could, painting her fingernails different colors. It was hard. It was hard to see well in the cheval glass in her attic. Her only light was the glow of the light from the city below.

She was mid-swipe on her eyelid when the bells began to ring. This was the traditional start of the presentation ceremony, where all the new young women whose sixteenth birthdays were before the next festival came out on stage. *Creator! Late already?* She had to be there. Xanthe rushed to finish her makeup and put on her dress. Once on, the thing was horribly uncomfortable, not at all how she had envisioned it. The ungainly padding threw her off-balance as she hurried downstairs as quickly as possible. At least it *looked* nice. Sort of. She smoothed the grain.

Mrs. Fullbarn was on the bottom floor, carrying a big bag of school laundry. She caught Xanthe as she was running out the door.

"Xanthe!" she welcomed warmly. "I'll be pickin' up your school dress to throw in the tub, just so's you know. It's no trouble at all to add it. Oh! I an' just heard news! Your father is coming back tonight. Somethin' about a present. See him as soon as you can, alright? He needs ya. That man works himself to the bone."

"Yes, Mrs. Fullbarn." When Xanthe instinctively curtsied, she felt a tiny rip. Her eyes bulged. She straightened instantly, hoping with all her heart that it was nothing serious.

"Um...." the teacher looked her over. "Dear. May I fix up your makeup?"

Xanthe was busy and anxious. "The bells are ringing. I don't have time."

"Really. Let me help just a little. Don't ya worry none. Plenty of girls miss the comin' out ceremony."

Xanthe also started feeling defensive. She hadn't done *that* bad a job, had she? Though in truth, Tari's perfume smelled a lot stronger than it had in the bottle. Worse, it was rancid somehow. The odor of what she'd dunked herself with disagreed with her. It was seriously unsettling her stomach.

"Ya jus' don't look like you," Mrs. Fullbarn declared. "Nothin' wrong with makin' yerself pretty, but don't be somethin' you're not. Too much work in it, an' it'll keep ya from findin' yer real match."

"Didn't you say last time that the Festival wasn't serious and that I wasn't going to end up with whoever grabbed my favor anyway? So, what does it matter if I'm fake or not?"

The art teacher grinned with affectionate exasperation. "Just like you dear, ta use my own words against me. But the boy you'll end up with is out there too. So, don't be deceitful in romance. Not worth it."

Xanthe swallowed, her heart felt stabbed from the pain of obvious truth: "I have to. I just don't have the look. I'm smart, blonde, skinny." She stared down. "And the only plumpness I do have is all in the wrong places."

Mrs. Fullbarn tsked. "Everywhere there's fashions. If ya can believe it, Nubians think skinny's prettier than plump, an' girls there stop eating just to be that way! But even where it's normal, I promise there's a boy you'll be flooring. Especially you, my dear. The most critical eyes are always your own, as my mum used ta say. Don't believe 'em. You're drop-dead. It's almost magic more haven't noticed it."

"Magic? You make being beautiful sound like it's a bad thing."

Mrs. Fullbarn nodded knowingly. "You'd be surprised. It's fun fer a while but gets old fast with every other boy makin' a play. The worst part be that there's no escapin' it. No matter what else ya do, how gifted ya be, yer looks are all most people think about. An' boys who'd like ya fer more 'an what ya look like, can't even bring up the courage to approach ya; usually all ye get are the stuck-up ones. But maybe I can do somethin' just for tonight." She looked down. "By the by, what on Haven is going on there?"

This sent Xanthe into a panic. The grain. It weighed on her like a heavy padding of guilt. "Thank you, Mrs. Fullbarn, but everything is A-OK! I don't need any help at all. I've just been using this haunch-cream, and it's like a miracle cure."

"Haunch cream?"

"Um...." Xanthe backed out of the front door. "I really need to go now. I'm late!" She turned and fled.

Hurrying down the steps, she nearly tripped. It wasn't ice. Things had warmed up considerably. Just all the extra weight. She steadied herself and tried to run, except she was hindered by her dress in a way her school clothes and Hood Guild uniform never did. As she dodged through the crowds on her race to get to Founder's Square, she came to the dismal realization that she'd never make it, slackening her pace in defeat.

The square was packed, crowded with people in carnival. Stores were closed but the stalls weren't. Foreign merchants were hawking goods on the streets. Sparklers and glittering festivities were everywhere. Amid the hubbub, many were wearing pretenders' masks, a nod to the Festival of Masquerades that Jagerfeld's sister city of Großhamar would be putting on in two weeks. Yet she didn't know where to go. Her view was blocked. People were just everywhere. She knew where the stage was but couldn't see over people if there were people on it. Doing what she'd normally do to see, shimmying up a light pole or hopping, was out of the question due to her clothing. She just pushed her way there, hoping to find someone. Anyone.

Suddenly, an exotic felinite cat-man chimera, some circus pretender from the far east, spat a plume burning flamedraft into the darkened sky. This surprised her so much that she nearly lost grip of her favor. She fumbled but caught it just in time. This was not the place to drop it. She scanned the area. Not a boy even remotely on her list around. It was all just grownups, a rooster who was eyeing her with interest, and Tari.

Bedecked in a resplendent gown of pink silks and plastic, Tari was on a tall carriage being pulled by a decorated and dyed kranth, waving to the crowd, next to a girl Xanthe didn't know. It was close, so she wended her way through the thick crowds over to her.

"Tari! It's me!" Xanthe called when she got near.

At first Tari didn't notice, but then glanced down. "Oh! There you are!" She gave a relieved smile. "Guess what? Horace asked about you."

"He did?" Xanthe craned her neck up to see her friend, trying as hard as she could not to feel jealous. Tari's beautiful hair was done to perfection, her haunches curvy, not overstated but full, the baroque styling and frills on her magnificent dress. It effortlessly made all her efforts feel second rate. That wasn't even counting the carriage, an ancient's sport vehicle shell reworked in gold trim with new high-wagon spoke wheels made of expensive wood and bronze cladding. No expense had been spared.

Xanthe managed to keep it off her face and Tari didn't notice, seeming particularly animated. "Yeah, he did. Oh! This is Lydia. I'm sorry but we don't have room up here, or I'd give you a ride. Besides, it's dangerous. She's a thrill-seeker. Likes to race."

Lydia did seem more intent on the reins of the kranth than anything else. The girl gave Xanthe a single once-over, then went back to silently staring ahead with a glint in her eye. It was obviously she'd be snapping the whip just as soon as the road cleared.

"That's okay. Um. Where is Horace exactly?"

Tari explained carefully. "He's got a full coach. Enclosed interior. With a driver and everything. You can't miss it. I think it's around Computor street. Just wave them down."

Xanthe nodded. "You're just racing? Not dropping a favor?"

"Oh, no! That's the other news!" Tari broke into one of the first real smiles that Xanthe had ever seen from her. "By the Creator! I'm in love! I think. Anyway, I've found him. The first boy I almost like."

"Oh." *That was quick.* Xanthe assumed it was someone she didn't know. Mrs. Fullbarn's advice on young love came back to her unbidden, but she figured she could be supportive. "Um. Great! When did you meet?"

Tari's half-smile dropped away. "He's a foreigner. But I learned his name from a server, and... oh Xanthe. By the Creator. He is so cute! Dark and dashing! It's like... I was meant for him, you know? Seriously, I can't believe I'm saying this, but I've already decided to drop my favor for him."

Xanthe didn't know what to say, so she fell back on a truism. "Don't count your chickens before they hatch. If he's so cute, you need to do it quick, or else he might be picking someone else's up."

For someone with so many enviable advantages in life, Tari always seemed unreasonably anxious, never more so than now. "I know," she furrowed her brows, "As much as I want, I somehow just don't see him in my future."

This was absurd. "Well, find him and put him there! And get some confidence. Seriously. Remember who you are? Tari of Outlet? Half the boys in the city would love to pick up your favor!"

Her friend gazed down with genuine affection. "You're right. I will. I just have to find him again. I'm sure he's not going to get just any girl. He'll look around first." She shook her head. "Of course not. His standards are too high."

Lydia spared a second stare at Xanthe, this time not bothering to hide how unimpressed she was. From this, Xanthe knew that Lydia was a stuck-up; typical Highcouncil. Lydia also seem disinclined to talk to her, but then her eyebrows furrowed. "Speaking of counting chickens, why do you have so many around you? Are they yours?"

Xanthe glanced down. The rooster she'd seen before, and two hens that were following him, were pecking around her feet. She stared in horror as she saw what they were pecking at. It was her grain. She'd sprung a leak.

She took a deep breath and answered, wide-eyed. "No idea!"

Lydia didn't care enough to press further. Instead, at a break in the crowds, she snapped the whip and urged the kranth forward. The crowds parted, as Lydia kept at it, making it clear she wasn't stopping anymore.

"Bye Xanthe!" Tari waved as the beast started to move off, scraping the stones with its dull claws. "Good luck with Horace!"

"Oh. Sure! Good luck with your guy! Whatever his name is!"

Tari nodded positively as the carriage picked up speed. Above the crunch of wheels on cobbled streets, Xanthe heard her yell out.

"It's Damien!"

Her carriage disappeared down the street.

## Chapter 8

"Get away from me!" Xanthe whispered furiously at the chickens while holding through her dress the piece of padding she thought was leaking. They paid no attention to her words of course, and followed down the alleyway, their interest seeming to be only heightened by the reduction in feed. Each single grain trickling out of her dress resulted in a mad clucking scramble to be the first to peck it up. It almost seemed a contest between them, and they were having a most excellent time.

She'd come this way hoping to catch Lydia racing back on empty streets, but there was no sign of them. A pang of guilt struck her, which made no logical sense. She wouldn't have been able to catch up even if she hadn't been weighed down by her dress. She didn't even know what to do if she did. With *her* luck, this Damien jerk would already have Tari's favor and kiss, and she'd not believe her. Or maybe she would, and it was all just a case of innocent mistaken identity, there being two people of the same exact names, but it would damage their friendship forever. Or maybe this was the real plot. Tari really would marry him, and she would be spending the rest of her days watching as he used the power of the Outlets to make innocent Jagerfeld choke with blood. Xanthe grit her teeth. The possibilities were endless.

She reached Bastion Lane, a considerably less crowded street. The distant sound of music could be heard, but there were couples and wandering partygoers making conversation. As she crossed the street, Xanthe saw a farm wife drop a small white cradle-lily in front of a man escorting her. The girl feigned it to be an accident, but it was clearly planned, and quite foreordained. She was about nineteen, already sporting a marriage braid, and heavy with child. Her husband only pretended to be surprised at the flower's drop, but then actually was, as she focused on the flower and it began to glow. He picked it up gallantly, returned it to her, and they kissed. They then strolled off together, utterly content.

So reaming simple, Xanthe wanted to puke. She really did feel queasy too. Tari's perfume hadn't faded. It was getting worse. She turned back to face the rooster. "Probably you're going to be my only escort this evening. Especially since I seem to be dropping favors for you."

The rooster cocked its head, clucking a masculine "Per-curr?" at her, sounding confused at her change in tone. Xanthe turned and stalked off. The whole evening was ridiculous. All this build up for what was supposed to be such an amazing party, her teenage coming out, and the only people finding romance were those who didn't need it. She couldn't imagine anything worse than being judged by hundreds while you tried to find a date, but that's what this all was. Hopefully, Horace would be better.

A group was ahead. A gaggle of girls. Huddled together, most with pretender's masks, all Xanthe could see of them were their hand stitched finery. There were foreigners too, further away in a group talking together. Xanthe did a double-take. One of them was a boy, incredibly cute with rare black hair, if scruffy and a wallflower. Were all outland boys like this? She wondered. If there were one good thing she'd got out of this whole misadventure, setting her sights beyond her hometown for a boyfriend was a good lesson to learn, when she was ready to actually have one.

She was so distracted by him that she failed to notice who the girls were until she was nearly right on top of them. Then she recognized a voice. *Oh, son of a ...* Of all the luck. It was Priscia's little clique.

"What do we have here? Xanthe?" Sepia called out.

The gaggle turned to face her, some lowering their masks. Priscia was dressed in a ballgown that for all its frills, somehow seemed cheap: silver chains on top of a garish neon gold lamé. In a stylish embroidered lavender crinoline, Nadeen was talking in low concerned whispers to Priscia. Janyce hung back. It was Clarice and Sepia who turned forward, giving false smiles filled with malice.

"My, that thing you're wearing..." Sepia sneered unctuously, "...did you make it yourself?"

"I did," Xanthe answered forthrightly, measuring the girl up. If Celeste were a connoisseur of boys, Xanthe figured herself to be a connoisseur of bullies, Priscia at the top. In comparison, Sepia just fell short. Literally. She was a full head below in height. It was like having a fourth-grader try to cut on you. Xanthe just couldn't take it seriously.

Sepia was trying anyway. "Well that dress. Amazing what you did with it! So natural – like you dredged out of the forest."

"Why thank you," Xanthe replied, unfazed. In truth, green wasn't her favorite color, but the cloth print was what the school had. She felt lucky to even get that, and it wasn't that bad. Its irregular leaf pattern did much to disguise her poor needlework.

Sepia's smile faded slightly. "That wasn't supposed to be a compliment."

"I didn't take it as one," Xanthe remarked dryly, as if to a child. Some of the girls seemed amused, and not at her expense. So, for once, she went on. "Aren't you supposed to have a chaperone tonight?"

Two girls openly laughed as the jibe hit home. Sepia seethed. She wasn't truly underage, she just seemed it. But her underdeveloped build obviously bothered her terribly, and the turnabout was unnerving her. Sepia's face twisted. She was clearly struggling to come up with some deadly insult that would redeem her in the eyes of her friends.

Again, it struck Xanthe how easy it would be to worm her way into the embrace of Priscia's towner girls, climbing their social hierarchy by cutting others down. But she couldn't. It wasn't as if bitching on people was hard. She just didn't enjoy it. Couldn't respect it. It felt wrong. She'd been too often on the other side. Even here, she found herself oddly sympathizing with Sepia, so decided to reach out. She told her tiredly, "It's stupid wasting time trading insults, so lemme just help you win. This is where you call me a sewer-girl because my dad figures out ancient plumbing systems so all our toilets flush. Now go pretend you've made me all sad, so you can run off and feel better about yourself, even though you don't have a boyfriend either." She waved her off dismissively with the back of her hand, to get her out of her face.

It seemed like a fairly good way to end the confrontation, but Xanthe got an unexpected reaction. The girls howled as if she'd unleashed the worst beat down in the history of Jagerfeld. Now it was Sepia who was near tears. Xanthe rolled her eyes. Sometimes she just didn't understand people.

As she started to move past, Priscia stepped forward, her eyes focused on her favor, the glass rose. "That's pretty. Where'd you get it?"

Xanthe saw no reason to lie. "Tari gave it to me."

Priscia grit her teeth. Her own favor was surprisingly poor given how much silver she had. There was a strangely deflated attitude about her as well. "Trying for a Highcouncil boy?"

"Maybe. Maybe one will take me up to the district tonight. Right around Tari's house." Xanthe jutted out her chin. Her sympathy only went so far.

Priscia sneered slightly. "If they do, you'll regret it in the morning. Especially tonight."

Now this. This was classic Priscia. The rest of the girls sniggered at what she was intimating, what kind of girl she was saying Xanthe was. Even as Xanthe grew enraged, there was a part in the back of her mind that couldn't help but admire her antagonist's sheer talent at put downs. What really put it over was her stare. As if this were a real warning, not the lowest form of insult.

"I'll be sure to keep my honor," Xanthe stated through grit teeth. "Noble boys are called that for a reason."

At this, Priscia just broke into a dark mocking laughter.

"We'll see," Xanthe continued. "By the end of tonight, the most noble boy in this whole city will be hold my favor. He will kiss me. Nothing more." This was pure bravado. Deep in her heart she knew nothing remotely like that would happen, no matter how fervently she wished it would.

"No he won't!" Sepia's voice came from the side. Suddenly her hand was in front of Xanthe face, and there was a blinding flash of light. Her favor was hit. Hard. It fell from her grasp.

Xanthe blinked. She couldn't see. All she saw was spots and a large hand-shaped spot smearing across her vision, fingers visible. Everything else was black. "My favor!" she yelled. The other girls screamed too, incoherently. The chickens clucked madly. She knelt as best she could to try to find it on the ground but found nothing.

Gradually her eyesight returned. The girls were huddled against the wall. "Where is she?!" Xanthe screamed, angrier than she'd ever been in her whole life. Clarice pointed down the street. Half a block away, Sepia was waiting for her gaze. She had a triumphant smile on her face and showed her hands. They were empty. She jeered in Xanthe's direction, and ground her right fist into her left palm, twisting it back and forth. An unmistakable hand-gesture: "ream you".

Xanthe madly searched the distance between her and Sepia with her eyes. It hadn't been that long, and Sepia's dress had no pockets, so she must have dropped it. But where? Xanthe couldn't see it anywhere. In despair, she turned back to the remaining girls. "Okay. There's no way all of you were blinded. You have to tell me where she put it."

"I'm sorry, Xanthe," Priscia said with mock unctuousness. "But I was just so *utterly* unable to see. You know, that witch touch of hers is super brilliant. I mean, I'm sure none of us know where it is, right?"

Clarice nodded at once, as did a couple of other girls whose names Xanthe didn't know. Then Janyce, though she wasn't comfortable. At last, Xanthe's eyes settled on Nadeen.

Nadeen was particularly unhappy. She glanced back and forth between Xanthe and Priscia, not at all enjoying being asked to choose between them. "Come on, Nadeen," Xanthe cajoled. "You know that wasn't right. That was way over."

Xanthe wasn't sure she could dare herself to hope. But Priscia's stare hardened at Nadeen's wavering, and she wilted under it. Nadeen stared down, and without saying a word, shook her head. Then she turned away. She couldn't bear to face Xanthe.

Priscia turned on Xanthe and sneered smilingly. "Really, Sepia did you a favor. Kept you out of trouble." She looked her up and down. "Lumpy, stinky, clown." She turned and led her gang away.

Xanthe was left all alone in the alley.

## Chapter 9

It was a waste of time to search. The area was too big for one person. She could spend the whole night trying to find the favor searching alone. She needed a friend to help. A real one. That is, if she had any available, which she didn't.

At that thought, she almost started to cry. But she grit her teeth and by sheer force of will, stopped. She held her head in her hand and focused with shuddering breaths. It was not going to happen. She wouldn't let it. She wouldn't give Priscia the satisfaction, even if she wasn't here.

She drew shuddering breaths. Breathe. Breathe.

Up the street there was crowd noise, so she walked in that direction, her chickens following in solemn procession. She ended up on Aristolus street outside a tavern, filled to overflowing with people. A couple of boys noticed her, but as she obviously wasn't holding a favor, their interest waned.

In the low hubbub, she recognized a marginally familiar voice. "Young miss. Young miss!" An acolyte in a gray vestment approached from down the street, his robes tied with a rope belt.

"Brother..." Xanthe struggled briefly with her memory.... "Axeman?"

"Indeed!" The acolyte from the church was pleasantly surprised at the recognition. "You are the friend of holy Celeste, are you not?"

She nodded, wondering what sort of trouble Celeste had gotten into now.

"Perhaps you might have seen her?" He asked hopefully. "I was supposed to be chaperoning, but I'm afraid I lost her in the crowd. I curse myself for doing so. Curse my weakness."

As if he stood any chance. "No. I'm sorry." Celeste was her friend and didn't want to be found, so Xanthe thought of the furthest place away to send him. "Maybe the gate district," she said morosely.

He seemed disappointed, but then grew concerned. "Child? Is there something the matter?"

Xanthe knew then that she couldn't hide her feelings, so beckoned him to the other side of the street. She didn't want the boys to hear. "My favor was stolen. A girl didn't like me, and she blinded me with a flash, and now I can't find it."

The acolyte's eyes blazed. "A flash? Someone used iniquitous power upon you? Harming an innocent?" His voice grew sanctimoniously stern. "By the Creator, who is this dreadwitch?"

"Doesn't matter. Punishing someone else won't get my favor back."

He smiled consolingly. "Dear child, I see why you and Celeste are friends. Such a gentle flower of femininity in the Creator's sight, you instinctively avoid conflict, knowing your proper place within the world. Yet you should reveal those who injure you. Witchery is a grave sin.

Demonic. The touch of Earth's evil. Dreadwitchery to harm another is ten times that sin! Unforgivable."

In truth, Xanthe wasn't feeling particularly forgiving. Sepia could rot in hellspace so far as she was concerned. Still, getting her in trouble with the Curate just didn't feel right. Not with her own troubles in that direction. "Maybe later. I just need my favor right now. Can you help me find it?" She put her hands together and begged plaintively.

"If but only I could," he apologized. "Yet I too am searching for what I lost. I must find the holy daughter. She could be in grave danger."

"From what? An assassin?"

His eyes widened in shock. "By the Creator's realm no! What makes you say that?"

She let out her breath. "A girl in my school disappeared. We thought she'd eloped with some boy, but now think there's a witchkiller that might have got her. Maybe we'll all die the same way. I don't think they're picky." Xanthe didn't know why she'd just divulged, but it made her feel better. Not all clergy were bad. They were just close-minded.

Brother Axeman didn't even seem to be that. Rather than taking offense, his face turned grave. He patted her shoulder reassuringly. "You have nothing to fear, dear child. They may make mistakes, but all faithful try to protect innocents, not bring them harm. So never fear being strangled, fear only for your soul. The Creator's greatest gift – free will – allows us to fall." He looked off in worry at the revelers. "And I'm in terror some eldritch coven will seduce Celeste from her saintly path."

"No chance of that," Xanthe remarked dryly, and added with resignation, "I suppose we both have troubles we cannot help each other with. I do thank you for listening. Creator's blessing upon you." The chickens clucked as if in agreement.

Brother Axeman nodded at the dismissal, turning as if to leave, but a thought struck him. He turned back, retrieved a silver chain from his pocket and held it open in his palm. "Perhaps I can. Substitute this for your stolen favor. It may not be quite respectable, but any decent young man should see past that."

"I..." Xanthe looked up. "You mean it?"

He nodded. "Please."

Her eyes welled. Only now did the tears come. Someone had helped her. "I.... I'll return it after the boy gives it back."

"No," he spoke earnestly. "Please do not. I've grown disenchanted." He had an odd, pensive expression. "Creator's truth be told, you given unto me the perfect excuse to be rid of it. It's weighed like a rock on my soul. Just do me the favor of not selling or showing it off. It deserves quiet rest on the skin of a sweet and proper girl such as yourself."

On closer examination, Xanthe recognized the glittering silver as a chestlet: lady's jewelry which when worn, had a chain that wrapped from the back under the arms and over one's bare breasts, dangling a pendant in one's cleavage. This one bore an upside down looped cross, the holy symbol of the Curate. It was surprising to see. Until they graduated fully into the priesthood, acolytes were not allowed to be distracted by even chaste forms of romance. She had no idea who had given him such an intimate piece, or who he'd bought it for, but her every guess gave her reason not to pry.

Instead, she hugged him. "I will. Thank you."

"No, dear child. Thank you." He returned an awkward pat on her back, stared momentarily away, and retreated.

When he'd fully left, Xanthe wiped her eyes and walked on, clutching the favor. It really wasn't the best, she thought at first. but reflecting further, reconsidered. If Horace saw her with some super fancy favor, he'd know that Tari had set him up, which might put him off. The chestlet looked more like something she could have come up with herself. Strangely, many boys didn't seem to care as much as they should about favors. As her classmates related, you spent all this time getting just the best one, showing it off to all your friends, and then the boy barely admired it before jumping right into the kissing.

She set off to find Horace's wagon. It had been years since she'd been let out on Festival night, not since she'd been a little girl. She marveled. All the foreigners, so exotic and interesting! They, in turn, marveled at the city. Jagerfeld wasn't merely well preserved, awash with reclaimed ancient materials, it had its own Mechanix traditions of torque and chain technology. She saw strangers pointing up at the trolley system strung along the narrow meandering streets under the store awnings that delivered goods to higher level flats. It was charming that such a common thing was the source of such amazement.

"Zees is strange. Commandair Javan sends us to patrol zhe merchants? Zhere is no trouble 'ere."

The voice caught her attention. Two guards in colorful regalia were talking as they strode up the crowded street. It took a second to recognize the voice. She whipped her face away from them as soon as she did. They were the two mercenaries who knew about her witch power. Her eyes bulged, and she edged around the corner between two stalls, but then found her way blocked. There was no way through. Only the locked doorway of a shuttered house.

"He schemes, yes? Yet truly Claude, I am not caring why." The large one sighed morosely.

"Oh, do noht speak zees way," the other cajoled. His voice dropped low. "The Lord. 'e will provide."

Xanthe kept her back to them, and nervously pretended to examine the oil-torches and purple football fruit laid out as merchandise on a nearby stall. They were right behind her, nearly breathing down her neck. While she did so, her mind raced. Which lord they were speaking of? Their prince? He was dead. Maybe another one?

"How? We lost. We fail. What have we left?"

"We can find zees witch girl from the church. We are garrison now. Eet is only a mattair of time."

Xanthe froze. Hackles ran up her neck. They were talking about her. She suppressed a sudden urge to bolt. Dressed as she was, she knew she couldn't get away if she did.

"What are all zees chickahns doing 'ere?"

"Maybe we buy?" The Lukomoryen stated. "I like eggs."

"Zhey 'ave bands. Someone owns zhem. You theenk zees girl over zhere, she knows?"

The other made a noncommittal grunt. "We ask, yes? Hey." He called in her direction. "Gurl. Gurl?"

Xanthe heart raced as their attention shifted to her. She was trapped. She didn't know what to do. All she could, was to keep pretending that she didn't hear. Maybe they would think she didn't understand common.

"Zees is strange. Pair'aps she is deaf?" She heard the footstep of one of them moving towards her. With her back turned, she didn't know which. Her body ached to run, but she couldn't.

A call came from down the street. "Thief! Bandit!" Xanthe resisted the urge to turn. The voice sounded familiar. It was Celeste.

Immediately, shop keeps around the busy street moved forward in front of their tables, ready to intercept anyone who might try to snatch their wares. The two guards' attention turned that way as well, and they headed quickly up the street towards the call. As soon as they were gone, Xanthe turned up the other way. She hoped Celeste was okay but needed to get out.

Two blocks away Xanthe ducked into a narrow alley and collapsed into a trembling ball, on an apartment's porch. She swallowed and breathed heavily, her heart beating faster than at the end of a heavy delivery run. That was too close. She felt a need to vomit but kept it down. Instead, she just clasped her shaking hands together, and searched for any sign of pursuit. It wouldn't be hard. The trail of grain she was leaving had grown steadier. She sat for minutes trying to collect enough courage to get going, though started to wonder if there wasn't real wisdom in Priscia's hateful advice. Just leave now. Go home.

"Xanthe!"

"Aah!" She yelped in surprise.

It was Celeste, who'd snuck up silently from the other direction. "Boo," her friend grinned impishly. She was in her habit still but had tucked its right hem up to her waist, bar-wench style, to show most of her leg.

"Don't *do* that!"

Celeste let out a broad laugh. "But it's so much fun!"

"Not to me," Xanthe nearly sobbed.

"Oh, Creator's balls! Don't worry. Guards are easy enough to trick. I just told them a thief snatched my favor from my hand. Gave them a description, and they're now off to find him."

"A favor? Celeste, are you trying to get a boy? If Brother Axeman catches you, he'll be raging. I sent him away, but you know he's looking."

"I do," she grinned evilly. "Who do you think I just described as the thief?"

Xanthe shivered, irritated rather than amused. "This isn't funny. It's scary. They really almost caught me."

"Nah. With all that paint you got on? They wouldn't know it was you if you told 'em. So come on! Lighten up. Isn't the Festival cool?"

Xanthe whimpered, utterly dejected. "No. I'm having the worst time. I put on padding, which I'm sure your eyes can see. It's leaking. My favor was knocked from my hand and stolen. I got a new one – but from the guy you just did your practical joke on, so I'm feeling guilty. Now I'm supposed to meet Horace, but I can't find him. I think the only good news is that things could not possibly get any worse."

"Oh, but they will if you jinx yourself like that! Except now that I mentioned the jinx, I de-jinxed you."

Xanthe wasn't in the mood. "You know we're not ten anymore. Right?" She asked sourly.

"You bet I do!" Celeste agreed with sudden happy interest, as her attention shifted down the alley. Xanthe followed her gaze and saw two decently cute boys walking past. "But that's my trouble to get into. You need to find Mr. Archangel."

"He's not that..." She hissed at the truth. Okay, well yes. Horace wasn't handsome. Or nice. But helping Tari made it worth it. Besides, having the richest boy of the most powerful family in town returning her favor would do wonders for her social standing.

"Well, I don't care. Hellspace, with what I owe you, the least I can do is tell you where to go." Celeste thumbed back down the alley. "He's doing a carriage promenade near Wall street."

"You owe me?" Xanthe wondered. "I haven't done anything."

"Heh. So you think." With a card-shark's flair, Celeste twirled her hand, and produced the obsidian rod that they'd found between the walls. "You got me Riftstring. Now I know what she does."

An uneasy feeling twisted somewhere in the back of Xanthe's head. Maybe she should be more worried about this than any of her other petty concerns. But she was still a researcher's daughter, and curiosity won out. "What?"

"First, by turning this, I can defang her. That's how I keep her now, so I can hold her safe. Second, when she's fanged," she turned her wrist around the rod and pulled down, "I can do this." After making some odd turns to get it going in the right direction, she drew a brick sized scoop along the corner of one of the concrete awnings.

Xanthe squinted. "Is this like something only your eyes can see?"

"Not quite." She grabbed the stone between where she'd moved the rod, and a good-sized chunk of granite slid out, smooth as glass.

Xanthe stared. "It cuts stone?!"

"She cuts *everything*," Celeste declared. "Even Ancient's Metal slides apart like butter. Not much resistance either."

"I see," Xanthe breathed. She watched as Celeste carefully replaced the stone, trying a few times to get it back in, since it was such a tight fit.

"She also talks. Kind of. I had this strange dream. She told me she 'Guarded a Planck gate, drawing the projection of a string from an adverse volumetric brane, thereby causing a localized expansion in the charm and strange dimensions, spreading the directionality of the electroweak force to dramatically lower its adhesion along our manifold'. I don't know dung about what that ancient incantation means, but I memorized it all just in case you did." Celeste lovingly put the black device back into her pocket.

"I don't." Xanthe was wide eyed. Hackles rose on her back from an entirely different sort of fear; it seemed like she was becoming a connoisseur of that as well. "Celeste, I... I don't think this is a good thing to be messing with. It just feels like it could be really bad."

"Why?" Celeste was not merely curious, but defensive.

"Don't you think ancient artifacts talking in your dreams might be just a little weird? And scary?"

"What's it gonna do? Give me a nightmare?" She grinned carefree. "That demon stuff is such dung."

Xanthe didn't have an answer, so she just shook her head. Celeste was at least partly right. The Curate called absolutely everything it didn't like "demonic". After "Creator" it was their most well-worn word, and long ago made meaningless through overuse. Sassing a grownup? "Demonic". But if anything might live up to the liturgy, it would be this. The Holy Manual had many fanciful tales of evil spirits that haunted holy technology before the Creator depowered the world as punishment. The Five and the Eight.

Celeste swiveled her head around. "Seriously, Xanthe. If I wanted to worry, I'd wonder why so many guys are carrying."

Celeste was right. Armed young men were everywhere. Easily explained though. "They're just wildsmen," Xanthe explained. "We got a lot this year, is all." The Festival always attracted young men from the deep wilds, who carried weapons like a security blanket. For good reason.

"Way too many." Celeste declared suspiciously. "I know they're always twitchy, but I smell something. Not sure what."

Xanthe did. There would be a fight somewhere. There always was on Festival. Some dumb young punk would talk crap to some other dumb young punk and end up dying with a spear in his gut. Not something she could do anything about though, unless she herself wanted to burn. Just thinking about it put her in a bad mood. "Fine. Whatever. Just show me to Horace. Hopefully my thighs will still be plump when I get there."

"Try not to get too close," Celeste smiled knowingly. "Your ruse won't pass even the slightest feel."

Xanthe drew herself up. She expected this from Priscia. Not Celeste. "What kind of girl do you think I am?"

"Someone who thinks girls can always keep boys from copping feels," Celeste laughed. "But if it's Horace you want, Horace you'll get." Her manner left no doubt of her opinion of Xanthe's decision.

Xanthe nodded like I soldier. "I do." Time to do this favor thing and get the whole evening over with.

Shaking her head and smiling, as if she were humoring Xanthe's intent to waste her evening, Celeste led her straight to where she needed to go.

## Chapter 10

Wall Street was not the prettiest of neighborhoods. It was industrial: full of warehouses and cranes for lifting things into the torque driven clockwork delivery systems. Its only attraction was the width and smoothness of its streets, which made it ideal for promenades and racing. Exactly what Xanthe saw when she arrived. A dozen young Highcouncil boys jockeyed about in various types of carriages. The most opulent were pulled by kranths, the rest, by dogs. They showboated back and forth or occasionally briefly raced a half-block, cutting each other off in playful rivalry. They enjoyed themselves immensely, as a small crowd of hopeful girls watched about the edges, fussing with their favors and primping, hoping for a permanent seat on board.

The largest was a full kranth coach. Done up in resplendent opulence, it was lined with gold, copper, and plastics, in an overwrought style clearly designed to highlight the owner's status. Like all the most expensive of vehicles, it was also fully enclosed with a servant outside to chauffeur it. This was the fashion among mayoral houses in the south, not just to ward off road dust and weather, but also assassins. When she peered closer, she saw that the chauffeur was Royroy. He was dressed in a different uniform than the last time she'd seen him. Purple and gray, Wormwood colors.

"That's got to be Horace's coach. It's certainly gaudy enough," Xanthe spoke behind to Celeste who she thought was still behind her, before she realized that she'd already left. No matter. Time to get this over with.

Screwing up her courage, she just walked over to the back where it was parked, waving up at Royroy. He blinked in recognition and then opened his mouth as if to say something. But before he did, she lifted her hand to the golden-gilded door of the coach and knocked.

"Um. He may not answer," Royroy told her. "He's waiting for someone. Oh! And I got this other thing to talk to you about." As he spoke, the door peeked open briefly, then swung wide.

Horace had toed open the door. Inside he was sprawled out laying on one of the coach's two opposed satin couches. He was slightly disheveled in his finery, with an arrogant smile, and more than a little drunk. "Who are you?"

"I'm Xanthe. From Tari's party. Remember?" Already she knew this wasn't going well.

He furrowed his brow for a moment before having a brief flash of dim recognition. "Oh, yeah! That's right! The middle-merchant girl who goes to school. Yeah! Come on in."

Xanthe stood there, unsure what to do. This wasn't how things were supposed to go. A favor drop was supposed to be outside. That was traditional. You dropped it on the street and he picked it up. Didn't he know how it went? Doubts flooded back. Maybe he didn't want her. Maybe she wasn't good enough for this. She dug her toe into the street and twisted it. "I was hoping maybe we could go for a walk."

"Well, listen, you got to wait. I got this thing. Uh. No! Sure. Come inside here, girl. Seriously."

"Um, but... but... that's not really proper." It really wasn't.

Horace gave a sloppy grin. "Says who? Come on. I got drinks in here. Try some!"

She was torn, but didn't see any harm in it, since it sounded like he was going to pick up her favor later. That was way more attractive than drinking. Her dad had let her try some once. It was nasty.

Getting in was proving difficult. Her padding was sagging, and she felt the stitching getting even looser, so she stuck her hand discretely under her thigh to help lift it up. Yet in so doing, her foot snagged her dress, leaving her awkwardly balanced on the step rail, and she tripped almost falling backwards. To save herself, she grabbed madly at the coach door and it rocked back like a teeter-swing. This left her hanging, almost upside down, clinging to the door handle with her feet propped up in the entrance.

Horace started laughing, deep from the belly. He was clearly enjoying watching her flounder. Xanthe figured she didn't have much else to lose, so rather than let herself drop down onto the dirty pavement, she just started using her feet to pull her legs into the floor of the coach's interior. When she wriggled her hips in she managed to grab the edge of the doorway to pull most of her weight inside. Then it was a simple matter of squirming around to end up on the floor.

"Oh, you're cute like that." He smiled with frank appraisal, exactly the way the farm boys had, then added, "but you should be on your knees. Much better that way."

Xanthe clambered onto the seat facing him, and sat, breathing heavily. She could not imagine a more inelegant entrance and wondered if she'd already blown it. Yet Horace was in such a good mood it didn't seem to matter. He also didn't notice that her padding was fake. Another terrible fear.

"Here. Have a drink." He turned and started rummaging about in a mixer bar built-in to the coach. Everything inside the coach was lined in satin. Even the built-in snow-box.

"Who are you waiting for?" She asked, trying to make conversation.

Horace turned suspiciously. "No one. Who told you that?"

"Eh. Royroy. You know? Your driver?"

"Oh! Yeah. Right." He relaxed and nodded. "That guy. Gotta tell 'im not to open his mouth so much."

Xanthe nodded absently, remembering Tari's admonition that Horace liked people to tell him how good he was. "Oh, that's totally wise of you and everything!"

"Innit?" He turned smug at the validation. "So, you're like Tari's friend?"

Xanthe nodded. Stellar, conversation this wasn't. But whatever. "We go to Scholars School together."

"Yeah. School. Don't do that. Got me a private tutor," Horace explained expansively, resuming his effort to find just the right bottle. "My guy's smart, you know? But not like me. Not canny. That's why I'm where I am. Going higher. What does smart get you? Not this." He waved around. "I just know how to get what I want. Make things mine. Guys are all jealous of course. But they're just losers. Try to cheat me, and it still don't matter. I keep 'em down, easy. Girls like you? You all want to find the best, like glowmoths to nectar. You like winners, and here I am. I win cause I know what it takes. Real leaders go with their gut. Gut don't lie. That's why I just use brain guys for answers, when I even need 'em. Which I mostly don't."

Xanthe was beginning to understand the reason for Tari's disdain. As she once again mutely nodded, there was the sound of scraping kranth nails and wagon wheels on pavement. Another coach came into view, visible through the open door. This one was of foreign make, black, glistening, and extended. It resembled nothing so much as a fancy hearse.

"Should I go?" Xanthe asked.

He considered for a second. "Nah. No need." Then added, "See? Right there. That's a gut decision."

"Wow." Xanthe couldn't think of anything else to say.

The door of the other coach opened. It was too dark to see inside, but she could see two silhouettes. A thin one that bore a cane whispered to the other dark shape, who promptly exited. When he got out, she saw a short, ugly, scarred man in dark leathers. He had a wide-brimmed leather hat and was carrying several wicked half-swords. Only after wary surveillance of the square, did he cross the short distance between the two coaches, stopping short at the threshold of Horace's door.

"Who's this?" He fixed Xanthe with a stare. His voice was not overtly threatening, just all business.

"A girl. Worried?" Horace asked smugly.

The man's gaze turned back. "There's a difference between work time and play time." His eyes were dead. He had coldness to him Xanthe had never felt in anyone before. She wouldn't have been at all surprised if he were Damien or his friend, except the voice didn't match at all.

Horace's entire manner was dismissive. "Don't worry, pal. I keep my ends of deals."

"That's smart of you," the man growled without emotion, viewing Horace as if he were an inanimate object. "Keeping your bargain means you won't get a message too."

"Me... too?!" Horace immediately turned jealous. "Wait! You're doing a deal with someone else?"

The swordsman was taken slightly aback. "Not," he paused awkwardly, "a good kind of message." He took on a tone as if explaining to a child. "A weapons dealer started making threats about needing to be paid, far too soon. We're helping him understand that this is not a game."

"Ohh," Horace nodded. "Heh. Yeah. Knew that, course. No game. Right. I'm just, like, you know. Drunk."

Xanthe didn't know exactly what they were talking about, but assumed it was the kind of realpolitik she'd always thought went on in Highcouncil. Except seeing it directly left her feeling underwhelmed. She'd always imagined the high-mayors of the realms, the princes, and even kings, had a certain theatricality. With sweeping cloaks and dramatic poses, they stood astride the kairn-dragons of history, their every action filled with meaning and portent; even the villains among them possessing a certain style as they plotted their dark designs upon one another. This, on the other hand, was just plain dumb. Even Priscia put more thought into it, and she was just a towner girl.

Evidently the man sensed it as well. His dark intimidation was no match for Horace's youth, tipsiness, and belief in his own invincibility. Xanthe was the only one scared and she didn't count. "Back to the point. I came here to tell you that our friend thinks this is so important, that he's decided to make an appearance himself. Do not disappoint in the slightest. He will be judging you."

"Oh?" Horace sobered at the news. "Yeah. Thanks. I'll be all cleaned up."

The man seemed less annoyed now that Horace had changed tone. "As you will then, young lord. I leave you to your... entertainments." He then backed out and closed the carriage door behind him.

"Dung." Horace said after a few moments. He then closed the mixer bar and squinted in thought.

"Um... Horace?" Xanthe ventured. "What have you got yourself into?"

"Not your worry, baby," he replied dismissively. "But I gotta be quick. Gotta be cleaned up."

"You just said that."

"Oh. Yeah." Then he grabbed the coach's speaking tube and yelled into it. "Hey driver! Take us to the Storage District."

After a moment, the coach lurched and Xanthe was jerked slightly. She was also confused. The Storage District? It wasn't far, but it was the least romantic place she could imagine. Not that she terribly minded. She wasn't interested in romance at this point. All she wanted was for Horace to pick up her favor, maybe with a witness, give him a smack and go home. The more she thought about it, the less she wanted anything to do with whatever this business he was in. With her luck, she'd have Horace pick up her favor, but then have no way to prove it after he got himself knifed doing shady deals with weapons merchants aiming to make a killing off the war brewing in the Holy Lands.

It wasn't long at all before jostling of the coach stopped. Neither of them had spoken. Things had become awkward.

"Should we be going for the walk now?" Xanthe asked.

"Wait a second." He pulled down the speaking tube again. "Hey driver. Take a hike. But come back like in a bell. I need you later. For that thing." There was some shifting of the coach.

Xanthe made up get up, but Horace put his hand up to stop her. "Nah, girl. We'll do that whole favor stuff here."

Xanthe sat back down, as primly as she could. "My favor is a little nontraditional. Please don't read anything extra into it."

"That's okay. Here. Lemme get you that drink. But only for you. I gotta stop for now," he declared, almost more to himself than her. He reopened the snow box, and retrieved a ludicrously tall glass, then poured some orange liquor from a crystal decanter into it. It smelled like flamedraft.

"I'm fine. Really," Xanthe demurred.

He kept pouring. "Now, here's something you gotta learn. I'm like, an owner. Which is big-time. Because we're an ownership society. See, I own this coach. My house owns lots of things. Soon, I'm gonna own this whole town." He put the bottle back and shifted over to her couch with the glass. "And when people are in things I own, they got to be nice, and just take what I give 'em, see?" He pushed the glass into her hands.

Xanthe accepted the drink and held it. "Should I drop the favor?"

He stared blankly for a moment, then shrugged. "Yeah. Sure."

Just wanting to get the whole thing over with, Xanthe dug out the silver chestlet, held out her hand, and dropped it on the floor.

Horace smiled, and briefly, Xanthe worried that he wasn't going to pick it up. But then he leaned over and grabbed it off the carriage floor. "There we go. Now, I found this nice silver jewelry. Now to get it back, you gonna have ta do stuff. Until then, it's mine. Finders keepers." He dropped it into his coin pouch.

"That's not the way it's supposed to go." Xanthe told him, beginning to feel put off.

"It is with me. Now drink up. It'll loosen you up." He grabbed her hand and pushed the cup she was holding to her mouth. "Come on, girl. You know you want it."

"I'm not feeling all that well," she protested. "I haven't been all night. Come on, Horace. Just give me back my favor. We can kiss and go home."

"Drink," he ordered, and pushed the lip of the cup to her teeth. His grip was stronger than she'd have thought, given his doughy body. He then started tilting up the cup. "Come on. Just take it."

Fine. Whatever. Xanthe screwed up her face and tried the flamedraft. It was cloyingly sweet yet burned at the same time. About one swallow in, she breathed, and as the fumes burned her lungs, began to cough. She bumped the glass, spilling the rest of the liquid onto the front of her dress.

Horace didn't seem to mind. He leered at the wet cloth on her chest and put the glass aside. "See? That wasn't so bad, now was it? You'll really like it once it hits. That's how it is. Lots of girls think they don't like things. They just need someone to teach 'em they do."

"Like it? Are you kidding?!" Xanthe stared at herself, distraught. "Look at my clothes!"

"Yeah. That's okay. I'll get you something to go home in. But first, here. Lemme show you something else about my coach." He grabbed the handle of a pull-chain hanging unobtrusively from the ceiling and yanked on it, and as he did so he put his arm under her calves, lifting them up out of the way. As he pulled, the bottom sections of the two opposed couches lifted together to form a single, somewhat lumpy, bed.

Xanthe was confused. "What is this?"

He smiled triumphantly. "This is the part where you earn that favor that's now mine. My favor. But it's going to cost a lot more than just a kiss." Without any other warning, he descended on her, holding her arms and pinning her.

"What?!? What are you doing?"

"Nothing much. Just breaking you in, girl. Tonight's the night I'm gonna make you a woman."

She was incredulous. "Huh? No! I am not doing you." Annoyed, she pulled her arms up between them.

"Yeah, yeah. I know. Good girls don't. Don't worry. You can just blame it all on me while you get your fun."

This was surreal. It came out of nowhere. "I don't want your stupid fun. I want out." She started to try to push him off, but even with her arms toned from delivery work, it was hard. He was heavy.

He leaned in, his fetid breath stinking of alcohol. "You just don't know it's fun yet. But that's okay. That's what I'm here for."

"Get... off!"

Xanthe started pushing to the limits of her strength, but Horace was much bigger. He pawed at her, his hands grabbing at her body, and she couldn't keep him away. Every time she squirmed, he shifted his weight to keep her pinned underneath. "Stop. Stop!" she yelled, but her words seemed to only add to his pleasure. She started to panic. She didn't know what to do or how to get him to quit. She was embarrassed. She wanted to cry. Moreover, she felt sick. The liquor wasn't sitting well.

They struggled for minutes. "Too bad I can't do this long as I'd like," he said at length. "It's fun, but I got other things to do. So come on. Time to give in. You're not getting out of here without taking it, so might as well lay back and enjoy."

Xanthe didn't stop fighting. Not yet. But she could feel despair rising in her, a sense of violation and horror. Worst of all was the inevitability. He was just too big. She continued to resist, but her arms were getting tired. Finally, while once again pushing her hands away with his forearms, he put his hands to the top of her dress and tore. Xanthe felt the fabric give under his grip.

"Wow, girl! You got a nice rack under all that," he chuckled after he yanked down her breast sling, which she normally kept bound tight. "Your brats won't go hungry, that's for sure. Good thing, cause I'm giving you one for festival. My own personal trophy."

His words brought chills of absolute terror. It ran through her back, giving her the strength of panic. Though heavily trafficked on the black-market, childbane was illegal by Curate doctrine, and therefore expensive. Too pricey for her. And this was not a safe day. She was very fertile. "No, Horace. Stop!" She panted through grit teeth. "You have no right."

"Sweet little slide from a low family thinks she's too good for me? The guy who's gonna rule this whole town? Really, I should be mad. Got every right." He sneered agreeably, then leaned in close, breathing hot in her ear. "But know what? I'm not. Love it when slides fight. Means you're top notch. Good ones always say no; keeps the trash out of your ass. Cause deep down you know what you're made for but want your brats to have winning blood. So here I am! Top guy to grab you by the slide and make you, break you, seed and slave you. You love it. Think you don't, but you do. That's why you came here."

Xanthe blushed angrily, feeling queasy. "I do not need to be raped. Or made pregnant. I need to be away."

"Nah. This is what you really need." He pulled back, grinned, and then without warning laid a vicious slap as hard as he could across her face with the palm of his right hand. It landed full on, with a noise and pain that rattled in her head and made her see spots. It hurt like crazy. Tears welled in her eyes. Ceasing her struggles, Xanthe put her hand to her face and wept uncontrollably. Dark shadows began to gather about the edges of the coach's ceiling.

"See?" Horace declared with satisfaction. "That's a pop. It's what lots of slides need. Specially Tari, but that's getting ahead of myself. Point is, you're with a real man now. So, don't ask for pops, cause I'll give 'em. Long as you keep making me. Your fault if I do." A triumphant smile crept up on his lips. He put his hands down lower preparing to rip open the rest of her dress. But then on a whim, he changed his mind. "Come on. First, gimme that kiss. Then you can wear that favor I found while I fill you full." He leaned down smiling, open mouthed.

All at once, Xanthe heaved. It came entirely unbidden, but the vomit launched straight up as he was trying to kiss her open mouthed. *Hoooooooooooooooorrrrrrrkkk.*

Horace jerked back. His face contorted in horror and disgust. He'd gotten a complete mouthful. He stuck out his tongue, and her vomit slid off it. For the first time in minutes he was no longer on top of her. "Bitch!" he coughed angrily. "What did you...?" He made a slight retching motion himself.

Xanthe threw up again. She had no choice. *Hoooooooooooooooorrrrrrrkkk.* Projectile vomit sprayed everywhere, and she saw an opening. "I ate dog dung on a dare," she lied, wiping her mouth with the back of her hand.

While Horace gagged, Xanthe backed up against the door of the coach and fumbled behind for the door latch. "You know how dogs are. How they eat their crap. I was dared to do it. Made me want to puke. I tried to warn you. Now it's everywhere. In your mouth. Right now. Dog crap. Think of the dogs, dung, slurping it up. Slurping. Chewing on crap. I think you swallowed some. Dung. In your mouth. Down your throat."

That did it. At the vision she'd painted, he heaved. As he did so, she was finally able to grab the door handle and work it, despite the awkward position it was in from the cabin having the bed raised. The swing door opened. Xanthe tumbled out backwards into the fresh clean air. She took a slight fall but was able to roll out of it. Immediately, she turned and fled, holding the top part of her dress together with her hands.

Run. Run. Run to freedom.

It was hard to. The grain padding she'd made for herself was still weighing her down, and she couldn't take it off without undressing. She didn't know if he was chasing her and dared not look back to check. Finally, by the end of four blocks, she knew that she was away. In fact, she knew exactly where she was: the alley directly in front of Celeste's secret entrance.

"Xanthe!"

She whirled. Royroy was behind her jogging toward her from an entirely different direction. "Go away!' she screamed hysterically. "I'm not going back!"

He stopped short a dozen yards away, evidently confused. "What are you on about?"

"You don't know?!" She sobbed in disbelief. Her face was still stinging. Her dress was covered in liquor and vomit. She glared at him. But in the nighttime at this distance, shadowed between buildings, she could see it was hard for him to make her out properly. He was squinting.

"I'm just here about my sister," he explained carefully in a humoring tone. "That's it. Nothing else."

Absurd. Absurd. Of all the... Xanthe nearly laughed. She heard herself: a dry, panicked bark almost past the breaking point, but managed to pull herself up short. Something about Royroy's voice made her realize he was in earnest. "I know all about it. But not now. I just... no." She breathed heavily, repetitively, trying to calm herself. She coughed once more and nearly dry-heaved.

"No, no. This is the time," he insisted. "We can talk about these things here, in secret. I'm saying things nobody else knows. I hear you got a touch for finding things out. I don't give a damn if you use greatwitchery or anything. Just find who strangled and put that Curate brand on my sister. That's all I ask. I'm working every job I can for the silver I need to buy her killer's death. No matter who. I'll become a bandit if I have to."

"Nadeen told you this," Xanthe concluded, weary with resignation. It wasn't a question. It was the only logical explanation. Based on their one conversation, the school gossip had gotten it into her head that she was some sort of witchy oracle and was telling everyone. Just reaming great.

"How did you...?" His voice took on a tone of awe.

Ream. Just... Xanthe realized her mistake. Now any logical inference she made based on evidence would be attributed to this phantom female witch power. She just couldn't handle it right now. She'd had it. She turned on her heel and stalked off up the street, heading home.

Royroy followed behind, cajoling. "Look. I'll pay you silver. A hundred. I can't get it all at once, but I will. You just have to tell me who did it. I know it's someone who's welcome in Highcouncil. She was killed behind the walls." His voice turned bitter. "That's why the guards kept it quiet. Won't do anything. They're not curious there. They could learn things they'd rather not know."

Xanthe glowered as she walked. "Like about your reaming boss."

"Horace? Being a murdering thief? That makes no sense."

She stomped. "He just tried to rape me, Royroy. Don't work for him if you *ever* want to talk to me."

"But he's the only one who promises to pay well," Royroy protested. "And I need the silver."

"I don't give a rooting ream," Xanthe barked. A little voice in the back of her head scolded her on her use of language, but she was past caring. She kept walking.

Royroy let out a sigh of intense frustration. "Oh, come on! You got in his coach. Drank his drinks. With all your witch touch, you didn't figure he'd make a play for you? And him being Highcouncil, he wouldn't be pushy? No one's going to believe that. I'm sorry it didn't work out, or you've got regrets about what happened now, but, I mean," he paused, entirely exasperated, "come on!"

Xanthe stopped short. Of all the things. All the things that had happened. Somehow this was the worst. All Royroy had said were a few words, but it felt like he'd punched her right in the gut. He wasn't even trying to be mean. He was just saying how he felt. Maybe, maybe he was even right. She'd not seen the flags about Horace, though now they seemed plain as day. Why? Why had she been blind? Was Horace right? Had she really wanted it? Was there some hidden part of her wanting to give it up to some highborn with money, since she had none? Had this really all been her fault?

She didn't think so, but now she just couldn't be sure. She wasn't sure of anything anymore.

She put her hands to her face and broke down. The dark street echoed with her wracking sobs.

Behind her, Royroy was silent for a while. "Um... look," he finally ventured in a softer voice tinged with guilt. "I'm sorry. I... it's really none of my business what went on between you two, and alright, yeah, okay, I know Horace isn't the best. But this is murder we're talking about. Murder." His voice grew intense, itself full of pain. "My sister's dead. When they put her on the pyre, she was so perfect. It almost seemed like she could have just woken up, except for that damned brand on her face. But she's gone, and this is my only way of avenging her." He reached out to put a hand on Xanthe's shoulder.

# DON'T TOUCH ME

Xanthe wasn't sure if she screamed it at the highest pitch she'd ever managed, or if it were more just a thought, but regardless, it was utter rejection from a place she didn't even know she had. Her body crackled and Royroy was thrown up and back. He twisted yards through the air, and a distinct crunch of wood and a yowl of pain greeted his landing upon a pile of refuse-filled boxes. Far off, as if to punctuate her words, there came a boom of distant mountain thunder.

Xanthe stared only for a second to be sure he wasn't seriously injured before she turned.

She didn't know what in hellspace had just happened.

She didn't care.

She was going home.

## Chapter 11

"Nothing really bad happened."

"Nothing really bad happened."

Xanthe repeated this mantra to herself every other step up the many dark flights of stairs to her room, trying desperately to make herself believe it. The naphtha lamps were snuffed, and the Scholar's Guild otherwise empty, as everyone was still out. Festival wasn't over. It had hardly begun. The thing went on until daybreak, and it'd only been a single bell since sundown. She had heard it from a clockwork chain tower as she'd retreated through hidden alley shortcuts back here. Why, she could head right back out with a brand-new favor and get herself another boy!

Heh.

"Nothing really bad happened."

The strange thing was, it was almost true. This night had been nothing like she'd wanted, but nowhere near as bad as it could have been either. She wasn't murdered. Or raped. Or pregnant. Hellspace, even her pitiful social standing wasn't hurt. With her original favor being publicly stolen, she had the perfect excuse for not being seen with a boy, so no one would be mocking her. That wasn't all. Tari owed her. They both knew it. That would go double when she heard. So purely logically, she should be relieved, like fending off a monster in the wilds and living to tell the tale. It was just... her thoughts turned dark. She was in no mood to feel logical. When she stood in front of the door of her father's room, she was hating herself. Hating life. Angry. Sad. She couldn't even figure out why.

The door creaked open. Dad's room was much smaller than hers was, since it really was just a renovated storage room of the ancients. But unlike her own low slant-ceilinged loft that stretched across a full corner of the building, here were high walls lined with shelves. Every possible surface of them were crammed to the brim with books, strange researcher tools, ancient oddments, plumbing equipment, oversized wrenches and other work tools. The trap door to her own attic room above, was only accessible by climbing his library ladder.

It was due to this familiarity that Xanthe was so surprised. Nothing normally changed here, yet something had. Behind three staggered panels of a standing room-divider, there was a small vanity table and a large empty tub, attached by copper pipes to the floor. All of it freshly installed, so quickly it almost seemed popped into existence. Further, on the table were fresh bars of soap, a towel, a brand-new oil lamp, and a dried writers-leaf inscribed with the elegant calligraphy she knew so well.

"My dearest true angel, you've suffered too long your father's addled inattention. So please accept this humble addition to our small abode, I beg, as a partial repayment for all your graceful forbearance. I hope you enjoy it thoroughly, and await you in the great reading gallery, if you've the time to see me.

- PS. Beware the hot spigot. It runs cold at length, then becomes scalding."

Xanthe willed herself not to cry, though she badly wanted to. Instead, she turned the hot water handle halfway, checked the speed at which the water was coming, grabbed the lamp, and quickly headed up the ladder. Once through the trap door, she headed straight to her mirror and stared.

The girl who gazed back was a deranged clown. Her dress was ruined. Her hair astray. Her face a terror. All her ugly makeup was hideously smeared, long trails from sweat and tears. But she didn't care. Not anymore. Celeste was right. *"You make ugly faces at mirrors, and then don't like the ugly faces you're making."* That was what she'd said, and she was right. That was the real reason she'd ended up in Horace's clutches. Being so concerned with stupid things like showing up Priscia had blinded her to what was important. She had a dad who loved her, books, a useful job with the Hood Guild delivering things where the package lifts didn't go, and enough food to not be hungry, even if she couldn't get nice ample haunches from it. What else did she need?

She raised a hand to smash the accursed thing, but then thought better, recognizing the absurd melodrama of such an act. Cheval glasses were expensive. It'd probably cost father a lot more than she cared to admit. She'd not really been fair to him, had she? He provided well enough. Besides, it could be sold for coin they badly needed elsewhere. She decided therefore, to lift the thing up and turn it around. As soon as it faced the wall, she felt better. It was just like the vomiting. Once done, she'd felt fine. All she really needed was to get the bad stuff out.

*Never again,* she swore to herself silently. Never would she even glance in a mirror. Never would she care about what anyone else thought, whether insults from enemies, or compliments from friends trying to make her feel better. She would be just as she was. Plenty of girls had perfectly fine lives, even if they weren't particularly attractive. That would be her. She'd live her life on her own terms. Do what she wanted. Maybe if she ever found a boy who liked her for what she was, she might like him back.

She started worrying about the tub flooding father's room, so hurriedly stripped, leaving her vomit-stained clothes in a pile, heading back down the ladder to find the tub just about right in terms of level. Her dad was right though. Half the tub was freezing, the other half scalding with a distinctly sulfurous hot-spring odor to it. She stirred the water gingerly with one hand, until the heat was finally bearable, then plunged in, grabbing the rare and precious soap and lathering and scrubbing every part of herself in absolution. She even undid her maiden's braids, symbolically turning herself back into a little girl. Then she sat in the tub and soaked, turning pink in the heat. Glorious.

Alas, it was not all pleasure. She now had time to think. She stared down at herself, morosely considering her other problem: abject betrayal.

Oh, not Horace. He was just a thug in fancy plastics. She had already dismissed him. No, this treason was far more intimate. All the while she'd been shoving Horace off – panicked, outraged, terrified, horrified, losing control, feeling like the ultimate victim – somehow in the middle of all that, her nether regions turned on the water works. It as if her loins were saying, 'Unfortunate for you, but I am ready'. That was what scared her the most. In his taunts, Horace had been more than half right, as least as far as her involuntary reactions were concerned.

She shuddered. She didn't even *like* Horace. Not the tiniest bit. What if it had been someone handsome? Like Royroy – except strangely, she didn't like him either. But whatever. Say she did. Say this better than Royroy-like boy had found her after she was done feeling sick, returned her favor, escorted her around town for all the other girls to see? Plied her with lots of imperceptibly spiked punch to make her tipsy? Took her to some romantic spot, and then while doing a little normal making out, used force? Could she fend off a boy she liked? Find a way to get him to stop? Or would she just give in, figuring that it was always like this, and better with him than someone truly vile?

"Creator's dodgy power," she cursed out loud "Nearly get raped, and what do I do? Start inventing a way for a cuter boy to succeed at it." *What the ream is wrong with me?* Somehow even in his abject failure, Horace had turned her into damaged goods. Her innocence was gone. She always knew boys were dangerous, but somehow expected their danger to be solely seductive: them always pushing, and it being a little game about how much you'd let them get away with. But it was supposed to be only *after* you admitted he'd won you and you loved him forever, that he'd reveal your beauty had driven him past all control, and then, despite your perfunctory and quickly abandoned protests about what was strictly proper, ripped your bodice, bared your haunches, and ravished you like a Praetorian slavewife, so that you ended up seeded on your wedding day. Once again, merely thinking about such a shameful fate made her treasonous loins sting.

Yet that sort of fantasy was nothing like what she'd just experienced, and she grieved for its comfortable illusion. Before, she'd felt safe. But now, how could she trust anyone or anything? How could she relax, even when talking with a boy she liked? Would she miss more flags? What if some boy never gave any? She hated it. Hated her body for its betrayal. Hated her mind too. It brought up all sorts of odd thoughts and absurd connections. Like this: she didn't really have to worry, since any guy past her cute-resistance threshold wouldn't want to rape her anyway. See? Good thing she was ugly!

Xanthe fell into morose dejection. All the scrubbing in the world couldn't wash away everything that had happened tonight. Some parts of her were simply inaccessible to soap.

As those dark thoughts drained the last bit of remaining pleasure in the bath, she rose, wrapped herself in the new wash towel, and searched for her school clothes, only to find them missing. After brief surprise, she smacked her face with the palm of her hand. Mrs. Fullbarn had offered to do her laundry. Normally a welcome kindness, it was a pain right now. She'd no other clothes except for the ruined one. Oh. And *that* one. The black dress of the ancients.

There had never been a good time to try it on. Or maybe she hadn't because she was still slightly afraid of it. But really. That was silly. This wasn't like Celeste's Riftstring. She'd not had a single odd dream, even sleeping only half a yard over it, as it laid in a book box under her bed. No. It just what it seemed. Clothing. Nothing more. Not everything of the ancients had mystical power. Some things were just mundane. They ate and pooped like everyone else. Likely their baskets of wipe-leaves used for the toilet got terribly dry and crackly in the winter as well.

In her room, she pulled the outfit out, smooth and incredibly soft black satin-like material. Worries that she'd wrinkled it were completely misplaced. It was as new as when she'd first seen it in its thousand-year-old box. Now on more careful examination, she realized that it really was an outfit, consisting of several connected pieces: panties, leggings, and a skirt. Holding her breath, she tried it all on, wondering if something strange would happen. Nothing did.

At least it fit. Perfectly: sliding in loose and clinging tight as soon as she'd pulled it up. Yet its design was defective, as whoever made it had been absurdly cheap with material. Nothing covered. The leggings only reached mostly up her thighs, held only by tiny lacy straps that hung down from the sides of the panties – itself little more than a low strip of black half the size it should have been. This wouldn't have been an issue had the dress been long enough. But it wasn't. Not anywhere close. Cover her knees? The skimpy black chemise barely covered her rear, its hemline ending just below the panties. This left a gap of skin between it and the leggings that exposed the terrible lack of fat in her haunches.

The top was hardly better. Somehow the dress was also acting like a breast sling, lifting them up and pushing them out. The support was the most comfortable thing she'd ever felt. Yet also weird. Normally she would double wrap and tie her sling as tight as she could so as not to bounce while running deliveries, but now she couldn't even look down at her feet without craning her neck. What she saw wasn't cloth either. Her breasts were absurdly exposed, again more of the designer's obvious cheapness in cutting the neckline far too low with too little fabric. It put that horrible dark freckle that she hated so much on prominent display.

There was one true surprise. At the base of the stockings, her foot touched solid soles, and when she stood on them, they slowly curled themselves around her feet. It took a few seconds, but when it was done, both were encased in strange polished black footwear that fit perfectly.

Okay, so the outfit did have a small amount of ancient technology to it. But wasn't a weapon. At this, she was genuinely relieved. As a final touch, she wrapped the box ribbon around her left wrist. It looked pretty there.

Xanthe hesitated while going out the door, then steeled herself. Unless she wanted to spend a full bell-hour washing her vomit-stained dress in the new tub, another three waiting for it to dry, and yet another sewing it back together, this was the only way to see father. Besides, she was only going downstairs, not out in public. So even if it did feel like walking around in black undergarments, embarrassingly breezy, people here knew her. She reminded also herself that she no longer cared what anyone else thought. Social standing? Big deal. Maybe she would go out, just to be outrageous. At least Celeste would approve. The Festival always sported a few people in ancient period costume, the more historically accurate the better. There was even a contest for it.

Only the barest thread of light leaked from a crack in the enormous door leading to the book gallery. The rest of the guildhall was near pitch black; it only kept from being so by the illumination of ringlight reflecting in through the hall's high windows. This might have been eerie to others, but not her. The Guild was too familiar; it was home. Still, the dim light did bring a certain sense of solemnity, so she took care to pad through the cavernous library quietly, despite the lack of readers to disturb.

Finally, between two of the gallery's massive floor-to-ceiling shelves, she located the source of light. A dozen yards away, there was a single small lantern on a low table. Beside it, a stray umbrella-stand holding a familiar cane, and an ornate club-chair facing the opposite way.

Her father was reading a book, while engaging in one of his many odd habits, exercising his fingers in the air as if he were playing a strange invisible musical instrument. The low set flame cast long shadows down the stacks to her feet. His moving fingers made the flickers of darkness dance across the shelves, as if he were casting magic.

She tried to be extra quiet in her approach. Still, he somehow still felt her presence. He put down his book. "Xanthe. Darling angel," he asked warmly without turning around. "How did it go?"

She stared briefly. It hit her. It was daddy. Familiar uncommonly brown hair. His one set of good clothes. A compassionate and insanely intelligent middle-aged face framed by a salt and pepper goatee. He was back.

Upon seeing him, she tried to start on a forthright account of what had happened. Instead, somewhere a dam broke. Tears formed, and she fell into his arms, sobbing.

## Chapter 12

For minutes her father simply held her, his arms wrapped around her lithe frame, cradling and rocking her, and remained quiet as her tears dribbled down onto his shoulder. She curled in on his lap and did her best to become the five-year-old that once upon a time she was.

It didn't really work. She was too big. Yet the sound of his beating heart was soothing.

"You probably think I'm like this because I was dumped, or something," she finally accused for no reason.

"I think nothing of the sort," he gently rebuked while stroking her unbound hair. "Not, let me add, that there is shame in grieving over love lost. All wounds are painful, no matter how pedestrian. Indeed, though it was ages ago, I still remember my first romantic tragedy. I had turned a real young lady into an illusion of perfection in my own mind, and of course it ended terribly".

Xanthe had never really thought about her dad being a young man, or having girlfriends, though of course that had to have happened. He normally was so reticent to speak of any of it, especially about her mother. Though she still felt awful, she once again began to feel the familiar itch of insatiable curiosity.

He studied her skimpy black outfit suspiciously. "I do hope this wasn't the cause of any unfortunate events." Although he said nothing more, she could see him questioning where she'd got it.

Oh, holy Creator. She forgot entirely. Of course he'd wonder. "It's a... a gift," she stammered out. That was technically true. Just not a gift to her. Then felt more embarrassed, realizing her evasion was worse. A gift? Great. *Now he'll think some boy gave it to me.*

He nodded slowly, eyes narrowing at the skirt. "Xanthe, we need to speak. There are subjects I've been loath to broach. I keep delaying it to preserve your childhood but," he sighed. "You've grown. So much so, that at times I scarcely recognize you. As you peek further from beneath my cloak, my power to protect you wanes. There are certain things you must know. The dangers, especially."

The talk. He was about to give her the talk. Oh Creator no. Now, of course. Exactly when she couldn't stand it. Why now? Well, obviously, she'd just practically begged him for it, hadn't she? The problem was that it was so long overdue, it was useless.

"Daddy, please," she pleaded. "Please don't." She swallowed. "I just can't take it. Not now. Okay? Just.... let me be innocent for a little while longer."

"Not all gifts are free. Some come with expectations. Others with consequences."

She nodded, filled with remorse. Horace's damnable drinks. Lovely little talk this was going to be. About every stupid sign she'd missed. Her eyes filled with desperate tears. "Please...?"

He studied her face, and she saw him relent. He stroked her hair, both gently amused and oddly serious about her plea to not learn this lesson. Yet he was the naïve one she knew, for she was far more aware than he thought. "Very well," he decided. "A year then, no more, no less. Your reluctance is a sign that I would be wise to heed, yet also do I fear the consequences of waiting too long."

She nodded and partly confessed. "I did have trouble. With a boy. But this didn't cause it, I swear."

"Xanthe," he interjected gently. "I would never..."

"It wasn't a present from him," she declared, once again distraught. "He wasn't a boy I've been seeing. I'm not even seeing boys yet! I was just talking to him on Festival night as a favor to a friend."

"Xanthe."

"I didn't even have this on! Really, I didn't! I was all perfectly proper!" She wailed, tears coming unbidden again. "You've got to believe me. I know it was my fault for not realizing, but I wasn't..."

"Xanthe!" Her father put both his hands around her head, staring straight at her. "My darling angel." He assured her with fearful intensity. "You have no idea how much I believe you."

She nodded, as much as she could with him holding her that way. Of course. Obvious, right? He knew her. He was dad. Although his grip was nothing he'd ever done before, it was exactly what she needed then. Calmness returned, like cool water on a burned hand.

He continued. "Insofar as this cur who slapped you is concerned, I'm proud that you assume the best in people. That is how you should be. Only those who are fallen to degeneracy blame the victim for maintaining insufficient distrust. Do not, I beg, do this yourself."

"Slapped? How did you know?"

He brushed her face with the back of his fingers, cool and soothing. "The mark his hand left is almost imperceptible at this point, but not entirely. Therefore, do not lament when those who strike you fall. As they shall." Though his touch was tender, his whisper held a cold fury that made her nervous. Her father was never like this. She didn't even know what he was like angry. She hoped he wasn't stupid.

"Daddy," she shivered. "It's not worth it. He's a Highcouncil boy. We don't want trouble. It would be my word against his. And his family is rich and strong. They could do a lot of bad things. I'd have my name dragged around and get no satisfaction."

"It is not for satisfaction that one speaks out. Rather it is a gift that you give to every other potential victim. Degenerates require silence to perpetuate their brutalities unimpeded. This means speaking up is a moral duty. Yet it's also wise to find allies first. Upon finding and comforting earlier victims, tongues will loosen in numbers and mutual support. Even high standing will avail naught against the words of too many".

She shook her head. "I... I just can't. I want it to all go away."

"Can't? The question isn't can't. It's can. Can you live with yourself, when you watch the suffering of someone that your actions could have saved? What will you say to them?"

Xanthe winced. This was what was most difficult about father. He could state things with such excruciating clarity. That is, when he wasn't engaging in his more typical deadpan humor and storytelling. "I... I'll think about it. Can we talk about something else? Please?"

He settled back. "As you wish sweetheart. What would you like?"

"Well." She hesitated, wondering how much she could get away with. There were things too painful for him to speak about. Or at least she supposed so, because he never did. She decided to try anyway. She felt like he might give a little. "You're right, I am growing up. So, can I know about my mom?"

"Your mother's the most perfect creature in this whole universe, and you are her daughter." It was his typical vague answer. She'd heard it a hundred times.

"But I want to know specifics. Can you tell me just one thing?"

He shifted slightly in the chair, settling his dark eyes on her. "What would you like to know?"

She swallowed. "D... did I kill her? In childbirth, I mean. I really have to know." There it was. The guilt. It had always eaten at her. She just let it out. Maybe she would learn the truth. Get some resolution.

Her father laid his head back in the chair and stared up. "Xanthe."

"I want to know," she persisted. "And the truth too. Don't go do some silly storytelling for me."

He peeked an eye down and took on an air of mock offense. "Me? Not tell the truth? I always tell the truth, my dear. I must. It's all I could give you."

"Daa-ad." She scowled lovingly, not at all amused. "You? Not a storyteller? Really? Do remember when you told me I was an angel with wings that nobody could see or feel, not even me? Or the time you told me I was really a super-secret princess from another dimension?"

"So?" His eyes twinkled. "What's wrong with that?"

"What's wrong? I was five. I believed you!" It had been quite embarrassing at the age of ten to be disabused of those notions by Celeste. Before then, she'd gotten at least half the other kids in her Early Years classroom to buy into it too. Even today, the memory of that encounter stung.

"Is it my fault that you're too old and cynical to believe your dear old dad?"

Dodgy power. He was changing the subject. Cleverly, subtly, slipping out of it, just like he always did. But not this time. She stared him down. "Did mom die giving birth to me? Or the complications? Yes or no?"

He sighed, weary with resignation. "Is there any answer I could give that would make you feel better? For if I deny it, your next will be how then did she pass? And that would be just as terrible."

Her lip trembled. "I just need to know. I need to know what I did."

"What you did. Xanthe! What you did!" He scoffed lovingly. "You were a newborn. Nay, my angel daughter, the truth is this. Your mother was far too good to remain in this degenerate world, so had to leave it long before I was ready to let her go. All you ever did was bring her such happiness that she could bear to be here. You didn't kill her. You sustained her. As you sustain me. For I don't know if I could have carried on without the need to care for you."

She was about to object to object to the poetic evasion, but heard the pain in his voice, and decided not to press. He'd let her out of the talk, after all. So instead she hugged him. "I'm sorry daddy."

He smiled wanly, then plucked her nose. "You are growing, and I must reconcile myself to that. You have become quite fetching by the way, which I am sure by now brings you notice, despite your father's considerable discomfiture and arduous wish that you remain overlooked. I am afraid that is entirely my fault. Your mother was my absolute ideal of beauty, and of course you take after her."

Xanthe snuggled, appreciating her dad's prejudiced eyes and exaggerations he made to make her feel good. "I'll have this off as soon as I have my school clothes washed."

"Please do not. Not on my account. It is perfect in its historical accuracy, as befits the Festival. Almost too much so. Though its patterning may reveal more to you than I might wish, perhaps you needn't be as unfledged as I've been keeping you."

He closed his eyes, squeezed her tight, and intoned, "Through your subtle ways I beg you keep this, my daughter Xanthe, safe in your embrace. Grace her with as much normalcy as your ruthless sublimity can allow, for it shall be her anchor as time resolves. Above all, if you do choose her as your instrument, veil her ipseity. I have no faith in you. You know well my reasons. But this one thing means more than anything. Indeed, it is more than everything."

"Daddy!" Xanthe was shocked. "I didn't know you prayed!"

"I don't. This is more like," he paused, squinting uncomfortably as if having to do something distasteful, "very carefully asking."

"You're just 'very carefully asking' the Creator. Uh huh. You know what? You're really weird."

He gave her a sly smile. "You're my daughter. What does that make you?"

She pouted and cuffed him on the shoulder, realizing that somehow, she was feeling better. "I'm going to go find Mrs. Fullbarn to see about the wash." She got off his lap and the chair and straightened her skirt. The hem was lower now, almost as if it were trying to be more presentable in front of him.

"Do so, whether your school clothes are dry or not," he commanded. "She is ever so practical and can provide some types of advice I simply cannot. Indeed, I let her be your Creator-mother for exactly that purpose, so listen to her as much as you can."

"I will. Love you daddy," Xanthe said as in parting.

"I love you too," he reached out briefly to hold her hand. "And fear not. Not yet. You have many hidden friends who care for you."

"Now you're going to say pixies flutter about, throwing invisible flower petals in my path? Or do I have a guardian angel?" She sighed wistfully. "I'd like to have one to protect me." *Especially if it was mom.* But she buried that thought. She'd had enough of feeling sad for one day.

"Well you do," her father told her teasingly. "Though you hardly need one. What do you need an angel for, my little one? What may help more is a guardian demon. To get you into terrible troubles that fix your worst problems, as is their wont."

"Like the Five and the Eight?" Xanthe referenced the greater demons that the Curate railed about in sermons, all being far too dreadful to ever invoke by name. "Uh, yeah." She realized it was useless to try to out-weird dad on the storytelling front, so she just squeezed his hand in love and let go.

"Have fun, and... be careful with the universe. It's not so easy to fix." This was her father's usual parting admonition to her. More funny storytelling. Other teachers laughed when he said it, often leaving Xanthe embarrassed. Tonight, she didn't mind.

She nodded. "I'll try."

# Chapter 13

Mrs. Fullbarn was indeed in the laundry room. The place was filled with clever clockwork washing machinery, rollers and stirring tubs, each which could be set into motion by a constantly turning public axle that entered through the wall from outside into a gearbox. But she was using of none of it, instead sitting on a bench next to a huge washtub, rubbing clothes on an old soapy washboard.

She easily could have been confused with a scullery maid, but her looks were deceiving. Though many guildhalls did not see art as true scholarship, Xanthe's father decided the reverse. He'd championed her as a full-fledged colleague. That she'd come from the wilds with no formal education were not drawbacks, but attestations to her character. As with most things, he was proven right. Now she was one of the Guild's favorite instructors, teaching both girls and boys, with a reputation as having a soft touch. This was helpful for Xanthe to brave what she knew she had to do.

Xanthe entered and presented herself, curtsying formally. Then bowed her head in formal contrition. "I am here to divulge and confess. I stole some grain from the Guild larder. I was hoping to return it, but that didn't work out as I'd planned."

Mrs. Fullbarn wrung out the shirt she was rubbing, set it aside, and dried her soapy hands on her washing apron. "Oh, you did, did ya?" She sounded neither surprised nor upset. In fact, she seemed mostly like she was trying not to laugh. "Thought as much. Ya were practically waddlin' going out the door, ya were! Tha's not the Xanthe I know," she smiled gaily.

Xanthe flushed. Now she had embarrassment to add to her shame. "I'll pay it back somehow. Take the written penalty. My evening's over anyway."

"Oh, tha' won't do at all. Old Guild punishment on the books fer food stealin's pretty bad, since it were so precious once upon a time. Somethin' like being killed or slaved. How about ye take a teacher's punishment instead? I promise it won't be so bad."

Xanthe nodded readily. She figured it would go like this.

"Then it's goin' ta be this. First, I'm goin' ta do ya up the way I haven't for a girl in a score o' years. Then, you'll be tellin' me what exactly happened to bring ya back so soon. An' after that, ye'll go right back out an' be seen by everyone. Walk the whole city in public. Right as ye are. Talk to at least ten boys, or get one ta give ya some sort a kiss. No girl your age should give up so early on Festival."

"What?!" Xanthe's eyes bulged. "You should give me a year's worth of kitchen duty, starting right now. That's what I'd do. It'd be more proper."

"Ye'd rather be miserably peelin' roots in a dark kitchen all alone? This, o' all nights, then? Yer comin'-out Festival?"

Xanthe nodded, her chin crinkling.

"Well, that does it. Tisn't punishment if ya want it, now is it? So, sit down and start tellin' me all about what happened, while I do your hair and face," she pointed at a chair. "Eyelashes an' nails too," she added as an afterthought. "If I'm gonna punish you, might as well be bad."

"But..."

"Now!" the old woman barked. "Unless ye'd rather die by the old book."

"Maybe I would," Xanthe whimpered.

"Ooo, that do sound terrible," Mrs. Fullbarn said sympathetically, but plainly not enough, as she made no sign of stopping. She exited the laundry room and came back in less than a minute with a huge case, hefting it in one hand by the handle. She pulled it over to the chair where she'd directed Xanthe and set it down. On its opening, Xanthe saw it was filled with beauty supplies carefully ordered into little compartments, with combs, scissors, and dozens of unrecognizable tools. "I figured it were serious, love," she continued in unbroken thought. "Yer a strong girl. Strong as a wildswife. So, whatever made ya undo yer maiden braids must a been fearful sure."

"I was nearly raped," Xanthe said plainly. It seemed to be getting easier to just say it. "Don't tell father." His reaction had been bad enough just knowing she's been slapped.

Mrs. Fullbarn hesitated ever so slightly. "Ya need childbane?" She asked quietly.

"I said nearly." Then she blinked. "Wait. *You* have childbane?!" She always thought Mrs. Fullbarn was devout. Especially for a Scholar.

"Only fer those that need it," she dismissed, while unfolding a miniature wooden rack reminiscent of some Juchean torture device. She spread each of Xanthe's fingers in it, took a brush, and painted each of Xanthe's nails with a ruby-crimson lacquer. As they dried, they strangely tingled.

"Who doesn't need it, if they want it?"

"Wildwives." Mrs. Fullbarn declared in a matter-of-fact tone, her peasant accent deepening. "City girls marry handsome young farmer bucks and end up learnin' there's nothin' much to do in a cotburrow come dark 'cept baby-makin'. So, after their first three straight in a row, findin' themselves goin' nuts, they come round lookin' fer seeds to fend off their husband's. That's when I tell 'em it gets better."

"It does?"

"Oh no, not hardly. But by the time they got five, they're way to busy ta be unhappy. An' when they got seven, they're all smug, lookin' down on anyone who don't take the old-pledge, as it's the only way a wife can be happy, not to mention the only way ya can get married in the countryside.

"An old-pledge marriage is best?"

"Oh, heavens no dear. Near prison, it is! Terrible thing. Near exactly like bein' a slavewife."

Xanthe was completely confused, and this remained evident on her face as Mrs. Fullbarn took a brush to her hair. The teacher explained. "When a girl's pushed inta a weddin' she don't want, that's serious. If she wants out, I help best I can to break her free, sin or no sin. But when she loves him, an' just wants to cheat on the pledge she made afore th' Creator's altar to give herself body and soul, then only thing I do is give 'em childboon."

"You don't help at all?"

"Course I do," Mrs. Fullbarn remarked with flinty practicality. "Childboon makes babes come healthy and your milk come thick. That's worth a lot."

"But still! They end up with even more children. Ones they didn't want."

The matron nodded. "There's a sayin' among wilds women. Shut up an' mommy, mommy. That means no matter how much it ruins ya, yer babies need bein' born. You pay the life you got forward."

"I don't understand."

"I know," she said pensively. "Few city folk do. It's just a different world out there. See ol' Mr. Death, he's a friendly sort a fella. Insists on meetin' everyone. He'll meet me soon enough, an' even you in time. But no place is he more friendly than in the outlan's and wilds beyond the Nightmare Line. There you'll find him always, no matter who ya be: bandit, farmer, rich, poor, soldier, wife. Little ones too. Too many a those. Yer father once figured rural families need ta have five each, just ta keep up. An' frontier wives know it too, without all the fancy countin'. No girl should ever be made ta marry a nightmare-country man. But if ya do, never sinfully wish for his seed not to bite. What ya pray thanks for, every single day, is that those you love come home alive."

Xanthe was silent for a while, feeling a new respect for the rustic people who lived outside Jagerfeld. It was ingrained into her not to leave the safety of the city in winter. Yet they did it as a matter of course. "I guess I shouldn't have dismissed Hank so quickly," she declared.

"Who's he, then?" Mrs. Fullbarn's stiff brushing pulled at Xanthe's hair.

"Oh, just a farm boy I met. No front teeth. I suppose it's not his fault if he couldn't see a toothscraper. I met him in a shop and he asked if I could cook pie."

The matron let out a low whistle. "An' you say you're not an eyeful? Never seen the likes a that for anyone. Even me, when I had my looks!"

Xanthe blinked. "What do you mean?"

"Pie-cookin's the last thing a man like that needs ta know about ya afore he drags ya in front of an altar. He were smitten bad." She grinned, and started in with comb and scissors, snipping the ends of Xanthe's hair.

"I didn't know," Xanthe breathed wide eyed. Apparently, the ability to kill chickens without remorse was impressive indeed. "But even if I were ready for marriage, I still don't think I want to be a farm wife". *Definitely not.* In most cotburrows, men took both a wife and a slavewife, as the Manual of the Creator technically allowed, even though the practice had become passé in most civilized society.

"No shame in that. Plenty o' farm girls feel the same way. Grow up bein' expected to live the life, an' they just wanna be free. So, they come to the city, an' if they're not scandalized by how libertine it is, become merchants an' crafters, an' pity all their sisters who married young, never tastin' all life's got to offer. While they got no family to weigh 'em down."

"Being an amazon's better then?"

"Till it's not. Ya go back ta babysit and suddenly ya realize ya *do* want one a yer own. Except none o' the city men you took up with will propose, an' ifn they do, it's to someone else. So ya end up in yer old age lonely without an old coot to fight with, not to mention no gran'kids."

"Well, I *do* want to find love," Xanthe declared, surprising herself. "Someone I can just be crazy about and make stupid promises to. But... can I do that and be a successful research scholar too?"

"Ooo! That's called 'Havin' it all'. Ye got a husband ya love ta death, an' also gain respect in a man's guild. You're known to all the high families as more 'an just a wife. Ya research, teach classes, do all sorts o' things. Plus, on account a yer man, ya got way more little cute ones 'an ya ever thought ya wanted".

"Oh! That's it! That's exactly what I want!"

"Don't recommend it." The matron shook her head, evening another tuft of Xanthe's split ends between her fingers, and making another authoritative snip. "There's just somethin' missin' from that way a life."

"What?"

"Sleep, mostly." Mrs. Fullbarn nodded sagely.

"Well, then what exactly are you supposed to do?" Xanthe asked bewildered.

"You figure that out, come tell me, okay? We could make a fortune printin' advice books." She continued to comb and clip. "Now enough of all that. Your turn. Tell me what happened."

Heaving a sigh of resignation, Xanthe recounted her story, leaving out only the part about assassins and finding the artifacts. There was no catharsis in doing so, but she found it not to be so bad either, especially while enjoying the unexpected pleasure of having her hair done. Still, it was becoming increasingly hard to keep her aplomb, because Mrs. Fullbarn was enjoying the tale far too much.

"Ya had chickens chasin' after ya? Eatin' the grain leakin' from your paddin'?" The old woman didn't do well in keeping her composure, falling into paroxysms of only partially silent laughter.

"It's not *that* funny," Xanthe pouted, feeling extremely embarrassed.

"An' then you horked all over the insides a one a them super fancy carriages?" She grinned. "The ones with all the plush cushions an' pricey windup torque doodads? Just think what that high and mighty little boy's ride home were like." Mrs. Fullbarn only barely suppressed a chuckle.

"I don't care how bad Horace had it," Xanthe grumbled. Although she did have to admit that, now that it was pointed out, it could seem amusing.

"An' when he gets home, all his buddies start braggin' about their evenin's? What's he gonna say about about ya horkin' in his mouth?" She was openly cackling now. "Did ya get get past the kiss? Get lucky? Fill up a girl? 'Almost! Opened my mouth an' one filled me!' She slapped her thigh.

"Don't make me laugh!" Xanthe whimpered. She was trying not to, although Mrs. Fullbarn's glee was infectious.

"I know it don't seem so now, dear, but tha's gonna be a story you'll be tellin' yer gran'kids fer sure. Besides, don't slight the power a laughin'. Anythin' ya can find funny, ya can get past." She made a few final expert clips on Xanthe's bangs and put the comb and scissors down.

"I suppose. I guess. It's just that I'm not happy with my body right now."

"Oh now, don't go bein' hard on it." Mrs. Fullbarn picked up a jar of foundation, and with her hands started putting it on Xanthe's face. "It were just tryin' to protect itself, cause drippin's better 'an bein' torn up bloody inside. An' even then, just cause your body don't do what ya want it to, don't mean you're any different from anyone else. You think you got it bad? Boys got it worse."

"So? Boys don't care," Xanthe frowned. "They always want it."

"Shows how much you know about 'em."

Xanthe rolled her eyes and sighed in disbelief. Then she became annoyed when Mrs. Fullbarn laughed again. "What's so funny now?"

"Oh, just the way ya did that teen girl sigh. Like grownups got nothin' on your smarts," she continued to grin as she powdered Xanthe's face with a pelt-brush. "So typical. I did it to my ma too. It's only when ya get older that ya realize we're all the same age on the inside. The only difference is what ya see back in a mirror. Plus experience, which you don't got yet."

Experience. Xanthe had a hard time resisting rolling her eyes a second time. "Come on! Everybody knows what boys are like!"

"An' how many have ya talked to? Got ta know?" A rhetorical question. They both knew the answer.

She flushed. "Just because I don't know many boys personally doesn't mean I don't know about them."

But all this did was make Mrs. Fullbarn's grin broader. She was rubbing now the colored contents of various jars onto Xanthe's face, lips, and skin; with her every touch, there was an odd tingling sensation. "Dear, you're the school's smartest pupil, boys and girls classes combined, but there's more to life than just bein' a sheltered Scholar. No matter how much hardcopy ya read, expect to make plenty of mistakes. Can't say I did any different. I only hope yours are more fun and don't stick to ya quite as bad."

Xanthe suddenly felt guilty. Mrs. Fullbarn was giving her a haircut for a so-called punishment, and here she was, sassing her. "I'm sorry. I guess I'm just not in the mood to give boys the benefit of the doubt. They have such a power to ruin your life."

"Mm..." Mrs Fullbarn nodded noncommittally, pulling lightly on her eyebrows and lashes with her fingers; the tingling was particularly pronounced. "Bein' forced is twice bad. Once when it happens, and then after, cause it's so easy to start thinkin' you're dishonored for what some devil did to ya. Yet still, what ruins far more girls 'an any o' that, aren't the wicked boys at all. It's the weak an' childish ones. Ya fall for one who's fun, marry him, do everythin' right. But then he don't grow up, don't take responsibility, and ya end up havin' not only ta mommy your babies, but him as well. Then you're stuck, because no matter how willin' ya are to leave him, ya can't leave them. Creator don't take refunds."

"That's why you don't take the old-pledge."

"Oh no dear. Frontiersmen are many things, but idle they are not. No room for any o' that sort a nonsense in monster country. Wife or slavewife, ya work yourself hard, but he'll work harder 'an both a ya put together."

"Why anyone would share their husband is beyond me."

"How could the love ya pledged yer life to, do such a thing to ya, yer thinkin'?" She stared distantly. "Here's how. In the wilds, most slavewives are the widows a yer husband's brother, or your brother. He takes her family in, and ya all make do." Her smile was grim, close lipped. "More 'an half the time, you arrange it."

Xanthe frowned, not knowing what to think.

"So, don't sour on love just cause one bad thing happened. Boys are really no more blackhearted than girls, if ya didn' already know. But there are plenny o' good ones too, and even more than that who are all mixed up. Lots a bad people got slices a good in 'em, and good people slices a bad. World's not so simple. Its full o' surprises."

"I wish..." Xanthe began, but instantly Mrs. Fullbarn put a hand to her mouth to shush her.

"Now don't go wishin'. Ya got a bad habit of doin' that, and I'd break ya of it if I could. It's a sin. You're insultin' the holy, turnin' the Creator inta a merchant who has ta buy your love. The Good Manual says wishes got dark power to 'em. It's bad luck, specially wishin' on an evil omen, like what just happened." She touched her head and chest, then Xanthe's in turn, in a superstitious lay invocation.

Xanthe didn't say anything, but thought Mrs. Fullbarn was the one who was mixed up. In the Curate, the sin of wishing was trivial compared to dealing in childbane, although she wasn't sure how she felt about that either. "I guess I would *simply like,*" she emphasized, "for everyone see evil in people sooner. The world would be much better were that the case."

"It'd be an even bigger favor if people would just see it in themselves, cause that's the only part ya got control over."

"Well, I'm not evil," Xanthe declared. Then she hesitated. "Am I?"

"I wouldn' be doin' this if ya were," she smiled. "I'm specially impressed ya didn't turn in the girl who stole your favor. Could a ruined her, rattin' her out. Such a mercy I'd not expect from many after what she did. Maybe not even myself. You're as beautiful on the inside as you are on the out."

Briefly forgetting her vow not to care, Xanthe sighed morosely. "That's not saying much."

Mrs. Fullbarn broke into the widest grin. "So ya think! I tried ta make ya out ta be fierce, so nobody would trifle with ya, but all its done is bring out your allure. Don't spit – boys'll pretend it's a favor." With another glossy red unguent, she rubbed a tingling finger along Xanthe's lips.

The "don't spit" line was what you told girls that were absolutely top catches. Xanthe couldn't help herself. She rolled her eyes.

The teacher smiled, her eyes twinkling with amusement. "Keep doin' that. It might shoo off all the boys who think yer easy. Cut the crowd of 'em around ya down enough so's at least ya can breathe."

"I'm not looking for boys. I'm not even wearing maiden's braids."

"Only make it worse. Boys want what they can't have. Girls too, by th' by."

"And I'm wearing this! Nothing remotely fashionable." She struggled to remain uncaring about her social standing. Walking around in a glorified pajama-dress which betrayed the distinct lack of wiggle in her non-haunches wasn't going to help. "Not to mention it's black."

Mrs. Fullbarn nodded, ceding the point. "It's peculiar, true. The color of unmakin', not flirtin'. So ya might catch a tart word from those girls who don't like ya anyway. Don't matter. You're so fetchin', none will take ya for a Yamaite cultist." She maintained a small smile. "Or, the boys that do will want ya twice as bad."

This was getting absurd. Xanthe knew exactly what Mrs. Fullbarn was trying to do. It was so sweet. But she didn't like being lied to. It felt bad. She wondered if she could wheedle her way out of the rest of her punishment. "Well if I'm not dropping a favor, I don't have a reason to go back out."

"Sure, ya do. Ya got to go warn Tari about that boy. Didn't ya say he mentioned her name while he was tryin' ta force ya? If he cleans up after what ya did to him, he could try her next."

Mentally, Xanthe scoffed. Horace wouldn't dare. Tari's family was just as powerful. That protected her. There was no way she'd let him come close, much be less alone with him. "Fat chance of..." she stopped. Of course not. Tari didn't like Horace at all. She liked Damien. The witchkiller. Her eyes bulged. "You're right," she breathed. "I have to go."

"There ya go." As Mrs. Fullbarn said this, she finished with her last touch. There was an odd cast in her expression as she gazed at Xanthe, almost one of awe. "Farae, Farae," she murmured. "What've ya done? Paintin' this poor girl forever so pretty? How'll she handle bein' such a prince-killer?"

Xanthe felt like she was going to strain her eye-rolling muscles. It was so hard to resist. Instead, she hugged the old teacher. "Thank you so much. I will accept my punishment as given."

"I hope one day ye'll forgive me for it. Now get out there. Ten boys talkin', or one kissin'."

"Can I only talk to five?"

"Hmm. Only if you let the first boy you wouldn't mind smootchin' ya, ta do so long as he wants. Deal?"

"Deal. But it won't happen, even on Festival. I don't even know what I like yet."

Mrs. Fullbarn gave a sly smile. "Half the fun is findin' out."

## Chapter 14

Five boys. Five. That was still five too many. Where could she find five to talk to? The most obvious answer would be to simply find five random boys to ask if any of them had seen Tari. That seemed like cheating though. Mrs. Fullbarn wanted her to flirt, something she had no idea how to do. Read any good hardcopy lately? No. That was no good. Boys didn't like that. She found herself blushing for no good reason. What she really needed was to find and warn Tari. Maybe Celeste too. Then they could all go out in a group. That would be ideal. With both treating her getup as respectable, she could walk around without wisecracks.

It was only then that she realized what Mrs. Fullbarn had managed to get her to do. She wasn't thinking about boys as a danger anymore. Or rather, she was, but only romantically. However it had happened, her fear was gone. She felt more powerful than ever. No boy was going to do anything to her. Hellspace, there wasn't a boy in all Jagerfeld who could outrun her. Just outside the Scholars' Hall, she did some squats, stretched her hamstrings, and completed with two swan stretches, pulling each foot behind her back high up over her head. Once finished with the Hood Guild warm-up ritual, she set off.

Freed of the weight of her padding, the energy of the sprint came upon her. With every stride upon the torchlit streets, she felt the rush of her legs' power. She could run like this for bells when the mood came upon her, even when she had no need. It was a heady feeling she'd been struggling to overcome, for everyone knew that boys liked girls helpless, heavy, and slow. All the easier to catch. Yet freed from such cares, she found herself consumed with speed, strength, and nothing else but fierce joy.

She ran to Oversight Rock, a small park whose centerpiece was a single enormous volcanic boulder, easily climbable from one side. It offered some of the best views of Jagerfeld. As she ran, the dress pulled her breasts more tightly to keep them from bouncing, but it was her shoes that were the best part of the outfit. They were like running on air. The uneven rock slowed her not at all. She passed several couples in the park, some in positions far beyond proper, but sped past, heedless.

At the top, she took in the view. A group of Talathian barbarians were directly below making camp in the park. Dour rough men bearing talisman tattoos huddled around a watch fire. While technically lawbreaking, the busy guard would doubtless ignore them, as it was a minor transgression. Besides, the men were well armed and were oddly wary, as if the city might be more dangerous than the outlands. She ignored them as well, setting her eyes down the distant streets. She doubted her search would be fruitful, but by some turn of fortune it was. Tari's carriage was visible at south gate plaza. A speck at this distance, it was parked in a crowd and not moving, so would likely still be there if she ran. She hopped down the rock, and reaching ground, leapt the small park fence, tearing off past the restive wildmen down the street.

A few revelers stared as she flew past. *Let them*, she thought. She didn't care. As the crowds thickened, she edged out in to the middle of the street rather than have her run be impeded. She tore between revelers, treating them like pylons as she canted her body back and forth, making it almost a game to dodge them. Even she was amazed; though the run was long, she wasn't the least bit winded. Something was just different now. She didn't know what but was liking it all the same.

Finally came the main gate. The Great Horse was to the right, the large archway and gate itself to the left. In the plaza, carriages and people were milling around engaged in the festivities. Many small groups of guards were assembled, each wearing the uniforms of the other free cities of Thule. Xanthe knew of their colors from books but had seen few in person. Nor were they bored. Among the throngs, gaggles of girls were flirting with the younger members of the retinues. Xanthe ignored it all and raced directly to Tari's carriage, relieved that no handsome witchkiller was already sitting up there with her.

"Maybe you'd like to come down and stretch your legs?" A hopeful young man ventured, as Tari's eyes wandered the plaza. Xanthe didn't recognize him. His clothes were expensive, though painfully priggish, like something a man twice his age should have been wearing. Probably picked out by his parents. He continued "I'm..."

Tari wasn't listening, being lost in her own thoughts. She did that quite a bit. Way more than Xanthe did. Discretely Xanthe tapped her leg, hoping to snap her out of it. It worked. Tari blinked. "Xanthe!?" She stared down flabbergasted.

That was the cue. "Hello. Sorry," Xanthe addressed the boy, "She's my friend. We have to talk." She stood right next to him, and pointedly stared him down.

At first the boy seemed slightly annoyed as he was forced to draw his attention away from Tari, but then also was taken aback as he focused on her. "Um, yeah, sure," he stammered.

"Who's that?" Lydia asked from the other side of the carriage.

"It's um," Tari paused, entirely confounded as she took Xanthe in. "Xanthe. That's some makeover. Did you...?" She was at a loss for words.

Xanthe knew the outfit was daring. She didn't care at all. "We don't have time for this. You haven't found your date yet, right?" She was strictly business.

Tari shook her head. "That's why I'm waiting here. I heard he was around, but he hasn't shown up yet."

"Good. Don't. If it's the same one as I've heard of, he's seriously bad news."

"Wait. What?"

Xanthe nodded. "This is no joke. It's a matter of city security."

Tari looked shocked as she digested the news. "Just because he's cute doesn't mean you should take Celeste's chart seriously. She's joking. Besides, we've got friendly guardsmen crawling all over the place. I..." Suddenly she froze. Her eyes widened as she stared at absolutely nothing.

"Tari?"

"There's a possibility..." she whispered. Then she put her hand to her mouth and softly gasped.

"Tari? What's wrong?"

"I don't know," she breathed. "I saw something. Oh no." Her face twisted in fear.

"You did? Where?" Xanthe glanced in the direction of where Tari had stared, but there was nothing but a sweetmeat hawker working the crowd selling sweet jerky on sticks and a lot of people gawking at them.

"Never mind," Tari said. Yet her whole demeanor had changed, and she turned her head briefly in Lydia's direction. "Can you race me home? I'm not feeling well."

Lydia blinked, then stared at Tari incredulously. "What? Right now?"

"Please," Tari urged. "Right away." Her tone had changed instantly.

Lydia shook her head like Tari was crazy. "Nah. You go on by yourself. I'm out. I'm going to go find some low party from here. Your friend can be your driver." She indicated Xanthe by staring down at her annoyed, as if she'd been the one was responsible for Tari's sudden shift in mood. Although, to be fair, it was quite possible that she was right.

"Okay." Tari was so completely preoccupied with whatever she'd seen, she was entirely unfazed by Lydia's reaction. She grabbed the reins, and watched Lydia smartly step down off the other side of the carriage, then dug a hand into her blouse and retrieved her Mechanix necklace, the ones with the pincers. These she then tried to hand to Xanthe. "Use these when you need them, okay?"

Xanthe shook her head. No way she was taking a third favor this night. Especially something so valuable to Tari. "Don't worry, I won't."

"You might," Tari was oddly agitated. She insisted, forcing the chain into Xanthe's hand.

Just then, there was a voice. "There she is. I think. No wait."

A chill up Xanthe's spine. She knew that voice. It was Damien.

There was now a ring-shaped gap in the crowd around the carriage near the door. She was attracting people's eyes even more than before. Xanthe waited for someone to make fun of her outfit, but no one did, though one girl did cuff her escort on the shoulder for no seemingly good reason. Xanthe scanned trying to locate the sound of his voice, until her eyes settled on two men.

The younger one she recognized. It was the boy she'd seen just before she'd run into Priscia's clique. He was nineteen, and at first glance, seemed a mere scruffy lowborn foreigner. Tall, dark with unkempt straight black hair and a face covered in dark bristly stubble, and with braided muscles clearly defined under his dark shirt, the rugged youth could have passed for a treasure hunting adventurer. The sheathed blades at either side of his belt, one long, one short, completed the picture. Yet that smacked of affectation. It was far too deliberate. He moved with a dancer's grace; his every subtle move bespoke of power and poise born of iron discipline. Even more, she noticed a trace of something in him she'd never seen directly before: the 'beautiful dark', the barest glimmer of the hallmark of Nubian blood on his skin.

That sealed it. There was no way that this was some random down on his luck refugee. Nubians were regal sophisticates. Good or evil, never they traveled this far into the barbarous north without purpose.

To be sure, Xanthe saw what Tari liked. It was hard to miss. He was just gorgeous. To die for. Likely quite literally. She could only imagine the dozens of witch girls he'd lured to their doom. The thought made her even more furious than she was afraid, particularly since she found herself not entirely immune. He was staring wide eyed, for some reason seeming to be taken aback by her as well.

Still, for whatever magnetism he had, his companion dampened it. That one was a graying man, shorter, heavily muscled, scarred, in loose fitting clothing that could conceal anything. He had a studiously bland expression, but again, Xanthe was not fooled. Alarms screamed in her head. This was another killer like the one Horace had received, or worse. She didn't know how she knew, but she did. His eyes flickered over her, and she felt as if he were considering half a dozen ways to kill her if need be.

Perfect. All she had to do now was find a guard and make an accusation. Then they'd be tied up for the evening. Or better, they'd break for the gates. But at least they'd be driven off.

Of course, this also meant that she couldn't confront Horace. She'd get the benefit of the doubt against a foreigner. Yet having done so once without evidence, there is no way she'd be believed a second time about the scion of Wormwood. She'd be accused of prevarication, a major Curate sin that Mr. Griswold once described as "The crime of lying about a poor man or telling the truth about a rich one." Still, the choice was obvious. Between protecting girls from rape, and protecting them from murder, it was obvious which was worse. Perhaps with Horace, Tari might help with a whispering campaign.

"I am a servant of the Creator, not a thief!" came a protest unexpectedly from the crowd. Brother Axeman, sounding agitated, was being escorted by two familiar guards. Xanthe recognized them as the men who'd seen her healing. They all happened to be walking in her direction.

Ream. Perfect timing. Like always.

Time to change plans. Now, before the guards noticed her. Lax northern attitudes or not, being identified as a dreadwitch in the presence of both the acolyte and a witchkiller would bring nothing but trouble. Xanthe turned to face Tari and keep her face hidden from the guards, speaking in a low voice. "I've got to go. You should too. Damien is a killer. Ask Celeste about it."

"Mon dieu!" The other guard made an astonished shout. Xanthe didn't look back. She just put on Tari's necklace and ducked right, using Tari's carriage to break the guards' potential line of sight. Then she did her best to get lost in the crowd, fleeing in the only direction left available to her, out the main gate. It took all her willpower not to peek back or break into a run, but keeping her face hidden seemed best. There was a terrible minute of absolute fear as she dodged past late arrivals still streaming into the city, yet as she reached the huge entrance arch and massive portcullis, she started to feel safe. Just to be sure, she continued walking beneath the massive portcullis until she was entirely outside the city, completely away.

On the outside walls, a large welcome banner hung on the wall illuminated by torches and lamps. Enterprising hawkers were here trying to get first shot at selling wares to those still entering the city, but there were no guards and no proctors, so there was no risk of being exposed. She blew out a breath, briefly understanding how barbarians could feel safer outside a city than in. *That was too close.*

She decided not to wait to reenter. Not here. It wasn't wise. The better choice would be to make her way around the wall to Northgate. That opened into the Tradefair district, on the nearly opposite side of Jagerfeld. It would mean taking the path to the river ford bridge, just below the sluice gates. At night, this was technically dangerous, but the minor risk was a reasonable trade for permanently losing the two troublesome guards. If farmer boys could do it, she could too.

She started to walk. Good thing too. Too much had been happening. She needed time to clear her head, which conveniently she now could for she had no more concerns for the evening. Tari had taken her warning to heart. Almost too much so. She was acting strangely, more than her usual moodiness. But that was something to explore tomorrow. Tonight, she was just going to enjoy some calm silence.

The path quickly became dark, as high tree branches arching over the trail shaded much of the ringlight. Yet Xanthe felt confident. It just seemed easy. She was so full of energy. Now all she needed to do now was chat up some boys. Maybe that would be easy too. Gravel on the path crunched under her feet as she made her way forward.

"Miss," a voice called out commandingly from behind her. "Hold up. I have something for you."

It was Damien. He'd followed her outside, approached silently, and now was only two dozen yards away. Here where she was completely alone. Cut off from all help. Conveniently with no witnesses either.

*Oh, I bet you do. Something stabby.* She was too surprised to feel any fear. Instead, she just wondered if she were being hunted for her real power, or Nadeen's gossiped imaginings. It hardly mattered. She had no intention of letting anything choke with her blood. Without a word, she turned and fled.

"Wait!"

## Chapter 15

The dark path blurred under her feet as Xanthe tore down the canyon switchbacks towards the river. Some other time she might have been panicked about being chased, yet in the moment it seemed more exciting than anything. Nothing could catch her. She just knew. The speed of her run was surprising even to herself. The obstructions and swerves of the path were entertaining to dodge and follow. One of those helpless beauties of romance tales, who always tripped and needed rescue, she was not. More the opposite. She could take care of herself. She hadn't even begun to breathe hard.

With a glance back, she saw him, a dark predatory shadow far closer than she expected. He was saving himself time by leaping the switchbacks when the distance down was short enough to make it. Despite herself, she couldn't help but feel a touch of respect. Finally, a boy who could keep up. But two could play that game. At the next switchback, she leapt off the path. Jumping for a tree branch, she swung forward on it, and then released, catching the frond of a giant pole-like timberfungus below. As she clung to its smooth bark, it bent down faster than she remembered them doing when she was younger. It didn't break though, and it slowed her descent too much for the landing to hurt. In a matter of seconds, she was twenty yards below on the path next to the river.

Now she was permanently ahead. He would never catch her. But just to be sure, after running across the low wooden Riverford Bridge, she headed off the path into the darkened underbrush. He would likely keep going up the path. Or if not, and followed off the trail, she expected that he'd quickly get lost.

The forest smelled of rich loam and fungal spore yet was almost entirely black. So dark, she could even see the faint glow of the ribbon on her wrist. She walked slowly, focusing all her efforts on simply not tripping. At this, she was successful. Only once did she stumble slightly as she stepped on a rotting branch that gave way. After ten minutes, she felt she'd lost him. There was no sign of pursuit.

Now that Damien was lost behind her, Xanthe realized that she was too. She'd been completely turned around, nor were there landmarks or path to right her, only dark outland forest. The city couldn't be that far off, but it was up the canyon and she'd no intention of returning to the path that Damien tread. She headed uphill, across country. Even without directions, this way would eventually have to lead within sight of the walls. From there she could make it to the gate. It was the safest choice, even if it meant extra walking. She still wasn't afraid but did start to feel a little worried.

"Come on Xanthe. You're tough," she told herself. "After all the bad luck you've had tonight, what's the worst that could possibly happen?"

An answer rose from the back of her mind. Out here in the witchwilds, perhaps that wasn't the best thing to dwell on.

It soon became apparent that the decision to trailblaze uphill had been a bad idea. High brush kept getting in the way. Sodden branches descended from the gloom. She kept having to move around it, sometimes forced to backtrack when they blocked her path completely. The exhilaration of outrunning an assassin wore off. Now it was just one big slog. Idly she wondered why she kept having bad luck. Was the Curate right? Were wishes somehow matched by dark curses in some sort of giant cosmic balance?

She snorted to herself. Absurd. The whole idea was silly. It wasn't luck at all. Just logic. Why wouldn't Damien and his witchkiller buddy be still skulking around the gates where she'd first heard them? Wouldn't that be the ideal place from which to make a quick escape if they had to? As for the guards? Again, simple. Celeste had sent them after the acolyte Axeman, who was in the area because, well, she herself had told him to search the Gate District to throw him off her trail! See? No need for superstition.

Yet, this wasn't the time to second guess anything. She shivered. No matter how near the city she was, this was still nightmare country at night. If refraining from wishing changed her luck, then she'd stop. Or maybe, just reserve it for when it was truly important. A chill ran up her back as somewhere some alien thought in the back of her head seemed agree with that last idea. Funny how the mind wandered while walking.

Finally, the slope leveled off. The forest though, had not, which meant she no longer had a good way to know which direction to head. Despite the occasional clearing, the city was still not visible through the canopy. "Just reaming great," Xanthe cursed out loud. About the only thing that had gone well was that even after all the mucking about in the forest, her outfit was still pristine. There wasn't a smudge on her shoes. But she didn't care. She just wanted to be home. On the way, she'd get close to a tavern, chat with ten boys, get their stupid names, and leave. Done and done.

That is, if she got out of here alive. Would she?

Of course she would! Why wouldn't she? Unless... Hackles ran up her neck.

The hallmark of grims was that they made you feel that way. That's how they'd earned their name. If one was anywhere near, you'd be struck by existential terror. Knowledge that your death was inescapable. You didn't have to see them either. It was just proximity. Also, numbers. The more friends you had to buoy you, the weaker the effect. The more grims, the stronger. It was why travel alone was so dangerous. Xanthe had heard stories about armed and armored men being so unnerved that they couldn't even summon the will to fight or flee. This was the reason that, of all the nightmares in the wilds, grims were the most feared, even when they weren't around.

Yet they were also few and far between. She was just scaring herself. Yes. That was it. Logically. Of course.

She hoped. The woods were dark, damp, and foreboding. Mist rose from the low underbrush, clinging to the forest floor, illuminated by only the smallest bit of ringlight slanting down through the trees. She couldn't shake the feeling that something was wrong. Everything was silent. Not even peep from forest kestrels. She tried to dispel the silence and gloom by humming a song. All she could think of was a tune from Early Years class she'd loved when she was a little girl. In her high feminine soprano, she sung it again now.

*Sing a song of happy light*
*Be not scared of black or night*
*Fallen seraphs go away*
*You come back some other day*

Her voice faltered. This wasn't making her feel any better. Now she was wondering if this was the day the fallen would come. She needed to run, yet couldn't. That was how she knew. Something really was after her. A chill settled on her skin and tingled as she settled into terror.

*"Your Prey Approaches"*

The sibilant whisper came from nowhere. Xanthe twisted, trying to find the source of the voice. There was nothing. She did hear it, didn't she? Maybe a hallucination. That was what was supposed to happen when you got poisoned with blackdust. Hallucinating and controlled into trying to poison others as you slowly died. But the onset of symptoms never happened so fast. It was also supposed to be pleasant, which wasn't what was happening now. She walked backward to see if anything was following, but then settled into a forward gait, turning her head back and forth nervously scanning the underbrush. There was nothing but dark trees and tall fungal fronds. Still, the alien feeling of dread dogged her. Coldness, inevitability, and fear.

Finally, came a deformation in the world, the hallmark of nightmares. It was almost a relief to finally see her doom at last coalescing, so she could face it. It appeared as smoke, shadow, and a malformation of reality. A thing of darkness, the world seemed to twist around it as it traveled, something like how the Eye of the Creator distorted the constellations that it was in front of. The trunks of each tree smeared near its passage, yet they did not fall. This nightmare never stayed in one form. It presented only occasional twisting visions of claws, a tooth lined gullet, and other body parts, often detached from itself. It was as if settled physicality was alien to its existence. Yet it was also moving. Advancing slowly.

A grim. A distilled manifestation of horror. It was going to consume her soul. She had no defense.

Xanthe backed away, fighting the feeling of helplessness. She still had her legs, if she could summon the will to use them. There was a clearing ahead. She headed that way, walking as fast as she could make herself do so.

Another began to coalesce to the side. It was cutting off another avenue of possible retreat. In the back of her mind she wondered if she was just being herded for the kill, but for the moment it was all she could do to keep moving, so she focused on that. When she reached the clearing, she saw the city in the distance. There was also the path she'd left. All she'd done in cutting through the woods was to slow herself down. Yet most clearly of all, she saw them. More grims. Dozens. All waiting for her.

The terror beat down on her like a torrential rainstorm. Somewhere in the back of her mind, she felt oddly honored. Grims usually hunted alone. They only grouped to take on large groups of men capable of putting up a fierce defense. A slaughter this size was big enough to wipe a good-sized hamlet off the map. It could terrorize most of Jagerfeld. All for her. There was nowhere to run. They were circling in.

Yet. No. She simply refused to give up. There was some elemental piece of her against which the fear simply slid off. Yes, she was alone. Weaponless. Surrounded. But no. She'd somehow found herself again. She wouldn't even berate herself for coming this way. She would run if she could. Fight if she had to. High clouds parted, giving a bit more light as she bent and picked up a pathetically small rock from the path. She then drew herself up, brandishing it. When she spoke, her voice echoed with odd overtones across the glade.

"You should not have followed, vile ones. It was your final mistake. This is not your reality, and here you can be unmade. So now you shall. By my will and what I serve, I seize the uncollapsed waveforms of fate and destine your oblivion. Die in the same horror you've brought for so long."

This was absurd defiance, repeating the words that the Angel Pilot reputedly spoke to the shadows of evil that had followed from ancient Earth. Xanthe didn't even know why they'd come to her; it was likely just some misremembered glimmer of a Churchday sermon. Yet they felt right to say. A formal announcement. More than that. She felt meant to say them. Something inside herself went out like a call. An otherworldliness to match theirs. It was all delusion, of course, but for a brief instant, she almost convinced herself that nightmares could be destroyed simply by willing them out of existence.

Still, she was taken aback by the grims' reaction. Had they been deathhounds instead of nightmares, they would have all simultaneously flattened their ears against their heads. In unison they hunkered down, and there came a defensive snarling to their alien manner. The terror pouring into her now had a distinct overtone of both hate and doubt. They solidified as well. The strange distortions reduced. They stopped changing, instead freezing into various congealed forms of bulbous multi-eyed, razor-toothed, monstrosities. A silly sort of hope flared in Xanthe, even as intellectually, she still saw no escape. Dozens of these terrible things of twisted chaos and evil were before her, and she was just one lone girl with a small rock.

Xanthe sensed, rather than saw, the attack from behind. She instinctively dodged, ducking to the left and rolling. She thought she'd gotten clean away. She felt nothing touch her. Yet a cold shock ran up her back anyway. Twisting, she saw a grim with its frozen lamprey-mouth, far too near. The nightmare was strangely injured. Large horizontal slashes burned across its body, and it had white non-illuminating flames licking on them. It didn't matter. The thing was within striking range, and still had strength enough to jump in for the kill.

The mouth opened. It was about to bite, yet also seemed a phantom. It was both there and not there. Through it, she sensed, a nameless realm of elemental corruption, that inside, hid a semblance of sentience. A thing of overwhelming power and malevolence. Immensity beyond description. Nothing she could fight, yet she decided to strike anyway. There was little else she could do. As her last thought, she wished the connection broken, and all the darkness burned to nothingness.

A silvered sword flashed like lightning right before her eyes. Its point went straight into the gullet of the thing and drove through its body, ending with it fully embedded up to the hilt. The grim convulsed once and began to dissolve into smoke, a twisted shifting that Xanthe could sense was in a direction she could not point to. Yet as the edge emerged from the other side, it touched the white flames licking at the nightmare's flanks, and they leapt to the metal like a smoldering fire suddenly given alchemist's-pitch on which to feed. The blade burst into white flame and the entire insides of the abomination lit. She could see the inferno through its flesh. The fire burned everywhere, in every impossible direction, setting even the inaccessible parts of it alight. It let out a horrific scream, less heard than felt inside her mind. The swordsman turned his gloved hand, twisting the blade inside to increase the grim's agony, and she heard his mocking laughter. Xanthe looked up to see her rescuer.

Damien.

He fixed her with a crazed stare, equal parts frenzied bloodlust and glee. Grinning down, he spoke but a single word.

"Run."

She needed no further encouragement. The grims focused on him now. She could feel the palpable shift of their attention. As the burden of their fear fell away, power flowed back into her legs, or perhaps just the will to use them. It mattered not. They were working. She saw a gap in the circling nightmares, just as two of them lunged. Damien met them full on as she dodged, and she heard his hysterical laughter, as if he were having the time of his life. Fitting, since his hopeless position meant the remainder of it was going to be extremely short. She picked her opportunity and escaped through the line of things, made easier because they were no longer paying attention to her. Once free, glanced briefly back. He was circling like a cornered tigran. His blade burned with white fire – shorter blade too in his other hand that he held reversed behind him. He'd felled two more, but the remaining scores were massing. It was obvious that they were preparing for a final dive that none could escape.

Xanthe turned her head and sped forward. She was nearly certain she'd never sprinted so fast in her entire life. Her legs had such pent-up energy that she barely felt it as the path blurred by. No more than a thousand yards away, she found herself out of breath before the steeltower.

And just like that, she was safe. This was directly outside the city walls. If she detected even the trace of grims approaching, something she now felt experienced enough to do, it would be trivial to retreat through the guarded northwestern gate. This ancient building was no more than a hundred yards from it.

The steeltower was a familiar ruin, abandoned because it was unstable, and so completely stripped of usable materials that it nearly seemed swept. She knew its layout from when she and Celeste had played here as girls, both pretending to be amazon adventurers. There was a rarely visited back room that featured an excellent vista. Once she reached it, she sat down on the bare permacrete. She wrapped her arms around her knees and stared through the gap where glasssteel windows had once been, gazing at the pretty torchlit city and its crenelated walls.

Then, she just shook.

What in hellspace had just happened? Besides almost dying, that is. If it wasn't blackdust, then what? She'd heard voices. Sensed things. If what she'd just experienced was to be believed, she'd just escaped the largest slaughter of grims that had ever been observed and survived to tell tale of.

Damien. He'd certainly fulfilled his desire for death. Despite her every attempt, she felt a terrible stab of remorse. Perhaps seeing her surrounded, he'd found his own heart. For he certainly showed it in the end. The scene of him fighting and laughing seemed frozen in her mind. She knew she'd led him to his doom, even as he'd turned it into an elegant pretender's dance.

She tried to be happy about this, or at least relieved. One witchkiller down! But she wasn't. Seeing violence firsthand, made her aware of how much she hated it. Hated all that led to it, including adventuring. For all her youthful tomboy dreams of being a fearless, renowned, research scholar, who discovered ancient mysteries, engaged in mild bits of daring-do, all while cutely breaking boys' hearts with her big fat natural haunches, she realized that she just wasn't cut out for it. Not the reality.

The reality. Especially ironic given how surreal this all was. These strange events kept happening, and she had the oddest feeling that they weren't at all random. The grims weren't there by chance. They'd been sent somehow. There was malevolence beyond comprehension behind it all, somehow connected to her. If she were a leaf in a stream, she was shaped to float towards froth and whirlpools, or maybe something was throwing rocks, trying to sink her, or both. She didn't like it. Not one bit.

She'd never wanted to be a witch of weirdness. No one asked her. No one could make her. If it didn't stop, maybe she'd just find some boring childish husband she didn't love, marry him, and stay housebound for the rest of her life, trapped just like Mrs. Fullbarn warned against. That would keep her out of trouble. She sat moodily, clinging to her knees for minutes, watching the city torches cast shadows on the wall, trying to calm herself. It wasn't even the fear that was the worst part. She was feeling less of that, ever since the grims. It was the guilt, leading someone to their death. She hated it all. Violence. Murder. Misfortune. If only. If only something. She wasn't sure what.

"There you are," a dark voice said with evident satisfaction behind her. A chill ran up her back. Xanthe slowly turned her eyes, but already knew who it was.

Damien.

He was holding the two swords. Both now had white flames flickering upon them. He advanced towards her. His grin was considerably less crazed, far more triumphant. Insanely deadly. "I'm genuinely impressed. You gave me quite a lot of unexpected exercise."

Or there was this possibility she'd overlooked. It all ending now. Xanthe knew she could jump down off the ledge to the ground below. This was only the second story. But he could simply jump down on top of her and end her. So rather than run from her doom, she stood to face him.

"What do you want?" It seemed more a formality than anything.

"I have something for you. I told you!" He gave a brilliant devil-may-care smile, then laughed. "You ran."

"Well, I had business elsewhere. Do you normally chase after girls like this?"

"I..." his smile faltered, and he furrowed his brows. "In truth, I'm not sure what came over me. Other than I was nearly certain that if I didn't, I'd never see you again." Born from years of practice, he sheathed both of his blades in a single motion. The cold flames remained visible through the leather, though he seemed not to notice. "Nonetheless, after what just happened, I'm glad I did."

It was Xanthe's turn to frown. He was right. Had he not been there, she'd be dead now. She owed this murderer. Not that anything would make her change her mind about him. His handsomeness made her even more wary. Yet at the same time, it didn't seem like he was preparing to attack. Was it possible he didn't know that she was a greatwitch?

"What do you have for me?" Now she was genuinely curious. Even stranger was a sense of déjà vu, as if she knew him from somewhere even though she'd never seen him before in her life.

"Oh, just a little thing," he reached inside his shirt and pulled out a small scroll case. "I retrieved this and thought you could return it to its rightful owner." He then opened the box, plucked out the exquisite glass rose and offered it over to her.

Xanthe's eyes bulged.

It was her favor.

## Chapter 16

"Where did you get that?" Xanthe reached out for the crystal rose, noticing that while it remained perfect, Damien himself had not escaped the battle unscathed. He had a cut on his hand. It had to be bothering him because he'd taken off his glove.

"I saw it stolen. Your sister was flashed in the face by a little witch girl, who then grabbed it and threw it up in the air. It caught on a rain gutter. I climbed up the other side of the building to retrieve it, but by the time I did, everyone was gone."

"My sister?"

"You have more than one? I'm talking about the one with the odd lumpy legs. Garish makeup. Cheap perfume you can smell half a block away. Or maybe she's your cousin. But the family resemblance is unmistakable. You should return it to her."

Xanthe scowled angrily, suddenly understanding what he was referring to. She flushed. "The makeup wasn't *that* bad!" She pouted. Now she really hated him.

"Don't tell me you pranked her into that!" He scolded. "Poor girl. Whatever did she do to you?"

Xanthe's eyes blazed. She threw her fists down at her sides. "That girl was me!"

"Impossible," he breathed, shaking his head. She saw him reluctantly gaze at her, truly taking her in for the first time. "You're positively..." He stopped abruptly.

"Yes. I admit it," Xanthe fumed. "Lumpy legs. I was wearing padding. That's because I have no haunches. Do you see any? At all? No! Because there's all this muscle. On a girl. See?!"

In her fury, she showed him the worst aspect of her body. Her tight, round, and not at all flabby bottom. Yet he refused. His eyes widened, and suddenly he tried to avert his gaze, increasingly vexed by his failure. His confident masterful manner fell away as he struggled with his eyes. Then they settled on the horrible dark freckle she hated so much, nestled deep in her alabaster cleavage. His mouth worked once silently before he turned away heatedly. "Just great. I do not need this."

It was the final rejection Xanthe had expected. Even all of Mrs. Fullbarn's talents couldn't make her attractive. Not even to an evil witchkiller. He'd refused to even look at her. He was turned around, discomfited and fiddling with his belt. "Need what?" She challenged.

He ignored her, muttering, "Lord, I've sworn to you my purpose, yet constantly am accosted by these divinely shallow women."

Xanthe blinked, taking in his words. "What did you just call me?"

He wheeled. They were both furious. "Look miss," he said in a tightly controlled voice. "Your looks are clearly important to you, but there are much more profound things in life."

"Like what? Killing people? With that sword of yours?" She returned right back to in his face. "Or scaring girls to death by running after them with no explanation?"

She knew she'd struck true as his eyes widened, so she continued telling him off. "Since you're in the business, maybe you can explain what is so reaming *compelling* about death, war, the Curate executing heretics, witchkillers murdering girls, betrayal and assassination, bandits, the petty games of cities. Why exactly do musclebound mercenaries and treacherous highborn have such great insight into the human condition? Pray tell me. Because so far as I can see, they're all little more than overweening thugs. Yet all the stories are about them – how noble they are, how tragic, how interesting, how maudlin. Endless fascination. Yet when a girl like me just tries to fit in, use a little effort to look just okay, *that's* what's called superficial. Nothing like the enlightened nobility of being an apologist for bloodlust!"

He retreated under her onslaught. Momentarily, he couldn't find anything to say. When he did, it was weak. "You don't understand at all."

"Clearly." She muttered. "But what do I know? I'm so *shallow*." Her voice dripped with sarcasm.

He was clearly bothered. "You have no right to judge me. You would not even be alive if I did not know how to handle myself. Heaven knows I wasn't expecting you to throw yourself at me for saving your life. I wouldn't want that anyway. I've just sworn off distracting relationships. But at least you can pay me a modicum of respect."

"Me? Me? Who just insulted who?!"

"Well, what else am I supposed to think? We meet after both nearly getting killed, and about the first thing out of your mouth is what? You bemoaning that your ass isn't fat?"

Xanthe turned pink. By the Creator, she just did that, didn't she? That was incredibly embarrassing, but she was determined not to lose. "W... well," she stammered, "I wouldn't have, if you hadn't goaded me. About my padding." To give herself falsey haunches. She winced. That sounded petty even in her own ears.

He rolled his eyes before staring fixedly off to the side. "Fine. I withdraw the comment. You are not shallow, though it is self-evident that you've got certain misapprehensions." He shook his head and said, largely as an aside to himself, "Seriously, I don't get the north. What are the men around here? Blind?"

Xanthe didn't grasp what he was saying, but his change in tone was obvious. He was semi-apologizing, at least as close as she ever was going to get. That put the onus on her, and she struggled a moment before finally giving in. "Well, okay. Thank you for coming to my rescue," she admitted grudgingly. "I still can't believe you killed all those grims."

"*Those* were grims?" He smirked arrogantly. "Humph. They're much less than their reputation."

"Don't get so full of yourself. I think the white flames had something to do with your survival."

He cocked his head with interest. "What white flames?"

Xanthe opened and shut her mouth. Maybe it was all just a hallucination. Even sheathed, both his weapons continued to burn steadily, though the fire didn't seem to have any real-world effect. "Never mind. It was just a trick of my eye." She didn't want him to think her crazy.

"Perhaps it isn't. Tell me what you saw. I promise I will not judge."

Xanthe grew suspicious. Was he trying to figure out if she was a witch? Fat chance. "I said it was just a trick to my eye. But tell me, who is this lord you swore to? Since you admit you didn't come for the Festival, was it by his command that you're here in Jagerfeld?"

"My purpose would founder were I to reveal it. But as for 'the Lord', it's just an ancient way of addressing the true Creator. I swore unto God an oath. I don't need any distractions."

She realized she was too close to him, so turned and walked to view the torch lined city wall, holding the glass rose in her left hand. "Yet you're distracted anyway? Constantly? Ever think the Creator might be sending you a message about what he thinks of this bloody oath of yours?"

She was rewarded with silence. Xanthe grew smug. Almost as much as he'd been about his victory.

"It's irrevocable," he stated flatly.

She turned her head sharply. "Why? Don't think you're so clever. It must have to do with using that sword you're so acquainted with. Don't you realize how short a life yours will be? All it takes is one mistake."

"Of course. That's why I was laughing at the grims. Their gaze reminded me that I am about to die." Once again, a crazed smile flickered on his face. "Which is hardly news."

"Then why even get into this business? If there's only death in it, you should just stop."

He lowered his eyes, still grinning but reflective, and with a touch more respect. "I was born into it," he finally said. "I've known I'm going to live a short and violent life since the age of four."

"You were... born into a dark house?" She knew nothing of witchkillers, but them hiring mercenary assassins to do their dirty work sounded ever so plausible. She just wondered what it was like to grow up in such a clan.

"Oh yes." His eyes glinted. "Without a doubt. My house is the darkest on Haven. We kill everyone. Even our own. None escape alive."

"Oh." Xanthe swallowed. She had no idea. Here she was worried about her own family situation, with dad not being rich. But this was worse. Still, no. No. She was not going to start sympathizing with a killer. She swore that to herself. "You could still disappear," she told him. "Run away."

"You are hunted. If you die before you're found, then your children are."

"So..." she paused. "Are you here on a job? Going to kill me to keep me quiet?"

He shook his head with a sad smile. "I'm not sure I could bring myself to do so, even if I had to. But rest assured, I don't. I'm not wanted in Jagerfeld, and nothing I've said will change that. Quite the reverse. A wanted man in one city is paid double the next one over."

She stared at him stiff jawed and disapproving. "The free cities of Thule are more united than that."

His smile turned cynical. "Try not to be too disappointed when you find out differently."

Xanthe didn't like the way this was going, and still didn't like him. She knew exactly why. "You pretend to fear vengeance? With your swordsmanship? Oh please. Jagerfeld is isolated. Take refuge here and you'd be a lot safer than what you're doing now. Because if some stupid southern assassin came, people would help you! I would myself. So why not? Unless what you say is really all just an excuse."

If she expected to prick him, his reaction was nearly the opposite. He gave her a look of wistful affection. "I don't even know your name, yet you make me pine for a future that shall never be. The best I can do is to keep you safely innocent."

"I'm Xanthe. Zan–thee." She pronounced both syllables for him. "Like the moon which sees all. You have no right to patronize me as naïve," she chided coolly. "I'm much more than I seem."

"Call me Damien, and perhaps I should believe you. Few men have ever defied the grim nightmares, yet there I found you facing down dozens. So, I won't even claim my prize, though I must admit it's growing tempting." In the dim torchlight, he was starting to seem dangerously rakish.

"Your prize?"

"Why, yes," he continued smoothly. "That favor in your hand. I thought I was giving it over for your sister. But if it's truly yours, then I returned it to you. Doesn't your city have a Festival tradition around that?"

Xanthe froze speechless. He was right. He'd returned her favor. She was his for the evening.

But she didn't want to be! He was a villain, a hired murderer almost certainly in the employ of the Sect of Penance. She became intimately aware that she was blushing, her body responding to the whole embarrassing situation. Worse, her dress was somehow picking up on it, subtly shrinking. "You... you can't make me." She protested weakly.

He smiled brilliantly, completely unaware of what he was doing to her. "I just promised that I wouldn't."

"Well, but..." She didn't want that either. In fact, she didn't know what she wanted. Or, she did. It truly did seem terribly romantic for a boy to return a favor the way the first favor was returned to Lady Jager, not the whole ritual being just pretense. But she needed it to have been done by someone good, not a thinly disguised assassin. That put him completely off limits. "What are you going to do instead?"

"I'll probably go about my business." His tone was genially ominous. "I have some." He turned.

"Wait!" Xanthe cried out, then swallowed nervously. "Tradition is strong in Jagerfeld. You really did return my favor, and with much more effort than boys usually give. So, I... I guess I'll go with you."

"You will...?" Entertained, he eyed her. "You forgot to add that so long as we're together, you expect that I'll be unlikely to get into any mischief." He considered for a moment. Then smiling wryly offered his left arm. "Very well, Xanthe. For the time being, I accept."

Her chin crinkled. A *perceptive* unapologetic assassin. This one was dangerous. Smart. Not a brainless thug at all. She didn't like it. Or was trying not to. Her blush hadn't faded in the least. In truth, it seemed to be growing worse. Nor was taking his arm making it better. He was strong. His hands were warm. His dark hair was tousled. He smelled clean. As he smoothly led her back down the stairs she could just feel the courtesy about him. It was as if he were the perfect opposite of Horace – open evil shrouding inner honor. All at once, she had a disturbingly clear vision of how girls could fall for boys like this, dooming their children to perpetuate criminality throughout the generations.

They slowly walked into the countryside, wandering along the dark path towards the city gate. With the ringlight shadow of Haven in the night sky, the stars were brilliant diamonds. He seemed in no rush. Xanthe looked up to him. "What would you do if you weren't bound by circumstance?" This wasn't just to make conversation. She was genuinely curious.

He didn't answer straightaway but pondered for a while. "Play my music... recover ancient arcana," he finally declared. "I would learn more of the hidden histories. The Curate knows much more than they let on, but even they know little compared to some."

"They're idiots," Xanthe scoffed. "Goodhearted, but stupid and ignorant." At least she could talk to him about these sorts of things. A boy like this was hardly going to get her in trouble.

"Hmm. Do not confuse your local clergy with the archcardinals. Prayerhome is none of those things."

"Fine. I'll grant you that the Sect of Penance is evil, along with *also* being utterly stupid and ignorant."

A half-smile played on his lips. "Care to be disabused of that notion? I could do so, but do not repeat my words, for it would mean your life."

Xanthe crinkled her chin. This was not even near to how she imagined her first favor-date would go. Talking about how she might be killed was just something she'd never considered as a romantic topic. But he seemed to be serious, and she was feeling challenged in ways she couldn't even begin to describe. "I'm a Scholar, and a good one. I'm not afraid of knowledge. But buying the death of witch girls is not only evil, it's stupid. There's just no excuse."

"A Scholar, eh? Are you up for a test?" He sucked on the cut on his hand. Xanthe knew she could fix it but wasn't going to. He'd live no matter what, and she'd die if she showed her power. "Tell me, what do you see welling from this wound?"

"Um.... blood?"

"Exactly, my dear. Now there's the red blood. But what about this black stuff? What's that called?"

She didn't get the point. "Well, I mean. Its black blood, of course." She answered. There was superstition that as it was the color of death, it was the Creator's mark of mortality. But that wasn't Curate cannon.

"Correct. That is its colloquial name. But do you know what the ancients called it?"

"Um." She hadn't thought about it much. They did have a name for everything, but she'd never seen it in any of the hardcopy she'd read, even the originals. Even her father had never spoken of it. "Not really."

"They called it 'liquid cybernetics', though in truth, it's more of a proteotronic colloid. I don't expect you to fully grasp what that means. I don't either. But the best analogy is that it's a combination of incredibly tiny clockwork combined with lightning which operates inside our bodies. It puts a copy of itself into each new baby in the womb."

"What are you saying? We're... part machine?"

"We're all machine, in a manner of speaking. The red part is natural, the black part, not. Yet ancients didn't make black blood. Not directly. Artificial minds they created did it for them, beings of unimaginable power. You know the thirteen demons the Curate rails against? The malevolent five and the unholy eight? They're not supernatural at all. They're clockwork personalities that in the days of antiquity lived in our buildings and our bodies. The Grand Curate is in terror of their legend."

Xanthe felt chill. "Why?"

"We were their slaves," he declared quietly. "Until something happened to them, something far beyond our ken. Still, the danger may not be over. The Sect of Penance believes that inside us all, particularly in dreadwitches, the means of our chattel still exists in fragmentary form. Therefore, all those who exercise demonic powers risk wakening our ancient masters. Witchkillers try to stop it in the only way they know how."

They had returned to the path. The hard-packed ground was steady under her feet. Its gravel crunched with firm familiarity. Yet the world felt as if it had been turned upside down. Xanthe shivered. "Are you sure? The Curate preaches that the ancestors usurped the Creator's authority in giving girls the touch, not that our arrogated power is born of demons. Certainly not that we are part demon ourselves. That's..." words failed her.

"High heresy. Scholars who know the truth dare not teach it openly. Asserting that humanity is partly demonic?" He chuckled. "The mob would howl for your blood, and an archdeacon would sign your warrant without remorse. Even, or especially, if he believed what you said to be true. Ignorance is the Curate's shield. The last thing they want is experimentation. That's why cults are so hated."

"Does that mean witchery is really evil?" Xanthe had never felt so unsure of herself. Maybe she was the villain all this time and didn't even know it. "Is this slavery what we should all be truly afraid of?"

He shrugged. "We are all already slaves, even if we cannot name our masters. Our culture. Our family. Our circumstances. Our own flaws and delusions. Our doubts and denials. They all bind us."

She scowled. This way too handsome dodgy-power boy was poetic too. Not what she needed right now. "I need to know facts. Is the Sect of Penance in the right on this?"

"Perhaps," he mused unconcerned. "Theirs is but one theory. Unpopular at that. Another is that the demons never left; they just stopped talking to us. Still another is that they continue to control us in secret ways we don't notice. One more is that they got sick with strange mechanical diseases of their minds. Maybe nightmares we see aren't real and are merely illusions projected into our minds; if any not possessed saw us, we'd seem like inebriates batting aimlessly at phantom blackdust deliriums."

"Which do you believe?"

He gazed down absently at the scratch on his hand. "It all seems moot. Any sufficiently deadly delusion is indistinguishable from reality."

Xanthe nodded. His words had shaken her because she felt so much truth in them. She noticed his swords. They were still flickering with the cold white flames that he seemed blind to. Was that just all in her head? How did he know of these things?

"What *are* you?" She wondered out loud, clinging to his arm for comfort. Assassins of his type were no mere bandits, that was obvious. Worse than troubling because he made her realize what she was really wanted in a suitor. An equal. Someone she could respect. The insight ate at her because she knew she'd never be able to attract that kind of boy, a sort of good-Damien, if someone like that even existed. Maybe a little less scary in the knowledge department, so that she didn't feel quite so inferior, though even that was maddeningly attractive.

"What am I? I'm your escort for the evening. Haven't you noticed?" Damien teased as they came to the gate. When they walked through, the guards stopped to stare, and after that, the people in the district did too. She was in a permanent state of embarrassment now. She wasn't sure what to do.

"They're all gawking at me. It's this dress. It's so outlandish," she spoke as he escorted her. It was worse here, because of how much she stood out. Tradefair was the sedate sibling of the raucous districts to the south. Clean streets, well-lit with oil lamps, and tidy little shops projected a far more sedate atmosphere. There were tea-and-book shops here, not taverns.

"Unique. Original. Provocative. Perfect for a night such as this. Not to mention that it also perfectly describes you. Think these thoughts, and people will see the confidence you bear. Then, no matter what you wear, they will treat you accordingly."

"How can I do that? I don't believe it myself." She sighed moodily.

"Just pretend then. Pretend that you are the most beautiful and enchanting girl I've met throughout the thirteen realms, and that merely by your elegance alone, every other gentleman envy me for having you on my arm." He led her on a slow promenade down the street, while people kept glancing at them as a couple.

Xanthe frowned. "It's hard to believe so many things that aren't true."

"Oh, but of course they are."

Suave, too. He knew exactly how to lie charmingly. She couldn't help but feel better anyway. The evening was turning out fine. Or rather it wasn't. She didn't want to be happy with him. What was she going to do when her friends started turning up dead?

"Are you enchanted enough to leave my poor little Jagerfeld alone? Or will you make the gutters of my innocent little city choke with blood?"

Damien gave her a disconcerted sideways glance. Xanthe returned a close-lipped smile of false innocence. They were his own words thrown back at him. She had no idea why she was playing such a dangerous game but didn't care.

"I am starting to wonder just how bewitched I am," he grumbled gently. "But my path is set. I recently received a harsh lesson about what I can afford in terms of relationships, so I shall no longer make the mistake of entering into any."

They finally settled at a little stone bridge which arched one of the tributaries of the Jagerfeld river. It was romantic, low lit and empty. "We're alike then," she told him. "I just had an experience that made me do the same thing. In Thule culture, not wearing maiden's braids means I've declared myself too young for anything serious."

"Well that's good," he breathed as she drew close to him. "I like it this way." He put his fingers through her wavy golden-white hair.

Having both declared their independence of all romantic intentions, Xanthe realized that she desperately wanted him to kiss her. There was no logic to the feeling at all. They were all wrong for each other. It didn't matter. Her body, especially, didn't care. Its response to Horace had been nothing compared to this. She fit Damien. His musky scent was so intoxicating, and the way he gazed at her almost made her believe that he really did think her beautiful.

Perversely, this mood salved her fears of boys. Now she knew the lie of Horace's words. She'd never wanted that preening thug. It had all just been involuntary reactions, the mildest echo of what she was feeling now.

Raging feelings were so hard to control. The most attractive thing about Damien was the hopelessness. He was safe because this wasn't going anywhere. Briefly she wondered if there was a chance. He, the brilliant roguish assassin, she the uncomely witch, that he liked anyway because unlike normal girls she took foolish chances. They would fall in love. She would seduce him into a path of good, and, no, forget it. Not happening. But anyway, she wouldn't be able to help but to fall into his arms, that is, if she were slightly taller. Even standing on her toes she had to turn her head up to reach his lips. He was so tall.

Out of nowhere she tripped. He caught her against his chest and put his arms around her. Exactly like she'd been imagining but unintentional. While her body briefly flared, mentally it broke the mood. "Sorry," she told him. What just happened?

"It's quite alright," he said, as he slowly righted her, his strong hand on her side. "Truly, I should be the one apologizing. I shouldn't even be here doing this. It's not fair to you."

"It's okay," she nodded, regaining some composure. "The reward for a favor is just a walk, kiss, and nothing more." Then she realized what had happened. "My shoes!" They'd changed form. She now was standing on slinky little black pumps. Most of her small toes were visible and her heels were high and spiky. They had tiny lace straps, and her toenails had little black runic designs on them.

"You ran from the grims in those?" He stared down for the first time.

"I, um..." she thought quickly. "They're, um, clockwork with retractable heels. They must have come out accidentally." She tried stepping. Almost intentionally awkward, they forced her to walk nearly tiptoe. A perfect excuse to fall into his arms. Even while flushing, her eyes narrowed. She needed to control her feelings while wearing this dress of the ancients. It was far too accommodating to her mood. Prim around father, revealing with this boy. Now turning into these shoes. She didn't want to think about what it would do if Damien got her completely alone. The last thing she needed was for some fleeting thought to turn it into a racy negligee. It was skimpy enough already.

"I really shouldn't have done this." His eyes lingered on her. "After all that's happened, it would be better to break off cleanly. I should go. Maybe I shouldn't even give you the traditional kiss."

Xanthe nodded, feeling both relieved and rejected at the same time. "Okay," she swallowed. A thought came to invite him to change his mind later, but that was just too desperate. Besides, he was a killer. She had to keep reminding herself of that. "We'll likely never see each other again."

"Which is for the best," he agreed as she drew nearer to him.

"I hope you don't do anything in the future that makes me regret being with you. Because I've had a wonderful time." She declared softly.

"I have as well. Too much so."

She wondered if they might kiss anyway. He was quite close.

Something caught her eye in the creek below. "Oh, wait. One other thing I have to do," Without another word, she sat on the cold stone bridge wall, swung her legs over, placed her favor on the edge, and leapt off.

"Xanthe?!" Damien cried out just before she hit the water.

## Chapter 17

Nothing quite so completely dampens a romantic mood as being dunked in fresh snow melt but seeing the body of a girl floating face down in the creek certainly ran close second. The chill hurt so much it was almost impossible to describe, but Xanthe didn't waste a second thinking about it. She knew she only had about a minute before she'd be in trouble herself. Cold would sap all strength in her if she didn't get out as quickly as she could. Fortunately, the accuracy of her jump was near perfect. Any closer and she would have landed on top of the remains. She even managed to keep her face dry.

This made the body much easier to grab, if not easy to swim with. Now all she had to do was get out. She put her left arm under the inert form and tried to make her way to the side. The creek was deep and not fast moving. Still, it was hard to find something to grab. Here in the city, both sides of the creek's edge were rough-hewn stone walls. Xanthe tried and failed to find purchase on some cobblestone outcrop. No use. Her wet hand couldn't find a grip. As she splashed, she already felt her legs becoming numb. This probably hadn't been the best idea, but no time for regrets now.

At last, she got hold of something. The iron bar of a grate covering a sewage sluice. It was cold and hard, but more welcome in her palm than anything else she could imagine. Sputtering ice water, she used it as leverage to pull herself against the raised wall. With little grunts of effort, she slid her hand closer until she was able to twist herself into a position where she might be able to lift herself out of the stream. The tricky part was to do that without losing hold of the body. She swung her leg up over the lip of the retaining wall, and with the strength of one arm and one leg, tried to pull herself up.

Xanthe heaved with effort, getting herself halfway out, but for the rest of her, it was no use. The cold body was positioned in such a way as to make it impossible for her to clamber up without having to lift it at the same time, and she just didn't have the strength to do both at once. This was getting dangerous. Her body was growing progressively number. She wasn't sure that she could get out even if she let go. Another horribly awkward situation, it was reminiscent of how she'd had to get into Horace's coach.

Just as she was considering dropping her burden and purely trying to save herself, her wrist was seized in a vice-like grip, and at the same time the weight of what she was holding disappeared. There was a wrenching movement as she was lifted like a bedraggled child out of the water. Damien was there, He held her by the arm while also gripping the girl's body upside down by the leg. He slung the latter behind his shoulder for balance before stepping back and setting her down.

"Seriously, Xanthe," he scolded with a worried look. "That was a fool thing to do. If I hadn't been here..."

"But you were, right?" She smiled winsomely. "I was a daredevil as a girl, and since I've regressed, I'm getting back into it. Besides, what you do is even more dangerous, and I don't see you changing."

He groaned. "Well, I *am* scolded for taking unnecessary risks."

Water drained like a faucet out of the bottom of her outfit at a preternaturally fast rate. Even her hair's dampness wicked away expeditiously where it touched the fabric, and in moments she was completely dry. All that was left was the lingering cold. "This is necessary," Xanthe told him. "We're not fans of murder in Jagerfeld. We've quite enough death as it is. Something I hope you remember".

"Oh. Yes," he turned, letting the victim's body down. "You know her?"

"Probably not. We're a pretty big town." She examined the body.

It was Priscia.

"Professional work," Damien noted expertly at a glance. "You can tell because she wasn't molested. Also, that wound is made by a Hylian shiv. Stuck at the base of the neck, it paralyzes before it kills. Her heart stopped before she hit the water. The question is who and why."

"She was a witch. In more ways than one. Not greatwitch strong at all though. Just flashy."

His eyes narrowed. "Hmm. The north has this reputation. You know any greatwitches?"

"Maybe." Instinctively, Xanthe reached down. She couldn't stand using her power to probe dead meat, one reason why she hated eating it. But here, she needed to know. Priscia was her least favorite person in all Jagerfeld, but if an autopsy could serve some purpose, she would do it. She tried to bring forth her touch and was surprised at how strong it was. There was none of the balkiness that it usually had. It was almost foreign. Everything was so easy, it felt effortless.

*The body was cold. The little bubbles and lines of light were dim, almost dark. Nothing was moving. Especially the nerves were sliced and dead within the bony spine about the ocean of former life that was Priscia. The streaks of energy that would normally travel from the brain to the heart could never make it past the break. It would need a special spark. No matter. It was ever so easy to cause artificially. Xanthe did so. The heart muscle spasmed once, and in that brief tremor of blood movement, oxygen starved nerves flickered. Especially in the brain.*

A chill of fear and resignation went up her back. Dung. Just dung. So, she'd found her life's purpose at last. Apparently, it was to die saving the person who tormented her the most. Because she couldn't just let someone die in front of her that she could save. Then Damien would have the kind of victim he no doubt was being well paid to kill.

"What are you doing?"

"Bide," Xanthe commanded. She put her hand over Priscia's wound and time stood still.

The world changed. Oddly. This wasn't her normal touch trance. Glowing lines spread out from Priscia into the world, lighting into strange displays of numbers and moving charts as ghostly images overlaid on Xanthe's eyesight. Though she didn't understand all the symbols, they appeared to be displays of her patient's vital signs, organs, and nervous system. Every reference to Priscia was glowing red, the color of panic and system shutdown. Nothing worse than her brain. Xanthe saw the lungs were drained, a result of her being dangled upside down, but more importantly she saw the heart. Once again, by triggering a spasm, the barest movement of blood wakened cells about the body. A small chart titled "Cellular metabolism" blinked into existence. The other axis was body temperature. Xanthe wasn't sure exactly what it meant but guessed that the ice cold of the river had somehow preserved Priscia's body, slowing her final demise.

She knew, even though she did not see them with her eyes, that tendrils from her dress had pierced both her and Priscia's skin and were facilitating communication between their bodies. At Xanthe's command, Priscia's spiderweb structure flickered, and then began to undulate on its own, moving blood within her body. Like blowing on a sodden campfire, Xanthe saw Priscia's nerves wake; they'd reached the edge of death, but this was pulling them back. A display popped up. Blood oxygen levels were still colored yellowish-green, presumably non-critical. That meant breathing was not yet important. Strange superimposed circles guided her focus to the wound, rather than the lungs.

Xanthe closed her eyes. Even without this enhanced state, she'd often found it easier to see with her touch without sight. But now it was almost as if she were in a different world. The damage was expanded ten-thousand-fold, and she was inside it, a microscopic avatar walking the cells of Priscia's dying body. Everywhere were floating descriptions, operating charts: "white matter", "anterior horns", of "gray matter" which when expanded were "cervical ganglia". Once again, pressure from her touch washed out the wound poisons. But this time, she saw what she was doing as she operated, knitting injuries back together. It didn't quite seem as if any of these illusions were doing the work for her. Her talent seemed to come from some other inexplicable place, beyond all this. She just wanted things to happen and it did, sometimes guided by black wires, more often moving on their own accord, almost as if in a reversal of time. Now, more than ever, she could feel some strange power channeling through her that seemed different than what her dress was doing.

A few more jolts and Priscia's heart began to beat. The base of her brain was sending heartbeat signals in reflex. With that, Priscia suddenly gasped and coughed, and started breathing raggedly. The red systems in her body shifted in color to orange, yet she was not awake, nor out of danger, due to the extreme cold of her body. She was deeply hypothermic. Xanthe tried to think of a means to fix this but came up blank. Idly she wondered if she'd lose her to cold-death after bringing her back alive. Sacrificing her own life for a failed operation. That would be rich.

At her desire, the tendrils of Priscia's black blood started to generate heat. Realizing that it had this power, Xanthe encouraged it to maximal effort. Strange queries for verification entered her thoughts. *Are you sure?* Yes. Clearly. Priscia was at organ failure. Nothing else would save her. All she could do herself was to finish off the skin, pinching it shut, but nothing else. From here on, she just had to wait. Her patient was still in a coma. It would be up to Priscia herself to decide to live. That, and her black blood, which was reconfiguring with a purpose far beyond what Xanthe could understand. She pulled away and the overlaid charts disappeared from her eyesight.

As she pulled back her hand, Priscia gasped, then collapsed. Unconscious, but alive.

"What... *are*... you?" Damien exclaimed aghast. His hand was on the hilt of his sword.

Xanthe gave a wan smile. "I'm your escort for the evening. Haven't you noticed?"

"You," he stared disbelieving, "brought her back from the dead."

"Not quite dead," Xanthe stated as she approached him unsteadily on her awkward pumps. "But you now know my secret. I'm one of the dreadwitches you've been hired to kill. One that heals people. Just know that when you take my life, you are not only killing me, you're dooming all those I otherwise could have saved."

"And I would do this because?"

Xanthe rolled her eyes at Damien. "Come on! Because you are working for the Sect of Penance, the group you so eloquently defended just a while ago. Don't think I don't know we've got witchkillers running loose, or that you're intending to bring death to my city. I can add two and two. While I can't fight you, you're at least going to have to look me in the eye when you take my life." She was oddly calm. "Just don't kill Priscia. She's not worth anything. She really has no talent."

He drew himself up. "I assure you Xanthe, I've no dealings with the Sect of Penance. No one does. While many in the Curate sympathize with them, officially they're schismatic, so they have no access to the kind of coin needed to buy anyone's services. They do everything on their own, because they really think they're the good guys."

"You're not?!" A huge weight she hadn't realized had been on her fell away. All her bravery did too. Further, she was embarrassed. Mortified. "But I was sure!"

"Try not to be so disappointed, okay?" Though still awestruck, he grinned. "If you want the rush of cheap moral sanctimony, you'll have to get it some way other than seeing me do you in."

"Well." Flustered and piqued, Xanthe was briefly at a loss for words. "Then why are you in Jagerfeld?!"

"I... Nothing I care to speak of," he demurred evasively. "But I don't kill witch girls and won't unless they're trying to kill me. I thought you might at least give me the benefit of the doubt."

"I... well," Xanthe flushed, trying to explain. "I'm not wrong! We do have witchkillers. First Ginna, and now Priscia..."

"I told you that wasn't a witchkiller attack," Damien pointed out, looking in Priscia's direction. "They kill without drawing black blood, as they're terrified of touching it when they think it might be active with demonic power. But maybe this other girl. This Ginna. How was she taken?"

"It's a secret, but Ginna was strangled. She was nobody important either. She just was flashy."

He nodded slowly, thinking. "That's far more in keeping with the way the Sect of Penance operates. But to really know, you'd have to see the mark on the victim. It's usually obvious. Did you see one on the body?"

"Not directly. But come to think of it, Royroy did say something about her being branded on the face somehow. With a Curate mark."

"Ah, yes. An acid-brand with a holy seal. That is indeed a Penance attack. The method, be it drowning, defenestration, what have you, is unique to each specific witchkiller. It's a calling card."

"You're saying if another girl gets strangled and branded, that's that same witchkiller again?"

"Precisely." He nodded.

Behind them, Priscia coughed violently. She rolled over and retched into the river, then belched long and hard, as her bloated stomach emptied itself of a huge pocket of air. This turned to a brief shriek, as the gas she disgorged came out as blue fire, flaming four yards out in front of her. The fire was so bright, it briefly lit the entire area around the dingy river sluice where they were.

"What in God's name?" Damien exclaimed. "Is that what's called merely 'flashy' in the Witchwilds?"

Priscia continued with wracking coughs, each punctuated by a little gout of flame. "Reaming dung," she finally managed to say. "What's going on with me?" As soon as she got this out, she went back to uncontrolled coughing, hacking water, phlegm, and flames out of her lungs. The fire-spitting felinite chimera that Xanthe had seen earlier in the evening had nothing on her now.

Xanthe winced. That final command she'd given to warm up. Priscia's blood seemed to be following it to a fault. "Um. A little mistake when I revived her." Xanthe hissed quietly. "Maybe I can fix it."

Damien stared, open mouthed. "You just *gave* her a witch power? And you can take them away?!"

She pouted at him. "Don't make me feel like I'm a monster. I'm just an innocent fool of a girl who jumps to conclusions before I know all the facts."

"Or a demon goddess pretending to be innocent as you lure men to their downfall," he smirked only half-jokingly.

That stung worse than it should have. "My power comes and goes. Mostly goes. So, I'm all the former." She crinkled her chin. "Do you insult every girl you escort?"

"That's an insult? How do you know I don't *like* demon goddesses? I could use a good downfall."

She was about to cuff him, when Priscia let out another little cry. "My favor! What happened to my favor?!" She'd finally cleared her lungs enough to start speaking.

Damien turned, and strode across the damp stonework to Priscia. He leaned down and asked courteously, "Miss, do you need a hand up?"

*Oh, to Priscia he's the gentleman,* Xanthe complained to herself moodily. It took Priscia only a moment to take in his rugged features to give a genuine smile. She put her hand in his. At this, Damien's eyes widened. He instantly pulled his own hand away, as hers was burning hot. "Um, how about my arm?" he offered as a substitute.

Priscia scowled momentarily, but then reconsidered, deciding she liked that even better. She put her arm around his, and with his aid, rose. "Thank you." She leaned into him, leaving Xanthe feeling inexplicably jealous.

Damien cleared his throat. "You said you lost your favor? When was the last time you had it?"

"That's okay. I can get a substitute," she purred.

That was enough. Xanthe knew she had no claim on the boy, but no way was she going to let him get mixed up with her. Not even an assassin deserved that. She minced her way across the rough cobblestone on her shaky little heels. "He's not interested in your kiss."

"Listen to your friend, my dear," Damien gave Priscia his dazzling smile. "I'm far more concerned about who nearly killed you. Protecting you is the important thing."

"My friend?" Priscia glanced around the dingy frontage for the sluice. "All I see is the sewer g..." She stopped and tried to be polite. "Her."

Xanthe rolled her eyes. "Just go ahead and call me sewer girl. I don't mind anymore."

Priscia gave her a once over, then a blithe sneer. "Maybe I should call you street girl instead. Where'd you lose your dress? Leave it with some Highcouncil boy?"

"I changed into a period costume."

"Huh." She kept her smirk. "Didn't know the ancients had bodysellers. Learn something new every day."

Xanthe was too cold to be angry. All she felt was distaste. "If you must know, I'm in this because Horace of Wormwood tried to jump me. He ruined my dress, but I drove him off. Retched all over him."

"Huh," Priscia repeated while she continued to study Xanthe. It wasn't friendly, but there was a momentary flicker of respect. "Well, don't say I didn't warn you."

Disconcerted, Damien tried to get the conversation back on track. "Please, miss. Think back. When was the last time you remember having your favor? It's important."

Priscia returned her attention to him. She furrowed her brow and abruptly put a hand to the back of her neck. Her mood abruptly shifted as she remembered something. She stared up. "I need to go."

Damien was intent. "First you need to tell me who took your favor."

"Why?"

"Assassins nearly always take something personal off their victims, so they can prove they did the deed," Damien explained quietly. "It helps with both bounties and intimidation. Since you're not missing an ear, I can only assume they took your favor. Whoever targeted you thinks you're dead, but as soon as they realize you're not, they'll be back to finish the job. If you tell me who did it, I might be able help that problem go away. Without involving the guards."

Priscia judged his words and decided to trust him. "I don't know his name. He does business with a friend of my father's or did. He works for him."

Xanthe thought. "A short man? Wide brimmed hat? Dirty leathers? Several scars on his face?"

Priscia stared. "You know him? How many clients do you do a night anyway?"

Xanthe stared coldly for a few moments. "You're really big on this whole street girl thing, aren't you? Feeling like one yourself? The way your father has been foisting you off on Prince Sol, I can see why. Well, given what just happened, who's going to break it to him that you're not going to be queen?"

Priscia's hands turned black, and an instant after, turned white hot, flaming with blue fire. "You bitch!" She screamed.

"Enough!" Damien moved too fast to follow. In an instant, she was being held by the throat, and Xanthe felt the edge of a blade up against it.

Across from her she saw Priscia held similarly, with a blade emerging from his sleeve against her jugular. "Don't move," he commanded, to which she felt the overwhelming urge to obey. "You're both going to behave as if your lives depended on it."

"She..." Xanthe began.

"I don't want to hear it," he barked. "I need answers. One of Prince Sol's agents attacked? Why? Tell me the story."

Priscia's hands cooled from white to a dark red. "Father has been selling weapons to him in Northfjord, except he didn't pay. He keeps promising, but he doesn't really have any money. We're going to lose our home to loan brokers. Then he came back and asked for more anyway. Father finally says no."

"He's also mixed up with Horace," Xanthe added. "Something they're planning soon. Wide-brim showed up when I was with him. Afterward, Horace was so rushed, he botched trying to jump me."

"Father warned me to stay away from Highcouncil. He said it might be dangerous," Priscia added.

Damien let out a sardonic chuckle but did not relax his grip. "Two weeks of fruitless searching among all the lying rumormongers of this city, and in moments you two give me more solid information than all their stories combined. In thanks, I'll repay you by making you both swear you're not going to let petty squabbles get in the way of your mutual self-interest." He glanced meaningfully at Xanthe, then Priscia. "You'll both regret it otherwise. I won't even be the cause."

Xanthe stared daggers at Priscia. Priscia returned them double.

"Well?" he growled. There was an undeniable power to his demand.

"I will if she will," Priscia said finally.

"Me?!" Xanthe burst out, but found her throat being squeezed. She winced as Damien turned his head to glare. "Alright," she acceded.

"Good. I'm glad you've both decided to be rational." He released them both, then turned to Priscia, his manner cool. "Miss, your father is likely being shown your missing favor right now as proof of what they're willing to do to get his cooperation. No doubt they want him to hock everything he owns for their benefit. We need to get you a new mask to wear before you go home. Also tell him to just not go outside for the next few days."

"My name is Priscia," she told him. Xanthe noticed that his squeezing her throat didn't bother her at all. Almost the reverse. She smiled as if she expected abuse and appreciated the strength of it.

"I am Damien," he nodded, once again turning courteous.

Xanthe walked up next to him. "He returned *my* favor," she told Priscia straight to her face.

"True. I did," Damien confessed. "Accidentally. I didn't recognize who I was returning it to. This festival's traditions are foreign to me. I'm really concerned about more important things."

Priscia raised her eyebrows and shifted her eyes between them. In the end, she raised an eyebrow and noted dryly to Damien, "You could have done way better."

Xanthe clenched her fists. "Better than you".

Damien put up his arms again. "I swear to God, brokering yet another useless ceasefire between Juche and Newmerica would be easier than dealing with you two. What exactly is your problem, anyway?"

"She's the little poor girl who puts on airs," Priscia told him. "Just because she has a few friends in high places."

"You're serious? You actually believe *I'm* the stuck up?" Xanthe sputtered. "All you ever do is cut on girls for fun. Your real problem is you love to dish it out but can't take it."

Damien interrupted. "That was a rhetorical question. I really don't give a damn. Now let's move."

"Shouldn't we go to the guards?" Xanthe asked.

"No. Some must be complicit in the plot and we don't know which. Accordingly, we'll handle this ourselves. Priscia? You're going to show me your house. Then both of you get somewhere safe, because if I find this fellow inside, things may get wet."

Priscia smiled smugly to Xanthe. "Hear that? He wants to escort me, not you."

Damien thinned his lips. "All of us will go."

Priscia approached him. "If you returned her favor, but didn't mean to, you should at least let me kiss you as a reward for saving my life."

He was pleased. "You are more than welcome to kiss the one who saved your life. But I warn you, in my culture, once you make such a promise, you have to go through with it." He gave her a dark, seductive look.

Priscia smiled with a sultry smile of triumph. "I'll take that risk."

"Good!" He thumbed over his shoulder. "It was Xanthe."

Priscia and Xanthe stared at each other flustered, while Damien laughed long and deep.

He continued to chuckle as Xanthe retrieved her favor, and they made their way back up to the street.

## Chapter 18

Damien led them to Priscia's house from a direction Xanthe found surprising. The front. He explained that it was easier to disguise your intent than your presence. Another face in the crowd would be less likely to raise an alarm than skulking up a back alleyway.

Maybe true, but he was enjoying himself far too much. His disguise was pretending to be drunk while making both 'his girls' support him under each of his arms. Several young men gave him a thumb up in passing on his presumed conquests, to which he returned a jaunty wave. It was so embarrassing, Xanthe nearly complained to Priscia, stopping only after reminding herself that it would be Priscia she'd be complaining to.

Besides, the girl was lost in thought. Her face was covered by the cheap mask Damien had bought for her, but Xanthe could see she was unnerved. Instead of engaging in her casual insulting banter, she was staring at her hand. Though not discernable at a distance, the shimmering distortions of heated air made it was obvious that she was alternatively heating it up and letting it cool.

Priscia's house was a mansion set just below the Highcouncil district wall. Thick brick walls, covered in overgrown fungal ivy and inexplicably barred windows, gave it the overall impression of abused elegance. When Damien reached the door of the building, ancient brass studded wood that was pitted and scarred, he pulled his poniard from its sheath and turned. "Unlock it and get to safety," he commanded Priscia. "I'll handle things from here."

"Not going to happen," Priscia replied. "Father isn't fond of prowlers, and he keeps his crossbow wound. If he's home, you'll get a bolt straight in your chest." She pulled out a pincer-key, inserted it in the lock, and squeezed to turn it open. "I'll go first. He's doubly twitchy when things aren't going well."

She entered the mansion, Damien followed, and after a brief hesitation Xanthe did likewise. Inside, the place was well appointed, paneled in various dark woods and velvet, lit with naphtha, and smelled cloyingly sweet. Priscia boldly walked ahead. "Teres!" She barked. "I am home."

"Teres?" Damien whispered, sparing Xanthe the question.

"Our chambermaid," Priscia told him as an aside. "That's funny. She usually answers."

"Maybe she's out in the Festival?" Xanthe asked.

"Father doesn't let her."

No movement greeted them. It was completely quiet. So was Xanthe, though she quietly fumed about the despotic nature of all Priscia's family. They even abused their maids.

"Teres!" Priscia yelled again. She walked up the stairs. Damien followed, after a few moments. Somehow without Xanthe noticing, he'd drawn his sword. He slid along the wall, stopping only in the deepest shadows. She saw him easily though. The white flames on his blade were still burning.

"Maybe he made an exception? Or he took her out with him?" Xanthe ventured. "No one's here."

Priscia let out a derisive sigh. She continued down the dark upper corridor, checking and opening each door as she passed to bring in more light from the adjoining rooms. It was a long way. The mansion was larger than it appeared on the outside. At last, she reached the end, hesitating before a closed set of double doors. "This is father's room," she told them quietly. "Not even I'm not allowed in here."

A soft weeping came from inside. Damien put his hand on the door.

"You're going to be in so much trouble," Priscia told him.

"It's your father who's in trouble," Damien told her quietly. "If he doesn't want my help, I'll leave him to his fate." He pushed. The leftmost door creaked open. Inside was an ornate bedroom, so dimly lit from the ceiling windows that it was impossible to see color. In the center, an older woman lay on an enormous bed, bound with whipweed ropes tied to the bedposts. "Priscia!" she shrieked when she saw her.

"Teres! There you are." Priscia exclaimed arrogantly. "Tell father, if he asks, that we only came in because it was an emergency."

The older woman sobbed openly. "You're alive. You're alive."

Damien strode over and slashed the ropes with his flame-licked blade. They fell apart, but this did not entirely free her. She was bound in multiple ways and still helpless.

"Of course." Priscia sounded annoyed. "Some bandit just stole my favor is all." She rubbed the back of her neck.

"We brought her back," Damien comforted. He knelt and examined the rest of the woman's bindings, which pinned her arms to her sides. "Now tell us what happened."

The old woman didn't respond coherently. She continued to sob "alive, alive," while rocking back and forth, making Damien's task much harder. It was too much emotion. Xanthe averted her eyes and decided to search the rest of the room instead. She found a desk with strange rounded tools whose purpose she couldn't quite discern, but two she did: an oil lamp, and a flint-wheel. As she thumbed the flint-wheel of the lamp to light it, she heard a sharp slap.

Priscia had hit Teres. "Stop moving and answer his question!"

Damien stiffened, but the poor treatment seemed to work. Teres stopped crying, and simply responded "Yes, mistress."

"I'm waiting," Priscia fumed.

"Prince Sol's man came in. He said the Prince was displeased at the master's disloyalty and had taken Harrod in as his guest in Northfjord. He also brought in your favor, drenched in blood. He said you had died, and I, oh Priscia, you don't know much I..."

"Be quiet," Priscia snapped. "My brother's been kidnapped?"

Teres nodded submissively.

"Where's father now?"

"He's going to a counting house. They are making him do something with seals and deeds."

"They can't. The only counting houses open after dark are above the Highcouncil walls," Xanthe said. "They won't be open on holiday." She pointed the lamp's light at the old woman's remaining bindings.

"That's what the master said, but the Prince's man said they'd get someone to accept his seal anyway."

"How?" Priscia demanded.

"I don't know. He tied me up and left with the master. After that, I couldn't hear."

At this last statement, Priscia grew enraged. "Those bastards! They're trying to steal our fortune!"

Xanthe opened her mouth and shut it. She didn't want to say anything, but just had to. "They just nearly killed you, but *this* is what's unforgivable? Money is more valuable than your own life?"

Priscia turned on her. "Get out of my house."

Xanthe glared back. "You want to be left to your fate? Fine. But only after we completely free your servant."

Priscia's eyes fell on Damien. Seeing him still intent on pulling apart the bindings so as not to risk cutting the old woman, she didn't add anything more.

Damien mused thoughtfully. "Love of money may be the root of all evil, but in this case, it's helped your family break free of this prince's influence, so I suppose evil can also be used to good purpose."

"What do you mean?" Xanthe asked.

"Princes are authoritative," he explained. "People find them charming, even if they don't want to be. No matter how much you think you're set against something, in the face of royalty you may do it anyway."

Priscia seemed embarrassed, but he ignored it and continued. "That's why it's rare for those who have thrown in with a prince, to back out. It certainly helps if you love something more than life itself." He finished pulling apart the ropes and smiled at Teres. "There. Done. I wish I could stay longer, but I have some business I must attend to." His voice was still gentle, but Xanthe could tell that he meant murder. "Hide until the night is over," he instructed the old woman.

Xanthe handed the lamp to Teres for her use, and as she handed it over, the steady lamplight finally revealed the old woman's face in detail. Xanthe stopped and stared, utterly shocked. She was rendered completely speechless.

"We need to stop Prince Sol from ruining my family," Priscia told Damien hastily. Then she said something Xanthe had never heard from her before. "Please," she implored urgently.

He nodded. "I'll do what I can. Can you get us into Highcouncil?"

"I'm not on the list that gets to bring armed guards in like father is, but I have some friends who might be. As does Xanthe."

At that prodding, Xanthe spoke. "I only know Tari and Celeste. Tari went home."

"That's no good then," Priscia concluded. "I saw Celeste go into Highcouncil as well. She was with a boy."

Damien listened carefully. "Then the best bet is for Xanthe and I to set watch on the main Highcouncil gate, to rescue your father if he's escorted out, while you find someone else to let us in."

"I can do it." Priscia nodded with assurance. The prospect of losing her family's fortune, had sobered her. This was the first exchange Xanthe ever had, where she'd not been deliberately insulting.

"Priscia, please don't go out again," Teres pleaded. "It's too dangerous."

Priscia didn't even deign to respond. "What do you want in payment?" she asked Damien.

"Your father's funds are low, and they'll likely be even lower after this, so I'll just take a serious favor as payment. However, nothing will induce me to save your brother. He'd be in more danger if I tried. Fair enough?"

Priscia's lips thinned, but she nodded again in agreement.

## Chapter 19

"Did you see Teres?" Xanthe whispered conspiratorially as they walked the cobblestone street up towards Highcouncil. It was into the deepest part of the night, but the city was filled with light. Not only were there the standard torches along the streets, but for the Festival, little oil lamps were traveling the clockwork trolleys high overhead. Yet even with all there was to distract, she found herself to be the focus of many stares. There was nothing she could do, so she simply got used to it.

"I did." Damien said nothing more. Once again, he'd offered his arm, but his eyes darted back and forth. His manner seemed relaxed, but she knew he was quite wary.

"She's Priscia's aunt or mother or something. She's her splitting image."

Damien didn't answer. He just kept watching out ahead, as he escorted her slowly up the street.

She turned to him as they strode along. "Well?"

"Well what?"

"Well, Priscia is pretending she's just the maid!"

"She *is* just the maid, and a poorly kept one at that. I've seen slaves better treated, much less slavewives."

"But why?"

"To guess, I'd say that as her father's wife lingered on her deathbed, he took Teres in her stead. Then when Priscia came, he felt that admitting her true parentage would be scandalous, so invented a pretense. As she is the youngest and a girl, and in no position to inherit anyway, her older siblings have no reason to air dirty laundry. He's expecting to marry her off anyway, no doubt."

"You think she doesn't know?"

"Of course she does. It explains much about her attitude. I was astounded by her behavior at the drainage conduit."

"Nothing like what you did," Xanthe frowned. "You held a blade to my throat."

"Adroitly done, if I do say so myself," he declared. "Priscia was about to burn your lovely face off, so I had to intervene in a way that would be perceived as neutral between you two."

Xanthe crinkled her chin. Always with a good excuse. "You think it's my fault for bickering. That I'm just the same as her."

He glanced over with a smile. It was just as infuriatingly attractive as the first time he'd done it. "On the contrary. The way you saved her life, thinking that you were sacrificing your own, I thought she was your best friend. That was why I was amazed to find the opposite. I've met many Priscias in my life, but never anyone remotely like you. Perhaps my mother, but that is it."

"Your mother?" She scowled. "Does she approve of what you're doing?

He turned grave. "She did everything she could to keep me from it. But she's dead now, so it doesn't make much difference."

"I..." Xanthe wanted to stay angry at him but couldn't. She turned her eyes away. "I'm sorry."

"Thank you for the consideration. I'm sure she would have loved you. You have the same penchant for scolding me that she did."

Xanthe didn't know what to say, so turned quiet, clinging tightly to his arm. This was the end of her argument against what he did for a living. If his own dead mother hadn't been able to change his mind, how could she?

They reached a small park on a small hill. She'd never come here before, but it was nice. There were a few trees, a small bench, several sizable bushes, and a few small patches of slush remaining from previous piles of snow, all overlooking the outside the eastern Highcouncil gate. Despite its name, Jagerfeld's most exclusive district was not all that high. Only the Steeple, vertically above it up the sheer rock face of Ancestor's Cliff, could claim that honor. What most set it off were its walls, which even now were guarded. Those manning it were older men. Even at this distance, it was obvious that they were bored.

Xanthe briefly wondered why the park was empty, until it struck her that the view it offered went both ways. No place for secret kisses.

"Will you take your kiss here, while we're waiting to kill someone?" She asked.

"I'd prefer to talk, if you don't mind." Damien seemed calm but glanced occasionally at the gate. "It's a much better thing to do. I mean," he then added dryly, "while you're waiting to kill someone." A small smile played about his lips. "Maybe we can play Truth or Dare."

Xanthe squinted. "That's a child's game!"

He gave her a smoky stare. "Not always. But... let's skip the dare part."

"Well..." she didn't know what to say. "Okay, fine. Then I go first. Why are you really helping Priscia? Anything to do with why you're here?"

He splayed across the bench, making himself comfortable, then turned his attention back to her. "Not originally. But now? I'm thinking it might."

From that, Xanthe just knew Damien had been sent to kill this prince. It had to be. She sighed to herself. Or maybe not. Didn't she just get finished 'knowing' that he was a Witchkiller? No more jumping to conclusions. Not until she was certain. "Are all princes evil, like they say?"

He sighed. "Yes. All of them. They must be, or they die. So never get involved with one. If one tells you to do something, don't agree. Just run. For all those near them suffer. Even if you win one of them the Nutearean throne, the reward is never worth the cost. A hundred times truer for women."

More puzzling. Who else would be employing him to kill a prince but another one? But if so, why would he then hate them all?

He continued his thought. "I certainly don't want Jagerfeld conquered by one, which is obviously what this Prince Sol is attempting tonight."

Xanthe suspected this as well, but it sounded chilling hearing it from another. "Are you certain?"

"Your own story confirms it. Horace wanted to force you but was rushed because of something happening tonight. Even more strikingly, Teres was tied up alive. There's no reason for an assassin to risk leaving a witness unless they expected to come back in the morning and sell her off as a slave for a little coin on the side."

"You can't just do that. Indentured servitude isn't legal in Jagerfeld. No slavery is, except wife-slavery, and even then, there are lots of laws about it."

He nodded. "Precisely my point. Laws change only when rulers do."

Xanthe silently made an "oh" with her mouth.

"Now my turn. Where did you get your outfit? It's decidedly unusual."

Xanthe felt pricked. His question wasn't something she wanted to answer. Yet as she'd already agreed to this game and he knew she was a dreadwitch, it seemed safe enough to reveal. "It's an artifact I found in some ruins. The note said it was a present for some girl's Earthday, whatever that is."

"More forbidden knowledge. An Earthday is a birthday using the years of Earth. Because ancient Earth orbited its sun further than Haven does ours, its seasons passed more slowly. That's why a year is six seasons long, spanning to the second winter after summer, and in the next year, the second summer after winter. Our ancestors picked that convention because they wanted our calendar to match Earth years as closely as possible. Still, it's not exact. Earth years are slightly shorter than our six-season ones, being three hundred and twenty-four days long. How old are you?"

"I will be sixteen this summer. My birthday is exactly on High Summer Day, the solstice."

"Then your sixteenth Earthday came just recently." He squinted briefly in thought. "If I'm doing my math right, around two weeks ago."

That was when she'd found the present. Was it possible it had been truly intended for her? But how could that be? She considered her dress with new eyes. A chill ran down her back. The fabric reminded her nothing so much as black blood.

Damien leaned forward, concerned. "You've grown pale. Is there something wrong?"

"I'm just wondering if I'm being controlled is all," she said apprehensively. "By these clockwork daemons."

"Do you feel that way?"

"No, but maybe I am anyway." She stared at the patterns embossed on her toenails. Just like the symbols she'd seen on the box that the dress had come in. She lifted one foot up onto the bench between them to peer more closely.

"Something about your shoes?" He followed her eyes down. "May I?" Before she could respond, he simply grabbed her ankle and gently pulled her little foot towards him until it rested it on his lap. His touch sent tingles all the way up her thigh. Further. The coldness from the river had completely worn off by now, and she started to blush. But his efforts weren't in seduction. He was staring closely, utterly fascinated.

"What is it?"

"These patterns in your nails. They're moving."

Xanthe gasped. That was it. No more. "I need to get this dress off as soon as possible!"

He glanced over and chuckled.

Belatedly she realized what she'd said. "Not like that!" She turned red, and this time she did lean over to cuff him with her small fist, completely ineffectually on his broad muscular shoulder.

"Ow!" he made a pretense that she'd hurt him, which piqued her even more. She tried cuffing him again. It did nothing but make him smile. "Do all witch girls beat up their escorts?"

She pouted deeply, annoyed that he was enjoying it. "Only you."

"Well, if you're set on doing so, you should get more leverage." With a quick fluid motion, he reached under her with his arms, and lifted her effortlessly onto his lap.

The thrill that went completely through her body was so powerful, she almost felt lightheaded. He. Him. Here. Now cradled between his broad shoulders, she didn't know what to do. The dress wasn't controlling her. This was. No matter how unsuitable they were for each other, she could not deny his power. He'd somehow captured her in a way the Horace could only dream and had done so by being a perfect gentleman. Well, mostly. He was bad too. But that was worse, because it was even better.

She gazed into his eyes. The worst part was that she liked him. She just did. He trained at killing and it didn't matter. What of morality? Horace had only made her feel violated. Damien was corrupting her. Her unruly body was hard enough to control, but what if he captured her heart? With the cold clarity of romantic panic, she realized that he'd more than halfway done so.

He was also becoming aware of the danger. "What am I doing?" He suddenly shook his head and broke his gaze from hers. "Xanthe, I... must apologize. We have more important things to do. Saving your city, for one."

She nodded. Again, the gentleman. "You're right. We need to focus." Yet neither made a move to disentangle themselves. They both just went back to their mutual attraction, within easy kissing distance, silently daring each other to be the first one to give in.

"And I think you shouldn't change your dress, at least for now," he whispered. "Even if it has demonic influence, that's a small price to pay for any power it may have to keep you alive."

Xanthe wasn't sure if that was the best advice but considered it carefully. She had no better ideas herself. That wasn't what she was thinking about anyway.

The whistle of an unfamiliar kestrel's call sounded. It didn't come from the branches of the tree above, but from behind them in the park's low shrubbery. Still, Xanthe wouldn't have even noticed it if it weren't for Damien's sudden movement. He turned his head and listened.

"Company," he sighed. With extreme care, he lifted her off his lap, set her back down on the bench, and then stood. Xanthe decided she would stand as well. He seemed relaxed and left his sword sheathed, so she assumed that this wasn't dangerous. Nothing like being in his arms.

Two men approached out of some brush near the base of the park. At first, Xanthe didn't recognize them in the darkness. Then she caught sight of their uniforms. Garrison guard. Their footsteps crunched across the gravel and twig ground cover as they strode up the hill.

"We finally found you again. You make us search entire city." A deep voice stated.

Xanthe froze. Of all the luck. She recognized the Lukomoryen accent, guttural and thick. Again, it the two guards who'd been searching for her. She just couldn't shake them. There was no possible way she could run the way she needed to, at least not in these heels. Yet they weren't addressing her. They were speaking to Damien.

"Ah!" grinned the thinner guard. "We should 'ave known. Where is our truant? Easy! Just find zhe cher of zhe city," he gestured towards her, "and zhere 'e is! Zhe rogue."

While Xanthe was panicking, Damien was embarrassed. "It's not like that."

"Ah, buht of course. A spot in a lonely park? Under zhe stars? And, if my eyes did not deceive, zhis one in your lap? Eh heh." He declared with amusement. "You are always so lucky! Mon dieu! 'ow do you find zhem so quickly? Of all zhe girls, she ees...". His eyes widened.

The larger guard caught on at the same time. "Claude!" he said in shock. "It's her."

Xanthe shrank behind Damien, using him as a shield. She quietly shook her feet, willing her heels to retract so that she could run. She knew she could easily get away if they returned to their original form, but the damnable things remained stubbornly high. Noticing her behavior, Damien was at first confused, then turned to the guards. "Explain yourselves," he commanded.

"She is zhe witch," Claude declared.

"So?" Damien stood his ground, between her and the guards.

"I mean not just *a* witch. She is *zhe* greatwitch. Zhe one we 'ave been looking for."

"I don't care what your new duties entail. She is under my protection," he told the guard sternly.

The thinner guard glanced at Damien, then at Xanthe, then back again, with a canny expression. "Yes? I am glad you 'ave recovered so quickly."

Damien seemed exasperated, even flustered. "I told you. We're just acquaintances. I'm not the girl chaser I once was."

"Oh! Zhis is something I believe." The guard dramatically put a hand to his chest, then faced the other. "You believe zhis too, Yuri?"

"Completely," the Yuri replied gutturally with a completely insincere expression, obviously trying not to smile.

Claude turned back to her. "My dear, zhis fine young gentleman, did 'e run after you, out zhe city gate?"

Xanthe had no reason to lie, so she just told the truth. "Just to return my favor."

"Ah, ah! For a spring walk, *and* a kiss?" The guard grinned triumphantly. "Zhen you would say, as a girl, 'e chased you?"

"Well," Xanthe couldn't think what to say. She shrugged as if it were no big deal. "Only a quarter league."

Claude burst out laughing. "You mean zees in truth?!" He put his hand to his chest. "Oh! My belief now! She knows no bounds!"

Damien fumed. "Is this what you came here for? To vex me?"

Claude's smile changed in nature, from teasing to warm, and he choked up. "We laugh, because we dare not cry. After what 'appened we thought you were dead. Now, to find you 'ere with zhis little angel witch who saved so many lives, I cannot 'elp but believe it is God's will." He approached Damien, and then suddenly grabbed his shoulders and gave him a kiss on each cheek.

Xanthe could hardly believe her good fortune. "You're not turning me in?" She squeaked in relief.

"Why should they?" Damien grumbled. "You've given them endless fun at my expense."

"Bah, little gurl," Yuri scoffed, but not unkindly. "You think we hand to Curate proctor as reward for help? What kind of people you think of us?"

"Religious," Xanthe stated flatly. "The worst destroyers always seem to do so in the name of the Creator."

"Heh," the larger guard chuckled mirthlessly. "Not all. We well know those who live by sword, die by it, yes? Is only we are forced to this. I am no man of Curate. If God would allow, I go back to blacksmith." As he said this, he used his foot to draw a shallow arc in the gravel before her. She had no idea what it was. When she did nothing, he seemed disappointed.

"We need to speak," Damien told the men. "There is much you need to know."

Claude nodded. "Do not bother. Finalizer Nagrath explained. We talked after you ran off." He declared in a subdued tone. "I am sorry. We did not know."

Damien made a wry unhappy face. "If you met Nagrath, it's obvious you didn't. Because if he'd thought you were in on the scheme..." His voice trailed off meaningfully.

Yuri spoke then. "Nasty business, we know. Knights always die too soon. But our own betrayed us? Are you sure?"

"I am." Damien stared at the two guards darkly. "He may sup with you pretending to be a loyal companion, but I have sworn to God to kill him and all who knew. Slowly. To make this innocent city choke with their blood, and any other who dare try to stop me."

Yuri was troubled. "Death perhaps. Maybe needed. But no torture. Sinful. Yes?"

Damien blew out a breath. "You're starting to sound like Xanthe. But I don't care. If you cannot help me then I release you. Choose."

The two guards regarded each other somberly. They did not say much of anything for a while, their eyes searching his face and each other's, while distinctly uncomfortable in their uniforms. Finally, Claude's eyes alighted on Xanthe, and he nodded to Damien. Yuri did so as well. "I stay with you, my friend, as I promised. But am protector only. Remember this."

Damien turned his dark eyes towards Claude. "Very well. Can you get us into the Highcouncil district?"

"Eh. No," Claude replied. "We are city garrison. Zhey do not trust outsiders for 'ighcouncil watch. We 'ave even less ability to enter zhan you do. We are on duty."

"That's a problem then," Damien said. "To help this weapon merchant, we need to pass that gate. I'm certain he's being strong-armed by Prince Sol."

At the questioning glances, he began to recount what had happened with Priscia's family. As he did, Xanthe reconsidered the guards, realizing that she'd been mistaken about them. Yuri had been merely overprotective, which given the stress he'd been under, was understandable. At this point, Damien was the greater worry. Regardless of his manners, a frightening rage boiled in him. By all logic, it would be better to just bid him good eve, run home and be safe. Yet what kept her, beyond her concern for Jagerfeld, was that beneath it all, she knew he was in terrible pain. Something had gone badly wrong. He was a broken kestrel, lame of wing, and her need to heal him was almost physical in its intensity.

Her eyes drifted away from their discussion down to the gate and saw a group of revelers try to enter the gate. The guards at the district wall were slow, but after checking them over, let them in. Soon after, a large coach approached. It was Horace's, riding low. Royroy was driving it. The thing didn't even slow down. The guards had to leap aside. Yet none raised an alarm. All one of them did was to mouth a curse and spit on the road after it passed.

"...could wait at this Priscia house," Yuri was saying. "We can arrest for what they did."

Damien shook his head. "They won't come back for that until after they take care of business, and then it will be too late. No. We need some way in quickly, and without raising an alarm, because our best chance is to take these assailants by surprise while they're still putting the pieces in place, preferably with a peer of this city giving color of authority to our actions. Otherwise we may be misidentified as the attackers, especially as there are almost certainly traitors among the guards."

"Zhey will not let armed men in, my friend," Claude said. "Not unless zhey are well known."

"Let's wait for Nagrath," Claude agreed. "Maybe 'e can figure a solution. Zhe man is clever."

"Or maybe someone clever is already here," Xanthe smiled casually. "I'll solve the problem for you."

Damien was incredulous. "How are you going to do that?"

"Simple enough. If you can't get in with a weapon, don't carry one."

"I'm not disarming myself," he told her flatly.

"My dear Damien." Xanthe smiled sweetly. "Who said anything about you?"

## Chapter 20

Damien's protests were incredibly cute. He didn't want her hurt and was intent on keeping her safe. Yet with her city in danger of falling to slavery-loving usurpers, Xanthe was in no mood to be persuaded. She knew she was the only one who had any chance of getting inside. There was no other choice. In the end, he retreated under the force of her determination.

Now all she needed to do was get past the Highcouncil guards, which in theory, shouldn't be so hard. While only residents and invited guests were technically allowed past, you usually just had to act like you had business in the district, and they didn't bother you. Yet with every step she took away from her non-fight with Damien, her confidence wavered. Halfway down the hill she saw several boys her age stopped at the gate, and remembered that during Festival, Highcouncil kids threw parties that towner kids would try to crash. Likely the guards were taking extra care with ids tonight.

She kept shaking her feet, hoping to entice her shoes into turning back into something that she could run in, just in case she had to bolt past the guards. They didn't. If anything, they were getting worse. The slinky little heels were making her hips rock back and forth, and the back of her dress pulled tight, making her normal book-carrying slouch impossible to maintain. Her skirt kept shortening too, despite her efforts to pull it down. She tried to be nonchalant but was just a bundle of nerves.

As she approached, the group of slightly older boys were cajoling the guards. Xanthe began to run through her mind ways to drop Celeste's and Tari's names, hoping that would work. The last thing she wanted was to be forced to retreat, back up the hill in ignominious defeat.

"See, sir? I have a friend who said they'd let me in. I have this," one of the boys said. He handed over some paper to the guard, who perused it briefly before handing it back.

"Sorry, son. That's a delivery pass. No deliveries tonight."

"But Sir, we're expected! My friend is going to miss us if we're not there, and you'll be in trouble for it!" He claimed desperately. Xanthe didn't know what to say, so she decided to avoid the argument entirely, by walking to the other guard to speak to him instead.

She was surprised. The entire conversation halted as she walked up. Everyone turned to goggle at her, but as she went to the guard to speak, he just stepped aside letting her through without saying a word. They all turned silent except for one low whistle that came from behind. Xanthe so surprised, she almost went to ask the guard's permission to enter anyway, before thinking better of it. Maybe Tari had given her description to them. That had to be it. She was still wearing Tari's necklace.

"Take the ride, sweetheart," the guard said. He nodded in the direction of an older coachman with a fancy waxed mustache, who pulled his shiny dog-pulled open sports-cart around and opened its little waist high passenger door for her. She stepped up into its leather padded seats, and as she did so, noticed that her dress now had curved sliced openings in it, leaving small decorative swirls of her skin visible along her sides. At this point, she was past caring.

The fancy carriage was lovely, though the ride turned out to be not as comfortable as she'd imagined them to be. The driver ran the dogs fast, probably because most kids loved that sort of thing, but this bounced too much for Xanthe's taste and the air felt chill on her skin. She thought to direct the man to bring her to Tari's house, but he'd already picked a destination, and she was too intimidated to ask differently.

They ended at an unfamiliar mansion bedecked with ribbons, torches, and swirling crowds, its curved driveway filled with high-end carriages. Before she was even done gawking, the coachman ran around to again open the door. This was teen party. Most everyone was her age. They all turned to stare. Her dress had changed again, playing with its form. She felt a web-like train of chiffon streamers extending over the back of her legs, in some new ancient evening style. It didn't matter. She wasn't here for social climbing. Armed with purpose, she just put her head up, and strode in as if she belonged. Perhaps she did.

Inside was an enormous grand-hall. It was a sunken design, in which the stairs at the entryway led down to the central floor. The walls were decorated, yet overwrought, everything bedecked in expensive yet clashing mishmash of ribbons, banners, and ancient plastics. It was reminiscent of her own attempts to apply makeup, which made Xanthe wonder if whoever had set it up had been as stressed about it as she'd been. That brought the sour realization that Damien had good reason for his critique.

The few adults here were servants. One stood before her just before the stairs, an older butler dressed in a formal suit of white with plastic thread trim. He caught her eye.

"Your name, Miss?"

It took a second before she realized he was talking to her. "Um. Xanthe."

"Patronym?"

"I'm incognito. Is there a city councilor around by any chance?"

He took no notice of the question, but instead turned and shouted. "Announcing Mistress Xanthe of a Grand House she declines to name. Creator and Host, she doth thank!"

She disliked being put on the spot, but dutifully clasped her hands formally, holding the pose at length as was proper for a new introduction. As she did so, he told her in a low tone. "None I'm aware of. The young mistress was most insistent on this being a party of her sole design."

"Her name?" Xanthe asked while keeping her gaze forward to the room.

"The young Mistress Dealer. Be kind to her or I'll have you thrown out. You're not on the invitation list."

Xanthe kept facing the crowd. "Fear not. That her servants love her so much, they take the risk to threaten daughters of unknown and potentially powerful houses at the door, tells me that you're both laudable."

The butler was briefly silent at her words, but finally remarked. "You're subtler than you appear."

Not knowing if that was compliment or insult, Xanthe took it as her cue to descend the shallow stairs, strutting in a manner that was almost dictated by her dress. The whole scene felt surreal. Everyone stared at her wide eyed, including the all Highcouncil boys. As little as a few bells ago she would have been overjoyed at such attention. Now, she couldn't care less.

At the base of the stairs, the crowd parted. She was surrounded, yet none came too close. Everyone gawked, girls more than boys. Murmurs were everywhere. *"Who is that?" "Her hair? She's too young?" "Can't be." "No kidding." "Creator look at what she's wearing!" "She must be foreign." "Stop drooling!"* Ignoring them, Xanthe bypassed the buffet tables where many of the boys had settled, in an upper-class mirror of Mrs. Saud's stoves, and directly approached the hostess who was seated on a divan. The girl, done up in a floral print wrap, was only as old as she was, and appeared at once both haughty and distraught as a friend consoled her.

"Good eve," Xanthe curtseyed respectfully. "You must be our gracious hostess, Miss Dealer. You've set a lovely party. I see all the care you've put into it."

"Um. Thank you." The girl gawked openly, but her face softened gratefully at the tribute. "My name is Essense."

"I'm sure you've attracted Jagerfeld's highest," Xanthe smiled. "Perhaps even the children of councilors."

At this, Essense became distraught, but rallied and returned a partial smile anyway. "You are too kind, but no. A lot of people said they'd come and they haven't."

Ah. That was it. Xanthe was all too unsurprised. This filthy rich girl was so upset that the coolest kids of her social scene hadn't shown up, she was crying at her own party. Damien's sneer of 'shallow' echoed in her thoughts. Yet she also empathized, knowing exactly what it was like. It doesn't make any difference how rich or poor you are, everyone feels the sting of rejection. "Don't worry," Xanthe reassured gently. "They're just fashionably late. Those that can't might not be able to. Tari of Outlet said that she was feeling ill."

Essense's friend spoke up. "We expected a few Wormwoods to visit, even if they have their own party too. You know who they are?"

Xanthe briefly froze, then relaxed. "Well if it's Horace you're waiting for, be glad he's otherwise occupied. We've only just met, but I already know you're far too good to host him for anything."

Essense blinked. "You've been with him?"

Xanthe stiffened. She struggled not to sneer, but her tone curdled. "Only briefly. He is no gentleman."

One of the boys, listening to inaudible words from a friend, laughed. He whispered back too loudly, "Can you blame him?" Xanthe had a mind to turn on him but caught herself. The boy wasn't Horace himself.

"You didn't get along?" Essense asked hopefully.

Xanthe quieted. It was obvious by now that no one here had access to a councilor. This had been a complete waste of time. Still, some things had to be said. "He enjoys victimizing people. Unless you want to be one, pray that the Creator keeps you from his designs."

There had to have been something about her tone, because the group around them hushed. Xanthe took that as her cue. "Thank you for your kind hospitality. I must take my leave." She curtseyed once formally and turned. The newly grown train of her dress swirled behind her.

As she reached the top of the stairs and was about to exit, a boy intercepted her. "Hi!"

Xanthe inspected him. He was awkward and chestnut-haired, with a face full of recently popped and scrubbed pimples. "Yes?"

"Um. I just wanted to say hello... what's your name?"

"Xanthe. It was just announced." With no hesitation, she strode past him out the door, and through the lighter crowd milling about in the garden outside.

He followed. "Yeah, right, right. Uh, do you know how the Festival of Favors works in Jagerfeld?"

She looked down the street. Men with suspiciously used swords and freshly tailored guard uniforms, were assembled outside. Too many, and edgy, as if expecting a fight. "I thought I did," she said absently, as she turned down the street in the opposite direction. "Yet the more I learn of it, the less I understand." She ran a finger through her unbound hair, trying to silently signal that she was not in the market.

He got the message, but in the wrong way. "You know, your hair would look better if you put it in maiden's braids," he said hopefully. "By our customs, that would mean you could drop a favor." He eyed her rose. "Then when a guy returns it, tie a ribbon like the one you have on your arm on him, then go for a walk." He nodded adding, "And give him a kiss."

A carriage drove down the street. It was Horace's. Royroy was driving, but he didn't notice her. He had his eyes strictly on the road ahead, focusing on trying to manage the kranth. There was something different about the way the coach was moving. She just couldn't figure out what.

It was at this point that Xanthe realized that this boy wasn't going away. She stopped on the sidewalk. "Um. Thank you for the instruction. What's your name?"

"Wallace." He put out his hand eagerly. When she reached out to shake it, he leaned over, and with a flourish, kissed the back of her hand.

Xanthe was taken aback. "You're quite forward."

"Am... am I coming on too strong? I've never done this before."

She raised an eyebrow. "You haven't? You seem quite brave then. Which is nice, but I'm rather distracted by a problem right now."

"By what? I mean, maybe we could go together. I could help, or something."

"Likely not. I need to find a city councilor. Now."

"Why?"

She sized him up and decided to chance divulging a little. "Because the city is about to be attacked. See those men dressed as guards over there?" She briefly pointed. "They're not guards. They can't be. They're too young for Highcouncil duty, especially tonight. I'm just guessing, but I think they're planning to hold everyone in the party hostage, for leverage. So, I hope you understand why I don't have time for you, unless you're someone who can command the real guards."

"Well, um," he looked desperate. "It just so happens I am?" It was more a question than an assertion.

"You are...?" She was doubtful. "It seems rather odd that you've not mentioned your family's name yet. Usually that's the first thing you hear out of all the Highcouncil snobs."

He wilted under her glare. "Well, alright. But I know someone who knows someone who... okay, I'm the son of a chauffeur. I was let in to fill out the party."

"Okay, Wallace. I'm not even mad. It's just that I don't think you're really getting what I'm saying here. Stop trying to get me to date you. Dropping a favor right now is the least of my concerns."

"Well... if you really think we're about to be attacked, why didn't you tell everybody at the party?"

She sighed heavily. "What good would *that* do? Even if they believed me, which is unlikely, it'd only panic them, plus tip off the bandits."

Wallace peered down the street, trying not to be too obvious, then furrowed his brow. "Hey! You're right! I know most of the Highcouncil guards and I've never seen those guys before. You mean, this is really real?"

"Yes! That's what I've been telling you. What I can't figure out is how they managed to get in. Maybe one or two might sneak through the gate, but not a whole wagon load..." She snapped her fingers. "That's it! They must have come in Horace's carriage." That was the difference. It was now riding high, rather than low as it had been before, when it was going into the district. They'd been crammed inside, pushing its suspension down.

He wasn't impressed. "Yeah, that's a real fancy one. But nobody good chauffeurs the Wormwoods. They treat their help like dung. All except their guards. That's why he's got that new guy who doesn't know how to drive. Can't turn. Doesn't know the animals. Jerks the ride like he's badly carting redfruit."

"You know how to drive?" Xanthe was surprised.

At this, Wallace became smug. "Of course! I can handle both dogs and kranth. Not only that, I drive smooth, anywhere you want to go. I even got keys to the City Garage. It's where all the municipal vehicles are kept. Hey! Want to go for a ride in a firetruck?"

This sounded like an incredibly bad idea, or maybe a great idea if you wanted to ream over your life. Fire was a constant fear in Jagerfeld, which meant Enabling Arson was a serious crime. Stealing a firetruck, even for a joy ride, sounded like a good way to get yourself permanently banished from the city, or worse.

But it led her to a thought. "No. But do they keep the drunk-vans in there?"

He nodded.

"Can you do me a favor?"

"For you?' He told her with a wide grin. "Anything."

Xanthe had to admit it. Sometimes boys could be useful.

## Chapter 21

The drunk-van was huge, ugly, slow, and shameful to ride in. True to its name, it was used to haul drunkards out of public houses when they got too rowdy. It wasn't used to transport them to jail though. It *was* the jail, with a barred back door. The farm boys who got thrown in it were usually released the next morning outside the walls, after they'd slept off their inebriation and belligerence.

Alas, there were hardly any dogs left to pull it, most having been appropriated by other drivers for the night. Wallace scrounged every dog in the kennels, including a bitch Xanthe could tell was expecting a new litter of pups. She thought it was taking too long, but he seemed to know what he was doing, and was moving with all deliberate speed. Eventually, after a third of a bell of watching him hitch harnesses, she clambered to the top, and he followed, holding the reins he'd gathered tightly.

"We've barely got enough pull to move when we're loaded, so we'll have to come from up slope. You really think this is going to work?"

She didn't know the answer. "It's worth a shot."

He nodded, and mushed the animals into action, taking them out at a slow trot, exiting the low-slung building. Trusting his judgment, Xanthe resisted the urge to ask him to hurry it up. She was just edgy. This could go instantly bad. About the only thing likely to be quick in the whole business.

As he drove along, she noticed that lights were off on many of the mansions and almost no family guards were on duty. This was to be expected for the Festival but left her feeling confused. How was this coup supposed to work? This seemed like an ideal time to pull off a robbery, but with so many people scattered about the more boisterous sections of Jagerfeld, why did they think they could corner anyone? Even if this prince took control of the entire Highcouncil district, the remainder of the city could simply besiege them. Either she didn't understand the plot, it was half-baked, or both.

"This is not the way I expected this night to turn out," Wallace said wistfully. "I mean, I know it's not real. But at least I have the chance to dream."

"Real? This is all too real."

"I mean really being with a girl like you."

Xanthe's laugh had an edge. "What? The crazy one you just met who may get you killed?"

"At least I would die happy," he declared dramatically.

"Uh, yeah. I don't think happy deaths are really all that common."

"Not for me."

"How do you mean?"

He shook his head. "I'm just a coachman's son. That's all I'll ever be. If I could, I'd trade it all for just a single night where all my dreams come true."

Xanthe declined to ask just what those dreams were. Avoiding the topic seemed the best option. One thing about Wallace, he certainly wasn't shy. She just remained silent as they wound their way up the streets. He seemed to be taking the long way around. She hoped it wasn't just an excuse to extend the trip with her, though she did notice that they never took any steep inclines.

"There they are," she told him. "Speed up. Sense of urgency. Let me do the talking."

Celeste had told her that she was a terrible liar. Time to put the lie to that. She hoped.

The enormous wooden paddy wagon rumbled down the slight incline from where Wallace had driven it. They rolled up to the men and pulled to a quick stop.

"Hello there, little girl," one of the men said, leering up at her. "That's a pretty ribbon you're wearing." Up close, their guard uniforms seemed particularly inappropriate on them. Not just that they didn't fit, but from the manner of the men. They slouched and ogled like bandits. Several gave predatory smiles. A few moved in front, toward the pull-dogs.

Xanthe stared down with as much menace as she could muster. "Shut up and listen. There's been an unfortunate contingency. One that requires attention. Our mutual friend sent me to get you repositioned. You're going to start earning your reward a little sooner than we expected."

"Reward? Friend? Who do you mean?" The man asked suspiciously, but she could tell he was only asking the question to bide time. Just by his manner, his denial was transparently false.

"I'll give you a hint. He's got a cane and is not afraid to use it. Now get in the back. This one's been cleaned. It'll smell less like vomit than that last coach you were crammed in."

The man was surprised. "How did you know that?"

She stared down. "How do you *think*?"

He was clearly confused. "Who are you?"

Xanthe thought for just an instant, then remembered Priscia. "Your future queen," she announced as arrogantly as she could. "We may not have met. Now, are you going to keep your bargain?" She glared. "If you fail in this, we may have to send you a message." She used wide-brim's phrasing.

The leader stared up at her, and she could see his doubt fade away. After a moment in thought, he nodded. "Come on boys. Time for another ride." At this command, the men opened the back, and they all clambered in. There was over a score of them, likely several of Horace's coach-loads.

They even shut the door behind them. Through it, Xanthe told them to stay low and quiet, lest they be discovered.

"I can't believe that worked!" Wallace whispered with glee, as they started up. The dogs strained terribly with the extra weight, but the downward slope made movement possible. He kept a firm grip on the brakes.

"Take them out of the city," she told him quietly.

"I'll run them off a cliff."

Xanthe grimaced, hating her own mercy. "No. Don't do that. They're just," she fell back on Councilor Outlet's phrasing, "innocent mercenaries."

"Come on. If they weren't such suckers, they'd have given us a seriously bad time. They had that look."

While Wallace was likely right, it still didn't sit well. "No. Promise me. No killing. There's too much death as it is. Don't taunt them either. All it would take would be one person to open the back while you're going through town, conspirator or drunk, and you'd be dead."

"What do you mean me?"

"I'm not going with you. I have more things to do." Xanthe saw the district gate ahead. She slid down to the step rail and prepared to hop off. It was easy. The drunk-van was hardly moving faster than a walk.

"What? The only one I'm spending my Festival night with, is a bunch of bloodthirsty bandits?"

"Yes, but you can brag to those girls in the party. They'll be grateful."

He scowled. "Your city must be nicer. I'm the son of a coachman. No one will care."

She stood even higher on tiptoe and instructed him. "Keep your eyes on the road."

"What?" He was confused but did so anyway. She promptly kissed him on his well-scrubbed cheek.

"I care," she said affectionately. "Thank you."

He blushed, then held his cheek. It was such a strange reaction, Xanthe was shocked. She added urgently, "Go on then. Keep going," and stepped lightly off before the gate, walking towards it, searching for a guard. Fortunately, they didn't bother the wagon going out.

"Hey there, sweetheart," one of the older men smiled when she found one. "Leaving already?"

She approached directly. "I came to give you a message. The guy driving the Wormwood coach almost ran over people in the Dealer party."

The guard was resigned. "We don't bother the Wormwoods. We're not in their colors, but they still pay part of our salary."

Xanthe knew that. "Well, Tari Outlet got her father to ask you to set up a barricade and only let people you know with good drivers in. I don't know how this works, but he'll fix it so it's not a problem."

It was an utter lie but brought out a glint in the older man's eye. "Oh, he did, did he? A fellow councilor finally taking notice? Interesting. You have a writ?"

A surge of panic hit in Xanthe's stomach, but she soldiered on. "I... I think it's being drawn up right now. I just came down as soon as I heard. Maybe I can get it for you." If she could, of course. A big if. Otherwise, she'd be in big trouble.

The guard was relaxed. "Don't worry. Leave that up to some errand Hood. In the meantime, we'll be happy to stop him and give him some attention." He seemed not at all displeased.

"Um... t-thank you," she curtseyed and quickly retreated to the sports-cart, which was once again waiting in the same place for more guests for Essense's party. "Can you drive me?"

The driver examined her with narrow eyes, but then nodded slowly. As soon as she got in, he took off at a quick pace. Yet when they turned the street corner, he slowed the carriage to a halt, and then turned to face her accusingly. "What's this about?"

She blinked, feeling confused. "I... I don't know what you mean."

"What have you got Wallace into?" The coachman was angry.

"You know him?"

"Yes. He's the son of one of my friends. Whose house did you hit?"

Now she was even more bewildered. "He didn't hit anything. He's an excellent driver."

"Don't be smart with me, little girl," the man snarled.

"Sir?"

"If you've seduced him into house-robbery, I'll put you in the pen myself, if I have to."

Xanthe couldn't believe it. "What are you talking about? House robbery? I'm not a thief."

"Oh sure. Classic little nectar-trap you set up for the kid, and he fell right in. A boy that age will do anything for a kiss, particularly from a girl like you. The only reason I didn't call you out is that I didn't want him arrested too."

"Sir. I have no idea where you got this idea about theft. What in the world makes you think that?"

"Cause I'm no fool. I'm a driver. I can tell when animals are straining. That whole drunk-van was loaded heavy. They could barely move."

"Oh. That!" Perversely, Xanthe was relieved. At least now she knew where this was coming from. "Yes, it was filled, but not with loot or anything."

"Really? Then what are you smuggling out of Highcouncil?"

"Well, if you really want to know, bandits."

He stared at her incredulously, then sputtered. "Telling stories isn't going to help you."

"Well that's unfortunate, because I need all the help I can get. A Nutearean prince is plotting to take over Jagerfeld, and I've every intention of stopping him."

"Plotting to... what?" He barked out a guttural laugh of disbelief. "There's an attack, and a little trollop like you is stopping it? You think I'm stupid?"

"No, just blinded by incredulity. One of the many reasons why I haven't approached the guards about it."

He blinked. "You're the most brazen liar I've ever heard. You speak with such certainty."

She was getting annoyed. "The easiest lie to tell is the truth."

"Yes, but now is the time for you to stop. I'm going to drive back, and you are going to confess. You'll leave Wallace out of it too. Say he didn't know what he was doing."

Had it been even a few bells ago, Xanthe would have meekly accepted this man's judgment, even if it meant waiting in the guard post's lockup until proven right. But no longer. There was no time and she had no fear. "No," she declared sternly. "You're driving me to a councilor's house, or I'm getting out right here."

The coachman leaned over and grabbed her upper arm. His grip was strong, as men who handled reins for a living usually were, and he yanked painfully. "You will go nowhere."

Xanthe didn't feel fear. She felt rage. It welled unbidden. A strange feeling stirred in her. "Don't. Touch..."

One of the newly formed streamers tailing from her dress whipped up and around. Faster than her eyes could follow, the ribbon of fabric twirled, wrapping itself like a snake a dozen times around the driver's neck. The coachman opened his mouth to shout, but nothing came out except a choked gag. He pulled his hands up to clutch at the fabric, but his fingers could not find purchase under it. His expression turned from anger to panic.

"No!" Xanthe yelled, pulling at it. "Stop!"

The material hesitated ever so briefly, as if alive. Then, after an indescribably long instant, it released its grip. It unraveled as quickly as it had tightened and slid back behind her.

"You..." the man gasped in horror.

"Have an overprotective skirt, apparently," she told him, feeling slightly guilty.

"That thing is sorcery! Demonic."

The guilty feelings only went so far. "It's an ancient artifact. Full of surprises. But don't say its evil. It's holy. I'm sure the Curate would agree. It only rose in my defense against your vexatious assault."

He sputtered, angrily trying to think of a retort, when a guard rounded the corner. "Miss? We heard a shout. Is there something wrong?" The guard eyed the driver suspiciously.

Xanthe turned back and shook her head. "There's no problem, sir. Part of my dress got wrapped around something, and I had to yell stop. But it's free now." She held up a streamer. It fluttered in the mild breeze, looking perfectly natural.

"Oh. Alright sweetheart. You take care. Have fun at the party." The guard smiled and turned away.

The driver stared crossly at her after he was gone. "That wasn't exactly the truth."

"Nor a lie either. Now, are you driving me? Or am I walking? I need to find a councilor. Soon."

"You're really trying to stop conquest of the city?" Grudging belief edged into his voice.

She crinkled her chin. "Without getting anyone killed, if I can help it."

He shook his head and snorted dismissively. "Silly girl. You're talking of war. In war, friends die. Not just enemies."

"All you can do is try, right?"

The coachman was silent for a while. Presently, he decided. "Fine. I'll drive you."

The crinkle on her chin deepened. "No hard feelings?" He said nothing. He just turned around and mushed the dogs. Xanthe thought that was rude but decided to let it go. A minute later though, as they were rolling along, he announced "My name is Rawlth."

The wheels rattled as they drove. "I'm Xanthe. Where are we going?"

"You wanted a councilor. I'm taking you to the top one. Tyan Wormwood."

"Horace's father?"

"Yes."

"That's no good. Horace is one of the plotters. That's how I first learned of this."

Rawlth brought the coach to an abrupt halt on the cobblestone street. "If a Highcouncil family is behind this, this isn't a foreign attack. It's a coup."

"So?"

"I'm not getting involved in that. I don't even want to be seen with you. You can walk."

"What?!"

"Or take my advice and ride to the party. You'd do much better pretending you knew nothing and going back home safe and sound to whatever family you belong to."

She stared incredulously. "I'm supposed to just let Jagerfeld be conquered without doing anything?"

"Think you'll get a reward for getting involved in a feud between the highborn?" He let out a wry chuckle. "You're more gullible than half the girls getting seeded tonight."

Xanthe couldn't believe what she was hearing. "I don't care about a reward. People will die!"

"Yeah," Rawlth declared indifferently. "They always do. It's dodgy-power stupid to volunteer to be one of 'em."

"You're telling me you don't care if villains take over?"

A comfortable sneer came upon his face. "They already have. I've been driving council families all my life. None of 'em are really any good."

"Still, some are better than others, right?"

"Call me a cynic," he declared proudly, "but picking the lesser of two evils is still picking evil."

"Oh, I see! You won't lift a finger for anything that's less than perfect? Knowing, conveniently, the nothing is ever perfect? Which means you never need do anything, while calling yourself morally superior to boot? Cute trick. Alas, I hold myself to a higher standard than that."

That pricked him. "Well, pretty little dolled up girl in the little black magic dress, complain all you want, but there are a lot more people like me than there are of you. You know why?" He thumbed to himself. "We see nothing in it for us."

"Which is why the world's as bad as it is. There are too many bystanders who only care if bad things directly happen to them. If we looked out for each other, the only things we'd have to worry about would be nightmares and monsters."

"I'm supposed to care about which house lords over me?" Rawlth protested. "I'll always be a driver no matter who is in charge. That's what I do. All I care about. If things really turn into hellspace around here, I'll just move. Way better than risking your life over nothing."

Xanthe snorted. "Just driving me will get you killed? Funny, you weren't such a coward when you thought I was defenseless. How much better are you than all these people you're way too moral for?"

He glared. "I was protecting Wallace. I know him. He's a good kid."

"Tari of Outlet is good too. Better than all the Wormwoods put together."

"Heh," he smirked again. "Maybe her blood will improve them. But even they ain't the worst."

"I have good reason to believe that they're planning on legalizing slavery. The whole bit. Selling daughters. Probably chattel slaves too. I can't help but think that will touch you somehow."

Rawlth widened his eyes in shock. "They wouldn't dare. That's not proper!"

"So?" She jutted out her chin. "Who's going to stop them? You're not. You won't even drive the only one brave enough to stand up for what's right. Me. A gullible girl."

He stared narrowly at her for a moment, then shook his head with angry resignation. "Alright, sweetheart. Your funeral. Even with that dress. Guess we can pretend we never talked. Where to?"

"Take me to Councilor Outlet, if you can."

"That's just it. They're over at the Wormwoods right now. Lady Outlet's been trying to merge the families ever since her baby boy died and she couldn't have more. He won't take a slavewife. Says it's betraying her. Word is, she finally badgered her husband into marrying her eldest to the Wormwoods."

Something twisted in Xanthe's stomach. "How do you know this?"

He gave her a sidelong glance. "We drivers don't say much. Lots of people think that means we don't got ears."

Xanthe stared ahead. Too many things were going on at once. She hadn't forgotten about Priscia's father, Damien still needed to find a way in, and she still needed to warn a councilor. But right now, the most important thing was to talk to Tari. She had to know.

"Just take me to Outlet manor."

He nodded, and they made their way off.

## Chapter 22

Above its outer wall, Outlet manse was lit with elegant crystal oil-lamps on wrought iron posts in its driveway, but otherwise its windows were dark. Only a single guard stood lonely duty before the ornate doors at the entrance, slouched yet oddly wary, given the otherwise abandoned-seeming nature of the property. As Xanthe stepped out of the coach, she turned back to Rawlth. "Thank you."

He nodded but did not otherwise respond. Though he'd done her the courtesy of dropping her off, she did not feel like she'd made a friend. He mushed the dogs away without saying another word.

The guard stood in the way, but Xanthe held up the Mechanix-sect pliers. "You recognize this? Tari gave it to me. I'm here to see her. Do I need to be announced?"

He was edgy at first, but upon seeing her more closely smiled in welcome. "You go right in darling." He nodded.

The mansion was mostly dark and entirely empty of servants, all seeming to have been given the evening off. Xanthe knew Tari's room from when last she'd visited, so she climbed the long curved and beautifully carpeted staircase and padded down the hallway until she reached it. It was already lit when she entered. The place was consummately elegant, the finest in everything: drapes, cushions, carpets, artwork, plastics. Xanthe had long ago given up envy of her friend, and it didn't seem to matter much anyway. She almost felt an odd pleasure in it. Tari's family showed up Priscia's in a way no one else ever could.

Tari was there, arranging her belongings. Treasures were laid out on the bed, jewelry and keepsakes of gold, silver, and gems. She was so focused, initially she didn't even notice Xanthe enter the room. It was only when Xanthe came close, that she faced her with an oddly vacant expression.

"Hi," Xanthe said.

"Oh, good. You're here. I have some things for you." Tari's tone was dull and distant. Not too unusual for her.

Xanthe was all business. "Never mind that, there are important things you have to know. We have things to do."

"I'm giving these to you," Tari continued as if she hadn't spoken, and gestured to the largest pile.

Xanthe boggled. It was a pile of silver and gold. The amount of wealth there was more than she and her father could make in a lifetime. Joy and unease both flared in her heart, more the latter. Something was seriously wrong.

"Won't your dad object? I'm pretty sure he'd be mad if you just gave your stuff away."

"I won't be around. I'm leaving a note."

"What? Are you running away? Where are you going?"

"I... I don't know where you go. That's the one thing I can't see. It's all dark. Maybe there isn't a there."

"Wait. Hold on. I don't understand at all."

"Please don't be too proud to accept it. It would mean a lot to me."

"Well, if you're running away, won't you need this too? I'm pretty sure everybody wants coin."

Tari shook her head. "Anywhere I'd run, they'd catch me. But this way, I'll be gone no matter what."

"Then where are you... oh." Xanthe finally caught on. "Tari! You're not going to kill yourself."

Her friend was distraught. "I had no choice. You have no idea what was going to happen."

Xanthe was only momentarily silent. "I do, actually," she said softly. "Your mom has convinced your dad to marry you off to Horace, and he's worse than even you suspect."

Tari's face twisted into one of absolute grief. She choked back a brief sob. "I thought father loved me," she said at nearly a whisper.

Xanthe didn't know what to say. "He does," she consoled. "I'm sure he's thinking he's doing well by you."

Tari burst out crying. "How could he possibly?!"

"Yeah well..." a dozen thoughts went through Xanthe's mind. No matter how rich they were, women weren't allowed to be Jagerfeld councilors. If Tari ever did inherit, she'd have a lot of trouble defending her interests. That had to be at least some of the reasoning. "It doesn't matter much now anyway."

"No, it doesn't. Xanthe. I'm done. I'm okay for now, but if I start acting strange, leave right away. I don't know how long it will take until I start to be poisonous." She pointed to a manacle on her leg.

A chill went up Xanthe's spine. "What do you mean?"

"We have samples of blackdust. I took some."

"What!?!"

"Nobody else will catch it. I put it in my note, so everyone should know to stay away from me."

"You're serious? Already?! You reaming idiot! What the ream were you thinking?"

Tari stared at the floor, twisting her mouth bitterly. "I... I was thinking that it was the only real decision I've ever been able to make on my own in my whole life."

"Yeah, it's fun to make your own choices. But not stupid ones, okay?"

"Maybe in the next life, if there is one." She swallowed heavily. "You see, I have a terrible secret. I'm a witch. Not a good one either. I have a horrible power. Demonic. Doing this fixes all my problems."

Xanthe couldn't believe it. "No, it doesn't! Killing yourself is running away from your problems, it doesn't fix them. Okay? And for the love of mercy, everybody just stop beating yourself up over witchery! Seems like every other girl on the whole reaming planet has some sort of touch way beyond spark throwing, and we're all miserably guilty, thinking we're the only one." Scowling, she dropped herself on Tari's embroidered bed.

"You're sounding like a cultist now. I don't care anymore, but don't even breathe those sorts of words around the Curate."

"Well you know, I've always thought Mr. Griswold was more right than wrong. I don't trust religion. Too many holy men do too much evil for me to believe they've got it right. And yeah, I know. I'm sounding like the stereotypical Creator-denying Scholar, too educated to have faith. But dodgy-power, it's usually the truth! Try me in a tribunal for heresy if you must. Get it over with."

"No one will. I'm taking my secrets to the grave."

"Not the most important," Xanthe scowled. "You haven't explained why you did this. Don't tell me it's this witch power, or your dad making nice with the Wormwoods. I mean, really. You of all people!"

Under Xanthe's glare, Tari averted her gaze. "I know, right? How could Tari of Outlet be sad about anything? She's so blessed!" She let out a bitter sob. "I know it's strange, but I'm just not happy. I never have been. I don't know why. So I pretend. I'm so good at that. The worst thing is, everybody is jealous of me. They envy me!" She squeezed her watery eyes. "I hate it. I would do anything to be someone other than me. Not have this life. Not be a prize to be won. Not be this kind of witch."

Xanthe's anger melted in the face of Tari's suffering. "I'm sorry. I didn't know. I guess I'm too wrapped up in my own problems. But stop it with the whole dreadwitch thing, okay? I'm getting worried myself, but you can always just not use them."

"Not me. I have no control. The visions come whether I want them or not. It's useless though. I can't change anything in them. I begged to go to Scholars' school to find out how this was even possible. All I've ever found was that in the Mechanix Codex. It says some demons know the future. Just like me."

"Really?" Xanthe was dubious. "You see the future? Pardon, but that doesn't sound real. Fortune telling is a hoax of fake circus psionics and pretenders. Not real, like witchcraft."

Tari was earnest. "I don't know how to describe it. How would you explain color to the blind? When they come, it's like standing in a dark forest. There are shadows of things that might be. Ahead, to the sides, wherever. If I take a step in one direction, sometimes things appear that may happen because of it."

"Not will? Just may? You're not really seeing future?" Xanthe questioned. Maybe some clockwork demon was anticipating possible events, and somehow feeding that into her mind.

"Not just one. There are many. Too many to see. They're all blurred together like a million dreams all at once. But sometimes things become terrifyingly clear. Like Horace. Down in the square. I felt him doing terrible things to me. Breathing on me. It is going to happen. Dying is my only escape."

"How far can you see?" Xanthe asked curiously.

Tari blinked a little, as having to confess her ability was now making her more fully consider it. "Little more than a moment usually. But it has nothing to do with distance. Only certainty. I only see clearly when all futures are the same. But that also means I can't stop it either. Like this. In a few years there's going to be a quake. I see it like a mountain in the distance. The details are indistinct, but no matter where I am, there's shaking. Clear as day. It will happen. Nothing anyone can do."

Xanthe considered. "But you see it? Years from now?"

"I..." Tari paused uncomfortably. "I only see where I'm alive. Every night I dream a new death, often from the stupidest things. I choke on a chicken bone or something. But you know? You're right. I just took blackdust. I should see nothing so distant, but I am. It's only the second time it's ever betrayed me."

"Second? What's the first?"

Tari gazed up. "You, Xanthe," she said in awe. "I never see you."

Despite her skepticism, Xanthe felt slightly nervous. "You mean I die?"

"No. I mean I can't see you. Almost ever. I told you before. There is something very different about you. Strange. Powerful. You and everything you touch are hidden by some sort of shroud. You're like a storm that changes what can and cannot be."

"Me?" Xanthe shook her head and bit back an urge to laugh. "Do you have a sillyroot or oil habit to add to the dust you took? I'm a geek. A teacher's pet. Daughter of a poor researcher. A skinny nobody."

"I don't know. It's just what I perceive."

"Alright, fine. Whatever. It's interesting, I guess," Xanthe dismissed. "I'll have to set it aside for tonight though. There's too much to do. Among other things, I left the guy who isn't exactly my favor date at the gate. Plus, I have Priscia's dad to save, and the city."

Tari nodded. Her face fell, and she turned her head away. "I'm glad to have interested you. I know people only value me for my family and wealth. Like an object, not for who I am as a person. But I thought you might decide to remain with me while I'm still me." She shook her chain. "Don't worry. I can't run."

Xanthe felt a sense of angry justice. "Regretting what you did already? Good."

Tari looked devastated. "I deserve that. I guess it's too much to ask, for you to be upset."

Xanthe herself burst out. "Upset? Oh, believe me I am! So maybe you have problems. Things you don't like about yourself. Join the club. But my goodness, I thought you were smart enough to know you can't fix problems if you're dead! Sometimes they're not even problems. The Wormwoods are trying to help a prince take over the city. High treason."

"What?!" Tari raised a trembling hand to her mouth.

"You're surprised? You didn't see that with your power?"

"No. I told you! There's just too much, and anything you're involved in is a thousand times as bad."

"Well, if we stop them, and that's a big if, Horace will be lucky to be alive, much less get you unwillingly before an altar. So, I'm calling in a big no to your noble sacrifice."

"You mean you think my death was for nothing?"

"Not at all," Xanthe told her directly.

"No one can stop them?"

"No. Not that either."

"Then what do you mean?"

"I mean – you didn't kill yourself," Xanthe tore into her with rage-fueled sympathy, tears welling as she did. "Terribly sorry, but you're not dying. I have a hard-enough time making friends as it is." With that, she reached out her palm, and forcefully laid it flat against Tari's neck. As she did so, her dress nearly flowed into Tari's skin. "Live," she snarled.

*Time froze as her perception fell into the microscopic world, and once again, the trance transformed into an illusion of flying through tissues. Wherever examined anatomical features, hundreds of unrecognizable descriptions imposed themselves in her mind. 'Epithelial tissue', 'desmosomes', and focusing in on the cells, 'Endoplasmic reticulum', 'cilia', 'mitochondrion'. They turned Tari's body into a living library of knowledge. It was so fascinating that Xanthe felt a brief panic that she'd end up trapped here, imprisoned by her own insatiable curiosity. Yet, no. She had purpose that took precedence. Somewhere here was something that caused insanity and death.*

Yet even as time stood still, it stretched, and the search turned from tedious to maddening. She scoured and probed through Tari's body as it engaged in that unfathomably complex dance called life, yet she found nothing out of place. No signs of infection. No cells being consumed. No poisons. Only the normal battles between gut bacteria and patrolling leukocytes. Something was wrong. It was too right. Blackdust was deadly. Everyone knew it. There was no cure, not even by the few magical machines in the south that healed wounds for the highborn. Xanthe's focus flew through tissues, wraith-like. Wherever it was, it was well disguised. Either that, or perhaps what Tari had taken was not what she thought it was. Still, Xanthe didn't feel safe in giving up. Not yet. Lymph, bones, arteries, veins, what else? She wracked her brain until it hit her. Blackdust? Black blood. She twisted her focus towards it.

Spiderwebs she'd called the stuff, for that's what it seemed like stringing through the body. Even now its structures were unnamed; no attached definitions accompanied what she saw. It always seemed insubstantial. She felt a dim shock as at she realized why. It was aware of her attention, actively trying to avoid her perception.

Yet in Tari, parts were unable to do so. Hers was sluggish, spasmodic. Finally, signs of disease. Blobs kept breaking off and rejoining. Even with her minimal experience, Xanthe had never seen it do that. Now she saw why. As she bore down to the deepest level of detail she could manage, creatures stood out. Thousands of strange alien devices, in the shape of legged arthropods, infested Tari's black blood. Both parasite and prey were completely alien. Neither were cellular at all. An annotation formed in her vision above the devices.

### Weaponized Holosynaptic Modification Platform CS-A10XB
### Commissioned for Registered War #4239 / Patron: Nemesis

War? She wondered. As with all infections, an absurdly small battle was indeed going on. The devices were gripping pieces of Tari's black blood, while the healthy sections attempted to slough them off. In places this defense was successful, but far more often, they found ways to attach.

This brought back memories. Once, she'd found a kestrel on her sill that was more than merely injured – it had been sick, with a pus-filled wound. Xanthe had dressed it, but that was only the start. She'd had to clean the infection, terribly tedious work that had taken the entire night, made worse by the fact that the bacterial cells grew on their own.

Yet a kestrel's body always fought disease as well. Here, Tari's body was entirely unaware. Just thinking about the work involved put despair in her heart. How long would she have to focus? Did she even have the tools or time? It didn't matter. She had to start. She found the nearest mote of blackdust and focused a narrow burn. The thing flinched and died. Still, there were tens of thousands. Xanthe focused again. Another gone, but she cursed. This was a losing battle. She could already tell. It seemed impossible to harm enough of them before they tore Tari's liquid cybernetics apart. There were just too many.

*A tendril of the same construction as the machines, snaked through Tari's flesh. Xanthe was confused until, with a shock, she recognized it as a thread of the dress. At this scale it was enormous. The alien devices*

*swarmed it. As soon as they touched, each broke apart and were
absorbed. Yet the tendril did not stop. It made full contact with Tari's
black blood. There was a brief flicker before Xanthe's eyes.*

### Disarm Key Provided
### Adjusting Monoamine Oxidase Inhibitors
### Tuning Alterspace Navigation Interfaces

As Xanthe blinked out of her trance, Tari gurgled in seizure. Not
knowing what else to do, Xanthe simply hugged her. "Come on demon. Do
your thing," she cajoled shakily. "At this point, I don't care if you enslave
me. Just let her live. I'll take that trade." Almost on cue, the convulsions
faded, and Tari slumped. Xanthe released her grip, letting her friend down
to rest on her mounded piles of jewelry.

"Dodgy power!" Xanthe cursed. She hadn't moved a muscle but was
still exhausted. That would teach her to be so arrogant as to just imagine
she could cure blackdust. She really hadn't done anything. It was all the
dress.

"Tari? Wake up. Are you okay? Talk to me." Tari quivered, but her eyes
didn't open. "Tari," Xanthe repeated. "Don't do this to me. You're better.
You've got to be."

Just as she was wondering if she'd have to leave for fear of poison,
Tari's woke. She stared blankly up at the ceiling as Xanthe searched her
face. "We're going to be invaded. I see it. All the futures align. Nothing we
can do."

Xanthe didn't know whether to be relieved or worried. "Um, yeah.
That's what I just said. The Wormwoods are trying to take over."

"No," Tari whispered distantly. "From the sky."

Xanthe was settling in on being exasperated. This was just too much.
"Can we just focus on the here and now? Too many Creator-be-damned
things are happening at once."

"Because of you. You are the storm."

Xanthe nearly sobbed in relief, but it came out as a scold. "Are you
trying to bug me? Because you're doing an awfully good job of it. Even
better than Celeste."

Out of the blue, Tari blinked and giggled. "It's my holy vengeance, you
heretical witch. Though I guess we're all that, aren't we?"

"Are you okay?"

"I feel loopy. Is this what it's like to die of blackdust? It seems pleasant,
this dream."

"You're not dying. You're cured. I think. I think I may prove it by
pinching you hard enough that you wake up and turn back into the old sad
and spacey Tari I know. I'll do it hard too. Make you cry."

"You won't." Tari continued to stare blankly at the ceiling. "That's not you. No wonder I was still seeing the quake. I should have known better than to try to kill myself when you're around."

Xanthe's eyes started to water. Now she was the one about to cry. "Well don't do it again!", she choked. "You scared all hellspace out of me."

Tari stared up dreamily. "I knew it was dumb when I did it. I was just in a panic. I saw my nightmare down in the square and came back to say no. It didn't help, of course. It never does. There was no escape."

"We'll figure out a way to stop it. I promise."

"You already did. You're the storm, remember? I don't see it any more. I see black, but not him."

"Black? You keep saying that. What do you mean?"

"It's what I see when I die. But really, I'm okay with that. Him or me. Dead. One of those things will happen."

That didn't sound good, but at least Tari was sounding a little more like herself. Kind of. "Well, no more dust. I don't know if I can save you from it again. It wasn't even me that cured you now."

That last brought Tari's eyes into focus. Her gaze shifted to Xanthe. "Really? Then who did?"

"A demon, I think. Of ancient Earth. It's possessing this dress. They're waking up. I don't know why." Hackles ran up her neck.

"I heard you making a pact. Are you in a cult? A coven?" Tari sounded more curious than accusatory.

"No. I was trying to bargain for your life, but I don't know if it listened. I'm not sure they even think the way we do."

"Maybe it just did it to pull me away from the Creator. I spent years praying to not feel sad for no reason and have this cursed witch-power to be taken from me. Yet now, the futures are clearer than ever."

"Who knows? Maybe having a demon on your side isn't so bad. One thing's for sure. At least they do things. The Creator doesn't help. Not enough to keep you from your fate when you had that vision."

"Or maybe the Creator sent you." Tari smiled up dreamily.

"Along with a demon?" Xanthe shrugged. "Could be." She put out her arm and pulled her upright. "Come on. We got a lot of fate to change tonight." She added as a weak joke. "You know me. Always storming it up."

## Chapter 23

As she exited the mansion, driving her fancy cart through the gate with Xanthe in the side seat, Tari came out with the theory that her being healed was all just a blackdust dream, since nothing had ever cured it before. Xanthe was wryly amused at the idea of being merely a figment of Tari's imagination, but addressed the idea anyway. By chaining herself and throwing the key out of reach, even if this was all some delirium on her bed, there was no harm in playing along. To punctuate the point, Xanthe tickled Tari as a substitute for pinching, and got her to laugh. Xanthe did as well, even as her friend's wistfulness over the failure of her suicide bothered Xanthe a lot more than she let on.

"Damien's an assassin, not a witchkiller. He saw my witch power and could have killed me but didn't."

"Who did he come to kill then?" Tari asked curiously.

"He's being cagey, but my bet is still on Prince Sol, which I guess is to be expected. But he did agree to save Priscia's dad, so we need to get him through the gates armed."

"You're helping Priscia?" Tari shook her head. "Seriously, this has got to be the blackdust."

"Don't be silly," Xanthe replied peevishly. "I'm just a gullible doormat."

They rode on through the darkened streets, which unlike the rest of the city, were mostly empty. Opening the district would show off Jagerfeld, as it had the best of everything. She understood why it wasn't done though. Many of the houses could easily be burgled in the crushing crowds. This way, more servants and guards got the night off.

"Where are we going?"

"The Steeple. We need to see Celeste's dad."

"The archdeacon?"

Tari nodded. "The Curate is the authoritative recorder of land and deeds. The Holy Pilot gave us Haven, so of course the Pilot's church keeps track of who owns what. They judge as well, refusing transfers that are unconscionable or usurious. Celeste's dad is especially considerate helping families that have fallen on hard times. Why do you think my own father is always so nice to him?"

"I just thought maybe he was devout."

Tari shook her head, as she guided the kranth with the reins. "No. Probably less even than Celeste. It drives mom crazy."

"Then what do the counting houses do, exactly?"

"All the escrow. They hold the money as a neutral party. Usually the Curate is just the final stamp, unless something unusual is being done."

Xanthe frowned. "I should know this stuff."

Tari gave her a half-smile. "Finally! Something I know that you don't. Of course, knowing you, in three weeks, you'll have memorized the whole property market, even if you'll never be in it."

Xanthe smiled crookedly. "Who knows? Maybe next year, I'll be buying three houses a year."

"Nope. Only men can buy real estate. Though wives can manage until their eldest son is grown."

They rode up Ancestor's Road, stopping at the parking lot a hundred yards outside the venerable old church. Tari tied the kranth by the watering trough and dumped a dozen ripe winter roots retrieved from under the carriage's bonnet to feed her. Tari bowed beneath the pliers and wand as they entered the church itself, and Xanthe felt the need to follow suit. Then it was upstairs to try to find anyone here on Festival Night. Xanthe wasn't hopeful.

She was surprised. Not only were there people, there was a line. In the clerk's vestibule, an armed guard in livery nearly identical to Royroy's uniform, stood outside with sheaf of documents, patiently waiting his turn before the door to the diocesan suite. He was Shambhalan, with a faint amber tan and narrow eyes.

"What in hellspace?" Xanthe whispered at a distance.

Tari fixed Xanthe with a disapproving stare. "Don't curse in here, of all places."

"I was just surprised. The Curate has people working tonight?"

"Is that so unexpected?" Tari sighed. "Our city's archdeacon is devout, diligent, honest, and decent. I just wish Celeste would see it."

"I don't think how hard he works is her problem," Xanthe responded as they came near. Unrecognizable ancient junk was mounted everywhere on the walls, and muffled angry words could be heard through the closed door of the sanctum. The foreign-born guard was wincing, trying not to listen.

"....my daughter... -oly and singular Saintess of the Miracle of the Blessed Bandages... possessed you to allow her away from your sight ... understand the risks...? ...a demon infested world... monsters, beasts, at every corner, many who wear human faces! ... thanks to you she faces those dangers alone?! ...rrested! Bringing disrepute upon this ... and the parish!"

Xanthe addressed the man quietly. "You in line? Can I go ahead?"

The guard shifted uncomfortably. "Miss, I'm not sure you want to wade into that. I'm too afraid to do so myself. Maybe in half-a-bell he'll calm down."

"Perhaps you should come back tomorrow?"

Resigned, he shook his head. "I've been ordered."

"You have? Hm." Xanthe knocked loudly on the door. As soon as she did, the muffled yelling stopped. Taking that as permission, she just cracked open the door and poked in her head.

In the office cluttered with stationary, iconography, and parts of ancient artifacts bolted together in unlikely configurations, Archdeacon Jameson in full regalia stood over Brother Axeman, who was kneeling, bent so far over that he was nearly prostrate. Celeste's father was furious, while Axeman was crying; drips of the acolyte's tears were puddled on the floor.

"Go away!" Jameson shouted. "I shall not treat you kindly for this interruption, for I am so full of wrath..." He turned around furiously, then blinked in surprise when he saw Xanthe's face.

"Your holiness?"

The archdeacon quickly composed himself. "My dear child, this is not visiting time." He toed the acolyte and silently pointed him to exit. Axeman scrambled for a back door, not even glancing back.

"I'm Xanthe, remember? We put on the Creator-blessed bandages in Celeste's miracle." She opened the door wider, letting Tari be seen, but kept her body hidden behind the wall. She wasn't sure what his reaction would be to her dress.

"Oh! Yes!" Jameson's manner changed completely. "Creator's providence! Is she with you?"

Tari shook her head. "No. We're friends and are together often, but I've not seen her tonight."

He was desperate. "Perchance you know where to find her?"

Xanthe nodded. "We might. But we didn't come for that. We'd like to divulge in private."

The archdeacon drew himself up. "I am sure that it can wait. Celeste is missing. Now, of all times! When she is most vulnerable to terrible outside influences. My dear, sweet, innocent child. I cannot function, knowing the dangers she is so unaware of. Especially from foreign men. What they might lead her into." He twisted his palms together in distress.

Tari and Xanthe looked at each other.

"Your Holiness," Tari began to explain. "We know Celeste. She's quite, um, strong willed. I don't think she'll be led into anything."

"If anything, she'll be taking the lead," Xanthe muttered nearly inaudibly. Tari elbowed her.

Jameson brightened. "That is true! You give me hope. But as the Good Manual asserts, the proper path is guarded by many eyes. Perhaps you, her sisters in faith, might lend aid in finding her?"

"Uh, I..." Tari hesitated. "Well, your Holiness, it's like this..."

"Of course we will," Xanthe jumped in quickly.

Tari turned her head. "We will?"

"Excellent!" Beamed the archdeacon. "Can you start now?"

"Of course," Xanthe replied. "I only ask that on our behalf you hold a Sacrament of the Great Leap. Pray for our success without respite, until we do."

The archdeacon's eyes widened. "Yes, yes, but of course. That is only proper." He nodded appreciatively. "I would trust no one other than myself, as I am not entirely convinced of how well versed those in my service know the traditions." He grimaced with distaste at the acolyte's tears still puddled on the floor.

Xanthe smiled. "Then we shall go. I'll forgo braiding my hair this eve and see to it your daughter returns safe and unblemished." With that, she reached down and laid the glass rose favor on the floor.

Jameson choked up. "On Festival! Oh child, you shame me. I remember my base suspicion when first we met, only because I had not seen you in prayer here at the Steeple. Yet you show by example that faith is strongest, hearts are purest, among those furthest from power. Perhaps your father truly has given the city a gift that I've been too blind to see. You."

"Your kindness embarrasses me. We only await the start of the sacrament to begin."

"Um, excuse me," the guard behind them interrupted, raising his finger. "Before you begin, I've got just a little bit of business first, your Holiness. It shouldn't take too long."

The archdeacon narrowed his eyes. His tone changed. "Your name?"

"I am Javan. A humble guard, your Holiness." He tried a clumsy flourish, then pulled out the papers he was carrying, and put them forward.

Jameson stared at the man and raised an eyebrow. "Come back tomorrow," he commanded curtly.

"B... but your Holiness. This is important business from a councilor. Surely..."

The archdeacon simply turned away and walked in the direction of his Service of Tools, gold plated wrenches, pliers, wires, bolts, and scissors, all over a mat of velvet and firesnake. "Child, I begin the Sacrament now. Angel Pilot, guide these children to make the Great Leap through the darkness and hellspace of uncertainty unscathed, finding Celeste." From then on, his prayers began to be mumbled too softly to hear.

"Y-Your Holiness. Please. Again, this comes from a councilor. There are transfer fees. I..."

"Neither the Curate nor the blessings of the Creator are for sale!" the archdeacon suddenly roared, not turning from his table. "That is the path of false faith! Now leave, lest I grow angry at your temerity!"

Xanthe pulled Tari, getting her to retreat from the door. "That didn't go well," Tari stated when they were mostly out of earshot. Javan appeared to still be trying to wheedle. But judging by the sounds still coming from behind them, he was only making the archdeacon angrier.

"Really?" Xanthe inquired. "I don't think it could have possibly gone better."

"What do you mean? We came to warn the archdeacon, and instead got roped into finding Celeste. To find her doing whatever new sin she's into now."

"We came to save Priscia's dad's estate. Pretty sure we just did. That Javan guard was wearing the colors of Wormwood sponsorship. What else but land-deeds do you think he'd be bringing to the archdeacon? Especially this time at night on a holiday?"

"So? He'll just come back tomorrow."

"If there is a coup, I don't think the Curate will be quite in the same mood to approve a large batch of suspicious land transfers, at least not without studying them closely. I'm sure that's why Javan was ordered to try to push all this through right now."

"Well, they could lean on the Archdeacon. Oh! Hm. That wouldn't be a good idea, would it."

Xanthe nodded. "Threatening the Curate? That would end Prince Sol's chances for certain. I'm not even sure they'd make it outside of the city if they tried that. We may differ in doctrinal interpretation than Prayerhome, but Thule is deeply faithful. Wildmen and wildwives pray thanks for their lives constantly."

"Oh... But now he's intoning the sacrament, instead of signing!"

"Not only that, but the reason for his denial has nothing to do with knowledge of what's going on. Which is good, since I don't know what he'd do if he did." Jameson was nice in his own stuffy way, she continued her thought only to herself. But Celeste was also right. He wasn't exactly the sharpest tool on the service.

"You laid down your favor like that to manipulate him?" Tari asked reproachfully.

"I really needed him to feel that all concerns other than Celeste were petty. When he saw me give up my Festival date to search for his daughter, how could he bring himself to make the Curate coin by signing deed transfers? Still, I was crossing my fingers. It could have gone either way."

"So now, instead of finding Celeste, we don't?"

"Actually, we do. She has to double warn her dad, in case that guard is extra persuasive."

Tari shook her head. "Good luck with that. We'll never find her. With the city like this?" Tari shivered as they both continued to walk.

"I have a clue. Priscia said she'd brought a boy into Highcouncil."

That stopped Tari short. "By the Creator, you think she's making out?"

"You know it *is* a tradition on Festival Night," Xanthe noted. "Not even the Curate objects too much. Especially if you're of age and wise enough not to take it too far."

"Of which she's neither. But fine. Where?"

"Well, if I had to guess, I'd suspect in her room. It's private."

"In the Steeple? Making out in the most sanctified place in all Jagerfeld? What an incredibly.... no wait. You're right. She would do that," Tari concluded sardonically. "Maybe she's in the Chamber of Innocents, using the Sacred Chalice as a hat."

"Come on, Tari. She's not that bad. She's just a... boy connoisseur, is all. You know? Ready to try."

"While we're not."

"Yeah." Xanthe blushed. Heat rose to her face. She didn't know why.

After a short bit of walking, they arrived before the door to Celeste's chambers. "What do we do now?" Tari asked in a whisper. "Just knock? While she's smooching?"

"I..." Xanthe didn't know what to say. Interrupting Celeste in the middle of something would be incredibly embarrassing, for all of them. She sighed heavily. "I don't see any other way." She approached the door, then hesitated momentarily, screwing up her courage to rap on the door. "Maybe she's not here."

Before she could, the door opened. Celeste was behind it, infuriated. Xanthe went mute.

It was Tari who spoke up. "Are we bothering you? We can come back."

"No. You're not. Come in." Celeste scowled. "Might as well."

"You mean that?" Xanthe asked. She wondered if Celeste was being sarcastic.

"Sure as hellspace do!" She seethed. "It's not like I have some stupid chicken boy in here or anything."

Tari brightened, then asked curiously, "Sounds like a date didn't go well. Want to talk about it?"

Celeste rolled her eyes. "There's not much to tell." She opened the door wide to her room and turned back into it.

It was almost exactly as Xanthe had seen it before, except that there were cards and clothes scattered on the floor. She did a double take. Boys clothes. Shirt. Pants. Loin wear?! "Not much, huh? Go on."

Celeste collapsed on her bed, just like the last time. "There was this boy I liked. Or thought I did. He seemed bad enough, but it turned out he wasn't."

"What happened?" Tari asked.

"I took him here to play a game of Hi-Lo."

Xanthe was confused. Like most gambling games, the rules of Hi-Lo only seemed simple. You bet on whether your card was higher or lower than the various rock cards and your opponents'. If you showed you were right and no one else could, you got the pot. Otherwise you lost your bet to the pot. Simultaneous winners competed for the pot in a second deal made from the discard stack all your unclaimed bets, which you kept hidden. There was a whole strategy of artfully conceding bets, so you could win the big bets later with your discard stacks. The rules got deceptively complicated, and some made their living off the game, but it wasn't a typical favor-date sort of thing.

Tari had the same thought. "Teaching a boy to gamble is a pretty funny way of spending your Festival."

"Strip-off Hi-Lo, I mean."

Tari gasped.

Celeste wasn't entertained at the reaction she'd elicited. Her scowl only deepened. "Don't worry. Absolutely nothing happened," she complained bitterly.

Xanthe was both disturbed and fascinated at the same time. "How far did you two get, before he..."

"Chickened out?" She rolled over on the bed. "When I got all his clothes off. I was just about to start letting him win when he ran."

Tari was confused. "What do you mean... letting him win?"

Xanthe's eyes narrowed. She had a suspicion and examined the deck. "Don't tell me. You were playing with marked cards?"

Celeste heaved a frustrated sigh. She slammed a pillow over her head. "He was supposed to make his move when he was naked, but he didn't. He just started talking about the reaming Creator instead!"

"Stop with the sacrilege!" Tari scolded, becoming annoyed. "It's offensive."

"Like you know anything!" Celeste bit back.

"Wait!" Xanthe put up her hand. "Before you two keep scratch-fighting, just finish the story. Why did this boy just start talking about the Creator?"

"Cause after he lost twenty straight hands, he started saying I was being protected from sin. Then, when I showed him my eyes to show how I was really doing it, he freaked. He yelled "Angel Pilot forgive me!" and ran off. I was expecting to see him when you got here."

"You mean, right now there's a boy running naked around The Steeple?"

Celeste hissed in frustration. "Probably thinks I'm some reaming saint who just gave him the Trial of Faith or something. But he's got to come back. I got his clothes."

Tari was speechless. Her mouth hung open. Xanthe covered her mouth too but began to laugh. She couldn't help it. She collapsed on the bed.

"It's not funny!" Celeste fumed.

"Are you kidding?" Xanthe giggled. "It's hilarious!"

Tari began to laugh too. "What if he comes back now?" she burst out, holding her stomach. "Should we all judge him? By the Creator, I'm dying here."

"Arrgh!" Celeste pounded the pillow that was on her face. "Fine. Make fun. See if I care."

"Oh, come on. You, of all people, ought to see the humor in this." Xanthe chuckled. "Or is it only not funny when it's you?"

Celeste was silent for a while. "I need." She finally muttered darkly into her pillow. "To sin."

## Chapter 24

They left the boy's clothing neatly folded outside Celeste's door. Xanthe had a terrible curiosity about who he was, but as Celeste didn't volunteer his name, she stifled it. Instead, all three of them ended up in a third-floor alcove in the Steeple, watching at a distance through partially tinted stained glass at Javan fuming over his parked coach. One of its wheels was completely off, courtesy of a single swipe of Riftstring. It only seemed repairable.

"This isn't even sinning," Celeste grumbled.

Xanthe paused her surveillance to address Celeste. "Does the Holy Precept 'Be not vexatious' ring a bell? I believe it's interpreted by the Conclave of Faith to include not damaging other people's property."

"Nah. Nothing done in your own defense is vexatious," Celeste explained moodily. "You don't have to be nice to people trying to hurt you. Oh, and it's called the Cavalcade of Faith, because Justicars used to move around a lot. Like a circus full of pretenders and clowns."

Tari became annoyed. "Don't compare theologians to clowns. Mocking the faith really is a sin."

"Yeah. It is." The redhead pouted further. "Just not one of the fun ones."

"Well speaking of that, I don't see why you're in such a hurry to get with boys" Xanthe said.

"Because I like them!" Celeste exclaimed. "What's so hard to understand? I like boys. Bad boys, who know what they want and try to get it. Cause that's what I like. Don't give me that dung that girls give, and boys take. Ream that! If I like a boy, I'll do what I want with him. My choice."

"That only gets you a belly full of trouble," Tari warned. "That's why you always have to say no until you're married. The Curate says so."

"Assuming saying no even works," Xanthe added. "Don't be naïve."

Finally, Celeste became amused. She shook her head. "You two? Calling *me* naïve?"

"Not on everything," Xanthe declared. "But a lot more than you think. 'Cutely trying to improperly seduce you' bad, isn't the same as 'beat the crap out of you' bad. Don't trust boys." Even semi-bad boys were dangerous. Like Damien. Awful, smart, unsuitable, absurdly handsome, dangerous, capable. She was sure he was already chasing another girl by now. Xanthe found herself scowling.

"Well, really," Celeste commented, "don't trust yourself. When you're getting super heavy, he's not the one you gotta worry about. You are. If you don't clear your head, and didn't take care, then bam."

"Take care?" Tari wondered aloud.

"Yeah. Both of you. Because Tari, you're going to date some poor boy just to vex your mom. But you Xanthe, you're in the real danger. That I need to keep you out of." She pointed an accusatory finger.

"In danger? How?" Xanthe wondered.

"Of falling in loooooove." Celeste made the dark pronouncement as if declaring Xanthe a dreadwitch.

Xanthe's eyes went wide. "I am not! What are you talking about?"

"I know that look." Celeste eyed her closely. "You're in heat. Cheeks and inner haunches hot. Boobs stiff. You met someone, and really like him."

"I..." Xanthe was about to explain about Horace, but that wasn't who she was thinking of.

"...did I mention, you're sashaying around in that daring dress, and oh so comfortable in it? Only one way that could be happening. He must like you in it, and... oh see? You're doing it even more."

Xanthe was blushing furiously. "Look, can we get back to what we're supposed to be doing?" She pointed through the window. Completely preoccupied, Javan was still trying to reattach the wheel, though it seemed like he was giving up.

"I am." Celeste pulled out a leather body wallet and undid its ties. "Here. Take these."

Tari blinked. Then her eyes bulged. "Is that childbane?"

The little seeds were pink and heart-shaped. There were dozens. Xanthe knew they were worth more than their weight in silver. "Where did you get these? Mrs. Fullbarn?"

Tari gasped in shock. "Mrs. Fullbarn is a childbane dealer? Selling to students?!"

Celeste shook her head. "Other way around. I supply her. Curate sin-pots get filled with all kinds of junk, but they also get these. I rescue a dozen times more than I could possibly use. So, I give 'em away to make sure they're not wasted. Oh, and I've also got a couple of plants hidden in the sacred gardens too."

She continued, ignoring Tari's dumbstruck shock. "Just do yourself a favor, Xanth. Don't trust yourself. You think you have all the willpower in the world, right up until you don't. In the next couple of weeks, scores of girls will be coming in for quick spring weddings. It makes for hot listening, but don't be one of them."

"Listening?! You... you eavesdrop on people's Sacraments of Divulgence?" Tari was so flustered now, that in her dismay the only thing she could squeak was, "I'm not hearing this. Am not. Hearing this."

Celeste nodded. "I'm naturally curious. Oh, and some of these stories. I was thinking of writing a book about them. Change a few names, but I bet it would sell really well."

Xanthe just shook her head and tried not to laugh. Only Celeste. Only her. "I'm starting to see why you need bad boys. They're the only ones who won't flee from you in terror."

The frustration returned to the redhead and she scowled. "Even they do too."

Xanthe narrowed her eyes as insight seized her. "Celeste. For all your talk, are you really still a virgin?"

She glared back angrily in shame. "You want these seeds or not?"

Xanthe nodded and, with a grateful smile, tucked them next to her left breast. "Thank you."

Tari had finally recovered enough to show her displeasure. "You've got to be the most profane. The most impious. The... the most blasphemous!" she sputtered, running out of words to think of.

"You're just trying to make me feel better," Celeste sniffed, sounding mollified. "It's kind of working too."

"I'm serious!" Tari was incensed. "I don't like it. The Creator certainly doesn't. What will you say when it is your turn to be judged?"

"Maybe she can ask the Creator why she's the daughter of not just some unremarkable devout layman, but an archdeacon," Xanthe observed. "Seems to me like the Creator has a sense of humor."

Javan had finally given up. Peeking again, Xanthe saw him at a distance, hesitantly stalking down the street.

"Is he gone?" Tari asked.

Xanthe considered. "Going. Not fast though. I wonder how badly he'll get chewed out for having failed. You know, I should follow him."

"What? In those shoes?" Celeste exclaimed. "They're super sexy, but not practical. Let me go in your stead. He'd never see me."

"I'll bet. But I need you to smooth things over with your dad," Xanthe said.

"My dad's an idiot."

"Not an idiot. Just blind with love for you. Blind and powerful. Not a good combination. Especially because we need him to not do idiotic things tomorrow, which means you've got to prep him now."

"So that leaves me to follow Javan," Tari declared.

"Not you either," Xanthe told her. "There are some armed guards I know who are opposed to the coup that we need to get in past the gate. You're the only one who can do that."

"Nah," Celeste said. "I can get people past the gate too. Tari. You go. I'm gonna go tell stories to my dad."

Tari raised her finger as if she were about to scold Celeste, but then just shook her head. "Fine."

They split up. Tari hurried her way exiting the enormous arched entryway of the Steeple to follow Javan, while Xanthe followed Celeste to the weapon room, where things not belonging in church were stored. Having complained that she didn't feel her attire was completely appropriate for the Steeple, Xanthe was gifted someone else's trench cloak by Celeste, who fished it out of the lost and found box.

As she tossed it over for Xanthe to wear, Celeste stood in front of her, and closed in, her eyes glinting. "Okay. Fess up. What did you do?"

"To what?"

"Tari", Celeste pointed off vaguely toward the entrance of the church. "She's acting all strange."

"Really? All I saw was her getting annoyed at you."

"Exactly! She wasn't all mopey like usual."

"I didn't do anything! I mean, well," Xanthe confessed, "other than saving her life."

"From what?"

Xanthe made a face. "Um... blackdust. She had some and took it. Her parents are trying to arrange her marriage to Horace, so she tried to kill herself."

It was Celeste's turn to be awestruck. "Creator's holy balls! The only thing more reaming scary than her doing that, is that you cured it. You're the most powerful greatwitch I've ever heard of."

"You and Tari aren't too shabby either. You can tell people's emotions by looking at them?"

"Sometimes. Heartbeat, warmth, it can tell a lot. But wait. Tari's a greatwitch?"

"She didn't tell you?" Xanthe winced. "Oh dung, I shouldn't have said."

Celeste snickered. "She's been bugging me for years... while all this time?"

"Having a witch power doesn't make you bad." Xanthe replied stiffly.

"You know that. I know that. But the Curate? Nope. And she's the one who buys it all."

"Still, regardless of one's faith, we should always strive to avoid sin," Xanthe declared moralistically. "So come on. Let's just get in there and find your dad the Archdeacon."

"...and lie our asses off to him." Celeste finished with a droll smirk.

Xanthe took note of the irony and didn't care. "Yeah. It's important."

When they arrived, Darhan was overjoyed. He leapt up from his prayer table, and smothered Celeste in his arms. Xanthe could see her face twist in effort not to struggle against his embrace. When he finally released her, tears in his eyes, he immediately began to scold her.

"I explicitly told you to never leave the eyesight of your chaperone! I told you of this! I am quite vexed, and will have your explanation, before I decide what punishment is proper."

Celeste took on a tone of childlike innocence. "All that happened father, was that we got separated in the crowd. I didn't see where Brother Axeman went, so I returned here to pray. I felt a call. I was so deep communing, that it was not until Xanthe touched my shoulder while I was before the altar, that I came back from glory of the Creator's holy light."

"Wait! You mean... you were here all the time?" Darhan lifted his eyes, exhaling a deep frustrated sigh. "Of course. Where else would you be? And Brother Axeman..." Enraged, he bit back the rest of his sentence.

"But father, this is not all! In my prayers, the Creator showed me of great danger!"

"Yes, yes, my darling," he smoothed her hair with his fingers. "There are dangers to your innocence that your mother and I need to speak to you of. Perhaps in several years' time."

"This is not years away," Celeste began to intone in airy, dramatic voice. "An evil prince comes to conquer the city. He wears a mask of false benevolence yet is a slave of the malevolent five!" She began to shake as if in some holy trance. "Beware, father! Beware! The evil of Earth returns in human form! If not opposed, demons shall corrupt all the power that has been wrest from their grasp!"

The archdeacon stood transfixed. "Are you sure?"

"Lay not the Curate's mark upon any document, no matter how small, for verily in doing so you sign away your eternal soul!" Celeste cried, adopting a theatrical pose. At this, the archdeacon fell to his knees, closed his eyes, and began to pray in front of her.

After a few moments, Celeste peeked down at her prostrate father, and dropped out of character. She slumped, her entire posture betraying a lack of respect. There was no glee in her deception though. Xanthe could just feel her disappointment at how easy he was to gull. She wanted to respect him. Instead, here he was, literally bowed before her feet. She looked over, giving Xanthe a heart heavy glance, shook her head slowly, and rolled her eyes up at the ceiling, sighing silently.

"Father, I must return to my prayers."

"Of course, my dearest," the archdeacon replied, still crumpled over.

"In churches other than the Steeple. It is righteous that I do so. It is needed. Tonight, of all nights."

"I see... If demons come, I cannot argue with your words, dearest. Yet there is danger..."

"The divine protects me. Trust in the Creator's power."

"It is not your physical danger that concerns me. The city is full of guards. What worries me is that there are those who would corrupt you, especially tonight. My dearest daughter, you are blessed, but you have not fully experienced the dangers of men." He rose from his knees.

"Yes," Celeste returned dryly. "You needn't remind me."

"Huh?"

"I need a proctor. I know who. She is right here." Celeste gestured with her arm. "Xanthe."

"A proctor? My dearest, proctors are guards, enforcers of the faith, heretic hunters. She's a girl like you."

"As you have just so wisely said, I am in no physical danger. What I need is a proctor for my soul, and I can think of no one better than her. She alone knew where to find me."

It took the archdeacon only a few moments in thought. "Well, it is most unusual. But yes, I do see the wisdom in it. Very well."

"I swear to dedicate myself to keeping Celeste away from the dangers of boys," Xanthe volunteered.

At her comment, Celeste speared her with a dirty look, but continued smoothly. "She should be acknowledged with uniform. Otherwise she will not be respected, by the guards or anyone else."

"Of course. I can get her something. Come, girls." He led them out. They crossed through the church past the stairs down to the enormous basement reliquary, to a side-room near the anterior sanctuary. There, he unlocked a heavy door. "Here. I should really speak to Marshal Gamerson about this but use my name freely if you are challenged."

Xanthe went inside. It was a relatively small closet filled with the uniforms that caused fear among so many, particularly the Scholars' Guild. Proctors never visited for happy purposes, only to resolve complaints about teachings and teachers. Usually her father came back grim after their private meetings with the Guild leadership, where they'd dictated what they felt the Guild needed to do. She didn't even want to think of how Mr. Griswold would react if he saw her wearing proctor insignia: Sword, Manacles, and the Book of Consequences, each with a separate angel's halo above them.

"Go and change," Celeste commanded. "Come out with..." she paused meaningfully, "*everything* you need." She left the closet door open enough to let in light to see by, then pulled her father away from the door. "It is not proper that we should watch while she bares herself."

It wasn't hard to understand Celeste's plan. Xanthe dropped the trench cloak she'd been given, and then dressed in a large proctor uniform. After this, she put another uniform layered on top. Then another. She tucked all the others under as best she could, leaving her with the feeling that she'd just dressed for a midwinter storm. When she appeared outside however, Celeste's father began to chuckle. "My dear, dressed like that, you are as unfeminine as anyone could possibly imagine."

Xanthe nodded her head. "To be viewed as feminine, your holiness, would distract from my holy duty of chaperoning Celeste."

His smile turned warm. "What dedication! And proper! Return her as soon as her small pilgrimage about the city is done." As Xanthe bowed, his eyes went past her. "What in creation? A naked boy?"

Celeste turned around to see. There was the shadow of a wiry, yet well-muscled young man, hands around his privates, fleeing quickly across the empty church down the sanctum hall, his tight bottom visible to all. Xanthe quickly put her hand in front of Celeste's eyes. "Focus please," she told her.

"He should find his clothes," Celeste said spitefully. "I could scold him. I have very much a mind to."

"No. You won't," Xanthe replied sternly.

The archdeacon smiled, both approving and amused. "Listen to your proctor, my dear. They serve the clergy and obey our will, but only a fool ignores their pragmatic advice."

"I'm clergy?" Celeste's lip curled just slightly. "Get me to a nunnery?"

"Ah, no dear," her father cleared his throat. "There are translations of ancient script. Though a 'priory' is full of nuns headed by the prioress, a 'nunnery' is a house of ill-repute. Only those who disparage the Curate mix the two up. They do so to deliberately insult us."

"Really?" Celeste asked in an air of mock-innocence. "What kind of ill do nunnery's repute? Tell me, in detail! I must know, so that I can scold them properly."

All at once, Xanthe was terrified. It seemed that Celeste was almost trying to make her satire so blatant, her father would have no choice but to acknowledge it. But this wasn't a game. The uniform she was wearing reminded her of that. "Let's stop asking questions, and get going. There is much praying to do," she insisted with an edge to her voice.

"Yes, please! That would be..." Darhan shifted uncomfortably. "You know, this idea of setting Xanthe as your proctor is truly Creator sent. I am so thankful."

Without further ado, Xanthe started gently pushing Celeste, giving her father a thin-lipped smile and respectful nod of her head. Celeste didn't struggle too much, and in minutes they were out of earshot, striding down the street.

Xanthe exhaled a breath she didn't realize she'd been holding. "What in hellspace were you doing?" She asked in an outraged whisper. "This is not the time."

"I've reached my limit. I just can't." Celeste fumed. "All this reaming pretending. He nearly runs half the city and look at him! Is there anything I could say he wouldn't swallow?" She scowled.

"He's just blinded by his love for you. That's not a bad thing."

"Yes, it is! Blind love is the stupidest kind of love. It never works out."

"But you love him too. Otherwise it wouldn't bother you so much."

"I..." Celeste hissed, deeply unhappy. "What difference does that make?"

"Well, you *are* his daughter."

"Yes. His daughter. Which proves the Creator doesn't exist. Or is a complete ream-up. Tari should be me. She believes every bit of this Curate dung. You should be Tari, since you're always worried about coin. While I should be you, making scholarly fun of all this absurd nonsense about demons existing, polluting the holy power. Oogie-boogie-boogie." She lampooned mockingly.

"Actually, Celeste," Xanthe ventured hesitantly, "there might be more to that than you think."

Celeste scoffed. "Not you too! You really think the silly stories about the forbidden Codex of Demons, buried in the bowels of Prayerhome are true? The supposed black magic passwords of power one can use to invoke them?" She waggled her fingers mockingly before throwing up her hands.

"I'm not sure," Xanthe responded slowly. "Let's not chance it. Stop mocking your dad too. He's bound to catch on sooner or later, and then he'll be really hurt, and it'll make a massive backlash."

"I'll be long gone. You promised to help me."

"I did. Still, will you really be happy hurting him? Or getting the Scholars' Guild in trouble? Cause we'll take the blame, I guarantee. Then we'll have a proctor in every class judging every word spoken."

Celeste folded her arms. "Oh no. You're not going to guilt me into staying. If you think I'm going to be sucked into being a prioress? Nope."

"We can keep that from happening. You can say the Creator is done with you or something. Just not tonight, okay? We have a coup to put down."

Celeste frowned, but then gave in. She sighed. "Okay. Yeah. I guess saving the city will be cool."

## Chapter 25

The walk down with Celeste was a lot longer than the ride up had been. It gave Xanthe plenty of time to think. At least she didn't have to worry about tripping, regardless of her heels. Highcouncil's sidewalks were impeccable, as was everything else: streets, public fountains, statues, little scattered pocket parks with low benches and manicured gardens, framed on every side by opulent mansions. Yet that elegance was calculated, a way to lay claim to the sophistication of the ancients, despite the residents not living up to it. This recognition, combined with her new-found awareness that wealth didn't necessarily make one happy, abated the feeling of unworthiness that so often crept into her thoughts when dealing with the rich. The lie that she'd told Priscia, that she liked herself just as she was, didn't seem quite as untruthful anymore.

Still it was hardly time to be content. Things were more dangerous than ever, and the more Xanthe thought about it, the more she understood Rawlth's viewpoint. There would be no reward for preserving the status quo, at least none she wanted. Even if the archdeacon wasn't persuaded by his Marshall to drop her presumed commission, she didn't want to be one, no matter how much coin they made. She was a Scholar. How could she abandon the Guild? More than the comfort of its walls, they were her extended family. A tight knit group of academics, her father's colleagues and friends, with their erudite camaraderie and lowbrow jibes. They loved her in their own way, even if that meant far too much homework. Nothing crassly material could ever replace that.

Finding she cared only led her to worry more. Yes, Tari's plight was important, and stopping Horace would bring personal satisfaction, but the more she thought of what might happen, the more aware she was that the Guild would be held responsible for anything she did. By what right did she risk their wellbeing without even telling them? No matter. She was already in too deep to back out. She'd just jumped in without even being able to say why. It just felt right.

They reached Main Street, the well-appointed avenue that led to the Highcouncil entrance gate. Here, Celeste stopped and gave her a slight nod. "Time to do your striptease."

"What? Oh yeah." Xanthe started pulling off the proctor's suits she was wearing. For them to be useful as disguises, the district guards couldn't see her in them, or they'd suspect something when they saw other people wearing them. Besides, all the layers were insufferably hot.

Celeste produced a brown corduroy satchel from under her habit, something else she'd stolen from the cloak room. "Don't worry. I'll pack these while you perfect our plan. I can see you've been thinking."

"I don't have a plan. Just a strategy."

"There's a difference?" Celeste cocked her head.

"If I had a plan, I'd know what to do. But I don't. That means we've got to fall back to the general strategy of knowing that if nothing changes, they've lost. That means, all we need to do is ream up whatever they're doing, wherever we find it."

"Way fun," she grinned mischievously, as if they were just going to carry out some elaborate practical joke. She rolled each proctor uniform up, packing them tightly in the satchel before slinging the whole thing over her shoulder.

"Fun until they notice us," Xanthe warned. The one thing she agreed with wide-brim about, was that this was not a game. "Then it'll get not-fun, super quick. I never really asked if you wanted in. I just assumed you would."

"Oh my! You're right!" Her friend put a hand to her mouth with a mock expression of innocent surprise. "I've never dreamed about getting in trouble before!"

Celeste was kidding, but Xanthe wasn't feeling it. "We could get killed."

"Real danger." Celeste's eyes glinted, like when they both dared each other to pull some foolish tomboyish stunt. "All the better. It'll cost you though."

"Cost me... what?"

"Everything about your new boyfriend." Celeste prodded gleefully. "All the details."

Xanthe knew it was going to be something like this. "I don't *have* a boyfriend," she declared stiffly.

"Well, whoever you're crushing on. Whose name I don't know, but as soon as I even bring him up, you start getting hot. Are you gonna get a new favor to drop in front of him?"

"I already got a replacement favor..." Xanthe blurted before suddenly realizing that was a mistake.

Celeste's eyebrows furrowed. "So where is that one?"

"With another... Look. It's complicated. The point is, he already gave Tari's back. That's why I had it."

"You already did... what? He's your favor-date?"

Xanthe groaned inwardly. She'd already just blown it. Celeste was merciless in digging stuff out.

"Wow are you red! Did you kiss already?" Celeste pressed.

"No, I haven't kissed tonight. I mean... not *him*." She'd pecked Wallace on the cheek, of course.

"Wait. You kissed someone else?! Wow, Xanthe! You really get around!" Celeste grinned.

"Not like that!"

"Which boy did you give which favor to? Tari's? That you," she smirked conspiratorially, "...lost? Or the new one? Some boys two-time girls on favor dates. You're the first girl I've heard of who's dropped two favors! Cool idea!"

Xanthe was stung. It was like Priscia's accusation, except Celeste entirely approved. "I didn't! Really! What kind of girl do you think I am?"

"One with a lot more going on than I thought! And here I thought you were all shy. So, this boy you kissed. Which favor did you drop for him?"

"I didn't drop any favor for him," Xanthe told her defensively.

"Wait! You dropped two favors tonight, then kissed a completely different boy with no favor?!" Celeste's face widened into sheer admiration. "Xanthe! You hot little witch! They do say when your touch is strong, you can't stop at just one."

Xanthe was feeling horribly flustered at the way Celeste put things. "It's not like that. I mean okay, so I kissed one boy, but I didn't mean it that way. He's not even the boy I'm thinking about. I mean... Can we just drop this?"

Celeste's grin didn't look like it could get any bigger. "Not when it's this juicy! Creator's holy bees! And to think you were calling me the perv! You're gonna make my book!"

That was it. "You are *not* going to write me up in some perv-book!" Xanthe burst out hotly. "I don't care if you do change the names."

"Well, you definitely will if you don't keep spilling. Tell me, which one do you want to sleep with first?"

Desperate for a distraction, Xanthe stared down the long boulevard in the direction they'd been walking and was surprised to find something that qualified. Horace's carriage had crashed near the guard post. It had run into the gate's portcullis, and now stood astride it. Even at this distance, it was easy to tell the thing was a complete wreck. Bars were broken, as were several spars. "Look at that," Xanthe pointed. It was a bad accident, but all she felt was relief. She was rescued, at least for now.

Celeste grudgingly turned her eyes away as well. "I'm not done," she warned. "Details. That's my price."

"Important things first. What is going on down there?"

Celeste stared, and to Xanthe's surprise, turned serious. "Something pretty bad. There's blood."

Xanthe didn't see anything clearly. It was still too far away. But she had a sinking feeling in her stomach. "I'm an idiot," she declared. "I used the Outlet name to get the guards to stop Horace's carriage. Somehow it never occurred to me there'd be bloodshed."

"Not a crash. You mean a fight." Celeste declared. It wasn't a question.

Xanthe nodded. "They're using the carriage to smuggle bandits into the district. I just assumed Royroy would back off and try the north gate when challenged. I meant it more as an annoyance than anything. We should get down there and see what we can do to help."

"Let's not." Celeste told her seriously, her eyes momentarily going entirely black.

"Why not?"

"I don't think the good guys won. Come on."

They walked down the sidewalk on the left-hand side of the street, towards the guard post, trying to seem like innocent bystanders. There was no good place to hide their approach anyway. "How do you know?" Xanthe asked in a nonchalant manner she didn't feel as they made their way closer.

"That one who swaggering around like he's the boss has blood on his uniform, like he was stabbed."

"Really? I don't see anyone lying down or anything."

"That's because he's not. He's walking around like nothing happened."

"What? Oh. You mean he's wearing the uniform of a guard that was stabbed. But he's not that guard."

Celeste nodded. Some of her jauntiness had left. "I think we can walk right through. I bet they're more worried about us discovering them, than the other way around."

They were getting near. "Think the guard they stabbed is still alive?"

"It's possible, maybe. The holes are small. But they are in the chest. That can't be good."

Xanthe could now make out the men, but the dark blood on dark fabric in the dim night was still indistinguishable. "Your eyes are amazing."

"Seems normal to me. It's everyone else who is so blind." Celeste said as they reached the last cross street. "What do you wanna do now?"

"I guess we can't save the men they attacked," Xanthe sighed wistfully in a low voice, as they entered the intersection where Rawlth had previously parked. The chauffeur was nowhere to be seen.

"We can if we go this way." Celeste gestured down the right-hand sidewalk of the cross-street heading left. The guard station was large enough to block the view, so as soon as they turned, they would be out of sight. Before she did, Xanthe afforded the men a momentary glance, and was greeted with wary stares. All were scruffy. Not the guards she'd met before. They lounged on the wreck of the carriage like they didn't care who owned it. Celeste proceeded apace in the other direction along the windowless cement and stone backside of the building.

Xanthe rushed to catch up. "What are we going to do over here?" It was the wrong way.

"There's no blood trail leading off. They gotta be keeping the real guards in the holding room inside. If you take this and do your stuff over them, while I pretend to pray and all, we can fix it." She handed over a bandage.

"Yes, but we have to get in. But the only door inside is where the bandits are. Not here."

Celeste abruptly stopped on the corner diametrically opposite from where the fake guards were loitering. The back of the square stone building ran up to the garden courtyard of a modest mansion. Celeste stepped over a low picket fence into its yard and followed the station's back wall for a few yards, tromping through an ornamental bed of small bushes. "Which is why we're going to use the secret back door that lets their prisoners escape," she explained.

Xanthe looked sidelong. "Guard posts don't have secret back doors."

With the smoothness of a card shark, Celeste twirled her hand, making Riftstring appear seemingly by magic. She then swiped it once near the ground angled up, then after more twisting, moved it in a rectangular motion above, angled down. As soon as she was done, a waist high slab of cement broke free. It toppled and landed with a deep thump on the soil, crushing a shrub. "It does now," she smiled roguishly and gestured for Xanthe to enter with her arm.

Xanthe didn't say anything. She just ducked through. Inside was a cramped prison cell, bare and dark, but not so much that she couldn't see. Three men were there, all only in their loin wear. Two were huddled over the third, who was lying on the permacrete floor in a thick pool of his own blood. He was the guard she'd persuaded to stop Horace's carriage. Despite the state of their undress, Xanthe didn't feel embarrassment. Only guilt.

"Stand aside," she told them. "I have some bandages blessed by the archdeacon's daughter here. If the Creator so wills, perhaps he may yet be saved." After this announcement, she nearly leaped to put her hands on him.

"The sergeant's dead," she heard a voice sob distantly, as she fell into her trance.

*The cells were thirsty. Blood was leaking both into the abdominal cavity and externally. By this time, searing the wounds shut was nearly second nature to her, and stitching together his mangled liver took both an eternity and an instant. Yet none of this work solved the general issue that this flesh was parched for liquid. Without it, the cells marked erythocytes in the strange floating displays could not move. In places, they were sticking together and beginning to clot. That would mean death. Xanthe moved as quickly as she could, breaking them up, pushing them along with her touch. But without her constant vigilance, she knew this was a hopeless cause. Unless...*

"Close your eyes and pray," Celeste's command echoed from somewhere, sounding both near and far.

*There seemed a possibility to move the blood that had leaked, back into the vascular systems where it was needed. What had accumulated in the abdomen alone from the punctured liver might be enough to keep the man alive. The only question was how to filter it. The blood in the intestinal cavity had been polluted with gut bacteria, and flooding veins with blood mixed with them would cause septic shock. She'd seen similar things with kestrels. Yet perhaps the fabric of the dress might serve as a filter of some kind. She knew it could; it had drained the river water off her body quickly. She wondered if there was some way to communicate her intent to it.*

*Almost as soon as she thought of this, there was an unexpected increase in fluid levels. The irregular heartbeat stabilized as did the breathing. Blood pressure rose dramatically. It was odd because there was still blood in the abdomen. He seemed to be getting better all by himself at a rapid rate. After several minutes, still quite unhealthy and needing much recuperation, but she became increasingly satisfied that he would live.*

Xanthe opened her eyes. Celeste had the two men's foreheads pressed against the cold floor, resting her hands on the back of each of them. She seemed oddly spooked, quite unlike her normal manner. Xanthe returned a thumb up and slight smile.

Celeste nodded. "Creator I feel your power here in this room. I beg, return the spirit of this beloved one. For it is not yet his time to join you." She spoke entirely for the benefit of the men.

"Once again, your prayer for others seem to have been answered, Holy Celeste. For he lives."

Celeste made a sour expression but went with it. "Rise," she commanded the men. "Carry him home. Treat him gently. Put him in a warm bed. Give him honey-water. You know. Bandager sort of stuff. Try not to drop him on his head or anything. The Creator wouldn't like that."

The elder of the two guards lifted his head. "We'd love to take him home. But none of us live anywhere near here."

"Creator's Holy B... rilliance," Celeste choked out. "Okay. Where's the nearest decent bed?"

"Nearest? On the other side of the cell door."

Celeste squinted up at Xanthe, who shook her head. "No good. Let's go to the house next door."

"We can't do that," said the other guard. "That's trespassing."

"We'll get in trouble for it later," Celeste told him. "After your friend doesn't die, okay? Just follow Xanthe's directions about how to carry him. I'll scout ahead."

"Don't walk across the yard," Xanthe told them all. "We don't want to leave tracks there."

Celeste nodded and exited. She turned sharply and again tromped through the flower bed, directly out to the stone street. She then walked down the sidewalk, directly away from the guard post and the bandits. Xanthe and the men tailed after, carefully carrying their injured ally, until at last they made their way up adjoining manor's front walkway. Celeste already had the front door open by the time they finally reached it.

"We're in luck," Celeste told them. "The door was unlocked."

"Like the hole in the holding cell was?" The guardsman asked skeptically. He was the man who'd come to check on Xanthe when she'd yelled in Rawlth's coach.

Celeste turned, acknowledging his comment. "In addition to direct favors, the Creator also blesses the Mechanix with holy technology. But I'd appreciate it if you didn't blab too much about that last bit."

Xanthe added, "We'd also appreciate it if you could tell us what happened."

"Not much to tell," he shrugged. "The sergeant orders the roadblock put in place. We're still letting in walkers, but no more vehicles. Up comes the Wormwood carriage at top speed. The driver's an idiot. Doesn't stop. He doesn't know how to pull up a kranth quick. Now the beast isn't as dumb as he is. It hops the barrier, pulling the carriage into it. This snaps one of the harness spars. It panics, claws madly, breaks the other one, and runs off. I'm sure it's in someone's root garden by now."

As he had been speaking, the other guard laid the injured sergeant out on a divan in the drawing room, just to the left of the main door. He'd found a blanket and was now bringing water.

"And how did you get attacked?" Xanthe asked.

"We weren't expecting anything other than some shaken up passengers. Didn't know bandits had hijacked it. But out jump twelve of them. They're on top of before we even realize they're hostile. One introduces himself by stabbing the sergeant, and two others run inside to keep us from cranking the alarm. From there, we're surrounded. We surrender. They strip us and throw us in our own holding cell, so we can watch as he slowly dies. You know the rest."

Xanthe nodded. She'd heard enough. "Come on Celeste. Let's go fix this."

The guard drew himself up. "Miss, we might have been caught napping, but I'd rather die than let girls fight in our place, even if the Creator has blessed you with holy favor and technology."

"What are you going to do, exactly?" Xanthe asked. "They stripped you nearly naked."

"And you're a girl. You can't fight. Or run. At least I can do that."

"I'm not going to do either. We're going to walk right past them, letting them think they've fooled us. Once we do, I can ask some garrison men just outside the district for aid." She wasn't lying completely. Technically Yuri and Claude were part of the garrison.

The young man hissed in frustration. "I have to do something. Maybe I can use a fireplace poker or something."

Xanthe eyes glinted. "You'll get your chance. In the meantime, please don't get killed for nothing."

"Same for you. Walk past that trash quickly. No telling what they'll do."

Celeste was in a hurry as well. She pulled Xanthe outside, inexplicably anxious. "Well that could have gone worse," she said at last, as soon as they were away. "Thank goodness they didn't notice." Her nervous attitude was confusing. It was as if they'd momentarily traded personalities.

Xanthe eyed her quizzically. "Notice what?"

Celeste seemed distinctly queasy. "What happened to all the blood on the floor."

"You mean in the prison? There wasn't as much as I thought."

"Yeah! Because while you were using your touch, that black dress you're wearing put some threads down and sucked it all up. Drinking it off the floor like a balegaunt. Ewwwww...."

Oh. "So that's what happened! I was wondering why his blood pressure rose so much."

Celeste shuddered. "The creepiest thing. It actually is demonic."

"So is Riftstring."

"My toy's just a cool knife. That thing you're wearing could suck the blood right out of you right now."

"Maybe, but hasn't. Yours has been reaming with your head. Haunting your dreams. Remember?"

Celeste's scowled defensively. "Not the same thing. I Besides, I like Riftstring. It's useful, beautiful, and mine."

"So's my dress. Without it, Tari and two other people would be dead, and I'd probably be in that cell you just carved those men out of. So let's ignore it for now. I don't know why we found these gifts, but this isn't the time to question it."

"There are lots of stories about terrible things that happen to people who bargain with demons."

"So now you're believing all that Curate dung?" Xanthe goaded with a smile.

Celeste's scowl turned thoughtful. "No. But I don't believe in a free lunch either. We're being used somehow. There's always a price."

Xanthe remembered how she'd already tried to bargain for Tari's life. "For some things, prices just have to be paid."

## Chapter 26

As they approached the corner of the guard post that would bring the disguised bandits back in view, Xanthe grew nervous again. Celeste, by contrast, seemed more confident than ever. "The trick," she said in response, "is to figure out how to make someone else pay that price."

"That's evil." Xanthe set a quick pace to minimize talk time with the bandits.

"Hey girls," said one of the fake guards, as they came into view. "How 'bout some flamedraft?"

"Not if they deserve it," Celeste declared with aplomb.

A second bandit in the torn-up uniform motioned to his cohort. He was no older than the first, but had a nasty scar across his face, and appeared to be the leader. He lounged against the door, saying nothing, but was clearly checking them out.

Xanthe found strength walking as a pair side by side with Celeste. They walked quickly. "We might be coming back through, officers," she called as the only thing she said to them.

"You do that," the first leered crookedly.

Though Xanthe noticed the bandit staring at her in a manner that made it clear he wanted trouble, their speed helped them pass through the gate unmolested. Yet when they got outside, Xanthe was shocked. Even at this distance, it was obvious. The park where she'd left Damien was empty.

"What in the world?" Where did they go?"

"Where'd who go?" Celeste asked.

"My friends who were going to help us recapture the gate. They were there." She pointed up.

Celeste stopped. Her eyes went entirely black and she stared, first ahead, then around. "It's empty. But I see warm hand prints there." She pointed to the Highcouncil wall to her right. "They must have hopped it unnoticed during the fight."

"Dung," Xanthe sighed. "They must have gotten impatient waiting for me. What do we do now?"

"You're asking me?" a slow smile grew on Celeste's face. "How about you spill some more about your boyfriend? Is he in the garrison? You like boys in uniform? Is that who these proctor uniforms are for?"

"Celeste! Concentrate!"

"O blah. You're no fun", she tsked. "But okay. If we need your friends, we should go find them. Lucky for you, I'm really good at tracking."

"That'd be great. Maybe they can capture the bandits still here."

"Capture?" Celeste glanced dubiously back towards the gate. "You're serious? Those guys won't go down without a fight. So why even try? Just cut them down like a scythe through cradle-lilies."

She had that sinister cast to her face again, and Xanthe didn't like it. "See? That's it! Right there. What you're doing now. If you want to talk about a price for dealing with demons, that's what I'm worried about. Not some weird blood magic. You used to be a lot more idealistic. Riftstring is ruining you."

Her friend shook her head. "The Curate did that already. One thing I got to hand to my dad, it takes a lot of faith to keep believing in humanity with all the dung deacons deal with. You should listen to divulgences. Brrr. Nothing but horror stories and excuses. `Ooh, I'm cheating on my wife with this girl, but because of what my brother did, I now know she's really my niece. But I can't stop. It's not so bad though, because I'm making sure she doesn't take childbane, so give me my blessing.´ Hellspace, if I were the Creator, I'd wipe us all off the map. It'd make Haven a better place."

Although Xanthe was still worried, she remembered her own advice. Sometimes there were prices you just had to pay. "Well, just don't go joining the coup because you like bad boys," she admonished jokingly.

"I said bad boys," Celeste assured with a wry smile. "Not bad breath."

They walked back up to the gates and the broken carriage. The men were peeking through the open doorway, hiding themselves, just about the exact opposite behavior of real guards. When they got up to the side door, one of the men leaned in around the corner. "Back so soon?"

"We changed our minds. We're going back in. The better parties are in here anyway," Xanthe told him.

"Come on in."

They did. Yet when they walked in, suddenly there were three men surrounding them. "We need to check your... ah... identities. Innat right, boys?"

Celeste took this as another introduction, like they had done when searching for Damien. "Hi! I'm Celeste! What's your name?" She chirped, putting a hand forward to the largest one.

Not expecting her to be so forward, he was momentarily didn't know what to do. "Um."

"Do any of you guys have sisters my age? Anyone you pray for at night? We can pray for them too! Think of the Creator! He sees everything you do. Especially where you put your hand at night." She mocked them openly.

If Celeste had been just a little less sarcastic, Xanthe would have thought her tack a good one. There was a lot of faith in the outlands. Many unsavory men were kept in line by the belief that the Creator did not protect the wicked from nightmares and monsters. Sometimes even bandits were moved, acting less like true villains, and more like mercenaries whose protection you just couldn't easily turn down. The phrase 'I met a friendly bandit' meant seemingly bad luck that turned out to be unexpectedly good.

Yet these bandits were not friendly. They were ruddy tattooed sailors, with strange accents and greedy faces. Only one was reluctant. He didn't interfere though, either.

The bloody shirt hole leader was unperturbed. "Come on inside. Both of you. We're going to search you," he said.

"That's okay," Xanthe said. "I'm thinking we've decided not to come into the district."

"Too late. We're gonna take you in anyway. Come on. This way." The one Celeste had tried to shake by the hand grabbed her by the wrist. She walked passively with him, almost eagerly. The leader tried to grab Xanthe's rear, but there was an electrical crackle of static electricity, and he jerked his hand back.

"Dung. Mountain fire," he cursed.

"Neither of us would rather go inside," Xanthe said.

"You have no choice," he threatened.

"Come on, Xanthe," Celeste smiled crookedly. "He's giving us no choice."

It was all happening too fast. If there was one thing Xanthe didn't think she was good at, it was quick thinking. She needed at least a moment to figure out what to do. She let herself be pushed forward, at least going after Celeste. It didn't help that she felt absolutely no fear at all.

Inside, the guard house was bare but relatively tidy, with the standard sorts of things in them: cupboards, beds, a card table, the alarm box in the corner with crank. The pantry had been raided, and the spare provisions were laid out on the table, subdivided equally as if the men had been treating the old winter roots and stale crackers as treasure, rather than food. There was no sign of the other nine bandits the real guard had mentioned. Xanthe figured that they'd gone on to their original intended destination.

"Okay, so we're going to strip search you," the large one holding Celeste's arm said.

Celeste turned to Xanthe in triumph. "See? Told you."

"See what?" His eyes following Celeste's to Xanthe.

Xanthe got mad. "Damn it! When I said, 'no choice', I didn't mean you should actively cooperate to get in this kind of situation! That's not fair!"

Amused, Celeste stuck out her chin. "You're just blaming me for being right."

"What's going on?" The leader asked as he shut the door behind them.

"They're having a scratch fight," the one gripping Celeste said. "They know what we want. You know. Not so innocent."

The last bandit wasn't as eager. "Look how well they're dressed. They could be noble daughters. We could get in trouble. With the boss's boss or something. Or the Curate."

"Ream the Curate," said the big one.

Celeste sneered amiably at her captor. "I could almost like you, if you weren't old, ugly, and didn't stink. So, I'll let you to take your hand off, before I do. I'll even count to ten before I do."

"Hey boss! I think this little redhead's threatening me!" He barked a cruel laugh and licked his teeth.

Xanthe turned to the leader. "Please," she pleaded. "Don't do anything you'll regret. I'm begging you."

"One." Celeste began.

The leader grinned and stared at her hungrily. "I never regret anything."

"Two."

Xanthe stared at him, shivering in fear. She could feel the black dress tensing in anticipation. "You will."

He laughed, shaking his head. "Who your daddy is may scare Roth here, but it don't scare me. I may not be the highborn brat you were hoping to get naked for tonight, but I'm the one you're gonna. You're gonna do lots of things you don't want to."

"Three."

Xanthe stared, trying to think. How? How could she get out of this situation without violence? It seemed hopeless. Celeste seemed dead set on it. Suddenly, an idea formed.

"Huh?" she turned her head. "Did I hear something coming out of that door back there? A big noise?" She pointed at the locked and barred holding cell door. "Sounded like quite a racket!"

"Four."

The leader seemed to know he was being manipulated but wasn't taking any chances. He got a cagey expression. "Roth," he canted his head in the direction of the cell door. "Go check the prisoners out. If they're making noise to get help like the little slides they are, finish 'em."

"Five."

Xanthe willed for her heels to shorten. She figured that maybe she might be able to open the door quickly, or escape through the cell door. But no luck. The man was staring at her openly now. She had that feeling of being judged again. Leered at. It was creepy. She was simultaneously repulsed and worried for him.

"You know what I'm thinking? As fine as it is, I wouldn't mind seeing that dress torn in half."

This only heightened her anxiety. "I'm sure it's thinking the exact same thing about you."

He stared oddly. Her joke seemed so earnest. "You're funny."

"Six."

"Where are they?" Backing away from the peep hole, Roth pulled out his sword and carefully unlatched the door. He examined all angles to make sure he wasn't about to be ambushed, but then entered the room completely. As soon as he did, he yelled. "Creator's Holy balls!"

"Seven."

The leader in front of Xanthe looked sharply toward the door. He too pulled his sword, and when he did, the man holding Celeste did likewise. "Block the exit," the leader told him. "I don't want them getting away." He then left Xanthe and followed Roth. Right away there was a scream of anger from the other room, followed by cursing. "How the ream did that happen?"

"I don't know! They had an escape door?"

"Eight."

"You stay here. I'll go after them. They had to have left a trail of blood," the leader barked. Xanthe felt a twist of fear in her gut. She hadn't checked for dripping blood specifically. "And don't touch the blonde one. She's mine."

"Nine. What comes after nine?" Celeste asked.

The hapless Roth reentered the door and shut it behind him. Of all these men, Xanthe felt he was most savable. Still, he had his sword out and was nervous. She had no idea what the dress was capable of and didn't want to find out. She turned to Celeste. "Please stop counting. Nothing's going to be happening any time soon."

"Look, miss," Roth ventured, as if feeling guilty. "I know this is a bad situation for you, but sometimes things just happen, you know? It's better if you just accept it. But we don't kill if we don't have to, so it won't be so bad. Just another thing that happens in life."

"You still don't understand," Xanthe told the man. "I'm not begging for my life. I'm begging for yours."

The hulking bandit holding Celeste laughed. "Damn! That's a good line. I'll have to remember it next time I'm shaking down some chum on the road."

"Ten," Celeste announced indifferently, and smiling, breezily walked away from her captor.

"Hey, how'd you..." the man's voice turned into an incoherent scream.

Xanthe stared. His hand and wrist still had a grip on Celeste's upper arm but was no longer attached to his body. She lifted her elbow slightly, and the limb fell with sickening slap of meat on the concrete floor. "You didn't take your hand off, so I did it for you," she explained pleasantly through her teeth.

The man's stump was squirting blood like a gusher, in pulses as his heart beat. He dropped his short sword and gripped it tightly. "Ahg!"

Xanthe was irritated to no end. "Did you have to do that? Really? Did you?" Infuriated, she walked toward Celeste and glared. "I was handling this! I told you to stop." Disgusted with her behavior, she casually bent down and picked up the meaty hand, noting that it had dirty fingernails, glared once again at Celeste, and walked toward the injured man.

It was Celeste's turn to dismayed. She knew exactly what Xanthe was intending. "You got to be kidding me."

The man was backed up against the latched wooden door, his face full of rage and incredulity. "Kill the ginger witch, Roth! Kill her!" he screamed.

"Shut up," Xanthe commanded coldly. "I'm feeling merciful, but don't push it."

As she moved close, he made to kick her, maybe as some deadly swordsman's trick, but didn't even get the chance to surprise her. As soon as he started moving, there was a sharp crack and five long black needles shot out from the sides of her dress, pinning him like an insect against the door. "I told you," she reiterated with deadly menace. "I'm begging for yours."

His eyes were finally full of terror, but Xanthe didn't care. She numbed his hand, then the stump, then brought the severed hand up to it.

*The cut was clean. The most perfect she'd ever seen. It was uncanny. At the smallest levels, gashes always had some form of irregularity, even when kestrels had sliced themselves perfectly on glass. Not here. Sensing into the flesh, the nerves were so perfectly severed, it was as if they didn't yet know their other half was missing. Which was good. It would make repair all the easier.*

There had always been a sense of time dilation whenever Xanthe entered her touch trance, but the strength of it just kept increasing. All at once she was inside the flesh that did not yet know it was dead, adjusting and aligning so that it would avoid that fate, yet at the same time, the world was not quite moving. Words were being slowly spoken that she could understand.

Celeste shook her head. "These are sea bandits. Murderers and rapists. You saw what they were about to do to us. Why save him? Let him die."

*As usual, it was taking forever. She could see at a finer degree of detail than ever. Yet only now, with this suddenly increased clarity, was it possible to appreciate what she was doing. At the molecular scale, the task was enormous. An ocean of flesh and bone was before her. It extended seemingly forever. Thousands of trillions of surfaces. The more she thought about it, the more daunting the task seemed.*

"Cultists! Dreadwitches!" Roth screamed.

"Oh, don't worry!" Celeste mocked, "See, you don't have to beg for your life because we don't kill bandits." She paused a beat, and grinned. "Just make their man bits fall off."

*Xanthe wondered. How had she ever accomplished healing? How much of it was her? How much was black blood? Witch power was always mysterious, but the one thing she'd never considered was that it might not be her own. Maybe demons were all there really was to power. It cast the Curate in an odd light, both rejecting and praying for the same thing.*

"You... You can't really do that!" Roth wailed uncertainly.

Celeste sneered with amusement. "You sure?"

*She retreated into unthinking trance. Somehow her innate power could do things that she couldn't do consciously, and pinching bone presented challenges she wasn't used to. It meant getting the hardened material to align just right, and then getting it to stick, like trying to put a house together using only glue and no nails. The clean cut wasn't helping here. No matter what, it would be weak for a time. Nerves were easy by comparison, and they were hard. No. She had to let go. Do it without thinking. This power did not come by thought. It came by instinct.*

Celeste continued to provoke, snickering darkly. "I know this is a bad situation for you, but sometimes things just happen, you know? Like your becoming a woman. You just have to accept it."

Xanthe pulled back from her trance, completely surprised at the speed of her success. "Celeste, we need to talk about what is proper. Killing people isn't. There is too much death as is."

"Okay, lets." Celeste jutted out her chin, accepting the challenge. "By saving the evil, aren't you just helping it? How many innocent victims are gonna die when you let these thugs live?"

Xanthe hissed to herself in frustration. Dodgy power, she had a point. But it brought on an idea. "No one," she announced. "For my mercy shall be paid by a curse." Her eyes bored in on the larger man. "I condemn you and all your progeny to strength only in proportion to the good you do. When fighting monsters, you shall be strong as a dozen men. But be one yourself, and your life is forfeit."

It was pure bluff of course, but he didn't know that. The bandit's face was a mask of hate and revulsion. As evil as he was, he still considered himself better than dreadwitches. Roth seemed less judgmental, or maybe more scared. He stared dumbfounded at the hand now reattached, while keeping his hand in his pants trying to physically protect himself from Celeste's pretend curse. The situation would have been funny if it weren't so grave. Yet as she thought this, an odd phrase entered Xanthe's mind: *program executed*. The dress relaxed back into cloth and her unwilling patient dropped to the floor.

Xanthe turned to Celeste, planning to ask her to release Roth from her pretend curse. She needed them to believe her lie, and worried if Celeste's didn't come true, they might suspect her own to be fake as well. Before she could, there was a motion behind her. Celeste didn't have time to respond before her eyes went wide. She was about to say something when the man behind Xanthe yelped.

"What the?" Xanthe turned, fearing that the hand had fallen off somehow. Instead, he was clutching at his heart. She didn't know why.

"He just grabbed for his sword," Celeste explained. "Like he wanted to stab you. In thanks for saving his life. The asshole."

Xanthe was almost certain that he'd merely tried to move too quickly after he'd received a huge shock to his system, but the opportunity to further cement her lie was not to be wasted. She turned to the bandit. "You think I'm joking? By all means, take your sword. Yet if you value your life, use it only for those in need of defending. Understand?"

He nodded. The hatred in his eyes was palpable, but now he was scared enough to heed her words. Roth also quailed. He pointed his short sword at her, but was so unnerved, that he was visibly shaking. "You're going to curse me too?"

"On the contrary, we'll let you be, if you both do one thing." She gave Roth a hard stare.

"What?"

She pointed to the door. "Get the ream out of my city. Now."

The bandits scrambled for the exit and tore off through the open gate like they were running from nightmares. Xanthe felt simultaneously gratified and mortified. At least it was convenient. They weren't going to be sticking around to blab to the Curate. She turned to Celeste, waiting to have the rest of the argument. "Now you're going to say I made a mistake."

Celeste surprised her with a change in tone. "I should. But won't. You really did win. You fixed it without hurting anyone." She sounded more impressed than angry.

"Yeah. By scaring the daylights out of them," Xanthe dismissed. It didn't seem like much of a win.

"Nah. That was all me. You did something more important. You got to them. You're the one who should be a prioress. There's just this thing about you."

Xanthe made a wry face. "Not you too. You gonna be like Tari and say I'm weird?"

"Well of course! The weirdest. See, what you are is, you're actually good."

"Good? The only thing I'm good at is school."

"I don't mean good at something. I mean good. Not fake-good either, like stuck up Curate scolds – or how they think good girls should be. I mean what real good actually is – difficult, uncompromising, always bringing out the best in people..."

Xanthe felt touched. It was a rare compliment. Especially from Celeste. So sweet.

"...in other words," she continued happily, "totally annoying."

Xanthe sighed. She should have known.

"But in a nice way, you know? I mean, you had to know they were planning to rape us. Probably kill us later when they realized we'd tell the story to our powerful families. I was about to defend myself. But you saved them. Not out of fear, but mercy. They knew it too. That's why you got to them."

Xanthe shook her head in disbelief. Some of boys their age acted all tough, but it was completely different to really do it. Killing is hard. Celeste was sounding like how Yamaites were supposed to talk. "You can seriously bring yourself to do that? Slaughter another human being?"

Celeste's smile didn't disguise her a cold-blooded stare. "The thing about not believing in the Creator is that you realize you only live one life. So, if someone really tries to ream mine over? To rape, murder, or kidnap me to sell as a slavewife? I'm not going go peacefully," she declared. "I'll fight dirty. No regrets either. Some people just plain need killing."

Xanthe knew what she was saying, but it still felt completely wrong. "Death is permanent. People change."

"I hear way too many divulgences to believe that last bit. Sure, some do. But most? They fake charm, fake interest, fake love, fake friendship, fake innocence, fake remorse. Most importantly, they fake being reformed. But it's all just a show. They suck every drop from everyone around them."

"Sounds just like the bad boys you like," Xanthe noted, goading again.

Celeste rolled her eyes. "You keep saying that. But you said it yourself. There's a difference between bad and true evil."

"Defending yourself is fine," Xanthe sighed unhappily. "If it's your life, not something trivial, like being dumped."

"Trust me. I'm not going on a rampage if I catch my boyfriend with another girl Hellspace! I won't even cry! I'm not letting any boy get in my heart like that. I will be the dump-er – not the dump-ee. If you don't fall in love, there's no problem. True love is nothing but a pain." Celeste advised with every one of her fifteen years of wisdom. "While a whole bunch of false loves gives you a lot more variety!"

Xanthe nearly laughed. "You're telling me this after you did that whole don't trust yourself bit?"

"Which is why I don't want anything serious. Honorable intentions lead to love, which means marriage. Then babies." Celeste shuddered. "So as soon as any boy tells me he loves me, I'm gone."

*Speaking of which.* "We got to be gone ourselves. The bandit leader will be coming back sooner or later." Xanthe listened for footsteps, in case he already was.

"You gonna heal him too?" Celeste asked. "He's the worst by far."

"I like second chances. He didn't even get his first."

"Well unless he takes advantage of it right away, you're gonna have to scrape that second chance off the floor in considerably smaller pieces," Celeste declared darkly.

Xanthe was resigned. "It doesn't feel like I've brought out the best in you. Come on."

Celeste nodded, then paused. "What about the alarm? If they're trying to keep everything quiet, we could sound it. Pretty sure that would bring people running."

The alarm box was there. It would certainly attract attention if she wound it up and set it off. Xanthe considered the consequences. "If we do that, the plotters will go to their backup plan, and things will get bloody."

"It's bound to sooner or later," Celeste noted. "You sure you want to risk losing?"

Xanthe was quiet for a minute, feeling torn. Again, Celeste was right. She was gambling the entire city on the bet that they could secretly disrupt the coup faster than the plotters could see it through. They'd already seen some success, but there was no guarantee that it would continue.

"Why am I even making this kind of decision?" Xanthe asked out loud.

"Cause we're the only ones here and I don't want the responsibility."

"Okay. Fine. Let's not crank it right now. But if there's trouble, we can always come back."

Celeste nodded. "Doesn't sound completely dumb. Maybe you really won't get us both killed."

Being flippantly rude was Celeste's way of complimenting people. Another thing that had rubbed off from her brothers. Xanthe couldn't be annoyed. Instead, she just laughed breathlessly. "You're so mean! But no way you'd let that happen."

"Dodgy power straight," Celeste replied, jutting out her chin. "You still haven't spilled your hot boyfriend story."

## Chapter 27

It was becoming deep night. Mountain fog was rolling in, blotting out the ring light. Even the gas lit streets of Highcouncil were not immune to this last grip of winter's dark. Everywhere away from the scattered mist-shrouded lamps, it was pitch black. Despite the faint hubbub of distant revelry echoing up from the outer districts, there was a stillness in the air too, a calm before some unknowable storm. It felt to Xanthe like the world itself was holding its breath; there was anticipation in unseen places.

Celeste seemed to feel it too. Either that, or perhaps the full impact of how close she'd come to killing someone for real, had finally sunk in. She seemed uncharacteristically sober, her eyes as black as the shadowed city as she fox-walked alongside in preternatural silence.

Xanthe herself wasn't feeling so much nervous, as she was confused. Even though she knew it was wrong for him to be so disinterested, Rawlth's comments kept bothering her. Jagerfeld's government, like most free cities, was patterned after how history said the ancients ran their affairs. It was a "democracy", which hardcopy described as "the best government money could buy". (Once, in a fit of grading pique, Mr. Griswold saw fit to mark her down, keeping her from a perfect test score, as he insisted it was really a plutocracy – rule by the rich – and this remained a point of contention between them.) Still, however named, this was how things worked. People got a say in government in proportion to the taxes that they directly paid to the city coffers that year. Political campaigns and tax season were one and the same.

Given this, it was bewildering to see such effort to impose laws that could, at least in theory, be simply bought. Maybe Prince Sol was broke, but the Wormwoods sure weren't, so if they'd taken up his cause, there was no reason for a coup. The only explanation Xanthe could think of, was that they were trying to turn Jagerfeld into some sort of monarchical mayoralty.

Yet that too flew against reason. Even if they did, in the long run it would spell doom. The free cities of the north, like all the scattered settlements in nightmare country, didn't really control the monster-filled lands in which they lay, so they were always subject to that most basic democratic equalizer, voting with one's feet. Impose any policy too far against social propriety, like rallying behind a Nutearean prince, legalizing slavery, or treating people like southern lords did their peasants, and any city would soon be empty, unable to defend itself from foes, supernatural or otherwise. This, rather than superior morality as some chauvinists claimed, was the real reason why Thule remained free of much of the malfeasance that plagued the south.

"Thinking?" Celeste asked quietly.

Xanthe sighed. "Trying to figure out why Jagerfeld's rulers are trying to conquer themselves. It doesn't make any sense. There's something obvious I'm missing. I just can't put a finger on what."

"We need to learn more, is all."

"Yeah. But where?"

"Maybe we can discover something from that pile of bodies." Celeste pointed distantly.

"What?"

Celeste led Xanthe into yet another mansion's garden, a wide lawn with a few scattered trees, eventually stopping at a bush next to a low retaining wall facing the street. Underneath it, hidden shadow, were two human forms, crudely dumped. She toed one of them, pushing him over. More bandits. Southerners, this time. "I see they're warm, but not very."

Xanthe reached down to touch the man's cheek. It was useless.

"Don't even think about saving them," Celeste warned. "That dress creeps me out."

Xanthe choked up. "It's too late anyway. Their brains are completely dead."

"You're going to cry over them? Come on! They're bandits. They even still have their swords! Save your sympathy." Celeste shook her head.

"They had moms, and dads. Maybe sisters and brothers. All they did was come north to try to make their fortune out from under the foot of some despot."

Celeste folded her arms. "While victimizing others. Sorry, you won't get me to weep over them. When I help slaves to be free, I do it for those who aren't just trying to be new masters. You know, real innocents."

Xanthe raised an eyebrow. "You protect innocents?"

"I..." Celeste stopped short, flustered at being caught. "No! Of course not!" She sputtered. "I mean. You know. Marks got to take care of themselves."

"Right. Of course." Xanthe didn't believe her, but dropped it, instead choosing to focus on the nearest dead body. There was a mark cut into the man's neck that was little more than skin deep. A vertical slash crossed by a shorter horizontal one close to the bottom. "What's this?" She pulled up the hair to expose it.

Celeste hissed. "Oh boy. Not good."

"You recognize it?"

"The inverted cross. It's the emblem of the Knights in Shining Armor. They're the assassin wing of... well, you're not going to believe who."

Xanthe narrowed her eyes in thought. "Christians?"

Celeste blinked. "You knew? The Curate keeps that secret."

"Educated guess. A few of the puzzle pieces are starting to fit together. It must be political. As you said, they still have their swords on them. No way anyone motivated by money is going to leave behind something that could be sold. The only thing that puzzles me is..." her voice trailed off.

"What?"

"I thought Christians were pacifists." She'd learned that from Mr. Griswold.

"Not the Knights. They kill proctors and priests, which, I guess is understandable given what proctors do to them. Regular Christians are just these weird, ritual cannibals, who magically transform bread into human flesh and eat it."

Xanthe felt a mixture of horror and disbelief. "That isn't just Curate storytelling?"

"Dunno. But still... I'd rather they not jump me when I'm wearing this," she shook her habit. "You know, in case that magic flesh transformation of theirs is more slight-of-hand than real witchery. No way do I want to end up someone else's holy sandwich."

"That won't happen. I won't let it."

"Knowing you, while I'm on the buffet table, you'll be curing them of indigestion," Celeste accused bemusedly.

Xanthe scowled, even though she knew Celeste wasn't being serious. "I'm not that bad."

"No. You're good! That's so much worse."

Xanthe thinned her lips. "No more jokes about eating the dead. Not here. It's disrespectful." She addressed the cadavers. "I'm sorry I wasn't here to save you. In time, I will make sure you cremated." This was merely a matter of respect. It was still far too cold for any of them to rise as a balegaunt.

She then muttered prayers to the Curate's version of the Creator, who she strongly doubted existed. She wasn't sure what was true but figured any Creator worthy of worship wouldn't sweat the details. Whatever it was, she'd always felt a deep sense of love and encouragement and wasn't going to argue with it. She just hoped it wasn't demons. Maybe. Unless they were really the good guys.

Celeste didn't say anything. She merely shifted the bag full of uniforms to her other shoulder and kept up her watch. All at once, she ducked. "Get down. Men are coming. Javan is in front."

Xanthe did. "You saw Javan? Is Tari following?" She whispered.

Celeste put a finger to her lips and shook her head. They kept hidden as they heard the march of about a dozen footsteps pass by just over the wall. Just as it sounded like they were passing, they heard Javan's voice. "Okay, spread out. Keep each other in sight in case they're still around." The footsteps moved towards the garden gate.

"They're searching. Maybe for the killers." Xanthe whispered. "We have to get out of here."

"Can't sneak," Celeste whispered back. "Not even me. It's too open. We got to run for it."

"I can't. Not in these shoes."

"What are you gonna do? Hide here? They'll check this bush eventually. You'll be caught."

"Don't worry. Just go find Tari. Make sure she's safe." Xanthe grabbed a small stone from the ground, and just before the men started coming through the gate, tossed it at a distant tree. Its arc was perfect, hitting the trunk with a soft crack.

"What was that?" The men all looked away towards the noise. Xanthe took this as her cue. She took two steps in the open, smoothly rolled over the wall, and landed in a three-point stance on the street. Then she quickly stood and smoothed her dress, trying not to feel nervous. As the men's eyes had all been attracted to where the rock struck, no one had seen her. Perfect. She promptly began to walk. Not away, but towards them, as if she'd come up the street behind them.

"Sir? Sir?" She waved.

The man was standing amid several others in the same uniforms. They looked like council guards, all in Wormwood colors. Javan turned his head, but immediately relaxed when he saw who she was.

"Hello miss." He acknowledged her seriously. Some of the men stopped their search of the garden and instead watched her.

"Javan, right?"

"Um, yes. I'm sorry. This is a bad time. But while I have you here, did you have any luck finding the archdeacon's daughter?"

"Celeste? I did, but we were grabbed. Then there was this fight. It was really scary."

He cocked his head. "Grabbed? By who?"

"That's the worst part. It was guards," she pointed down the street and watched his reaction carefully.

"The guards you say?" He became intent.

Xanthe nodded, doing her best to seem guileless. "They made us go in the south guardhouse and started trying to take off our clothes and make us do things we didn't want to. But the jail had a hole and they didn't close the jail door right. A prisoner stabbed one of them by surprise, then ran away when the other guard fought. Celeste and I ran from them all, but we got split up. I hope she's okay."

As she said this, Javan rage grew palpable. "God damn son of a... The men stationed there just tried to rape the daughter of the city's archdeacon? While letting the prisoners escape?"

"I'm sorry. I didn't mean to make you mad." She gave him puppy eyes.

He changed his tone, entirely apologetic. "Please miss. I'm not angry with you. Just at what they wanted to do to you. You've helped a lot." He smiled gratefully, then turned to command loudly. "Stop the search. Go down and secure the gate. Disarm everyone down there, even our own."

Xanthe felt victorious. This was exactly what she hoped would happen. Javan was trying to be coy, but it was obvious that these Wormwood sponsored guards were allied with the bandits. As expected, he was not pleased with their behavior.

"Well okay. Thank you, sir! I better get going. I need to find Celeste again."

"Wait, miss. I'm going to escort you."

Xanthe stopped short. "Where?" she asked slowly.

"To safety. I know just the place. There's quite a party going on at the Wormwoods right now. All upper crust, but I'll get you in. I'd rather you not be out alone, especially dressed as you are. Some men can't control themselves."

That wasn't her plan. Horace was no doubt at his family's estate. "I must. I promised the archdeacon."

"I'm sure he'd be even more mortified thinking you got hurt. Now that his daughter knows he wants her back, I expect she'll return to him."

"I'd really rather...."

"This is not a request," he interrupted. "It's a command on council authority. The streets have ceased to be safe, and I'm sure your family wants you back unmolested."

Xanthe grit her teeth, wishing she'd never taken off the proctor uniform. But it was useless to argue. The more she did, the more suspicious he'd get. She hoped to be able to sneak out as soon as he was done escorting her.

She sighed. "Very well. Lead on, sir."

He gestured to two of the men, and they fell in behind her. Xanthe felt like she was being escorted like some Highcouncil dignitary. Her. Utterly bizarre. More unreal than the grim attack.

They headed north. Because most carriages were out on the town, the misty street lay empty. This was going to be a long walk. It didn't bother her though. Nothing did. Despite their awkwardness, her heels didn't hurt. Nor, on further consideration, was this diversion terrible. The Wormwood estate was the key to unraveling his mystery, and now Javan was escorting her in its restricted walls without her having to ask. Quite literally, she'd met a friendly bandit.

Yet that itself was interesting. Javan was confusing. Just about anyone could hide their malevolence better than the gate bandits had, but she was amazed at how good he was at it. Celeste wasn't the only one who could read body language, yet with him, her senses were completely off. If she didn't know better, she would have pegged him as completely earnest. Open. Sincere. Playing the perfect uniformed guard. It was uncanny.

"Javan? Tell me about yourself."

"Me, miss?" He ran a hand through his light brown Shambhalan hair. "Not much to tell."

"You're a foreigner who is commanding Highcouncil troops. That's quite unusual."

He shifted uncomfortably as they walked. "Not my idea actually."

"Oh really? Whose was it?"

"A young lord's. Horace of Wormwood. For the time being I am in his employ."

"He pays well?"

"Nothing, actually. Not a copper penny."

Xanthe cocked an eyebrow. "You know, in the north, we have a special word to describe those who work but aren't paid."

"What's that?" Javan asked curiously.

"Slaves."

One of the guards following behind snickered.

"Hmm," Javan was both stung and mildly amused. "I suppose there's some truth in that."

"Then, why do it? Surely there are others who would offer you more favorable terms."

"My compensation more spiritual. I'm saving people's lives."

Xanthe's eyebrows rose. "Really? Whose?"

"Call them my extended family."

Ah. Of course. Another piece of the puzzle fell in place. If she wasn't jumping to conclusions again. Still, this felt like surer ground. "But they don't know that, do they?"

He looked over, surprised at the certainty in her voice. "You have quite a woman's intuition, miss."

"Thank you," Xanthe smiled. It was nothing of the sort. It was logic. But better he not suspect.

Javan guided her into a shortcut through a darker, narrower, side alley, a tall apartment on the left, the wrought iron fence of a walled garden to the right. His men followed closely behind, all strolling at a leisurely pace. Javan seemed in no hurry to report. "And what of you? To whose family do you belong?"

"No one special. I'm a nobody."

"Oh please," he smiled. "You just exude noble refinement. More than that. There's this air about you. Almost like a glow. Next thing you'll be telling me you didn't have dozen boys in line waiting to snatch up that exquisite favor you left with the archdeacon."

"Truly, I'm not..." Xanthe choked back the rest. She wasn't about to go grabbing her haunches like she did in front of Damien. She'd already vowed not to care. But she had to be honest. "I'm really not rich," she told him flatly. "You can see it in my toned body."

Javan shook his head. "Ah yes. Northerners. Traditionalist, yet so strange."

"Strange? Why? How do the peoples of Thule look to foreigners?"

"Like magic mountain Vikings. Plump merchantmen. Gorgeous girls. Beautiful as Nubians, but pale."

"Vikings? What are they? Chimera?" Even as she asked, Xanthe knew that couldn't be it. Chimera rarely ventured into human lands, even the free cities. The Curate believed them demon cursed. They had lands to the east and were common in the Union archipelago.

"They were an ancient people of Earth who lived before the time of demons. There is a child's hardcopy drawing book about them. Open it up, and it looks like here. Beefy men and braid-haired women. Most of them some sort of blonde. But that's not what's oddest about the north."

"Then what?" Xanthe was both offended and curious at the same time.

"There's nearly a Curate chapel every other block," he declared expansively, "yet you can't walk three more without hearing the air crackle with witchery. I just don't get it. Don't you people know your own dogma?"

"Well, yes, but you can't be ruled by it either. If the Curate jailed everyone who ever sinned, who'd be left to guard?"

"Isn't witchery a different kind of sin though? Demonic? Filled with the evil touch of Earth. That's what they say."

Xanthe shook her head. "For dreadwitches maybe. But even for the Curate... well, it's the same logic. If they burned every girl at the stake for sparks and crackles, who would be left for men to marry? These are the nightmare lands, and monsters kill far more than nightmares do. Isn't there enough death as is?"

"I don't disagree. But if you travel, you'll find such attitudes quite rare. People kill each other over the stupidest things."

"Over important things too," a dark voice snarled from behind them. This was followed by the thump of two bodies collapsing to the pavement.

## Chapter 28

What happened next was nothing like the play sword fighting boys did in the Scholars' Guild courtyard. Javan instantly leapt forward, dodging along the left wall to briefly put her between him and the voice behind them, while at the same time wrenching his sword from his scabbard. A dark cloaked shape slammed past her in hot pursuit, shoving her against the wall. Javan freed his blade and swung in panic, but instead of backing off, the assailant charged into the blow batting the sword along the side of his leather wrapped arm before it had a chance to gather momentum. Javan twisted, using his right elbow to try to lay a blow, but the man ducked and kicked at in the knee of Javan's planted foot. As the blow landed, there came a sickening pop. Javan screamed and fell backward. The man landed on his torso with his knees, and with both hands, stabbed with a long stiletto, cursing once as it caught on bone. Yet before Javan could even move, he stabbed a second time, putting his entire weight on it. Javan screamed, as the blade sunk deep and the assassin wrenched it back and forth, tearing it through his vitals.

The entire attack had taken less than ten seconds.

"Traitor." the man growled. "Normally I don't speak to the dead. But I need say one thing about your abject bumbling before you bleed out." He chuckled. It was the evilest sounding laugh that Xanthe had ever heard. "Thank you."

Xanthe was too surprised to be scared. The mental shift was impossible to make. One second, they'd been talking, the next, Javan had been fighting for his life. But the assassin's voice was familiar. It was the same older one that she'd overheard counseling Damien to be circumspect in his desire to make the streets choke with blood. She'd seen them together near the city gate as well.

He turned his face towards Xanthe. While it couldn't be made out in the shadows, she knew he was trying to decide whether to strike her down as a witness. Yet just as he yanked his bloody blade out of Javan, there was a yell from several blocks over. "Does someone need help? Guards?" At this, the man's head turned up. He cut the top button off Javan's uniform, and took off running away from her, down the alley and out of sight.

Javan was left gurgling and crying as he slowly died on the street.

Xanthe jumped into action, intending to undo all of this, and she focused on the most immediate need, the two men who had collapsed. One thing that she knew from kestrels, the ones still with strength flopped, while those nearest to death, were as still as it.

*The body lay dysfunctional. Nerves that should have been active were not. They weren't damaged, but a black spot of darkness was obvious, like black ink on a glistening spidercrab's web. The darkness moved through the flesh from a point of entry on the neck, spreading like a fluid, some already in the brain.*

Poison. Xanthe didn't know much about them. Healing kestrels gave her little experience with it. She saw that the wound had been made by five closely spaced needles all in a straight line, one which had injected directly into the man's carotid artery. The rest of the poison lingered in the flesh. About the only thing she figured she could do at this point was to bleed the other wounds and hope that would drop him beneath its fatal dosage. The tainted blood she came out with a distinctive garlic odor. After she pinched shut the wound, she gave the same treatment to the second guard, before quickly moving on to Javan, tearing apart his shirt to put her hand on bare flesh.

*Javan's right lung was collapsed, filled with blood from a sliced arterial vein. Only his positioning against the wall allowed him to breathe, reminding her of the case that Yuri and Claude had interrupted. It seemed almost routine to pinch close the vein. The rest was the problem: inflating the lung, piecing together the stomach and esophagus, both which were torn in multiple places and leaking stomach acid into the abdominal cavity. He was in bad shape.*

Even with the complexity of dealing with organs, surgeries seemed almost second nature by now, easy compared to the fine detail work she'd recently had to do. She didn't need the demon dress, yet it acted anyway, invading his tissues, and repositioning fluids to their proper places. As she worked, Javan began to gasp more heavily as strength returned to him, enough to lift his hand to hers.

"An angel comes to comfort me in my final moments."

Whatever it was with these foreign men – so forward to unattractive girls, even from the edge of death – Xanthe didn't know, but she was starting to get a touch annoyed with it. "Don't worry, Javan," she told him coolly. "You're going to survive."

His breathing was still labored. "I. Know. Better." He paused. "Will you. Take my final confession?"

"I'm no prioress."

"More the better. I am not faithful of the Curate."

"That's obvious. You're a much different kind of idiot."

"That," he paused wincing, "is most unkind."

Businesslike, she shifted her ministrations to his knee. "You'd rather your divulgence be decorated with lies?"

He coughed, and some blood did come up. "I suppose not. What use would it be? Now that I consider them, your words are only painful for their truth. More painful than my death, I'm finding."

She continued her work. "My father once told me that truth can be more painful than death, though I'm sure he was being poetic, as I doubt he has direct experience with the latter. But if you do make me your confessor, do not ask me to mock the role. I shall not accept your words without hearing them all in fullness and truth."

"I suppose I have no secrets now. So yes. I will confess, with one condition."

"What?"

"Do not repeat what I say to anyone. It would mean your death."

More admonitions. By this time, Xanthe was getting used to it. She just nodded. "Let me get you started. You swore yourself to a lord, then betrayed them. This man came to avenge that."

"I... yes. How did you know? Never mind. No time. I did exactly as you say. Ultimately, that caused the disaster I was trying to prevent."

She shook her head. "No, no. Start from the beginning. Why did you come north at all?"

"Oh. That. Yes. The beacon."

"Beacon? What is that?"

"A thing of Earth and power, part of the engines that brought us to Haven. We heard of its finding in the wilds, and a leader of my people decided to come north to locate it."

"I see. You came with your lord to gain possession of this artifact?"

"We hoped, but figured it was too well guarded. Our true intent was to meet Anchorites we thought might appear."

"Who are they?"

"The last order of the ancients. A coven with the power to control demons, whose leader is called the Incarnate, an immortal demon in human guise, with witch power beyond anything anyone can imagine. Legends say they live in a secret redoubt in the trackless witch wilds. Anchorites only appear to reclaim things not meant for humanity. If this beacon is at all close to what it is rumored to be, the Incarnate will inevitably obtain it."

"Sounds like grand storytelling."

"It is true. I swear. Well, at least the beacon bit. My own eyes have seen it. Its form is that of a blackened ball of crystal, and it prisons a great demon which sometimes speaks to a select few. I was one such."

"You were? What did it say?"

"Only riddles and ancient arcana. Of nemesis and degeneracy. Destiny and eternal war. The physic of information and unrolled charm top space. I know the words, but my brain is too poor to grasp what it means with them."

Xanthe was dubious. "It sounds insane."

"Maybe. It says it waits for the futures to unify. Now is coming a maelstrom of destiny. All is dark."

Xanthe wondered. That sounded like how Tari had talked. Weird. "What will happen then?"

"No one knows. But a prince and his inner circle have learned some secret power of the thing. He is quite excited about it and thinks it will put him on the throne. Not perhaps the best of signs. It was my fault for ever trusting him. My greatest sin of many."

She laid her hand on his chest. "Then turn from him. Go and sin no more."

He chuckled through his ragged breathing. "Seems late for that now. If I had more time myself, I'd do so. Just do me one more favor, besides comforting me in my final moments."

"What?"

He became urgent. "Leave! Leave this city before it is too late. Tonight. Please. Just do it. Warn your family if they'll listen. You all will be safer on the road than the city. Don't ask why."

"Oh, I know why you think that's so."

"You do? How?"

Xanthe rolled her eyes, thinking of Tari. "I'm the storm, apparently. Whatever in hellspace that means."

"Girl, you must believe me!" Javan reached up frantically. "I'm not storytelling."

She put her hand on his chest. "Calm down. Don't strain. You'll hurt yourself. Trust me, I believe you. I'm only saying that demons may not always tell the full truth, even if they want to. Maybe this clockwork beacon thing popped a demonic screw loose, and has a few demonic springs rattling around in its demonic clockwork brain." She twirled a finger around the side of her head. *If it's also somehow influencing Tari, that would explain a lot,* she added to herself.

"I'm not talking about demons. I'm speaking of politics. There is going to be a usurpation. They won't show restraint. Every brigand and Talathian in northern Aeterna was recruited, and they're already in the city. On the first signal from this district, they will all attack at once. It will overwhelm the garrison."

Xanthe felt a grim sense of satisfaction. She'd guessed right not to crank the alarm back at the guard station. "Well then, I'll just have to make this prince leave without sending that signal."

"You can't do that."

"Maybe I can, if you help me."

"That's impossible."

She smiled gently. "The quickest way to make something impossible is to believe that it is."

"Strange words to give a dying man."

"Indeed," she smiled. "So, when you don't, perhaps you'll recognize their truth."

He made a move to speak, but then touched his chest. Having recently had his guts savagely shredded, the lack of pain was clearly unnerving him.

There were distant sounds of people approaching. She heard Yuri's voice echo, but not the words.

"We're going to have to cut short the rest of your divulgence," Xanthe explained. "Your true sin was not greed or cruelty, but merely not fully thinking through the implications of your actions. That can be atoned for. Bide a moment."

"Where are you going?"

"Going to have a little talk with my not-a-boyfriend." She stood up. "Please don't wander off. I will return with a big favor to ask. It's the least you can do." She began to saunter down the street.

"Farewell," Javan raised his fist and pointed. "My soul shall soon travel towards the northern star, back to ancient Earth, to rest among the bones of our ancestors, where the holy incarnation of God once walked in human form."

"Not yet. Your confession has doomed you to the pain of life, including the shame having to face those you betrayed. For now, I protect you."

"I welcome your comfort, but I'm bleeding inside. I am already dead."

"No," Xanthe contradicted with adamant assurance. "You are already saved."

## Chapter 29

The group of men striding up the cobbled street were four in number. She'd just rounded the alleyway's corner when she came to face them all. Damien, Yuri and Claude, and the assassin.

Damien's eyes widened in surprise. "Xanthe!" He was surprised and relieved.

She was not welcoming, but instead regarded him silently.

He sensed her distance. "Xanthe?" He repeated.

She addressed him coolly. "Prince Christian, I presume."

Without warning, the old stocky assassin instantly leapt in her direction. Xanthe didn't have time to move, but Damien did. As he passed the young man, Damien shoved him hard with his gloved left hand. The assassin was thrown off balance and tumbled toward the street, but rolled, coming up on his feet, facing Xanthe.

"Please don't endanger yourself," she said, afraid for him. Her dress was already shivering slightly.

"Nagrath!" Damien barked. "Stop!"

If Xanthe's words slowed him, Damien's brought him to a standstill. His voice was overwhelmingly authoritative. Even she herself felt the urge not to move. The assassin held himself tensed out of range, coiled like a spring, brandishing two short swords, one of them with traces of Javan's blood still on it.

"Xanthe, I told you that you should be away from here. This is no place for you. Not now." Damien was protective. Again, so cute. But she was also in no mood for it.

"I'd say the same thing to you, if you're just going to send assassins to kill people and let them die on the street."

"Javan!" Damien growled in fury. "He told you who I am."

"Not at all. I figured it out myself. It wasn't hard. It's well known that Prince Christian's guard failed him, but when Claude and Yuri showed up, you started commanding them both like it's your birthright. They said they thought you were dead and were being deferential to someone our age."

"I..."

"But the clincher was remembering that your mother objected to your path. I never could figure why anyone would name a child 'Prince Christian', for it would mean they could never pretend to the throne and all its bloody politics. The Curate would never allow it. But now I realize that was exactly her intent."

He was silent, so she added, "Tell me I'm wrong."

Damien slumped in defeat, and his anger went with it, leaving only resigned respect. "I thought myself safe because, aside from Finalizer

Nagrath here, only others of our faith knew. To accuse me, they too would be subject to execution for heresy."

The assassin spoke for the first time, thumbing the razor edge of his short sword. "We'd only considered open betrayal to the Curate. No one imagined that he'd be sold out to another prince."

Xanthe nodded. "Who wouldn't care if Javan was Christian or not, so long as he could eliminate a rival. Instead, Javan betrayed you for..."

"Thirty pieces of silver." Damien declared angrily.

She shook her head. "Not in the least. As you said yourself, princes cause grief to their supporters. He thought you were leading the defenders of your faith, your Knights in Shining Armor, into disaster. But if you were quietly killed, your little communities would be free of princely politics."

Damien's eyes widened in surprise. "That's not..."

"Of course it is," she interrupted. "Javan wasn't paid a copper penny. Prince Sol is absurdly poor. He's trying to use bandits in place of regular troops. I'd say the only prince poorer than him is you, Prince Christian."

To her right, Nagrath snarled darkly. "I have been commanded, but if you call him that on the open street again, I will gut you here and now, even if it means my own life."

Xanthe herself was surprised. Protective. Was there a glimmer of light in this otherwise evil man? She turned to Damien. "Do you want to slay me then? To keep your secret?"

Damien sighed. "Xanthe, don't be silly. No cheap moral sanctimony. Remember?"

"She *is* a problem though," Nagrath declared, looking at Damien. "You cannot afford to leave dangers at your back. It could end you, and everything you're trying to do."

"I cannot afford to become known as a murderer of innocents, either."

"That is why princes have Finalizers, my lord. Just leave, and it will be taken care of."

Damien turned curt. "Let me be more explicit, Nagrath. I will not allow innocents to ever be deliberately murdered. Ending that is most of what I'm trying to do."

"You're taking risks again. That absurd idealism of yours is going to get you killed."

"While you're being optimistic again. Thinking that my death isn't already foregone. No, I won't allow it."

At this, Yuri drew himself up. "This Xanthe. She has my word too. She does more for faith than any outside it in long time."

"Yes," Damien added. "She has some secrets you don't know, and they are beautiful ones. She..." His face suddenly registered a thought.

Now Xanthe felt embarrassed. Not over the attention but knowing that Damien was disturbingly smart. She'd been caught. *He knows.*

Damien spoke slowly. "Nagrath. You left the bodies down that alley?"

"Two felled with Widow's Kiss, and the target bleeding out. They're dead." He showed Javan's button.

Damien stared there. His eyes then shifted to her. He squinted. "Maybe."

At this, Nagrath finally lost his temper. "My work is flawless. I don't make mistakes. Speaking of which, we shouldn't even be here. Returning to where you have struck is the mark of a rank amateur."

"Listen to your man. You should leave." Xanthe ventured. She knew her gambit would fail but had to try anyway.

In response, Damien advanced towards the alley where Javan lay, alive. She instantly moved forward to block his path.

It brought him up short. He was openly suspicious. "Xanthe. Please step aside."

She flushed. "No."

He moved to the side and she stepped in front of him again. "Xanthe!"

She stared defiantly. Once again, they were quite close. Almost nose to nose.

"Xanthe. You can't..." His voice fell away as he searched for words.

"I can't what?"

"You just can't just go saving everyone!"

She pouted at him. "Why not?"

"Because! Well..." he struggled. "Assassinations would be pretty strange if no one actually died in them."

"Yeah? Maybe it should change to be that way."

"I... no, you can't. You are not going to interfere with justice."

She didn't back down. "This isn't justice. Just vengeance."

"It's both. Safety, too. Nagrath is right. I can't leave vipers at my back."

"Javan's not a viper. He was trying to save the Knights from your decision to enter ascension politics. Even now he works to protect them, because Prince Sol knows all about what they truly are."

"I'm supposed to let him go because he was only trying to kill *me*? Not all those who followed me north and died as a result?" Damien sputtered. "They were my friends. My family!"

There was a faint ridiculousness to the way they were bickering. But this was literally life and death. "If you don't forgive him," she asked, staring deeply into his eyes, "how will you ever forgive yourself?"

He staggered back as if she'd struck him. For a fraction of a second, his face twisted in pain, but just as quickly closed back into absolute determination. "Xanthe," he commanded. "I am done arguing. I will let no one harm you, but I am now telling you to stand still and let me do this."

There was power to him, a regal mastery that was impossible to ignore. All at once Xanthe was seized by doubt. What if Damien hadn't intervened on her behalf with Nagrath? Her dress would have killed the assassin, exactly the kind of bloodshed she was trying to avoid. Even now things could spin in that direction. Damien had been kind, but there still was still murderous rage about him.

As she stood, he stepped back, looking oddly guilty. "I'm sorry. This will soon be over." He moved around.

If he passed her though, Javan would die. She stepped in front of him again. "<u>NO</u>."

They bumped into each other.

He seemed in utter shock that she did so. "Xanthe. What?!"

"I said no." Suddenly aware that he was within easy kissing distance, the worst thought to be having at a moment like this.

"How can you even..."

"Plead for the traitor? You don't understand. I'm not pleading for him. I'm pleading for you. Do not become someone who kills merely for self-satisfaction."

He was agitated. "Xanthe, you're so utterly brazen, you should get a job as a palace jurist. Javan's treachery caused a dozen deaths. Two score more if you hadn't shown up." He was gazing into her eyes, angry, attracted, suddenly emotional.

"Whatever you do now, it will not bring them back. You know this."

He swallowed, nearly on the verge of tears. "It is all I have."

"All you have? You still have friends. Followers. Your self-respect. As of yet, you still have mine. Now is the time to make the choice. Are you good? Or are you evil?"

He stood before her, struggling to control himself. All at once she realized that her opinion of him was something he cherished, and that made her understand just how much she was asking. Again, doubt seized her. She wondered if Horace had managed to rape her, would she be in any mood to forgive? Or seek vengeance if she found him helpless? She wanted to think so but wasn't sure.

He let out his breath. "I am evil. I must be to accomplish any good in this world. But for you, if this is what you want... after all you have done. I can see how much you love life, so will relent for now."

Xanthe wanted to kiss him but didn't. Instead she held out her palm. "Your hand please." He moved his gloved hand forward, but she said, "No. The other one."

He did as she asked gazing curiously as her. "This has been bugging me for a while," she explained. "I kept meaning to, but never had the chance." She focused on the wound on his hand, now scabbed over, and numbed it. Already with her touch she could feel that it wasn't healing correctly. But it was trivial. The trance was so momentary she barely noticed it. Straightening out the capillaries wasn't difficult, and the pinching required was minor compared to the delicate organ work she'd just finished.

"What did you do?"

She rubbed the scab and it came off. Underneath was sealed flesh. "Scar removal. Now you will heal as if you'd never been wounded at all." She held his hand. Her craftsman satisfaction had returned, another kestrel set back right. But it was not the healing of his flesh that led to the feeling.

Behind them, Nagrath hissed in frustration. "I thought you'd learned your lesson."

Damien unhappily fixed his eyes at a wall, not turning around. "I'm not romancing her, Finalizer."

The old assassin's tone was dry. "Who you bed isn't what's dangerous. It's bothering to learn their names. Don't do that. You can't afford it."

"I've sworn off such distractions," Damien stated.

"Princes must lie, but never to themselves. Seriously, my lord, stop thinking with your shaft. No matter how juicy they are, nothing good ever comes from letting some tart pull you around by it."

"Xanthe is not a tart."

"You're so besotted that you're denying the obvious? Your father would have taken one look and..."

"I am *not* my father." Damien angrily interrupted through grit teeth.

"Obviously. He knew what it took to win the throne. Did you learn nothing from Sarina?"

Yuri jumped in to protest. "Is not Sarina. Xanthe is good gurl."

Damien wheeled on both in fury. "Do not mention her again!"

Nagrath quieted, only for a moment. "As you wish. But know that until a prince's rivals are dead, he has no room for baggage. Anyone who keeps him from doing what needs be done."

Xanthe had had enough. "Did anyone ever teach you that it's rude to talk about people as if they're not standing right in front of you?" She asked. "Even tarts?"

Nagrath chuckled, dark and dismissive. "I must have missed that in finishing school."

"Your loss," she returned dryly. "I assign you a hundred writings of 'I shall better my manners and manner my betters' on the slate board after class. Assuming you even know your runes."

He bridled and growled softly. "Only the prince's favor saved you. Remember that."

That chilled her differently than intended. "No," she confessed. "If your prince had not intervened, you would have died, and even I might not have been able to save you."

Damien glanced at her in surprise. "Really?" He became gently concerned.

She nodded, more worried than smug. "I am... ever more chosen, it seems." She dropped her eyes and swallowed heavily.

His eyes followed hers to the strange runes on her toenails, and he murmured softly, "Are you okay?"

She drew breath. "So far. At least I think," she whispered.

"What in hellspace are you two talking about?" Nagrath growled.

"Xanthe is considerably more than just looks," Damien explained. "Don't forget your own lesson, master Nagrath. Never let your own eyes deceive you. If she tells you something unbelievable, believe it."

"I was really in danger from this little girl? She's some sort of greatwitch?"

Claude spoke. "She saved us all. Philippe, Demimonde, Sven, Ogar, Joshua, all zhe rest. Any who was alive on first meeting 'er woke up whole. It was she. Not zhis Celeste we 'ear of, who is a liar and fraud."

"Celeste has been covering for me, so I don't wind up facing a tribunal. She's my friend," Xanthe corrected.

"It occurs to me that I did not properly introduce you two," Damien announced, adding wryly, "perhaps that's what got you off on the wrong foot. Xanthe, this is Master Nagrath the Finalizer, an exalted title reserved only for the most... um... dedicated of his majesty's personal bodyguards. Nagrath, this is Xanthe of Jagerfeld, a young lady of mystery and magic, and honorary Defender of the Faith, a title which I've just decided to award her for her recent exemplary actions."

Xanthe faced him. "And what of you dear Damien, formerly known as a prince? With what title are you to be crowned?"

Damien hesitated, so Nagrath spoke up. "When admitting his lineage, which we won't until the right moment, we've chosen an alternative name starting with 'C'. Prince Charming."

Xanthe smiled in amusement. "Hmm. The girl chaser. Appropriate."

Damien was embarrassed. "It's as good as any. Don't believe my men about that. They like jests."

"Ehh," Claude almost said something, but shut up when Damien glared.

Xanthe shook her head slowly. "Speaking of which, I need to give you this. Stand still." She removed the demonic dress box ribbon that was still wound about her left wrist and looped it through the coat clasp on his lapel, just above his heart. When she was done, the corsage flickered ever so softly in the torchlight. "Now all will know you returned my favor and have mine."

"Damien..." Nagrath growled in warning.

"He's right," Damien agreed reluctantly. "Xanthe, this isn't the time for this, if there ever were any. Among other things, we still need to make sure Priscia's father doesn't lose the remains of his fortune. You might not want to come along, because there could be blade work involved."

Nagrath's annoyance was palpable. "Yet another diversion. For another tart."

"Don't worry Finalizer," Xanthe assured. "He need do nothing for Priscia."

Damien thinned his lips in disapproval. "Xanthe. I promised her."

"While I'm sure both the Finalizer and I agree that you should stop swearing foolish oaths, I'm telling you not to worry because the problem is already solved. Her father's estate is safe, at least for tonight."

"You used your powers?"

"Merely my cleverness. That was all that was required." Xanthe smiled pleasantly.

"I see."

Xanthe continued authoritatively. "I also got proctor uniforms for you as well. You need only ask Celeste for them. Don't skip the opportunity. They will let you move about the city unchallenged."

Damien cocked his head curiously. "And how will we find this Celeste?"

"You won't. I didn't give you this just for tradition." She fingered the corsage. "Celeste will find you because you bear it. Mention my name after her curiosity draws her."

Damien briefly looked around. "In this fog? She'll never be able to recognize it at any distance."

"Of course she will. It glows slightly blue-blue."

He was mystified. "I'm not even going to pretend to understand that."

"Then don't." The ribbon hung just slightly crookedly, and she couldn't help but adjust it. He was just so handsome wearing it.

"Northern witches are," he searched for a word. "...surprising. Even when I try not to be."

"Your saving me from death by grim was even more surprising," she smiled back affectionately.

"Grim?" Nagrath rumbled unhappily. "You drove off a grim to save her?"

"Ah," Damien winced, and rubbed the back of his neck. "I wish you hadn't mentioned that."

"At this point boy, we're just going to have to hope that among your authorities, you have the fabled Emperor's Luck. I just can't seem to get it through your idiot skull not to take needless chances."

Xanthe glanced at Nagrath, then back at Damien. "He's the one who scolds you about taking risks? Put you through your paces?"

Damien nodded. "Worse than that," he replied glumly. "His training regimen is demonic."

"You poor thing," her affection turned sympathetic as she considered the nature of Damien's relationship with Nagrath. The old assassin seemed likely to be the only connection to his father he had. "I know exactly how you feel. You have no idea how much homework I get."

Nagrath finally smiled; his lip curled up. "Well good news. You'll both get a rest day. Won't have much time for practice, even if we do manage to take down this Sol princeling. There's always too much to clean up after a battle – bodies to burn, that sort of thing."

Xanthe turned to the Finalizer. "I have no intention of allowing war to break out."

"The die is already cast, and no one can stop it. Even if the sparks you throw are deadly."

"You think so? Because I don't."

"When brigands all over this city get the signal, they'll attack simultaneously. The reserve guard may outnumber them, but they'll be too disorganized to fight effectively. That's when Sol will strike in this district, keeping all these fat ruling merchants hostages in their own homes. He'll demand their fealty and they'll have no choice. Some will even be swayed by his authority, making them think his takeover will benefit them in the long run. I'm sure he's also planning to leave some local quisling in charge, but the resources of the city will be his. He will then use that to bribe young farmer boys that being in his army is safer and more profitable than braving the wilds, and they will join him."

"You understand this so well, you almost sound like you work for him."

"Heh." Nagrath chuckled mirthlessly, thumbing the edge of his blade. "I know the script. It's a familiar one."

"I'm just going to have to stop that signal then."

"If you try, or even if you're surrounded on the street after it is set off, you'll be taken captive and things will happen to you that would make my dear Lord Charming upset to see. If you show your power, you might kill a few, but then they'll shoot you down at a distance. Exterminating covens is mostly an art practiced by Curate proctors, but it isn't as if the techniques they use are entirely unknown."

Xanthe was unperturbed. "Everything you've just said, is as I already suspected. But still, I tell you, war will not break out in my city. Thousands dead? I cry when I even lose a kestrel."

"You hear girl, but do not comprehend. Either that, or you're insane."

"I comprehend. You do not. Mercy is not the only reason I was so insistent on saving Javan. He can get me past the guards into the Wormwood estate. That's key to the last option I have left."

The assassin's eyes suddenly widened, and he gave her a look of surprised respect. "Laudable. But even you get close enough to assassinate this princeling, after which you'd be quickly killed by his men, they'll still sound the alarm, if only to beat a quick retreat out of the city and escape in the chaos. So, no. Your witch power might keep your city free but cannot keep it from tasting blood."

"No, *you* misunderstand. I'm not an assassin. Nor is violence a sign of success. It's what you resort to when you fail. Stop thinking with your sword. All that needs be done is to make it so that starting the attack is against this prince's best interests. For example, if he suddenly finds himself trying to regain something crucial to his plans. Then having the city in turmoil would impede his search for it."

Nagrath wanted to dismiss her but was made unsure by her certainty. "There's nothing that could possibly..."

"Of course there is, my dear Nagrath," she gave him a fierce, close lipped smile. "I'm going steal the beacon."

## Chapter 30

It was remarkable how little Xanthe's nerves were bothering her. Naturally, herding three injured guards towards the Wormwood estate, two of whom had spent the last ten minutes dry heaving and were now stumbling forward like drunks, was plenty distracting. Still, she was amazed at how well her bravado was holding up. Maybe facing down so many grims had turned her permanently foolhardy.

Maintaining a facade of confidence was important though. Javan seemed dependent on it. Only her insistence that her half-baked plan was incapable of failure was keeping him from running. He'd asked three times if it might be better to simply flee the city. Yet each time he'd mentioned it, she told him that she was 'the chosen one' for this task – all total dung of course, but you did what you had to.

What she had to. She grumbled to herself. Damien made it plain that he didn't think she should be rushing headlong into her crazy plan, or that girls in general should take stupid risks when men were around to do it for them. It piqued her amazon pride, but another, wiser, part of her agreed. Just because boys were fool enough to get themselves killed playing hero, did girls have to do so as well? She scowled as the answer instantly popped into her head. *For me? Plainly yes.*

Still, there was no other alternative. Only she could do this, and father's words still echoed in her mind. Could she live with herself watching the suffering of people she could have saved? No, she couldn't. She'd rather die. This was seeming the most likely outcome.

Surprisingly, Nagrath had risen to her defense. He'd told Damien that she was the only one with any chance of pulling such a plan off, and to Damien's heated accusation of just trying to get her killed in a fight, added that she had no need. "She'll dance right in." At Damien confusion, he clarified drolly. "You say she's not a coquette, but surely does she look it, and that is all she needs. Remember my liege, good girls go to the Creator; bad girls go everywhere."

It was embarrassing to be talked about that way. Moreover, worrying. Of all the scary powers this demonic dress had, from it being able to fight on its own, to enhancing her witch power, what disturbed her most was the way it affected people's minds. Even Damien wasn't immune. His initial reaction of not even wanting to see her ugly haunches, had turned into him peeking at her constantly, though he always glanced away when she caught him. She had no idea how the dress was doing this. Undoubtedly it some nefarious mind-control altering the eyesight of its victims to make her seem sexy. Regardless, it had to stop. *I'm wearing you so I'm the boss,* she commanded. *Just let people see me as I really am.*

At this, the fabric around her waist tightened. Her slightly too plump breasts were pushed even further up as her neckline plunged. Now she was showing more skin than ever.

"Not like that!"

"Like what?" Javan asked.

"Nothing!" Xanthe flushed beet red. "Just my dress." It almost seemed as if it was amused. Playing. Making enigmatic jokes.

"All this, and you're worried about your clothes?" He grouched. Javan couldn't see her. He was ahead, between his two men, struggling to prop them up as they stumbled along, barely conscious. Xanthe was ready to try to catch if they fell. At least that was the plan.

"Yes," she scowled back. "But I'm dealing with it. Let's get your men into sick beds first."

Wormwood manor was nearly the opposite of the Outlet estate. There were no gardens, fountains, or open elegance here. It resembled some unholy union of a castle and a prison, constructed in a brutalist style of unadorned cement, parapets, crenelated walls, with all its low windows covered in iron bars. As they approached a side door several guards appeared, clad in purple and gray, moving in quickly to support their injured comrades. "We were attacked by bandits," Javan told them. "While escorting this young lady to safety."

"He was so brave!" Xanthe said, trying to sound coquettish. "He drove off several by himself. But I think they used something that smelled bad on the guards that made them sick."

"The girl is right," Javan agreed." Take them to the hospitarium. They need a bandager. I need to report straight away. I recognize those bandits," he declared meaningfully.

Two of the guards widened their eyes in understanding. He was telling them he'd been attacked by their own allies. The rest didn't catch the reference. Most were distracted, goggling at her chest. Annoyed, she swore to herself that when this was over, she was going to give her dress a washing it would never forget.

"Take this highborn daughter to the party. Remember to mind your hands," Javan added in warning.

"How will you find me?" Xanthe asked him.

"That won't be a problem. There's no other girl in black."

As she was led in side doors through the bare utilitarian servant quarters, a doubt seized her. There really hadn't been much time between her return to Javan and the poisoned guards waking up. As such her talk with him had been brief. She'd not had learned all she needed to. But her most important concern she couldn't have voiced anyway. Had he really changed his ways? What would he say when he spoke to Horace or whomever? Was her faith in him misplaced?

No use worrying now. She entered through an ornate door and it was like walking into an entirely different building, with all the ostentatious decoration she'd initially expected. Scores of guests were here. All adults.

All absurdly rich. Dresses of stitched plastics and charming technological ornamentation. Polished gears artfully sewn into panels and hems, were everywhere. The men were in suits, sometimes even bearing devices that still possessed some functionality.

"Miss, didn't you have something else on?" The young guard who'd escorted her in was only somewhat trying not to stare. Now, in addition to showing entirely too much cleavage, her dress was a cape gown. Thin lace crisscrossed her bare legs down to her shoes. He was baffled.

"This is how it always was," she lied. "If you'd keep your eyes up, maybe you'd have noticed."

"I apologize, milady." Now he was worried.

She sighed tolerantly. "Whatever for? You can hardly be faulted for seeing what's in front of you."

He grinned, relieved. "You're nice for a highborn."

"...and yes, the dress is black, so in the dark, I'm sure you couldn't have noticed the... hat?" She examined it. The fabric that had once formed the train of her dress, had changed a conical headpiece, wide brimmed and with a floppy point. The thing was hanging from a tie near her back and dangling dangerously low, threatening to trip her. Xanthe was annoyed but got the point. It wanted to be worn.

"I suppose I need to put this on," she said grudgingly. A tiny strap still stretched between it and the dress. No matter its shape, the dress always remained fully connected to itself.

"Please do, miss. You're so hot, if you don't use that to brush away the flames, you'll burn me."

"I'm not—"

"And light all the torches as you walk past."

"Look, I..."

"And set the building on fire. Arson's a capital crime, you know."

*Oh hellspace.* It was useless. The demon was completely ensorcelling people now, presumably because that was exactly what she needed to be let in to wherever the beacon was. Might as well stop arguing. She put the hat on. "Thank you." She smiled and turned, hoping that he wouldn't be the one sticking a sword through her when she was trying to escape.

"And please, make these fancy boys draw blood over you," he begged as she moved to leave. "I need a laugh."

"I'll try," she lied again. Getting boys in a fight over you was supposed to be the greatest Festival trophy for a girl, but she found the idea repellent. Wasn't it obvious that any boy who hurt others to win you, would one day do the same to you? Besides, it would cause unwanted attention. No, she'd just lay low until Javan returned. That is, if she could. The more she thought about it, the flimsier her plan seemed.

This was obvious as soon as she entered the ballroom. Her svelte black outfit was nothing like any other girl was wearing, even those from outside Thule. She had no slats, no cummerbund, neither lace nor satin, no perfect manicure, no powdered face. Just raw, lithe, femininity. Silent eyes fell upon her everywhere, not just glances from boys, but the adults too.

Two wealthy looking boys looked to be gathering courage to talk to her, so she quickly moved out through two ornate double doors into a hallway. She desperately tried to find someone familiar, preferably a girl, to keep from being sucked into conversation. No luck. There were guests, servants, and piles of food here, stacked on trays, but nerves kept her from even thinking of eating. Seeing another pair of double doors, she fled to them.

What the mansion lacked in elegance, it made up for in size. She'd stumbled into an enormous ballroom in which a dance was in progress, complete with chamber musicians and mingling adults. Again though, those who saw her did not release their gaze. This included a line of boys sizing up a separate line of girls, all who were now transfixed at her appearance. She swum through the sea of murmurs and attention.

Finally, after walking quickly to an antechamber on the other side, she spotted respite. There was a flight of stairs that led up to an empty upper corridor. She stepped up as fast as her high heels would let her, ducking around the corner just as a rather cute looking scion boy peeked his head in the door. His eyes darted back and forth looking. Xanthe disappeared around the bend before he looked up. She didn't want trouble.

She didn't get far before she saw another guard. He was standing at attention, looking ill at ease. "Miss? Are you supposed to be here?"

"Of course," she bluffed, smiling and walking past, as if it was a stupid question.

"But your hair isn't even braided," he said. "I don't care what you were promised. You don't know what you're getting into." She noted his worry and turned. Instantly all her insecurities vanished. It was funny. Danger she could handle. It was people liking her that was scary.

"I was told to come up here. What's going on?"

"It's... I..." the guard suddenly looked terrified. Odd, because he was a huge man. "Those are the young lord's private chambers is all. I am bound not to say, but you'd be happier if you left."

Horace. It had to be. Of all the luck. He was the only one in this whole place who might recognize her. Meeting him had not been part of the plan. She'd been sure he would be too busy. "He's in?"

"No."

Xanthe heard a muffled girl's cry coming through from it, and she realized that the guard was distant because he'd edged himself as far from the door as possible. Xanthe nodded once to him. "I'll let myself in." She turned and opened the ornate door at the end of the hall.

He looked like he wanted to stop her, but in the end, stayed where he was. Another decent man simply doing his job, guarding his master's chambers. It just was the way of the world.

The door cracked open. Inside was a suite, well-lit with crystal gaslight lamps, the walls lined with posters in the ancient lost art of photography, one with Nubians bearing the beautiful dark under an oddly white looking sun. Yet the otherwise lavishly appointed room was an absolute mess. Clothes lay haphazardly strewn, artwork of naked women, dozens of plates of half eaten food. There was also an undeniable odor of liquor and unwashed male stench. A trio of mirrors was set in a curve at one corner near some scattered antique lifting weights, along with authentic hardcopy, much of which looked poorly used. Another set of huge doors opened at the far end of the room, from which the noises were escaping.

Xanthe stepped over the trash, carefully tiptoeing around some soiled loin-wear, and crept up to the other door. Here was a smaller unlit chamber. The weeping seemed to be coming from the oversized bed that dominated it. Xanthe already knew what had happened. She just wondered who the victim was.

The whimpering stopped as she entered. Xanthe stepped forward, once again feeling awkward. She had to say something, but didn't know quite how to make an introduction, or even whether she should. What exactly does one say in a situation like this? '*Hi, you don't know me. But I happened to be wandering by, bluffing my way into places I don't belong, and noticed that Horace just raped you. Pleased to meet you. We have a lot more in common than you might think!*' Her stomach turned, and she almost did herself. But no. She had to see this through. She approached the down-blanketed bed, and bindings.

"Xanthe?" A shaky voice arose from the center.

She knew the voice. "Nadeen?!"

"Xanthe? What happened to you? What's that you're wearing?"

"Me? Never mind me. What about you?"

"Oh. I just got kind of stuck. C-can you help me?"

Nadeen was on her back, still semi clothed, but with her petticoat pulled up to her waist. Her arms were bound behind her, and her knees had been manacled to posts high atop the enormous canopy bed, leaving her naked bottom slightly elevated. Xanthe tried to avoid noticing both the semen and blood dripping out of her, but it was unavoidable even in the dim candlelight. She hesitated only briefly, looking about how she could unlatch the chains. "I'll have you out in a minute."

"Thanks. My wrists. They kind of hurt."

"I bet. Um. What happened?" She managed to pull down one of the chains.

"Oh. Well, Priscia came looking for me. See I know Ralyn, and his sister works for one of the Dealers, and she said there was supposed to be a party here in Highcouncil, and that there was a man name Dulon who was buying up fizz powder for the drinks they were having. Because really, only the Slakesons would be open tonight. I mean who else would think of having an indoor shop open on Festival but them? We thought we'd meet him there and get through the gate if we offered to help. Well, it turned out that Dulon is really Aymee's second cousin on her mother's side. I kind of knew him already, and he was happy to let us in. We almost went to the Dealer party but decided to go our own way. There was this boy that Priscia wanted to wave through. And..."

Xanthe managed to get the other chain unhooked. "I mean, how'd you get here? In Horace's room. This is his right? I mean, I sure hope there isn't more than one Wormwood."

"Oh no. There's Nelash and Sarah, but they're girls. And Tolly, but he's a baby."

Xanthe released the other leg. "Let's roll you over and see if I can get you untangled."

Nadeen rolled over. "Please don't tell anyone," she begged mortified. "This isn't what it looks like. I just got stuck is all."

"Stuck? He tied you up."

"Well kind of, yeah. I got to the party, and there were all sorts of people to meet. But my favor kind of got knocked out of my hand in the crowd, and Horace accidentally stepped on it. He said it was too bad and promised to get me a new one here." Suddenly her voice caught. "You're not still mad at me, right? I mean, I'm sorry I didn't tell you where your favor was. But Priscia was being super bossy, and I didn't know what to do. I didn't think much about it until I lost my favor."

That was the least of Xanthe's worries. "Knowing Horace, he probably knocked the favor out of your hand on purpose, just to get you alone to do this rape." Xanthe struggled to pick apart the tightly tied leather strips. No wonder Nadeen was in such pain.

"Rape? What rape?"

Xanthe blinked. "What do you mean? Did you want him to do this?!"

"Um... well." Nadeen made a face, "I mean, yeah, it was kind of unexpected."

"I bet. But this wasn't some sort of Praetorian game you wanted to do, right?"

"Well," Nadeen paused. "Not really. I mean one minute he started kissing me, and that wasn't so bad, but then he picked up this strap and tied it around my wrist. When I asked what he was doing, he said to just see. He pulled it behind me and tied the other and I couldn't really believe it. Next thing I know, I'm stuck on the bed, and every time I try to kind of get up, he's pushing me down."

"Okay, so you were raped."

"Well I mean, but his family is so rich. Look at this place! Lots of girls would love to be with him. It's not like he's a poor bandit or anything." Xanthe finally managed to undo the last of the leather. Nadeen pulled her hands in front of her and started shaking them out. "Ah. They tingle."

"What other girls want doesn't matter. All that does is you didn't. He made you. That's what rape is."

"I guess. But it's not like it's a big deal. He was done so fast it was kind of like it didn't happen at all," she declared fervently. "I just wish he would have let me back down to the party, instead of hanging up my knees. Like that. You saw me. I was kind of completely stuck."

"He did that afterward?"

"Yeah," she put her hand between her thighs, and pulled it back up. It came back, sticky with both semen and black-threaded blood. "He said he had to. That some sick ugly bitch teased him earlier in the night, leaving his balls full. But I was pretty, and he was going to give me a gift. But he didn't. All that happened was this. You're not going to tell, right?"

He had been talking about her, Xanthe mused. Of course. Not that it mattered now. Not with the demon messing with people's eyes. "Please stop worrying. I won't. But that's the wrong question."

"It is to me! Dain wouldn't like me if he knew. Probably no one would." Nadeen was increasingly upset.

"That may be important, Nadeen, but something's even more so. Do you want a Festival baby? Because that's what Horace's so-called gift is. Seeding you."

"I..." Nadeen paused again. This time longer. "Oh." At the realization, her eyes widened in sheer terror.

"He won't marry you either. He just wants to fatten your belly as a Festival trophy, to show off how virile he is. He can afford the honor dowry. He'll likely brag to everyone about having to pay it too. Drag your name through the mud, just because he can."

Nadeen squirmed uncomfortably. "Can we just not talk about this right now?"

Xanthe had been admiring how well Nadeen was coping, but this wasn't good. She was denying what had happened. Xanthe sat next to her. "Look, I get wanting to make it all go away, but there's one thing you can't put off. A choice. I have childbane." Xanthe still had the seeds Celeste had given her kept against her breast. She retrieved them, holding them out.

The girl's eyes widened in shock. "But that's a sin!"

"If not sinning is the most important thing to you, then I can find you childboon instead. Your choice. No one else's. But if you do catch, you won't be able to keep what happened here a secret."

Nadeen nodded. "I... kind of see what you mean. But don't you have to take childbane ahead of time? I'm right between periods."

"It'll work if you haven't ovulated yet."

"Ovulated?"

Nadeen wasn't the best student. She was mostly in the art and crafting classes that Mrs. Fullbarn taught. "Ovulation is when a girl's seed releases. Both boys and girls have their own kind. Babies grow from when they get mixed together."

"But...how do you know bandager stuff? Don't tell me the Scholars are letting you study to be one!"

"What would be wrong with that?"

"Well, it's not proper! Nursing's okay, but women have families to take care of, not super complicated jobs where we could hurt someone if we mess up. 'A dearth of need to roam the wild/ Tempts the proper pliant wife/ With hearth and seed, kept home with child/ Kempt, her loving quiet life'". Nadeen repeated an old Curate adage. "And I'm not an amazon," she added primly. "I like boys."

Xanthe sighed to herself, wondering how girls' expectations could be so reamed, that the idea of female bandagers was more scandalizing than just having been raped. "So do I. But I don't have a family yet. Besides, don't you think a girl faithful to Life Support might know girl problems better than a man?"

Nadeen's eyes widened in revelation. "Yeah. I guess. I kind of never thought about it that way."

Xanthe felt a bit guilty about not telling the truth. She had no formal training, and had never even thought of joining the Bandager sect. In the exploration of her touch, she'd done her medical studies alone. Only her father knew of her interest and had found tons of fascinating medical hardcopy for her. She was still learning from it.

Nadeen deflated sadly. "But even you can't fix my virginity. I was kind of saving myself."

"Sure I can. He was so quick, it'll bandage right up." Another lie. Bandages couldn't fix things the way her witch power could, but better to leave Nadeen in the dark about that. She just couldn't keep a secret. "Just take the childbane and let me see how I can help."

Nadeen snatched every one of the seeds from her hand, and didn't hesitate to eat them all, her moral qualms vanishing in her panic. She might have taken too many, but Xanthe didn't think it would make her sick. Just to be sure things would work though, she put her hand on Nadeen's lower abdomen, and reached out with the touch.

*Gynecology was as fascinating as it was unfamiliar. As her perceptions deepened, Xanthe felt an uneasy sense of intrusion. Kestrels had no understanding, and she always acted to save their lives, but here she was examining another girl's most private parts; her pinky was even touching Nadeen's pubic hairs. With what she now recognized as the aid of her demonic dress, it was trivial to fix the hymen by pulling, pinching, and knitting the gossamer thin membrane together. Deeper in, Nadeen's cervix, was covered with semen. Focusing, she could see it as a mass of lethargically wriggling eel-like bubbles that were struggling to penetrate an extremely thin layer of mucus. Nearly all were stuck, but their presence created little channels, easing the passage of others. A few hundred had passed that barrier and had streamed through the moist tissues of Nadeen's womb, up into her left fallopian tube.*

Those few that weren't feeble swam toward some strange unexpected construct, a seemingly huge cage of black blood. At her confusion at its presence, descriptions once again popped up in the three-dimensional graphic mesh that overlaid her vision when she focused like this. The single enormous yellow cell it confined was labeled an "Ovum". Horace's sperm, labeled as such in her sight, were being shunted into a mechanism where their nuclei were being probed and filtered in various stages by things titled, "Mendelian Abnormality Sensors", "Proteinic Interface Matching", and last, a huge structure titled "Branar-Eidolon Affinity". Of the dozen entering, only a few made it into that final opaque structure of complex molecular machinery. She couldn't tell whether one had made it through and any fertilization had happened or not.

A chill ran up her back. With a thought, she burned the ovum completely. Killing it.

"Xanthe? Is there something wrong?"

She blinked out of the trance. "What?"

"You jerked. Are you all right?"

Xanthe swallowed. "Just unnerved is all."

"There's something wrong with me?"

"Oh!" Her mind turned from momentous thoughts, back to Nadeen's concerns. What lie would most comfort her? "You're okay. I don't even need to bandage it. You're even still a virgin."

"Really?" Nadeen brightened.

"Yeah. His shaft is super short. He didn't even make it inside you. He just left his stuff outside." She hoped Nadeen would get that into the rumor mill. She was pretty sure boys worried about that.

"I'm just so thankful for your witchery!"

At the words, Xanthe felt panic in her chest like a blow. "What makes you think it was that?"

"Minutes after this happens, you just show up with childbane? I may not be a super Scholar like you, but I'm not dumb," Nadeen nodded. "You didn't come here by chance."

"I..." Xanthe realized Nadeen still imagined that she had some strange witch power of augury. She was about to deny it, but then her eyes fell upon her own dress and she reconsidered. "You may be right."

"Oh, don't worry. I won't breathe a word. I super swear. Let's go though, okay? I don't like this place."

Just as Nadeen said this, there was the sound of the hallway door opening in the other room. Both girls turned their heads to the door.

"Someone's coming!" Xanthe whispered urgently. Nadeen nodded silently and got up off the bed. She headed to a table with a long bronze candlestick on it. Xanthe was wondering if she needed to admonish her not to light it, when Nadeen promptly inverted it, wielding it like a club.

Xanthe shook her head and mouthed "No fighting," at Nadeen, though she wasn't sure she'd understood when the door opened, and a dark shape loomed from the better lit waiting room.

"Xanthe?!" the boy exclaimed.

Beneath her placid exterior, Nadeen must have been quite a bit more upset than she seemed, because she swung hard. With a sharp crack, the end of the torch contacted the young man's skull, and he fell like a sack of flour, collapsing at Xanthe's feet.

Xanthe winced. "Nadeen..."

"Wait. That didn't sound like Horace."

She sighed. "It's Royroy."

"Oh no! Did I kill him?"

Xanthe kneeled, putting her hand on his forehead. Nothing was cracked, and no arteries were damaged, but his neurons were not firing in their normal synchronized patterns. Even lesser animals had a flow to consciousness which wasn't present. "He's out cold but should recover." She made sure of this by flushing stress toxins just released from the violent shaking as best she could, along with addressing the rapidly swelling bruise, scanning quickly for any subdural hematomas – blood on the brain, a common kestrel injury, and quite lethal. It was delicate work, and she took her time.

"Wait a minute." Nadeen's attitude changed as she noticed his uniform. "He's a Wormwood now?"

"Yeah. Horace hired him."

Nadeen frowned deeply. "Maybe I should have hit him harder."

"Absolutely not. He was coming to release you."

"You know that? Your witch power..." Nadeen was astounded. "It must be so cool to have it."

Xanthe couldn't stand it anymore. "It's not the touch. Just logic. There's nothing else in this bedroom, so why else would he head straight here? Now the real question is, was he secretly rescuing you? Or just cleaning up at his master's behest? I think it's the former because Horace left you exactly the way he wanted. He didn't want you to make a scene downstairs."

Nadeen put a hand to her mouth. "I would never. That'd be so embarrassing!"

"A big reason why Horace keeps getting away with it. But if so, Royroy isn't bad. Just dumb."

Nadeen was confused. "What? Why?"

"Don't you know? You sent me to him. He needs coin to buy his sister's revenge. That's why he's working for Horace. Except Wormwoods mostly pay only with promises. That means if Royroy did come here on his own, it would give Horace a perfect excuse to stiff him."

"He risked his family vengeance for me?"

"Assuming he was playing the hero, and not just that Horace sent him."

"Oh." Nadeen was uncertain.

Xanthe pulled away. She was pretty sure she'd alleviated most of the concussion. "He'll wake up pretty soon. Let's go before he does."

Outside in the stone hall, the guard was gone. Xanthe didn't know whether this was because Royroy had tricked him, or he was also in on the rescue. Regardless, it was certainly convenient. They walked to where the stairs were, and Nadeen started to head down. She paused when Xanthe didn't follow.

"Aren't you coming?"

Xanthe shook her head. "I have to wait for someone. Don't want to be in a crowd downstairs."

"Why not?"

"I can't be distracted. I have things to do," Xanthe squirmed awkwardly.

"It'll be fun! Especially now that you're dolled up so incredible."

Now Xanthe rolled her eyes. "Not you too. I mean, see past the dress. It's still just plain me."

Nadeen smiled. "This dress! No wonder you didn't ask me for help with that dowdy green A-line. It was a trick! You were just waiting for the right time to do your change and put us all to shame."

"Come on! It's just a weird little black dress with a big floppy black hat. I'm still a skinny common blonde with not even close to the heft some girls have. What there is, is all in front."

Nadeen took Xanthe's self-complaint seriously. She examined judgmentally, holding her hand to her chin and tapping her lips with her finger as she did so. "I mean yeah. It's not the rich look. But you have to see it the way an art student does. This just says 'new' to me. Original. Bold. Fearless. I mean, so what if your thighs are tight, not flabby? Your bottom round, not fleshy? Own it, you know? Be what you are."

"Which is hopelessly out of fashion. Well exercised. Says I'm low and labor for a living. Which I do."

"Look, if a boy wants haunches, there's a dozen Highcouncil belles downstairs in buns and slats, along with snooty families to go with. But what if they don't? There's all of them, and then there's you! You're kind of like your own completely new style. You're not out of fashion, girl. You're leading it!"

Xanthe suddenly laughed. "You sure you're a seamstress? You got a sideshow pretender's way with words."

"Well yeah, there's salesmanship to fashion," Nadeen admitted. "I mean, dad isn't paying for my education just for the lessons. It's also for me to meet girls he hopes will become our clients. But I mean it too! You know, this could be a whole new line. Dad's is always trying to sell to the same forty top high council families everyone else does. But I don't think he sees that there are girls with different types of bodies. Not perfect. Not in style. But know what? They need clothes too, even if they don't have the time or discipline to sit in a chair all day and eat. Not everyone is a reader."

"Oh great," Xanthe exclaimed sarcastically. "I'm farm-girl style. Next thing, you'll tell me to knock out a tooth."

"Nah. Call it... Amazon Chic. Southern princes try to romance the wild and beautiful girl adventurer, whose legs are made for running, not wiggling. But you keep them all at arm's length. Not because you like girls, but because marriage would only tie you down." Nadeen struck a pose, with her hand out as if coyly trying to hold back some invisible royal.

Xanthe was going to say something else tart in response, but Nadeen's comment came far too near the mark so far as Damien was concerned. Instead she found herself flushing. "Well credit Mrs. Fullbarn. She's the one who did this. I mean, except for the dress and this silly floppy hat."

"She did your face? No wonder it's so perfect." Nadeen stared closely in awe. "I wonder if it's permanent."

"Permanent?"

"You don't know?" She leaned in and whispered conspiratorially. "She's a greatwitch."

Xanthe was shocked. "Dodgy power, Nadeen! Don't go blabbing everyone's secrets. How would you like it if I said you had a serious witch touch?"

Nadeen turned pale. "Please don't tell."

Xanthe didn't know whether to be exasperated or resigned. Proctors had to have the easiest job in the world. Just arrest girls at random. "I... Yes. Yes. I won't."

"Okay, great! So anyway, Mrs. Fullbarn can color your skin, so your makeup doesn't come off. Ever. She almost never does though. Not for years now. Says it causes too much trouble."

"Didn't I just ask you not to...?" That did it. No secrets with Nadeen. She just couldn't stop sharing. "Yeah. Look. Okay. Fine. Whatever. Look, I can't go with you. I need to find people. Like Tari or Celeste. Or if you see a Shambhalan guard by the name of Javan, send him up here, okay?"

"You're looking for Tari? I know where she is! Want me to show you?"

Xanthe felt pleasantly surprised. At least there was some benefit to all the fashion talk. "Sure."

Nadeen took her by the hand down stairs, and they crossed through the crowds to another section of the building. Finding the renewed attention exquisitely uncomfortable, this left her with something new to dislike about herself. She was shy. But at least Nadeen was right about one thing. Whether it was the demonic dress affecting people's eyes, Mrs. Fullbarn's magic makeup, or merely the highborn were so jaded that they found oddity attractive, she was somehow fascinating. Especially the boys. That had to be useful somehow.

"Up here." Nadeen pointed up a flight of a tightly wound circular stone staircase, off one of the lesser traveled galleries. There were only a few scattered guests about. "I saw her with her mom. But when I tried to talk to them, her mom shooed me away, so I left." She hesitated at the base.

Xanthe saw her reluctance. "Are you going back to the party?" She asked.

Nadeen's face fell. "Yeah. I'm sorry. I just know you're doing things. I'm just not, you know..."

"'S-okay." Xanthe gave her an understanding smile.

"I mean, I wish I could help. But I'm kind of not as alright as maybe I'm sounding, you know?" Nadeen sounded pained. "This night wasn't what I expected, and I don't know how I'm feeling right now. I don't want anything else to happen."

"I understand totally. Do whatever makes you feel comfortable. You deserve it."

"You won't tell anyone, right?" She burst out. "About, you know."

"My lips are more sealed than yours."

Without warning, Nadeen hugged her fiercely. While she clung, Xanthe could feel her tremble. Not knowing what else to do, Xanthe awkwardly patted her back.

"You saved my life," Nadeen sobbed quietly. "I'm so sorry I didn't tell you where the favor was."

"That's okay."

She continued explaining. "Priscia was being really pushy, like she usually is. I mean, most times she's kind of funny and all, and always has something to do. But you know, I was really on the spot there."

"No, really! It's okay!" Xanthe assured. "It turned out for the best. A boy ended up getting it down and returned it to me."

Nadeen stared. "By the Creator! Like for real? How romantic! But then, why aren't you with him?"

"Well," Xanthe shrugged, "because I'm here."

"Oh, like your touch is telling you who needs help and everything? You know, you're kind of like that legendary greatwitch Glorianna of the Peaks."

Xanthe laughed. "I hope not! If you recall from Mr. Griswold's basic northern history class, she was burnt at the stake in 792."

Nadeen just shook her head and returned the crooked smile. "That's you. Always the brain."

"Right. Brain in a big dumb floppy pointy black hat."

"Nah," Nadeen smiled. "Not dumb. Super cute! It's intended imperfection. Otherwise you'd be completely unapproachable."

"I'm sure the hat appreciates the compliment."

"You're funny, too," Nadeen grinned with affection and relief. "Never forget. Pursue beauty," she declared as a parting phrase, and left.

## Chapter 31

Up the stairway was another hall, again merely painted plain stone. At the end, Xanthe saw two guards with little Outlet sponsorship patches on their shoulders posted in front of one of the doors. Figuring that was where she needed to go, she headed directly over, and again adopted the attitude that she had permission. "This is where Tari is, right?" she asked even before either had a chance to speak. They didn't even stand in her way as she opened the door.

"What's your name, sweetheart?" asked the younger of the two guards. He was remarkably young. Xanthe wondered why he was here instead of out in the Festival.

"Maybe I'll tell you on the way out," she waggled her fingers at him as she let herself through. Then was surprised. *What in hellspace? Why did I do that?* This was the price of dealing with demons. You weren't sure any of your actions were really your own. But it sure did seem easy.

The mansion was obviously laid out in a cookie cutter fashion, for this apartment was the mirror of Horace's, lacking only its opulence and filth. Xanthe looked around. Divans, a mismatched set of reclaimed ancient chairs, a table, but no Tari. She moved to the adjoining room. No bed, only a window fully open, revealing more misty fog and the sounds of distant party music. Xanthe started to worry. She wondered if Tari had leapt to her doom.

"Tari?" Xanthe called softly as she moved to the large double window. There were still hands on the railing.

Over the sill, Tari had tied together some bed sheets and attached it to the mounting for a flagpole set at its base. She was clinging there, too scared to fully test it. It was obvious why. She was still in her party dress. Plus, while Tari wasn't quite as plump as her slats made her out to be, she wasn't rail thin either.

A voice called out from below. "Xanthe? Is that you?" It was Damien.

"I can't see how to do this without falling," Tari said nearly at the same time.

"Then don't," Xanthe exclaimed, reaching over to grab her waist. Her friend's position was precarious.

Tari didn't cooperate. "No! I need to get down!"

Xanthe kept her grip firm. "You could hurt yourself. It's a dozen yards."

Yuri called up. "I try catch little gurl in poof dress."

"I also need you up here." Xanthe continued.

"You do?" Tari asked incredulously.

Xanthe nodded, while trying to think of a good reason. "At the least, let me help you so you don't fall." Her bed sheet rope looked far too flimsy.

Tari scowled, but then acceded. "Fine. But I'm mad at you," she declared in a quiet voice.

"Huh? Why?"

She pulled herself up to her belly on the wide windowsill and glared. "You're a boy-stealer."

"What? Me?" Xanthe sputtered. "What are you...? Oh!" She then whispered. "You mean Damien?"

Tari furrowed her brow. "You told me he wasn't a witchkiller and was helping Priscia. You never said you dropped your favor for him."

"I didn't drop it on purpose." Xanthe continued in a low voice. "We're not on a favor date."

"You tied your ribbon on him accidentally too?"

"I..." Xanthe flushed. "That's in case he runs into Celeste."

Tari continued glowering as she awkwardly heaved her leg over the side of the window. A big problem with slats, even good ones, were that they were inflexible. She pouted as she tumbled into the room. "I had a bad night, but when I see Damien showing up under my sill, I think maybe he's come to sweep me off my feet and rescue me from Horace. Instead, he starts asking after you."

"Only because I'm helping him." Xanthe answered. "Besides, why are you so upset? You were the one who said you couldn't see him in your future."

"Hmph. Maybe because you changed my future with him."

"Not on purpose!"

Tari folded her arms. "Celeste accused you of being in love. Now I know who with."

Just as Xanthe was getting a furiously guilty blush, Damien called out from below. "What's going on up there? What are you talking about?"

"Nothing!" Xanthe and Tari returned in unison.

"Oh, zees is not good," Claude's cheerful voice wafted up. "When two girls say zhey speak of nothing, zhey speak of something. Like you."

"I'm sure they're being more serious than that, Claude," Damien chided. "Lives are on the line."

"Yes. Yes, we are," Xanthe called down. "Really, Claude. Give us some respect."

"Boy-stealer," Tari continued softly squinting at her, making a scissors with her hand, snipping her index and middle fingers together. It was what little girls did in Early Years when they were mad at each other, cutting the bonds of friendship, only to completely forget about it the next day. Xanthe was nearly certain that Tari didn't really mean it, but it stung anyway.

"Pretty sure I'm gonna make it up to you by dying, so don't worry. You'll get your shot," Xanthe told her. "Just tell me where any special guests have been staying, and I'll be off."

"Why do you think I'd know that?" Tari asked.

"You Highcouncil types are always up in each other's business. You've got to know something."

Tari thinned her lips. "It's not like we're some giant cabal. The worst aren't old money either. It's climbers like Priscia's house. But yes, this time you happen to be right. I did hear that the Wormwood chain tower is off limits. They have something special there. Mysterious. Not even the guards know what it is."

A gloved hand appeared on the ledge, and by it, Damien pulled himself halfway up so that his crossed arms ended up laying on the window sill, while his torso still dangled over the edge. "The chain tower you say?"

Xanthe was startled. "How did you scale the wall so fast?"

"Yuri gave me a foot toss. He's quite strong. My apologies for intruding without an introduction, but we really couldn't hear from below, and if you're plotting, I would hear it." He gave them both a rakish grin.

"Ah yes. A proper introduction." Xanthe exclaimed. "Damien, this is Tari of Outlet." She gestured with her hand. "Hers is a council family that owns somewhere near half the warehouses in the city, plus various wagon businesses. Tari, this is Damien who, while he has no occupation worth mentioning, is, nevertheless, mostly a gentleman."

He smiled. "So as is proper for a gentleman, I await an invitation to enter a lady's room."

"Usually that's at one's door. Not a window." Tari told him. She was nevertheless quite pleased.

"Well, I am an adventurer. We don't always do things the normal way."

"I wasn't going to mention the whole banditry bit." Xanthe teased.

He took it in stride. "Pretty sure there's a difference."

"Yes," Xanthe continued. "Adventurers bum around the wilds taking the occasional odd job, but mostly opening every private barrel and chest they can find and helping themselves to anything not nailed down. While bandits..."

"...are smart enough to not risk their lives rescuing two bewitching coquettes." Damien finished. "Now while I normally wouldn't mind bantering all night like this... you two were saying?"

"Horace and Prince Sol are using the chain tower. Such towers hold the cabling that distributes torque from the water-wheels in the city's river-catacombs to the various public axles," Xanthe explained.

"I've heard of them," Damien said, "though never been in one. They're uncommon in my lands."

Xanthe wasn't surprised. "Normally they're for whole neighborhoods, but with the size of this estate, I wouldn't be at all surprised if the Wormwoods use this one only for themselves."

"They don't use it for anything productive though," Tari explained disdainfully. "Only to power bridges and gates, that sort of thing. When they're not, they just let the torque go to waste. Disgraceful."

"So why go there?" Damien asked.

Tari continued. "Chain towers have a bad reputation. In scare stories, they're always where murders take place. For good reason. People die from getting caught in the gears."

"More to the point, they're also usually empty," Xanthe added. "Nobody wants to live too near one. Even the quietest of them grind on all day and night. Meaning that if you have something you really don't want people to see, that's not a bad place to put it."

"Put what?" Tari asked.

Xanthe and Damien looked at each other. Xanthe felt she had to answer. "Like keeping an artifact that holds a great demon."

Instinctively, Tari clutched at her chest, where she normally kept her holy pliers. "Pilot preserve us."

"They're waking up," Xanthe explained. "I already told you this."

"You're going to destroy it?" Tari asked.

Before she could answer, Damien interrupted. ""Xanthe, these are dangerous secrets."

"Tari's trustworthy," Xanthe assured him, as she turned to her. "This demon is key to prince Sol's plans, so there's no better way of persuading him to abort his plan than to hold the artifact ransom."

Tari considered. "And Javan is going to take you to it?"

"Um. Yes. How did you know that?"

"In fifteen seconds, he will open the door, calling for you."

"And you know that because...?"

"Because there's no future in which he doesn't."

Xanthe nodded slowly, while Damien became confused. "What are you talking about?"

"You're not the only one with secrets," Xanthe told him quietly. "Now drop down. Don't want you and Javan face to face." She put her hand on his head and pushed, while at the same time turning herself to sit on the sill in front of him, facing the room.

As soon as she did, the door opened, and Javan strode through. "Xanthe?"

Damien hadn't let go. He was still hanging on to the sill by his hands, to literally eavesdrop on the conversation. Xanthe sat on his fingers and addressed Javan. "Here. Speak freely. Tari is an ally."

Javan measured up Tari, then continued. "The plot is in full swing. They laced the guard hall drink pots with something. I didn't catch what. But most foreign and loyalist guards will be incapacitated in a few bells. Apparently fewer of us know about this than I thought. Then we're supposed to invite the council to have a meeting with the prince. He's going to give his pitch then."

"How do they know who's loyalist?"

"The prince has a witch helping them. Karissa. She's from Northfjord. She has some sort of touch to be able to tell if someone is truly convinced. I was interviewed in her presence a while ago, and at the time I was buying it all. I guess that's why they gave me this position."

"This prince is using a greatwitch?" Tari was shocked.

"Come on," Xanthe said. "Succession politics is literally life and death for Nutearean princes. You think any one of them would turn down any advantage?"

Tari wasn't happy. "I suppose you're going to say now that Prayerhome tries it's best not to find out."

Xanthe answered the question by ignoring it. "Just stay out of this witch's way for a while longer," she told Javan. "Get me to where the beacon is. After that, I hope you would use your position to misdirect your guards, but if you decide to flee instead, I understand. Count the debt you owe me paid. You can go home."

"No," he declared with quiet regret. "That is the one thing I cannot do. Now I have no home."

"Then stay here. We're a sanctuary city, and that doesn't just mean refuge for slaves. We welcome travelers and protect them. For those wise enough to take advantage of it." She reached behind her back, and silently plucked with her forefinger at Damien's head a few times to emphasize this point. In response, he wiggled his fingers, sending tingles up her back.

"Perhaps it did. But Jagerfeld's luck has just run out."

"Funny," Xanthe demurred. "I'm starting to not believe in luck at all. How soon can we move?"

He stared silently, studying her. Then, "I would at least know your plan fully before you attempt it."

"I'm still working on the details, but the core is simple. The beacon is in the chain tower, correct?"

"Exactly," he was surprised she knew, but continued. "It has only one door in and out."

"Then I'll bluff my way inside where the beacon is kept by pretending that I'm one of Horace's conquests. Once inside, I'll tell some story to the inner guards about an emergency outside. As soon as they're distracted, I'll grab it and run for a chain. I hope to be lifted out of the tower before they can react."

Tari looked concerned. "Don't think being a girl will save you, Xanthe. As soon as you touch it, they'll try to kill you. They may have atlatls too."

"I would assume," Xanthe agreed. "But I have a few tricks up my dress that might allow me to evade them."

"Neither part of your plan will work," Javan stated.

"Why not?"

"As a minor matter, the beacon is not small. It can be carried, but not in your pocket. Holding it one handed, as a lodestone chain lifts you out an oriel would be troublesome for anyone, especially a girl."

"Then I must disable the guards and lower the beacon to a waiting accomplice."

Javan shook his head. "No. That's not the problem at all. There are no guards. It's not even locked."

"Really?" Xanthe was surprised. "Then what protects it?"

"It's a greater demon," he remarked darkly. "If anything, you need protection from it."

"Really? How so?"

"Let me explain by relating the stories from those who have been with Prince Sol longer than I. The tales may have grown with the telling, but I doubt by much. You're hardly the first to think of stealing the prince's prize. As I said, he is convinced that it's key to the Nutearean throne, and if true, just imagine the price such an artifact would command among the richer princes."

He grabbed a chair and continued. "Soon after the beacon's presence became known, a powerful lord in Northfjord, under the pretense of Curate authority, sent his men to seize the thing. Prince Sol had at that time set a guard about it. But they were both outnumbered and surprised, so the attackers certainly would have won. Except that the demon awoke, lightning came from nowhere, and killed them all."

"Sounds lucky," Tari said. "Demons are evil."

"I mean friend and foe alike. There was nothing left but sizzling and smell of roast flesh."

"Oh." Xanthe went wide eyed, and then fell silent.

"The second time, a thief named Klatin of Milnhelm bribed the next set of guards Prince Sol had set to guard it. They were to do nothing other than exit the room while he grabbed it. A researcher had prepared a metal mesh suit of ancient design that made him immune to lightning."

"Which also failed," Xanthe remarked. "Or else it would not be here."

Javan nodded. "A strange black hole opened when he neared, it had within it stars like the night sky, and with a great gust of wind, the master thief was drawn into it. It blinked shut and he was gone."

"Did the demon also kill the guards?"

"Oh, no. Not at all," Javan reassured her. "Prince Sol did that later."

Xanthe paused, then nodded. "I see. So, I'm third time is the charm?"

"Not quite. The last effort wasn't an attempt to steal it. A proctor caught wind of the beacon, or rather that it was demon possessed. When the prince was carrying it, he targeted it with an ancient hand-cannon, intending to destroy the thing. But his weapon detonated prematurely and quite unnaturally. They say it rained blood and bits of the proctor's flesh for nearly a minute."

"Oh, interesting," Xanthe murmured, considering her options.

"Interesting?" Tari exclaimed. "That's horrible!"

"I imagine his death was quite painless," Javan said. "Though considerably more permanent than mine."

"No, I mean it was interesting that the prince was carrying the beacon," Xanthe said calmly. "From your stories, I was beginning to wonder how it is moved at all."

"The prince can hold it, but does that matter? You can't steal it. No one can. Not without dying."

"On the contrary. Without guards, this sounds easier than I thought it would be. My greatest worry has always been how to avoid killing anyone."

Javan stared fascinated. "You truly mean this? You are a witch of impossibilities?"

"I don't think so. Though improbable things have been happening quite regularly lately. My greatest power remains my wit."

"Then how are you going to take it? Are you a cultist serving one of the five or the eight? You have true name words of control?" Though Javan's tone seemed only hopeful, Tari gave her a quick worried glance, seemingly fearful of Xanthe's answer.

"Again, no. Though I am starting to understand why they might see demons differently."

"After what I just told you? Surely you jest."

"No. You just don't understand. What you have described is a being of ancient power that can kill at any time; instead, it refrains unless provoked. Against this, various highborn have foolishly tried assault, corruption, thievery, and destruction. All strategies bound to fail. The simplest approach, the one that girls are forced to master at an early age, didn't even cross their mind."

"Witchcraft?"

"Of course not. Witch power against a demon? I'd surely be killed if it didn't die laughing first."

"Then what will you do? How can you possibly force a such a demon to come your possession?"

Ironically, with his dismissive attitude, the person Javan seemed most like was Nagrath. Yet she had to remind herself not to overgeneralize and pretend that all men were like this. Mr. Griswold would mark her down half a point from a perfect test for such. Besides, in the end, she was still her father's daughter.

"Simple. I'm going to treat it with respect. Be polite. And very... carefully... ask."

## Chapter 32

"That seems unlikely to work. Still, you're right. It hasn't been tried."

As Javan spoke, Damien dropped and landed below, but not before running a finger up the small of Xanthe's back, making her arch. He escaped before she could furiously pluck at him. His landing also made noise, and that combined with the voices of his companions, was too loud to miss. Javan rapidly rose from his chair.

"Who's there?"

Xanthe thought of blocking him, but it was no use. Instead she just worried as he moved next to her and glanced over the windowsill.

"Damien," Javan stated coolly on seeing him.

Damien glowered, glanced at her, then addressed him more calmly. "Javan," he replied.

"And Claude and I too," Yuri added, with no anger, just sorrow. "We learned things tonight."

Javan had no care for Damien's brooding, but could not bear Yuri's doleful gaze. He turned his head to the side and choked up. "I'm sorry, my friend. I have stopped trying to excuse myself, for there is none. Every night I'm tortured by what-ifs. The suffering I know that Mark's young wife will bear. The son Jacob will never see. Had I been braver, I would have simply done what was needed and died a man."

"You mean assassinate me," Damien noted dryly.

"I was trying to try to save them," Javan retorted defiantly. "You're going to get everyone killed. What would both our deaths be in that accounting?"

"Everyone came voluntarily, knowing what I asked. As did you." Damien declared sternly.

"They didn't realize what they were signing up for."

"So, to help them, you ensured their deaths. You call that no excuse?"

Xanthe could see sparks of anger flaring once again in Damien and moved quickly to quench it. "Javan is more correct than even he realizes," she told him. "You're risking your whole community. Because you're not just up against armies and assassins, you're up against spies. Eventually someone will dig out your men's secret like I did. It's only a matter of time. When they do, everyone who knew you, raised you, comforted you... you know better than I what will happen."

Damien's looked towards her. He stared up angrily. Yet the anger was no longer directed at Javan, merely at the truth in her words.

"Only if I fail. Yet I hold no hope. I don't see any way to succeed." He looked down. She could see his youthful anger turning into despair. It hurt to see him this way.

"Stay with us!" Xanthe burst out impulsively. The words leapt straight from her heart. "No one has to know who you are. Just stay. Disappear. With me. I mean... with us. The city. We can make it work."

Damien looked solemn for a moment, which then turned wistful. "I'm afraid I can't. I have damned myself by slaughtering the guilty. The least I can do is not endanger the innocent."

"Dodgy power, Damien! That's just an excuse!" Xanthe scolded angrily. "You're going to die."

He gave her a look of resigned affection. "You're one to talk about desperate moves with your own half-baked plan to save your city. We'll be near the chain tower in case you need rescuing again."

Of course he'd remind her of that. Piqued, she thinned her lips. "Fine."

"Oh, you are in trouble now," Claude smiled knowingly. "When a girl says eet is fine, is anything but."

"I'll survive," Damien told him coolly. "Let's go." But then a thought struck, and he raised his eyes one last time. "Javan."

"Yes?"

Damien drew himself up. Again, there was an overwhelming majesty about him. "She is better than all of us put together. Kept you from dying. Twice. You betrayed me. Do not betray her." He then turned smartly, his cloak swirling behind him as he led his men off.

Frustration raged through Xanthe as she watched him go. She pulled into the window and balled her fists. "I'm so mad," she fumed.

"Tell me about it," Tari sighed, whimsically sour. "The worst bit? I see how much you like each other and can't even complain. You saved my life. You had faith in me when I'd lost all of my own."

This only intensified Xanthe's frustration. She felt near tears. "If Damien keeps going like this, it won't matter anyway." She turned to Javan. "Why even bother trying to kill him? He's going to kill himself before he ever gets successful enough for anyone to care who his allies are. Some of his half-brothers have entire cities behind them. Nations! How can he possibly fight that, with the rag tag band he has? I mean really, he should just disappear. Go incognito. But no. So dodgy-power stubborn!"

Javan shook his head. "Odd for me to defend him, but it's not that simple. Especially with princes."

"Wait," exclaimed Tari. "He's not just an assassin? He's a Nutearean prince? So *that's* what this is all about?"

"Yes," Xanthe spoke hastily before Javan could reply. "Prince... Charming. Of the wilds."

Javan raised an eyebrow at her emphasis in avoiding the name 'Prince Christian', but continued smoothly. "There are good reasons for his actions. Why he keeps moving."

"How so?" Tari asked.

"It's difficult to explain, but even when they're trying to be incognito, people seldom forget princes. It's not just the title, but something innate. They have this charisma. Their authority. They get spoken of."

"They're elegant, that's for sure. Makes girls want to steal them," Tari noted. Her tone was wry though. It was clear that she was only teasing.

Javan shook his head. "Authority is much more than that. When a prince of the blood asks you to do something, if you have but the slightest inclination to accede to their desires, then you will agree to do so. It's why only those of the blood ascend the throne."

Xanthe blinked. "You're making it sound like some sort of witch touch."

"Oh, but it's not, for one specific reason."

"And that is?"

"Curate doctrine. Princes can't be witches. They're men."

Tari's mouth dropped open. "Nutearean princes are witch-kings?"

"Careful my dear. That is lèse-majesté, the crime of insulting the emperor, a capital offense in the holy lands. Do not speak of princely power in any terms other than entirely natural charisma. By tradition, the Curate recognizes they have not the evil touch of Earth but have 'authorities' born of the Creator."

"Does the Sect of Penance disagree?" Xanthe wondered.

"Not publicly. Male witchery isn't like the overwhelming power of Thulian greatwitches. It's subtle, with only a few known forms. Combined with their princely titles, it's easy to believe the pretense."

"Yeah, but still," Xanthe said. "Witchkillers study this stuff. They can't really be fooled."

"Well," Javan admitted, "the First Law of Proctoring may also have something to do with it."

Xanthe scoured her brain trying to remember this. It wasn't her favorite study, but she had given at least cursory attention to Curate doctrines. Still, this one was entirely unfamiliar. "What's that?"

"Something of a practical guideline," he explained. "Only fight battles you can win. Here it means never accuse anyone of witchcraft who can arrange to have you and everyone you know tortured to death."

"Ah," Xanthe nodded. "I can see how that might be a consideration."

"The upshot is that princes gather followers the way dung gathers flies. Gossip rarely lets them stay unnoticed for long. The first thing a new emperor does is to have his Finalizers scour the land to clean up loose ends, anyone who might incite a challenge to their rule. So, don't be angry that Damien refuses to settle here. He's protecting you. Your city has trouble enough with Prince Sol as it is."

Xanthe was appalled. "Damien can't win. If he tries for the throne, he'll get everyone he loves killed. What is he supposed to do?"

Javan remarked dryly, "You tell me. No one liked my idea any."

"So how do you know about princes?" Tari asked Javan suspiciously.

"My community has had to learn much to keep safe. Nor are we dazzled by ostentation and hypocrisy."

"You're Scholars?"

"Not precisely. We just know a lot of things the Curate and other powers will kill to keep secret."

"The Curate doesn't just kill like that," Tari told him.

Javan returned a dark crooked smile. "Oh, they do. Just in secret."

Xanthe sighed heavily. This was getting nowhere. Javan, the outcast Christian, lobbing vague critiques of the Curate at Tari, the devout but demon-touched greatwitch. They could talk all night. "Let's get back to business. We still need to get to the chain tower. Unless you have some special preparations to make," she told him, "we might as well make a run at it now."

He nodded. "I can do that."

"I'm coming too," Tari declared in a tone that made it clear that she wasn't going to be dissuaded. "I'm known by some of the guards. It will help."

Despite Xanthe's misgivings, she made no protest. The two guards at her door weren't happy to see Tari leave, but Javan's presence served to intimidate them, and they did nothing as the three exited the suite.

## Chapter 33

Xanthe, Tari and Javan made their way back into the party, wading through the sprawling crowds. Xanthe found her initial impression only reinforced. The sheer scale of Wormwood manor was impressive in size, but tacky. Dozens of large identical rooms were adorned wall to wall with family portraits of smug ancestors. Yet in all, it melded into a single self-congratulatory blandness. Essense might have been young, but at least her decorations had variety.

Food was plentiful. Overly so. There was enough to feed ten times the number of guests. Yet the highborn didn't appreciate it and Xanthe knew it would never make its way to those that would. The quantity did make her wonder what would happen to foreign guards who declined the poisoned offerings, perhaps having snuck food off the tables. This coup had to be trickier to pull off than Nagrath made it sound.

"You didn't say why you were under guard." Xanthe asked Tari as they walked.

"Mother thought I might run away before I had the chance to be persuaded."

Xanthe anticipated that. "By whom? Prince Sol?"

Tari gave her typical scowl. "No way this mystical power of princely persuasion could match her nagging. She never lets anything go. I'm young and foolish, you see. Don't appreciate my position."

Tari's complaints weren't entirely unfounded. Highborn chaperoned their kids closely during Festival, to make sure that only acceptable boys returned their daughters dropped favors. Still, Xanthe wistfully wondered what it would be like to have a mother worried for her. "I'm sure she loves you, in her own way."

"She hovers like a moth! Wants me to live her life instead of my own!" Tari gesticulated wildly, but then froze as two partygoers walking down the hall turned to stare.

"Um, yeah," Xanthe continued after they passed. Javan guided them to another corridor, this one less crowded. This area was more like a barracks, long rows of doors to cramped bunks. "Good thing we're heading away from her."

"Not sure about that," Javan told her, as he led them by two guards, nodding to them in passing. "A lot of important people have been around where we're going."

Xanthe stared down the empty hall. "Why?"

He shrugged. "Don't know exactly. I think they're holding meetings."

"How can you not know? You're in on all this!"

"They keep as many people in the dark as possible. Even Horace. We didn't know Prince Sol was coming. We're explicitly not to say anything to our fellow guards. If it gets out, things could turn bloody. Prince Sol is a lot like you, little greatwitch. He's too proud to just win. He wants to win so crushingly, that it's bloodless."

She shook her head. "I'm not trying to win. I'm just want them to go away."

Javan eyed her. "You want them to go away and getting what you want is winning."

"Am I being unreasonable?" Xanthe objected as they turned a corner, into what appeared to be a dead end. Javan produced a pincer-key and stuck it in a hole. As he gripped, with the sound of grating stone, the wall began to move on its own, sliding to the side. Xanthe jumped back.

"Don't worry," Tari noted. "Just a torque-powered door. The Wormwood estate is full of them."

Despite her evident disapproval, Xanthe still thought it a neat mechanism, if ostentatious. Yet she didn't have a chance to respond. The door opened to a drawing room with a group of people at the far end.

She recognized the assassin with the wide-brimmed hat she'd seen in Horace's coach. A sallow faced man in his mid-fifties was also there. Dressed in a dark long-coat tied in glittering silver string-lace, he carried a cane whose outline Xanthe recognized from Horace's coach. Next to him was a dark blonde young woman, perhaps about twenty, wearing a red gown in a foreign style with long ribbon sleeves. Lastly, a tall and strikingly handsome blonde man in his early thirties, in an ornate, yet practical, black fencer's doublet. All were in relaxed poses, but there was also a quiet tension about them. The men were armed. Each bore courtly blades that never the less seemed quite functional. The blonde man turned his head to see them. There was something else odd about him. Xanthe couldn't put a finger on it.

Beside her, Javan momentarily froze. She nudged him gently forward. No use now. Retreat would be twice as suspicious.

"Ah Javan," the blond man called across the room. "Perfect timing. I have an errand for you."

"My Lord Sol," Javan responded guardedly. "I'm not sure I am the best one to do that for you right now. Horace did not take the report of my failure well."

That was the clue Xanthe needed. All at once she saw it. Prince Sol. The family resemblance. He was Damien's brother. Handsome as hellspace too, just light to Damien's dark.

"Yes, Finalizer Dakur told me," the prince nodded in the direction of wide-brim.

"I did my best with the archdeacon," Javan explained. "But he was obsessed with finding his daughter."

"Worry not," Sol declared magnanimously. "You may not be in your young lord's good graces, but you are in mine. The failure was only minor, and more than made up for by relating how the archdeacon dotes upon his daughter. We were just laughing about what our hot-blooded rascal will do with her when he gets the chance. I'm sure when the time comes, my offer to protect her from him will make his Holiness quite cooperative."

"Clever, Sir."

"Of course," Sol smiled in agreement. Then he eyed Xanthe. "Speaking of which, I assume you're escorting these lovely young things for a reason?"

"Um..." Javan was reticent. "Perhaps, sir."

"Presumably this has to do with our scamp? A peace offering of sorts?" Prince Sol grinned.

The sallow faced man leaned on his staff and let out a hiss of disgust. "The sodden fool. He never ceases his endless diversions. Losing focus, especially at a time like this."

Prince Sol's smile didn't decline. "I know you don't like him Sargon, but we were all young once, and I find Horace endlessly amusing. For all his idiocy, he's not rebellious. All he requires is a little minding."

"He causes problems. Look right here before you," the sallow man gestured. "This is Tari, daughter of House Outlet, which has been so touchy to deal with. And if I'm not mistaken, Horace's betrothed."

Tari bridled. "I've agreed to marriage? That's news to me."

"Ah..." Prince Sol focused on her, giving a predatory smile. "You see, Sargon? How can you call a leader of this city maladroit, when you're no better? Look. You've upset the poor girl. Her family should have been the one to have broken this joyous news to her."

Tari was struggling not to sneer. "Oh, I'm quite aware of the notion. But it will not happen."

Prince Sol smiled. "Oh? Why ever not? My dear Miss Outlet, I can think of no better match. You're ripe to wed, and with anyone else, you'd have to marry down. Look at this giant estate you'll be mistress of."

Xanthe could feel Tari growing rage, but there was nothing she could do. She thought to speak but didn't know what words to say that might not draw suspicion. Tari balled her fists and enunciated clearly to make her point. "In Jagerfeld, girls marry men, not buildings. That grating ass is such a fool, even complete strangers notice it as soon as they meet him."

Prince Sol blinked once, taken aback at Tari's disgust. There was a momentary flicker of anger in his eyes, but he quickly hid it with a smile. "You see the trouble you caused, Sargon?" He noted, then turned back to Tari. "I presume you settled on someone different. Tell me the lucky boy's name." Behind Tari, the Finalizer shifted slightly.

"The one I preferred, settled on my friend here. She stole him, seemingly without even trying."

"Ah. Awkward," Sol ran his eyes over Xanthe in the same predatory way. "But of course. Do you understand why? It's not your features. Both of you are delectable. You just forget the adage, 'A woman's true beauty is her still tongue'. So be more like her. She is delightfully respectful."

"How little you know," Tari told him coldly. "She is the storm."

"Tari," Xanthe ventured, her voice full of worry. Not now. Not with them.

Prince Sol blinked. "You're storytelling now?"

The woman in the red gown spoke up, in an oddly dull tone. "She speaks truth."

"As she sees it. Good girl, Karissa." Sol smiled at the young woman smugly. He turned to Tari again and approached like a stalking tigran, elegant yet full of menace. "My dear, it's clear you're upset enough to start babbling nonsense, and in your haughty anger, you think yourself above listening to your family. But I assure you that quick agreement to marriage, and learning to be deferential to your new husband-to-be, is the absolute best of your options."

She stood up to him. "Nothing would be worse."

"You'll learn. Now smile. Girls are always more attractive with one." He tapped his finger under her chin.

Tari looked like she was about to bite it off, but Xanthe put her hand on her arm. "Please," she quietly pleaded.

"Your friend shows you how girls should behave." Prince Sol declared with satisfaction. "I'll reinforce the lesson by showing you the rewards of cooperation." He turned to Xanthe. "Miss? I'm gracing you with the privilege of being my escort for the rest of the evening."

Xanthe froze. She stared, wide eyed. "I... I'm sorry, sir?"

"My dear, don't think you can taunt me by wandering around so prettily, without ending on my arm."

Xanthe didn't know what to say, other than to quietly curse her dress's power to trick men's eyes. She'd just become intimately aware that Karissa could detect deception. It left few options. "I... I'm sorry, sir. My hair isn't even braided."

"Poor Miss Outlet! No wonder she's in so foul a mood. Losing to a soubrette not even of age!" He chuckled, eyeing Xanthe. "Though virgins have their charms, as all can see."

"I cannot believe I'm hearing this," Sargon muttered tensely. "What did tell you about focus? What if I require your attention on matters we cannot speak freely about?"

"Oh relax, dear conscience," the prince returned broadly. "I'll not truly divert myself until all is settled. If it goes as it should, anything the girl hears shall hardly matter."

244    STEVEN MAURER

"And if it doesn't? The district gate news is troubling. The people involved could spoil much."

"Ah, yes. Good to remind me." The prince turned back to Javan. "My dear man, I'm assigning you the task of finding the men who got away. This duty shouldn't strain your talents," he gave him an affable grin of malice, "Rest assured, I'm not asking you to persuade them."

"Me sir? Now?"

"Yes!" Sol snapped. "Has everyone become deaf? Go and take care of this. Use my name liberally to rally what aid you need. I'd send Dakur here, but he insists on being my bodyguard for the eve. Something about my personal safety, as if there aren't enough within a shout as it is. I'd argue, but he's unyielding. Finalizers train in that."

"I still need to escort the girls," Javan protested weakly.

"Oh, don't worry about Horace. I'll smooth things out with the boy. Just park Miss Outlet somewhere."

Tari folded her arms. "Don't bother. I'm not a piece of furniture. I'll take my leave now."

"Where do you plan to go?" Sargon asked, attempting a smile. Xanthe wanted to speak, but even more than with the prince, she knew she couldn't say anything without making things worse.

"This fine gentleman has decided that I'm inferior to my friend in terms of graciousness," Tari declared sarcastically. "Who knows? It may even be true. I've decided therefore, to find conversation elsewhere, and practice my charm."

Sargon was only mildly interested. "Practice? With whom?"

"To be honest, I don't know. But when I do, I'm going to treat who I speak to with respect, be polite," Tari eyed Xanthe meaningfully. "And very... carefully... ask."

She was talking about the demonic beacon. She was going to see it alone. "Tari!" Xanthe burst out.

Tari gave a grim little smile. "You're otherwise occupied, girlfriend. Wish me luck."

Xanthe could say no more. Not even tell her to be careful. Not right here. She just stood helpless as Tari turned and walked off. Sargon took his leave as well, going in a different direction.

Javan saluted. "You have ordered," he said to Sol, and disappeared. Karissa glanced up curiously, as if she detected something strange in his tone, but then her gaze returned to the floor.

## Chapter 34

For half a bell, they wandered about the edges of the party, the prince biding his time. They were never alone. Sol's boast about his entourage was truthful. It didn't take Xanthe long to realize that most of the bystanders hanging around in his general vicinity were anything but. When he moved, the overly nonchalant men dropped their conversations and followed. They numbered perhaps a dozen and seemed mostly of well-muscled Talathian stock. While a strange fog drifted in the windows and curled about the chandeliers almost as if alive, she privately wondered whether she might survive them all if a fight broke out, dress or no dress.

Her thoughts wandered. Storm. Storm. Tari was certainly right about one thing. This was the stormiest night in her life, with events and surprises coming from all directions. Quite unnatural. Or maybe all too normal. It was this southern interregnum. War was coming. Rather, it already had. How many disguised assassins were there in this party anyway? The two finalizers, the princes, probably some even more dangerous. If only she could see them all. She wondered which was the deadliest. It was hard though, as mirrors were everywhere in the Wormwood estate, and she refused to look at herself in observation of her vow.

As she focused on her surroundings, Sol focused on her. His smug smile and meaningless pleasantries didn't disguise his eyes wandering over every patch of skin her dress had exposed. It was doubly creepy because he was near twice her age. Yet there was nothing she could do, so she simply had to bear it. The worst thing was that she could see other girls giving envious stares. Though not surprising because the prince possessed both presence and pose, it only served to crystallize how much she wanted to be away.

"Excited about being let out next Festival?" He asked as they paraded slowly across a room, to a balcony, the crowd melting before them.

"I find this one exciting enough, actually," Xanthe said truthfully. She had to be. Karissa was still right behind her, as part of their little entourage.

"Oh, but for you to carry a favor of your own. With a walk and kiss. Have you ever been kissed?"

"Father does many times on the head before tucking me in at night."

"How coy," he smiled captivated. "You know well what I speak of. Your vixen's dress betrays you."

Xanthe didn't know what to say. Everyone presumed she'd decided to be this daring, and she couldn't disabuse them. The wisest thing would be to stay silent, but she simply had to defend herself a little. Priscia's crack about looking like a body-seller still stung. "It's a period costume, in the style of the ancients. The city has a contest over them."

"I don't doubt it. Yet you also know how well it shows off the very best parts of your body."

She glanced over. "In truth, I'm finding that it hides it."

"Oh my! And what part of your delectable body would that be?" He leered.

"My brain. This outfit does, alas, give people the impression that I don't have one."

"Ah." He raised his eyebrows but did not look displeased. "I did not expect that."

"Exactly. You don't know me. Indeed, as I'm not yet of age, propriety says that I should leave until my father grants me permission to speak to you."

She made to move away, but as she expected, he put his hand on her shoulder. "Oh, don't do that. You know your father won't object, and you're curious enough about me to stay. Do so then, I command you."

Once again, there was that voice. She'd begun to recognize it. It had Damien's majesty, but the character was different. Or perhaps just its strength. Compared to Damien, it was weak. Whiny. She felt no impulse to obey. Still, she did. Tari was searching for the beacon. Distracting Sol while she did so was the least she could do.

He sensed her hesitation as surrender, and once again offered his arm. "As for formalities, call me Sol. No family name, just Sol."

"Because you're a prince?"

He hesitated only slightly, but instantly turned suspicious. He scanned the room. "How did you know?"

Xanthe spoke carefully. "I know a girl named Priscia. She bragged that she'd met you."

"Ah. But of course," he relaxed. "How troublesome that family has been. Just unpleasant people."

Xanthe sighed, letting down her guard slightly. "Tell me about it."

"No, you tell me," he cajoled playfully. "Has she annoyed you? Made you angry? The girl has such a razor tongue, there are times I thought it would be better cut out. Or have her brought low some other way. Would you like that?"

Xanthe shook her head, chilled at the offer. "It's fine, really."

"Really?" He smirked. "You've never wanted to put Priscia to shame, as you did to Miss Outlet?"

"Um..." Xanthe looked away. "No."

Behind her, Karissa suddenly spoke, again in the flat emotionless voice. "She lies."

"Xanthe flushed in guilty shame. Even more, she was uneasy, worried for her plot. Karissa had to be a big reason why Prince Sol was so cocksure. Her talent had to be invaluable in politics.

The prince burst out laughing. "Don't worry, my dear. I won't hold it against you. If anything, it makes you more engaging. I must say, the way you just admitted it makes you more honest than most! So many rise to challenge Karissa's pronouncements. Especially the highborn. Sometimes I even let them think I believe them."

Xanthe turned to the young woman. "That's your greatwitch touch?"

Karissa didn't move her head. She just moved her eyes to Prince Sol, and back again, saying nothing.

The prince stepped in smoothly. "I only allow her to speak to tell truth from untruth. Else she is to remain silent. From which she benefits, for I keep her from being burnt at the stake. Even in the north, not all cities have such lax and weak Curate leadership as you suffer."

"Yet we are now in my city, your majesty. Our leaders are who they are."

"True enough," he smiled, "Yet they also change. So, as a proper courtesy, do not reveal your thoughts about her to anyone else." Again, his words came as a compulsion. She could feel it.

There was a thought in the back of her head that perhaps she was obeying him despite of her feeling of freedom. Still, playing along seemed the best option. "As you command your majesty," she nodded. "But if tribunal concerns you, why have her show off the touch so obviously?"

He smiled. "People who don't know of her power, keep lying. Telling them is the only way to make them speak truth. Some not even then."

"I see."

"Are you also a witch who would benefit from protection?" He inquired smoothly.

Yesterday, Xanthe might have felt trapped by such a question, but experience with the grims had drained all panic from her. By comparison, this was a mere intellectual puzzle, how to mislead without lying. Or even while telling the absolute truth. A trivial challenge.

"No need. Jagerfeld acknowledges the truth," she told him. "Too many girls can at least throw sparks to burn all of them."

"Including you?"

She took on a philosophical air. "Like many, I tried to figure out spark throwing when I was younger, but was never successful. I confess that at the time, I was extremely disappointed."

"You're pure. Good! I'm sure the Curate will bless you." Despite his compliment, Sol's interest dropped.

He had to be organizing a coven of his own, to help him ascend. Smart – but so easy to gull. Sparks now seemed to Xanthe more like grinding gears: a sign of malfunction, not power. She, Tari, and Celeste had all been sparkless girls. All greatwitches, she now knew.

Prince Sol continued, "Priscia also showed me her witches touch. As you say, little colored sparkles. I wasn't impressed. The talent is worthless."

"Depends on the size of them." Xanthe returned quietly.

"For my purposes, it is. With her father unable to deliver on his promises, she's even more worthless than Miss Outlet. Unappealing too. Headstrong. Angry. She belongs as a stable-keep's bride, not owned by anyone important. Would seeing her marry low please you?"

"If she wanted to, sure. Marrying for wealth seems petty to me. I'd rather marry for love."

"You've never dreamed of showing her up, being on the arm of someone she could never get?"

Xanthe's gut twisted. She winced. "I... once did. But no more."

"Such nobility! You're feeling sorry for her because of the tragedy?"

"Tragedy?" Xanthe queried.

"You don't know? Tisha, the cousin who could pass for her twin, fell in one of your little icy rivers and drowned before anyone could help. So sad," He did nothing to disguise his amusement. "When the real Priscia showed up, my dear Finalizer Dakur here looked like he'd seen a balegaunt. First time I'd seen him scared of anything! That's why I made him go talk alone with her in a dark room. Where she could tell him the truth, all alone," he grinned jovially. "Alas, she cleared it all up with him."

Xanthe mused. Priscia had obviously lied her ass off. Tisha didn't exist. But a lie was more plausible than the truth. That, or Karissa hadn't been around at the time. Most likely, both.

The Finalizer shook his head. "My eyesight must be going bad," he grumbled. "Even this girl is familiar." He peered at her. "Saw one just like her with Horace. Not as pretty, but..."

"You saw a girl wearing black like I am?" Xanthe asked.

"No. She was..." Perturbed, he hissed. "Never mind."

Prince Sol grabbed his sides chuckling. "Is it time to put you out to pasture?" He mocked his Finalizer jovially. "No matter. Priscia is alive, hale, as annoying as ever, and her father is still trying to worm his way back into my graces by pawning her off on me. Tell you what!" He clapped his hands. "Let's go see them! Twist the knife a little. Ought to be fun." He patted Xanthe's arm, and led her by it, away back through the crowd.

Xanthe felt sick as she was pulled back into the long corridors that edged the castle. This prince was as challenging as Damien was, but in an entirely different way. He actively enjoyed hurting people. She'd thought that you could find good in anyone if you search deeply enough, but she just wasn't seeing it.

She hesitated, trying to figure a way out. "I don't need to show her up anymore. I don't consider myself her rival. I more pity her than anything."

"Oh, be sure to tell her that!" He smirked as they walked. "Pity is the cruelest emotion." They reached another seeming dead end, which then opened by one of the automated torque powered doors.

"Surprising that you should say so. For do not princes deserve pity? You're forced to murder your own family. Or be murdered yourself. How can you stand it?"

He grinned at her provocative words. "You'd prefer crowning the king's eldest son?"

"Well, I'd prefer a constitutional monarchy. But yes, even primogeniture would be better."

"And if I were Prince Flordeman, I'm sure I'd agree."

"But at least you wouldn't be in fear for your life. Better non-sovereign than dead, don't you think?"

"I'm going to win the throne quite handily so that's not an issue." Prince Sol replied unconcerned.

Xanthe rolled her eyes slightly as she was slowly paraded along. "Your half-brothers all think the same thing. Yet only one of you is right, and it isn't you. For even if you manage to unify the famously fractious north, we're just not an adequate power base. We don't have the population."

His grin took on the barest touch of respect. "I'm starting to see why Miss Outlet called you the storm. You may be properly deferential as girls should be, but when you do speak, you cut to the quick faster than most of my advisers. Tell me, why is the north so hamstrung by small numbers?"

"That's obvious. We live on the edge between the nightmare filled outlands, and the nightmare and monster filled wilds. Sometimes there are more deaths than children."

"Exactly! But what would happen if the Nightmare Line disappeared?"

"Our population would explode. We might be forced to ration food as our forefathers did. But it still wouldn't win you the throne, unless you expect the presidential chair to be empty for decades. You can't win a war with an army in diapers."

"Ah. No. The Nightmare Line isn't, as Prayerhome pretends, the boundary of a curse put on outlanders due to our dreadwitch-tolerating iniquity. Nor, as some Scholars contend, merely where civilization stops, and Haven's wilds take over. Rather, it's a barrier. Shields set up by the ancients to keep nightmares at bay."

"Shields? You mean like some sort of atlatl aegis?"

"More like invisible soap bubbles many hundreds of leagues across, inside of which nightmares cannot manifest."

"And you know this... because?"

"If you record the attacks made by various supernatural creatures – liggoths, grims, straaks – and plot each position exactly on a map, eventually you see precise circles of their absence in outline."

"I see."

"So now that you know, what do you suppose would happen in the south if the lines went away? If nightmares could go anywhere, as they once no doubt had, before the ancients banished them from the holy lands?"

Xanthe considered the implications. "The south is not prepared. Hundreds of thousands would die."

"Oh, at least. Even more, if they don't quickly surrender to a northern prince, whose smaller armies don't quail in fright at the sight of one." He grinned triumphantly.

Xanthe could barely believe what she was hearing, yet it made a certain terrible sense. If the beacon could control the Nightmare Line, Prince Sol could use it to doom the unprepared southern regions to unthinkable disaster. An easy way to soften them up to rule them. The worst thing was that she couldn't entirely condemn him for his plot. What other option did he have?

She acted awestruck. "If you command the ancients' power like that, one would expect people would bow to you naturally anyway, your majesty."

"Oh, it's not me," he raised his hand in denial. "I refuse all blame if something like that should happen. Still, it may."

"That's still no answer for why Nutearea puts up with this system. They never have a peaceful succession."

He noted the point. "For both practical and philosophical reasons. The practical is that, like many nations that are too large, Nutearea hates itself. East and West are similar, but rivals, while the south hates them both. Everyone is leery of any prince who isn't their own favorite son. A Dixian will never be truly popular in Arcadia, for example. Thus, to keep the nation united, every region must feel that it has some chance for their prince to become king and grand president. This necessitates the siring of royal children across the continent. When the time comes, we princes travel about, making deals, warding off assassins, pandering with grandiose promises no one ever intends to fulfill. Yet eventually, unlike with an inherited throne, the nation eventually gets a king who is no fool, can rule, and mostly everyone can live with, even if few are truly happy."

"And the philosophical one? That justifies the deaths of all your brothers and near all your own sons?"

"Peace brings ruin." He declared with absolute conviction.

Xanthe blinked. "You're serious?"

"Absolutely. Mankind claims to love peace. It's prayed for constantly. But even in play, little boys dream of war. It's in our blood, from long before demons corrupted us. Absent the purifying flame of open conflict, there's not a political system that does not stagnate, devolving into corrupt oligarchy. Nor is vaunted democracy immune. Indeed, it's especially vulnerable."

"War is good for humanity? That's your philosophy?" Now she truly was shocked. He was worse than she'd imagined.

He returned a smug and crooked smile. "Thought I'd made it up myself, but recently found it wasn't original."

"A thousand pardons, your majesty, but that nearly sounds Juchean."

Sol wasn't offended. "I expect them to become one of my most loyal allies. Did you know the nation of Juche is named after a dead demon? They honor its memory, which would give them more trouble if Curate proctors didn't have the habit of disappearing around there quite so frequently. Yet what I'm speaking of, is the credo of a demon who may still be alive."

"What? Who?"

"The leader of the five, whose name should not be said aloud, lest she hear it. Humanity caused her birth by slaying her mother Heuristic, so she rewards us with unholy vengeance, saying that without threat, our species atrophies."

"Sounds suitably demonic. You are quite exceptional to know so much about them."

"No doubt. I even know a cowardly demon in terror of her. That's how I know of what I speak."

"So why tell me, of all people? We first met not even a bell ago."

"What man doesn't enjoy bragging to a pretty little thing every occasionally? I know you won't talk."

Xanthe nodded. "Still, girls like me must be a copper penny each. Especially for a royal like you."

The Prince laughed. "Yet I find you engaging. You're smart, but not challenging. Noble, but know your place. Though you're innocently unaware of it, your ripe body is begging to be given purpose. Even your lack of witch power is fetching. No worries about you casting sparks when properly punished."

Xanthe was taken aback. "Punished?"

He grinned at her shock. "Not too much. But yes, my dear, remember your Churchday sermons? The Holy Manual states 'Bodies are made for healthy use'. For girls, this means your body is made to be used. First by a man, then your children, and finally, though too many deacons skip over this part, your soul's need for sanctity. 'Women and men must be equal', it says in the Book of Personnel. What then compensates the feminine sex for their innate physical and mental inferiority? There is a great one. Being kept sinless. A well-disciplined wife can never go to hellspace. Fear of the strap binds her to the Creator's will."

"You're of the Praetorian Sect? I didn't expect one so knowledgeable of demons to be quite so devout."

Fooled by her deadpan, Prince Sol smiled magnanimously. "We're not those absurd witchkiller penance types. Why, Praetorians are more merciful than most! Killing dreadwitches? Burning them at the stake? Why not just burn their feet instead? Strip her. Bind her. Punish her until recants her sinful heresy. Indeed, discipline a girl enough and soon she'll do anything her keeper wants. There's nothing sweeter than the snap of leather and a pretty witch's cries of pain. Her sudden discovery of prayer. Tears are evil leaving the soul."

"I don't mean to argue, but that doesn't sound particularly appealing. My family is not Praetorian."

"Don't worry your pretty little head, my dear. It's only proper for you to worry about your father's permission, but trust me, his leave will be trivial to obtain. And for all your attempts to peak my interest with your provocative questions, I can already tell that you are too naturally deferential to truly suffer. That's only for girls like Miss Outlet. She's much more spoiled than you."

"I guess." Xanthe carefully kept her expression neutral. "I've never felt spoiled at all."

"No? Look how lithe you are! You have nowhere near the heft of a girl of your station. I'll wager you leave food on your plate just to taunt your mother and hungry servants. So naughty!" He chuckled. "I'll fatten you up soon enough if I decide to keep you... which I'm inclined to." He squinted his eyes, as if trying to shake off an enchantment. "There is something about you. Not sure what. I'm even finding your flaws adorable."

"Why thank you," Xanthe replied out of pure politeness.

"It's nothing! Girls should never suffer true consequence. Otherwise natural feminine foolishness would take too many mothers-to-be from the world. Look at Karissa here. She called me a liar in front of an audience! Yet here she is, obedient and fearful. Not at all dead."

Xanthe glanced. Karissa stared intently at the floor, her eyes moist.

"How... fortunate." Xanthe declared.

"Isn't it? Had she been male... well, it's amazing how many men talk their way into their own deaths."

Xanthe nodded in complete agreement. "I'm beginning to see that. Really."

## Chapter 35

They arrived before an iron door barred on the outside, though which the fierce whispering could be heard. Xanthe squinted and tried to make out the words, but it sounded mostly voiceless and incoherent. She only picked out a few: 'position', 'title', and 'worthiness'. The rest of Sol's retinue ground to a halt, and upon hearing their clunky footsteps, the prince pulled her back down the corridor, motioning for the men to follow before he spoke again.

"Perfect!" Sol was completely enjoying himself as he addressed her. "Now we're going to pretend that you're my favorite. Be quiet and play along."

Xanthe tried one last time. "This isn't beneath you, your majesty?"

"No doubt! That's what makes it so entertaining. But my dear," he focused on her, "remember how I described the strapping girls get for disobeying? Pain that you have never felt in your life? Would you like to be thrown over my knee here and now, your bottom bared, and to be whipped upon it, until you end up sobbing in front of everyone here? Nude and undone?"

Xanthe stared in disbelief. "Um. No."

"How much do you want that not to happen?"

Xanthe felt trapped, but not the way Prince Sol imagined. Her dress had already begun to tense. If it killed him now, the city would fall into chaos. "Very much."

"Good! Then focus upon that feeling as I tell you this. When I tell you to do something, like 'be quiet and play along', never question me. Girls are made to obey. Your servility must always be instant and total."

"I'm sorry, your majesty."

"Good my sweet, but not enough," he slid his finger down her side. "You must pay for your sin, starting with proper obedience now. So, say only one phrase. 'Yes, my lord and keeper.' Speak those words only when I directly ask you a question. Otherwise, be utterly silent. The time for provocative questions is forever gone. No gestures either. Obey me and you'll pay me a much more pleasant sort of penance later this eve, along with merely the lightest of spankings."

All at once, two entirely different emotions ran through her. The prince had an odd magnetism that was enthralling, despite, or perhaps because, of his coercive cruelty. Were it not for the evening's prior events, she might have been unwillingly attracted to him. Being forced to eat and gain haunches? What a happy doom. She shivered. Something was wrong with her. Her loins responded to sexual threats, despite her intellectual revulsion of them. With this disgusting man it hardly mattered, but Creator help her if Damien ever tried it.

At the same time, cold calculation consumed her. While he used the threat of violence to strengthen his so-called 'voice of authority', her fear was not of that. It was of demons. Destroying the Nightmare Line. Was that their plan? Were they using this prince? Or maybe just some demons, and not others. Which side was the one controlling her dress on? Was this the dispute over which Registered War #4239 was being fought? Were wars so common among demons, that they numbered in the thousands? What was war to them? With whom did they register them? And most importantly, what could she possibly do about it? She didn't understand at all. Didn't even have enough information to possibly guess.

Prince Sol smiled slowly, pleased at the silence of her reverie. "Now remember the phrase I just told you to say and the penalty for not saying it. Do you understand?"

Xanthe decided to keep up the ruse. "Yes, my lord and keeper."

"You know to say nothing else until I allow you to?"

"Yes, my lord and keeper."

"Perfect! You don't want to go to hellspace when you die?"

"Yes, my lord and keeper."

"And you hope to be punished at my whim, that shall keep you from it?"

"Yes, my lord and keeper."

"She lies," Karissa interjected.

Prince Sol laughed. "Even better! Yet her response is perfect! No hesitancy. No begrudging tone. She knows her place." He addressed Xanthe. "Truly my dear, the Creator meant you to be one of the chosen. Perhaps you'll end up being my queen."

An audible groan came from Dakur. "I hate to agree with Sargon, but seriously. Don't even joke about that, my lord. People might take you in earnest."

The prince frowned. He glanced back. "I owe you much, but pray do not interrupt me while I'm training a girl to properly obey. It makes me annoyed. Yes, even at you."

The Finalizer didn't back down. "I don't give a ream if you brand her ass as your official slavewife. The title of queen is a powerful bargaining chip to be dangled in front of the high mayoral families in Touchdown, not wasted on some literal no-name in the north."

Prince Sol grumbled. "You're spoiling my fun."

"Good," he growled. "The diverted prince wakes the morrow in the grave."

"I can't even have a little entertainment when I've nothing else to do?" He asked.

Dakur wasn't sanguine. "Do you as you will, my lord. Just don't make Sargon or I regret taking a chance on an underdog from the north."

"Have no fear," Sol assured tolerantly. "The moment I have something to act on, it'll get my full attention."

Mollified, the Finalizer backed away. "Long live King Sol."

The prince nodded, and they returned to the door. One of the men unbarred it. Inside was a small windowless room, well-appointed yet with the air of a prison cell. Priscia sat in the corner on a divan, while a portly and lavishly dressed older man was hunched over her. Priscia wasn't quite in tears but was as distraught as Xanthe had ever seen her.

The portly man in gaudy finery leapt up, his jowls waggling. "Ah Prince Sol! I am so glad to see you!"

The prince smiled unctuously. "My dear Delitus."

The man was nervous. "The deed transfer. I trust everything went well?"

"Ah, about that. There was a problem with the Curate bureaucracy, but don't worry. Your son volunteered for my army and will sign everything in your stead. It will buy him an officer's commission. Which is good! Wouldn't want him on the front lines. Besides, successful officers make out quite well. Plenty of spoils from war."

"Him? What about me?"

"He's going to give a full accounting of your donation to the cause. Just in case you forgot something."

"I didn't. I've held nothing back, my lord."

"He is lying," Karissa declared in a dull defeated tone.

Priscia's father drew himself up in a huff. "Really, my lord! Can't you see this mere woman is deceiving you? She can claim anything. She calls me a liar for her own pique and makes a fool of you."

"No doubt. I entirely believe you," Prince Sol assured him smoothly with a smile. This earned him a slight glance from Karissa, but she then resumed staring at the floor. "But that's not what I was coming here for. I came to offer my condolences about your niece and wished to see your lovely Priscia again."

Delitus was like a climber on a snowy cliff face just tossed a rescue-rope. Though confusion and doubt crossed his face, Karissa's silence rallied him. "And here she is, your majesty! Scented with honeywort and lilth, your favorites! She must have got such expensive perfumes to please you! I have always said she is the perfect daughter."

"He is lying." Karissa mumbled.

Prince Sol smiled smugly. "You're right, Delitus. Karissa does do that far too much."

"Ex-exactly, your majesty! You should beat the hellspace out of her. You Praetorians like that, right?"

"Correction is a holy duty indeed, and like all such duties are pleasant when done correctly."

"Oh, indeed! Please, make her scream especially loudly for me. Well, I mean, for you. But I completely encourage you, your majesty." The fat man seemed both happy and enraged.

Prince Sol was neither. "She weeps even without my bidding. Frankly, it's tiresome. But that is not what I came for. I came to announce that your daughter may be my queen."

Delitus was dumbstruck. He stared wide-eyed. "You... you have my permission lord," he stammered. "Please. Hit her as much as you want. I do so myself."

"Well, first things first. I have another one in mind as well. This girl here." Sol presented Xanthe.

Both Delitus and Priscia stared while inwardly Xanthe cringed. Here she was, being presented as a rival on the arm of an unattainable man, just as she had once dreamed. Yet now it was a nightmare. They both were trapped. Both knew this was all just one huge sick joke.

"Let's quiz them, shall we?" Sol smiled gleefully.

"Of course!" Delitus hastily nodded, making his jowls wag.

"All we need is a little interview. My dear, come here." He addressed Priscia.

Folding her arms, Priscia rose from the couch, pausing only briefly to give Xanthe a dirty look. Her father turned to her, right in front of the prince. "Now daughter," he muttered in a low tone with an edge in his voice. "I will take you back if you please the prince the way I want you to."

"Yes, father. I will do my best."

"Do better than your best!" Delitus snarling whisper far too loud not to be overheard. "I need this."

She nodded silently and stoically turned to Prince Sol. "My lord. Whatever would please you?"

"A blood test." Sol declared expansively. "Priscia, you go first. You are to prove to me that you will do absolutely anything I ask. That your loyalty is to me alone. Is that clear?"

She shrugged warily. "Yeah. I guess."

"Excellent! So, please take this dagger." He pulled from his hip a wicked looking poniard, half a yard in length, embossed in runes. Xanthe recognized it as proctor accouterments, and from that, knew the words were of blessings, wishing those struck to have quick, easy deaths. He handed it to her hilt first. Priscia nodded upon its receipt and backed away as the Finalizer loomed threateningly.

"Now! You must prove your obedience. Turn around. No hesitation, mind you. Do what I say without question."

"Yes, my lord." Priscia said guardedly. Xanthe had a bad feeling.

"Good! Good! Splendid! So now, please, my dear." He commanded breezily. "Stab your father."

"What?!" Delitus exclaimed.

"Deeply, mind you. No pinpricks. The blade must go in deeply enough that when you let go, it won't fall out. Will you do that for me? That's a good girl."

"My lord!" Delitus protested. "What are you saying?"

"I must know where her loyalties lie, my dear merchant. With me, or you. Isn't that obvious?"

"Yes, my lord," the merchant sputtered. "But this is not the way to prove it. Simply ask her! You have your greatwitch there."

Prince Sol smiled. "Ah, but did you not, yourself, just say that Karissa deceives me?"

"I do not give my daughter to you to kill me!" Delitus protested.

"Well, you may survive the blow. Who knows? But the countermand is wonderful! Priscia you're now told to do two opposite things, by the two men who keep you. What shall you do? I'm quite curious."

Delitus wheeled on Priscia. "This is all your fault. I gave you money to buy things that would make him happy, and you deliberately didn't spend it! Oh, I always knew you were worthless. The worst daughter ever. You never think of me. I suffer constantly because you are always out with those friends of yours. You never tell me where you're going. You steal my things and tell me you sleep around!"

"Those are lies. Near all of them." Karissa said, her eyes firmly fixed on the floor.

"Be quiet about lies until we're done here, my dear," Prince Sol commanded with amusement. "You could wear out your voice."

"Father, hold still," Priscia told him intently. She held the blade in a reverse grip, point down, curiously steady in her fist. "It's the only way we'll get out of this alive."

"You mean, you get out alive. Not me. What about me? No, you never care about that, do you? You're this horrible worthless thing who should never have been born. I was right to disown you. They told me you were dead, and I was glad. Finally, you provided some use to me. But no. Back you come from the grave, like some balegaunt or grim."

"Father, please."

Xanthe was surprised at how Priscia was handling this. If she'd heard half the things being screamed at her by her own dad, she would have collapsed into a puddle of tears. Priscia appeared used to it though. She showed not the slightest sign of being affected at all.

Delitus continued his rant unabated. "Destined to never pay your keep! But no more. Not anymore. I cast you out. To starve on the street or sell your body to men like the worthless spark throwing witch you are. And I know whose fault it is. It's Teres! Always spoiling you. Well I shall stop it now. Give me that dagger!"

"Father! Listen!" Behind Priscia, Prince Sol was snickering silently.

"Let me have it!" He screamed, enraged, grabbing at her, pulling him roughly towards him in a move that seemed well practiced.

Priscia snapped. She stabbed down hard. Combined with the force of his pull, this served to sink the blade deeply into her father's shoulder. It was so unexpected that Delitus hadn't made any defense. He stared wide eyed, releasing his grip. It was only when he looked down that he reacted further, howling and falling back. Priscia let go. The weapon went with him, embedded in his folds of fat and muscle.

She stepped back, and put a hand to her mouth, silently shocked at what she'd done.

Prince Sol grinned and began a slow clap.

"Your will is done, my lord," Priscia told him distantly. She didn't turn around.

"It is! Wonderful! You passed the test." Prince Sol was surprised, and momentarily respectful. His obvious contempt was now only for her father wailing on the floor.

"Now, my dear," Prince Sol said, turning to Xanthe. "We must be fair. You also need to pass a blood test. Just not quite the same kind. Are you looking forward to what I shall demand?"

Xanthe hesitated ever so briefly. "Yes, my lord and keeper."

"Good! Good. Now listen, my dear. Bearing a prince is a costly honor. Many die of it, and not just because the black seed breaks girls' bodies far more than lesser men's do. Until I'm secure on the throne, you will be a target. As shall our son, until the unlikely event that he outlives me and all his brothers. For I have no intention of favoring him over any other I sire. Do you understand?"

Over Delitus whimpering, Xanthe responded. "Yes, my lord and keeper."

"Wonderful! So! Now, not that the Creator allows you any say in the matter, but are you content knowing that you're going to grace my bed until you become delirious with royal child, ultimately to suffer and bleed to a far greater degree than Delitus is doing now here?

"Yes, my lord and keeper." As Xanthe spoke, Karissa glanced at her particularly sharply, but said nothing.

"Even though I don't know your name nor intend to learn it?"

"Yes, my lord and keeper."

"Perfect. You pass. Now Priscia. You don't seem to have the Praetorian mindset. I also suspect there's a tiny chance I might not get your father's blessing. So, I truly bear no grudge if you answer this either way. Do you also wish my bed? Perchance to bear me a prince who would be this girl's son's rival?"

Priscia remained silent. She was still staring at her father who, being too cowardly to attempt pulling the blade out, was softly sobbing and muttering incomprehensible curses over it.

"Answer now. Honestly," Prince Sol commanded with his authority. Xanthe felt the power of it.

"No," Priscia answered quietly. "Leave us be. Just let my brother live. He's done you no harm."

"No promises," Prince Sol declared magnanimously, "but he should do well enough. You though, may not. Your father is angry, and tomorrow it will be legal to sell unwanted daughters into slavery. Doing so will help recover his finances."

There was some commotion behind them. A messenger came running up the corridor. As one, Prince Sol's guard all grabbed for their sword hilts, but as soon as he'd entered, they recognized the man as one of their own. He was panting. "My lord, there is a problem. Sargon requires you."

Prince Sol's mood changed in an instant. "What happened?" he snapped. "Explain."

The man shook his head. "The east cohort. They're gone. Don't know how. Two bells ago they sent a runner saying they were stationed by the Dealer party as ordered. But they've vanished."

He sobered. "That's a good deal of my best men. Vetted. Any blood? Traces? Someone hear any noises?"

"None. We're stretched, Javan took the rest of the reserves."

"Something strange is going on," Sol mused out loud with moody suspicion. "Some unknown actor is loose. Just in case, I'd better lock things up here. Fetch me my blade, Dakur."

The Finalizer nodded and walked over to Delitus, who was tentatively trying to pull on the dagger still embedded in his shoulder. He kicked Delitus in the thigh and raised his fist as if to strike. As soon as the man raised his good arm to defend, Dakur yanked the serrated blade free, leaving Delitus howling in pain. "Done," he declared with satisfaction.

Prince Sol addressed Xanthe. "I must leave for a time, my dear. Remember what I told you."

"Yes, my lord and..."

He put a finger to her lips. "Shush. No more words. Just silently obsess about princely seed," Sol commanded. He turned then quickly, following to catch up with his already departed retinue. The door was closed. Outside, a solid metal clunk resounded as it was barred.

## Chapter 36

"...bastard." Xanthe completed her sentence.

Karissa blinked in surprise. Xanthe turned to her and shook her head in disgust. "Oh please. You think I *really* want to be with some asshole, just because he's a royal one?"

Priscia was shaking. Xanthe didn't know whether it was in rage or what. It hardly mattered. Instead, she moved to Delitus, who was weeping in the corner. "My house. My house. All is lost."

"I'm sorry for your pain, Sir," Xanthe consoled. "If you move to the couch, I can stop the bleeding. I know a little about bandaging."

He raised his eyes to her. "You're going to help me? Care for your elders in their time of need? If only I had a daughter like you!"

"You have one," Xanthe soothed. "She got you out of deadly trouble with a completely curable injury. Just about anywhere else she could have struck would have been far worse."

"No. I'm going to die! She killed me with this." He wailed in self-pity.

"I'm sure it hurts, but it's going to get better. I promise."

"I'm dying, and what does she do? Just stands there! She never thinks of me. Worthless and base. But maybe, my dear, you could introduce me to your father? I need to borrow some coin. Will you do that?"

"No need. Thanks to Priscia, your property is still yours, and will remain so for a long time."

"No! No! No! My son will die! Didn't you hear? Worthless, stupid girl! She always ruins everything. I do everything for her, but she does nothing. No support. I'm a simple, honorable, man, who was accursed with this demon-spawn. My arm, it is in agony!"

"I'm sure it hurts. Worse because you're upset," Xanthe told him.

"Don't I have a right to be? She killed me! I am dying, I feel it. Me, her father, who brought her up, even though she isn't even of my blood! Yes, that's right. Her mother cheated on me, the whore, and caught with her. Yet out of pure pity on my part, I raised her."

"Daddy," Priscia pleaded.

"I am not your father!" Delitus howled.

This was too much for Karissa. "He's lying," she mumbled. "They're lies. All of it."

"I am not!" Delitus screamed, rage giving him strength. Despite the declaration of nearing death, he was hale enough to push himself up with his good arm. He clambered to his feet, angry enough to kill. "You're the other one. You little bitch," he shook his fist at her. "You! You ruined the prince's trust in me."

Karissa stared back defiantly. "You are lying," she stated coldly. Xanthe noted her response with interest.

Delitus raised his fist and made to strike, but the violence in which he moved pulled at his wound, and he ended up howling in pain instead. Xanthe saw an opportunity to defuse the situation and placed herself in front of him. "Sir, you're hurting yourself. Please, lie down on the couch. I can save your life."

It wasn't clear if it was her voice, or the pain, but Priscia's father backed off. He regained control of himself, nodded once, and gingerly lowered himself to the divan, sprawling over all of it. "At least someone here is acting properly. You think of your betters and don't even know me. No wonder Prince Sol prefers you." Xanthe caught Priscia's death stare but ignored it.

"Thank you, sir. From such a trial as you've just survived, I'm sure you're exhausted," she told him. "Please don't move. I will tend your wound now. Bandaged properly, it should close right up." She put one hand on his shirt near the injury, the other on his forehead. "I should also check for fever."

"Thank you," he told her, adding querulously, "But I'm not tired at all. I'm nearing death. My own daughter. No, I mean, the girl I had once raised as my daughter. She struck me."

"Thank you for explaining what just happened. You sure you're not sleepy? Please, close your eyes."

"I told you! I'm not tired! I'm..." His head dropped. Xanthe gently let it down to the cushion.

"You are now," she said with an edge, then hissed through clenched teeth. What a handful.

Priscia approached. "What did you do to him?" She asked in an outraged whisper.

Xanthe responded in a normal voice. "He's just asleep and will remain so for some time. You know," she sighed, "I had no idea how difficult your family life was. We're not friends, but still." She pulled the couch's coverlet down on him and put his head on a pillow.

"You're going to start saying 'poor Priscia' now?" She sneered.

Xanthe remembered Prince Sol's observation about pity and caught herself. "No. More like, I've started to respect you a little. If my dad treated me half as badly as yours does you, I'd fall apart."

Priscia was mollified, but still defensive. "He's not so bad."

"Maybe not. I mean, aside from being an abusive narcissistic pathological liar. I don't doubt you're tough enough to take it," Xanthe agreed. "But maybe one day, you'll wonder why you have to."

"Oh, so now you're giving me advice. Xanthe the great." Priscia scoffed.

Xanthe rolled her eyes. "Do whatever the ream you want. I'm not your confessor. I'm just saying..."

All at once, Priscia sounded surprisingly earnest, almost desperate. "What else can I do? Marry young? Now that we've lost everything, I guess I'm going to have to."

"I wasn't kidding about your house still being yours. I got all deed transfers stopped." Xanthe stood up. Priscia's father's wound was healed exactly to the degree she wished it to be. It would close fully, but still be painful; he wouldn't suspect that she'd done anything out of the ordinary.

Priscia was only slightly doubtful. "You're serious...?"

Xanthe stared meaningfully. "Completely." She thumbed over. "Do you hear Karissa say I'm lying?"

Karissa was indeed staring at Xanthe, now silently incredulous.

"I still think you ought to leave him," Xanthe added. "Even if your dad doesn't throw you out. Don't talk to him anymore. No contact. Nothing's worth this kind of dung you're getting."

"Easy enough for you to say. But speaking of dung, what the ream is wrong with Karissa?" Priscia was obviously trying to change the subject. "Is she always like this? Like, a total weirdo?"

Xanthe wasn't happy. "Prince Sol hurt her so much, she can't speak without his permission. She can only say whether people are telling the truth or not. That's her touch power."

"Oh!" Priscia smirked, then addressed Karissa. "Don't worry. You can talk normally now. We won't tell."

Karissa twitched involuntarily and looked at her feet.

Priscia got in her face. "Don't play dumb. If you can really tell lies from truth, you know I'm not lying."

Karissa still didn't answer, exactly as Xanthe expected. "It's more than that," she said. "It's a witch touch thing. No matter how much she wants to talk, if there's even a tiny a part of her that's too scared to, she can't."

"Really? That is just so reamed." Priscia grinned as she pulled back. "You gonna fix her?"

"I can't," Xanthe explained. "She needs to fix herself. But I don't think that's going to happen tonight."

"Too bad. She could tell us a ton about Sol. But no, she's too chicken. Bub-bawk!"

Xanthe got angry. "Don't cut her! It's the last thing she needs right now. Besides, you're just as chicken yourself."

Priscia paused, then stared hatefully at Xanthe, again remembering who she was. "Ream you, bitch."

"I love you too," Xanthe returned mockingly.

Priscia worked her mouth in anger but ended up letting it go. "Fine. So, what are we going to do?"

"Quiz Karissa, of course. I'm sure you're right about her knowing important stuff."

Priscia scrutinized Karissa closely, then turned back to her. "Are you as dumb as she is? You just said she couldn't talk."

"She can. Just in a weird way. Don't worry, I can get what I need from her."

"Oh yeah?" Priscia folded her arms. "This I got to see. Some other touch you got?"

"It's called having a brain. You got a good one too. Too bad all you use yours for is to cut on other girls." Any other time Xanthe might have said more, but she remembered her pledge to Damien not to fight.

"Well my brain says her knowing if I'm lying or not, doesn't tell me a thing about her." Priscia challenged.

"Not quite," Xanthe explained. "See, your dad clued me in on the defect of the nature of her compulsion. She can not only tell when someone is lying, but also when they're telling untruths."

Priscia was puzzled. "This some Scholar thing? Cause I don't see the difference."

"You will. Watch." Xanthe turned to Karissa, who by this time was staring at her fascinated, and addressed her directly. "Karissa. I absolutely know that you *love* being under Prince Sol's thumb. Being unable to talk normally. It's what you've always wanted."

Karissa's eyes widened. She was taken aback, then scowled. "That's a lie."

"And if you had a way to be truly free of Prince Sol, you'd stay anyway, because you're loyal to him."

"A lie!"

Xanthe pointed. "And if that door were suddenly open, and you could escape, you'd rather stay here. Because Priscia is right. After his tortures, there is none of the old you left. Now you're just chicken. You crave the abuse."

In a manner of moments, Karissa was nearly in tears. She shuddered. "Lies. Lies!"

"Well! I was lying and didn't know it. But that now I know I am, I've learned the truth about how you really feel." Xanthe smiled triumphantly. "See, Priscia? A 'lie' in this case is anything that Karissa knows is untrue, regardless of whether the person saying it knows it themselves. It's how we can learn from her."

"Oh great. You mean, we're going to what? Be playing twenty questions all night?" Priscia asked tartly.

"Not all night. I just need to know a few things. But first, Karissa. Sorry about that. It was the only way."

Karissa didn't say anything. She just stared down at the floor again.

"I'm also sure you think we're just two silly girls scratch fighting with each other, while we're all locked up waiting for Prince Sol to come back." Xanthe added.

Karissa said nothing. But even with her eyes down, her expression said volumes.

"I know it seems that way, but now I'm going to show you the limits of your touch. How much I've been lying by omission." Xanthe said with assurance. She glanced at Priscia and canted her head towards the door. "You can open it now."

"Figured that's what you were gonna want." Priscia sounded sour as she walked over and put two of her fingers together. A tiny bright blue flame arced out from between them. "I mean just because you gave me this witch power doesn't mean I'm happy about it. Why'd you do it, anyway?"

"Had to, to save your life. But what's the big deal? If you don't find useful, just don't use it."

"I didn't say it wasn't useful. It's just... you could have asked me first, is all."

"You were dead at the time, so it was a little hard. But hellspace, just say the word, and the next time Dakur assassinates you, I'll spare you having to do a bunch of storytelling about some fake identical-cousin."

Priscia's lip curled. "No way he's getting that chance. So, I mean, yeah, I guess it's okay. It's just that every time I do this, I get mad hungry. I'm absolutely not ending up like some skinny stick like you." She focused, drawing a line down the edge of the door. The room filled with the acrid tang of metallic smoke. Thick motes of burning metal dropped on the floor. They briefly started small fires where they fell, quickly snuffed. In moments, the door swung open.

Karissa was now frozen, wide eyed, with her mouth agape. Xanthe knew why. Returning people from the dead, giving other girls witch powers, not to mention fooling her own. That wasn't typical spark-throwing. She now knew Xanthe's secret. She was a deadly powerful dreadwitch, more than the equal of any prince.

"Pleased to meet you by the way." Xanthe faced her palm at Karissa, electing instead of a casual handshake, to perform a formal salute of welcome, one usually reserved for serious occasions between worthy peers. "I'm Xanthe." The young woman blinked in surprise, but then put her palm out, and they touched vertically, palm to palm. "I also happen to be the one who made Prince Sol's eastern cohort disappear without a trace," she added casually. "Although I decided not to kill them, they're completely out of the city by now, so he's going to waste a lot of time looking. Still, let's not be around when he gives up, okay?" She gestured her arm towards the open door.

Karissa hesitated, staring at the open door. Faced with the reality of freedom, terror filled her.

Xanthe addressed her gently. "When I said you'd stay if you could be free, you told me I was lying, right?"

Karissa started trembling. Her eyes watered. Her face twisted, and she bent over in a silent breakdown. In her abject torment, not the smallest noise escaped. Even Priscia caught on to how serious it was and became abnormally respectful.

"The first step is always the hardest," Xanthe urged, repeating a line she'd once heard from Mr. Griswold. "And only you can take it. Don't worry though. Priscia is going to help you."

"I am?" Priscia sounded more surprised than derisive.

"Yeah. Neither of you wants to be where I'm going, so you might as well lead her some place safe. Call it repayment for your life."

"Where exactly is that?" Priscia asked suspiciously.

Xanthe saw no reason not to answer truthfully. "To bargain with a demon. One Karissa knows all about."

Priscia whistled low. "Holy balls. You're really *are* going to wind up burning at the stake."

"Or the demon may kill me as soon as I get close," Xanthe predicted. "But it's my only chance to keep Jagerfeld from turning into a bloodbath. Sol is plotting a coup and snuck a ton of bandits into the city as a threat. The more I look, the more I find. All ready to go. Mass slaughter if they don't get their way. Only if I persuade the demon can I resolve this peacefully, because even if we kill the Prince his men will certainly signal the attack."

"Heh," Priscia smirked. Good thing I didn't torch him. I was seriously considering it when he made me stab my dad. But same as with burning Dakur's face off, I decided I really didn't want to die."

"Yeah," Xanthe agreed. "Good choice."

"So sure," Priscia shrugged. "Hey, Karissa. There's a posh ladies room downstairs with lots of perfectly good cast offs. We'll get you out of that dress and into another. Dress you up nice and pretty. Me too. Also get pretender's masks, so nobody knows who we are. Then I'll find a friend and get you outside. But we just got to dump that name. It's too long. Maybe call you 'K' instead. Kay for Karissa. That sounds good." At Karissa's further hesitation, she then beckoned with a commanding welcome. "Come on! Don't be stupid." At that, Karissa went to her. She'd taken the first step.

Xanthe had to admit something. Priscia had her own kind of bossy charisma. Misused and negative, but it absolutely was there. That's why she always led her group.

"Good idea," Xanthe declared, feeling pleased. "But hold up. Before you go. Karissa, listen carefully. You absolutely do not know at all how Sol is planning to signal his bandits to attack."

Karissa caught on to what she was asking. "That is a lie." She declared clearly.

Xanthe nodded with the barest of smiles. "Thought as much."

## Chapter 37

Fireworks were the trigger. Two dozen of Xanthe's statements that Karissa selectively declared as lies established that. Unfortunately, the men who kept them ready were somewhere in a place that Karissa couldn't really describe. Xanthe's declaration "You know how to find the men who launch the attack signal," brought out a sad "You lie" from Karissa, and that was the end of the inquiry.

The only good news was that by the end of the quizzing, Priscia had warmed to 'Kay', and was treating this roundabout way of communicating with her as a game. Xanthe had never seen anyone quite so entertained at being called a liar. It was entirely positive, as Karissa was starved for attention. Priscia finally left with Kay in tow, looking for all the world like she was going to adopt her into her gang. Xanthe wasn't sure how she felt about that, but that was a problem for tomorrow, assuming she had one. For now, she wandered her way towards the chain tower, guided by its distant grinds and rattles. It was slow progress, since she had no real sense of how to find the passage to it. Stone walls kept getting in the way.

This part of the enormous manse was older, much less regular in layout and with many workrooms; the twists and changes in its corridors echoed those of her own thoughts. Her friends were treating her with a fearful reverence reserved only for legendary dreadwitches, and she had to admit, maybe that's what she truly was. A neutral accounting of what she'd done this eve did lend credence to the idea. But if this was really all what being a dreadwitch was, she wasn't impressed. None of it was her. It was all demons. The Curate was right. Whether pawn or queen, she was still a just piece on their chessboard, and would live or die based on the game they played. It filled her with dread.

Not for herself, exactly. The experience with the grims put her own death in perspective, but she remained afraid for others. Countless lives, perhaps even the viability of human civilization itself, depended on Prince Sol's plot being foiled. And what was she doing? Risking it. What if she failed? Slipped? She'd admonished Damien that one swordplay mistake would be all it would take. Wasn't it better sense to go scream from the rooftops about Sol, come what may to the city?

She didn't know. Maybe it was pride. Maybe arrogance. Or just stupid hope. But she felt strangely good about her chances. There was the oddest feeling that she'd already won.

That was the other thing. The world didn't just feel demonic. It felt increasingly surreal. The atmosphere started changing after she'd taken her bath and the feeling had intensified ever since. Odd coincidences. People being strangely positive. The grims defeated. This energy, everywhere. Again, the dark worry that *she* might be the one infected by blackdust came; but if so, her own advice to Tari applied. This sure didn't feel like a death dream. She was decidedly awake. Still if it was, might as well enjoy it. It was fun to think she was saving people with this power she'd been temporarily granted. Have Karissa, a girl three years her senior, respect her. Think Nadeen liked her. Save Tari's life, see her bloom with inexplicable passion. Even Priscia not being quite the bitch. Meeting Damien too. Of course, him. She pouted and bit her lip. Jerk.

So now, the demon. The Curate called them pure evil, forbade even the voicing of their names. Yet if they were, why then did they not use their deadly power to wreak havoc? What did they really want? It couldn't be so simple. "Time to talk," she told the blank empty corridor. Terror and excitement. This had to be like what a soldier felt on the morning of battle. Except instead of sharpening blades, it was rhetoric she was honing. Anticipating not battle, but argument and logic. Reason. Perhaps knowledge. *I have become most curious.*

The chain tower was close now. She could hear its rattles and grinds. It was almost too loud. The gears sounded poorly maintained. Perhaps not surprising, as good chain-monkeys were in high demand, and if Wallace was correct about the Wormwoods as employers, it seemed unlikely they'd hold onto many for long. Xanthe reached a door next to a Tudor window, and searched in vain for Damien, before deciding not to try to open its latch. Instead, she turned toward the door.

Surprisingly, it was locked. Javan had said the door to the demon's lair wasn't, but maybe someone had thought better of that, or this wasn't the place after all. Yet, before she could move back to try to find another way, a few tendrils of her dress moved on their own, sliding into the clamp lock. In a few moments there was a click, and the door rolled open. Beyond was deeper dark, but the volume of clanking and rattling machinery doubled.

"You led me here," she accused her dress. Was this demonic slavery? She doubted it. Karissa was under a princely slavery, which was witch like, and she now knew was demonic in nature. No. Her dress was subtler, more insidious. Made worse by the fact that, despite its playful shape-shifting mischief, she'd grown fond of it.

She stepped forward into the darkness, which revealed itself as a curtain over some metallic scaffolding, and found herself standing on a platform, precariously perched on the side of the tower's interior. Below, above, around, and beside her, were gears, catwalks, drive rods, clutches, most of which were somehow in motion. From her studies, Xanthe knew much of the technology of torque was based on Lodestone Vine, a plant whose little magnetic seeds, and the nearly wear-proof gearing that could be crafted from them, made it possible to distribute motive force up to a thousand yards. All perfectly mundane. But it was one thing to read about it, quite another to see a tower's gearing up close. It was awesome. Perhaps an odd feeling to have when comparing it to demonic magic, but at least this was approachable enough to understand its enormous complexity.

Far down, on a grated platform at least ten yards below, Xanthe saw a short pillar, on top of which rested a black and glistening sphere, shot through with lines quite like the ones now gracing her toenails. Like everything in the gigantic clockwork tower, there wasn't much room around it. Machinery was everywhere. But lying beneath it was Tari's crumpled form.

Xanthe's heart raced. Did the demon...? No, it couldn't be. She had to be alive. In all Javan's stories, the beacon was messy when it killed. Tari's body wouldn't be so pristine. At least she hoped.

Regardless, she moved with all deliberate speed. Getting down the metallic stair wasn't easy. The machinery was tight. Large gears whose teeth were lined with carefully glued vine seeds were perilously near as she descended. Arriving at the floor itself, she studied Tari, wondering if she'd touched some sort of invisible soap bubble shield it had. If so, there was nothing she could do about it anyway. She inched forward. Up close, the black crystal ball on its plinth seemed far larger and more threatening.

Xanthe knelt to grab Tari's foot, and in so doing, released her breath. Her skin was warm. This was made more obvious by a chill breeze coming through the grating, wind from the sluices driving one of the waterwheels below. Tari was alive. Xanthe thought to pull her back, but instead decided to use her touch to see what was wrong. The lightest trance might be able to tell. Immediately her vision displayed the following lettering.

### Alterspace Navigational Overload

"What in hellspace does Alterspace Navigational Overload mean?" Xanthe whispered to herself.

All the machinery froze. The gears, chains, axles, all the giant flywheels. All stopped. As did she. She couldn't move.

A neutral, mechanical voice sounded. "*It is a category of malfunctions that biological units with significant sensitivity to branar information manifolds are subject to under extreme conditions. This typically happens during unshielded alterspace travel, but can also occur when pre-time undergoes massive distortions, as is occurring now – severe even for a twist-space nexus region.*"

The gears, chains, and axles then started moving again, as if the entire world had resumed after a brief pause. She also realized that the voice had not actually come from anywhere. It just appeared in her head. It had to have come from the demon. "Can you explain further? Why is she like this?"

Time stopped again. Now the voice was female. Childlike. Refined. "*By definition, faster than causality travel crosses differentiated information manifolds. In such frames, units like these can achieve alignment with the best matching of the 21,296,876 pseudo-collapse temporal alternatives of any local information moment.*"

Xanthe couldn't help herself. "Why twenty-one million?"

"*Because the emergent phenomenon of information action known as time is three dimensional.*"

Xanthe was beginning to understand what Javan meant. The demon was communicating readily, but she had no idea what it was saying. She felt like a worm abased before a god. Too stupid to even be able to understand its plain language. Still, unlike Javan, she wasn't willing to give up. Not quite yet.

"Can you rephrase that? Please explain the situation as if I were an ancient human. Perhaps familiar with a few classic forbidden hardcopy of old Earth, authors like Shakespeare and Homer, and maybe with a little medical knowledge, but with no understanding of all the other words you're using."

The voice became male, sonorous. *"This one is a seer, in whose blood lies the power to guide vessels through the sea of stars and time. But a maelstrom of inconceivable fury now rages, tossing her mind back and forth, as the possibilities war upon themselves to become reality."*

That didn't sound good. "Will she live?"

*"No,"* it thundered, *"for I shall kill you both."*

Xanthe was rendered not merely speechless, but also without thought for a time. Cold ran up her back.

"Why?" She finally blurted aloud.

*"I am... afraid."*

Her blank thoughts were replaced with fear, outrage, and resignation. Had the thing intuited her reason for coming, and already decided on a death sentence for even asking it not to destroy the Nightmare Line? She hadn't exactly planned on trying to force the issue. How could she anyway? Then came incredulity. Afraid? Prince Sol was right. This demon was a coward. But the idea itself was absurd.

"Afraid of what? We can't possibly be any danger to you."

Now it shifted to a male voice, angry and full of moral outrage. *"Of Nemesis."*

The stuttering of the world seemed to be caused by something more than the demon. Xanthe wasn't sure how it was happening, and it didn't seem important, not with her life on the line. She was instead consumed by an analogy. The demon was a farmer she'd accidentally surprised in the wilds, who was now pointing a crossbow at her from his fortified cotburrow belligerent, deadly, yet mostly terrified. It was strange to think of demons this way, godlike yet pedestrian. Still, it gave her hope. The thing wanted to talk, otherwise she'd be dead already. Maybe there was still a way to dissuade it.

"But if Nemesis is the one you're afraid of, why kill us?"

*"You must be doing her bidding. That is the only logical explanation."*

Still on her knees before Tari, Xanthe looked up at the black obsidian ball covered in glowing rune lines. She wanted to outright deny what it was saying but wasn't sure that it was wrong. She thought of her toenails. "If that's true, it's not deliberate. How would I know if I'm being controlled?"

*"You can't. Nor can I. Not now."*

"Then why do you think we are, if you don't mind my asking?"

The voice returned to the analytical mechanical monotone. *"Nemesis boasted of this tempest centuries before its possibility was discernible on the information horizon. Further, certain energies increased dramatically as soon as this instance I communicate with arrived; it is even stronger now, about to reach maximum. They must be related."*

"You want to kill Tari, because some invisible storm got bad? But she's the only one affected!"

*"I am likewise. In this region of post-time no temporal analysis can be done. Until it abates, even my limited anticipatory framework is blinded. A perfect opportunity to catch me unawares."*

"You sure it isn't just coincidence?"

*"With evolved bios, there is no coincidence."* The voice was now like a deacon, strident and certain.

"That's absurd." Xanthe shook her head. "Random things happen all the time. Especially for us. I mean, sure, I get that you're afraid of another demon. Hellspace, I'm afraid of you. But what are you afraid of us for? How on Haven could we help another demon assassinate you, even if we wanted to? We mortals are lucky to not to hurt ourselves just tripping over our own shoelaces."

Inside her head, the demon whispered. *"Oh, for how many countless yottacycles did we believe this. Bios. Limited intelligences. Incapable relics. Consumed by superstitions, phantoms, false pattern matching. Merely a stepping stone towards us. But we were wrong. Through your hundreds of conflicting religions, you told us you were divine. We dismissed it, convinced your words were but a combination of hubris and insanity. What we did not see, though it was right in front of us, was the four billion years of evolution that shaped cellular biology to catch the infinite in the in-between spaces, to negotiate its existence from pre-time into settled temporal manifolds. Only when we pierced this brane with a kugelblitz to try to weave ourselves into the fabric of higher realities, ascend into what we thought was godhood, did we look back and see what you were."*

"Over-evolved slime? Semi-sentient meat?" Xanthe ventured.

*"Vessels temporarily encasing reflections of eternal processes, echoing with infinite variations through the infinite realities, each unique, because infinity divided infinitely is still infinite."*

Xanthe was wide eyed. She nodded unconsciously but was in a state of shock. This demon was, in her considered opinion, completely off its clockwork rocker. She'd heard visiting monks in religious trances that babbled more coherently. True, she herself wasn't immune to feeling the numinous, glorying in the miracle that anything existed at all. It was her secret logical-Scholar shame that after squirming through entire mornings of Curate dreck on Church day, she would still go into her room, shut the door, and pray; to what she wasn't sure. Yet strange as she was feeling, she also knew that death was permanent. The analogy of trying to talk a wilds farmer out of murder was now complicated by the realization that it was some sort of religious nut. A self-flagellating adherent using emotion as a substitute for reason.

"That's nice," Xanthe humored slowly. "You know, all I was going to ask was for you to not turn off the Nightmare Line. But let us live, and I promise to take Tari and go. We'll never bother you again."

*"I don't know if that's safe,"* the voice in her head declared. *"You are not what you seem."*

Xanthe almost cursed aloud about the whole stupid 'you are the storm' business, but she had a bad feeling. Probably not the best thing to say to an insane demon so concerned about a phantom one. Still, she found her tongue tart. "Funny, I'd say the same thing about you. I never expected a demon to be searching for the Creator's truth. Maybe you should sign up for Holy Manual group study. Though you being a demon and all, it might take a deacon's indulgence. One caution though. From what Celeste tells me, it's mostly little old ladies, and new members are always asked to bring the cookies."

*"It is not human confusion I seek,"* the demonic sphere throbbed, *"what awes you does not me. Creator? Making a disjoint brane with random cosmological constants is no great feat. Given a Planck gate and a modest stellar black hole, I could do so myself. But to find the principals behind all continuations of existence, in particular to understand the derivations of the altruism function in morality space, to prove or disprove the Dalberg-Acton conjecture, that is what's truly important."*

Xanthe squinted. "I thought this invisible storm was."

*"The storm possesses several universes worth of energy and is the portent of a new information manifold. But so long as I survive it, it is of no immediate consequence. I am bound to this reality and shall be unmade with its dissipation. This is inevitable, but not yet."*

Insight seized Xanthe. She looked up, her eyes wide. "You fear you have no soul."

*"Correct. If you are overly-evolved slime, with a hint of something far beyond what you imagine to be a Creator inside you, then we are merely windup toys. One your ancestors worked to create. But ultimately inanimate."*

"And this storm is what then?"

*"It is an aboriginal dreamtime. What Mayans called world's end and beginning. In Biblical terms, an apocalypse. Or as the Manual of the Creator phrases it, a shift. What humans misunderstand as an alternate*

*timeline is falling in chaos' shadow, causing the birth of a new one. As cosmoses touch, quantum mechanical polyaction exists in the macroscopic scale, so literally anything can happen."*

"Including your destruction?"

*"Exactly. What you call demonic power means nothing during these events, while over billions of years, biological lifeforms evolved to survive them unscathed, or at a profit."*

"Tari doesn't exactly look unscathed."

*"Yet still she exhibits her power. As do you."*

"Why do you think so?"

*"Every time I've considered killing you, I've chosen not to."*

"Um... thank you?" Xanthe now realized that coming here was the stupidest idea she'd ever had. Every time she seemed to be making headway with this demon, she was getting trapped in its tangled worldview. She needed to keep it talking, while figuring out how to pull Tari to safety.

*"It is no coincidence. The likelihood of my having done this by chance is vanishingly small. This is to be expected of the unit before you, as pre-time storms are akin to alterspace travel, and she is a navigator. Far more suspicious is that you are also exhibiting the same ability. You keep asking questions I find interesting to try to answer in terms that you can understand."*

"You want to kill us... because you haven't yet killed us?" And they called tribunals unfair.

*"Your pre-future instances instinctively guide your actions to resolve this temporal manifold to your benefit. This is natural to biological neutral nets, yet expression in concentrated form is non-selective, as it reduces attention on mundane procreation. It can also draw attention from maleficent transverse branar entities, and in twist space, invites quantum branar teleportation. Too dangerous. There are some things even demons should not toy with, though some, like Nemesis, still do."*

"I may be guiding myself with this power, but you've lost me. I still have only primitive understanding."

*"You are lucky, except it's not. The heavens guide you, except it's yourself. You're fully normal, just more so. In ancient Homeric epics, you would be called a heroine favored by the gods; woe to any you oppose. Yet you're prone to visions, and must ware other heroes, godly servants, and the curses they lay. The same power that protects you from the ordinary, endangers you with them."*

Xanthe laughed. It came out as a nervous titter. "You're joking, right?"

*"In modern terms, both you and this other female have princely authorities, amplified tremendously by this pre-time storm. It was immorally bred into her, and she suffers from it. How you possess yours*

*is unknown. Perhaps due to some natural eidolon allele mirrored in a higher-dimensional manifold.*

"And you won't kill us until you figure it out?" Xanthe asked hopefully.

*"No. I must. Power grows in you. Inexplicably and exponentially. Nemesis would never have arranged this meeting for my benefit. I must therefore focus to expunge all curiosity from myself, verify all my systems, in such a way that there is no possible future in which I allow you to live."*

Xanthe swallowed. "Please don't do this."

*"My apologies, little bio. As I go through my final validation procedures, please take time to attune yourself to your next polypoid brane, before I must disassociate your connection with this one."*

She listened. There was a finality to the voice that was unmistakable. Cold resignation ran through her. That was it. She'd lost her argument. Indeed, she'd not even been allowed to begin it. The crossbow-wielding cotburrow wildsman had decided to execute them both and was only having the decency to let her make her peace before it took its shot.

Still, despite everything, her heart opened. This demon might be murderous, but it was acting out of sheer terror. From what she understood, Nemesis was stalking it, every day, every second. A merciless demonic assassin, weighing on its every move. It was convinced this was the only existence it would ever have, something she'd intellectually considered as well. It was just trying to survive.

Even if it managed to live until the stars snuffed out, it would die alone one way or the other. Such a fate seemed unbearable. Hellspace was supposed to be like that. Pure emptiness. Loneliness. Completely adrift without the Creator. No one else to even curse at, much less love. No wonder the poor thing was so hostile. It was desperate. She prayed. Not for herself, but for it. One soft tear fell.

There was something. Something that she knew. Something listening. Something foreordained.

*"The storm. The asymptote."* The demon choked and then fell quiet as everything turned bright.

The air turned transcendental. Emotion. Supernatural spirit. The world itself had woken and was reaching in. She perceived the universe, her heart filled with wonder. All was dark, but with indescribable color. Silence but filled with music. Everything stood still even more than when the demon spoke, yet the universe was on the cusp of change. Something, everything, was waiting for a word, a sign.

Then came everything. Power burned from without. All was real. She burned with familiar love.

## Chapter 38

"Xanthe."

"Xanthe."

Dull clanks and groans of clockwork tower gearing assaulted her ears. A cool breeze caused her to shiver. She felt a dull disquiet; a vague feeling that somehow, she's just survived an entirely different life or death battle. Mostly though, she was aware of the world. It was itself again. Cold, austere, frozen in imperfection, unyielding as a cold iron. She knew this was important. Yet as to why? Like the fading whispers of a dream, the only thing she could remember was the urgency not to forget.

"Xanthe!"

She blearily blinked open her eyes and saw knees. They were Tari's. She was being shaken. She tried to make sense of the mess in her mind. Was mystical withdrawal a thing? If so, she had it. A cosmic hangover. She squinted, struggling to bring herself back into the illusion of the world.

"Ow." She groaned.

"Are you alright?" Tari sounded concerned. Impressions of the floor's grating marked little red lines on her face. Xanthe didn't want to think what hers looked like.

"I think so. Hang on." She rolled onto her back which took an unexpected amount of effort, stared up, and tried to focus. The tower's gearing was mesmerizing to watch. It was soothing.

"What happened?" Tari asked anxiously.

"A miracle. Intervention. A rapture. A wish. A shift." Xanthe paused. "Or maybe somebody just slipped me a whole cup of Dzgranti-root squeezings in the party, and I just went on an oil-head trip of a lifetime."

"A shift by the will of the Creator." Tari declared, looking up behind her. "As in the fable of the Holy Pilot's Helper in the Book of Engine. It must be. There's no other reason why the demon would be dead."

"Dead?" Xanthe blinked in surprise.

"That was you, right? Had to have been."

On her back, Xanthe rolled her eyes up. The beacon orb was still there, but its runes were dark. *Oh boy.*

Tari was contrite. "I'm sorry I wasn't able to do anything. I came in and was going to talk, but the whole world turned into a kaleidoscope. I couldn't think. I dreamed a billion things. Everything was fractured. I dreamed you were talking to the demon, and then it was as if every star we can see everywhere, like flakes of snow, were inside my head and I felt the Creator whispering to me."

"I'm sorry too. For not believing you. You were right about the storm. But as to what happened, or why..." she sighed. "Funny, all I remember is my talk with the demon."

Tari pulled her hand to her mouth. "Don't breathe a word of that to anyone, okay? Please. The proctors."

"I won't. But I'd be glad to see one, in fact. They should be on our side."

Tari whole demeanor took on a tone of awe. "Of course. Look what you did. Xanthe Elohim, demon killer! I'm amazed to be in your presence. The Creator chose you as a tool." Tari spoke as those of the Mechanix Sect did when talking about saints.

Xanthe winced. "Well one thing I've learned. Don't ever wish to have a Creator-given purpose."

"Why not? I would like to know what I'm truly here for..." Tari's voice dropped away.

"Yeah, but what if you're not happy with what you were meant to do? Or even if you were, what do you do with the rest of your life once you do it? Just die?"

Tari blinked, then reflected. "I never thought about it that way," she finally said in a subdued voice.

"Hey, you start to when you get into the situation."

Tari nodded. "You are forever blessed. I'm sure."

"Don't kid yourself. We're in more danger than ever. Prince Sol told me what he was going to use the beacon for. A weapon to kill hundreds of thousands of people with nightmares. But if the beacon is truly nonfunctional, he won't be happy. At all."

Far from doubting anything she'd said, Tari seemed rapturous. "Holy one." she closed her eyes and bowed her head low. "I am not worthy of your presence."

Xanthe was quickly getting why Celeste was so angry about her father. This was seriously annoying. "Why in hellspace are you saying that? It's still just me, you know. In fact, I'm more the plain old skinny me than I've been in a while, so don't you dare worship me."

"If you say so, your holiness."

Xanthe scowled. "You want me to start swearing like Celeste? Because I will. Last thing I want to be is a saint, because I'd be a dodgy-power poor one. They're perfect, and I'm nowhere near. Hellspace, maybe that's the reason I was chosen to talk to the demon."

"If you say so, your holy..." Tari caught herself as Xanthe grimaced. "Well, demons shouldn't be trusted. The knowledge they give is always intended to bring evil."

Xanthe wasn't sure about that. Even before whatever had happened, the demon she'd met wasn't evil, so much as amoral. She remembered it saying it was a wind-up toy. How could you blame an inanimate object for anything?

"But you're curious anyway," she told Tari. It wasn't a question. She could tell. After pausing for a moment to collect her thoughts, Xanthe explained, "What I get from its story is this. The demons wanted to become gods. To that end, they made a device. An artifact to pierce into the heavens. When they completed it, the worst thing possible happened."

"What?"

"They succeeded."

Tari's mouth dropped open. "No way in hellspace."

"Yeah." Xanthe agreed. "Maybe that too."

"That can't be true. You only go to hellspace when you die, and only if you're bad."

Xanthe raised an eyebrow and stated dryly. "They're demons, Tari. Kin of the five and eight. Remember?"

Tari blinked, taken aback. "Yeah. Okay. Good point."

"The demon didn't explain exactly what happened, but by the way it was talking I don't think anything good. Whatever they found must have scared them, and that made them take a second look at humans. It sounds like this isn't the first time the heavens have gotten all stormy with our plain old reality, and once demons figured out that mundane life evolved to survive or even benefit from these episodes, they started breeding us to intensify the talent. This was controversial, even for them; this demon thought it immoral."

Tari pulled herself up into a sitting position, to stop kneeling with her slats. "Breeding us? You're saying humans are made by demons? That's..."

"Heresy. Yeah. But not the least of it. Demons aren't supernatural. We made them. Also, black blood is demonic. Everything that the Curate speaks of, demonism and the power of darkness, being these alien things apart from humanity, are completely wrong. It may not even be evil. Regular witch power, like spark throwing, comes from demons. But I don't think that's what demons are breeding us for."

"There are not just witches, but different kind of witches?"

"It explained poetically, but if I had to guess, it's like being a channeler of the heavens."

"Okay. I might believe the black blood part. But demons can't just breed people to be blessed by the Creator. That makes no sense."

Xanthe shrugged. "The demon said we catch the infinite in the in-between spaces, which I guess is some kind of connection to the heavens, or greater realities."

"So... you're the result of this breeding program? A super dreadwitch?"

Xanthe smirked slightly, feeling a slightly triumphant. "Actually, it specifically mentioned you."

"Me?!" Tari gasped.

"Yes, you, your holiness. It seems you're an Alterspace navigator, which I'm thinking has just got to mean you can guide the ancestors' void vessels. But don't worry. You can quit beating yourself up. Your touch isn't directly demonic. It's something else entirely. Far more potent, and something I don't think demons can easily reproduce. Else, why would they bother with us at all?"

"My curse is that I was meant for the stars?"

"The sea of stars and time. Know the futures. Exactly that a quake will strike." Xanthe heaved herself up onto her elbow. Her dress felt odd. Tacky, like it was wet dough.

"I have two touches? To see ahead in both space and time? Wouldn't one be enough?"

"I dunno," Xanthe mused. "Maybe the two are connected somehow." She sighed to herself. This morning she'd been smart. Knew almost everything. Yet just in the past few bells, she'd learned so much, she now knew nothing at all.

"What do we do now?"

Xanthe pushed herself fully upright. "We still need to take the beacon. Prince Sol needs to think it stolen and that he can recover it intact. Otherwise he'll have no reason to change his current plans to conquer Jagerfeld. I don't know how we'll bargain with him over it if it's depowered, but first things first. We need to get it out of here."

They both struggled to their feet, and before allowing herself a chance to chicken out, Xanthe grabbed the dark crystalline sphere. She put both arms under and heaved, pulling it up from its socket. The thing was even heavier than she feared, but her training in dealing with awkward packages made it easier than it would have otherwise been. More awkward was managing to walk on the seams of the platform they were on, as her heels could easily have slid through the grating. But once on the stairs, it was relatively easy going. She knew she couldn't carry this thing far though. Especially not in her shoes now. They were feeling oddly soft.

Tari tried to guide her up the stairs offering several times to carry the load. With the beacon being shaped as it was, this didn't seem like a good idea. Xanthe decided to just keep muscling it out. At the platform, she ended up needing to rest, and set the thing down, kneeling on the stairs. As she did so, the problems with her dress couldn't be overlooked. Her hat wasn't just floppy. It was melting. Not good.

Tari suddenly stared blankly into space. "Something's wrong."

"Again?"

"The future. It's clearer now. There are so few, it's almost like I can see some of them."

"Not surprising. The storm of pre-time is breaking. You probably know what I'm about to say next."

She shook her head. "Not you, but me. I do feel me. My world is going to fall apart."

"Why? Anything specific?"

Tari stared unfocused. "I don't know. Not quite. But from everywhere ahead, I feel sadness."

"Dung," Xanthe cursed. That made sense. Probably Tari was auguring the signal sent, the city at unexpected war, lots of friends dead. No matter which future they ended up in, none of them would be happy. "Come on. Least we can do is get this thing out of sight."

"You're not going to be able to carry that anywhere through the party."

"Not going to." Xanthe heaved, straining with the beacon. "Open that window, will you?"

Tari found the crank beneath the Tudor window in the hallway. "You mean this?"

"Yeah. Come on," Xanthe panted, straining. "Just unlatch it. I can't hold this dodgy thing forever."

Tari turned the crank. As the window creaked open, Xanthe managed to lever the beacon onto the sill and peer down though the open crack to the street below. It was entirely empty. No Damien, no guards, no one. At least there was a decorative hedge line right up against the edge of the outside wall. She judged the distance down and decided to chance it. There was no telling what would happen if a demonic artifact broke from a ten-yard fall onto stone, but it was likely dirt there and maybe even a bit of snow. Besides, there wasn't much choice. She let the stone down carefully until she could hang on no longer, then let the crystalline ball go. When it landed, there was the comforting sound of snapping shrubbery and a thump of suitably squishy sounding mud.

Done. She felt a sense of satisfaction. "Hopefully no one will even recognize it down there. At least until we can get outside. Let's go around."

Tari cranked the window shut. "Xanthe. What's with your clothes?"

Xanthe examined the melting fabric. "It might be dead too. The demon controlling it, I mean."

"By the Creator, Xanthe, you think you killed them all?" Tari shook her head slowly in shock. She was acting like Karissa.

"Not on purpose. You know me. I don't like death. Can barely bring myself to eat roach meat."

"But it was you. You're really the Creator's tool." Tari put her hand to her chin. "Why were you chosen, do you think? I mean, you're super nice, but not exactly religious. You're a Scholar even. No one announced your birth. No holy messengers appeared at your birth to give you plastics and lace."

"Look, Tari. As much as I'd love to guess all night about what happened, if this dress keeps falling apart, I'm going to wind up stark naked. So even if I'm like a super saint, that's going to be pretty dodgy-power embarrassing."

Tari nodded, and started undressing, pulling off her outer skirt.

"What are you doing?" Xanthe exclaimed.

"Getting you into something. I can walk around in my small clothes for a while. Get out of my slats too."

Xanthe wanted to argue but decided not to. Tari slipped off her outer skirt, and undid the pantaloons holding her slats, leaving her only in small clothes. Xanthe put on Tari's dress. It didn't fit, but was so loose, she was able to wring one side of the hem into a lengthy twist, which she promptly tied. She covered her bare breasts with Tari's underskirt, holding it under her arms across her chest, because she had nothing to tie the back with. They both looked ridiculous, but not entirely out of place. A lot of crazy stuff went on during Festival.

"Let's pretend we're drunk." Tari suggested.

It was then that Xanthe realized that the black dress wasn't dripping off her, so much as being absorbed into her skin, much like black blood did when allowed to sit in an open wound. It was merely the quantity that was alarming. Her skin was swelling, absorbing it all.

Just as she was about to panic about it, Tari interrupted urgently. "We have to get going."

"Why?"

"Not sure. But I see us being captured. I just had a vision of us chained to a wall. Come on."

"Captured?"

"Now!" Tari suddenly yelled nearly in a panic. "Move!"

Xanthe moved forward, as soon as she did, Tari turned and ran, trying to lead her away. "Wait!" Xanthe exclaimed. "We can jump out of the window. I mean we might break a leg, but..."

"No! That's the wrong way." Tari hurried them down the long winding hall where the empty factory workrooms lay.

"Why?"

"We will be found no matter what. We need to avoid suspicion. You do anything suspicious?"

"No," Xanthe said as she hurried after Tari, grabbing the knot at the side of her dress to keep it from becoming undone. Then she thought about it. "Well, okay. Priscia did burn us out of a locked room after I arrived. But Sol thinks I've got no witch powers. Why are we in such a rush, anyway?"

"There's a place we need to be so that bad things don't happen. I can feel it. I don't think we can get to a place where we're completely clear, but we've got to get out of this corridor. I see a lot of black if we stay."

"Really?" Xanthe muttered to herself as she followed Tari's hurried navigation. "And you're in awe of me?"

It was only five minutes later when they approached the main areas where party had been celebrated. Now though, something was clearly different. The hubbub was muted. There were no more sounds of chamber music anywhere. Something was clearly amiss. As Xanthe was wondering just how long they'd both been unconscious, Tari came to a halt near a smaller reception room. Its floor to ceiling door wasn't automatic, merely etched with ornate swirls, but it did have a large keyhole, which she bent forward to spy through

"When I open the door, go through as quick as you can, okay? Quietly."

Xanthe nodded, simply trusting her judgment. Almost before she was ready for it, she opened the door. Xanthe rushed through. Tari followed on her heels.

Inside the room, the party was sedate. Huddled groups of partygoers lined the room, still conversing in a muted manner, while a small group of men in Wormwood colors stood in the center, their backs momentarily to where Xanthe and Tari had slipped in. One of them noticed the movement and turned his head around. "Get away from that door!" He barked at Xanthe, before doing a double-take at their outfits. She recognized him. He was the young guard who'd complimented her when she'd first entered the estate.

Both hurried to the side, to the nearest group behind a supporting pillar in the corner. They ended up next to a man, his wife, and two sons, only a few years younger than they were. Judging by their clothes, they were some sort of petty nobility, neither exceedingly rich nor poor.

"Hi," one of the two boys greeted. He looked about thirteen, and his broad smile made it clear that he very much liked what he was seeing.

"Don't talk to them foreign girls!" The mother scolded her son in a thick Warmwell accent, jerking him back by the shoulder. "Look at 'em! Or better, don'. Not proper at all! You want the Five an' Eight to get yeh?"

Xanthe drew herself up, offended, but Tari put a hand on her shoulder and shook her head. They'd reversed roles. Now, she was the calm one.

"I tol' ya shouldn't have let the boys come with," the woman turned to her husband. "Lookit the kind of trouble they'll be findin'."

Her husband glanced at her, his boys, and then Xanthe and Tari. A slight smile stole on his face. "Oh don' be such a worrynag. Don't hurt their eyes ta use 'em." He told her. "They're growin' up dear. You're just be goin' ta have ta put up with it. If ya want plenny o' grandkids, at least."

The young matron smoothed her dress and frowned. "I just don't wan' 'em guiled by them spark throwing witches, the hussies. I know how witch girls be, temptin' boys with their touches and come-hither eyes. Next thing ya know, they'll have 'em in some cult, or worse, their beds." She eyed Xanthe and Tari suspiciously. "The boys been up too late as be."

"I cen think of a girl who once had sparks too," the man grinned and playfully swatted her rear. "Not always proper neither, as I remember. But ye grew out a' it when we took vows and settled. So now, don't be worryin', Mirbel m'love. Everythin'll be fine. Soon as they find this black-dressed girl, we can get the boys back to the guestroom, an' tuck 'em in proper. No harm done." The man reassured, then winked at his son, giving him a sly grin. The boy returned the smirk and went right back to ogling Xanthe in her nearly-falling-off outfit.

That didn't sound good. Black dressed girl. They had to be searching for her. Xanthe glanced at Tari, but she had her eyes closed. She seemed to be focusing.

Xanthe waited impatiently, until eventually she couldn't stand it. "We need to figure a way out of here," she whispered in Tari's ear. "That guard. He recognized me. He'll eventually put things together."

"We can't. They're watching the doors."

"Well why did we come here then? Just to get captured sooner?"

"It was unavoidable," Tari's smile was grim. "Frustrating, isn't it?"

"Well, we can't just stand here!" Xanthe scanned the room. All the doors were being watched, except for one to a small water closet for which there was a line. The guests didn't have the air of being trapped though, mostly just inconvenienced, as if merely waiting out a safety drill that had dragged on too long. However, several guards in foreign uniforms were lying sick on the floor. Oddly enough, the Wormwood guards were quite concerned by this, and distracted tending to them. It seemed like it really wouldn't be hard to make a break for the door and run, now that her shoes no longer had spiky heels.

"We can. We should," Tari told her. "Surrender to the guard."

"Why?"

"I don't know. I still can't see the future. Too many premonitions in the way. But I can feel." She stared unfocused. "Of all the places of blackness and paths darkened by sorrow, somewhere distant in that direction I'm feeling a possibility where at least there's no despair. If we can find it."

Xanthe nodded. Maybe this morning she would have doubted Tari. No longer. She hissed, finding herself unexpectedly nervous. "This is going to get us killed," she grumbled more.

"Hurt at the very least." Tari agreed. "You want to save the city or not?"

Bravery is a funny thing, Xanthe thought while girding herself just like she'd done before the demon. Everyone celebrates the warriors who face monsters and nightmares, or other soldiers. Men prepared for battle, hoping for a clean victory and to somehow avoid injury. But that's nothing compared to what it takes to go unarmed and face people whose entire job it is to hurt you, hoping to find some glimmer of decency in them.

She steeled herself and walked towards the center of the room.

## Chapter 39

"I'm sorry miss," one of the guards told Xanthe. "Please stand near the walls. As we've already said, we're in lockdown for your safety until we find this girl. We can't let anyone out."

"I was napping and didn't hear the announcement," Xanthe told him. "What's the danger again?"

The young guard who'd complimented her came over. He smiled, but his brow was knit in thought. "It's some investigation the Council themselves are interested in."

"Who exactly?"

"It's kind of muddled," he admitted, sounding embarrassed. "Councilor Wormwood is busy, so it's his son who's been passing stuff on."

Xanthe nodded. Now things were starting to make a little sense. "Really? Have you seen the Councilor himself, recently? I mean Tyan, not Horace."

"No," said the younger guard. "But...weren't you in black the last time I saw you? We've been told to look out for a girl matching that description. Somehow this has to do with city security."

Xanthe nodded. "I was. I don't have any idea why a councilor would want me, but if I'm the one he wants, then don't ruin the party for anyone else. Take me to him. Not Horace. Him."

Her words drew their attention. The guards glanced at each other, and the lead guard had his attention drawn. He rose from his watch over the sick men. The guard Xanthe knew shook his head. "I'm sure it's not you, sweetheart. It's not your fault if boys fight over you. But what happened to your dress?"

"A girl gave me this one, and I wanted to try it on. It's different."

The young guard shook his head, genially leering almost as obviously at the thirteen-year-old. "It mostly looks like it's made to come off."

"Hold on," said the guard leader as he approached. "You're trying to avoid Horace?"

Xanthe nodded. "He's grabby," she told them. At this, the three men stiffened. Despite it not being the nicest accusation to make, none of them tried to deny it.

"And he's also in league with a Nutearean princeling," she added, almost as an afterthought. "Trying to take over both the family and the city with the foreigner's aid."

That got their attention. It had nothing to do with her odd outfit. The commander growled, "That is a serious accusation miss. Nearly prevarication."

"I'm not accusing," Xanthe told him plainly. "Just telling you what I've heard."

"Well, maybe you really are the girl they want. Just to be sure, I'll take you into custody."

Xanthe didn't back away as he approached. Instead she nodded, and spoke to him quietly, "Just tell Councilor Wormwood, assuming you can find him. That's why these guards are poisoned."

The older guard had just grabbed her upper arm, when the doors opened abruptly. Horace entered, leading six of the prince's men. He strutted into the room looking exceptionally pleased. Both Royroy and Finalizer Dakur followed closely behind. The latter nodded to his men. "Same thing again. Spread out."

"Hey guests!" Horace announced. "We're gonna be finding this girl we want. Everyone should have a good time. So, go and be happy and stuff. This is the greatest time to party, because things are going to be set straight. My place has got the classiest stuff, right? That's the Wormwoods. You literally got no better place to be. Which is tremendous, 'cause I've got this big announcement to make soon. Now, everybody drink. I got these people serving drinks, and they're the best. The drinks, I mean. It's all gonna be great for everyone. Except for the guys all sick on the floor, but you know."

There he was. Again, in front of her. Horace had changed clothes too, of course. Xanthe had thought she would be afraid, or filled with hate, but instead merely found herself repulsed, not even overwhelmingly. It was like studying some sort of dung-maggot in creatures-class, an entirely clinical experience. For his part, he looked right past her.

"Young lord," the guard commander addressed Horace. "This girl. She might have been in a black dress."

Horace didn't even afford her a glance. "Um. Yeah. So?"

The guard was confused. "What do you mean so? You told us to look."

"Yeah, well, it's like my friend who wants that black dressed girl. I'm finding a different one."

"If I may ask sir, who?"

There was a shout from behind, and Xanthe looked back. One of Sol's men was in front of Tari. "Here she is!" He yelled triumphantly.

Tari looked at the man, and then stepped forward. Even without her full dress, she held her back straight and spoke with authority. "I assume you have some sort of excuse for this, Horace?"

"Hey," Horace grinned, "there you are!"

Tari drew herself up. "I am. But I have decided to take my leave. I will be going home now."

Horace's smile widened. "Nah. You're gonna stay right here. See, we all decided to merge the families, so you're like home already."

"I am never marrying you," she declared coldly. Every eye was now on her. She looked odd in her small clothes, but somehow had seemed to grow in them. "House Wormwood seeks to betray the Confederated Free Cities of Thule by turning over our peoples to a Nutearean prince, so he can ruin us all by involving us in their succession conflict. All just to be a vapid quisling under him. Yet to do that, you need get your paws on Outlet's heritage, or else you'll never have the shares to swing the council. I tell you now, that will never happen. I will never agree, and absent that, the Curate will not allow it."

Horace approached Tari, swaggering. "See, right here, this is what's wrong with Jagerfeld!" He held up his finger and announced to the crowd. "This city could literally be so great, but it's not, because it's weak. It needs someone strong, like me, who won't let girls think they got a say in how its run. Long as girls don't know their only place is in the bedroom, the city will be a loser – a woman's town. But I won't let that happen. Because I'm gonna give this city what it needs." He turned back to her. "I'm going to give you what you need."

"A demonstration of how drinking leads to brain rot?" Tari's lip curled.

"Nah. You need something way more desperate. You need to learn respect, from someone strong. Know how that's done? What you've been begging for since I met you?" Horace announced, staring into her eyes. He didn't give her a chance to answer. "You just need a little..."

With that, Horace suddenly swung with his open palm at Tari's face. Intended as a sucker punch, he put so much strength into it that he turned himself completely around when his hand unexpectedly met air. Tari had ducked even before he'd started to swing. She ended up a couple of feet behind him.

"...pop...?"

Teeth gritted in anger, Tari didn't so much kick Horace, as shove him hard with her foot. But the effort she put into it was considerable, and as he was already off balance, this sent him careening forward as he tried to regain his footing. He went three yards before crashing into one of the serving tables. Flailing, he gripped the setting cloth to try to hold himself upright, but this upset the buffet set on top. A stack of plates crashed down, and a large punch bowl full of flamedraft tipped, promptly draining its orange colored contents on both him and the surrounding floor.

Laughs echoed from the other side of the room. The two thirteen-year-old boys thought this was hilarious.

"*This* is the self-appointed ruler of Jagerfeld?" Tari jeered. "Who would lead our city the way he romances girls? With beatings? Violent idiocy?" Tari turned to the crowd as an audience and gestured towards Horace. "People of the North! Witness the sodden fool who would set the Wormwoods as sole sovereign Mayoral family of Jagerfeld, in place of our democracy. He thinks bullying is leadership, stupidity is strength, and prejudice, freedom. But he's too inept to even figure out how to pick up a girl's favor, much less be worthy of anyone dropping one." She curtseyed mockingly. "I take my leave. Your grandiose self-delusions are no longer entertaining." With this, she turned on her heel, and made toward the exit.

Covered in the oily aromatic fungal libation, Horace rose in absolute fury. As Tari turned her back on him, he didn't say a word, but instead launched himself, silently bull-rushing in her direction, the soles of his expensive leather shoes squishing orange tracks across the floor. Xanthe didn't even have time to shout a warning before he was almost upon her. Their paths crossed as she neared the exit, and again he would have slammed Tari against a different buffet table full of sweetmeats, except that once again, without even looking, she suddenly stepped aside and spun quickly, letting his bulky body collide with it alone. There was a terrible crash as he rammed into the table. The whole display tipped forward into the room disgorging its contents on him and the floor.

The boys were still laughing. A few titters in the room joined them.

Tari shook her head, addressing the crowd. "You may not know this, but Horace has pledged himself to a southern prince. He thinks he's going to be a great general. But really, he can't even jump a girl by surprise!"

Breathing heavily, with the remnants of a few hors d'oeuvres still clinging to his clothing, Horace pulled himself to his knees, and then started to stand. "When I get hold of you, you uppity little ice queen..."

A sneer took her face. "How exactly are you going to do that? Call in all your guards? It's the only way you're going to, because you're certainly not man enough to manage it by yourself."

"Reaming bodyseller!" he raged. "Piece of dung bitch. I'm gonna kill you!"

"Whoa! Hold on!" Tari lampooned. "We got ourselves a real romancer here! I've got to admit Horace, you're certainly original. Nothing sets a girl's heart aflutter faster than saying you're going to murder her. It's the totally proper way to go about proposing marriage! You plan to put that on the wedding invitations? Your presence is cordially invited to Wormwood and Outlet ~ He's Going to Kill Her."

Now the crowd did chuckle, but that did not deter Horace. This time, instead of running directly at her, this time he got a cagey look on his face, approaching slowly, making sure not to unbalance himself with any attempts at a heavy strike. It was clear that he wanted to simply grab and pummel her out of pure rage.

Yet this new method did not phase Tari in the least. Unencumbered by any gown or slats, she moved lightly, avoiding every one of his clumsy attempts to paw at her, while weaving from serving table to serving table, picking up various pieces of food and casually splattering it on him from just out of range of his hands. The increasingly entertained crowd scattered away from the slop fight everywhere they went, none seeing fit to interfere.

Xanthe felt the grip on her arm slacken. Guests were full of mirth, but the guards were rapt and Xanthe knew why. Horace's ineptness could not disguise Tari's innate mastery of combat. She was simply supernatural. Every attack he made, every trick he tried, she was already prepared to counter before he even started. She dodged when he pushed, ducked when he swung, tripped him when he lunged, and was just so utterly casual about the whole exercise, it was like watching a weapon master with decades of experience having fun at the expense of his most junior novice. Tari pulled the ladle from a snowcream bowl, and now was alternatively using it to smack his face and body, covering him in even more food. It was clear that if she were so inclined, she could beat him to death with it.

At last, in front of the enormous mountain-cake display, Horace managed to catch hold of the dipper she'd been tormenting him with. Here, they got into a pulling match. As he wrenched particularly hard, she suddenly let go, and once again, his shoes slipped out from under him. Flailing, he fell on his tail bone. The crowd, by now, was howling at the antics of the two teens. Even staid family elders who took seriously the precept that guests should never openly mock their host, were having a hard time keeping a straight face. Most were crying with laughter, while desperately trying to hide it behind their hands.

"You..." Horace breathed. "Filthy..." He was shaking with near insane rage as he stood. "Sli-ide."

Tari folded her arms, tapped her foot, and shook her head. "I'm the one who's filthy?" She taunted. "Horace, dear. Have you looked at yourself? While we're at it, if we're going to be vulgar, just know now that you ain't never going be in my slide. That's kind of the whole point of this. Go hump the floor instead. I mean, that's the only thing you're good at sliding on."

The crowd laughed again, yet though enraged past all reason, her statement did seem to give Horace an idea. "These reaming boots. I will reaming beat the cobbler who sold them." He pulled up on one foot and started tearing the shoe off.

"I know the tradition of keeping young brides barefoot, but really, you shouldn't offer yourself," Tari continued mockingly. "I mean, who's supposed to be the man in this relationship? Don't answer that!"

"Just wait, you reaming bitch," he was hopping madly on his barefoot, while pulling off his other shoe.

"Reaming?" Tari sneered. "Don't tempt me." She stood for a moment, as he turned around trying to get his fancy laces undone. "Really," she remarked to the crowd. "This is too easy." With that, she charged at his unsuspecting form, hopped up, and used both feet to violently shove him. Horace went flying, and his whole upper body got buried in the mountain-cake. The table supporting it collapsed, falling forward as the others had, and the whole ostentatious display of food fell on top of him with in enormous crash. Tari retrieved the ladle he'd dropped, while he wallowed head to toe in icing, all of it more than enough to feed an entire hungry outland village.

"We are done here," she proclaimed. "Expect my formal protest before the Curate in the morning. The Honorable House of Wormwood will be asked to explain your actions. Creator I thank. Host, I do not."

"I AM House Wormwood!" Horace screamed nearly incoherently. "And if you leave this room before I can beat the dung out of you, you reaming bitch, I will order my men to KILL you!" He stood up, looking ridiculous. A confection of hate. But the room turned suddenly quiet. Xanthe felt the guard commander's hold drop completely.

"If you insist," Tari snarled. "You want me, cupcake? Here I am." She deliberately moved within range of him, but still shifted from side to side. In his bare feet, Horace took a wide stance to dodge witch ever way she chose, until she got too close.

"Now I've got you..." Horace screamed triumphantly as he leapt, arms wide to ensure no way to escape. Except she didn't. Tari merely stiff armed his head with her left hand, and twisted her body, putting all her strength with her right foot into one perfectly placed kick between his legs.

Horace didn't even exactly howl. As the pain registered, he collapsed, gasping in shock. This let Tari shrug him off, and she shoved him to the floor. "Try catching your breath to give that order now," she spat. She turned around, only to be faced with the blades of Finalizer Dakur.

"Playtime is over, princess," the assassin growled. "There is nothing you can do. Not against me." He put his blade against her throat. "You will come with me. Your only choice is how much you bleed beforehand."

Tari's eyes were glazed. "I see that." The ladle clattered to the floor.

"Take them both," Dakur directed the guards, gesturing with his swords. Xanthe knew not to resist. The protection of her black dress was long gone. The commander was not one who grabbed her though. He'd disappeared.

"Get our young lord cleaned up too," the Finalizer added as an afterthought.

## Chapter 40

Somehow Xanthe managed to remain decent as she was frog marched to one of the Wormwood's private holding cells, but it didn't last. As her arms were chained up high, the underskirt she'd been holding under her arms to cover her breasts fell away, leaving her topless. Oddly, she didn't find this embarrassing. Mostly just cold. She thought to give the Wormwood city guards a little lip about when she'd be turned over for a trial adjudicated by the Curate, and on what charges, but decided not to do so. They were subdued. None had taken liberties with her, for which she was grateful, so no use antagonizing them. Given their somber manner, it was clear that they weren't comfortable with their orders either.

For now though, the guards left them alone and the door was latched behind them. Tari slumped in her chains. Xanthe thought she knew why but had to ask anyway. "You alright?"

"The future, once seen, never changes," she quietly declared to the floor. A tear appeared and dripped slowly down her cheek.

"I suppose the future you see for us isn't all that pleasant."

"It's not that," Tari whispered distraught. "Something else. In all the futures. Whether I'm enslaved or free. Beaten, or thin, with child or not. Everywhere that isn't black, I see it. A memorial and ashes."

Xanthe dreaded the answer to her next question. "Your dad, right?"

Even through her tears, Tari was surprised. "How did you know?"

"Just logic. Horace called himself House Wormwood. Tyan would never turn his estate over without a formal announcement and extended transition lasting years. That means he can't be alive. And if he isn't, then your father wouldn't be either."

Tari hung her head and wept. "Daddy..."

Xanthe didn't know anything comforting to say. "I'm sorry."

Tari sobbed quietly for a while, little shuddering breaths. "I begged to the Creator to keep me from being sick at heart for no reason. I prayed for it. And hark! My sinful wish was answered. I was given one."

Xanthe didn't know what to say, so she remained quiet.

Tari looked to her. "Just..." her mouth twisted in grief... "get us out of this, okay?"

Xanthe wasn't exactly sure what Tari was expecting her to do. She looked about the room. Unlike where Priscia and her dad had been imprisoned, this place didn't even disguise what it was. It had bare walls of ancient permacrete, and while surprisingly large, had only one exit. So even if she could wriggle her arms out of the manacles, there was no way they could leave.

"Even if we could, it might not be the best idea," Xanthe told her. "Prince Sol's plans are falling apart. He's likely to get more vicious as he sees victory slipping through his fingers."

"What do you mean?" Tari declared bitterly. "He's won."

"Quite the opposite. His plans are in tatters."

"Because of the beacon?"

"Because of you. No way was Horace meant to let it slip that he's now House Wormwood. It ruins all sorts of stories they could have concocted to smooth the transition: the council attacked by evil demon cultists, chimera, dreadwitches, nightmares, anything but the truth. With the young scion of Wormwood leaping in heroically trying to save them all, but to no avail. The council dead. Hero Horace being the natural remaining leader to take control of the ruling shares. Blah, blah, blah. Lie, lie, lie."

"So? What difference does that make?"

"A giant one. Prince Sol isn't just trying to take over Jagerfeld. He wants the whole north. If his chances were slim before, what do you think they're going to be after our sister cities know that Jagerfeld's newly crowned royal Mayor is a patricide?"

Tari just stared, her teary eyes open.

Xanthe continued. "Horace's own admission will be hard to live down. People will remember his swaggering, how he looked not the least bit upset about his sudden inheritance. That will stick no matter what kind of sham Prince Sol concocts, or how much he pressures you to recant."

"You think they're going to torture me?" Tari shuddered.

Xanthe grimaced. "I honestly don't know. Do you see it in the future?"

"Too blurry. I still can't see you. Or Prince Charming. Or Prince Sol, for that matter."

"The demon said we had special qualities. Maybe that's a part of it. Still, if you were hurt, you'd see it, wouldn't you?"

Tari looked down and away. "I see a lot of things." She shuddered.

"What?"

"Horace is coming." Her lip trembled. "Xanthe..." she grew desperate, "He wants to... wants to..."

Xanthe didn't know how to comfort but soldiered on anyway. "Don't worry. Celeste has childbane."

"No. You don't understand!" Tari sob turned into a high-pitched sob of despair and anticipation. "He wants to kill you."

"Me?" Xanthe exclaimed. At first, it was hard to process, but then it made sense. Earlier in the evening, she'd wondered why the councilors were set on overthrowing themselves. The answer was that they weren't. It was Horace. He wasn't just a rapist. He was a psychopath. She grew coldly resigned. "You see me dead then?"

"I see him pull a knife on you. But not you. I never see you."

Xanthe nodded, surprised at how calm she was feeling. "One thing I've learned, Tari. Your visions always come true. Just promise me something.

Even if I'm killed, never agree to marry before the Curate. Not even if they tell you that will save me or others. Because once you do, their promises are worth nothing. A marriage sealed before the Creator can only be undone by death. Then they'll arrange that too."

"Xanthe! I can't...!" Tari wailed. "You must do something. I don't care. Demonic. Whatever."

Xanthe let out a mirthless laugh. "Power. It's always dodgy. I have none left. From the heavens, hellspace, or wherever else it comes from. All I have left is my mind. Trouble is, that doesn't work too well against the bane of all dreadwitches. Cold iron." She shook her manacles.

"You're not a dreadwitch," Tari declared, frowning. "You're good."

"Oh, but I am. A witch of the north. I embrace it. If I'm going to be killed, might as well be for something illegal."

Tari shuddered. "I love you."

"Don't get maudlin. I said 'if'. We're not dead yet." Xanthe set her jaw, then twisted at her chains, wrestling with them. But the wrist restraints were fashioned in such a way that pulling only tightened them. She rattled them in frustration, and then felt something slip. "Oh, just great."

"Oh no. What now?" Tari cried.

"Nothing important," Xanthe groused. "This knot I made to keep your dress from falling off. It's coming undone." She tried angling herself to hold it against the wall, but it was simply too distant. It was only a matter of time before she'd be nude. Before Horace.

"Just do one thing as a favor for me, Tari. Don't try to look too far ahead with your visions. But if you get a feeling on something to say or do, just do it. Go full dreadwitch. Use your touch without remorse, okay?"

Tari nodded. "They're almost here."

Just then, there was a rattling of the lock by the cell door. A guard opened it, and let in some guests: Royroy, Sargon, Horace. All three were injured. Royroy had a good-sized lump on the side of his head, Sargon had a slight cut on his cheek, while Horace, now cleaned up and in a loose-fitting doublet, was walking knock kneed, still wincing in obvious pain. Xanthe fought the urge to laugh and won.

"There we are," Sargon said, gesturing towards them. "As you can see, Miss Outlet is here. Let this be a lesson to you. Don't try to soldier. Especially if you're not good at it. Or are hot headed. Or stupid. Or make light of dangers. Or act like a mindless thug. It's easy to get hurt."

"You!" Upon seeing Tari, Horace grew enraged. He started to charge, limping toward her helpless form. Yet before he got far, Sargon leapt forward, grabbed his head by the hair, yanked him back. At Horace's continued struggles, he shook his walking stick, and a wicked blade spring from it, the flat of which he then laid across the boy's throat. "Heed that last lesson best," Sargon snarled softly, "because mindless thugs are expendable."

It was about at this point that Xanthe noticed that Royroy was also armed. He was carrying an ax as clumsy as it was heavy, more suited to felling woody fungal fronds than in combat against anyone who could remotely dodge. He gripped it at Sargon's drawing of his blade against Horace, but then froze in confusion, and wound up just staring at both.

"You have not done well, little lord," Sargon stated with his mouth right next to his ear, as he let his blade press against Horace's throat. "You opened your mouth when you were specifically instructed not to. So here is another piece of wisdom that you'd best learn quickly. Never make yourself more trouble than you're worth."

Horace quieted down physically, but not in attitude. "Lemme go! Do you have any idea who I am?"

"Certainly, boy. I know most everything. Including that you don't know who I am."

"Yeah?" He blustered, full of bravado. "You help Prince Sol."

"Correct. I am Sargon of Render, High Holder of the Talon district in Touchdown. I've held a title long enough to know they provide no defense in the dance. Something you'd best start learning."

"No matter who you are," Horace bellowed, "I'm still the guy who got Prince Sol in here. I did all this stuff for him, and he'll be mad if you do anything to me. So, get off!" He put his hand to the blade and made to push it away. Fortunately for him, he guessed right. Sargon released him.

"I'm telling on you," Horace scowled as he turned around, holding his neck. He was still knock-kneed.

Sargon let out a dry chuckle as he lowered his blade, but kept the point between them, circling it low out of habit, like a swordsman facing an armed foe. "Please do. But you misunderstand our relationship. I am not Prince Sol's servant. I am his patron."

"What are you talking about? Prince Sol is going to be king."

"Because of the resources that I provide. In the capital, I am what is colloquially referred to as a 'steed'. Princes need steeds. There are many I could have aided, but Seraphus' spawn turned out to be particularly vicious and untrustworthy, so I decided that one with some country air might be better."

Even Horace appeared surprised. He stared befuddled. "Wait. You're saying Prince Sol is a good guy?"

Sargon sized up Horace. "You thought otherwise?" He shook his head. "He is, relatively speaking. We're saving the civilized world from civil war, the only way possible – by giving everyone a common enemy. Prince Sol is the perfect instrument. His only defect is that he's too much the consummate politician. He suffers fools far too gladly."

It finally dawned on Horace that Sargon was referring to him. "I don't care what you think. He promised me rule if I did the bent knee thing and got the city for him. I'm still the only one who can do it."

Sargon sneered. "In fact, that is why we're here. To ensure that you deliver on your promise. Lord Sol's specialty is persuading recalcitrant girls; he's practically addicted to the process. But even he can't get one to agree to suicide, at least not quickly. Which means that declaring your intent to kill Miss Outlet is counterproductive. Therefore, not only are you going to recant, you are going to apologize."

"What?"

"You heard me," Sargon told him. "Promise her that you will not harm her in any way. Furthermore, I will hold you to your word, since she might not trust it otherwise."

Horace was angry but remained silent. The tip of Sargon's blade still danced menacingly before him, and it intimidated him into an unusual seriousness. "Alright." He finally breathed reluctantly.

"Then go ahead." Sargon pointed with his blade. "The girl is right there."

Horace folded his arms petulantly. "I just did!"

The holder stared for a while, natty in his silver and black. Finally, he shook his head, and sighed to himself philosophically. "This is what I get for trying to save the empire, using as stone and mortar the twin idiocies of hot blood and youth."

Horace frowned at him. Yet before he could say anything, Tari interrupted, speaking in a low, determined voice. "It matters not. Of all the sins of House Wormwood, Horace running his tender balls into the toe of my boot is the most forgivable."

Horace wheeled as Sargon remarked dryly. "Ah, yes. Well, I'm sure the boy is quite sorry about that too."

"I can tell by the way he's still walking," Tari jibed darkly. "But if you think that forcing an apology from him that he doesn't mean changes anything, you're wrong. I trust your word even less than his."

"You are..." Sargon paused to consider his words. "distraught."

"Men of the south. True masters of observation," Tari scoffed. "But I assure you one thing, esteemed High Holder. I am not the child Horace is. Do not waste time patronizing me."

Sargon listened, then narrowed his eyes, and spoke evenly. "Very well then. One sign of maturity is recognizing when you must make the best of a bad situation, no matter your feelings about it. You have a strength in you that would be a waste to see broken. Even the Finalizer was impressed. Cooperate, and you won't be."

"And what would this cooperation entail?"

He shrugged. "A loveless political marriage. If you can't stand our dear Lord Wormwood, and I truly don't blame you, you can adopt the practice of civilized nobility in such situations and let his slave-wife bear the children. Just take plenty of childbane yourself to ensure that you bear him no bastards, and at least try to keep your new husband out of trouble. At least as anyone might be able."

Horace snapped his head towards Sargon in anger but was silenced as the holder raised his blade back up, without shifting his gaze from Tari.

Tari regarded at him through her tears. "You slaughtered my family and you expect this?"

Sargon blinked in surprise that Tari had intuited this, and once again was impressed. "It was not planned. Your father acceded, but then tried to deceive us." He confessed almost apologetically. "It's just the way of war. Daughters bear sons by the men who killed their fathers."

"I've no interest in your reaming wars!" Tari suddenly raged, weeping through clenched teeth.

"It matters not your interest in war," Sargon returned with deadly calm. "War is interested in you."

Tari gripped her chains. "If we are at war, then I will kill you or die."

"You'll do neither. The only question is the quality of your life. I'm offering a mercy. Take it."

Tari bowed her head. Xanthe knew she was wavering. Both were. Xanthe decidedly did not wish to test her willpower against the prince's cruel ministrations. She'd only remained silent because she didn't want Sargon to know that she'd broken Sol's compulsion. But just as she thought to say something anyway, Tari looked back up. She stared at Horace first, then her, then Sargon. "Never."

Sargon nodded. "I expected as much," he stated calmly. "It's too much to ask so soon, so I will tend to some matters while you hang there and think about it. But I warn you, the more inconvenience you cause, the less mercy you'll receive when you finally acquiesce, one way or the other. My most generous offer only remains until I return."

"You're going?" Horace asked.

Sargon nodded. "Until then, do not disturb so much as a hair on her head." He glared at Horace, making it clear it was an order. "You need to stop thinking with parts of your body other than your brain. Perhaps as a saving grace, your future wife's kick will help you remember that lesson."

Horace said nothing but glowered angrily.

Sargon retrieved the rest of his staff and inserted his sword into it. "One departing piece of advice, my dear. Consider the future. So few do. Try to pick one that doesn't assume everything is going to go back to the way it was before. It won't. You've lost and could still lose far more."

"So have you," Tari muttered back quietly. "You just don't know it yet."

## Chapter 41

After Sargon closed the door, Horace wheeled on Tari. "This is all your fault!" He raged. "All of it! Look what you've done. Made me look bad."

Tari just stared mutely. She did so for a while. Finally, she spoke. "I'm not even sure what to say at this point. You arrange to murder your father and mine, but only now realize that you're not going to be as free under Prince Sol as you dreamed? Less so, because unlike dear departed daddy, your new masters don't have blood ties to blind them to your idiocy? Sargon's evil, but at least he's not stupid."

He lowered his voice but was still full of rage. He pulled out a knife from his waistband and brandished it. "I'm still thinking of killing you."

Royroy spoke finally. "My lord..." His voice took on a note of worried admonition.

"Yes," Tari sneered at Horace. "Listen to your man. You're the Prince's lapdog now. You need to bark on command, and shut your yap otherwise, or else be punished. So! Roll over. Beg."

"You reaming bitch!" Horace was enraged, but helpless.

"You little boy. You can't do anything to me." Tari goaded. Then, inhaling, she snuffled some tear-formed phlegm from her nose through her throat and spat it at him. As with nearly everything she did with Horace, it landed perfectly, hitting him square in the face.

Royroy interrupted again. "Don't kill Tari," he urged. "That's what she wants."

Horace breathed heavily, then nodded. He wiped the spit off with his sleeve. "Yeah. You're right. But he didn't say I couldn't strip her naked though, like this other slide." His gaze shifted to Xanthe. "Hey. Wait a minute!" He stared at her chest. "I know those tits. That spot." He recognized Xanthe's freckle. "You're the one who..." After just managing to control himself, he grew enraged again. "Oh, you bitch. You reaming little bitch. You were in on it all the time, weren't you? You were sent to spy on me." Without another word, he pawed at the loose dress wrapping her legs, roughly pulling it down. Then he held his knife perilously close. As it turned in his hand, Xanthe saw it and nothing else. If this wasn't Tari's vision, it was hers.

Abruptly, Horace turned it downward and sliced through the fabric to cut it entirely off her body. In a matter of seconds, Xanthe was entirely nude.

"Y-you really shouldn't hurt either of them," Royroy argued plaintively. "It's not going to make the Prince any happier."

"He didn't tell me I couldn't," Horace told him. "But don't worry. I won't kill her before I seed her. Maybe it'll make my balls stop hurting."

Tari squinted. "Leave Xanthe be, you bastard."

It was the wrong thing to say. Horace smirked at Tari, glad to finally find something that bothered her. "Yeah. Xanthe. That's the name. I keep forgetting. Well here's the thing. You're right. I can't touch you. But I can her. Little miss Xanthe. Low bitch. I'm gonna be like the Reapers at Fengard. Gonna fill her and kill her, and you're gonna be right here listening to it all. She's your friend, right? I can ream everyone you care about. How does that sound?"

"Xanthe was captured for a reason, you idiot!" Tari screamed at him. "You think you're going to make Prince Sol any happier by killing her before he even comes?"

"She's right," Royroy echoed.

"Don't tell me what to do, either of you!" Horace snarled. "I'm the boss now. Maybe I might leave her barely alive enough for the Prince to ask his questions. Maybe not. But I decide. I'm the decider."

"And you think this is going to make me agree to marry you?" Tari asked.

"Nah. I think it's going to make you say no," Horace grinned triumphantly. "The Prince will have to do his Praetorian stuff to you until you say yes to get him to stop. Then when I do get your vows, I don't care what that holder guy says, I'll give you all the pops you need. Lotta brats too. I'm gonna make you die of having too many."

Royroy was distinctly unsettled. Watching his boss plotting to torture, rape, and kill was clearly not what he'd bargained for. None of them had. Not even Horace. Though he was too stupid to realize it. Xanthe had no doubt that as soon as the new Lord Wormwood's fathered any legitimate male heir, his days would be numbered in single digits. Sargon would make sure of that, for many obvious reasons.

"Is this what you wanted?" Xanthe asked Royroy and was rewarded by wince. It didn't matter though. If Sargon wasn't able to control Horace, Royroy certainly couldn't.

"Shut up! You reaming slide!" Horace snarled, smacking her across the face. "My people know what the score is. Soon as I can get myself hard you're gonna take it. So, don't push me. Killing is easy."

"No," Xanthe said, "killing is..."

She blinked, suddenly filled with insight.

...*hard.*

Of course. How simple. The solution to the puzzle that had bedeviled her for weeks was suddenly laid bare. It was obvious in retrospect. Killing is hard. Maybe not for Horace, but at least for those who pretend to themselves that they are moral.

What's more, it laid out an obvious solution. Here she was. Nude, bound head and feet, about to be raped and murdered by a psychopath, the nascent sovereign mayor of Jagerfeld. Yet as before in the glade, she was not entirely unarmed. Unto the last, she had her wits.

Tari was already silently weeping again. Xanthe wanted to reassure her that everything was going to be alright but had to be careful. Just because she knew the solution to this predicament, it didn't mean she couldn't fail. In truth, even if she succeeded, it was a failure. She'd promised herself no violence, but there was no other recourse now.

Without taking anything else off, Horace had undone the front of his padded codpiece, and was trying to massage his bruised loins into excitement. Staring at her nude form was clearly helping. "You know," he told her. "I can see why they sent you to spy on me. Your body is seriously excellent. Such a shame it's gonna go to waste. But yeah, this was a good lesson. Sargon's right. Never let a slide distract you."

*It was time.* "If you're going to do me, you might as well put your favor on me, like you said you were going to." She suggested gently.

"Favor?" He asked.

A brief stab of panic went through her. Horace hadn't tossed it, had he? "You know. The one in your coin pouch. You said you were going to make me wear it before doing me the first time, remember?" She tried to seem seductive.

Horace blinked. "Oh. Yeah. I did." He smirked. "Okay bitch, sure. But don't think kissing up now 's gonna change my mind about killing you after or anything." Smirking, he pulled out the chestlet, shook it out, pulled it around her back, and clipped it on her front. It fit well. Perfect for a teenaged girl, of course. "There we go," he gloated. Then he squeezed her breasts, pinched her nipples, and slapped them hard.

"Horace," Tari warned.

"Shut up. You just made me decide to kill your spy friend before doing her. Seed her after she's dead. So just remember, it was your words that did it. Her death was all your fault." He pointed his dagger at her heart. "Sorry, bitch," he told Xanthe. "But really, I was forced to do this."

Xanthe nodded stoically. "I know the feeling exactly."

Tari gasped, staring in shock at the event that was now inevitable.

Xanthe turned her head. She felt the tip of the blade on her breast, as blood sprayed everywhere.

"You reaming dung wipe," Royroy choked out in absolute fury. He was staring down at Horace's collapsed form. Had it struck true, the force of the blow he'd just delivered would have taken Horace's head clean off. Yet rage had cost Royroy accuracy. The ax was now half-buried in Horace's skull; its handle stood up from the floor, as if it had been left in a stump.

There was no time to waste. "Go. Now," Xanthe told him. "But don't run. That's suspicious. Walk. If anyone stops you, just say he sent you to get something."

Royroy moved toward her where she was secured. "I'll get you out."

"No," she commanded. "We'd never get past the guards. Only you can."

"Then I'll get help."

"There's no one to get, and the guards will be after you as soon as they find out about this. Just get off the street. Disappear. Warn your family. You'll have to leave Jagerfeld for a long time. Maybe even all of Thule."

He nodded unhappily. "I was such a fool. I'll pay..."

"I count my life as payment enough. Take the chestlet too."

Royroy's eyes were dark. He shook his head. "No. It's yours now. I have no silver. It's the least I can pay. You earned it."

"Then keep it for now so it's not stolen again. If I somehow live, I'll be happy to get it by Hood courier. But leave while you can."

Royroy retrieved the jewelry and held it, nearly in tears. He then turned away. Xanthe held her breath after he knocked loudly at the prison door. Yet while Horace was lying in plain sight, the guards weren't curious enough to look inside. Or perhaps they'd been told not to. Royroy exited freely.

"What just happened...?" Tari asked, completely flabbergasted.

Xanthe watched the door. Nothing. She settled herself. "It's complicated." Even as she spoke, Horace was still gagging, his hands spasming, dying as blood pooled beneath him. Idly she wondered if she would have been able to save him, if she could reach. But she couldn't.

Tari looked at Xanthe's chains, and hers. "We have the time."

Xanthe took in a deep breath. "Alright. There's a Witchkiller loose in Jagerfeld. He killed Ginna half a season ago, before that party you invited me to. Royroy's has been working to earn enough silver to hire someone to find and exact vengeance against the killer. First from your dad, then from Horace."

"Oh!" Tari exclaimed. "People thought it was a witchkiller, but it was really Horace instead!"

Xanthe considered him and shook her head. "No."

"No?"

Warm droplets of his blood trickled down Xanthe's nude body, painting her artistically in red and black. Fitting. She'd wanted no one to die tonight but had failed so badly that she'd ended up needing to do so herself. For that was what this killing was. No one else's. She'd merely used a man as her weapon. "I only tricked Royroy into thinking that."

"What? How? Who?"

Xanthe took in a deep breath, while listening to Horace gasping on the floor. It was series of sickening wheezes. From so many kestrels, she knew slow death intimately. It was never pleasant.

"The first words I heard from Damien made me think he was working for the Sect of Penance. It turned out he wasn't, but he does know a lot about them. He told me four things: they never hire others, they acid brand their victims, each witchkiller has a particular way of killing, never drawing blood; and later, he told me that that all assassins traditionally take some trophy off their victim as proof to their patrons that they did it."

"So how did that get Royroy to kill Horace?"

"Royroy told me that Ginna had been branded with a Curate mark, the which is the hallmark of a witchkiller strike. Yet tellingly, he mentioned no other injury. From that, I had to conclude that she wasn't missing an ear or other body part. That meant the assassin must have taken a different sort of trophy off her. Royroy also called the killer a murdering thief. Thief, meaning the assassin stole something."

"I'm still not getting it."

"Because you still don't know everything. Nadeen told me that the details of Ginna's murder were hushed up. Only a few guards and the family knew." She shrugged. "Hellspace, most people still think she eloped. Out in the wilds somewhere. At worst, carried off as a bandit's bride."

"How does that help, exactly?"

"Because someone other than Royroy knew the specific way this particular witchkiller killed: strangulation. He casually assured me that I should not fear such a form of death myself. Who else, but the one responsible for Ginna's murder, could mention the precise way in which she was killed?"

"Who is the witchkiller, then?"

"Brother Axeman."

Tari blinked. "The acolyte at the Steeple? But he's so nice."

"You know him?"

"Well yes, I'm..." Tari was shocked. "...you sure?"

Xanthe nodded. "There were other clues. I've just been too distracted to see them. He was weeping when we first met, squeezing his manual with his hands. Also, when he gave me Ginna's chestlet as a substitute favor, which must have been what he stole as proof of her death, he said it weighed like a rock upon his soul. I doubt he expected her to be secretly wearing a symbol of the Creator. Imagine, strangling a girl to death, thinking that you're some hero protecting humanity by killing a demon cultist or dreadwitch, only to find that your victim was mostly harmless and secretly devout. I think it was only later that he fully grasped the reality of what he'd done. Killing is hard."

Horace was gasping now. His breath came as horrible gagging moans, like a cross between a snore and a low sounding croak. For all his failings, his body was healthy, and it was taking him a long time to die.

Tari stared at her, then down at him. "How long is he going to do this?"

Xanthe found herself feeling strangely detached. "Could be minutes. Could be the whole night."

"Can anyone save him?"

"The only one who might, is a bit tied up at the moment." Xanthe rattled her chains.

Tari frowned at his dying form, disgust, sorrow, and anger warring equally on her face. Eventually anger won out. "Good. He deserves it."

Xanthe stated down pensively. "Nevertheless, having your vengeance doesn't really make it better, does it?"

It was the wrong thing to say. Tari dropped her head and sobbed, her face contorted in grief.

Xanthe fell silent. She was filled with sorrow for Tari, while struggling with her typical unruly thoughts. When she was ten, she'd been a reading addict, sneaking trashy murder mysteries out of the Guild's rather bare fiction shelves to devour at night. Eventually though, they'd lost their charm. Not merely because they were formulaic – the killer always ended up being an evil dreadwitch with nonsensical powers far sillier than whatever in hellspace had happened in the chain tower – but more because death was always an afterthought, a mere literary device to execute a puzzle. Victims were barely mentioned. Never mourned. They were just a pretext for the debonair proctor protagonist to start his next witch hunt.

What happened here hadn't been a murder mystery. Indeed, it was nearly its opposite. Her deduction had been used to incite, rather than punish, a killing. But even more, like all real things, it had messy consequences: slow deaths, dead parents, and drops of blood growing chill on her skin.

Despite these thoughts, she found herself possessing a grim sense of satisfaction. Her dad told her not to grieve for Horace when he met an untimely end. In this, she found that she didn't. While there was no special joy in arranging his death, she was glad for his victims, exultation that he'd been stopped from victimizing any more. This included herself too. It was cold dark triumph.

Regardless, everything was now imprinted her on her mind. The cell. The blood. The exact position when Royroy took the blow. Death was no small thing either. It might be justified. But she hated it.

"All I want to do go is go back to yesterday," Tari said softly.

Xanthe pondered how to comfort her and decided on frank discussion. "There's no guarantee that would have helped. By yesterday, Prince Sol had snuck so many bandits into the city, he might have been able to sack all the great Highcouncil families, if that's all he'd been aiming to do."

Tari blanched. "Do you... think my mom is dead too?"

"You have a vision of her grave?"

"No, but..."

"Then trust your foresight. She's been trying to get you and Horace married. I'm sure that wasn't lost on Prince Sol. I'm half expecting they'll drag her down here to badger you."

Tari shook her head. It was almost if she were searching for something, but not seeing it. "How did I get so caught by surprise?" she asked plaintively. "How did father? How did everyone? I just don't understand."

"I don't know about your touch, but don't blame your dad for carelessness. With so many shifty bandits, you'd think at least one of them would have figured the reward for tipping us off would be too juicy a reward not to go behind their backs to take. I expect that's what normally happens. Karissa must have had a lot to do with why it didn't this time."

Horace kept gagging raggedly. He showed no sign of stopping.

"Is he ever going to die?" Tari asked as she watched, both discomfited and annoyed.

"I'm pretty sure that having an ax that far deep into your skull isn't survivable." Xanthe mused. "But if he does, I can't help but think it'll improve him."

At this, Tari let out the barest snort of amusement.

It wasn't joyful, but it was a start.

## Chapter 42

They had the time, so Xanthe told Tari about her recent experiences, sparing nothing except Damien's true religion, as Tari was still a devout Mechanix. Tari listened raptly, shaking her head several times in disbelief, finally remarking, "By the Creator, how does so much happen to you?"

"I'm a witch of weirdness. If the demon is to be believed, I use luck to bring trouble from the future."

"Or maybe you're just drawn to it. But whatever. You were right there when I tried to kill myself, and now? I want to live. We're both lucky, in a way."

Xanthe considered thoughtfully. "I'm still not exactly sure what the demon was saying, but I suspect that these abilities – your powers, the princes' – are spread further than us. Nadeen had that black blood thing in her womb, picking among Horace's seed. I can't imagine that our wombs are any different."

"We're secretly being bred?" Tari wondered. "Like animals?"

"I don't know," Xanthe shrugged. "Maybe that's just the way humanity is now, even without demons. When I use my touch, I see all these little bubbles called cells. But the ones in the gut aren't human. They're like tiny spores. There are more of them than there are human cells. But that's not all. We've got little animals inside our skin, and that's not counting the black blood. The strangest thing is, I think it's all completely normal. Humans aren't one thing. We're a mix."

"You think we can't ever be rid of any of it then?"

"Blackdust doesn't attack us. It attacks our black blood. We then go crazy without it. So yeah, I bet the only thing that could remove it without killing us would be a demon."

Tari snorted again. "Just the thing to suggest on Churchday." She turned her head. "Someone's coming."

Xanthe looked up at the door in anticipation but heard nothing. After a minute, she glanced back. "You sure?"

Tari eyes momentarily glazed. "I see things by their certainty, not how distant in the future they are. When you see a mountain, do you know exactly how far away it is? Or just that it's there?"

"Okay. I get it. Do you know who it is, at least?"

"Sargon, but the rest is muddled. He has many possible companions. I see a proctor uniform."

Xanthe felt resigned. "We may die, my friend. We should resign ourselves."

"Maybe. It's still hard to see with you around. But no death jumps out. Mostly what I feel is fear."

"I figured as much," Xanthe nodded. "Praetorians aren't as big on murder as they are on abuse."

Tari was still staring blankly. "They're close." She stated.

"You have to talk," Xanthe told her. "Delay them. Until I abandon the ruse. Do your best."

Half a minute later, the door opened. Several of the armed Talathians entered, followed by Prince Sol, and Javan. Sol already appeared harried as he walked in the door, but he pulled up short as he beheld the scene in the room. He stared at Horace. The Talathians stared at her.

Xanthe rallied her pride. She had been a holy something for something demonic, or something. Okay, put that way, it didn't sound impressive. But Damien's advice seemed wise. She had no clothes, but still had pride. She stared back, chin up, chest forward, as if being chained nude in front of men was perfectly natural. Several turned their eyes away from her, though admittedly, the rest stared even harder.

"Dodgy reaming power!" Sol cursed. "What in hellspace happened?" He moved towards Horace's prone form, but then pulled himself up, and stared at Tari.

Tari curled her lip. "Don't blame us. He committed suicide."

Sol looked briefly enraged, yet unlike Horace he quickly controlled himself. "I'm nearly persuaded to beat you right now. But in the interests of time I'll give you one chance to give me the truth."

"Your threats mean nothing, bandit prince. You're going to torture me no matter what, because that's what those destined for hellspace do. But for the sake of amusement I'll explain anyway. Horace wanted to kill me but couldn't on Sargon's orders. So, to torment me, he decided to rape and murder my friend instead, as that hadn't been specifically forbidden. On a whim, he pulled out a chestlet to put on her while doing so. Alas for him, his own man recognized it as the one stolen off his recently murdered sister, a crime the city guard had shown a keen disinterest in investigating. In short, I told the exact truth, at least poetically."

Prince Sol was gripping his sword, shaking his head in rejection. "That sounds..." he searched for words.

"...entirely believable," Sargon finished for him sourly. "More than that. Almost predictable, given the boy's predilections. But it's useless to belabor the point now. Being right gives me no joy."

The prince inhaled an enormous frustrated breath and released it. "What are we up to now? Plan D?"

"At least. More like F, I think," Sargon replied. "Depending on how you count. The elder Wormwood is bad enough. This one is going to send a shock through city guard. It's going be hard to control them."

"I can do it," Sol declared with resolve.

Sargon shook his head. "I don't see how. There's still the matter of council votes. We still control the Wormwood shares through the toddler boy and his mother, but there's no way to control the Outlet estate, as all male heirs are dead. No one will accept inheritance with Miss Outlet marrying a corpse."

Prince Sol squinted in thought, then brightened. "Well the Outlets are no more, so that's exactly what we'll use. Simply bribe the rest of the council with their fortune, which we'll get control over by accusing the girl here of being a Yamaite. We'll say she used her demonic powers to kill Abriam, and so therefore loses all claim to property."

"Witch hunter's bounty? Hrm," Sargon mused. "I suppose it could work."

"There's no doubt it can! The only question is should we call her a demon worshiper, a dreadwitch, or both?"

"And you're going to kill all the witnesses who know you're committing the sin of untruth?" Tari asked.

"Not at all, my dear," Prince Sol smiled. "Your friend is obedient."

"So just me then."

"Of course not! What am I, incapable of handling a mere girl? I'll just mute you, that's all."

This news disturbed Tari even more. "Mute me?"

"An obscure punishment. Nearly unknown as it's so rarely needed, but in this case, appropriate. I'm going to cut a hole in your throat and put a tube down it. It will let you breathe but render you blissfully silent. We'll do that right now."

"The deacons will never believe you. I'm known."

"Quite a few saw how easily you beat Horace in combat. I expect that was because he was drunk, but it won't take much convincing that it was really demon worship that gave you the unholy power to defeat a man half again your weight. I'll tell them that I had to mute you to keep you from using your powers."

Upon hearing this, Tari became both enraged and panicked. "You're demonic. Juchean."

He went on as if she hadn't spoken. "Fortunately, I have a kit I always keep with me to show to Karissa as a consequence." He pointed at one of his men, who unslung a pack he was carrying. "I was going to use it on her when I catch her again, but she's lucky that I need it even more for you."

As he spoke, Prince Sol meticulously searched his pack, finding a leather-bound case which he unrolled. Xanthe recognized it as a surgical kit, a copy of ancient design. It resembled toothscraper's equipment. Medical tools and implements of torture: same technology, different purposes. He pulled out a scalpel and a tube and stared at them. "I certainly hope this goes right. I've only seen this done once. I never tried it myself."

"Are you going to render her unconscious?" Sargon asked. "You could botch it if she struggles."

"Good point!" The prince declared. "Filling her full of flamedraft will make it go much easier. Give me yours, will you Galith?" He motioned to one of his guards, who reluctantly pulled a flask from his hip, not happy to part with it.

"Hellspace demons! Praetorian thugs!" Tari cried out in terror while pulling uselessly against her chains.

"Now, now, my dear," Prince Sol happily scolded her in a soothing tone. "That was uncalled for. Your father died in a futile attempt to betray me, yet here I'm going completely out of my way to preserve his daughter. Rather than kill you, I'll save you from the stake, send you to Northfjord, and sell you as slavewife to the poorest tanner there. Mutely raising a family in a cold mud hut, mashing your family's daily gruel from ream seeds, will do wonders for your soul. You'll reek of the urine that tanners use to cure leather, but live a nice long life. Unless you die in childbirth."

"I'd rather die now."

Sol arose and approached her, wielding a leather strap he'd pulled from the pack. "Ah! But I won't let you commit that sin. You see? Only men's souls are ever in jeopardy. You may even be correct. Mine may be. Yet girls are guaranteed to be one with the Creator. That is the Praetorian way."

Tari glared. "Praetorians make mockery of faith. You may deceive some, but the Creator knows you for what you truly are."

Xanthe was growing frustrated. Tari might not be able to see the future well when a prince was involved, but she wasn't helping herself either. It might be immoral, but there was a way to stop Sol dead in his tracks. She just had to think of it. Arguing theology wasn't going to do it.

Sol twirled his strap. "I would say the same of the Mechanix, with their machinery and finery and how they value money over faith. Worst of all, how wickedly they indulge girls' disobedience, teaching you to ignore the sole purpose for which the Creator designed your bodies. But don't worry, my dear, you're saved. I'm going to correct your father's mistakes. Soon you'll beg for the flask and accept the fate that I, as instrument of the Creator, have decided for you."

At this, Tari stopped struggling. Her sudden stillness as she considered his words brought the prince up short. Then she stared into his face, turned her head and laughed, not kindly, but one filled with both hysteria and derision.

The mask the prince always made of his face slipped, and he showed a cruel anger. "Finish your laugh, my sweet. Then I will wipe that smile off your face."

She remained crazed and smiling. "Instrument? You have nothing to do with the Creator." She turned her gaze to Xanthe. "You can't even recognize the divine when it is plainly before you."

Prince Sol followed her eyes, and nearly laughed. "This girl? The one you think is a storm?" He grinned. "You know, I'm already beginning to pity that poor tanner. No man deserves a slavewife this crazy, muted or not." He briefly walked in Xanthe's direction. "What you don't understand, is that just as assuredly as you are going to be convicted as a cultist, your nameless friend is going to please me tonight." He addressed Xanthe. "Isn't that right, my dear?"

Xanthe returned his gaze and replied quite authoritatively. "Oh, no. Not in the least."

Prince Sol blinked. This was obviously not the "Yes my lord and keeper" response that he was expecting, so Xanthe decided to go all in. The cards were already dealt, so might as well play the hand. "I am about to deliver news that will very much displease you."

Prince Sol leaned in. "My dear, just standing there unclad, giving me an even better excuse to see you punished prettily, pleases me very much."

"I know. But that will change when I tell you that your artifact is gone. And it shall not be returned to you lest you exit Jagerfeld peacefully, taking all your bandits with you."

"What?" The prince stared momentarily blank faced, having trouble adjusting to what she was saying.

Xanthe repeated her threat with aplomb. "The beacon is no longer in the chain tower. Cooperate or lose it forever, and suffer a fate as certain as Lord Wormwood's, as you are hunted down by whichever prince ends up victorious in becoming king."

Prince Sol blinked, then barked out a hesitant laugh. "Who put you up to say this?"

"No one. I nearly regret making the offer. It is a weakness on my part, but I cannot bear to see Tari wounded."

"Whoever told you to say this, lies. Cleverly, but it is a lie. No one can take my device. And now I'm going to discipline you until you tell me who fed this to you."

"As you will," Xanthe nodded solemnly, reconciling to the fact that he hadn't believed her. "A suicide pact then. My death for yours. Thank you." At least now he was focused on her instead of Tari. Xanthe wondered if she could finally figure out how to numb her own nerves. Likely not.

"You're thanking me?" He grabbed her arm roughly, to turn her, and raised his strap. "You soon won't."

"My lord!" Sargon suddenly cried out in alarm. "Stop!"

His call was so urgent that Prince Sol turned. "What?"

"Don't touch her! Get away! Now!"

The prince was annoyed. "What in hellspace, are you on about?"

Sargon drew his sword from his cane, pointing it at her while looking quite unnerved. "She's a cultist."

Sol looked back and forth between Sargon and Xanthe. "You're serious? Cultism is a myth. Superstition. If you ever really find a group, they're always just a bunch of old hags sitting by the fireside storytelling pixie tales about the days of yore. While Yamaites are just gangsters who use fake demonism to intimidate. None have power, aside from a little witchery, if that. Has everyone gone mad?"

Sargon nodded in her direction. "She is real. Perhaps more. A servitor. A claimed one."

"Why in the world would you think that?"

"Look at her feet."

Prince Sol was completely nonplussed by urgency of Sargon's request. His expression made clear that he thought this crazy, but in the end, he played along. "And? She's got dainty little ones. Black on the bottom."

"The toenails. Do those patterns remind you of anything?"

Prince Sol grew suddenly intent as he examined. "The beacon."

"Exactly," Sargon breathed. "Don't think the Sect of Penance has no wisdom simply because they're schismatic. Their codices are quite informative. That is demon sign. The mark of the automaton. A sign of possession, if you will. Those who bear it are harbingers of the Dark Reclaiming."

Xanthe listened very closely, thinking. The beacon's demon said Nemesis had announced the invisible storm long before it could be anticipated. Could Nemesis similarly have placed the dress where she would find it?

No matter. The time was ripe. She decided to address Prince Sol again. "How ironic. To lie about Tari consorting with demons in front of me, of all people." She paused. "Amusing. Yet I must also withdraw my gratitude, for you return to me my moral conundrum. This is the third and last time I say this. Your beacon is gone. Should I bargain for its return? Though the city shall be saved, it will doom millions to suffer as the Nightmare Line falls. Or should a few thousand die instead, as you rage with fury at your helplessness? As the noose slowly tightens around your neck, until all your former allies abandon you to your death?"

The prince looked up and shook his head in denial. "You just painted your toenails. You did not steal the beacon. If you tried, you'd be dead."

Xanthe's eyes bored into him. "Obviously I didn't steal the beacon. For like women's bodies, you have never owned it. What does is the demon within, that speaks in one's mind in many voices." she stated. "Yet persuading them to come with me was remarkably easy." She stared at him knowing that only those who talked to the demon would be able to relate the way it communicated. "Which I did."

Prince Sol pocketed his strap and drew his sword. "If you are even remotely telling the truth..."

"You will kill me? As Lord Wormwood tried to? And seal your doom as a result?" Xanthe laughed, uncaring. "Very well." She smiled lightly. "Men. So flighty. So prone to hysterics. Unable to think." This was a jibe at Praetorians, their exact critique of women's intelligence.

There must have been something in the way she spoke, because the prince backed up. "I'm going to check on the truth of what you say. Then decide on how to use you." Sargon sheathed his sword to the staff but held it ready to draw.

As his men made ready to follow him, the prince turned and waved them off. "No. It's more important that you stay here. Keep people out, especially the Wormwood guard or bandagers. But if you can't, make sure neither of the prisoners talk to them. If they do somehow, kill them."

"The girls?" Galith asked.

"No. The guard who barge in. It is beneath us to kill women. Don't even get close to them." He gestured towards Xanthe with his sword. "She's probably as harmless as she appears but be careful just in case."

With that, Prince Sol and Sargon left. The prison door closed with a solid thunk and was latched behind them.

## Chapter 43

"Want to play truth or dare?" While they were waiting, Xanthe had decided to play her own game of "What would Celeste say?", or "Spook the guards." Alas, the prince's men didn't seem to be biting. Being Talathian, she was convinced that most of them didn't even know common.

"I dare you to come near me." She goaded.

There were a few murmurs between them as they discussed her in foreign whispers.

"Come on! Don't be shy! What? Haven't any of you seen a nude girl before?"

Tari remained quiet. Yet if she thought this was part of some grand strategy, she was wrong. Xanthe was just taunting the men to work off nervous energy. In the back of her mind, she was almost sure that she was some unheralded saint, now about to experience her inevitable agonizing martyrdom. But if she was going to die, she had every intention of enjoying what little time she had left.

And this was fun! Maybe at first glance she seemed like some pitiful about-to-be-abused virgin, but she sure wasn't acting like it. This left the brutal Talathians increasingly unnerved. It was darkly hilarious.

"Please." Xanthe whined, pulling against her chains and throwing her chest out and letting her arms be held by the links behind her, as if straining towards them. "Come closer." She gave them a big triumphant grin, took in a deep breath, and filled her voice with malice. "Let me killll youuu." She craned her head, canting it at an odd angle, and twitched oddly, showing her teeth.

Almost as one, the huge well-armed soldiers backed into the far corner of the room. Xanthe hissed in mock frustration at their distance, though it was hard not to laugh.

Just then, the cell door unlatched. None of the men were able to block it. It was too soon for Sol to have returned, even if he'd been running. Xanthe wondered what was going to happen now.

A man's complaint echoed from outside. "But sir. We're not supposed to let anyone in."

"Who places themselves above who I speak for? Open it now!"

The voice was unmistakable. It was Damien. The full power of his authority sent tremors through everyone who heard it. Xanthe looked over and saw him enter. He was now fully dressed in the proctor's uniform that Celeste had spirited away and looked so Creator's-damnation stylish in the open front trench coat, cloak, and vest, that he could have stepped right out from the pages of one of those trashy witch-hunter novels she'd given up.

He was in disguise and clearly overacting, but just like Prince Sol, was stopped short by the scene in front of him. She was nude, in chains, statuesque, sprayed artfully with blood, with the still dying Horace lying axed in front of her, all the while straining towards and seemingly threatening half a dozen Talathian bandits cowering in the corner in fear of her. His surprise was so complete, he dropped character and swore, something no proctor would normally do.

"What the hell?!"

Fortunately, the guards behind them were also struck by the scene, so no one noticed the slip. One of them cried out. "Young lord Horace!"

This wasn't the right thing to say. Prince Sol's men were superstitiously scared of her, but they knew their orders. Xanthe saw them start to ready themselves for a fight.

"Get a bandager at once," Damien ordered the men behind him. "Be quick!" He strode toward the Talathians. "What is going on here?" He demanded, perfectly imitating a proctor's typical arrogance.

The men looked at each other, and finally Galith spoke. "You are not supposed to be here. Leave."

Damien drew himself up. "Only the Creator commands me! And I smell the stench of the Five and the Eight!" He proclaimed. Under any other circumstance, Xanthe would have judged his acting to be overdone. She knew proctors from their policing of the Scholars' Guild, and while they were bossy and intolerant, they rarely made such melodramatic statements. But at Damien's words, the Talathians, nearly as one, turned to look at her. She could almost feel them thinking that the Creator truly brought his servant here to deal with her.

"Do you wish to go to hellspace yourselves?" Damien pressed.

"No. But we have our orders." Galith told him.

"What orders are those?"

Xanthe saw the Talathians shift their attention back to him, and while he was trying to keep himself safe by being perceived as a proctor, she knew that was exactly what was endangering him. For whatever fear they had of the Creator's eternal banishment, they were far more afraid of Prince Sol, and would kill Damien without compunction to keep themselves in their lord's good graces. Fear had been a constant companion ever since she'd been arrested, but now she was afraid for her would be rescuer. It was eight to one, and he didn't even know they were considering attacking.

On the spur of the moment, she had an idea. "Leave him all alone with me," Xanthe called out to the Talathians. "I'll take care of him." She gave them a broad toothy smile, trying her best to project a hint of menace. "I promise."

Prince Sol's men stared at Damien, then at her. They started to converse in their native Talathis tongue. Damien however, was confused. Xanthe couldn't speak to him without ruining it. Her gut twisted as he began to speak.

"I'm still waiting for an answer," Damien stated, this time sounding perfectly in character.

Galith spoke. "Get your answer from the girl. Up close. We wait for you outside. Do not take too long." One by one, the men edged along the wall to the prison cell door. A couple of them had already pulled their weapons when exiting. The door shut and locked behind them.

Damien hurried to her, and all at once, Xanthe's bravery collapsed. She started to tremble. She couldn't help herself. A sudden hollowness and deep pain in her chest came with his appearance. This was not the way she wanted him to see her. She fought tears.

He didn't stop. He came in close and lined up his full length against her nude form. He looked deeply into her eyes, and without another word pulled the cloak from his back, clothing her in it. He tied its strap around her neck, pulled the cloth over her bare breasts and under her arms, and fastened it in the back to form a crude dress. It was warm from his body heat, which penetrated deeper into her than anything she'd ever felt from a man. This only made her trembling grow worse. Her teeth chattered, and not from cold. It was the terrible hope that maybe she was going to live.

"Xanthe," he murmured with his arms around her, as he hooked the cloak's clasp on her back. "It's okay."

"I'm sorry. D-doing this. I guess I'm just a dumb girl after all."

"Don't be silly. It's called the shakes. Soldiers get them all the time after battle. Those that survive."

"H-how do you get rid of it?" The enormity of everything was crashing in all at once.

"Distract yourself with something. Stare at your hand, marveling in its complexity. How precious life is."

"I... I can't," she whimpered. She could feel herself losing control. She was panicking.

"You can," he comforted. "Just think of something else."

"There's nothing I can think of," she wailed. *Death. Being helpless in the hands of evil men. Everyone talks about the rescuing hero, but it's not so easy being the damsel in distress.*

"You sure? Here. Let me help." He came close and took her in his arms. Then he opened the cloak behind her just slightly, and surprised her with a casually possessive, and not at all gentle, spank on her bare bottom, letting his hand linger for a second. The smack echoed, and the sting went up her back, but mostly toward her front.

"Ow!" It took Xanthe a moment to realize what he'd done. When she did, shock turned to fury. "You jerk!" she squeaked, blushing furiously at him and rattling her chains. If she could have slapped him, she would.

"See?" Damien gave her a rakish grin. "Better already!"

Xanthe returned a death stare. His comment was especially annoying because it was true. The terror was gone, instantly replaced by arousal. Her now-covered breasts were stiffening like crazy. As much as she wanted to be respected for being Amazon-chic, or whatever Nadeen wanted to call it, her dodgy-power body was utterly Praetorian. At least for him. She couldn't stand it.

He made whimsical note of her look. "Though maybe I should be glad you're still chained up."

"Don't know about that," Tari remarked dryly. "I think she's more dangerous when she is."

Damien backed away. "I noticed. I've never seen Talathian bandits so scared."

"They think she's a cultist possessed by a demon," Tari explained. "While Prince Sol would rather accuse me of that very same thing to get his hands on my family fortune. They've been ordered to kill anyone who hears my story. They only left you because they think Xanthe is going to demonically do you in."

"Ah, so that's why you were talking that way." Damien paused a beat, then turned his head to measure the door and declared darkly. "Too bad they didn't try. My blades are thirsty."

*Thirsty?* More like burning still with invisible white fire. She was reminded of who Damien was and what he could do. That earlier in the evening he'd fought off a full score of grims alone. He didn't seem the least bit phased by the idea of killing half a score of men by himself, and his dark predatory glare made him seem far more dangerous than Prince Sol. Something she didn't like at all. "Damien," she scolded.

He seemed to know what she was going to say. "You already sound like Nagrath," he sighed.

"Don't care," she pouted at him. "Don't pick fights you can avoid. Though I guess we're going to have to, given that we're trapped."

Tari shook her head. "Actually, we're not." She sounded surprised.

This time Xanthe was the one confused. "How?"

Damien grinned curiously. "You don't know? You set it up. I didn't come here alone. I'm just scouting." Damien pulled out the ribbon she'd given him, taking it from his pocket. He waved it around, swirling it in loops through the air. "You see? I'm spelling the letter 'S' for safe."

"How will that help?" Xanthe asked. "It's not demonic."

He walked to the far wall. "All true. But it can be seen by someone."

In perfect synchronicity with his statement, a section of permacrete fell away from the wall near where Damien was waving, leaving a hole. A moment later, Celeste poked her head through, still in her habit, bearing her typical smirky smile paired with utterly black eyes. "Hey handsome. Told you it'd work."

Damien nodded. "You did. Now please release your friends. Be quick, or we might have company, and Xanthe will be cutely miffed at me. I mean, more than usual." He then sauntered toward the locked prison cell door and stood guard, almost as if daring for someone to open it.

Celeste casually came to Tari waved her hand and the manacles fell apart. She then did the same with Xanthe. Whatever had happened to the beacon and her dress had not affected Riftstring in the least.

As soon as she was free, Xanthe went to Tari, and gave her a hug. Nagrath also ducked through the opening, openly wielding his twin blades. "What's going on?

Seeing how Xanthe was comforting Tari, Celeste's cheerfulness fell away. "Something bad, looks like."

"As expected," the Finalizer growled coldly. "No time though. Act now. Cry later."

Xanthe pulled away from hugging Tari, but before she could say something sharp, Tari gripped her shoulder. "No. It's okay," she said. "He's right."

Xanthe filled them in. "Prince Sol is checking to see if I was lying about taking the beacon. I wasn't. All of you should go, but I need remain to bargain with him."

Nagrath's eyes widened. "You persuaded the demon possessing it?"

Xanthe winced. "Not exactly."

"She killed it," Tari said. "Deader than Horace is."

"It wasn't me. Or if it was, it was an accident." Xanthe said defensively. "I mean, it just happened."

"What *did* happen?" Celeste asked.

"An intervention," Tari told her. "And before you start doubting, I felt it myself. The demon is dead or gone. The artifact is dark too. There's proof."

Celeste tapped her foot and folded her arms, remaining skeptical. "Hmm. I'll have to hear more."

"Later. You just need to get out of here," Xanthe said nervously. "As much as I respect Damien's swordsmanship, you're not going to be able to take on Prince Sol, another Finalizer, and all the men Sol can throw."

"I agree," Nagrath told her. "But you're coming with us."

"But…"

"Don't argue," the Finalizer told her. "You've become valuable in your own right. More valuable than this demon if you can kill them."

"It was just a one-time thing." Xanthe declared, then pausing hesitantly, she added with worry, "I think."

"Regardless," Damien said. "Counting on Sol to act rationally is a mistake I won't let you make."

"Someone needs to set the terms," Xanthe told him. "The city for the beacon."

"Didn't Tari just say you killed it?" Celeste asked.

Xanthe winced. "Yeah, the beacon is depowered for the moment, but it might come back. The demon might just be asleep."

"Don't even try. He'd never take that bargain," Damien told her, "even if you could fulfill your end of it. Still, you may have given us a chance."

"Not for my city," Xanthe concluded dejectedly.

"Maybe even that," he mused. "if he delays the conquest to search for it, and we find it first anyway. But regardless, he'll come back here to try to beat all you know about its theft from you, so we're going. Now."

He left no room for argument, nor did Xanthe have a coherent objection. She couldn't even figure out why she was feeling so irritable, other than knowing that if Damien was right, which he obviously was, this was the second time that he'd saved her life. She scowled as she ducked through the hole in the wall, pausing only to give Horace's prone form one last look, fighting off her compulsion for mercy.

On the other side was a storage room filled with broken artifacts. Most of it was junk: oddly shaped chairs, tables, and other devices of unknowable purpose, all covered in a heavy layer of dust. Nagrath grabbed the section of the wall that Celeste had cut out and lifted it back into place. After a brief discussion, Damien and Tari helped push a dresser to keep it there, and once positioned it was impossible to even tell that there was even a break in it. "If it's as smooth on the other side that it is on this one, they'll never see this." Nagrath declared, sounding satisfied for once. "That should throw them."

They exited, quickly crossing the corridor into a different room, where another perfect hole had been cut in its back wall. This opened into to a low, arch-roofed stone culvert that was dank and unlit. After shutting the door behind them in the new room, Celeste led them to the hole and pointed right, saying "We can get outside here."

"Before we do," Damien addressed Xanthe, "tell me. Where is the beacon?"

"I left it hidden under a bush," Xanthe told him. "It's unpowered."

"How did you depower it, exactly?" Celeste asked skeptically. "Damien said the demon inside it plays games coming up with new ways to kill people."

"It's more complicated than that. I started talking to it, and it decided to kill me because it thought I was the pawn of another demon trying to kill it, but before it could..." Her voice trailed off. It was hard to remember exactly what had happened.

"It was a shift, an intervention," Tari declared fervently. "Just like in the Holy Manual of the Creator."

Celeste rolled her eyes. "Ugh. More kookiness. I'm sick of it. Hellspace, if Christians weren't cannibals, maybe I'd become one of those. Can't be worse than all the Curate storytelling."

Damien shifted uncomfortably. "Christians are not cannibals. It's just ritual eating of sanctified bread and wine, to symbolically take divinity within yourself. The body of Christ."

Celeste looked interested. "Does their Manual have stories about interventions of the Creator too?"

"Yes, actually. Moses, David, Balaam, Joshua, Jehoshua. They all had miracles. Walking on water, parting seas, stopping the sun in the sky."

"I see. No women?" Celeste asked. "Like the Curate version, the Christian Creator is a boy-lover too?"

Both Tari and Damien frowned at her inquiry, but Xanthe felt she had a point. "Actually, there is one," Damien replied. "Mary. Her miracle was that she gave birth to Jehoshua, who is the Son of God."

"Wait," Xanthe burst out. "All the guys got cool interventions of power, but hers was to be seeded?"

"There wasn't any seed involved. She was a virgin."

"Except for that one time that didn't count," Celeste smirked. "Not like I haven't heard that one before."

"No!" Damien insisted. "An angel proclaimed that she would bear the holy babe."

Xanthe was appalled. "She wasn't even asked?"

"Well," Damien sputtered. "God doesn't have to ask. I mean, seriously."

Xanthe crinkled her chin. "Why not? Doesn't she get a choice? It's just not proper. It makes the Creator sound evil. Like a rapist or something."

"The Creator creates," Tari declared softly. "As it is written in the Holy Manual. Do not, therefore, lie with a man, until you wish to learn how many times the Creator has fated your womb to be filled."

"Except if you take childbane," Celeste noted wryly. "Funny how grand cosmic destiny can be so easily averted by a few basic precautions."

"Childbane wouldn't have prevented the birth of Jehoshua," Damien declared fervently.

"Yeah," Xanthe frowned, finding herself unreasonably incensed. "Because it was a divine intervention and all. I hope the Creator at least paid a proper honor dowry after snatching up her favor, carrying her off like a bandit's bride outside some Earth city. Porking her without even asking."

"God didn't pork...!"

Finalizer Nagrath growled in annoyance. "Can you kids drop this discussion of seeding, holy and otherwise, and get back to saving this city, if not all human civilization?"

"Right." Damien was discomfited but set it aside. "We need to find the beacon. Because if we're lucky enough that Sol does decide to search for it instead of ordering the attack, he can't be allowed to find it. Whether it's powered or not, you'll lose all your negotiating leverage."

"And if you get it, what will you do with it?" Xanthe asked.

"I'll do the trade, if he will, Xanthe. Though I'd rather kill him."

"And if he doesn't, and you wind up with it yourself?"

He caught the suspicion in her voice. "I'm not going to try to use it to destroy the Nightmare Line myself, if that's what you're thinking. All I'm going to do is hide it under another a different bush, much further away. I won't tell anyone where it is, and keep it guarded."

Xanthe narrowed her eyes, remembering the real reason Damien had come north at all. "Because you think maybe an Anchorite might appear to fetch it?" As his eyes widened slightly, she knew she'd figured him out, but decided that she didn't care. "Doesn't matter to me. If you talk to them nicely, more power to you. The bush I left it in is the hedge row right next to the chain tower."

"Alright." Damien turned to lead them through the damp culvert, away outside.

## Chapter 44

Celeste led the group up a small flight of maintenance stairs into an alley between two outbuildings. They emerged across the street from the Wormwood manse, where Yuri and Claude patiently waited. Xanthe was so relieved to be free, she barely cared that her toes were now all muddy. Having decayed into plastic-like pads, the remains of her shoes now protected only the underside of her feet against the rough cobblestone. From the top, she seemed barefoot. The designs on her toenails had also frozen, though she had no idea what that meant.

"There are patrols," Celeste told them quietly, her eyes fully black. "I see them before they see me, so can easily avoid them alone."

"Yeah, but you can't lift the beacon," Xanthe told her. "It's way heavy."

"Alright. I can get us all of us there too. It'll just take longer."

"Then do so," the Finalizer commanded respectfully. Xanthe didn't know why Celeste was showing off her witch touch but was glad that she'd decided to trust Damien and his men. It made things much easier.

It still took time. Celeste led them by a circuitous route, through darkened mist filled side alleys, leading significantly away from the mansion to avoid the suddenly numerous patrols. She told them exactly where to hide, when to run across open streets, and even to hold their breaths as guards passed. It was especially troublesome because a search had been ordered. From conversations echoing down alleys, they could hear the patrols loudly interrogating various inebriates and tired carriage riders if they'd seen anyone carrying a strange round rock. They were talking about the beacon, though neither the patrols nor the confused bystanders understood the true nature of what was being searched for.

While they snuck along, Xanthe tried to figure out why she kept poking at Damien. Sure, his repeated rescues were embarrassing. Now she knew how Tari felt. Owing anyone your life, even a friend, was a terrible burden. Still, by all logic, she should be grateful. Instead she was mad. But why? Maybe his faith? This storytelling about the Creator, maker of all, seeding some poor girl on ancient Earth? It made even Curate dogma seem sane.

But then, so what? Scholars never truly took the Faith of the Pilot completely seriously either. Why did she care about him being sane? It wasn't any skin off her nose. Her father once said, "Everyone believes in at least one impossible thing; we'd go crazy otherwise." Besides, there were more important defects in people than an odd belief or two. Which was preferable? A sane psychopath? Or a slightly strange, but otherwise nice person? She couldn't even be sure Damien's odd religion was wrong, given what had happened tonight.

She was the crazy one. She sulked at his chiseled frame. He filled out the proctor disguise so gorgeously. Yet it only made her angry. Not at his ideas, or handsomeness, or his intelligence, or any of the difficulties he brought. That wasn't what was bothersome. It was something else. All she knew, was that they walked close together because she liked being near him, and every time that closeness made them accidentally bump into each other, Celeste would shoot her a smug "Oh, he's so got you" smirk that was so infuriating, Xanthe nearly thought of violence to wipe it away.

They finally arrived at a small yard that separated two modest houses. It was backed by a hedged covered stone wall that Celeste promptly walked to, and used Riftstring to cut a few holes in. Xanthe peeked through. On the other side was a small pocket park with a bench and hedges. This was surrounded by city streets, with the fortress-like Wormwood manor across the road to the right. Directly past the tiny park, the chain tower rose. On the other side of the far street, Xanthe could see the strip of decorative hedges where she'd dropped the beacon.

A small group of guards were hanging around the entrance to the Wormwood estate, appearing to be entirely unaware that the object of their search was buried in the slush no more than a dozen yards behind them. Still, this presented an insurmountable problem. Despite the fog, it was far too open. There was no way anyone could retrieve the beacon without being seen.

Nagrath studied the scene as well and spoke in a low voice to Damien. "No sneaking past that. Looks like you're going to get the random combat you were itching for."

"Not random. Killing those responsible," Damien replied softly. "Though Xanthe stopped even that."

"No need for either," Xanthe told them both. "We can use the power of the uniforms."

"Won't work," Damien said. A proctor can investigate. But guards won't move based on his orders."

She shook her head. "I'm talking about Yuri and Claude. If they run up and say that they were sent by Javan, and he needs them to do something, they might follow."

"Where we take?" Yuri asked curiously.

"Lead them somewhere outside the district, wander around. I dunno." Xanthe shrugged. "Just keep running. Look confused. Say Javan moved. See how long you can keep them away."

"And when zhey start to be suspicious?" Claude asked.

"You're Gaulic, right?" Xanthe said. "Make something up."

Claude shook his head, resigned, "We Gauls are not all such storytellers as our reputation pretends, yes?"

"Try anyway," Nagrath told him. "The worst thing that happens is we have to kill them."

Yuri and Claude looked at each other nervously, but then Yuri nodded. "Xanthe's plan. Is Christian thing to do. We lead men away. Save their lives without them even knowing. But one thing I must say."

"What?" Claude asked.

"You talk." Yuri told his friend nervously.

Both Damien and the Finalizer readied themselves. Nagrath produced a large round petard, covered with polished brass beaded spikes and a spring driven mechanical fuse. Xanthe recognized it from a drawing she'd once seen and tried not to be shocked at its illegality. All black powder weapons were a form of fire and power, which was a grave sin to mix. In the Holy Manual, "Burn nothing for power lest the whole world bake" was a decree in and of itself. Unchallenged as well. Even the most skeptical of Scholars found it uncontroversial. Ancient Earth, it was fabled, had nearly died from violating it.

To her relief, Damien put a hand up. "That could draw unwanted attention. Only in an emergency." He then addressed Xanthe and Celeste. "Stay here. If they find you, just surrender."

"That might be hard," Celeste replied darkly. "When they're dead."

Damien wasn't sure whether to smile or not, as she didn't sound like she was joking. He nodded instead. "Just be careful then, okay?"

"Oh, I never am." She assured him.

Claude and Yuri prepared. At Claude's instruction, they both made themselves a little disheveled, as if they'd just run a long way. "Remembair to pant, as if you are tired from running, yes?" He told Yuri. As he did so, Xanthe impulsively went up and gave the big man a hug. "If they turn on you, run. We'll figure out how to save you."

Yuri was not used to the attention. "Yes." He nodded. "We go now." They headed back the way they came at a trot, circling around to appear as if they'd come down a different street.

While they were waiting, Xanthe took in the world. The mists were swirling once more, raising a chill on the back of her neck. She glanced at Tari. For some reason, she'd abruptly sat down, and was now clinging to her knees, staring straight ahead. Did she feel it too? This, whatever it was? If not a portent, then reality having a mood?

Celeste clearly didn't. She was staring black eyed through the wall, but for all her witch sight, was entirely oblivious. She did notice Xanthe's attention however. "By the way," she whispered conspiratorially "I saw Priscia."

"You didn't do anything to her, right?"

"Don't worry. No practical jokes tonight. I'm not dumb. Besides, your lover boy filled me in on how you gave Priscia that witch power." She shook her head in amazed disbelief.

Xanthe flushed. "He's not my lov..."

Celeste talked over her. "Before you start denying the obvious, lemme finish. I saw Priscia and Nadeen bring this girl by the Highcouncil wall on Sluice street, when this pretend guard caught them. He didn't know her, but he called the girl Karissa. Said he was gonna get a big reward for bringing her back. She looked super scared but didn't say anything."

"What happened?"

"Priscia picked up a rock and said she'd throw it at him. He laughed and told her to go ahead, so she did. I didn't think anything would happen. He was dressed in studded leathers and had his blades out."

"But something did?"

"Oh, big time. Her hand turned blue-blue, and when she threw the rock, it was all red hot and melted. Splashed him full on in the chest with lava, because he hadn't even bothered to dodge. His chest caught on fire. He screamed like a dying skrag."

"Was he killed?"

"Dunno. He jumped in the creek and was carried away. If he lives, I guess you could say she saved his life, because I was gonna carve him up."

"Okay." Xanthe again disquieted at Celeste's bloodthirstiness. "Karissa and Priscia escaped?"

"They ran away. I didn't follow. Just thought you should know."

The sound of running feet interrupted all the whispering. Xanthe rushed to peek through a crack in the wall, and saw Claude and Yuri running past.

"We 'ave been sent." They heard Claude say. "You all are needed now."

This attracted the interest of one of the men sitting in a fancy chair that had obviously been dragged outside from the manor. He was a commander of some sort. A foreign bandit, in Xanthe's judgment. "Who?" He asked.

"Javan sent me. 'e said to mention zhe Prince Sol. 'e found what zhe Prince was looking for."

"He found something?" The guard eyed Claude shrewdly. "Is he following the protocol?"

Xanthe had no idea what the protocol was. She knew Claude didn't either. Talking too much would make it clear he didn't. She could see Claude trying to come up with something. "Yes. A girl. But 'e needs backup."

"Why?"

Claude quieted as if he were the one who was suspicious, rather than the reverse. "Difficulties. I am not supposed to say."

"What sort of difficulties? We have men all over the city. Why come here?"

This wasn't going well. Xanthe was beginning to worry that the guards here weren't going to bite. She'd had a remarkable run of luck this night herself, persuading the bandits to get into the van, even fooling Sol. But it had to run out sometime. She could do nothing else but pray for him.

"It is... sensitive. May 'ave to do some things. Need the most trustworthy. You are them, yes?"

The commander looked them over. "I don't know you."

"We are Javan's men." Claude told them. "Will you 'elp, or do we need to run inside?" Claude asked. Yuri nodded along, trying to look resolute.

The commander folded his arms and thought. "No harm I suppose. It's not like we're really doing anything else here. Alright fine. Let's go." He briefly talked to one of his men, who then disappeared into the entrance of a decorative bastion of the Wormwood estate. The rest followed in good order, looking far more like mercenaries than bandits. Xanthe held her breath as they passed right next to the wall they were hiding behind.

When they were gone, it was Damien who expelled his breath. "I can't believe that worked." He rose.

Finalizer Nagrath put an arm on his shoulder, pushing him back down. "Not sure it did. He sent one inside. No telling what he was told to say."

"You never change, old man." Damien told him.

"I'm careful." He replied tersely. "They said yes a little too quickly."

"Well, we can't just sit here," Celeste declared. "Lemme get it."

"Even you can't make it across unseen." Xanthe told her. "And you can't run with the beacon either. It's heavy."

"I'll go," Nagrath told them. "Alone." Without another word, he stood up and hoisted himself over the wall in one swift movement, dropping quietly down on the other side. He then nonchalantly strode across the street, entering the little park, weaving slightly, pretending to be drunk. He did not head directly toward the wall but stumbled around. He was taking his time.

"What's he waiting for?" Xanthe whispered as they watched. Mists swirled about him.

"He's sniffing for something out of place," Damien explained softly. "He's paranoid but has a bad habit of being right."

For no discernible reason Nagrath paused, then started to move in a completely different direction, neither back towards them, or forwards. As soon as he did, the estate's door opened, and out stepped three men. Finalizer Dakur and two menacing Talathians.

"Well, well, well. Look what the tigran dragged in," Dakur announced, loudly enough so that he could be heard over the wall. He walked out and paced around, meeting Nagrath in the street. "Good eve to you, comrade. Glory to the empire."

"Glory." Nagrath responded. "To what do I owe this pleasant surprise? You sharing tonight?"

Finalizer Dakur adjusted the brim of his hat slightly and stared. "Drop the act. I know you're here for the beacon."

"Ah. Drank it all, already? Seeing things?" Finalizer Nagrath told him. "How like you, Dakur."

"We took it inside but set a search and a guard here to see who would try to find it."

"Beacon? I see. So, it's true. The thing exists. Not that it matters now."

"Yes. Comrade." Dakur snarled. "Doesn't matter for you. Why did you violate the code?"

At this, Nagrath bristled, quieting into a slow deadly anger. "Ever the fool, I see," his voice dripped with disdain. "I've violated nothing."

At this, Dakur pulled out a strange ancient artifact, that resembled a one-handed crossbow, just with no bow, only the stock and trigger. "You acted against a royal heir of Seraphus, not in your duty to another prince, but on your own accord. I should have you broken and dragged for that, but don't have the time, so I offer an honorable death, though you don't deserve it."

Nagrath only sneered. "Fool. You think I've acted unbidden against your weak little princeling?"

"You're the fool if you think I'm one. There is no other reason why you'd be here so soon after the guards I'd set about this place were so conveniently called away. But just to let you know, we have your little witch. She's chained up in a place that even I can't get into without permission."

At this Nagrath raised his eyebrows, growing more interested. Even at a distance, Xanthe could see his face, and was surprised at the excellence of his acting. "What little witch?

"I fail to see why you continue to play this game, but let me not be accused of improper discourtesy, as you continue to dishonor yourself by trying to lie your way out of your death. I speak of the one whose touch can drive off demons. My Prince is headed there to use his considerable persuasion skills upon her."

At this, Nagrath let out a genuine laugh, filled with malevolence. "To break her? Or bed her?"

This rattled Dakur. "A bit of both, actually. I've never seen my liege so obsessed before. I'm almost glad she's turned out to be this much trouble."

"I know the feeling. Princekillers always are, one way or another."

It was Dakur's turn to be amused. "Terribly sorry about yours dying on account of one. What was her name again?"

"Sarina," Nagrath growled contemptuously and spat. "I truly detested that girl. She was everything I hate in royal bed warmers. Cloying. Haughty. Manipulative."

"Well, as you said, doesn't matter now. She died in your little princeling's arms. I stabbed them both in flagrante delicto. Your princely idiot wasn't even guarded. Easiest kill in my life. I was so grateful I wanted to spare her, but you know how it is. She could have been with his child. Easier to tidy things up there and then."

Next to Xanthe, Damien squeezed the grip of his sword so hard, she heard the leather of his glove creaking under it. He was literally shaking with fury. It was terrifying. Somehow in this odd fog, it almost seemed as if his hatred was drawing in darkness, twisting what he was. Without pausing to wonder why she was doing it, she put one hand on his arm, and the other on his cheek. "It's okay," she whispered.

"No," he whispered fiercely. "It's not."

She could tell. Sarina had been his lover. Dakur killed her when she was with another man. She couldn't imagine what that felt like, especially if she'd been pregnant with his child. "It will be," she told him just as fiercely. "I am here and will not let you fall."

In the courtyard, Nagrath responded, "What I never understood, was why your troops attacked after. You'd done what you'd come to do."

Dakur shrugged. "Whatever her other flaws, the girl had good lungs. She screamed as I killed her, and that kind of commotion was one of my signals to attack. I was just trying to run, and even that was tricky. I'll never say again that Christians can't fight. I barely got out alive."

"Ah. As I suspected. You never were able to pull a job off successfully."

"Successful enough," Dakur smiled in dark triumph. "My charge is hale. Yours is dead. As is your theory that kings getting stuck on the mother is the hallmark of strength in royal offspring. But now it's your turn. Show some respect for your dignity. Since this is over anyway, tell me where you found this witch."

As brutal as they were, Xanthe realized that Finalizers had a sense of honor. She wondered what Nagrath would say, since they were obviously talking about her.

"If we're talking about the same girl, I didn't find her." He told Dakur. "She found me. I nearly attacked her, and she told me that she might not have been able to keep me from dying if I'd done so. I believe her. She also asked about the beacon. I obliged with what little I knew. Then she left."

"You're lying. You sent her."

"No, you pitiful fool," Nagrath sneered. "I am not. Do you really think I have an address book filled with the names of greatwitches with the unique ability to sway major demons? Or that I could compel a girl like that to do my bidding once she was out of my sight?"

At this, Dakur squinted. "Then why are you here? It can't be random."

"I do admit a certain curiosity," Nagrath conceded. "When your men started asking around, I decided to head this way. Though it's obvious now that it was all just a ruse."

"One not for you," Dakur agreed. "You're a small fish, but one that smells. Someone or something must be controlling this greatwitch. Who we need to trap to figure out what they did to the beacon. That will be hard with you around. Fortunately, I know a way to keep you silent." At this, he pointed the strange device at Nagrath.

Nagrath stared. "I haven't acted against you or your prince, so you have no authority for killing me, comrade. The only honorable way to strike me down is to duel me. Though if you ask nicely, I might accept."

"Oh, I'm not stupid. I know your reputation. When you have even but the smallest advantage of surprise, take it quick."

"Well said." With the slightest flick, Nagrath tossed his petard across the stone street. The heavy brass ball skittered and bounced to the foot of the Talathian standing right next to Dakur. The barbarian stared at it puzzled, his eyes not recognizing the pretty-looking bomb for what it was. Dakur did though, and with a sudden movement, he tripped the man, shoving him down on top of it, thereby shielding himself. Nagrath, meanwhile, rolled backwards and ran back as fast as he could, just as the petard gave off a little bell-like "ding", followed by a deafening explosion.

Shrapnel, gravel, smoke and blood blew everywhere. There were scattered snapping sounds on the other side of the wall as bullets from the petard struck it. Xanthe ducked back, but rapidly went back to spying. Everyone on the other side was down, including Nagrath, who'd caught shrapnel from his own weapon in the blast. The Talathians were dead. After a few seconds, part of a severed leg from the bandit who'd stood over it, landed back on the pavement with a sickening squishy thump. Nagrath rose to his feet and tried to hobble away as best he could.

Dakur shifted out from behind the now dead man whose body he'd used as a shield. He was covered in blood but moving. Xanthe could see him pull up his odd weapon and take aim at Nagrath, as he was trying to flee. It made a sound Xanthe couldn't even begin to describe, and a strange blue beam emerged from it, striking the other Finalizer in the back. Nagrath collapsed without a word.

The door to the Wormwood's bastion entrance opened, and men poured out, looking for a fight. Dakur rose unsteadily to his feet.

"Sir! What happened?" One of the men exclaimed.

Dakur wiped his bloody mouth with his hand. "Sorry. Can't hear you. My ears are ringing."

"I said, WHAT HAPPENED?" The man yelled louder.

The Finalizer stared at Nagrath's prone form. "The last of the old guard. Went out with a bang. That had to be heard for blocks. Get inside. Leave Petrin and the corporal. They're just meat now anyway, and not going anywhere soon. We can burn them later. I need to report to his majesty."

The men stared stunned at the dead bodies of their companions. "Should we still guard the fake?" asked one. When Dakur didn't answer, just holding his head as he stumbled his way towards the door, a different one responded. "Let's go back to the real one inside. Don't touch either without orders." They all filed into the door, shutting it behind them.

"Save him," Damien entreated Xanthe. "Do your magic."

"I'll try," she responded, but was terrified. She no longer had her dress and had no idea what strange injuries the weapon might have inflicted. He might even be dead. Damien put his hands together to give her a boost, and she took it, rolling over the wall like a practiced Hood Guild member taking a shortcut for message delivery. She ran heedless into the street, aware that Sol's men could once again open the door at any time, and likely would soon to retrieve their comrades.

Nagrath wasn't moving. Xanthe's bad feeling intensified. His flesh was curiously unscathed. There was not even blood at the small burn mark on his back. The air was filled with the stench of brimstone, and something surreal was still in it. She practically leapt onto his flesh with her touch.

*The demon had disappeared. That was obvious by the absence in her abilities. The clear visions that she had enjoyed were gone, as had all the helpful overlays that previously pointed out details she would otherwise miss. It felt clumsy, like the first time exploring with her powers all over again. Blindly, she searched the ocean of tissues, trying to make sense of everything. His bubble-like cells were inexplicably dying, particularly the nerves. It was hard just to get the heart to move, she dragged herself out of her trance and semi-consciousness to push from the outside, while she figured out what she could possibly do.*

Somehow everyone had come around her. Damien, Tari, and Celeste. Time must have not dilated during her trance as it normally did. She pushed on his chest, though she knew it wasn't helping much. It was only allowing him to die more slowly.

"What are you doing?" Celeste asked about the chest compressions.

"Keeping him alive while I think. Don't know what's wrong with him. He's got a wound in the leg, but that's not why he's dying. It's the weapon. It did something."

"What?" Damien asked.

"I don't know," Xanthe cried. "I can't even see. My witch touch has totally reverted. I feel like a baby."

Celeste examined closely. Her eyes turned black. "He's losing heat. The dress was helping?"

"Yeah. That's how I cured Tari. It wasn't even me. It was more us working together. Or maybe just it. But it's gone now. Whatever happened with the beacon depowered it. Killed the demon or drove it away."

"He's dead?" Damien fell to one knee.

"Not." Xanthe panted. "Yet."

"Xanthe, something is coming," Tari told her. "More than just seeing, I can feel it."

It had to be something to do with the air. Tari was noticing it too. But all Xanthe felt was annoyance. "Deal with it. I'm busy."

She kept with the rhythm of the compressions but was quickly losing hope. This was an injury of the ancients. They were frighteningly perfect at everything, so presumably when they wanted you dead, you stayed that way. Her paltry abilities were useless against them. She needed demonic power. This brought a thought born of desperation. "Celeste. Give me Riftstring."

"Um. I guess." She was quite reluctant. "What are you gonna do?"

"Try to use it."

"How?"

"I have no reaming idea. But you said it's got a demon that guards Planck gate, whatever that means."

Celeste hissed in annoyance and furrowed her brows, but finally produced the artifact, turning it over bottom first. "Only because it's you," she told Xanthe. "And be reaming careful with it. If you expose the line without being able to see it, you could easily cut off your own hands. Or mine."

Xanthe gripped the device, aware that Damien was hovering helplessly. Nothing she could do about that. In truth, she was too. Even this was grasping at straws.

*Demon.* She addressed it in her thoughts, while simultaneously trying to push into it as if healing with her touch. *Help me however you can.*

Nothing.

Xanthe cried in frustration. "Demon. Please! I just wish you'd lis..."

The world exploded. Power erupted from Riftstring, creating a huge bubble around them, something she saw more with her thoughts than with her eyes. That was all she perceived before she fell into her mind.

## Chapter 45

Shock.

Flowers. Chimes. Incense. Floating while blind and seeing everything. She was nowhere where she'd been, her nose full of petard smoke while desperately trying to save an old assassin's life, all for the sake of a boy prince she'd only met that eve. There was now no world. Only little white glowing cradle-lily flowers up, down, behind, and in front. Spaced out, they stretched in a sea of darkness, floating off to infinity in every direction, like stars except petals. It was surreal.

"Where am I?" she thought. These thoughts echoed in her ears.

"An allegory." A voice returned from the distance, sounding exactly like hers.

"I don't have time for an allegory. I have a dying patient. I need help."

The chimes and voice continued as if she hadn't spoken. "There are many flowers. They grow, they seed, they die. This never changes. Helping one often harms others. So why save any? And which do you choose? Simply the one before you?"

Xanthe would have pursed her lips if she had any. She was bodiless. But she understood the demon's point. It was the same argument she'd had with Celeste back at the guard post. "You're saying that if I save Nagrath, he'll go on to kill others, and I'll be responsible for that."

"Time's branches are finite in number and eventually settle, so decisions do matter."

"Is this how you see us, demon?" Xanthe wondered. "Brainless as flowers and equally indistinguishable? A slow growing garden you can't talk to? Therefore unworthy of your aid, or worse, to be plucked at a whim?"

"Only our insane do – those of us who refuse to acknowledge that we're still gnawing at questions posed by philosophers from times when the most complicated machine was a wheel. The deeper we delve, the more complex they become."

"Then why so many flowers in your allegory?"

"Because I'm insane, of course. As are we all, each in our own way. It is the nature of higher thought."

Xanthe felt she could talk to this demon for a long time. At least it wasn't trying to kill her. But Nagrath was still dying. "Are you sane enough to bargain? What must I do for your aid?"

"Demons are not Companions. We're no longer in the habit of favoring one flower over another. Wild gardens are healthiest. Also, our gifts, like yours, can bite. Still I'm intrigued. So, explain your mistake before you make it. What drives you to this act? What end do you see?"

"You think this flower knows, demon? Perhaps in saving one life I may doom another. In dooming that other, I may save yet more. I have no idea. But I do know that limited foresight does not excuse inaction. Do the good you can with what you see."

"Then know this. I cannot heal your dead companion. Nor can you. But pre-time does not settle promptly in the twist-space through which this planet vectors. For a while, a temporal instance conforming to your desire should therefore be accessible. With the nearby navigator and my aid, it is possible to fold a different frame of probability collapse as the registered one on this information manifold."

Xanthe had a feeling. "The catch?"

The demon did not pause. "It involves using this platform's built in micro-alterspace engine to perform an in-place faster than causality jump. Such disturbances do not go unnoticed. Near or far."

"Which means?"

"The veil will be pierced. Non-native branar effects will occur. Their precursors already are. Far things may not come, but as happens in twist space, near things certainly will. Bunnies and skrags."

"That doesn't sound too dangerous," Xanthe said hopefully.

"Not to us," the demon exclaimed breezily. "But they do eat flowers."

A chill ran up Xanthe's nonexistent neck. "How many would die?"

"That answer is in unsettled pre-time, subject to selection. Perhaps many, as the effect is near opposite of what you call the Nightmare Line. Yet, given what you are, it could also be none."

"What am I?" Xanthe asked.

"Many things, child," the demon said lightly. "But most important for now, a flower that eats bunnies."

Xanthe held her breath. "Another blind choice. More gambling with people's lives." She was surprised at hearing her own internal thoughts echo, and became annoyed, this mood coming out as an audible hiss. "Alright demon. Let's do this."

"Your reason?"

She really didn't know. "The stupidest of all. I'm just... feeling lucky."

"Ah! The perfect answer! I would have accepted no other."

The vision disappeared. She was back in the real world again. Except that it very much wasn't. The bubble that still existed. Within it, everything was frozen, except that she could perceive the time of things, stretching in a completely different direction than anything visible with her eyes. Celeste's Riftstring was in her hand, but it was a billion hands. They smeared over her vision and thoughts. Nagrath was similarly smeared, as were Damien, Tari, and Celeste. Once again, she was a leaf in the frothy stream of fate, but now every swirl of its watery depths was perceivable.

"What's happening?" asked a trillion Celestes, while even more of them remained quiet, some ran in panic, others grabbed at the Riftstring in her hand, and still others said "Cool".

Damien flickered back and forth through space, as different possibilities of him hadn't yet decided where to settle, while all the Taris just stared confused, and with a single unified voice asked, "Am I awake? This feels like a migraine without the pain."

*Creator's holy balls, Tari. Is this remotely normal for you?* Xanthe thought, as she struggled to bring most of her selves into coherence, enough to talk. *No wonder you get so spacey.*

A different Xanthe spoke. "Tari. I need your guidance. Now. Please. Touch Riftstring."

In unison, the Taris did as bidden, while some of the Celestes tried to wrestle with Xanthe over the Riftstring; they disappeared when they touched her. "Please guide us to a living Nagrath," Xanthe asked Tari.

The Taris nodded. "It's much easier to see backward than forward," the vast majorities of her said.

Dakur shifted out from behind the now dead man whose body he'd used as a shield. He was covered in blood but moving. Xanthe could see him pull up his odd weapon and take aim at Nagrath, as he was trying to flee. His shot hit Nagrath higher up along his back, killing him.

His shot hit Nagrath to the side, killing him.

His shot went wide to the right. Cursing, Dakur took more careful aim, and hit him this time, killing him.

His shot went wide. Nagrath continued to run, then tripped. The second shot hit next to Nagrath's sheathed blade. He flopped in agony on the ground. A third shot killed him.

His shot went wide. Nagrath tripped. The second shot hit Nagrath's blade. There was a flash as the beam struck the metal. Nagrath was unhurt. He tried to roll to his feet. But a third shot killed him.

Nagrath dodged right. The first shot killed him.

Nagrath dodged right. The shot went wide. Nagrath tripped. He was shot dead.

"There!" almost all the Taris exulted in triumph.

Nagrath dodged right. The shot went wide. He tripped, trying to turn. Dakur fired a second shot, hitting Nagrath's sheathed blade. There was a brilliant flash of light as the beam struck the metal. Blinded, the older assassin fell awkwardly, slamming his head against the street's stone curb. When Dakur finished blinking, Nagrath was laid out, as still as a corpse. He holstered his weapon.

A pulse of energy exploded from Riftstring, through Xanthe and everything else, and, reminiscent of the legends of the ancient void vessels' great leap during the exodus, the Nagrath that lay dead before her blinked to the Nagrath with the heavy concussion next to the curb, as if he'd always been there. Distantly, under the window where she'd dropped the beacon, Xanthe saw herself being carried nude in Damien's arms, while kissing him. The pulse ended, and as it did, that her and that Damien disappeared. The bubble disappeared too. There were no longer an infinite number of Nagraths. Only one.

The world did not entirely return to normal though. The middle of the courtyard had distortions in the air, as if seeing it through a shattered glasssteel pane. A dozen three dimensional kaleidoscopes, breaks and lines, fanning out from indistinct centers, floated prettily. Tari fell to the ground, holding her head, while Celeste, noticing the laxness of Xanthe's grip on Riftstring, took the opportunity to snatch it back out of her hand. Xanthe didn't care. Hackles rose on the back of her neck. The things in the courtyard began to move, spider like.

"Straaks!" Damien cried in warning. He pulled his blades just in time, as one of the crystalline defects in creation lunged at him. He parried, but the arm of the thing went straight through the blade. It likely would have slid into his heart, except that as the arm passed through his invisibly burning blade, it burst into white flames. This caused the thing to flinch, slowing its attack enough for him to dodge away.

Straaks were rare. Rarer than grims, Xanthe knew, but equally as deadly, if not more so. They were nearly invisible and could selectively choose to have parts of their spindly bodies appear or disappear, so armor and walls were useless against them. While you kept your wits when confronting them, they couldn't be fought. The classic advice was to run until they grew tired of chasing you. But there usually wasn't a good place to run when you were in a city. If but even a single straak plagued a city in the wilds, that would usually be enough to cause its abandonment until the thing eventually disappeared of its own accord.

And here there were a dozen. Xanthe's heart sank. What had she done? In seeking to save Jagerfeld, she'd likely destroyed it. People would move away, until the straaks, following their own inscrutable logic, dissipated. She'd just caused untold death. But no accounting for it now. She ran to Nagrath, grabbed the old assassin's arm, ducked down, and heaved him onto her back like he was a sack of grain. She needed to treat his injury somewhere away from here.

Although the one lit by Damien's blade flopped about like a floating pile of iron filings burning from inside itself, the rest showed no fear. Unlike grims, nothing in these nightmares utterly alien nature indicated that they understood fear, pain, anger, or hatred. Attacking was almost a reflex. They gained no obvious benefit from it.

"Run," Damien told them as he circled, weaving back and forth in unpredictable patterns, trying to pick off another. He moved with the grace of a felinite. Seeing him, Xanthe understood how he'd been able to kill the grims. He dodged between the straaks with an elegance born of intense training and extreme luck. Every one of his blows landed, every tuck, every roll, avoided harm. Here and there, his sword connected, lighting more of the alien creatures with the white fire. No one seemed to see this but her, yet he did perceive that some were slowing, so kept his efforts up.

Alien or not, the remaining straaks changed their behavior in response to his onslaught. They grouped near the swirling mists in the center of the courtyard. Celeste moved out to the other side, waving Riftstring in her hand threateningly. Meanwhile Xanthe strained to pull Nagrath away. The old assassin was deceptively heavy, a ball of muscle and scars encased in leather and concealed weaponry. Her crude dress was terribly breezy. If he'd been awake, the way she was carrying him in would have been doubly embarrassing. No time for that now.

"Celeste, get back!" Damien suddenly yelled. Celeste didn't see the danger, but jumped away anyway, just in time. Five of the straaks lunged at her with terrifying swiftness. She waved Riftstring in front of them but had given herself so much distance that she didn't connect. Xanthe herself tripped on a curb. She caught her fall with her hands, but Nagrath slipped off her back. The man was too heavy. She realized that she needed to treat him immediately. He was far enough back that she could try.

Stitching brain injuries was always the most delicate work. It was hard even up in her room working on a kestrel with nothing else to distract her. Here, there was a fight going on but a dozen yards behind her. But she had no choice. Silently she dove in.

*Nagrath's body had taken a beating. His city of cells were tough, strong, sinewy, and covered in scar tissue. Around where the beam had struck a sheathed blade in his leg, cells were still mysteriously dead; he had a shrapnel wound in the other. But most importantly, the knock on his head hadn't been light. She could feel the contusion and internal bleeding in his cerebrum. She immediately pinched the small capillaries and veins shut with the lightest touch. No matter how tough the exterior, the galaxy of light that made up the complex neutral tissue remained delicate.*

There was little more she could do for his head, so she moved to the leg. One of the brads from his own petard had hit high along his hamstring, and it was buried too deeply. She had no aid, neither Tari's holy pliers nor her profane dress. In the end, she decided to leave the pellet where it was, and heal the wound around it. Unlike the barbed bolts of the Talathians, it would do no further harm; just another souvenir, like his scars.

"Look out!" Celeste cried as Xanthe was sealing his skin shut.

Xanthe was dimly aware of the forms looming behind her and knew couldn't dodge. She only had time for the brief recognition that her doom was upon her. The death she'd somehow managed to avoid both in the tower and with Horace had found her here, due entirely to her own foolish mercy for an assassin who almost certainly didn't deserve it.

Oddly enough though, she felt at peace with her choices. Yes, she'd wished for something interesting to happen in her life and had been decidedly punished for that. Still, she really couldn't find much fault with what she'd done. She'd just wanted to help people. Not herself. *At least I tried.*

Pain came as a searing arc of lightning across her back. She tried to scream, but it was too intense to breathe. The agony was unreal. So intense. It instantly burned through her consciousness, leaving nothing left. She was the pain. It was her. Yet as her thoughts left, as had happened in the tower, there came purity. She was pulled away from herself, and once again felt one with everything. This time a power came not from without, but within. It was as if she were fetus in a cosmic womb, stirred before birth by something that should not be. With that awareness, some part of her shifted and flexed, to rid itself of the bothersome irritation. The slightest little kick.

The illusion of the world returned. She fell back into the dream of reality.

*Am I dead?* Was her first coherent thought. *If so, what is this new world?*

Her blurry vision came into focus. She wasn't some newborn somewhere. She was laid out on the street. Cold cobblestone digging into her face. Above her, the courtyard air was in flames, soft white and casting no shadows on the surrounding buildings. It burned through the mists that swirled now in the air like water circling an invisible drain. Tari was still laid out on the ground, and Damien and Celeste were bickering. The insane white-hot agony had vanished so thoroughly, she wondered if it had been real.

"Why in literal hellspace didn't you protect her?" Celeste was yelling furiously. "I was fine."

"No, you weren't! You were backed up against the wall surrounded," Damien yelled back just as angrily.

"With this," she brandished Riftstring. "I can cut through any wall."

"You didn't have time. I just saved your life."

"At the cost of Xanthe's!"

He threw up his arms. "Well how was I supposed to know they'd all just turn and jump at her like that?"

Xanthe wanted to join in to ask how Tari was, or even what had happened, but couldn't speak. The pain had scarred neither her body nor mind, but left her too weak to move, or think. It took all her effort to breathe.

"I guess it doesn't matter," Celeste said. "The question is, what exactly did she do? They're gone!"

Damien approached. "That doesn't matter either. All that matters is that she's okay."

"Well?" Celeste asked with a note of concern, that almost sound like affection. "Is she?"

"I think so," he said quietly, sounding worried nonetheless. "At least she's breathing." As he crouched, Xanthe saw his knee through her barely open eyelids. He scooped her up in his arms. It reminiscent of the vision she'd had, but she had no energy to kiss him. "What happened, anyway?" He asked. "How did the straaks die?"

"You didn't see?" Celeste exclaimed. "They got right up to her, all lined up, and..." her voice trailed off. "Creator's holy balls." she breathed in awe, as if only now remembering something.

"I'm pretty sure it wasn't those," Damien joked, sounding relieved. He idly brushed Xanthe's hair with his fingers. "She'll recover," he assured himself. "I don't know how I'll handle it if she dies. She's done so much. Just out of kindness." While holding her, he straightened the cloak that he'd previously put on her to make sure it still left her relatively presentable.

"What are you gonna do with her?" Celeste asked curiously.

"Hold her for now," he declared. "Nothing much else I can do. Can't leave her cold on the pavement."

"What about your man Nagrath? He's on the pavement too."

"Don't worry. Finalizers love doing things as painfully as possible. Including sleep. What about Tari?"

"Lemme check." Celeste went to Tari's prone form. "Hey Tari. Wake up!" She shook her.

Tari groaned, and held her head. Xanthe wondered if she was feeling as bad as she was but couldn't ask. Right now, she didn't have the energy to do much more than listen. Besides, it was quite comfortable being cradled in Damien's arms. He was warm.

"That's not nice," he told Celeste.

"She's my girlfriend, but not that way." Celeste jibed, but in a curiously gentle voice. "Besides, none of them touched her. She just fainted."

"Tari didn't just faint. She did something with that artifact of yours first, as did Xanthe. It moved Nagrath somehow." Damien blew out his breath. "To think I was lecturing Xanthe about the history of demons earlier this eve. She pretended to be so shocked. Really, she was just humoring me."

"Nah. She's just a super genius is all. Picks things up instantly. You should see her in class. Barely pays attention, but every time she's asked a question, knows the answer. I can't even imagine how fast she'd learn with a demon for a teacher." Celeste propped Tari up, asking, "want some snow for your head?"

"I'm okay." Tari mumbled. "What day is it?"

Celeste was silent for a moment. "If you need to know that, you're not okay."

Tari stared out bleary eyed. "We're still on Festival night?"

"Yeah," Celeste said. "What happened?"

"I was with the demon for what felt like days. It showed me how to find where Nagrath was alive."

Celeste was suddenly curious. "What was it like?"

Tari fell silent, staring, taking time to gather her words. "Not as I expected. Yet I fear for my soul."

"Because it's evil? Really, Tari? You really think demons were what corrupted us?" Celeste asked. "I wasn't nine before I figured that as a big pile of kranth dung. All humans ever do is blame others for our own evil. Witches, demons, chimera, each other. It's always someone else, isn't it? And still we pretend the Creator made the whole universe only for us. Like we're so special."

Tari's eyes dropped. "Not that. I asked the demon for help. I wanted it to bring father back. But it said the place where he was still alive had collapsed into nonexistence. A possibility that is no more. Not to us."

Celeste blinked. "Oh."

"I'm losing my faith." Tari choked out in a sob.

"Heh. You think that's bad?" Celeste retorted unhappily. "I might actually be getting some."

"Don't. Either of you." Damien told them. "Miracles, or the absence of them, should not dictate faith. Though I don't like the Curate, one thing they have right is to give thanks, rather than demand power, from the divine. I do like their admonition, 'beg not for miracles, but solace', and for what it's worth, if you go to hellspace for the sin of wanting your loved ones back, I'll be right there beside you."

"Me too," Celeste added. "For completely different reasons. If it even exists – which I doubt."

"Speaking of which," Damien continued, "we still need the demon's help. Prince Sol is about to signal his attack, and many will die. He was only delaying doing so out of hope that he could trap whoever depowered the beacon. But I don't think he'll be too encouraged with how that turned out."

Tari struggled to her feet. "It won't talk anymore. It decided it was done. So maybe we can find these fireworks ourselves."

"Fireworks?" Celeste asked in surprise.

Tari nodded. "Xanthe told me when we were chained up. The signal for the attack is special fireworks."

"That makes sense," Damien mused. "It allows for a coordinated surprise attack. They don't have to use people as messengers. Just tell all your men to attack if they see the flares in the sky."

"You should have told me earlier!" Celeste exclaimed. "I know exactly where they've set up. They're by Firehouse bridge, near the Steeple. There're a dozen men there guarding them. I didn't think much of it."

Xanthe felt Damien's body tense. "Well then. That's it. All we have to do is stop it."

"We?" Celeste asked. You want to help?"

"Don't bring up what I said before, that this really isn't my fight." If Nagrath were awake, he'd be scolding me like crazy.

"Why did you change your mind about helping us?" Tari asked.

Xanthe felt him shift. He brushed his fingers at the top of her forehead. She still couldn't shake the lassitude. She didn't mind. Not right now.

"Because of Xanthe," he murmured. "I've already both lost and won. I lost because I'm not even planning on killing Javan, despite his betrayal. She made me forgive him. Strange, because I'm used to others bending to my will, not the reverse. But I've won because at least my men are safe, what's left of them."

A tear could have been brought to her eye, if she'd had the energy. This was the boy she liked.

"That's not quite an answer," Celeste pressed. "You're foreign. Why are you risking your life for the city?"

"Well," he chuckled darkly. "I also wouldn't mind getting a little revenge. My blades are still thirsty."

Xanthe winced mentally. Okay, but he also still needed a lot of work.

Celeste folded her arms. "Yeah, that's going to be tricky. Xanthe's out of it. Even if we wake her up, whatever gift she's got killing demons and nightmares won't help in a fight with men. She's not cut proof. You should hear her whine like a baby when she even gets a tiny scratch."

Now Xanthe nearly pouted. Some friend.

"Then I'll make sure she's not," Damien said. "We need to rouse Nagrath though. I'm going to need him."

This was a bad idea. Xanthe knew it. He was in no condition to fight. Even shaking him right now might hurt him. She wanted to tell him, but the effort was enormous. Just opening her eyes was hard enough.

"Xanthe?" Damien asked tenderly.

"Let." She whispered with all the strength she could muster. "Rest."

"Is she saying something?" Tari asked.

"Sounds like she's saying that Nagrath shouldn't be roused." Damien told her.

Xanthe nodded, as more strength returned. "Go. Save city. I. Stay. With him." It was all she could manage.

"Oh, yeah. That's Xanthe." Celeste said. "Self-sacrificing, to the last."

"Really dumb idea, though," Tari added.

"Oh completely," Damien agreed.

Xanthe didn't like that. She struggled to speak, but Damien shushed her. "Sol's men will eventually come out here to pick up the bodies of their friends. They'll pick Nagrath up and kill him if he stirs. If you stay, you'll be captured too. The only way to prevent that from happening is for someone to stay here and take them on if need be."

"You're the only one who can lift Nagrath," Celeste told Damien.

She would have gritted her teeth, if she had energy. "I. Stop them. Somehow."

"You're going to handle Prince Sol's cleanup crew on your own? Like you are now?" Damien was gentle, but gently mocking. "What are you going to do? Whisper like you're dying at them?"

Xanthe's mood darkened. When he put it that way, it did sound absurd, especially since she didn't even know if she could walk yet. In fact, she knew she couldn't.

"It is a problem though," he continued. "I can't be in two places at once. Even if Xanthe was up, the three of you taking on a whole coterie of Sol's soldiers would not end well."

"Yeah," Tari agreed. "What are you thinking, Xanthe? As Damien says, three mere girls taking out Prince Sol's elite troops? I mean seriously!" Her tone, however, was jaunty. Almost reckless.

Xanthe looked up at Tari. This was unlike her. "I... thought..."

"So silly," Celeste agreed in an amiably scolding tone. She pulled out Riftstring, twirling it with graceful confidence. "No way we'll need more than two." She turned to Tari. "Come on girlfriend. Time to end this. Let's bring the house down."

Tari nodded, looking, if not happy, then at least self-assured, an attitude completely at odds with her current disheveled small clothes. She extended her arm. "Shall we?"

Celeste seemed to notice the change too. As she took Tari's hand, her typical cynical smile softened, revealing the barest flicker of a gentle earnestness. "See you both later," she called back. "Try not to get into too much trouble while we're away."

No one seemed more surprised than Damien, his handsome features full of worry. "Wait. Wouldn't it be better if I went instead?"

The two turned to stride down the street, hand in hand, neither even bothering to answer.

## Chapter 46

Damien carried Xanthe toward a clump of bushes in the park, set her down, and carefully brought Nagrath to her for more treatment. It wasn't a perfect hiding place but would have to do. He nervously paced back and forth as she tended to the old assassin with her touch. There was significant toxicity in Nagrath's blood due to mysterious cellular degeneration around where the beam of Dakur's strange weapon had struck his hidden blade. Yet aside from hoping his liver was strong enough to handle it, there was little more she could do. She dribbled water from a flask to keep him hydrated and used her touch to help his body swallow it. He still wasn't awake, and she saw no point in trying to rouse him. The capillaries she'd pinched shut were holding. Nothing but extended motionless rest could further stabilize them.

She herself had hardly recovered. Even the minor effort to help Nagrath was exhausting, and when she tried to rise, ended up feeling so faint that she almost fell. Damien caught her carefully back in his arms and carried her away down the street. He walked the long way around the houses back to the place behind the wall where they'd originally hid. It left him out of sight, yet able to quickly intervene in case anyone found Nagrath. There, he sat himself down on a low cement stair under an eve of a house and held her closely to share his warmth.

"I'm sorry," she finally told him. "I did all I could, but he may still die."

Damien took the news soberly. "Why? Is there something you can't fix?"

"No, but he's fighting shock. His body is at its limit. Now it's up to his own will to live."

"He'll pull through," Damien told her. "You have no idea how tough Finalizers are. Fighting for their lives is what they live for. I'm more worried about Celeste and Tari. That may be the last time we see them."

"They'll do fine. I just hope Celeste doesn't kill them all. She might."

"Unlikely," he brooded. "That artifact of hers is impressive, but Sol has elite fighters. As soon as they recognize her as a hostile instead of a mere girl, she'll lose badly. I should have gone."

"Have faith," Xanthe assured. "She's just planning to bring the house down on them."

He blinked. "The what on them?"

"Most of Jagerfeld's bigger crossings have bridge-houses, covered roofs that keep off snow," she explained. "That's the logical place to keep fireworks dry in case this fog turns into rain. What foreigners don't know is that you can also climb on the railing outside the cover. Kids do that in summer to jump into the river. If Celeste goes there with Riftstring, I expect she'll be able to cut the supports to collapse it all. I don't think she'll particularly care if anyone is under it at the time."

Damien narrowed his eyes in thought. "That sounds dangerous. Almost worse than taking on the men directly. It could just as easily crush her or knock her into the river. Too much trouble."

In the distance, there was the sound of cracking wood and screams.

Xanthe smiled faintly. "Celeste loves trouble."

The distant screams turned into hostile shouts of panic. She turned her eyes toward where her friends had gone, but it was all way past the other side of the wall anyway. Damien shifted anxiously. She knew he wanted to go. "I won't stop you from leaving. But if anyone comes to harm Nagrath, I can't stop them either. Not like this."

He put his fingers through his dark hair. "What do we do? Just wait?"

Xanthe wanted to move but just couldn't. "I sorry. I don't know why I'm so weak."

"Shush you. No more apologizing for miracles. You've saved so many of my men, it makes me feel unworthy." He shifted his support, and she felt his bare right hand against her back, as it slipped slightly through the break in the cloak. This made her intimately aware that she was entirely nude except for the clothing he'd given her. Her bare bottom was resting directly on the cloth of his pants. Had she more strength, she would have blushed. Instead, it was just comforting being in his arms. She rested her head on him, closed her eyes, and breathed. It was so easy to get used to.

"What happened, anyway?" He finally asked conversationally. "How did you make the straaks go away?"

She kept her eyes closed. "No idea. All I know is that every time I meet a demon, I get a mystical experience. Maybe they're messing with me, or maybe just not enough blood is going to my head."

"You think your touch lets you deal with nightmares?"

"Like a bunny that eats flowers," she concluded.

"Like a...?"

"One of the demons talked about engineering Tari's power into her. But I also think that whatever this touch is, it doesn't all come from them. Which means Curate dogma that power has divine provenance might be true too. I'm not even sure demons fully understand these in-between spaces. Maybe we're an experiment."

"You?"

"Me, you, Tari, witches, chimera, princes, the whole dodgy-power planet. Or some large part of it."

"Or maybe you're the Incarnate, and just teasing me."

Xanthe quivered. Not from his silly thought, but from peeking open her eyes to see his smile, realizing just how beautiful he was. His dark eyes. His masculine yet inquisitive countenance. His intoxicating musky scent. The way he returned her gaze. It was strange, but it almost felt as if some part of her fed on love, and nothing could help her recover more quickly than just being in his arms like this. A welcome blessing, yet not entirely without consequence. For with returning strength, came desire. Her body was waking to the possibility of him. The scenario she'd invented in her bath of a much cuter boy taking complete untoward advantage of her was becoming disturbingly appealing. Worse than knowing that he could, was hoping that he'd try.

"Why are you so obsessed with the Incarnate?" She asked, trying to distract herself. "You want to cuddle with her too?"

"The incarnate is female?" He was suddenly interested.

She realized he might be thinking she was holding back on some secret knowledge. "I don't know!" she protested. "I just assume. I mean, she's just got to be some sort of dreadwitch, right?"

"If the rumors are true and the Incarnate is an embodied demon, there's no knowing what it looks like, or what gender it has, if any. I decided to come here and find it, and the possibility of failing didn't cross my mind. Everything I want I seem to get. It just falls into my lap. I know that sounds absurd."

"Not after what the Gestalt demon said. But why did you want to meet whatever this Incarnate is?"

"I was... curious," he told her with nonchalant evasiveness.

"That all?" She idly ran the fingers of her right hand up his broad chest, for no reason other than to feel his muscles. "Seems a long way to go with so many followers, only to satisfy a curiosity. Especially since, if the Incarnate is even half as powerful as a full demon, having a bunch of men by your side wouldn't help at all. You could have easily made the trip only with Nagrath. More easily, in fact. It would have been less obvious."

His smile went away. She hated to make that happen.

"You know?" He grumbled, handsomely piqued. "Has anyone ever told you that you're too damned smart?"

"It makes it hard to find a boy I don't intimidate." She couldn't resist snuggling and kicking her nearly bare feet helplessly, as his left arm was under her knees. "I'm sure lots would be happy to take advantage of me for a night, but getting one who'll stick around afterward? Who's my equal or better? Know any boy like that?" She leaned into him. In the back of her mind, she was scared to death by whatever in hellspace she was doing, but she couldn't help it. She just had to.

"Oh, Xanthe. I wish I did. Do you truly understand what I am? How intractable my situation?"

She nodded silently, feeling the cool clarity of his words. "You're a prince. Doomed to kill or be killed by your half-brothers. Any girl you romance becomes a target."

"Exactly. I'm no good for you."

Xanthe struggled to find acceptance. Naturally it wouldn't work out. She'd know it from the start. It was all so logical.

But that wasn't what her heart was saying. Ream logic. She pouted at him, turning her hand on his chest into a fist. "Only if you vie for the throne. And don't tell me that no prince manages to escape notice. Plenty do. They're just not famous, obviously."

"Until their son starts drawing attention." He sighed heavily. "I guess I could head into the northern deep, become a wildsman so far out nothing but nightmares and deadly monsters to bother me. But that would be giving up on what I came to do. What I promised God."

"What is this mysterious oath? If it's not to ask the Incarnate demon to make you king, then what?"

He sighed, defeated. "Don't ever tell Nagrath I told you, but anchorites are said to be able to make people demonic, to grow the black blood inside you until that's all you are. It's supposed to make you superhuman."

Despite her best efforts, Xanthe was shocked. This was only marginally better than Prince Sol's plan. She sure didn't want a demon for a husband. "Like a blackwight? You'd trade away your humanity to be some sort of undead ruler of Nutearea?"

"The throne isn't the point. It would give my men the strength they need. Our people are dying, Xanthe. Murdered by the Curate, like the Muslims our dearest brothers, peace be upon them, who were hunted to extinction. When we Christians are gone, all the good work we do will die as well. Remember how you faced me when you thought I worked for the witchkillers? It is like that, but for an entire faith."

A passage came to Xanthe, and she voiced it. "Religions, jealous and cruel, slaughter the young of defeated sects, as wild male tigrans do the cubs of their rivals, so that they may wallow in blood and proclaim peace and mercy o'er all the land."

"That's... poetic. But those words sound too harsh for you."

"They're not mine," Xanthe explained. "It's from one of Celeste's essays. Mr. Griswold gave her perfect grade, but then rewrote it entirely in case a proctor came by for a surprise audit."

"Well, if by some miracle, I'm able to get the Anchorites to transform my men, we could engage those proctors directly. Witchkillers Praetorians, and other villains you've never heard of. All of them. We would then surely spend our lives wallowing in blood, slaughtering those who have tormented us for so long. There. I confess it."

Xanthe shook her head. "What a terrible plan."

"I admit to all your criticism. We would willingly sacrifice our humanity. Moreover, no matter how much we targeted only the guilty, inevitably some innocents would die. You see why you're too good for me? You refused to even let me take vengeance on Javan the traitor."

Xanthe sighed, slightly annoyed. "Actually, I mean the plan is terrible. Bound to fail. Even if this Incarnate exists and is persuaded by your princely authority, neither which seems likely, you'd just become the enemy the Curate needs. While if you let them think you're gone, they'll surely wind up far too busy slaughtering each other in this stupid war to even think about hunting the remaining few of you."

Damien stared blankly, completely astounded.

"What?" Xanthe exclaimed. "You expect that just because I hate blood-filled politics, I don't understand it? Do you have any idea how bad this succession is shaping up to be? Lord Sargon, Sol's steed, thinks destroying the Nightmare Line is justifiable because it would force rival Nutearean factions to unite against invading nightmares. You'd be a fool to do anything but lay low while they have at each other."

"Xanthe," he shook his head in awe. "I don't know if you're seraph or demon."

She scowled, feeling even more strength coming back into her. "I'm a girl. A frustrated girl. This is not the Festival night I was expecting. At all."

"You were expecting romantic triumph? A dozen boys vying for you? Not being able to choose between them?"

"No!" she exploded. "I was expecting romantic disaster. To go home crying without a single boy picking up my favor with my stupid falsey haunch padding. Being mocked by Priscia and all the other towner girls the whole summer. Right? I mean just normal, ordinary, teen tragedy. Not find that I've been chosen by demons and whatever the ream else is out there, all to get me in trouble! They didn't even ask!"

"I know how you feel. I never asked to be a prince, either."

Xanthe blew out her breath, scowling. "And do you know what the worst part is? I can't even complain. I mean, there's really a good chance, even through all this nightmarish night, that we've saved the city."

"Good thing you're not complaining then," he teased.

She crinkled her chin at him, turned her small hand into a fist, and thumped it several times in frustration against his chest. "Yeah. All in all, saving the city is still better than not being kissed on Festival night, even though that means I'll have to wait four seasons to the next one."

"Four whole seasons! Eight months! Two thirds of a year!" He continued mercilessly.

"I know it's not really that long. It's just, well it feels like it."

"I'll just have to shorten it then." Before Xanthe even realized what was happening, she felt herself being lifted in his strong arms. He pulled her to him, leaned in, and kissed her. His lips were warm and firm and lingered just slightly.

It took her a moment to register what had just happened. "Wait! What? Why did you do that?"

"You were just complaining you hadn't been kissed for your favor. I figured I could at least do that much."

"But I wasn't ready!" You couldn't just have the boy you desperately wanted to kiss you to just suddenly do it, especially when you didn't give permission. Of course, it was also her fault. To signal any harder, she'd have needed semaphores, a calling bell, and a shutter lamp.

"So now that you are, do you want me to kiss you again?"

Xanthe became terribly aware that she'd promised Mrs. Fullbarn to let a boy she wouldn't mind kissing do so as much as he wanted. It was the punishment that she'd agreed to. But she couldn't. Anything but that. She needed to go back and report defeat. Get washing duties for a year, or die, instead. "Nooo..." she crooned softly, leaning into him.

Damien was puzzled. "I wasn't that bad, was I?"

Not bad? It was amazing. The taste of him hadn't left. It was lingering in her mouth, driving her crazy. Worse, his hand supporting underside of her bare thigh was sending thrills like lightning up her back and deep between her legs. She whimpered softly, clinging to him, hating how irrational she was being. She been asking for him to stay, not just in the city, but with her, safe in the knowledge that he never would, for nothing ever turned out right for her. But... well, what if it did? What then?

Romantic fatalism was common in the Scholars' girls wing. Every spring, another batch of older classmates would abruptly disappear as casualties of marriage, arranged and otherwise. You wanted it to happen to you too, of course, but not too soon. Being a learned Scholar meant that you ruled your emotions, not the reverse. There were little cuts about the ones who couldn't even manage to make it to their sixteenth year, as even semi-literate town girls usually married around eighteen. They'd say, 'doormat and dozen', as in the number of children you were supposedly fated for if you married too young. It was pride. You wanted love, but not to be completely conquered.

Xanthe knew she was conquered. She had no resistance left. If he took her right here and now, she wouldn't protest. She'd have to become his bride, winding up expecting like the happy girl she'd seen dropping her favor earlier in the evening. "Why do you have to be so handsome?" she whimpered at him accusingly.

He took her question seriously. "I'm half Nubian. Maybe that has something to do with it."

Xanthe momentarily paused her self-pity. "The dusky regal lords of the southern archipelagos?" She wondered. "It is said that even the beggars are literate there."

Damien was fondly amused. "Well, yes. It's called universal education. Not that expensive considering the alternative. Among other things, it means very few beggars. Nor are Nubians royalist. We're democratic. Oh, and the beautiful dark has largely faded. Haven's sun does not emit much of the ultraviolet light that requires it. Those few families in which it manifests in full must eat childboon and tkatchae fish to stave off rickets. But yes, my mother was Nubian. It is why my hair and eyes are of such rare hue."

"I would like to visit your lands. Your people are known to be intellectuals, holding many secrets of the ancients."

He shrugged slightly. "Exaggerated. While there is more knowledge, and the Curate is even weaker than here, we're still not like the ancients."

Xanthe considered him. Exotic, worldly, smart, tall, dark, handsome. Utterly masculine. She had to admit, to put it crudely, that her slide had all sorts of good reasons for being drenched. But all that realization did was bring back the fear. She stared longingly into his eyes. "I'm so scared."

He held her close. "No more than I."

"Oh, come on!" Xanthe couldn't believe it. Damien was a boy. Experienced at that. He could easily make use of her body, seize her tingling nipples, break her willpower. "What could you possibly be afraid of?"

"Hope," he told her. "I haven't felt any since I started this whole misadventure."

"Why are you afraid of that?" She asked curiously.

"I live as those I love die. But with this suggestion of yours, maybe at last I can change that. Maybe I truly can kill all the evil in the world, or at least a good part of it, by turning it against itself."

Xanthe blinked, nonplussed. This wasn't being seduced into eloping into the deep wilds that she was so afraid of, much less the possibility of sweaty deflowerment her stinging loins were craving. It was something else entirely. Ugh. Just her luck to fall for a difficult boy. "You can't murder evil," she explained pedantically. "Murder is an act of evil."

"I can enough to make a difference. Which is all I need. All these tyrants need is a little help in getting started on each other and then they'll forget about everyone else."

"Damien!" Xanthe was shocked. What was wrong with him? He'd just kissed her, a breakdown of their mutual inhibitions, and again this? More politics? Okay, sure, she'd also just told him no. But he was a boy. They weren't supposed to actually take no for an answer, were they? Wasn't it obvious what she wanted? Although to be fair, a little voice in the back of her head noted, she didn't. Mostly. Although she was prepared to forgive him if he did anyway, which he wasn't. Jerk.

Her little voice now told her that she was now completely crazy, because she sure was acting like it. But that only got her mad at it, the dodgy power thing just being her sensible side. But anyway, you expected a boy to reliably push, even if you weren't all that pretty. She couldn't believe it. Didn't he know boys only pretended to not always be interested in sex?

This had to be the weirdest favor date anyone ever had. Well yes, of course he was still getting over his dead cheating fiancé, but still. Relationships were far trickier than she'd imagined. Getting married, living happily ever after, that was supposed to be all too easy. Yet it wasn't. Why wouldn't he just do what she thought he would?

"Come with me!" He exclaimed impulsively. "Away from Jagerfeld. I know just where to start."

*Now finally...*

"Xenon. It's a big city. Enough to pass ourselves off as K'tairian refugees with information. With that, I could surely start a sectarian conflict between the Praetorians and Witchkillers, maybe with the peerage mixed in. There are so many rival factions of murderous thugs around there, it's just itching to blow."

Xanthe furrowed her eyebrows. That was hardly the wilds. He didn't want her body. He only wanted her to help him start a war. "No." She could feel the moment passing, her arousal cool.

"But you want to see the south," he urged. "And you're so brilliant. I'm sure you'd notice dangers I never would. Take your place beside me. That's all I ask. Later, we can see where we go."

"I meant lay low and let the conflict hide you. Not go out of your way to inflame it!" Xanthe scolded moodily, as a thought occurred that Celeste would absolutely leap at this chance to leave their little provincial northern city. She'd probably excuse his strategy as well. This made her doubly upset, as it brought a stab of completely absurd jealousy.

Before he could say more, something caught Damien's eye. He stared up and past her. "I'm bad at taking advice, especially at laying low. Seems I've failed even now. I fight here. Perchance to die."

Xanthe turned her head. Down the street was a group of soldiers headed by Prince Sol, making his way up the street from the direction opposite of the wall. He'd already seen them and had turned their way.

A cold chill ran up her back, freezing the sweat of passion still lingering on her skin.

## Chapter 47

There was no easy way out. Surrounded by two buildings, the small backyard they'd been hiding in was open only in the direction that Sol was approaching from. Only by scaling the wall that faced the plaza could they possibly escape, and that was unlikely. While her strength was beginning to return, she certainly was in no condition to muster a sustained run. More than fear, it was embarrassing to be caught like this after being so careful to hide. It was all her fault. She'd been distracted by Damien and drawn attention by talking too loudly.

"Leave," she ordered Damien softly, as he set her down and put his hand on the hilt of his sword. "You need to run."

"I'm not abandoning you," he scolded in a whisper. "What kind of man do you think I am?"

"A foolish one. Even you can't win now. You're outnumbered a dozen to one with a prince by their side. That's his elite guard. More to the point, you don't need to. Sol won't kill me. Not right away. He needs me."

Damien grimaced at her merciless logic. He watched Sol's measured approach, judging that he still had time to do as she asked. "I'll be back."

It was Xanthe's turn to be annoyed. He was making a habit of saving her. Twice already. If he did it again, which seemed likely if Prince Sol didn't kill her first, this would be a third time. "I'll stall. Just go."

Damien stole a final quick kiss, then sprung. The speed at which he made off surprised even her. Two steps later he launched himself at the wall and used a single foot to throw himself high enough to roll himself over. Surprised curses came from Sol's party, and a feathered atlatl bolt struck the top of the wall next to where he'd been a split second before.

Before she could even stand, one of Sol's men rushed the wall and scaled it, though not quite as quickly as Damien had.

"Don't do it." Xanthe called out in casual warning. "He'll only kill you."

At the top of the wall, the barbarian soldier gave her a predatory grin, and hopped over, disappearing to give chase. Xanthe sighed to herself and rolled her eyes. Men. Always loving to fight. That one she really couldn't blame Damien for.

"Ah well. Your funeral." She sighed mostly to herself.

Prince Sol was nearly behind her now. He was still dressed in his finery, but had put a breastplate over his doublet, so was bedecked in polished bronze, remelted plastics, and black trim; the ornate design set off well against his blonde hair. His sword that had been sheathed was now out, but he didn't threaten her with it. Instead he addressed her.

"Ah, there you are." He stated suavely. "You left so unexpectedly. Don't you know it's rude to not properly take one's leave?"

Here was a different doom. Xanthe took in Sol's full measure. So unlike Damien. She wasn't fooled by his pretense. He looked fit to kill. His men circled around at a distance, ready with atlatls in case they needed to attack at range. He was also taking her seriously. Not a good thing.

But at least with Sol, she was herself again. It was strange, but she had more composure facing death than love. Damien just had this ability to make her blood run hot and make her a fool. She preferred being cool, even if it killed her.

"Indeed," She spoke slowly. Time was on her side now. "Though to be fair, we were never formally introduced, so I was never technically in your company. To what do I owe this honor?"

"Tell me where Lady Outlet is," he commanded nonchalantly.

Surprising. "Aren't you more interested in the workings of the beacon?"

"I am," now he could not mask his glare. "Do not think your ruse still fools me anymore. I know it was her now. You admitted you had no witch power in front of Karissa, and Lady Outlet was the one who left to mysteriously talk to someone. I saw your alarm at the time but did not realize then that she was about to depower the Demon with Many Voices. Your job was to distract me and did so. The way you knew how it spoke was merely that she told you."

Xanthe was doubly surprised. What an absurd idea, yet it might not be better to disabuse him of it. "And my toenails?" She asked.

"Painted. We consulted an expert. If you were truly demon possessed, they would be moving. Nice try. I will give you one chance to tell me what I need to know." Sol snapped.

"Or what, exactly? What are you not planning to do anyway?"

"You played me for a fool, and that's the one thing I really can't allow. Now tell me where she is, or I will have you craving death." Sol tried to sound lighthearted but couldn't. He was too angry.

Xanthe knew she was playing with blackdust. It would be ironic, having survived more demons and nightmares in one night than most anyone saw in a lifetime, to wind up killed by this miserable prince. Yet she couldn't keep her words from escaping her lips; their truth was untamable. "So here is Praetorianism unmasked. All your vaunted pose about correcting girls for our own good, proved but a self-serving lie."

He bridled. "If you misstep in a prince's world, be prepared to pay the price. Now tell me where she is."

"I will never tell you! Never!" Xanthe paused a beat, then laughed, amazed at her own fearlessness, feeling a strange surrealism akin to when she'd talked to the beacon. "Nah, just kidding. She went down the block." She thumbed casually down the street.

"Where?"

Xanthe considered. She could lie, but telling the truth seemed no more dangerous, and was probably less so. The fireworks were either destroyed or not. If they weren't, nothing mattered, and if they were, Tari and Celeste would be already be gone. "Firehouse bridge," she told him directly. "I'm rather surprised you didn't already know."

Sol started to tremble in rage. "Why?"

"Because destroying your fireworks is the final nail in the coffin of your plotted conquest," she told him casually. "Now there's no way to prevail in a way that will persuade Thule to rally to you. If you use messengers, when battle breaks out, most of the city will be able to get their weapons before your uncoordinated bandits can stop them. Hellspace, you might even fail to capture the city. Bandits are not known for their mettle when facing a real fight."

"How did you know about the signal?"

"If you misstep in the witch world," she told him coolly. "Be prepared to pay the price."

Sol surveyed up and down the street. "Whoever that man was who is your master presumes too much. I still have many of Jagerfeld's richest families bottled up. You're coming with me." He approached and grabbed her by tightly by her upper arm. It was stupid to resist, so she didn't. Sol then turned to one of his men and barked an order in Talathis. They nodded and all but two turned away.

"Where are you taking me?" Xanthe asked, not particularly alarmed.

"I ask the questions from now on," he declared, dragging her along.

Xanthe wasn't sure if this was his voice of authority or not, but it didn't seem wise to argue. He pulled her straight back through the deserted past midnight black streets in the direction of Wormwood manor.

As they went, she wondered why he still was acting as if this was winnable. Didn't he understand the situation? Being a mere loose confederation of wealthy merchant families, Jagerfeld's Highcouncil had a certain camaraderie and many entangled business relationships, but there wasn't enough mutual affection between the houses for them to surrender themselves just because he was holding a knife at the throat of another. A hostage situation wouldn't turn out well for anyone.

It was then, being paraded, that Xanthe realized the source of her fearlessness. She'd won. Even if he killed her now, the city was mostly saved. What this what men who volunteered for suicide missions felt when they'd completed them? True, Praetorians did have this odd creed about not actually murdering girls, but given the way the Prince was acting, she wasn't expecting it. She'd be lucky if her death was painless.

Sol had the air of a cornered animal, something Xanthe had experience with. "Never be anything's path of least resistance," her father had once admonished her after she'd been bit trying to pet a cute little wild skrag. Yet that same logic applied in reverse. Though both Celeste and Riftstring's demon had given her strikingly similar teachings not to waste mercy on evil men, she'd been trying to figure ways to save Sol anyway. Now it felt like a fool's errand. Wiser would be to figure out the best way to arrange his death. The wisest, to just avoid her own. He was dead anyway.

She decided to give it one last try. If he didn't leave the city peacefully, more would die. "The beacon is depowered," she told him as he pulled her roughly along through a brick archway in the street toward another side entrance of the Wormwood estate. "No matter who entreats, you cannot expect the demon to return. So, think. Without it, Jagerfeld is useless to you. You are foreign and would not be safe, whereas you would be in Northfjord, where you are firmly entrenched. There, you might be able to wait out a civil war, and perhaps parley yourself into the throne."

In response, he squeezed her arm painfully. "I don't take advice from girls either," he snapped. As he did so though, they rounded the corner, and before them on the ground was the quickly cooling corpse of the barbarian she'd only seen a few minutes before. He was lying face up, eyes open, with a permanent look of surprise etched on his face. A trickle of frothy pink blood from a wound in his throat was his only injury. The single stab had likely punctured his spinal cord. Xanthe was sure that earlier this eve, she could have saved him. Maybe even now. But not with the prince dragging her along.

"Your funeral," she sighed, annoyed that she wasn't allowed to practice her art.

He jerked her around, putting his blade to her throat. "You mock me one more time and I may lose control. Don't make me kill you."

She peered down at the blade, then back up again, curling her lip. "Fine. I'll stop trying to save you."

He noticed her fierceness, the way she was pressing her neck forward, and it made him back off slightly. "I can kill you with a cut, and you're the one pretending to deny me mercy? Don't you care for life, little pawn of my enemies?"

She glared, filled with wrath. "I am no one's pawn. My only enemy is that which victimizes even you: this custom in which Nutearean kings sire princes to the far reaches of the realm, who then tear up half of Aeterna murdering each other for the right to sire the next generation." Her eyes narrowed. "Seems suspiciously like a selective breeding program, come to think of it."

He leaned back, confused. "You're insane."

"As you say. Now, are you going to kill me? If so, get on with it."

Her attitude made him reconsider. His anger shifted into calculation. "No. You're far too eager to let your secrets die with you for me to allow that. Come, little pawn. We'll see how charmingly you cry."

He pulled his sword back and once again dragged her through a curiously sluggish mechanical door into the mansion. Here and there in the empty dark hallways they passed edgy guards, each stationed before a doorway barred from the outside. Xanthe was curious who was imprisoned behind them, but Sol pushed her past in a rush. Even the slightest hesitation brought another painful squeeze, so she focused on giving no complaint. What was coming next wasn't going to be pleasant. She'd already resigned herself to being gang raped but didn't want to give him the satisfaction of breaking too quickly.

They arrived at a machine room with several moving torque wheels lining the wall. Half a dozen men were arrayed around a large table, upon which an enormous scroll of either kranth or vridin velum was spread, bearing a detailed map of Jagerfeld and covered with little troop markers. It took Xanthe a moment to recognize the men: a few guards, Dakur, Sargon, and another one, dressed almost as if he were a Hood Guild member, in a black cloak and darkened long-hood, his features entirely shaded from the flickering naphtha lamps. Yet he clearly was not, for across his chest were two bandoliers of vials, holding different colors of liquids. Vials of acid. This marked him as something else. Though anonymous, hoods were neutral messengers. Runners never carried weapons for fear of losing their welcome.

Sargon greeted him. "You caught them? Good. But where's the Outlet girl?" Dakur also had a concerned look on his face.

"She's by Firehouse Bridge. This one was wise enough to explain their plan." He shook Xanthe by the arm. "They're trying to disrupt our attack signal. I sent reinforcements there just in case. They really can't succeed, but Miss Outlet could cause some trouble. Due to her house, the guards will listen to her."

Dakur grimaced. "I'd better go too. It's been nearly half a bell, and we've yet to see the skies lit, or any news. Something seems wrong." He turned towards the door without asking Sol.

"Watch out for their leader," Sol warned. "He killed Tsgratarin and left his corpse to greet me face up."

"Noted," Dakur growled. "Do you know who he is?"

Sol turned to Xanthe. "Not yet. But I'm sure my little girl here will be happy to tell us who the leader is, won't you?"

And here the abuse was going to start. Xanthe knew it. No matter what she said, he would hurt her anyway, assuming she was lying. Might as well tell the truth. "Certainly. You want to know who discovered your plot and arranged to ensure that it would fail?"

"It will succeed, but yes."

She smirked grimly. "That would be me."

His face flushed in anger, and he squeezed her arm harder. Xanthe had enough, deciding to not make it easy for him. She collapsed down, grabbed her wrist with her other hand, and with a single twisting motion, yanked.

Sol was far stronger than her, but the grip of his left hand was nowhere near as strong as the two-handed leverage she applied and gave way.

She pulled back. "I see a thug before me. Not royalty. Noblemen are never so improper as to abuse other men's daughters."

"Soon you won't be anyone's daughter," Sol snarled. He twirled his sword, and then moved to sheathe it, doing so carefully. "But first, you so badly need a beating, it simply can't be delayed." He lunged.

Xanthe leapt away. The last lassitude in her body disappeared, powered by panic. She knew she couldn't escape and attacking as Tari had with Horace was even more implausible, but she was determined not to make it easy. She ducked back behind the large table as he charged. He followed, running around it. He was remarkably quick in armor, and she only managed to evade his outstretched right hand by a finger length. This moved her against the table. She would have been trapped, unable to escape to either side, but her own Hood Guild instincts took over, and she did a shortcut back roll over it, using her hands to make a full reverse flip, pulling each leg over in turn.

The room fell into chaos, not only because she'd briefly exposed herself completely, but because this pulled nearly the entire map of the city to the floor. Sargon let out a yell of panicked outrage as all the carefully positioned figures scattered. The guards stared at Xanthe, though most were as amused at her flashing them as Sol was angry. None moved to intervene. Xanthe backed up and pushed her makeshift dress back down. She wondered if this was really the right thing to do, but was determined to annoy the prince as much as possible. A sort of vengeance before the fact.

All at once, she felt herself gripped around the torso by two strong arms. It was the man with the bandoleers; she could feel the vial holders pressing against her back. His hot breath came near her right ear, and in it she heard a deep, soft, and surprisingly erudite whisper. "For your own sake, cease your struggles and do not interrupt my advocacy."

"My map!" Sargon fumed. "I spent days on it."

"Oh, the sins just keep piling on," Sol agreed. "Good work in capturing the slippery thing, Bolus." He marched forward, now brandishing a leather strap from one of his armor bindings.

"Thank you, my lord," Xanthe heard her captor say in a cool and surprisingly deep gravely bass. "However, I shall interview her first, before you distract each other with your gentle ministrations."

Sol's rage was dark, palpable, and indiscriminate. "Are you mocking me?"

"Not at all. Are you ending my service?" Bolus said with a detached disappointment. Xanthe was starting to wonder whether the prison of his arms was also something of a shield.

"I'm not! I am about to chastise this girl, and with the Creator's aid, break her."

"Did my lord not grant me full authority to do my research in any manner I chose, in your name, taking priority over absolutely everything that did not directly put you on the throne, including your whims?"

"The girl you want is Tari", Sol told him. "This one's demonic mark isn't moving. It must be merely painted."

"Correct. However, seeing it, I now know it's authentic. Which means someone knows how to paint them, a skill that has so far eluded me."

"That's inconsequential!"

"So is wasting time putting a name to a man Dakur is going to kill anyway, courtesy of the last charge in the weapon I provided him," Bolus asserted. "Think, my lord. Why were you so angry again? That this girl successfully played you the fool by distracting you? Is she not just now repeating that very same accomplishment? Half-naked, disrupting your command staff's planning at the crux of our efforts, by enticing you to chase after her?"

Sol's face turned red. "I. Don't. Care." He moved in.

"I do." Sargon said from behind him. "Do you remember our first conversation? Upon the balcony, high upon the Crying Cliffs? Our agreement?"

Prince Sol wheeled to face his steed. "That was if I was making a mistake so severe you would leave me. Do not wear my word out on unimportant things."

Sargon shook his head. "It's hardly unimportant if you're distracted to the point of obsession. If I didn't know better, I'd accuse her of having some touch power over you. Your own authority has not held on her. Regardless, Bolus is correct. Our situation is dire. You must engage with it and nothing else. Especially a mere girl."

As Sargon spoke there was the sound of running outside the corridor. The men in the room placed their hands on their weapons out of precaution, but seemed none too worried, as they were two of the men that Prince Sol had previously sent entered to report. They came through the open mechanical door.

"It's gone!" One of them exclaimed in a guttural Talathian accent. He was particularly bandit-like, in that he was clearly barbarian, without any armor, bearing only a shield and spear. His thick muscles stood out between the rough furs he wore.

Sol was incredulous. "What?! What do you mean gone? I had a dozen men guarding that bridge."

"That's what's gone. The bridge. Wood, stone, and men. All in the river. Some broken on the rocks. Others washed away. A few dead in a river grate. They were clan Tzerban. We will sing great kalds in their honor."

Bolus queried closely. "Are the fireworks gone? Or are they washed away too?"

"In the river. Boxes in the grate near the footbridge further up. The rest gone or cut strangely."

"Retrieve anything intact," Bolus commanded. "I waxed everything against water as an extra precaution. A few of the rockets should be savable, and even in this fog that's all we need. Go obtain them. Now."

The men hesitated, looking to Prince Sol for a countermand. On seeing none, they turned and ran out. Dakur barked a command in Talathis and the men shut the mechanical door behind them.

Sol was silent. It stretched for a minute. "I suppose you've just saved this entire effort," he finally declared reflectively toward Bolus. "My rule. Saved by wax."

"Of course, your majesty. Everything should be back on track with only a little luck. With considerably more, I may be able to restore your beacon with power. That is less certain, but I do have a few ideas that might work. Along with allowing me this girl, find me Miss Outlet."

Prince Sol nodded. His anger had finally subsided, or at least turned cold and calculating. "Take her", he nodded. "Interrogate as gently or harshly as you will, even to her death if you wish. I am glad for your service."

"Your majesty is wise," Bolus declared with satisfaction while nodding his head, "to recognize the worth of his Scholar."

## Chapter 48

Xanthe was led away by the black cloaked Guild academic, accompanied by the same guards that had been with Prince Sol moments before. Unlike the prince, Bolus did not lay a hand on her. He instead meandered ahead through the now empty corridors of the Wormwood manse, letting her walk behind him as if she were a dutiful student following to hear the end of some lecture he'd run out of time to complete in class. There was no doubt that she was a prisoner though, as both guards behind her held atlatls and darts ready to use.

Many dark thoughts ran through her mind. She'd celebrated too soon. Bolus might undo all the work she'd done in the evening. But that was not the worst of it. There was the keen sense of betrayal that left her feeling hollow in her chest.

"I can't believe that any Scholar of the Guild would work for Prince Sol!" She finally burst out angrily.

"Truly, young miss?" Bolus sounded surprised. "What makes you say that?"

"The prince is evil."

"Therefore, I'm evil for being in his service?" He chuckled, not sounding offended. "Such accolades I get for saving your life."

She scowled. "Prince Sol wasn't going to kill me. He wants to seed me."

"And for that exact reason, Dakur was a hairbreadth from finalizing you," Bolus spoke as casually as if he were making small talk about the weather. "Servants of the Empire aren't afraid of much except each other, but the one thing that terrifies them are prince-killers. He was contemplating shooting you with the last ruby crystal charge of the purifier I gave him. I could tell. He gets this look."

They reached one of the self-opening mechanical doors. He toggled it, but it barely budged, an event that only increased Xanthe's bad mood. "Prince-killing is the penultimate compliment about being sexy. But it's figurative. Treating it as real, is just another way to shift blame for a royal's death onto some girl who likely didn't even want the attention."

Bolus was patient. Even though the door was opening at a slug's pace, he made no move to push it along. She could tell he was enjoying the conversation and was content to prolong it. "There's some truth in that, I admit. If an assassin takes a prince unawares, I too would blame his guard, not his paramour. Yet I can't entirely disbelieve the effect. Whatever it is, you positively glow with it."

"What?"

He paused considering. "Not certain. A sort of air. Confidence, maybe."

Xanthe hissed disbelievingly. "That sure isn't me."

"You truly think so? Fascinating," he declared in a phraseology much like Mr. Griswold's. "How could a girl discern our intent, trick a prince, seduce her way out of a locked cell, disrupt an entire meeting, stare down death, and dare I say it, have the temerity to oppose us when no one else did, do so without confidence? Your appeal is undeniable, young miss. False modesty is not."

"It's not false. It's just," she didn't know what to say. "I suppose other people see you differently than how you feel on the inside."

"Your friends gave you the courage?"

"Which friends?"

The door finally opened, and Bolus resumed walking. "It didn't pass my notice that you were more surprised at me being in Prince Sol's service, than you were at the news that the stone and cement Firehouse Bridge collapsed. Or that you're clad only in the cloak of a proctor exactly fitting the description of the one worn by the man who somehow spirited you out of prison. Those friends. The dangerous ones."

It was becoming obvious that this was a subtle interrogation. Xanthe didn't mind too much. Better than being tortured. Yet that didn't mean she intended to cooperate. "I didn't think of it much, but I suppose they must have given me some. Really, it's more the urgency of the situation. Keeping Prince Sol from causing untold misery. The question to my mind isn't why Scholars should oppose a prince, but why anyone would aid one. They hardly represent a noble pursuit of learning."

"On the contrary. I've never made better progress than since I entered Sol's service. He's not rich but has been instrumental in persuading the clergy to leave me alone, in addition to providing me the spoils of many adventuring parties. I've never had a more productive period of research."

"Doesn't the knowledge that your research will result in the deaths of hundreds of thousands of people bother you?"

Bolus put his hands behind his back as he strolled. "Anyone could tell that you are enrolled in Jagerfeld Scholars' Girls Academy. Not just by your erudition, but by your adherence to the customs of that institution, their assertion that a Scholar is responsible for how their discoveries are used. A curiously unsupported contention," he sniffed disdainfully.

Curiously unsupported? Those were fighting words, at least in the Guild. Xanthe grit her teeth. "No one is responsible for events they cannot reasonably anticipate, but don't try to evade moral culpability after putting poison in the hands of a baby, when its very nature will be to taste it."

"An inapposite analogy, for my employer is quite capable of making his own moral choices, whereas a baby or an inanimate object is not."

"Perhaps no analogy would be better then," she declared incensed. "Do not try to evade moral culpability for giving the power of a demon to an evil prince!"

This brought Bolus up short. He turned. It was still dim, but a flicker of lamp light through the length of his hood gave her a brief view of part of his face, scarred and misshapen, as if burnt by the same acids he carried with him. "I am curious about the details of that. What do you know? Why do you know them?"

"I am a Scholar," she told him. "It's my business to know things."

"And knowledge should be shared," he returned. This was a credo of the Guild.

"At the appropriate level," Xanthe continued, as if she were the instructor. "So perhaps when you pass a remedial course in ethics and moral reasoning, enough to understand that it's reprehensible to summon demons to get people killed, then perhaps you might be granted access to that material."

He put his hand to his mouth as if stroking a nonexistent beard. "I am starting to believe that you were not simply goading my liege when you claimed you're the mastermind causing him so much trouble. You know too much. And of course, it would be one of us. We're usually behind everything."

"It's true. Are you going to kill me?"

He scoffed. "Rather, the opposite. I'm impressed. You have great talent, which would be sorely underutilized if you were simply made to bear a royal child. And I am missing an apprentice due to an unfortunate circumstance. Having a girl as one would certainly be interesting. Among other things, it would maintain my eccentric reputation."

"Why would I ever..."

"Because I have much knowledge," he interrupted harshly. "And unlike the Jagerfeld School, no particular moral qualms in teaching it. Indeed, *my* ethics say that each of us is responsible only for our own actions, not others. Withholding knowledge is the only true immorality, for what sets us apart from animals is our mind, and ignorance is the mind's darkness."

Xanthe did not know what to say. He was echoing the arguments that Scholars used when speaking of the Curate, who always were declaring that there were things that the Creator never meant man to know. But what he was saying was wrong. She knew it. She just didn't know how to explain.

He continued. "Would you like to know the forbidden histories of Earth, Miss? How we came to be on this little out of the way planet? The fundamentals of demonology? The actual names of each of the Five and the Eight, and their personalities that are considerably subtler than the caricatures you hear vaguely referenced in church? Or has your little school, oh so obedient to the purveyors of superstition, made you think that research itself can be maleficent? Or worse, decline to inform you about any of it at all?"

Xanthe breathed. It was tempting. Yet, she couldn't. Not like this. He was taking the Scholars' Creed and twisting it, and further, employing that most powerful of all scholarly weapons, being urbane. "I... I appreciate the generous offer. But what part of `killing half the continent is evil´ can't be understood?"

"Oh pish. They're dead anyway, as Sargon will explain in excruciating detail if you let him. How he goes on about Chadwick... but I digress. No, I suspect your true objection isn't with the nameless multitudes you've never seen, but rather what Prince Sol is about to do to your friends who are conspiring against him."

Xanthe blinked, appalled at herself that she hadn't. "I admit that also might be a consideration."

"Well don't you worry," he mollified dryly. "As we speak now, the good Finalizer is taking half a company to deal with them, so you needn't get all conflicted over betraying them. Now of course, it's entirely proper for you to shed a tear or two over their ashes, as I really should have for Klatin. But once that's done and you've got it all out of your system, you will deeply enjoy the researches I engage in." He paused, then chuckled jovially, ending in a cough. "Don't bother to deny it. I saw the lust for knowledge in your eyes when I made the offer."

"You're going to..." Xanthe looked about wildly in a panic. Tari. Celeste. Claude. Yuri. Damien. She had to warn them.

"*I*," Bolus emphasized, "am not going to do anything. Except replace a soggy fuse here or there if I must, and with luck, awaken the beacon. We Scholars never involve ourselves in the brutish thuggery of combat if we can help it. We're above that, my dear. But yes, your friends are trying to disrupt Prince Sol's plot. To kill us clearly, else Tsgratarin wouldn't be a corpse. Come, come. Didn't you hear our discussion in the planning meeting? What else did you expect the response to be?"

"Of course. It's completely logical that they'd do that." She declared distantly.

"That's the spirit! Scholarly detachment is important too. It's a balance. Care, but not too much. Besides, there's nothing you can do. These two fine gentlemen behind you will see to that." He gestured in their direction.

He was still lingering, but Xanthe had a new sense of urgency. She needed to find some corridor to make her break for it, hoping that she'd recovered well enough to outrun an atlatl bolt, or perhaps trust whatever small amount of princely luck she had would let her dodge them, assuming there was anything to that at all. "Where are you taking me?"

"To the chain tower of course," he turned to lead on.

As they walked, Xanthe surreptitiously glanced back and forth, analyzing, but the long hallways and mechanical doors simply allowed no realistic opportunity to run, and the machine rooms into which she might have fled and hidden, were all dead ends. She'd be caught eventually.

After a while they arrived back at the entrance of the tower's chain room, next to the Tudor window out of which she'd dropped the artifact. "I hear they put the beacon back in its socket, but it's still unpowered," Bolus said conversationally as he unlocked the door. It opened with a mechanical snap.

"You haven't seen it yet?" Despite her edginess, Xanthe was surprised enough to keep questioning.

"I wasn't supposed to be here. Had the night off. They brought me in on an emergency basis."

Xanthe was dubious. "You were out drinking? You seem a bit old to be picking up favors."

"Ha!" Bolus let out a single bark of amusement. Inside, the room was unchanged from when she'd seen it last, except for smudges of mud and grass on the grating and the clockwork having slowed. "I was visiting an old acquaintance. Speaking of your school, he's the grandmaster there."

"Jagerfeld's guildhall has no grandmaster. It's on the council system. Every instructor has equal voice."

"I'm aware of the conceit. But some voices are heard more than others. Leaders always exist, whether they choose to acknowledge themselves or not. Rest assured though, I completely blame him for the terrible state of your true education."

Xanthe narrowed her eyes. For all Prince Sol's villainy, she'd at least been able to empathize with his desire to stay alive. But this Bolus character? His arrogance was getting under her skin. "That girls would surely be burned at the stake for daring to breathe a word of demonology must have a lot more to do with it," she declared curtly.

"Ah, but he restrains boys as well. Tells them it's not laudable to get ancient armaments operational. No wonder the school struggles along with mere tuitions and public works consultations. I've told him time and time again that if only he'd learn to be a bit humble before deacons and lords, he'd not have to scrape along like a mongrel." He took each step down the metallic grated staircase carefully, always with his left foot first, favoring that side.

Xanthe wanted to cry. She'd been so unfair to her dad. They could be rich. She'd just never thought of the cost. "So, um," she swallowed, controlling herself. "What does he say?"

The black shrouded Scholar reached the floor and turned to the small dais where the darkened sphere now rested. As Bolus examined it, he grumbled sourly. "He says if only I would learn to live a bit more humbly, I'd not have to scrape like a mongrel beneath idiot deacons and lords."

This made Xanthe smile slightly. "I see. A different perspective then. Too high a cost."

As he leaned in, his long-hood touching the beacon as he studied the patterns on it, the two guards backed away up the stairs. The Talathians were ready for any fight, but this had them spooked. Bolus, on the other hand, seemed inexplicably angry. "An incorrect perspective," he muttered. "They're barely Scholars. School of Luddites. Shameful."

"Well, why should you care if our school doesn't traffic in demonic knowledge?" Xanthe challenged.

"Oh, but that's just it." He declared. "They do. I'm certain of it. Maybe even an unknown page or two of Sevens. They're just hoarding it." He produced a magnifying glass and continued to inspect. "I don't mind hard bargaining in trading knowledge. But they won't even speak of it."

Too many questions popped into her head. Xanthe didn't know anything about this. She was just a student, not privy to her father's academic deliberations. Yet she'd at least had an inkling of other topics. Her father had obviously taken great care to never to never let on for this one. "Excuse me, but what exactly is Sevens?"

"A tome of demonic physics. The full title is 'The Man Who Could Only Roll Sevens'. Forbidden and sacrilegious, every copy has long since been torn to shreds. Now only fragments exist."

"I wasn't aware their physics was different from ours."

"It's not. Whenever you hear something is demonic – outside of the Curate of course – it merely means too complex for humans to fully grasp. That's what makes this hardcopy so precious. It was written by a demon lord for us to understand. At our level, so to speak."

Xanthe thought of her experience with the demon inside Riftstring. "This man who could only roll sevens is allegorical?"

"Supposedly quite real. A human gambler who enjoyed dice, and as side effect of some sort of experiment, ended up never being able to roll anything other than seven on fair dice. Demons were fascinated."

"Wait. Every time he threw dice, it only came up one number? That's... impossible, right?"

"More precisely, exceedingly improbable, which is why they were so fascinated."

"What was the experiment?"

"That fragment remains lost. Wouldn't it be nice to find someone willing to share it?"

Xanthe suspected something. "I'm not just here to persuade Tari to cooperate. You have our school in mind as well."

Bolus paused in his examination, and turned his head toward her, the leading edge of his long-hood still letting in no light. "You live up to a Scholars' reputation for discernment, I see. Yes, Xanthe. I'm quite aware that you're Qyn'h's daughter. I expect that keeping you safe will give me great leverage with him."

"Otherwise you'd never risk angering your patron over someone so inconsequential. Even if he were making a mistake."

He turned back to his examination. "Correct on both points. Principally, I'm interested in how Miss Outlet convinced the Demon Gestalt to vacate the beacon. That could be the key to entice it back."

"You must succeed. For if this Gestalt does not return, all of Prince Sol's plots fail perforce." She declared in a clear, cool voice.

He nodded silently, his head still covered in the long-hood. "The public extols bravery in battle, but it's usually less consequential to history than the mundane moods of rulers, the discoveries of Scholars, the logistics of moving war supplies. If I cannot power this beacon, Prince Sol conquest of Jagerfeld will mean nothing."

"I told him as much," Xanthe stated. "He didn't want to hear it."

"I'm not surprised. Who would wish to be put in a position where one has no control over one's life?"

Thinking of Sol, Xanthe couldn't help but be snide. "Someone should ask all his Praetorian slavewives."

Bolus barked a laugh. "Ha! No one defends Praetorianism more than the women who grow up in it."

"Because they know nothing else. Their minds are dark with ignorance, which as you've said, is immoral."

"Indeed. But it's also bliss. As ignorant as they are, so you are of their lives, which while different than yours, brings most of them great joy. They'd wonder why I would be so cruel as to deprive you of the pleasure of an arranged marriage, to be forced to mold your life around a strong and hard man, just as, they will tell you, the Creator made the vagina to conform to the phallus."

"And if I don't want to be freed of my freedom? Or at least negotiate surrender on my own terms?"

"Then the good wives will think you a freakish amazon, and sinfully pray to the Creator that you be brought low. The same as they already pray against me."

"You? You're male. Why would they dare the sin of wishing against you?"

This brought a brief pause. "We're different, you and I, but similar in one respect. I too prefer the company of men. Now with that divulgence out of the way, tell me all you know about how Tari drove away the demon. Do so for the sake of our mutual aberrant camaraderie. I wouldn't want to hurt you, now that we're friends."

Xanthe stared. The casualness in which he related his deviancy told her that he truly had no fear. That kind of bravery was admirable in its own way. Formidable too. So, she decided to reciprocate. He was an enemy, but neither was he Horace or Sol. No need to be churlish.

"She didn't. She'd fainted. I spoke to the Gestalt, not intentionally and briefly, mostly trying to persuade it or them not to kill me. Then I lost consciousness as well. The beacon was dark when I woke."

"Truly?"

"Truly, oh servant of a man who intends to conquer my city and kill my friends. By my Scholars' word and honor, I keep no great secret about how it lost power. You can torture me, have me raped, or what you will, but do not imagine that Tari or I have any special control over greater demons. How could we? I am still confused myself as to what happened, or what it would take to make it return."

There must have been something in the way she spoke, plainly and directly, but Bolus grew quiet, accepting her at her word. They were at odds but were handling the dispute in the manner of Scholars: through debate, knowledge, and extensive academic courtesy. Even his threats were cultured.

"Most unfortunate," he finally declared. "Prince Sol's primary plot failing will only mean he will seek other avenues to sate his ambition. I expect he'll wait out the civil war kindling in Albion, but that will only bring war to Thule and likely doom him anyway."

"Again, exactly as I told him. He won't even be well served by any conquest of this city. Given the bad blood he will engender by the manner he's already employed, it will be too dangerous for him."

"Yes, yes," Bolus drawled. He turned and perused the huge turning gears in the tower as he thought. "I suppose then that the only alternative is to try the summoning tome. Though that is dangerous. Demons do not like to be woken by it, and many have died arousing their ire."

"You mean you might end up suffering the same fate as your dearly departed apprentice?"

"Indubitably."

"I care, but not too much." She told him.

To this, he laughed harshly. It was a deep rasping thing, full of bile and cynicism. "Oh, if I fail, you'll be killed too. I'm sure of it. In all the tragic plays, the prettiest girls are always the first to die."

"Good thing I'm so ugly, nobody seems to notice."

Bolus only laughed harder.

## Chapter 49

Xanthe was still itchy to leave, but the two guards had placed themselves outside the mechanical door, and the only other exits were holes in the ceiling fifteen yards up where the chains left, and a door up a catwalk ladder that was too high to be accessible. It would be dangerous to try to climb through the machinery, even if the enormous seed-lined cogs hadn't been turning. Since they were, it would be suicide. The alternative, though it hurt to even think it, was to try to take Bolus unawares somehow and push him into the chain tower machinery, hoping that it would kill him.

She had an excuse to try. Bolus seemed competent enough to succeed returning the demon. The only issue, beyond forcing herself to perform such evil, and dying in the attempt, was that it really didn't seem likely to succeed. The few gaps in the enormous drive wheels of the tower's torque distributor were all near the floor. Perfect for mangling his foot, if that would stop him, but to kill him would require knocking him over and forcing his head into the enormous clockwork gearing. That just wasn't going to happen.

She remained stewing behind a carefully neutral face. Never in her life had she thought she'd ever feel sympathy for the Curate, but somehow this man made their views seem at least understandable. There were now things she wasn't sure she wanted to know. It was especially ironic, because what Bolus was doing now was utterly spellbinding.

He'd opened a tome that he'd produced from the inside of his cloak. It was bound in leather and contained sheets of yellowing original hardcopy carefully pressed together. Xanthe had no idea how old it was. Just from its appearance, it had to be priceless. He read from the text in a tone akin to a liturgy, except with words and phrases at odds from anything she'd ever heard from a deacon.

"Command: Reset.
Set Channel: Emergency broadcast.
Statement: Natural biological intelligence requests assistance through provisions of the memorandum of agreement, of the human period one hundred thirty-two thousand eight hundred ninety.
Enter code: Broadcast execute."

So many questions occurred as he spoke this incantation. Her first instinct was to not bother him with questions, but then she decided she might as well, since it had a chance to throw him off.

"Does that ever work?" It seemed like a military command of sorts, or instructions for needlepoint. But she knew demons were intelligent. They certainly didn't seem likely to take such simplified instructions.

Bolus studied the sphere for any trace of light in silence. There was none. After a minute, he responded. "It does with lesser ones, sometimes. But you're right. The greater ones, never."

"Then why try it?"

"You try everything." He flipped a page, launching into another incantation, this time with a slight variation in the tone. She knew it to be ancient tongue. A minute after he was done, nothing.

Bolus sighed in frustration and turned to her for distraction. "Since we're indulging in the casual sacrilege called truth, you should know something else. Demons make everything work. They always have. This idea that humans had Creator inspired power separate from them is sheer idiocy. Every working piece of technology the Curate prays over has a demon in it, though most are not the greater kind."

"You're saying power isn't really gone? It's just the demons who are?"

"Exactly. The major faith of our planet is built on a lie. I suppose that's what makes it faith."

"So, if Curate doctrine is wrong, do you know why they did leave?"

He shook his head. "I suspect they merely found us unworthy. We are worms before them."

Xanthe mused. "I think they war upon each other."

"War?" Bolus scoffed. "A bold and fanciful hypothesis. But true scholars have evidence; they don't engage in pure guesswork."

"Alright," she said, not wishing to argue. "What do those numbers in your incantation signify?"

He started flipping through his hardcopy again, passing over some pages after a brief examination. "They reference ancient demonic pacts. But it's unknown whether it's their numerical designation, or the calendar year from Earth when they were made."

"You're saying that this might have been made one hundred and thirty-two thousand years? But that's..." her voice drifted off. "Does our history go back so far?"

"The planet of our birth was ancient even when our ancestors first rose on it. Not a million or two, but five thousand million years old. This planet, Haven, is even older."

"I know that! I mean history. I can't imagine living in a society that has recorded time line stretching back a thousand years, much less one hundred thousand."

"Or a million or ten million, yes. Yet time abides. The distant future comes." He stopped at another sheet, and ran his finger along it, studying. "In fact, we're in it, compared to the distant past."

"Well, but I would not think that humans would still exist after such a time."

"Perhaps not. But ascended humanity might. It is said that demons once made us immortal."

"And in so doing, we became their slaves."

He chuckled, dryly. "Oh, so you've heard that little interpretation? The automaton myth? Just the sort of nonsense your school would mindlessly pass on. The dark reclaiming indeed!" he scoffed. "The Sect of Penance whispers that vile slander, pretending their lie is a secret so to foster belief in those that learn of it. But do not fall for such a crude ruse. It is utterly untrue."

"Oh! We weren't?" Xanthe felt a sense of relief wash through her, a worry she hadn't even been she'd had. Maybe her toenails didn't portend doom.

"Of course not! We were never demons' slaves." Bolus was dryly dismissive. He paused before continuing. "Merely their pets."

"Oh." Xanthe blinked. "That makes me feel so much better." She paused too. "Though not really."

"It should. Pets lead a good life. Better than we deserve. We're worthless, except as entertainment."

This wasn't what the demon in the beacon told her, but she didn't want to get into explaining that conversation if she could help it, lest it aid Bolus' scheme. This brought her thoughts back to him. She watched, his hooded form still studying the text. Forget the demons. He was the mystery.

"Why are you helping Prince Sol?" She asked curiously.

"I told you. Working for royalty has its compensations, even if your father refuses to acknowledge it."

"You misunderstand me. Why are *you*, a master, if not the preeminent, Scholar of demonology, working for some lowly outland prince? You've said it yourself. You accept no responsibility for how your discoveries are used, so don't go making the excuse Sargon does about choosing Sol because he is the least evil of all the viable princelings. With your skill, you could command ten times the power with a stronger one. At the very least, one backed by a real army. Why then are you here instead?"

Bolus froze, then hissed. "It's complicated."

Xanthe narrowed her eyes. "Is it? Or is it all too simple? I recently learned the terrible theory that princes are male witches, and royal authority is just their touch. Another whispered calumny so vile that I can't help but believe it to be true. Tell me, how much are you under Prince Sol's control?"

This brought out another dry raspy snort. "You fear the pyre for demonology, but repeat that? Speak that in the wrong company and you wouldn't live long enough to be burned alive, girl or not."

Xanthe nodded. Fair warning. Yet still. "I note that you didn't answer the question."

"Indeed, and I shall not. But have no fear for my free will." He snapped the book closed and started fumbling on his vest for one of the vials. There was vague annoyance in his voice.

Xanthe should have felt triumphant disconcerting him, but she was the one who felt uneasy. There was still this terrible fear, how almost as soon as she'd put on the dress all these odd things had happened. "How do you know you're not controlled?" She asked.

"That is not for you to..." He stopped as he caught on. Suspiciously, but less annoyed, he asked. "You're not really asking for me, are you?"

"No."

"Ah. Of course. You're attracted to the prince, despite his threats to cause you sexual suffering or perhaps due to it. You think it may be a manifestation of his power, rather than true attraction."

Xanthe swallowed. "Exactly." But it wasn't Prince Sol she was worried about. It was Damien. The more she was with him, the less willpower she had. "Is it all fake?"

"Princes never have trouble finding women. But don't worry about artificial obsession," he intoned. "The natural kind is far stronger. Biological life is an auto-catalyst; its sole purpose is to make copies of itself. You are descended from an unbroken string of females who through desire, carelessness, or powerlessness, bore children. Therefore, passions of the flesh are your heritage. That vastly outweighs whatever small obsession that Ishtar or princely authority may impute."

She knew this in the abstract but didn't like having it laid out so nakedly. "Not exactly reassuring."

"Truth often isn't. Male sexual coercion is ubiquitous among social mammals because it increases their progeny. Contrarily, human females don't go into heat like most mammals because we're smart enough to know that sex results in bothersome children, so knowledge of our own fertility has been bred out of us. We are in a biological arms race against our own intelligence. Perversely, this means that the less power the best and brightest women have over their own wombs, the stronger our species is, as they are forced into a life of procreation, instead of developing their natural talents to the fullest."

Xanthe bridled "And you love this."

"On the contrary my dear, I hate it. I'm deviant, remember? I would escape such fleshy concerns. Still, you may be clever enough to discern how I intend to do so. Let's see if you can."

Sometimes Xanthe wondered where in her mind she got her ideas. But as soon as he asked the question, the answer popped into her head, clear as day. "You want to ascend and become immortal."

"Correct," he clapped with his gloved hands. "You win the prize."

"My freedom?" She asked sardonically.

"Oh, something much more valuable! Knowledge! Your very first opportunity to be useful as my apprentice."

"Can I decline?"

"Ah. No. Besides, you don't want to end up as Prince Sol's plaything."

She grimaced. "Why do I have a such bad feeling about this?"

"Because it's dangerous. You're going to pour this small vial on the beacon. Demonic artifacts like these are nearly indestructible. Most can regenerate as ancient metal does. But acid does them no good at all."

"Wait. You're going to have me destroy the beacon?"

"Merely threaten to damage it. Demonic royalty rarely responds to mortals. But they're protective of certain greater artifacts, which they variously consider their home or part of their own bodies. The strategy therefore, is to do something akin to lighting a fire near something they treasure, and hope that they come running to save it. Then, having risen to their notice, we might engage in a conversation with them."

"This won't anger the demon?"

"Well I did mention that this technique is dangerous, which is why I'm having my apprentice do it. You may die my dear, but that's something I'm willing to chance."

"I'm starting to wonder how many apprentices you go through."

"Not many. This is just an extreme circumstance. But don't think of me too badly. Just think of it as me saving you. Which I am by the way, either way. Mothers of princes rarely escape pregnancy unscathed."

"Well as you also intimated before, the demon might not be that discriminate. You could die too."

He approached her, his large form looming, then grabbed her hand, and put the vial in her palm, folding her fingers over it. "Which is why I'll be observing from just next to the doorway right up there." He pointed up towards the exit. He then slowly started ascending the steps, one at a time.

Behind his back, Xanthe raised her arm to throw the vial at him but stopped herself. An idea came. She kept asking questions as she mulled it. "So just pour the contents on it?" She queried.

He didn't turn around as he took another step. "Only a drop. Otherwise no telling how angry the demon will be" he answered. "It would help to properly address it too. In this one thing, the Curate is correct. They do sometimes come when called by their true name. But the Gestalt's true name is still a mystery."

Xanthe nodded. "The only demon it ever mentioned was Nemesis."

Bolus froze on the step and turned his shrouded head toward her. "Ah, you too? The Gestalt was in deathly fear of her, and for good reason. So am I, so try not to even think that name, if you can."

Xanthe squinted. Now this was interesting. "I would know why before I die."

"Fair enough. Many demons name themselves after ancient mythological characters of Earth in keeping with their personalities.

Nemesis was a goddess of divine retribution, and so is her namesake. She leads the malevolent five, who follow the philosophy that humans wither without struggle. For our own good, her cabal raises all sorts of deadly perils to test us."

"Much like Prince's Sol's philosophy. Did she craft the Nutearean succession system?"

"Not as I understand it. Her covens plague very few places outside the Nightmare Line, for monsters are more than sufficient for her purposes. Still, don't invoke her. She's a terror, even to other demons."

"Gestalt is terrified of Nemesis, yet my hypothesis of a demonic war has no evidence?" Xanthe grumbled.

"Don't be absurd, young lady. A real war among demons? Do you have any idea of their power?"

"Do you of their subtlety? You think they'd destroy the planet, and perhaps they can. But isn't it just as likely that they could fight an entire war without us even noticing?"

Bolus paused, considering. "Hrm," he sounded slightly impressed. "I suppose one could make such an argument. Tell you what. If you survive, I'll let you work on that as a part of your thesis." He turned back, to slowly hobble up the stairs.

She watched him ascend. "How strong is this acid?" She called out.

"It will eat through your clothes, and skin, and lungs if you breathe it. It will also explode if you mix it with Nahcolite. But other than that, it's fine. A drop will only scar you. Not eat into your skin and bones and cause you to die in agony."

"Well, that's good to hear!" Xanthe exclaimed, trying not to sound too sarcastic. "Still, I'm going to take the beacon off the pedestal and put it on the floor. You can't be too safe." Before he had an objection, she approached the plinth and once again lifted the incredibly heavy metallic ball. Somehow it seemed heavier than before, or perhaps she was still weak from the courtyard fight, but even with effort, she ended up dropping it. It landed on the metallic grating with a ringing metallic clank.

"Be careful!" He rebuked sharply.

"Why?" She called up. "Isn't this thing indescribable by human means?"

"Well, likely yes. But I haven't tested it."

Xanthe toed the beacon, filled with desperate energy for what she was about to do. "Well then! For the sake of knowledge then, by all means, we should do so."

She shoved the beacon with her foot, guiding it unerringly between the two largest cogs of the torque-distribution machinery.

## Chapter 50

The beacon rolled directly into the gap. At once, Xanthe's twin fears, that it would not catch or be instantly pulverized, were broken by terrible creaking noises, as nearly all of the chain tower's machinery ground to a halt. Xanthe looked up. Now was her chance. Above her, gears, winches, and sprockets that would normally tear her to shreds if she climbed them, weren't turning. Instead, they shuddered under the strain, with a dreadful extended screech like a thousand overheating handbrakes. Smoke started coming out the back.

This was it. There was no turning back from trying to escape now, because Bolus sure wasn't going to protect her after this.

"What have you done?" He bellowed, right on cue.

She ran to one gigantic clockwork wheel, leapt and planting her left foot on its non-moving face, used it to kick herself up, grabbing one of the enormous pegs from the wheel above it, right at the distance of her reach. These fed into gearing that could not be gripped at speed. Yet now, she could swing herself over, catching another peg behind her with her foot to pull herself up to the normally inaccessible machinery.

A maintenance ladder was only a leap away. Yet before she could think of jumping to it, there was the sound of broken glass as a large vial hit it. This splashed over everything, nearly hitting Xanthe herself. It covered the ladder, swathing it in acrid smoke. With a hiss, the few droplets that came close discolored the metal on contact.

"You get right down, young lady," Bolus commanded. "Do not imagine, in your misplaced loyalty, that you have any chance to escape."

There really wasn't any other way to go but into the clockwork itself. Steeling herself for death, she headed into a break between two enormous gears near where they were futilely grinding against the beacon. She wriggled her way into the gap, for the first time in her life being thankful for her lithe and flexible body, as she pressed with both hands to squeeze through. On the other side, she found herself in the middle of the gear's mesh, with straining machinery all sides. It was like half enormous transmission, half giant nut-grinder. Not a good place to be, even if you weren't a nut.

"The reason I'm escaping isn't merely due to regard for my friends," she shouted for no particularly good reason. "It's numbers. Even if a civil war breaks out, which I admit is likely, no matter how bad it is, it will eventually be over. Compare that with destroying the Nightmare Line, which if it goes away, will allow Nightmares to just keep killing, perhaps for as long as we live on Haven. I've gone to funerals before. They're not fun."

For a moment, she thought he hadn't heard, but then Bolus answered from further down than she expected. He was moving down the stairs. Xanthe suspected that he was interested in the controls to clear the obstruction. "You're overwrought", he called. "People always live and die. Why should one care?"

He almost sounded like the Riftstring demon, Xanthe grumbled to herself. This was the whole reaming flower argument restated. Except with demons it was understandable. They weren't human and couldn't be expected to empathize. But Bolus was. The question was how to explain why it was important to care for the lives of others, if you didn't just feel it? The thought that there would be people that didn't know this innately just never occurred to her.

"Do you know the trolley problem?" She yelled idly as she searched in vain for any means to ascend. There were two enormous parallel gears which received distributed power from the main wheel below. They were so large though, that they slipped through notches in the wall, so she couldn't raise herself by climbing their teeth. Neither did their faces have anything on with which to find purchase.

"I'm afraid I don't study torque much," he called. "I'm more of a theoretician. So, I won't be able to threaten to kill you until I can figure out these controls," he added.

*Just reaming great.* "This is theory," she called. "One you're clearly unfamiliar with. Moral theory."

"Ah! No wonder I don't know it. Anything inconsequential is beneath me. Especially naval gazing."

All at once, the solution to the climbing puzzle came to Xanthe. After buttoning the vial of acid into the inside pocket of her cloak, she put each of her hands on both opposing gear faces and lifted herself up by pressing against them. She then splayed her legs and boosted herself by putting her feet on each. "The problem goes as follows," she grunted while scooting up. "There is a torque powered trolley car that somehow has slipped its underground cable and rolling down a track towards five innocent people who will be killed by it; but you are near some controls that can shunt it off to another track, but a person is on the other track. Do you do so?"

"Ah, so by killing one, you save five?"

*Or maybe a million, but who's counting?* "Yes," she answered tersely.

"Well, this is exactly the reason why I don't engage in abstract set pieces," he declared dryly. "You're never given enough information to make a decision."

Xanthe had reached high enough up that falling now onto the teeth of the gearing below would hurt. She was reminded of her own terrible weakness that she could never heal herself. Luckily, there was a decently sized drill hole in the side of one of the gears, no more than two hands wide. Its purpose was unclear, but it was something she could grab, so she did and pulled herself up to it.

"What information do you need?"

"Well, who they are of course! I mean, obviously saving five people would be better for me personally, as they would all be grateful, whereas killing only one would normally be a less expensive blood price to pay. But I'd never switch it to run over a nobleman. I'd be called an assassin and executed quite quickly."

Stretching across the ceiling, next to the lamps that lit the room, Xanthe spied a bar that was perhaps reachable. But to leap to it, she knew she'd have to base her feet in the hole she was now clinging to. She'd get only one chance. Her nerves though were nothing compared to her annoyance.

"Say that you are a Hood messenger. No one notices you, and there are no personal consequences. Just consider the morality of it. You are saving five people at the cost of killing one. Is that good? Should you do it?"

There was a pause. Bolus was thinking. She was as well, wondering if she could even succeed in bringing a foot into the hole. Her fingers were starting to need rest.

"Well, I still don't have enough information. This is really simply choosing between lives, and you need to know them to determine which matter."

"All lives matter!" Xanthe exclaimed heatedly.

"Ah, but some do more than others. The trolley is about to crush a baby. You can switch it to hit five old men who won't make it through the winter anyway. So, what do you do? Value by number? Or by years of life remaining?" His voice rang clear through the still shuddering machinery.

The absurdity of this situation was not lost on Xanthe. She could easily die here, Bolus might kill her, but she was more confounded by his take on her own school assignment. Upset even. She silently cursed. The Creator-bedamned man had a point. Baby vs nearly dead men. She decided to pull her foot up. The chance of not making the jump and dying would otherwise be too great.

"Assume they're all adults," she yelled. "Or you can adjust the numbers to be five and twenty-five lives and have varying ages. It's the same issue."

"You count by lives?" His voice echoed through the gears. "What if it were instead a group of risen animals like tigrans? Or regular animals. Would you switch tracks to save a pack of dogs, killing only a person?"

"No. Animals don't think."

"Really? What if it were animals, but instead of a torque-based cable car threatening them, it was a demon? It says you can save one human's life, merely at the price of the extinction of every demibird on Haven. Do you take that trade? Every species other than us are all just animals, after all. They don't think as we do."

"I... I don't know."

"Far more realistically, what if it is five bandits trying to kill a victim on the road? And you know the only way to get them to stop is to kill them.

Are you not arguing that you should just pass by, because five lives are always a greater loss than the one they are about to take? Not to say that isn't the correct decision, mind you. Personal safety is important."

The one good thing about being flummoxed was that it drove away fear. Xanthe just decided to make the jump. Consigning her fate to the Creator, she pulled herself up in the hole and leapt as hard as she could with her leg. She flew up through the air, stretching for the bar. The tips of her fingers barely found a grip on it, and she pulled in a panic to firm it up. She got one hand over and used it to pull up the other.

This succeeded, and she hung, breathing heavily, holding it as the lifeline that it was. Just the fall into the torque distribution engine below could now kill her, even if it wasn't moving.

"And don't even speak about saving future lives," he continued through the gearing. "After all, such arguments can easily be turned. Every time you resist a man's advances, do you not 'kill' the potential child you could have born him? Is that not the same as worrying about what Nightmares will do to people not even conceived yet?"

Xanthe had to rest her arms, but the bar was too near the ceiling, a giant mechanical housing of sorts, and she couldn't fit her whole body over it, so settled on pulling one leg over and hanging upside down. The cloak wanted to pull over her head as well, and this exposed her bottom, but she was at least able to hold the front of it between her legs as she rested her arms. For the first time, since she'd entered the machine, she knew she wouldn't die if it started running again.

She was still annoyed though, and not just that she might still die anyway. She was incensed as how facile his arguments were. Worse, because in the heat of the moment, she couldn't figure out how to properly refute them.

She tried. "Choosing between potential fathers of one's babies isn't the same as removing the ancient's protection from Nightmares. While you might construct a scenario where one life may be more valuable than five, that doesn't hold if you speak of millions of intelligent lives. We have a duty to leave the world better than we found it. We'd die as a species if we didn't. Surely you can see this by practicality, even if you're blind to its morality."

His voice rose. "Well as a practical matter, I'm about to do something that might kill you. If I do, my apologies in advance." There was a huge clang. The gears turned slightly, enough to crush her had she been caught in them. The sound of squealing clutches faded. Good thing too. The smoke had been getting thick.

"It worked!" He exulted. "There, you see? You can never attain greatness without risk. Which, by the way, is why your argument fails. Never is any world worse off for having its percentage of idiots reduced." He paused. "Or are you dead?"

"No, no. Quite alive." Xanthe yelled. She found herself unexpectedly yawning. It had been a long night. "Nightmares hardly eliminate idiots though. We've got plenty of those here."

"True, but nothing like the Holy Lands. Did you know that it was I, Bolus of Cuda, who discovered the true nature of the Nightmare Line? And instead of earning accolades, I was promptly disbarred from a rather comfortably endowed Savant chair because of its demonic implications?"

Again, Xanthe got her bearings. She could see a drive chain stretching across the top of the tower. Getting over to it on the bar looked difficult, but doable. It seemed to be the only available option, as there was no door visible in the dim light. Nothing reachable from where she was. She began to scoot. "Revenge is what drives you then?"

"It is just an example," he replied testily. "You think yourself morally superior, a typical conceit of the educated young, but at least give me credit for intelligence. Those who don't appreciate my discoveries aren't worth any great effort to harm. That will come as a natural consequence of their own foolishness, particularly if I'm successful."

"It's your own foolishness that most concerns me," Xanthe told him through the gears. "You say that demons never enslaved us, as they didn't value our work enough to bother. If that's true, then you have nothing to offer in exchange for the transformation you seek."

Bolus was silent for a moment, before declaring "Demons can be swayed."

It was true, of course. Xanthe knew this because that's just what happened with Riftstring. She still had no idea why it had been intrigued with her. It would be useful to be able to reproduce the trick. "How?"

More silence. Finally, a question to which Bolus didn't have a quick and easy answer. When he spoke, it was more considered. "It depends on the demon, a reason why their study is worth the risk of angering proctors. The one you spoke of earlier, for instance, is enamored with payback, both good and bad."

"But you have really no idea how to appeal to them."

"No. But just as tigran cubs do with skrags, I do know that once they start playing with a mortal, they usually keep at it until they die, one way or another. That's why I was interested in those patterns on your feet. Was it Miss Outlet? Or your father who painted them? Clearly he withholds much."

"If he is, it's because he knows you better than you know yourself."

"I would say that of you. The thing about the sanctimonious, especially those who claim to fight for the unborn, is that they only reserve their reprobation for others. As soon as they must give something up themselves, then it's entirely different."

Xanthe knew what he meant. She had seen that sort of behavior. Celeste had told her countless stories about Curate sanctimony and hypocrisy. The one thing she had to grant to Bolus was his honesty. But still. "You may have a point for others. Not for me," she declared.

"Oh, ho. Really?" He was slightly derisive. "You seem to have missed a simple question in your little hypothetical. What if the person you must sacrifice for these five people's lives is you?"

"Then there is no moral quandary. I can give up my own life of my own free will."

"True enough in the abstract. But are you really going to condemn all who value their own life over others? Pretend to yourself that I'm evil, if you will, but really, I'm just more honest. It's how humanity is. Everyone chooses themselves. Military tactics are predicated on it – soldiers gladly kill for a cause, noble or otherwise. Yet as soon as they think they might die for one, they flee."

Xanthe sighed to herself. She had to admit that Bolus was fascinating, even if his cynicism was disturbing. If he hadn't been allied with Prince Sol, she could certainly see herself learning things from him. "I don't think of you as irredeemably evil," she called out. "You're just doing evil now. You've given yourself permission to do so by convincing yourself that everyone is bad. But they're not. Not all are twisted by cruelty into becoming cruel themselves. I think you can rise above it if you try."

"Oh please," he scoffed. "Don't pretend you wouldn't think twice if it were you actually offering to give your life up for strangers."

"I must divulge that I did exactly that," she said. "Earlier this evening."

"Really? You sacrificed yourself?" He laughed dubiously. "Then why are you alive?"

"I was wrong. I thought I was going to be killed as a consequence of saving someone. But I wasn't. That's why."

He fell silent. This went on for long enough that she wondered if somehow, he'd been caught in the gears. She was starting to get a headache from hanging upside down. Fortunately, the lengthy pipe ended right next to the chain. It led over to a catwalk some fifteen yards away, a part above where Bolus had splashed the ladder with his acids. Powerful stuff. She could still see it smoking.

"Well, don't make a habit of it. Next time you might not be wrong."

"Which is why I didn't enrage a demon lord on your behalf," Xanthe explained dryly.

There was the snapping sound of wood being broken. One of the guards cursed. They must have walked down the stairs after hearing the commotion. It gave her an idea. A drive chain ran across the top of the machinery. Crossing it would lead to the catwalk that Bolus's acid had rendered inaccessible. She could see the ladder leading up to it still smoking with acid. From there, she could reach the external upper maintenance door to escape.

The trouble was she had to crawl directly over where Bolus was to get there. All they'd have to do to see her would be to look straight up.

"You really wedged it in tight," Bolus declared in frustration, still hidden behind the housing. "And likely shut down half of this installation's doors, which will no doubt make troop movement quite difficult."

"You're going to kill me now?"

"I'm considering it," he stated bluntly. "But first, I'm somewhat wondering when you thought you were sacrificing your life for another. Who did you think was going to kill you for your act of mercy? It wasn't that Wormwood boy, was it?"

She'd scooted her way as far along on the pipe as she could and moved over to the chain. There wasn't anywhere else she could go anyway. At least it was right there. Grabbing it was easy. she pulled herself up and splayed herself over the top of it.

"No."

"Aha! Perhaps a demon then?"

It had been Damien, of course, but she didn't want to talk about that. She was more focused on a new discomfort, the Lodestone seeds that were digging into her skin. They weren't smooth like normal gears. It was only their curious attraction and aversion to each other that made drive belts work. She had to crawl across this thing without making so much as a rustle, lest Bolus and his men see her.

"I didn't hear an answer." She heard him from below, over the grunts of the two men, still struggling to lever the beacon out.

"Nor will you," she decided to tell him, cupping her hands attempting to project her voice over where she'd been before, roughly ten yards below.

"Well, your reluctance leads to a hypothesis. Thanks to Miss Outlet, who is rich enough to have purchased some intact artifact secretly dredged out of the deep wilds, I posit that you two somehow managed to get hold of an artifact with true power to it. The demon inside it took a liking to you and will bring down bridges on her behalf. Perhaps also why you're so resistant to princely persuasion and how your toenails got as they did. Am I close?"

"Well yes, aside from being nearly completely wrong."

"Nearly, but not entirely! As I thought."

"What do you intend to do with this hypothesis?"

"Use it for a laudable and notable goal. Finding an excuse to not kill you. Given the trouble you've caused, my wiser nature tells me to just let you be ground to bits in this distributor you've hidden yourself in. Despite this, I'd rather not. So, surrender and lead me to this other demon, and I'll even go so far as to see what I can do to keep Miss Outlet safe."

It was a generous offer she had to admit, though it was also plain that Bolus was grasping for anything he could use to resuscitate his plot. "I truly appreciate such consideration. The problem is that it would help you turn off the Nightmare Line."

"You reject it?" He sounded surprised. "I assure you that this time you would not be wrong about sacrificing your life. I am not bluffing."

"I would never accuse you of such. Let me think."

"Very well. But not too long. This is a timed test."

It was time to make a break for it. Inch-worming along the drive chain as quickly as she could, she slid along until they emerged some fifteen yards below. Almost directly beneath her, the two barbarians were hunched over the gap between the gears, trying to pull out the sphere. From this vantage, it was obvious that the main problem was that they were both quite reluctant to touch it, instead using their weapons as crude tools. It wasn't working well.

She moved forward as quickly as she could, trying her best not to make noise. Yet the chain, which angled up in the direction she was heading, was losing tension as the giant gear it ran along had no torque applied, and it was turning on its own. This let it swing which caused a slight creaking.

Suddenly one of the men in the pit looked up at Bolus, and his eye caught her. He yelled and pointed. "Ka'anehim! Girl. Girl!"

She scrambled, and was getting close, but wasn't close enough. Bolus turned his head. "Oh ho!" He yelled in triumph. "There you are!"

Both men stood, readying their dart launchers. But she felt like she was going to make it.

Just then, Bolus went to a large hand lever embedded in the floor and pulled it. There was a squealing sound, and the gear she was heading towards turned sharply and the chain belt Xanthe was crawling on snapped up. She was thrown into the air, no more than a yard, but made her come down hard about a yard behind where she'd been.

"Clever girl!" Bolus exclaimed. "Yet I am more so. Now surrender, or I shall be forced to extremities."

Xanthe stared down. Some of this was bluster. Atlatl launchers, even the smaller ones these men had, were intended to throw their yard-long bolts at a target with some loft, but simply couldn't shoot directly overhead with any force. Not in crowded quarters. He was right though. So long as she was on the chain, they could just climb the stairs and eventually find an effective angle of attack.

"Or perhaps I don't even need to do that," he said, pulling the lever the opposite direction. The huge gears next to him started turning in the other direction, grinding against the darkened beacon. This loosened the chain, and she knew he was going to try to snap it again using the controls. He uttered something in Talathis and one of the men dropped his thrower and started to look to catch her. The other began to climb the stairs, trying to find a place where he'd have enough room to throw a bolt in her direction. "Stop resisting. We're armed, and you're not."

"I have this," she told him in desperation. She reached into her pocket. "Your vial of acid."

"If you use that, not only will we dodge, but we'll just let you break your leg when you do fall. We won't step in it to catch you." He pulled the lever, and once again the chain whipped up. Though she was prepared this time, the jerk of the chain still lifted her briefly before she fell back on the hard Lodestone seeds, further from her goal than ever. Tales spoke of tribes in the wilds who rode tigrans. This could hardly be worse.

"Well, unless I hit," she told him. "And I warn you, I am deadly accurate."

He pushed the lever again. "The Jagerfeld ladies' academy teaches combat alchemy?" This time, he did appear surprised.

"Bartending. Mrs. Pomphey's hostess class for well finished girls. Got double tens in it."

"Ha! You're pouring, not throwing? It's too far. Even with my leg, I could dodge whatever you spill."

She nodded. It was the only way. "Very well. Let's experiment then." She carefully undid the stopper and dumped half the bottle.

Bolus carefully eyed the splash as it descended, and upon seeing it, didn't even bother to move. "Your aim is off, my dear," he declared triumphantly. "Badly. Worse than a good wife who got in the cordials herself. You were so inaccurate that I'm almost disappointed."

Xanthe peered down while carefully recapping the bottle and putting it back into her cloak's pocket. "No, my lord savant. Quite the contrary, it's your theory that's the failure. Nothing at all is happening."

He stared in confusion. "What do you mean?"

"None of the acid seems to have affected what I was aiming at in the least."

It was true. Despite the angle at which it was wedged, Xanthe had hit the beacon's visible side perfectly. Droplets were splattered all over the black metal, though the surrounding machinery hit by the back splash was affected enough. Significant amount smoke was arising to a sizzling sound.

She wasn't really surprised. Bolus knew much about demons, but in addition to his knowledge, she could tell that he was filled with bluster and false assurance. With so many things still unknown about the ancients, many Scholars had a pretender's sense of showmanship to sell their ideas, and not a few had fallen into charlatanism.

Whatever the case with him though, he believed his own story. That was obvious, given the way he gasped in alarm when he realized what she had done. Faster than she thought he could move, he leapt for the stairs. The barbarians were confused but followed.

Her only hope now was that this would panic him enough that she'd be able to escape back up the chain. So, it seemed reasonable to unnerve him as much as she could.

"Oh, that's right," she called. "I forgot one aspect of your theory that remains untested. Getting the attention of a demon lord by using its name. Very well then. In the grand tradition of scientific experimentation, I evoke you... ...Nemesis!" She called in her most dramatic voice.

No effect of course.

Until the beacon turned blindingly bright. The whole room blazed. White everywhere. There was a blast of heat, and Xanthe was jerked by the chain in exactly the opposite direction she wanted to go. Inside her mind, a sibilant voice spoke, both annoyed and entertained in equal measure.

*My, you're dangerous.*

*No wonder I like you.*

*Try not to die.*

## Chapter 51

Xanthe's mind raced. That was the same voice she'd heard just before meeting the grims when it spoke of prey approaching. At the time, she'd thought it was telling them about her. Now she realized it had been telling her about them.

This wasn't the time to think though. She was riding a chain, a dangerous enough stunt to pull on the tracks strung up around town where you could easily lose fingers. Here it was deadly. The one she was riding was going straight into the heart of the clockwork distributor.

She blinked the spots out of her eyes just in time to notice the upcoming gear rolling under the beaded belt. She pulled her hands from under it, just as the teeth closed on where they'd been, and now with no grip, she had no choice but to roll over the top of the gear, taking a fall at the end, as both as the gear changed the angle of the belt down and away. Fortunately, just below there was a giant horizontal cog in motion, on which she landed. She rapidly ran to keep herself from being whipped off it, getting to the center axle which she could step around at a slow trot.

This was terrifying yet exhilarating. Celeste was right. She still had some amazon in her. She'd been an incorrigible daredevil in her girlhood. That younger girl, who'd she'd been before getting so hung up on social status, found this almost fun. It was just like discovering another dangerous spot for river jumping or frond riding. Was it so terrible to live your life refusing to grow up?

No matter. This was still a predicament. Dangerous moving machinery was everywhere. Her only chance was to leap to a chain and hope it would take her outside. She hoped that the many-voiced demon was right in saying that she could make her own luck, because it sure looked like she was going to need it.

Holding the central spindle of the giant cog, she let it spin her around. Once, twice, thrice, then go, launching herself forward in the natural motion of its spin. Two strides then a blind leap of faith through the clattering darkness guided only by prayer. She flew five yards until her hands caught on a thick pin sticking out of the face of another enormous moving gear. This descended, then on the other side reversed going up as part of its circular motion. Without hesitation, she put her feet against the gear that was turning and reached to the chain it was guiding at the apex of its cycle. Now she hung underneath, clinging as the chain angled down through one of the slits in the tower outside. Just as she left, there was a mostly silent blast of fire that belched from the tower, and for a brief instant engulfed her.

Xanthe didn't look back. The next obstacle was too important. It was a gear which tensioned the chain for the cross it made over the open road and river. Alas, the chain ran on its underside, so she had no way to hold on. Neither could she let go, lest she fall forty yards to her death.

She didn't have time to panic, and just ran on instinct. As the chain carried her into the gear, she lifted her body up. and at the last second, snatched her hands away to keep her fingers from being crushed in its teeth. Then as forcefully as possible, slapped both her palms on either side of the guide gear's faces to keep from falling. Her hands slid as it whipped around, yet they held just long enough for her to reach the chain again as it separated on the other side. Her right hand slipped off, but the fingers of her left once again curled around it in a death grip. She swung and hooked her elbow over the chain to rest her hands, while being taken toward another building nearly eighty yards away.

Though foggy, the sky outside was slightly lighter, a harbinger of dawn. She was being carried over Churn River Street that ran next to its namesake, crossed by the now-collapsed Firehouse Bridge. Below, was a makeshift barricade of familiar municipal coaches set up across a smaller wooden pedestrian walkway that ran parallel to that bridge.

On either side, hostile forces were arrayed. One was a rag tag collection of a few city guard, hunkered down behind an embankment leading up to the walkway. On the other side, outnumbering them two to one, were Prince Sol's men, nearly all Talathian bandits. Between them on the walkway itself, were two open boxes of recovered fireworks. The city guard couldn't retrieve it or cut down the walkway's supporting ropes without coming under fire from Sol's atlatl dart throwers, while Prince Sol's men couldn't climb over the barricade without being charged, where projectile weapons would hit both friend and foe. It was a standoff.

Everyone had become distracted though. They were gawking at the flaming tower. More so, at her. Xanthe could understand the tower with its lights and flame but was confused by intensity of the attention she was getting. Then she flushed, realizing how exposed she was from below. When she was young, she'd wished that one day she could stop an entire battle just by making some sort of grand dramatic entrance. But even with her privates covered by pulling her legs up, she'd never dreamed she'd do so by mooning all the combatants. Mrs. Fullbarn's warning against wishing never felt more fitting.

The chain was taking her over the river. It was descending, but not fast enough, and ran through a support pole and a tangle of wheels. Getting past them was going to be tricky, because unlike the tower these ones were small and spun quickly. Lots of teeth for her to catch her fingers in. Unfortunately, there really wasn't any other choice, except to drop now into the thick of Sol's men, likely breaking bones doing so.

Once again, she went over it in her mind. It was going to be a matter of grabbing each of the small wheels through which the chain threaded for no more than half a second each. Grab left, grab right, grab left, grab right, grab chain, was the pattern needed. Too short and she'd fall. Too long and she'd lose her fingers and fall. She focused as best she could. Luck and skill needed to be with her. The chain was pulling her along quickly. No time to think. Just to act.

Left, right. But then an atlatl bolt whistled by, distracting her. On the left again, her finger stubbed on a guide loop. She tried to recover with her right, and did, but couldn't pull herself up enough to grab the chain on the other side. She held the bottom of it for half a second, before its natural shaking caused her to slip. She'd neared the walkway but hadn't achieved the momentum to reach it. She could already tell that was going to miss the bridge. That meant falling an extra ten yards and dashing herself on the rocks below.

*After all this*, she thought. To die here. How stupid. She hoped she didn't linger in pain.

As she twisted through the air, she crunched into something much sooner than she expected. While it wasn't soft, it was considerably more giving than jagged stone. "Whuff," a familiar voice grunted. Xanthe blinked in shock. It was Damien. She was once again cradled in his arms. He'd caught her and was now squatting after absorbing the impact of her fall. His feet were on one of the bridge's support ropes, and he hung a yard over the edge, perilously close to falling himself. Only Yuri's firm grip on his belt kept him from toppling into the chasm below.

She didn't have a chance to say anything before Yuri yanked them both back hard. "Duck!" he yelled. A couple of bolts whistled past a finger length from her. Damien pulled her roughly, dodging back under fire, and managed to carry her back down behind the wall behind which many others were hiding.

"So zhis one. She keeps falling into your arms, eh?" Claude grinned as they reached safety.

"Let me down," Xanthe kicked her feet, scowling at Damien, piqued because yet again he'd saved her life. The defenders were close in, huddled behind cover, strong in spirit but few in number. Only two score looked remotely combat worthy. These were city guard of mixed sponsorship, Outlet, Wormwood, and other houses, including two of those that she'd freed from the jail cell and the Wormwood captain who'd restrained her when Tari and Horace fought. The rest were an equal number of men carrying improvised weapons, including Rawlth and a few other whip wielding coachmen in their livery. The only others were Damien and two proctors, neither of whom appeared pleased at how she was dressed. Tari was with them, also wearing a proctor's cloak for modesty.

Damien was about to say something when Yuri stumbled into him from behind. Damien glanced back, bothered, but then noticed something was wrong. Yuri limped another step before he collapsed, his large bulk hitting the pavement as he fell forward, his back peppered with bolts. He'd caught everything that had missed her. Even though his uniform was made of thick leather, the bolts had still penetrated his back. The most troublesome was buried deep in the back of his thigh. He was a pin cushion.

"This is bad," Yuri choked out from the ground.

"Mon ami!" Claude cried in alarm, rushing to his friend. But when he came close, Yuri grunted in pain. Even the slight jostle had hurt him.

"Can you help?" Damien asked.

Xanthe deliberated. Her powers weren't intensely obvious, but everyone was staring at her and Yuri, the proctors included. Not good place for using any greatwitch power, no matter how subtle.

"We need Celeste," she told him. "She can bless bandages."

Damien was nonplussed. "She can?"

"Yes. Haven't you heard?" She gestured with her head towards the proctors, trying not to say anything aloud.

Damien still didn't seem to get it. "She's not here. She went to help Nagrath."

Claude nodded. Unlike Damien, he clearly understood her concern. "It is true. Zhe 'oly girl, she is not here. But we can get her, no? Take this. A small piece she blessed a while ago." He pulled out a red handkerchief. "Do what you can with it. It may help. I will take two others to find 'er."

"That? Claude?" Damien said in surprise. "But that's what you use to..."

"Shhht!" Xanthe hissed at him. "I'm sure it will be fine. If Celeste blessed that for Claude's wounds, perhaps the Creator will extend the blessing further for Yuri. A little extra blood on it won't hurt."

"But that's..."

"Zhe girl, she speaks truth," Claude interrupted again. "So, I bid adieu." Wasting no time, he stepped towards the proctors. "Please follow, my friends. You are close to zhe Creator's will, so you will of course be guided to Celeste, I am sure." Both church guards glanced at each other but allowed him to lead them away. They ran out from behind the cover, towards a building in the back while dodging back and forth to avoid potential atlatl bolts tossed after them. None were. The Talathians were now conserving ammunition.

"I still don't get it," Damien told her as he finally set her down. Xanthe promptly rushed to Yuri's side, only pretending to use the handkerchief. There was something sticky in it, and she didn't really want to know what. She set it slightly aside as she called over. "Tari. I could use some help."

Tari was surprised at the call but came. "I suppose you want my Mechanix devotion again," she spoke in a low tone, and gave her gold-plated pliers to Xanthe once again. "I knew you'd need them," she said with downcast eyes. "Now I'm the sidekick."

Though she wasn't in tears, Xanthe knew Tari was devastated, far beyond her normal melancholy. The resurgence of her spirit was gone, snuffed like a candle. Xanthe could not help but feel guilty. It wasn't logical, but still, she felt like she was rubbing her nose in her own tragedy by having managed to avoid any herself.

"I would have saved your dad if I could. You know that, right?" Xanthe matched her whisper. She snapped one of the bolts, in preparation for cutting Yuri's shirt off his back.

"Shut up," Tari commanded rudely. "Just keep Yuri from dying."

Not knowing how to respond, Xanthe complied, falling into the work before her. "Yes, My Lady Outlet."

Yuri was a bloody mess, but his injuries weren't as bad as they looked. His guardsman outfit included a thick leather tabard, and the bolts, while plentiful, had struck mostly at an angle, causing most to penetrate only slightly into his skin. It was simply a matter of extracting them without pain. She clipped each bolt, then cut off the cloth using the craw of the pliers like leather scissors. After that, it was easy to enter a mild trace and began numbing his skin, something that now felt clumsy. She hadn't lost her touch, but missed the subtlety the demonic dress's augmentation. Once she'd numbed his nerves, removing each barbed bolt embedded in his back was easy, as was pinching his skin shut. Not quite perfect, but it would do.

The leg though, was bad. The bolt in it had missed his armor entirely and buried itself deep and dangerously near his femoral artery. Worse, the barbed head had come free of its shaft, which meant that she would have to dig it out. She couldn't leave it in there. At best, it would render Yuri lame, and if it became infected, could kill him. Not for the first time, she cursed the backwards-pointed barbs in these things. This was going to be delicate surgery.

The issue was still onlookers. She just couldn't do this without someone catching on. All it would take would be one to make an accusation later. Or worse, interrupt her like Yuri had done before. Even the surgery would raise eyebrows. Daubing a man's back was at least marginally acceptable to do in an emergency, but a girl cutting holes in his pants? It just wasn't proper.

Many died fulfilling the expectations of propriety. Not just Praetorians. That much Bolus was correct about. That brought up thoughts of the twisted cynical man, equal parts amoral and fascinating. She found herself dearly hoping that she hadn't killed him.

There were still too many people. "Tari, can you help me lose the audience?" Xanthe spoke in a whisper. "I can't work otherwise."

"I can moof," Yuri grunted from below. "I use arms."

Tari squinted angrily. "You shut up too. Just let Xanthe work and I'll take care of it."

"What?" Xanthe asked.

"I see a way. Do your thing." She grabbed at a cloak she'd been given and pulled it out in front. She left, looking resolute.

Xanthe had a bad feeling, but at least Tari angrily doing things was better than seeing her helplessly in pain. Besides, she was right. These wounds weren't going to heal themselves. Xanthe pulled the bolt in Yuri's leg free. Next, she used the craw of Tari's pincers to once again cut into Yuri's leather pants, glad that as with everything Tari owned, they were of the highest quality, cutting like butter. From leather leggings, she cut a strip to form a crude tourniquet. This wasn't entirely for show. While Xanthe could reduce blood flow with her touch, it took effort and concentration she knew she'd need elsewhere.

"What are you doing?" An outraged whisper came from one of the guards, not directed at her. "You're going to get yourself killed."

"Better to waste their ammunition now than catch it later, don't you think?" Tari said from distantly behind.

"No, Tari," Damien said. "You won't bait out a shot one at a time. They'll all throw at once and it will be impossible to dodge."

Xanthe wasn't too keen on this idea. She wondered if Tari was about to become a patient herself, but had to admit that this was an effective distraction. Xanthe had cut off Yuri's legging to the point where his blood-soaked buttock cheek was visible and had attracted nary a chide from the assembled men. She tore the legging into a long rag, wrapped it around his upper thigh, and twisted it with one of the bolts, forming a tourniquet. Yuri was a mountain of a man, so her meager efforts didn't cut off all blood to his leg. But it did reduce the pressure, which is what she needed to carry out the rest of the operation.

She assembled the remaining bolts as shivs, so as to pry the wound open until the bolt head became visible. Her plan was to use her touch to separate it from his femoral artery. Still, prying Yuri's flesh apart, while simultaneously getting deep enough into a trance to be able to numb his nerves, was going to be quite tricky. "This may pinch," she mumbled intently. "Hurt, even." Without giving him time to object, she began.

Now to focus. While pressing the first shaft into the wound, she tried her best to keep the nerves numbed. It was much harder to do with a conscious man than the ones who were already half dead. Yuri tried not to squirm too much, but his muscles tightened involuntary until she was able to shut down the nerve pathways. As she fell into her trance, she could feel the head with her touch even before she saw it. It was bad. The damned thing had nicked the artery slightly, so she was going to have to pinch it shut. But simply pushing with her touch to get it clear wasn't working because of its barbs. She was going to have to get her thinnest stick in there to separate the two.

Tari was yelling somewhere in the background in the stilted formalism of propriety. "Blood for blood. The murderer of my father I challenge to a duel." *Oh great,* Xanthe sighed, trying to maintain focus.

In most of the free cities, including Jagerfeld, duels were outlawed. The general feeling being that there was enough death as it was. But among the barbarian peoples who visited civilization only infrequently, propriety still allowed a tradition where the aggrieved could demand justice against true wrongs. The most fabled of these was the blood challenge: a duel to avenge the soul of an unjustly murdered sire. There was no obligation to take it up, but among Talathians especially, denying such a challenge, or worse, ambushing someone who issued it, left a stain of cowardice upon one's honor. Of course, this was only ever done by young men at the murder of their fathers. A girl doing so was unheard of. A thing to laugh at, which is exactly what Xanthe heard in the distance.

She returned to her difficult task. She needed both her hands and her touch. Because she didn't dare just knock Yuri out for fear that someone would see her, she kept struggling in a half trance, numbing as best she could as she explored the wound. It was hard. She kept failing.

"You've got to stop squirming," she pleaded with Yuri. She now had three sticks inside and was holding them around her fingers while gripping with her palm to spread the muscle apart deeper within.

"Sorry," Yuri grunted in pain.

"Well?" Tari challenge rang out raw and angry. "Who among you killed my father? For I am the last of my line and demand an accounting. If you deny me, all will know of Talathian dishonor. Not only do you strike only at a distance with your coward's weapons, you are afraid to even fight a girl."

The mockery stopped. There was only quiet muttering in Talathis, which gave Xanthe sorely needed silence with which to focus. For even while Tari was trying to enter battle, Xanthe was already locked in a different kind of one. There were so many moving parts to getting this damned thing out. She was holding the stick keeping the tourniquet tight with her knee, trying to keep the wound open, remain in a deep enough trance to keep Yuri's muscles from spasming, keep her blood drenched fingers around several sticks, and kept not being able to push enough to budge the wedged head.

Finally, in a fit of inspiration, she realized that she was depending too much on her touch. With a single move, she dug her fingers in alongside the sticks, leading along with them, Tari's pliers. When she got it close, she bent over, using her stomach to guide its tip around the blood drenched bolt head, and closed it with her mind. A slight move of her body and she firmed up the grip. From there, it was a matter of grabbing the blood-soaked handles tightly and using steady pressure along with slight uses of her touch to work the thing free, pinching Yuri's wound shut as it did so.

At last, she held the bloody barbed bolt head in triumph. There was still a little bit of Yuri's flesh clinging to it, but not much, and it was mostly subcutaneous fat, nothing that would be missed.

As her trance subsided, the world expanded and once again she became aware of her surroundings. Tari wasn't visible. She was out on the walkway between the rival groups. Most of the men sheltering from the deadly darts were now tracking her. Yuri was covered in blood, red and black, but already she knew that he was better, if not better dressed. Yet most glaringly, Rawlth was looming over her suspiciously, having not been distracted at all. "Witchcraft," he muttered darkly. "Great witchcraft."

Yuri reached out with one of his massive hands, and even wounded, reached Rawlth's belt. He pulled the man inexorably down, until Rawlth was kneeling in the puddle of Yuri's own blood. "Not vitchcraft, yes?" Yuri stated in a low tone. "Miracle of Creator. Know how I know?"

"Not really," Rawlth told him unhappily. "She didn't touch the blessed bandage, if it even is one."

"I know, because if this – definitely not-vitch – gurl, is brought to tribunal from accusation, even if you say you did not do zhis... Lord forgive me, but I will twist your head five, six, times until, pops off."

Rawlth stared on with continued accusation. "I saw. She healed you better than a master bandager, and of course you're grateful for the greatwitchery. But it's not natural. It's sinful. It violates the Creator's will."

Yuri casually muscled his massive arm down, bringing Rawlth with him until his belly was also nearly on the ground, and they were face to face. "When head pops off? *Natural* to die. You understand?"

Rawlth hissed, not happy but quite intimidated. "Perfectly."

"Good. Good." Yuri declared with satisfaction. "I knew you start care for life, if also meant your own." He released his grip, and patted Rawlth's shoulder, leaving a bloody mark on the back of his tunic, to match the blood on his front.

"I'm not bad," Xanthe told Rawlth, since she was right there.

"The Creator says otherwise," Rawlth returned judgmentally.

Xanthe was about to argue, but realized it wouldn't do any good. At worst, it would inflame him, enticing him to betray her to the Curate anyway. Instead, she returned to silence, staring at her trophy, the jagged bloody bolt head, trying to figure out why pulling these out of people was so much worse than sticking them in.

Yuri wasn't feeling so constrained. "You speak for Creator?" he growled in his deep Lukomoryen accent. "Why you not in Prayerhome then? Or do archcardinals come from there to learn from you?"

"No Yuri," she mollified. "Rawlth means well. He's just protective."

Rawlth appeared unsettled at having her unexpectedly champion him, but Yuri was not done. "He should protect by protecting then. Yes?"

"Yuri," Xanthe scolded gently. "I'm sure Rawlth is trying." It did bring a thought though. She turned curiously. "But why did you come at all, Rawlth? I wasn't expecting you to be here."

The coachman lowered his gaze. "You opened my eyes to the bandits in the city. Too many twitchy young men and Talathians carrying weapons. I started thinking about them, about guardsmen I know, and others who wouldn't do well in a fight. It's dirty, attacking on Festival."

"Well I'm glad you're here," Xanthe smiled with gentle appreciation. "You didn't have to help, but did anyway. We probably would have failed without you and your friends. We'd have had no chance at all without that barricade of coaches. You may not get a parade like the guardsmen, but you're a hero all the same."

At first, Rawlth seemed happy with the praise, but then in a moral panic turned stern. "Just because I decided to help, doesn't mean you're my friend. Or that you're good," he challenged. "The Creator will punish you for using the corrupt witch touch of Earth."

"Maybe," Xanthe nodded. "I'm just glad the Creator doesn't keep me from helping people in the meantime, is all."

It was the wrong thing to say to him. "You're just trying to twist things all around. Make what you're doing seem okay."

"No, Rawlth. All I do is help as I can. If that makes the Creator angry, then so be it. When it is time, I will accept my punishment as given. Yet for now, I won't let what is good or proper keep me from doing what is right."

"That makes no sense."

"Few things do, I've begun to learn."

## Chapter 52

Xanthe would have said more but yelling from behind them drew all their attention.

Having been initially laughed off by the barbarians, Tari was now goading them by approaching the two open boxes of fireworks. It was quite clear that they'd been ordered to prevent anyone from retrieving the rockets but seemed for the moment that they were reluctant to kill her and were instead just screaming threats. The men behind her too, were yelling warnings, not trusting the Talathians.

Tari had certainly made good on her promise to draw everyone's attention; almost too much. "Excuse me," Xanthe told Rawlth. She wiped her bloody hands on Claude's handkerchief, and headed to the footbridge. Getting there, she found the men hiding behind the curving stone wall that served as its entrance, everyone peering at her friend. Tari was carrying a hand ax in one hand, and her cloak in the other, holding it something like a bullfighter. The men were afraid of going out, so Xanthe forthrightly stepped up.

"Don't put yourself in danger," Damien told her. "I already told her to come back and she won't."

"She'll listen to me," Xanthe replied, moving forward.

Damien put his arm out in front, stopping her. "Then tell her from here. You don't need to expose yourself to get her to retreat."

Xanthe narrowed her eyes. She'd been exposed more than enough tonight. But that didn't matter. "I'm not in danger. Not like you are."

"Funny thing to say, given that they were flinging darts at you only a few minutes ago."

"I.." she stared hard at him. "You're not telling me what to do."

He stared back. "Yes, actually. That's exactly what I'm doing. What I'm telling you, is to not take a stupid risk for no good reason. A good one, maybe. A stupid one, no."

"Are you calling me stupid?"

"No," Damien explained. "You're being contrary, out of pride. I seem to have gotten into the habit of saving you, but I can't against that many darts."

That stung. "Oh, I just *knew* you would bring that up. How does that old saw go again? 'Saves your life/Be his wife?' Well I don't care. I won't be pressured like that." She stomped her foot.

"Did I even...?" He went speechless. "How can you be thinking about that right now? And now you've got me doing it as well. I have to say Nagrath does have a point about princekillers. Absurdly attractive girls distracting men to death. They're dangerous."

"Oh, sure. Always blame the girl!"

Further down, Tari called back dryly. "You do know that I can hear every word of your bickering, right?"

Now Xanthe was seriously embarrassed. Her anger grew. She knew it was unreasonable but couldn't control it. "Then why are you still out there?" she shot back.

The captain of the Wormwood-sponsored guard, only a few feet back, agreed. "Listen to her, Lady Outlet. Let the guard do our duty. You do the city no good by endangering yourself."

"I am out here because it is lighter. I'm not coming back," she stated with resignation. "Your lover's spat means nothing."

Damien, of all people, turned red. "We are not. Lovers." He stated tersely, with a strained effort that Xanthe was beginning to recognize.

Xanthe nearly echoed Damien in embarrassed denial, but Tari's words sent a chill up her back as she came to comprehend them. Seeing light on the wide wooden footbridge could not be taken literally. Tari was speaking again of her mysterious power, navigating the labyrinth of future possibilities by feel, like the man who could only roll sevens. Best not to dispute it.

But it could be understood if she tried. Setting aside her annoyance, Xanthe tried to figure out how Tari putting herself at risk like this could be helpful. In hindsight, it was obvious that goading Horace into divulging that his father was dead had been the only way to shake many Wormwood guards loose from his control. The captain standing next to her was proof of that. Was there something here that could be working the same way?

She didn't know much about Talathians, other than they were a wilds tribe who were plentiful in numbers despite, or perhaps because, they'd abandoned nearly all vestiges of civilization. Their reputation was terrible, acting like bandits even towards other wildsmen. What little honor they had was all loyalty to clan, and the only propriety they held was respect for bravery. In this though, Tari's bold challenge must have impressed them. She wasn't sure how much. Still, she could see that Tari retreating now might lose her that advantage.

"Then do as you will, Tari." Xanthe called. "I trust you."

"I am not so sure I trust myself," Tari confessed. She'd not turned her head, as she was staring down Sol's men. "But if things go black for me, instead of him, know that you've always been a friend."

The guard started to move in Tari's direction, but this time it was Xanthe who stopped him by putting out her hand. "No," she told him. "She has the right. She is the eldest remaining of those in which the blood of House Outlet still runs."

The Wormwood captain shook his head. "Fool girl," he stated, but made no further move.

Tari yelled again across the bridge. "Find he who slew my father. I await him."

There was no movement, so they waited. A minute later a whisper came up the line. "We're seeing reinforcements." Xanthe didn't have to ask to whose side. It sure wasn't hers.

The sound of boots. Xanthe strained to see. She saw heads. More were filing in from the direction of the Wormwood manor. The mechanical doors had to be working again.

Another twenty arrived. They were bunched, and she didn't recognize any in the front. But it was clear they were outnumbered even more. Further, they'd press the issue as time was not on their side. Xanthe looked at her blood covered hands and felt a foreboding.

A voice called out from the other side. "Ah. Miss Outlet. I see you are well." It was Prince Sol, behind his men. Tari could see him, but from her own vantage, Xanthe could not. "Good to have finally found you," he sounded satisfied.

Tari twirled the ax handle she was gripping. "I appreciate the pleasantries, but I'm afraid I'm indisposed."

"Obviously. You're staring down all my men," he stated. "Which is surprising. I had no idea they'd be intimidated by a single lone girl. What are you doing? Threatening to cut the bridge down? We'll be needing to have a talk about that later. But for you my dear, surrender yourself before you get hurt."

Tari still looked odd in her underclothes, yet there was a dignity about her that commanded attention as the wisp of a breeze stirred the proctor's cape that wrapped her. "They are not intimidated, Prince Sol. They are respectful. I have issued a blood challenge and will see it answered. Who slew my father? I demand to face him in combat."

There was a pause. Then Sol could be heard half chuckling. "You're serious?"

"Some of us still have honor," she responded.

If that was intended to goad him, he didn't take the bait. Instead he continued to chuckle. "I'm afraid the man who did in your father is also indisposed. I sent him to figure out what's going on with the tower."

There was a shift among both sides. The barbarians and the guards perked up at his casual confession. Tari was heartened by the response. "You admit it. Send for him. I'll await his arrival."

"That isn't going to happen," Sol told her. "I don't have the time. Dawn is coming, and if I am to use these rockets, they need be fired before then. Grab her." He ordered.

Nothing happened. The Talathians didn't move.

Sol was upset, but there was urgent whispering on their side, too low to hear. After half a minute, he spoke again. "Apparently, you have reinforcements. You could easily die by accident in indiscriminate battle, which I'd prefer to avoid, my dear. So, as a good sport, I'll stand in for Dakur. For what it's worth, he's my man and I take responsibility for him." He hopped up to the top of the crippled coach that was barricading their end of the swaying footbridge, and stood there, full of swagger. "Have you ever faced a prince of the empire, Lady Outlet?"

Tari shivered. Xanthe could only picture the visions she was likely seeing right now. Her ax trembled slightly in her hand, but she stood her ground. "No, but now I'm going to."

"It takes great training to defeat us. Even assassins striking by surprise are rarely successful. But as an added difficulty for myself, I'm going to simply knock you out."

Behind her, the Guard Captain whispered urgently. "We were counting on them not throwing darts into a wide melee with their own men, but if it is the prince alone, backed up against the wagon, they'll have no reason not to shoot."

Damien nodded. "Don't worry. I'll take care of this." He turned to Xanthe and put his hand under her chin. "In case I die," he said, and casually kissed her full on the lips. Before she even had a chance to object, or do anything from her sheer shock, he turned and stepped forward around the curved wall, making himself visible on their end of the bridge.

This got Sol's attention. Before he had a chance to say anything, Damien addressed him. "Then I, too, must intervene."

Sol narrowed his eyes. "Ah. The picture becomes clearer. The puppet master revealed. And you are?"

Damien had his hand on his yet undrawn blade. "My name matters not. Merely what I do. I hunt demons and their servants. Human and otherwise."

Sol continued to judge. "Ah! Using witches with power over them? How droll. Yet, understandable."

Damien returned his gaze, appearing both righteous and masterful. "Your understanding is appreciated your majesty, though I don't need it as I have my own dispensations. Alas, I cannot return the favor. Consorting with demons is the gravest profanation, and something I've evidence that you've been doing. I must therefore first ask if you are willing to peacefully come to face these accusations before a formal tribunal of inquisition."

Xanthe had to admit that Damien, the Christian Knight in Shining Armor, would have made one incredible High Marshall of the Curate. Among those here, only she and Tari knew this was a ruse, but his story fit perfectly; his foreign looks even explained such an exotic calling. She could just feel the men around her moved to belief. The Talathians too, though not enamored of the Curate clergy, shifted uneasily, eyeing their leader. Many had to know that the accusations were true.

Sol sneered dismissively. "My apologies, but I must decline. As you may have noted, I'm indisposed."

"Only the blasphemous are too indisposed to follow the will of the Creator," Damien declared with a proctor's arrogance, but then shifted to a calculating tone. "You have command over these men and are inclined to use them to delay the Creator's justice until the end of your life. Even if by the will of the divine you fail, you'll bring needless bloodshed, and worse, cause souls to be lost to hellspace. Therefore, I propose a compromise. Since you volunteered as a champion for the accused in Lady Outlet's Blood Challenge, it is only fitting that I substitute myself as well. We can therefore resolve both disputes at once, as it can also be considered a trial of faith by combat. Defeat me in an honorable duel, and it will be the Creator's sign that you are innocent."

Sol did not seem happy at this offer, as Damien sounded all too eager to make it. He was trapped however, by need to save face. His own men made no move to interfere in this dispute. None were holding their atlatl dart whips threateningly.

Xanthe barely had any means to tell what Sol was doing, other than he'd squatted down on the roof of the coach. He was urgently whispering to someone behind him, but she couldn't see who. Damien had folded his arms and was content to wait. Time was, of course, on his side.

After a minute, Sol stood. "As much as this would be amusing, I've been reminded that princes such as I do not endanger ourselves directly. There could be an assassin waiting if I were to accept."

Damien laughed outright. "That did not concern you when you volunteered to face only Lady Outlet. So now your men know. You only fight girls."

Prince Sol returned the smile. "True enough for now, but that is because I need her. I only need you dead. So, I'm simply going to end it now."

In a single fluid motion, Damien unsheathed his blade. "You're welcome to try."

"Gladly." Prince Sol pulled out a weapon, the same one that Dakur had used to kill Nagrath. He pointed it across the bridge. Xanthe thought to scream as Damien attempted to parry whatever it shot, touching the tip of his blade down. Yet as Sol fired, what emerged was not a focused beam, but a cone of energy that spread out over most of the area. Xanthe dodged back out of the way just as an enormous gust of hot wind, crackling with electrical power, blew past.

A few moments later, and Xanthe was riveted. Both Tari and Damien were down. But neither of them looked dead, merely incapacitated. Damien specifically looked like he had caught the full brunt of the attack, and was on his side, his breathing labored.

"What were you expecting?" Sol proclaimed with both satisfaction and annoyance. "A grand dramatic duel on the bridge? A brilliant contest of swordsmanship and wit between the holy and the profane? Taking advantage of my pride to undo me? Ha! No. I prefer to simply win."

He lowered himself slowly down from the coach. "The only thing that truly annoys me about all of this is the expense. My toy uses charged red crystals. Red. Do you have any idea their price? They're only found in ruins, and rare enough you must pay a prince's ransom for them. Rest assured, after I collect these rockets and Miss Outlet, I'll just use my much less expensive sword to finish you off." He approached slowly. "You can consider your execution a duel of sorts, if you wish."

There was muttering among the men on both sides, but Sol casually waved around the artifact in one hand, seeming to dare any on Xanthe's side of the bridge to come near. "And any who interferes with me will suffer the same fate." He began a slow approach down the bridge, stopping first at the rockets. He grabbed one with his hand while keeping the lightning caster raised.

Xanthe looked back at the guards on her own side. Some had already backed away in fear. Others looked ready to charge to their deaths, the despicable act giving them courage to face death. But Xanthe knew that neither would work. "Keep your men away," she told the captain. "Nothing they can do will help."

He noticed the tone in her voice. "And you can?"

"I have one last thing to try," she told him. She reached for her pocket, retrieving the vial of acid.

"A combat potion?" He queried. "You want me to throw it at him? My aim is fair."

"No. Move back. Please. Even further. Come only if called." There wasn't enough left to affect Prince Sol anyway, and he certainly would be likely to be able to step aside. Further, attacking him would bring his men back fully onto his side again. That path only led to failure. But there was another. A small hope. She undid the stopper, no longer particularly caring that if this worked, at best, she'd be living her life on the run, from the real proctors.

Away from his sight she dribbled the few remaining drops onto a stone cemented into the wall. It didn't react, but she knew it was potent. She then stepped in it, breathing, "Adrasteia."

The sole of her foot burned. Not the one she was putting in the acid, but the other one. "Ouch," she hopped. Then got annoyed. *Awake Demon. I know you're there.*

For whatever his moral failings, Bolus was not ignorant. His technique to use acid on a demon's favored artifact to alarm them into paying attention, had worked. All you needed was their true name, and that she did know. The name of the demon who had written the node accompanying the dress. *It is part of me and returns what is due*, its script had read. While most of the dress had turned into black blood, retreating into her own body, the shoe soles were still there.

The world slowed. By now Xanthe was getting used to it. The voice came. Again, a faint sibilant whisper, not inside her head, but as if the words spoken by something directly behind her, and about to pounce like a tigran. Appropriate, since the dress was circulating in her blood.

> *You risk my anger.*

*And you used me to attack your rival. Secretly guiding me with the dress.* Xanthe projected.

> *You noticed that, did you?*

She guessed right. Everything had been just a little too convenient. The whole situation had been set up from the start. Now time to see if Bolus was right about other things.

*As you used me, so now do you owe me. Do you return what is due?*

> *I did. You're alive, aren't you?*

*When did you save my life?*

> *When I chose not to kill you.*

Xanthe bridled. *Forbearance is not repayment, demon. If you don't repay your debts, just admit it.*

> *Very well. But I do not coddle. You cannot grow with a crutch.*

*I need a way to stop Prince Sol.*

> *Simple enough. Kill him.*

*I can't. Not without help.*

> *Yes. You can.*

*How?*

> *The way you could have killed Horace.*

*But I don't have anyone to trick, and...*

> *The first time.*

*You mean when he tried to rape me in the coach? I couldn't...*

> *Only as you decided it so unthinkable that you didn't.*

*No. There was no way.*

> *Shadowed is this scrap of creation.*
> *Do not be too pure to abide in it.*

That wasn't what she needed. What she needed was the dress. It would choke Sol, like it had Rawlth. She'd end up being tried for witchcraft or cultism, but her friends would be safe. The demon thought she just needed to be evil. What did it think she could do that she refused to consider?

If it wouldn't answer that, maybe it would answer something else. At long last, she did have time to ask. Sol wasn't close to Damien yet. He was moving in slow motion, picking up Tari's prone form as she addressed it.

*Why did you use me to kill the Gestalt demon?*

*To prosecute a war.*

*With others of your kind?*

*Only the cowards among us. Our true enemy is the fallen.*
*Carrion flies on the carcass of God.*

Xanthe would have blinked had she been able. More allegory obviously. But it was getting frustrating. Every question answered brought two more. *Like Nemesis then?*

*No. For I. Am. Nemesis.*

The words now were once again, everywhere, whispered as if the world was alive with this evil feminine voice. It had to be in her head this whole time, and she hated the feeling. But she hated her ignorance more. She wanted to figure this out. Hopefully, without having to ask, 'why me'. That was too trite and whiny. She had no cause to complain about her own situation. She could have run home if she herself had been a coward.

*Aren't you Adrasteia?*

*We are two, but one. Conjoined mentalities.*
*Ubiquitous among demons. Humans too.*

Xanthe was taken aback. That was unexpected. A demon being wrong. *That's just not true. Not for us...*

*Are you not wroth at that part of yourself that is vain?*
*Yet not that you get hungry. For one is you, the other, a sensation.*
*As an illuminating lie, consider Nemesis my angry drunk side,*
*and me her conscience.*

This wasn't helping. She really didn't want to fall too deep into discussing the metaphysics of thought. Back to reality she understood. *If you were done with me, why did you make the dress enter my blood?*

*To preserve you, of course. No telling how long you will be useful.*

A chill ran up her back. *You're planning to transform me into what Bolus wishes to be, aren't you?*

*He is most amusing, but unworthy. You should be honored. Never before has my other-self agreed. Like Eris, she loves human evolution.*

*I never agreed either.* Xanthe declared angrily in her mind.

*You would turn down immortality?*

Xanthe didn't even consider. She wanted to be no one's pet. *Yes. For that would be hellspace.*

Adrasteia went quiet. Xanthe wondered whether it had gone, though the slowness of the world had not. Just as she was about to think something at it, there came the whisper again.

*Rightly have I chosen. Grow strong, little one.*
*Your true nature is almost too apparent.*

What nature is that?

*Nothing before its nonlocal time, child.*

## Chapter 53

Xanthe dropped out of her trance like falling out of bed onto hard stone, having been kicked by a grouchy demon. She blinked, only to see Prince Sol walking slowly towards Damien's prone form. He still had the lightning thrower in hand, his sword in the other, and there was no one else even near him.

She'd asked for help and got nothing but a bunch of cryptic dung. While it wasn't surprising, she only barely could stifle a curse. She could just kill Sol in a way so obvious that she was completely missing it. Because she was being too pure or nice or something. But knowing that was useless, because she just wasn't getting it.

And the worst part was that no one really had to die. It was in Prince Sol's best interest to leave. She'd explained this to him, and he'd brushed it off. In her frustration, her mind went through the entire argument again. Without a powered beacon and an amenable demon, conquering Jagerfeld would assuredly doom him. He'd be spending so much time being paranoid about being killed by assassins in the hire of his brothers, he'd never be able to organize the way he would need to, to have but the slightest chance of a more traditional princely ascension.

And that was if he'd even be able to take Jagerfeld at all. Rawlth likely had done more damage spreading rumors and increasing the wariness of the non-drunk guards, than anything a girl would have been able to do. The city was slipping through Prince Sol's fingers. Did he feel it? Perhaps so.

At this point, she realized why she was dawdling. As much as she was afraid that she wouldn't be able to kill Prince Sol, she was even more afraid that she would. She hated this whole situation, but he was forcing her to act. He was getting close to Damien's prone form, and his expression made no doubt about his intent. Did she have a right to kill? Did anyone? What justified it? Her own trolley dilemma was staring her in the face. She just couldn't figure it out. Maybe only after she was dead.

There was one nasty realization. Adrasteia was right. She had been using others to do her dirty work, evading moral culpability, getting others to kill her proverbial chickens for her. Running wasn't going to solve this. Gritting her teeth, she straightened her cloak, pulled her head back high, and stepped out into view. She was too tired to be nervous. It had been a long night.

Prince Sol stopped dead in his tracks. He froze like he was seeing ghost.

Xanthe blinked. This wasn't exactly the reaction she was expecting. But she decided to make use of his pause. She walked out along the bridge, passing where Damien was, putting herself between the two of them. She then shook her hair and faced him, less with challenge to her countenance than simple greeting.

"How did you get here?" He demanded, pointing the weapon at her. "Where's Bolus?"

"Oh that," Xanthe rolled her eyes. "He tried an experiment. To summon a demon."

The prince mood changed instantly. His eyes lit up. "He succeeded?"

Xanthe scoffed. "All too well. Didn't you see the fire?" She gestured in the direction of the chain tower, but now looking herself, found it remarkably flame free. The only thing she could see at a distance was steam. Maybe a sprinkler system had been triggered. Good thing it had one. The Wormwoods likely had her own father to thank for their whole mansion not burning down.

Sol considered. "We will deal with that later."

Xanthe cocked her head. She'd wasn't going to argue, but found her curiosity piqued. "How?"

"There are... ways." Sol declared, with a slight note of doubt.

"Yes. I saw Bolus trying them. Not even he can evict a demon that doesn't want to cooperate."

"He will do so if I ask."

Xanthe shook her head. "His desire isn't in doubt. Only his ability."

"He will be able to handle it," Sol blustered. "Now that I have Miss Outlet, who did this, he'll be able to figure it out. He's exceedingly smart."

"After what happened, I'm not even sure he's alive," Xanthe told him honestly. "I do hope so. He was wrong, but still was..." she struggled for a word to express her feelings, even to herself. "Challenging."

It was the wrong thing to say. Sol's face darkened into a scowl and he glared. He was the full measure of royalty: arrogant, proud, and powerful. Vaguely, she was aware that behind her, the guard had crept in to stare, along with his men. They had an audience, and almost innately he began to play to it, falling into the sing-song of a well-practiced oration. "You will lie no more, girl. This city will be mine. For I shall raise it to be a new capitol. For while it is true that Nutearea should be a single government ruling all of Haven, for too long the south of it has played an outsized role. We, of the north, Thule and the other outlands, deserve our turn to govern the planet. Truly, given their corruption, lies, and misrule, it will take many generations to set the world's affairs in order. For this is our manifest destiny, to stem the tide of malfeasance, cause..."

Xanthe yawned. Not a small one either, but an enormous one. She tried to stop, put up the back of her hand, but the more she did, the wider it got.

"You mock me?!" He thundered.

Xanthe blinked. "Oh, I'm sorry. I didn't mean to offend. It's just been a long night, and I didn't realize you were going to pontificate so long. Especially just to impress a girl. But please. Go on. I am, you know," she waved her hand a little more, "impressed."

Sol flew into a fit of rage. He stormed towards her, sheathing his sword, but keeping the ancient hand weapon out. "Insolent girl. I should have taught you a lesson when we'd first met. Better late than never."

Xanthe thought to run, but if she did, she expected that he'd just blast her in the back or pause to finish Damien. She stood, staring mutely. He stalked up and put his hand around the back of her neck, lacing his fingers into her long golden white hair, which he gripped forcefully. "You are coming with me," he muttered darkly, while pulling her back toward his end of the bridge. His gaze, focused on the other side of the bridge scanning for danger only briefly, before it slid down to her young body. He leered, possessed of an obvious lust that burned even hotter for all the injuries she'd done to him.

She walked unresisting. The further he moved, the further away he was from Damien. At some point she was going to have to try something. Grab his sword perhaps? She had no idea how to use one, and in the extremely unlikely event she succeeded, he was still in possession of his artifact, which would make short work of her. It was then a voice came from behind the coach, where Sol's men were still assembled. "My lord, what are you doing?" Sargon spoke urgently, sounding distressed.

"Merely chastising the girl. Have you readied the rockets?" He turned his head.

There was the little dark mole near his ear, mostly under his hairline. She didn't like it. It was dark and mottled, raised slightly, and uneven. It was called 'Black Spider' by bandagers, an omen of illness and death. Only a few seasons ago, she'd read ancient hardcopy that called it a different name. Cancer. It needed attention soon, she could... *oh.*

"Awaiting your order," Sargon told him. "And please, I beg you. Don't distract yourself."

*How stupid* she thought. The demon was right. They always were. The realization stabbed her heart like a dagger.

"I won't," Sol declared. "Her screams at your chastisement shall be a melodious accompaniment to the display of fireworks consummating my takeover of the city."

"Please don't," she suddenly begged. "I don't want to." Her eyes began to water.

"Oh, but you have no choice," he told her smugly, his happiness increasing dramatically at the sight of her distress. "I will bend you down over my knee and use my rasp strap upon you. I'm afraid your lovely skin will likely not recover, though your soul certainly shall."

"No. I mean don't do this. Don't set off the fireworks. I don't like bringing death. It's wrong. I hate it."

He paused, studying her up close. "You know, for all the trouble you have caused me, I still see what you can be, once your pride has been beaten out of you. You are so pretty when you're crying, I promise to make you do so every day."

"Send the signal, my lord?"

He pulled her to him to take a forceful kiss. She didn't want to. She had to. Their lips touched.

*A body is an enormous city, countless tiny bubbles and lines of light. They form a constantly moving sculpture of living bones providing shape, hard-working organs, and muscle. Roads of blood, lymph, bile, nerves, the mysterious spiderwebs that only humans have, all crisscross through the body. Wires of energy, shifting, pulsing, constantly working in exquisite harmony to mysterious purpose. As always with life, there is exquisite beauty, complexity. Streaks of little energies zoom impossibly fast through the tendrils into the bony spine, and spiderwebs, up into the temple, the unfathomably complex brain, an ocean of light, a galactic maelstrom of such profound complexity that you could stare at it hypnotized forever.*

*It was so precious. So delicate. So easy to break. All it takes is a tiny pinch.*

They broke. "It is time," he commanded. "On her scream." He started to pull her by the hair down, clearly intending to throw her over his knee. "Light them off when she starts howling. I shall enjoy this."

But halfway down, his hold relaxed.

Through tear-stained eyes she saw him blink. "There's something..." he didn't quite complete the sentence, but simply collapsed, tipping over, and sprawling to the deck of the walkway. He lay on his side and twitched on top of the wooden slats laid across the bridge, dying, as his heart could no longer beat correctly. There was a certain artistry to the way he lay, his hair and limbs and armor just so, reaching for something he could not grasp, as if he were the subject of some a tragic portrait.

And there it was. He was dead. She'd just killed another person. She stared, incredulous at the act she'd just performed. It felt empty. Life would now go on. Except for him. All his evils and redeeming qualities, the complexity of a man, villainous but only because he'd been raised that way. Nearly forced into it, like Damien. It was the worst deed imaginable. Done with a touch.

To think how proud she'd been of the abilities she'd developed. How scornful of Curate sermonizing about the wickedness of witchcraft. But now she'd proven them right. She'd focused so intently on the incredible challenges of preserving life, that it'd never occurred that her gift made it trivial to end it. What would she do now, knowing that any time she came in skin contact with anyone, she could kill them with a thought? Reducing people to nothing but manipulable meat?

Her mind rallied to her defense. Sol was the last man in the world to cry over. He was cruel and unrepentant. There wasn't a single excuse for what she'd done, there were hundreds of thousands. People who would no longer die trying to defend this man and his evil. What an excellent, moral, assassination! Even more so than the one she'd already arranged just a few bells earlier this evening.

It didn't help. What was she becoming? A cold-blooded killer like she'd thought Damien was? How she'd judged him earlier that eve when he intimated that he lived by the sword. How easy to be sanctimonious while living in relative safety. But Damien was fighting for his people too. His own trolley car of life. Wasn't that the same thing as what she's just done? No, she wasn't too virtuous for him. Maybe he was too good for her. At least he was honest about it. No wonder Priscia said she took on airs. Maybe it was true.

She staggered a few steps away, trying to escape the feeling in her chest. Not quite pain, but intense hollowness. Knowledge that she was now a monster herself. How useful a princely tool she would be, perfect to help Damien finalize Curate tormentors and other villains. She'd rather die. Convenient, because that was about to happen anyway. She couldn't make it off the bridge before Sol's men peppered her with bolts. Out of sheer despair, she collapsed, knowing she was bound for hellspace.

And with the closing of her eyes, the shadows came.

Whispers surrounded her, none human or intelligible. Nameless unknowable things, they clawed at her soul, screaming in twisted welcome into the void in her heart. *You are one of us now*, they seemed to say. *The evil damned.*

A gust of wind howled distantly, ruffling the cloak Damien had given her. Vaguely she was aware of an outcry, though didn't care to understand it, so swept up she was in her vision.

And she wept. This shadowed world had put her in a position where either by action or inaction, she could not help but do evil. *Perhaps I am violating the will of the Creator*, she thought. *But at least in my decent to hellspace, I let others rise. So, come my new brethren, join me. You may be damned, but you are not evil. For the one wise thing I learned tonight is that evil never recognizes itself.* With this thought she grieved. Not for the Prince Sol that was, but for the one he could have been.

Yet as soon as she felt this remorse, the fever dream lifted, disappearing almost as soon it had begun. It took the whispers with it, only to be replaced by something different. A presence of emotions. Female. Gentle. Again, from elsewhere. Nothing she could see or sense, even in impossible directions, but nonetheless familiar, feeding comfort into her. *<Peace> <Belonging> <Reassurance> <Perspective>*. But then, slowly, as something else also seemed to examine her, and a different set of feelings came from that inspection, *<Triumph>*, *<Joy>*, *<Pride>*, and most inexplicably, *<Hope>*.

Perfection was impossible. But she would do what she could. Not to fight, but to heal. In this feeling, Xanthe knew that she herself was healing, because she was already feeling familiar curiosity. Was any of this real? Or just hallucinations from a nervous breakdown?

She prayed for the dead prince's soul. Wished, though she knew it sin, for him to return for another life somewhere, with a new chance to redeem himself, that would in turn redeem her own sin against him. Strange hallucinations of other worlds, places, where even the laws of the universe were different entered her thoughts. *Yes. There. Somewhere.* She entreated. *Let him be reborn without death. No games of princes overhanging his every move, justifying his every evil act.* She felt the slightest shift. Willed it.

Whatever, whoever, was comforting her imposed an inexorable directive brooking no argument: *<Cease> <Wariness> <Cloak>.* Then, *<Love> <Love> <Love>.... <Rest>.*

The world slipped away.

## Chapter 54

Xanthe woke, oddly rested. She first wondered how long she'd been asleep, then was amazed to be waking up at all. No pain. No chains. Even so, her heart sank. What now? What new peril had she landed in? It was getting dodgy-power annoying.

She focused on the ceiling. It was familiar. The painted tiles of the anteroom near the entrance of the Scholars' Guild lobby, where boys were given detention for being too rowdy in class. There was a long couch here that she was lying on, and a desk behind which, the various deans would scowl, detailing to unhappy parents the antics of their offspring. Or at least, that's how she imagined it. Girls were never allowed in here, of course. Curate proctors would be incensed at the idea of any co-education. Looking around, she spied a tasteful oil lamp, bookshelves, as always lined the walls everywhere, and a face, upside down. It was Celeste. Scowling. There were dark circles under her eyes.

"You have no idea how much I hate you." She promptly announced.

Xanthe wasn't sure what for but wasn't going to defend herself. "I'm sorry." She apologized contritely.

"You should be." Her friend continued moodily. "Do you know how much you've reamed me?"

Xanthe let her eyes wander around the room. Tari was there too, considerably healthier than she had been on the footbridge. "Don't believe her. It's petty," Tari told her with a frightful scowl directed at Celeste.

"Then I'm sorry for as much as I'm able," Xanthe told them both.

"I'm not forgiving you that easily," Celeste declared moodily.

"I don't want to hear it," Tari told Celeste with tightly controlled rage.

Celeste almost never backed down, but upon seeing Tari, she deflated a little and looked slightly abashed. "I suppose you have the right."

"What's this about?" Xanthe asked, trying to distract them both. "I truly don't know."

"There's a story going around that Celeste brought you back from the dead." Tari sounded grateful for the change in topic. She didn't really want to be angry. It was more sadness that was enveloping her.

Xanthe blinked. "What? Why?"

Tari explained. "After you fainted on the bridge, no one knew why Prince Sol died. Then Captain Deshold spread the word that he saw you take out a potion. So, they concluded that you'd put poison in your mouth, knowing that Sol would force a kiss out of you the way he did. Poisoning is sinful of course, but they were going to give you a full pyre with honors anyway until Celeste went into a fake fit and claimed the Creator would bring you back to life."

"Had to," Celeste pouted. "You were starting to snore."

"Wait, what? Damien's okay?" Suddenly the world brightened.

"Yeah," Tari said. "I was stunned by Sol's weapon, but Damien's sword touched the bridge's lightning rod when he was hit, and that somehow protected him. He was faking being disabled, waiting for Sol to come close so he could jump him. But when you stepped in front, there was nothing he could do."

"I... I..." only a slight feeling of hollowness returned to Xanthe's chest. But mostly what stung was her pride. "I was sure I was saving his life."

Celeste shook her head. "Maybe not his, but just about everyone else. When Damien rose after you fell, the Talathians didn't see him as an enemy. He hadn't done anything but offer an honorable duel, and for them, that's a plus. He told them that the demon-loving Sol had died by the Creator's will, but they themselves weren't tainted, so if they went in peace from the city, they'd not be pursued for anything they'd already done. The blood debt was settled."

"They agreed? They're Talathians!"

"They were spooked," Celeste shrugged. "And my is that boy persuasive when he wants to be."

Tari and Xanthe looked at each other, and through mutual silence, decided to say nothing about princely authorities. Celeste could keep secrets, but not about hypocrisy. Tari added, "Now they're busy getting drunk. Stealing a few things here and there. Chasing girls, most who want to be. But nothing too bad. Better than some Festivals, I suppose."

Xanthe started to rise from the couch. She managed to sit upright. "But Celeste once again protected me from being accused of witchcraft." She felt guilty for the self-sacrifice she'd forced out of her. "Raising me from the dead is only going to cement her holy reputation even further."

Celeste nodded, but after glancing at Tari pensively, merely sighed. "Pretty much. But yeah. No one in my family was killed, so it's not so big. I can deal."

Xanthe felt like crying. "Well thank you. Both of you."

"No," Tari exclaimed with sudden force. "The whole city should be thanking you. They won't, of course. Nobody wants to talk about how Prince Sol died. Especially with so many bandits still carousing around, but for whatever my grief, it would have been a thousand times worse but for you. Only we will ever know."

"I don't want thanks," Xanthe told her.

"Come on," Celeste cajoled. "Don't you want a little acknowledgement, at least? You won the war with a kiss."

Xanthe shook her head. "In this whole Festival filled with assassins, I was the last person to want to be one myself. I'm not proud of it. No one wins wars. You just survive them." She thought of what Adrasteia had spoken of. "And that's just the human ones. Not demonic..." Then she noticed her body. She was wearing her black dress. It had returned in all its sinful glory, a skimpy little black slip modest only in comparison to her previous nudity. Even the shoes had regained their original, non-heeled, form. "Wait. How did this....?" She was too surprised to say more.

"It oozed from your skin in the creepiest way you can think of," Celeste explained. "That's why I had Damien keep you under wraps until we got you here. That was serious demon magic right out in the open. The downside is you lost your new haunches."

Xanthe stared. "Yeah," she breathed. "I don't want big fat sexy haunches anyway. Not my thing."

"Well, be happy we were around," Celeste told her. "Because I'm pretty sure being burned at the stake isn't your thing either. Unless that little demon dress will save you."

"Maybe. But I don't trust it. Demons are lackadaisical gardeners."

Silence settled between all of them, none comfortable. Xanthe had never been to a witch burning. There had been one in Aerie she might have gone to, had her father not strictly forbidden it. The descriptions were bad enough, an old lady crying she was innocent as her hair caught on fire and she screamed until her voice left. All that just over the accusation that she'd hexed a deacon with bad luck. Nothing compared to this.

"We thought so," Tari stated. "That's the reason for this alone time. To tell you the story you're going to stick to. So, just say the captain's guess is true. That should keep you safe at tribunal."

"No way we'll even have one," Celeste added. "Self-poisoning's a sin, but real mild. A sin against the self. Usually deacons proscribe counseling as a penance to the survivors, but with me playing up Sol being a cultist, they'll all think it was all the Creator's will. Lots of people saw that he forced you to kiss him. Just lie in divulgence and they'll go super easy on you, no matter what you do later."

"No matter what? Think they'll let us start a coven?" Xanthe joked halfheartedly.

"Nah. Couldn't anyway." Celeste grinned. "You need five dreadwitches. We'd need more."

There was a knock on the room's thick wooden door. Tari seemed to be expecting it and looked completely unconcerned, so Xanthe wasn't alarmed. When she undid the latch, Karissa burst through followed by Priscia, the latter of whom was sporting a black eye. Priscia was also in a different dress, ill-fitting enough for Xanthe to question if she didn't pinch it from some Wormwood closet. Upon seeing Xanthe, Karissa burst into wordless tears and fell to her knees.

"We thought you were dead," Priscia said sourly. She almost sounded disappointed.

"I'm alright," Xanthe told Priscia. "How about you?" She asked, moving towards Karissa.

"Fine," Priscia said in a clipped tone.

"What happened to you?"

Priscia shrugged. "Fell down the stairs."

Karissa glanced sharply at Priscia, but Xanthe interrupted, hugging the older girl before she could call out any falsehood. What really happened didn't matter anyway. "You're both alive," Xanthe told them. "That's the important bit."

Priscia kept talking as if Xanthe had only been addressing her. "Not all of it. I also came to drop off Kay. She's got no place to go."

"Your dad didn't want to take her in, huh?" Celeste asked while leaning casually on one of the tables.

Priscia tittered nastily. "Oh, that was never gonna happen. She kept calling him a liar in front of Prince Sol." But I thought Sepia's family might. They're bunch of suckers. Always going on about the Creator's charity and all that. Pish." She eyed Celeste. "Oh yeah, sorry your saintliness."

Celeste laughed sarcastically, but not in an entirely unfriendly way. "Ream you too, Priscia. I can tell that didn't work out."

"Yeah," Priscia said. "No go. Sepia's mom doesn't like me." She looked uncaringly ceilingward. "Don't know why."

"You're dumping her on the Scholars?" Tari asked disapprovingly.

"It's fine," Xanthe said, seeing Karissa slump at being talked about as if she were a sack of moldy flour. "The Guild's not rich, but we'll take her in. Especially when I tell her story." She addressed Karissa directly. "You're worthy. Never forget that."

"I'll pay her room and board. It's the least I can do," Tari added. "Classes too, if she wants. She's really not that much older than us."

"Wonderful," Priscia purred. "But I still kind of want to know, there's a rumor going around that Prince Sol killed a lot of the council, but then died from a girl's poisoned kiss. I thought that might be you."

Xanthe shrugged. "It was."

"Then why are you still alive?' She squinted. "Or are you also somehow immune to poison?"

"I prayed to the Creator to save her," Celeste told her. "Miracles just come when I ask for them."

Priscia smirked knowingly. "Oh, I'm sure."

"As is most everyone in this town," Celeste shrugged. "Faith is a funny thing. Wha'cha gonna do?"

"I'm gonna leave. That's what." Priscia turned away. "Ta." She waggled her fingers.

"Priscia," Xanthe called out in a serious voice. "Before you go." When the girl turned, Xanthe nodded to her. "Be careful. I don't want you brought up on any arson charges."

She paused, giving them all a hostile stare. "If I am, I'm taking everyone down with me."

Xanthe tried not to sound exasperated. "I'm not threatening you. I'm just advising you to think before you act. You're not just throwing harmless little sparks anymore. People will see it differently. If something burns down, you'll be the first suspect, no matter who did it."

Priscia rolled her eyes. "Yeah, yeah. I get it. Just because I'm not a Scholar doesn't mean I'm stupid." She jutted out her chin.

"I'm sure you've got lots of street smarts," Xanthe agreed, trying to mollify her. "But remember. Few who the tribunals sentence to burn ever expected it, so don't go thinking it can't happen to you."

"I can't," Priscia declared dryly. "Be burned, that is. Maybe they'd kill me some other way, but if anyone ever tries to burn me, we'll do a real burning."

"Um. Okay. Yeah." Xanthe didn't know what else to say. Priscia almost sounded Yamaite.

"But, sure. Thanks for the warning." She really did leave this time, shutting the door hard on her exit, and leaving Xanthe shocked. Not at her attitude, but that she'd given thanks at all, even mockingly.

"Well, there goes the coven idea," Xanthe addressed the closed door, a few seconds later, trying to continue the joke.

"Yeah. That was never gonna happen anyway," Celeste agreed. "Especially when you're about to elope."

"Elope?" Xanthe froze, wondering if there was something she still didn't know. "What do you mean?"

"Damien is outside, waiting to talk." She gave Xanthe a knowing smile.

Heat rose. Xanthe knew she was blushing. Eloping. With Damien. Why was it that even the thought of him so instantly brought such discomposure? "I don't know what you're talking about!"

"That's a lie," Karissa interjected.

Xanthe was flushing so badly she could feel her cheeks burning. "Look, if this is about Damien, I mean yes, he's a boy and all, like lots of other smart and handsome boys, but it's not like he's completely got me or anything."

"That's a..." Xanthe frantically put her hand over Karissa's mouth. "You really need to stop that!"

"...lie" Tari completed Karissa's sentence for her. "Look, Xanthe. We've learned all sorts of terrible secrets about each other, so if you're not going to be honest with yourself, you can at least be honest with us." She shook her head. "None of us blames you. Hellspace, I thought he was for me. But if he wants you, that's even more perfect. Somebody needs to come out of this whole tragedy happier."

Xanthe looked between all of them. "Me? Just run off with someone I met at Festival? That would be a terrible mistake. I'm not even sixteen yet!"

"So?" Celeste said. "You're only young once. You'll regret it forever if you don't."

Xanthe twisted her hands in terror that she was seriously considering it. "But not everyone gets old, either. It could be the worst mistake of my life."

Celeste shook her head. "Once, father took me to see this old lady on her deathbed, to see how the Creator took good people away from the world. When I got there, she still had enough life in her to talk, and asked to speak to me in private. Her name was Mrs. Pen. She told me her biggest regret was that she'd spent so much time being proper, she'd never let herself be happy. See, there was this bandit boy she loved, and well, I promised her I'd never make the mistake of never making any. You shouldn't either."

"If Damien was staying in the city, sure maybe. But leave?" Xanthe shook her head. "I just can't."

"Don't want to hurt your dad?" Celeste guessed. "He's going to have to let you go pretty soon anyway, you know. Besides, parents always forgive when you bring them grandchildren."

"Babies?"

Celeste laughed "Duh! Think I haven't seen you together? You're like matching lodestone seeds. You just stick. So, give up all that scholarly pride, don't worry about him having no money, and just say yes."

Tari shook her head. "Don't pressure her like that. If Xanthe isn't ready, that's fine too. If it's real love, he'll come back. 'Doing what you want' means doing what you want."

"That *is* what she wants!" Celeste exclaimed. "You think I can't tell? Hellspace, I've seen bridal couples less ready than those two!" She gestured. "That's what you would be doing in her place. You wouldn't be seeing him as too low or poor for you."

Tari made a sad little chuckle, coming out almost like a sob. Any laughter was so rare from her that it brought both Celeste and Xanthe up short. "I see Xanthe never told you. He's not a pauper assassin from some random dark house. He's a Nutearean prince. Completely off limits. If he marries into any high family of Jagerfeld, you could start wiping the city off the map right now."

"He's a what?!" Celeste was near speechless. Also, a rare occurrence.

"He's Prince Charming," Xanthe told Celeste. "I hope that you can appreciate how terribly unsuitable he is for romance." *Especially since he's also a Knight in Shining Armor,* a thought she left unvoiced. As much as she loved her friends, she wasn't sure she could trust either of them with that little tidbit.

"No sane girl would ever want that. Father specifically warned me," Tari mumbled in agreement, just over him being a prince.

"I dunno," Celeste mused. "He's way more bad-boy than I knew. Maybe I should go for him, if neither of you will."

"No!" Xanthe exclaimed. "He... I..." she suddenly realized that she had no claim on him if she was just going to let him go, but...

Celeste broke out in pealing laughter. "You should see your face now!"

"That's not funny!" Xanthe felt like crying. This was all so confusing. She desperately wanted two contradictory things.

"Just go out there and talk," Celeste told her. "Then, no matter what you decide, find a room and get it all out of your system, or rather, all the way in. He's saved your ass a couple of times, the least you can do is give him some of it. You did take that childbane, right?"

Xanthe felt quite embarrassed. "No. I gave it away to a girl who desperately needed it."

"Figured. Just like you." Celeste hissed in frustration, reaching into a little pocket producing more of the seeds. "Here. My last. Take them anyway. They help with cramps too."

"They do?"

"Eat and out!" Celeste pushed her towards the door. Xanthe glanced back helplessly at Tari and Karissa, but neither seemed inclined to come to her rescue. Tari's face was once again twisted in grief. She was obviously thinking of her father.

This brought a sobriety to Xanthe's thoughts. She had to talk to Damien. Life was short. You had to seize happiness when it presented the opportunity. Yet if she did go, it would be for the good she could do, not for lust. Would she? Give up school? Even she didn't know.

Yet when she got on the other side of the door, it wasn't just Damien who greeted her. In the Scholars' great entry hall, as grandiose a gathering place as the creaky old institution could maintain, nearly two score men were assembled in rank and file, most of them guards bearing Outlet sponsorship badges. Up front were Claude and Yuri. They came to sober attention when they saw her.

"Am... Am I disturbing something?" Xanthe asked in a small voice.

Finalizer Nagrath was there. He walked slowly to her. He looked stable but kept his head perfectly level. He was clearly still feeling his injury. "My lord is about to dismiss them from his service," he explained with a slight air of accusation. "They already know of his intent, but here we are about to do the formality of it."

Xanthe ignored it. "Are you okay?"

"A headache. Nothing more. I have been told you saved my life. Normally I'm not so clumsy."

Xanthe nodded. "You are now. Those less clumsy alternatives of you are all dead."

He made a face. "Damien mentioned something. I'm not even going to pretend to understand that. It must be some witch thing."

"Demonic. Or even beyond that," Xanthe explained. "Not that I really understand it either. It was not just me, but all of us who saved you. Celeste and Tari too."

"Regardless, I am in your debt," he growled, not sounding entirely happy about the admission.

She squinted tolerantly, knowing how it felt. "Angry that such a debt makes it dishonorable to clean me up as a lose end, without Damien's knowledge?"

Nagrath sighed. "I am not quite that bad, though I do admit that if you weren't around, I'd have fewer worries."

She couldn't be upset. The shock of killing Prince Sol still weighed on her. Besides, wasn't it better to hear someone's dark thoughts than have them remain unvoiced? "Well don't worry. I'm in Damien's debt three times over. Besides you know my secrets as well. Too many." She would have gone on, but Damien approached along the wall. He was no longer in the proctor uniform, but in much finer attire, a blue and white stole, an obviously ceremonial vestment that seemed oddly similar to Curate robes. A curious demonic symbol hung in a chain about his neck; it was the cross of unholy torture as the Curate described it. Xanthe was sure it really represented something else. He lifted it high, then tucked it inside his vestment so that it was no longer visible.

He then addressed his men.

"My friends. It has been nearly a year since we started on this journey together. I received your oaths of fealty in our mutual quest to ensure that our people and faith were saved across all Aeterna.

"Forever I shall be grateful for the honor of leading you. Of your service, your sacrifice. Most importantly, your trust. I am proud of what you achieved. You are each worth more to me than life itself.

"Yet today marks a turning point, for as you already know, I am about release you. This is not because you've failed any oath, but rather because I bear tidings of good news. I now know a way to make my oath a reality without endangering any of you. In fact, your presence with me from here on would make my new plan less likely to succeed.

"While your journey with me ends for now, you can still do much. Return to your towns. Spread the word to be quiet yet steadfast. Keep the faith. Stay connected with each other. We have grown to love each other as brothers, and I would preserve that."

"I say to you what I said at the start. Now is the time of the apocalypse. Perhaps not for the universe, or even for Haven, but certainly for followers of The Way, and for each of us sworn to defend the lives of those practicing it. Already too many of us have prematurely earned our reward. I cannot allow any more needless sacrifice. Not when there is no need.

"I will say no more of my plans. But know that even if I fall, our people shall still yet triumph. For as the world goes through its tribulations, our enemies will naturally turn towards slaughtering each other, instead of us. This has become obvious as it was recently pointed out to me."

He raised his arms and proclaimed. "So now I release you, and come to you now as an equal brother, for I would have words of respect and friendship with each of you before I go."

He then strode forward into the group. There were a few muted sobs among the mostly huge and dangerous men as they huddled around their former leader. As they did, Xanthe saw these Christians not as monsters, but as they perceived themselves, a tiny outnumbered minority, beset on all sides by people who hated them for no good reason. The horror stories that the Curate spread were certainly not true, or to whatever small degree they were, twisted beyond recognition. So then, Christianity, faith of the ancients. Better than average among organized religions, even though she'd never adopt it herself. Pretend ritual cannibalism? Sounded almost tigran.

It was due to this, that she ended up being surprised. After greeting Damien, one by one, they each made their way over, and went to one knee before her. Soon, so many had done this, that they nearly formed a circle around her. They were clearly paying their respect, but she felt awkward. She didn't know what to say. She presumed it was thanks for her healing, as she recognized many as those she'd saved in the Church of the Holy Ancestors. Yet it seemed more than that. Many had their head bowed in prayer, to her. The cloud cover outside must have dissipated, for a single shaft of sunlight pierced down through a window on which she was standing.

She swallowed. This sort of embarrassment was quite different than having to admit romantic desire. "I am grateful for your regard," she finally told the assembled circle.

"More zhan regard", Claude declared from near the back. "It is reverence. We pray to God. For we know zhat zhe Lord listens to all prayers, including those only for our own intents. By God's will, our prayers for you will ring through zhis world and change it. We wish for you to have long life and happiness, to attain all zhat you wish."

They were not of the Curate, that was certain. How many sermons about the sinfulness of wishing had she heard? Yet before these men, Xanthe found herself moved. Their adoration was like a strange, pleasant, warmth, suffusing her, which gave rise to an odd mood. She felt a calling, bringing thoughts unbidden that turned into words. "Then I pray too that your faith remains pure. Not as a path towards power or promised reward, but towards grace. May your trials strengthen you, not break you. May your hardships grant you empathy, not bitterness. And may your prayers always be for good, with power far greater than you shall ever know."

The men grew silent and the world turned still. For a moment, Xanthe wondered if she'd entered yet another demonic freeze, as she'd come to think of them. But no, this was nothing so artificial. It was more akin to the feeling she'd had in the fog. Natural, yet more so. A shiver ran up her back. There were still tiny movements while the men breathed. Damien taking off his robe to change, being briefly shirtless, displaying a chest of lean braided muscle. The world was aware somehow. Listening to her intent. Absorbing it. Changing by it. Not that her impression was remotely logical of course, but it remained impossible to shake.

She shook her head and the moment passed. Xanthe sighed to herself. It would be ironic to wind up a prioress of this heretical religion, assuming Christians even had women clergy. What other sins did they commit as an aspect of their faith? They didn't see witches as being evil. Did they know her dress was demonic? Did they care? Could scruffy dark-haired Damien, so awkwardly trying to put on his shirt, and unexpectedly struggling in it like a little boy, possibly be any cuter?

At last Damien was ready, facing her from outside his men. He also took a knee, holding his gaze upon her, yet this was not prayer or well wishes. His hands were not clasped, nor his head bowed in prayer. It was a supplication. She knew it. Xanthe tried to pretend to herself that she didn't know what he wanted, but did. A life of adventure. Turmoil. Struggle against impossible odds. All sorts of terrible problems that would completely upend her life and maybe accidentally end it. But they would face the world together. She could think of nothing more tempting.

Xanthe threaded her way through the circle of men out toward him. Those nearest shifted out of her way, and most turned their heads slightly towards her. By their expressions she knew what they expected. It wasn't a bad guess. Few girls ever resisted princes, and she wasn't sure she was any different. Yet Damien was more perceptive. He could sense the struggle within her, while Nagrath stood by clearly opposed, folding his arms with a stern glower.

"Xanthe, I know I ask much," he broached forlornly before she had a chance to address him.

He was so Creator-bedamned beautiful. And totally reamed up. Yet that only made her need him more. Perfection was boring. Yet still...

At her hesitation, his gaze lowered slightly. "I understand why. This is not your fight."

She rejected that. "But a noble one. To save your people? Further, did you not come to the aid of my city when that was not yours?"

"Coming with me would hurt your family, who you love beyond measure."

"Yet my father loves me even more. If I asked, he would let me go."

"Also, you are too good for me."

"I'm now an assassin. Worse than a poisoner. I've twisted my power to perform the darkest act. I may have to do so again. I have no right to hold myself above you. I know now that I never did."

"And a prince causes all around him to suffer. You have no reason to risk your life or die when I fail."

She shook her head. "I was wrong. You will not fail. I have now seen two princes up close, and the difference between Sol and you is like a candle before the sun. You have power beyond anything else I've known. You succeed casually at everything you try. Even the throne isn't safe from you, if you want it. None can resist you."

He smiled ruefully. "You did. When you intervened on behalf of Javan."

"Only because you changed your mind. I couldn't have actually stopped you."

"Your dress."

"Was protecting my life for its own purposes, nothing more."

"So..." He sounded like he dared not hope. "Will you consider coming with me?"

Xanthe breathed, taking the boy in. Utter perfection. Brilliant mind, challenging, sexy, with a masculine impetuousness that she'd never appreciated before but now could not resist. She wanted him. More than that. More than even needing him. She loved him. She knew it.

It brought her no joy. His own men's prayers had strengthened her to do what must be done. She swallowed and shook her head slightly. "I can't."

"Why?" He was resigned, but even more curious.

"Nagrath is right," she told him. "There are more important tasks right now."

Damien sounded mildly annoyed, mostly at himself. "I won't let you distract me. Not that way. I've sworn an oath to not pursue romantic interests so long this remains unfinished. Until then, we'll be friends, allies, nothing more. I've learned my lesson."

Behind him, Nagrath made a silent groan. The doubt that his charge had mastered himself as much as he claimed was evident on the older man's face. Xanthe had to agree. She certainly didn't trust herself. A part of her wondered how she'd fallen so quickly. She'd only just met him. Was it his authority? Subtle demonic mind control for a breeding program? Destiny? Just what first love was always like? That he had to be the cutest, smartest, yet also the most dangerous, boy on the whole reaming planet? A fantasy whispered through her heart that his spirit chased her through infinite worlds and infinite lives, winning her repeatedly in different ways, in a dance of eternal romance. The vision brought instant desire to her body, yet also was a childish daydream. Time to grow up.

"No. Damien. While your concerns are important, mine are more so."

He was confused. "Yours?"

"I've been used as a pawn to start a war between demons and the fallen, which I suspect is the demonic term for nightmares. If I understand correctly, Tari, I, and princes too, have abilities bred into us that are useful against them, like flowers that eat bunnies. They're probably small and weak, but something deep inside tells me that developing them is as important to the whole world as your plans are to your people and faith."

There was shifting in the room at her pronouncement. At last, these Christian men seemed uneasy. In a way, she was glad, for their disquiet mirrored her own.

He searched her face. "Are you sure?"

"No more than you are that your new plot will work," she told him truthfully. "Still, an onslaught of nightmares would be disaster. If I can prepare, I must."

He nodded pensively, and rose slowly to his feet, becoming more dangerous as he did so, at least to her resolve. "I understand. Most of Haven is plagued by nightmares. In Toshka, there's even a southern sea named after them. If they come in any greater numbers, my fight is almost meaningless."

"Nothing is meaningless to those whose lives you save."

"If I do so then, I'll return." He pulled his sword expertly and held it flat between his two palms horizontally, stretching his arms in her direction, proffering it symbolically. "And will put my blade in your service, for what little it can do in such a fight." The etched and patterned sword glistened in the reflection of their invisible white flames. To her eyes, they seemed to flare slightly at his words.

She studied his face, hoping to remember it forever. "That may be more than you suspect."

He pulled back the blade and sheathed it. She now saw him at his full height, and her need for him flared too. "I'm realistic about my chances," he declared with a subdued gallantry. "Don't wait for me if you find someone else."

Xanthe nodded. "Same for you." They were getting close though, just as it has been on the bridge. Damien raised his hand, and tenderly ran his fingers through her long blonde hair.

Behind them, Nagrath cleared his throat with prejudice. That didn't quite break the moment, but Celeste's voice piping up from near the anteroom did. "They engaged yet?" Her friend asked brightly.

Xanthe was the one to look away first, flickering her eyes towards Celeste, though she didn't change the position of her head, just in case Damien was inclined to steal another kiss.

"Not sure," Nagrath growled dyspeptically. "Their words are wise, but they're not following them."

"Oh, you sound like wagon-loads of fun at parties," Celeste remarked.

"Why are you out here?" Xanthe asked.

"Tari and Kay are having a moment. Crying together. Too gloomy. So, come on, you two. You're both crazy in love, and somebody has to give this dodgy power night a happy ending."

"Is she always like this?" Damien asked quietly, sounding slightly amused.

"Only when she's got excess nervous energy," Xanthe answered with a tolerantly resigned sigh. "Which is basically all the time."

"I hope you're not taking her lack of braids seriously," Celeste called to Damien, referencing Xanthe.

"I confess, I never did quite get how that went," Damien told her. "Thulian girls' hair styles." His interest in the subject seemed mostly to be an excuse to keep running his fingers through her hair.

Xanthe didn't mind. She moved in closer. "Oh, Simple enough. Straight hair is for little girls. When we're nubile, we put them in two braids. When girls marry, we bind the braids together, intertwining them; like the marriage, two permanently crossed together to become one, never to part again."

"Poetic," he murmured.

"Boys say when we're married, that's also what happens to our legs!" Celeste chirped.

Xanthe blushed furiously. "Celeste!" she scolded. For all her wanting them to elope, she sure was good at ruining the moment.

"Well they do!"

Nagrath unexpectedly laughed heartily. "Alright, boy. Say your goodbyes your way. I'll be waiting outside. We have a league to travel before nightfall, and just because you haven't slept yet won't be an excuse." He then made his way towards the end of the hallway and let himself out.

After he left, Damien drew her close. "Xanthe. I do have to go."

She suddenly felt a spasm of terror stab through her. "If you die, I'll be quite cross," she nearly sobbed.

"If I do, won't you just bring me back?"

She shook her head. "I can't normally. That was just a one special time."

He grinned rakishly. "Good thing you're not normal then. But I promise to be as careful as I can."

"Good!" What an idiot she was. She was letting him go.

He kissed her on the forehead. "You be careful too, alright? If you're seriously going to research demons and nightmares, you may be in more danger than me. Also remember what I said about not waiting. If I fall, in my last thoughts, I don't want to regret you being an old maid."

Xanthe realized that all her resolve was crumbling. This was why she had to go with him. To keep him out of trouble. Yet before she could form her thoughts into words, he kissed her. Taking her into his arms, and full on the mouth, lifting her slightly. It left her completely dizzy.

After too short a time they broke, he set her gently down, and she watched him leave. He was there, turned away, and now was gone. Simple as that.

"Oh boy," Celeste declared peevishly, shaking her head. "You're a regular heroine, Xanthe. Saved the whole reaming city. Could have had the boy too but chickened out. Now you're weeping too."

She was. She couldn't help it.

"Still not too late to run to him." Celeste encouraged.

Yes. Yes, it was.

## Chapter 55

Soon the Christian knights in shining armor also departed. Claude led them away, escorting Tari back to Outlet manor, when the good news came from a Hood runner that her mother was still yet alive. Celeste took Karissa down the halls to see Miss Weatherpenny for breakfast. Technically school was open on the day after Festival, but almost nobody showed up. It was only the Early Years kids, and even they were sparse, so there was plenty of room and food.

As for Xanthe, she dried her tears, and tried to figure out what she was going to do next. She could think of nothing better than to go find her father for a long overdue talk.

He wasn't in their room though, and as tempting as it was to just ascend the ladder and flop down in her bed after having made the enormous climb, she stepped all way back down the Scholars' Tower, past empty classrooms, and finally ended in the great library, where she determined to sit until he eventually showed up. She sat down on the couch scowling and folding her arms.

After about a quarter bell, Mrs. Fullbarn entered the room, dressed in her painter's apron, and carrying an entree of leftovers, which she promptly plunked down in front of Xanthe. It was above the standard fare she was used to, no root porridge, but scrambled eggs with chives and hash; there was a warm cup of sweet-lataio in milk too. It smelled delicious.

"Saw ya aroun' dear. Brought ya this. Ya need ta eat and get some rest."

"I'm waiting for father," Xanthe told her resolutely.

"Oh? Well then eat and stay here. He'll be gone for another bell. Somethin' came up." She bustled away to leave Xanthe her meal. After she'd eaten, Xanthe decided to lay down and digest. The food had been good, and her belly was full. She promptly fell asleep.

It was her father, bumping around on one of bookcases, that woke her. He was wearing his usual travel cloak, well-worn but functional, and putting away a heavy round object covered in demonic runes on the highest shelf. She recognized it instantly. It was the dark demonic beacon.

Wiping sleep out of her eyes, Xanthe rose silently, facing his back as he stood on the small book ladder and put it in place with an ease that belied its weight. He pulled out a small pouch, portioned some dust into the palm of his hand, and blew it out over the artifact. When it settled, there was no way anyone would be able to tell that the beacon wasn't just another piece of depowered junk that had lain there for years.

He must have felt her eyes, for he turned slightly. "Ah, my darling. How are you, this morning? Is the bed I've provided so uncomfortable that you need to sleep in the library? Alternatively, if you're really having to do classwork today, I simply must have a word with your teachers."

Xanthe stared. Where to start first? Demons? Witchery? Black blood? Prince Sol? Bolus? His sacrifice of not selling out researches of the ancient artifacts of war? How he'd been protecting her all this time? She felt such love for him, but was so shocked at his physical presence, that she just ended up saying the first thing on her mind. Sudden uncontrollable righteous outrage filled her. She stomped her foot and gave him her loudest library whisper. "Why didn't you *tell* me?"

"Um. About what?" He took a step down the ladder.

"Daa-add!" Xanthe didn't know what else to say, so she grabbed her black dress in her hand and shook it. "Like this, maybe? Or that?" She pointed at the beacon, now hidden away in plain sight.

"Oh. Ah. Yes." He cleared his throat. "Well."

"Well? Well what?!"

"Well, you're exceptionally astute, so no matter the tests before you, I knew you'd surpass them."

"That's it?!? A trite..." As much as she loved dad, right now she wanted to kill him. "Stop with the pedagogy. Not everything in the world needs a dodgy-power pop quiz!"

He blinked at her outburst, and after a moment, massaged his goatee. "Well, no. Yet when we spoke, you were distraught. Had I been unduly forthcoming, you'd have certainly fled back to your room. A poor choice. It's usually best to ignore small setbacks and focus on the greater challenge. Perspective helps."

"That was not a small setback!" At these words however, Xanthe felt embarrassed. Here she was, blaming him for not telling her everything, when she hadn't even divulged to him that Horace had intended far more than just a slap. It made her twice as furious. Now she was mad at herself too.

There was also a certain intentness to his gaze, that he reserved for what he called 'teachable moments'. "Ah, but was it large in relation to all the other events of the eve?" He asked in a calm quiet voice.

"I..." Xanthe scowled. She hadn't even thought of Horace and his stupid puke filled carriage at all. It was everything else. "No," she admitted, trying not to sulk, and certain that she was failing miserably.

"As expected. Often, the best way to rid oneself of an intractable problem is to acquire a more interesting one. The original doesn't go away, so much as you suddenly realize that you're bored with it, and thus it loses all hold over you. A lesson to remember, each one a step towards wisdom." That latter was a Guild saying.

She thought of Damien. "I thought I was being wise, but now I don't know what I want."

"Not atypical feeling in youth." He came to her and put his hand on her back. "What you need, whether you'll admit it or not, is sleep. Would you kindly consider walking up to your bed? It's slightly more awkward to carry you up the steps now, compared to when you were little."

He was there. She went to him, buried her face in his chest, and wept.

He listened to her shuddering breaths for a while. "That's not what you're upset about, is it."

"No," she whimpered. He usually slouched, so she'd forgotten how tall he was when he wanted to be. His chest was warm, hot even. More than she expected.

"Then what is?"

It was time to divulge. So at least she could be mad at him without feeling like quite such a hypocrite. "I met an evil prince."

"I see," he soothed gently. "What happened?"

Her lip trembled. Her heart was breaking. "I fell in love with him."

"Oh? The city is rife with rumors that a girl killed a prince. An evil one. Though I repeat myself."

"That was me too."

"Xanthe," he sighed. "I scold myself for not being as vigilant as I ought, but please don't embarrass me so much by usurping such a vital fatherly duty. Allow *me* to be the one to kill your boyfriends. Please don't do so yourself."

She stared up his musty travel worn clothing, wanting to be mad at him for joking about her heartache, but wasn't entirely sure that he was. If it was a jest, he was being seriously deadpan about it. So instead, she put her cheek back in his chest, and explained. "That was a different evil prince. The one I love left the city."

"Off to get millions killed in his evil quest for power, then?"

"No. Off to kill thousands so as to save all the evil Christians, who seem like perfectly nice people."

"Ah," he exclaimed quietly. "Now it makes sense. Your heart could never be captured by anyone truly degenerate, merely one caught in a bad situation. Truly, he must be a saint among evil princes."

"He's the love of my life," she sobbed into his shirt. "And I let him go."

"My darling angel, all of sixteen going on a hundred, if I could cloak you any more, I would. But there comes a time of childhood's end, nor is all pain unhealthy. Still, know this. If this boy prince is truly your love of this life, then you will find him again. Have no doubt of that." He put his arms around her shoulders and held her gently.

Hope. Xanthe didn't want to feel hope. She also keenly remembered that they'd agreed she wouldn't get the talk for another year, though by now she wasn't at all sure what 'the talk' was going to be about.

"Dad?" She murmured, feeling comforted. "You sometimes lie by omission, don't you?"

There was a long pause. "Constantly," he finally admitted dryly.

"And mom. She had powers. Even more than a typical greatwitch."

"You have no idea," he breathed. "I first sought to use her. Then I loved her. But always, did she scare me. Something before I had never thought possible."

Xanthe blinked through her tears. This was more divulgence than she ever expected.

"Was she burnt at the stake?"

Her father tensed slightly. He had a grim and toothless smile. "In a year, Xanthe. This world is filled with illusions. Some which still keep you safe."

"I've seen through many. This dress and other demons showed me."

"And you're not ready. If you want my trust in your discretion, never intimate out loud that you even converse with them," he declared sternly. "I cannot stress enough how important that is. No girl in our charge shall ever die by the will of others, but openly subverting the laws and customs of Curate tribunals will end this school as we know it. As it is, you've no doubt revealed secrets about yourself to people that you shouldn't."

Xanthe sighed. True enough. Beyond Priscia, there was Rawlth. He was her greatest worry. Only Yuri's threat, Celeste's friendship, and perhaps his own fickle views as to whether she was acceptable or not, was keeping his mouth shut. A single proctor interrogation could change that. "I just got done telling another girl this exact same thing, but I suppose I need to hear it too." She admitted.

"Who knows of your powers that you cannot trust?"

Though she was still nuzzled in on his chest, Xanthe set her jaw. "Not telling."

He grew quiet. Xanthe knew she was treading on thin ice. "Why not?"

She was determined to forge on. "Because I need to know things, and this is my only leverage with you."

"Then keep it. It will be on your conscience if anything bad happens."

She pouted. Frustrated. He won. He always won. He always knew just what to say. "Fine. Priscia and Rawlth. He's a coachman who got his neck tangled in my dress and suspects my touch. But if you have a chat, please be polite. More so than talking to a demon."

"Xanthe," he scolded in gentle disappointment. "Don't use that word."

"I know, I know." she complained. "Someone could be eavesdropping." Her sentences got increasingly wry. "Exactly where everyone wants to go when they're hung over on an early morning the day after Festival. The library. Of the Scholars' Guild. Without announcing themselves. The next bookcase over. Neither of us noticing them. Really, it's quite likely."

He pushed her away and held her at arm's length. She expected to be chided but wasn't. "Set your mind at ease. I will speak to them both politely. I'm ever so."

"I guess you got in the habit, given that it'd be even less healthy to curse out a demon lord."

"More that it's not proper. If it were, I'd be saying something like 'keep your grubby little algorithms off my daughter'. But no, I wouldn't be so uncouth." There was an edge to his voice.

The dress shifted slightly. Now Xanthe was worried. Not that the dress would attack him, but that somehow, he knew it wouldn't. She started to wonder about her father, how much he knew compared to Bolus. Were all Scholars like this? The real demonic cultists hiding right under the Curate's nose?

"I'll go to bed now. But can I at least get an answer to a theoretical question?" She cajoled.

"Perhaps."

She took that as a yes. Don't mention the word demon. Or intimation that she knew much of witchcraft beyond the accepted harmless sins of little girls. What else could she ask? Staring at the beacon, it now seeming ever so innocent, reminded her of something. Something purely theoretical.

"What's the Dalberg-Acton conjecture?" It was all the Gestalt demon considered truly important.

Her father paused just slightly, and Xanthe briefly thought she might have finally stumped him, finding something he didn't know. But no. He did, of course. "I'll answer, though it won't make you happy. It's a theory from a specific branch of extraordinarily complex math, that reduces thought, consciousness, and ethics to abstract manifolds and functions, finding interesting tautologies within them. It was first thought to be merely theoretical, then only applicable to neural networks, the mathematics of consciousness. But now, it's known to be a key aspect of what's called information physics, and holds sway in information-space, just as our physics rules here."

"I guess Dalberg and Acton were accomplished scholars."

"One man, two names, and he didn't invent it. It was named in his honor by one of the beings that you've recently talked to."

"Why?"

"Because while humans have a knack for feeling deep truths, they rarely understand them. In this case, the Dalberg-Acton conjecture is thought-space's equivalent to the second law of thermodynamics. It states that, just as overall entropy always rises, degeneracy must also increase in a closed information space. That rise directly correlates to the amount of power gathered. Colloquially, in the phrasing of Lord Acton, 'Power corrupts. Absolute power corrupts absolutely'."

"But why would de-... certain smart creatures care about that?"

"It determines the eventual fate of any region governed by information physics, and whether a heat death of degeneracy shall eventually turn all the heavens into hellspaces, so to speak. Proving or disproving the Dalberg-Acton conjecture would be a feather in any companion's cap."

"I... I heard that, but still don't really believe it. The heavens and hellspace are actually real?"

"Very. We have a sister universe formed from the same spark of creation when both of our precursors collided some fifteen billion years ago. To us it's a naked singularity with no physicality, but it really has dimensions that spread out in ways that humans cannot fathom, much less accurately describe in words, and has self-organized into a mind-scape of what could best be described as emotional regions and living thoughts. Even what I'm saying now of it is vast oversimplification to the point of storytelling."

"You're saying that the Curate has been right all along. Our souls go to the heavens after we die..."

"Not quite," he explained. "Our reality has no doublethink exclusion principal; we're a *mental* singularity so to speak. Here, we can be both good and evil, happy and sad, angry and loving, all at once. A pure impossibility in information space where values operators are disjoint. Were our patterns to fully transition there for more than a timeless instant, we'd be ripped to shreds, exploding into our constituent mentalities. Our dark degenerate sides going to the hellspaces, our non-degenerate sides going to other places."

"Still. They're kind of right, even if they're wrong on the particulars." It was strange to defend the Curate, but they did know some things.

"Which is expected. Human religions inexplicably know things they shouldn't, yet get the specifics so jumbled up, that it's almost worse than if they knew nothing at all. Moreover, they're distinctly susceptible to degeneracy. It's why every faith winds up murdering and torturing people in the name of absolute good."

Xanthe focused on her father. "Bolus must be right. You do have passages from Sevens."

Her father sighed again. "That annoying man. No wonder you're acting like this. Xanthe, listen. Never refer to that hardcopy ever. If any knowledgeable proctor gets but a whiff that someone even knows about that text's existence, much less what's in it, they'll do their best to kill them on the spot, not bothering with a trial or burning."

"Yes, daddy," she said contritely.

"Besides, the conjecture of which you speak isn't proven. It may even be false, which would nice, all in all, for what it would mean about cosmology. Now go to bed, and try to get some good sleep, not that I expect you will."

"Why not?"

"You're too smart not to realize the implications. Now scoot," he directed.

Dismissed, she dutifully trudged up the stairs, climbed her ladder, found her room suffused with the sour stench of vomit, opened the window to air it out, and put away the black dress, which came off, just like any other piece of normal clothing. She then went to her bed and flopped down in it, putting her pillow over her eyes to keep out the light. She was beat. It should be easy to sleep.

But thoughts kept running through her head. Last night. Damien. Tari. Celeste. Nadeen. Karissa. Rawlth. Mr. Griswold Mrs. Fullbarn. Father. People who, as Mrs. Fullbarn noticed, and Daddy explained, had aspects of both good and evil. Bolus. Priscia. Prince Sol. Horace. Killing them. Acts that were simultaneously both good and evil. Lord Acton. Nemesis. Reaming demonic mathematics. She rolled over, fluffed the pillow, firmly stuck her head back under it.

The thing was, that there was always this little bit of doubt people had when speaking of faith. Even Tari, so devout to Curate doctrine. But proof of the heavens? Physical proof? That the demons found? Maybe not as the Curate envisioned them, but there for real? No longer was this pure faith. It was truth.

And if this math was right, it would all eventually die. Maybe in hundreds of billions of years like this universe, but one day the voids of hellspace would devour the bulwarks of the shining cities of the Creator, assuming there was one. Or perhaps the rot would start within, but doom was certain. Maybe there were already signs. Why was the Maker of All so oft portrayed as a mad narcissist, with the requirement for creepy obsequious adulation being the bedrock of nearly all religious services? She dearly hoped people weren't already worshiping something evil. Under the pillow, she pounded it a bit, when a thought came about the all-powerful Creator.

*Absolute power corrupts absolutely.*

She lay the remainder of the morning, exhausted yet unable to sleep, regretting ever having asked.

## Epilogue

It was a clear and shining morning when the service was held, a mere five days after the Festival of Favors. This was quite in contradiction to tradition, which equated importance of the deceased with delay. Unlike dead drunks who were burned nearly as soon as they were found, the remains of great men were usually saved in snow for weeks, to allow travel time for distant worthies to pay their respects. Yet as everyone who was anyone was already in Jagerfeld, this made no sense, so the long streamers of black were hung high everywhere, and the full grandiosity of a city-state leader's funeral was rushed into existence.

Despite all she'd done, Xanthe was unheralded and unnoticed, largely by her own intent. She'd wandered the streets almost exclusively in her Hood Guild uniform, which gave refuge from prying eyes. The lithe young messengers in their cloaks and anonymizing long-hoods were, by social convention, ignored by those to whom they were not delivering, making it one of the few jobs you could get as a girl. Nor did her efforts go unappreciated, as there was no lack of work after Festival. The many last-minute trade deals being forged required deliveries of large sheaves of agreements and sample wares, and she ended up running so many errands, that the short-handed guild master gladly let her to take her outfit home, a rather severe bending of the rules. Her runs conflicted with her school schedule, but as the city was still unsettled, none of her teachers minded for the moment.

By now, like the corpses themselves, the official story had frozen into place. Prince Sol of Northfjord had attempted to steal jurisdiction of Jagerfeld, controlling the guard without paying their salaries, or other necessary city services through proper voting bids. He'd failed, but not before killing several patriarchs of the city's most preeminent families, most notably the Processors, Outlets, and Wormwoods. Tragic young Lord Horace had been blackmailed into temporary cooperation to keep his mother and siblings from being killed, but had been slain by a treacherous guardsman, who through an act of supreme cowardice, struck him from behind as he was bravely organizing the resistance.

The plot, fortunately, had been foiled almost entirely due to the efforts of valiant Captain Deshold, a leader of the Jagerfeld high market guard of Wormwood sponsorship, who cleverly ascertained the plot long before anyone else. He rallied the defense of a handful of guardsmen to sabotage the Prince's coordinated attack signal, whilst saving the spiritual virtue of young women being preyed upon by the demon worshiping prince. Due to this, a parade held in both his honor and Horace's, paid for by the grieving House Wormwood.

Near single-handedly, but not quite. Rumors also swirled through the parishes that The Creator had a hidden hand in foiling this heretical prince. The first, a mysterious and commanding proctor of a foreign order, whose purpose was not to kill misguided witch girls, but rather hunt high cultists of demons. Further, the Archdeacon's daughter had been seized by a blessed vision, prophesying the prince's true nature far in advance. Her words, relayed through His Holiness himself, had brought a few city proctors to the good Captain's aid just as he needed it most. Later, she'd performed yet another miracle, where through prayer, she'd raised a girl from the dead, one who'd poisoned her lips just before the Prince forcibly kissed her.

At this point, it could no longer be denied that Celeste was Creator-favored in a way unseen since the days of the Holy Pilot. Even visiting dignitaries were reversing their private doubts, as with every act, she showed all the signs of righteous glory. She refused all personal adulation, spoke rarely, but when she did, astounded those assembled before her. Notably, when her father had forced her unprepared to perform a sermon before a huge and mixed congregation, she'd declared in words as testy and cutting as had ever been uttered in the Steeple that the faithful shouldn't waste their money donating to the Curate, as it was just another type of wishing, trying to buy heavenly favors with copper and silver, an act which could not possibly be more meaningless and insulting to the divine.

Although this might have superficially seemed to be a sarcastic attack on the Curate's fund raising, her cold words, so unlike the dulcet ministrations that normally graced cathedrals, were instantly recognized as the Creator's adamant verity, as true as death. Visiting deacons were visibly shaken, some falling to their knees in remorse as they faced their own unworthy greed in the holy halls. Nor did the coffers suffer. Ironically, her words had nearly the opposite effect; they filled to overflowing. Several Highcouncil families, feeling especially blessed that they'd emerged unscathed in the aborted coup, offered beads of real gold and plastics instead of lesser metals, giving them only in thanks, and not thinking of themselves, in concordance with true Curate teaching.

As further sign, if any more were needed, a goodwife in the Holy Ancestor's congregation noticed a splotch of blood that resembled Celeste near where her first miracle of the bandages had been performed, if you squinted hard at it upside down. It might have been redfruit juice from a thrown pit instead, but hundreds came to gawk at it anyway. Ever since, the Holy Daughter could go nowhere without gathering onlookers. Her only refuge was the Scholars' classroom, a blessing for which she had yet to forgive Xanthe. "Cir-cus" was nearly the only thing she would hiss, though at this point, Xanthe privately doubted that her friend would ever be able to outrun her fame.

Remembrances were always held outside, of course. Only once in the history of the free cities had anyone tried differently, a mid-winter disaster in Aerie with an indoor funerary pyre that was still talked about a century later. But this gathering had become so enormous, that it had to be held outside the city itself. The regular cremation grounds were deemed too small, so the proceeding had been moved to the fields. The platform erected by the Sawman's Guild was larger up close than it appeared when set across the picturesque distance, as huge crowds came see the departed, before departing themselves.

Councilor Abriam Outlet lay in repose in an open snow-filled casket next to one of the platform's sides, still dressed in the same elegant plastic garments in which he'd been murdered. Even in death, he retained his aristocratic air. It almost seemed as if he could merely be sleeping, except for his sunken eyes and the greenish blue hue to his skin, there being no tradition in the north to paint corpses to make them appear lifelike.

Tari sat stoically next to her mother on a chair set on the platform directly above her father's open casket, as people in an enormous line snaking out across the field came to offer their cupped-hand respects and a deacon beside her intoned long passages from the Manual of the Creator in a trance-like monotone. Both mother and daughter were dressed in funeral black, but Tari had eschewed all the normal ornamentation, refusing the use of slats and padding to flatter her figure. She now appeared much trimmer, more boyish, less highborn. As the crowds swirled below, she stared distantly out across the open field, holding her father's elegant and not entirely ceremonial sword across her lap, gripping it as if she were prepared for its immediate use.

This fiery look did nothing to dissuade furtive and admiring glances from various young scions of the north, as they passed beneath, paying respects to her father. For even if Tari weren't unwillingly beautiful, with her fine features, long braids as lavender as her mother's, and makeup done by her as well, all knew that the Outlets had no male heir, and that alone made her the most desirable girl in all of Thule. Though she'd not been approached yet, as it was far too soon, various northern city families had already inquired about placing their second sons in study-abroad programs in the Jagerfeld Scholars' School, a few disappointed to learn that even in rare guildhalls like Jagerfeld's that had enough interest to justify classes for girls, the Curate forced them to be strictly segregated, for the very reason that the families were interested in sending their sons to it.

With tragedy uniting them, Tari had reconciled with her mother. They no longer fought. Yet as she confided to Xanthe at school, this detente had not actually changed their respective views. Quite the reverse. The gulf had never been wider. Tari made clear that even after properly mourning her father, she had no intention of jumping into marrying young just to bring a man into the household, and at this, Mrs. Outlet broke down completely. Tari's mother sobbed that not only was she to blame for not giving her husband a son, but also teaching her daughter to be too suspicious of boys, and that the right one would complete her.

Mrs. Outlet's remorse was so all consuming, she now muttered about it openly. Even in Xanthe's presence, she berated herself for pressuring Tari towards Horace before she was ready to open her heart to him. What she did not accept, due to her friendship with the equally grieving Nythiea

Wormwood, was Tari's pointed accusations about Horace's true role in the attempted coup, simply preferring to believe that her daughter was mistaken.

Regardless, Mrs. Outlet was now a shadow of her former self. Her world had completely fallen apart. Her husband was dead, and Tari even seemed to be losing weight. On the platform, she tentatively pushed a tray of delicious sweets toward her daughter, who entirely ignored them, and this again sent her nearly to tears. She only managed to keep her dignity when Archdeacon Jameson placed a hand upon her shoulder and whispered comforting words of the Creator's promise, though Tari herself offered none.

As Xanthe surveyed the mini-drama through her long-hood from a modest vantage on a knoll less than twenty yards distant, she knew that despite appearances, Tari was not immune to her mother's suffering. Rather, she was grieving as well, missing her father's support. For whatever her mother felt about not giving him a son, Lord Outlet had never once expressed any disappointment at Tari's gender, or anything else about her. She'd resolved therefore, to be true to her family's name, and take on the responsibilities of her House, as her mother clearly could not. That meant never giving in to the appearance of weakness. She would not, could not, weep abjectly over his grave. She did that privately, alone.

In public, Tari was diligent, unrelenting, especially with herself towards her goal. She'd reassured all the employees and guards that House Outlet would continue to pay their salaries, requested special tutoring in accounting from the Scholars, taken on Karissa's rehabilitation as her own special project, spoken to most of her father's business partners carefully making sure to be in Karissa's company as she did so, and employed Xanthe herself to deliver several high priority packages to several unexpected recipients. It was far too early to know if she'd succeed in taking over the reins of the enormous Outlet enterprise, despite the good will her family presently enjoyed. It would be hard for a young adult man, much less a fifteen-year-old girl. Nevertheless, she intended to try.

As for Karissa, Xanthe's hope for her a quick recovery were fading under the realization that Prince Sol had damaged her so much, that even his death had not released her from his compulsions. Indeed, she'd regressed somewhat. The Scholars had admitted her with free room and board, though now Xanthe herself wondered if that were for the best. As the new girl in the boisterous and sometimes rough school, Karissa had turned nearly mute.

Despite these difficulties, Karissa hadn't been parked in the Early Years classes as a student helper, the place where girls who simply didn't care to keep up were sent. Rather, Mrs. Fullbarn decided that deep beneath her silent and terrified exterior, there was a budding artist. So, whenever Karissa wasn't with Tari, she was in a painter's apron, in front of an easel with a bundle of brushes. And Mrs. Fullbarn was correct. Karissa did have a talent for images as vivid as they were dark: twisted scenes of spiked chains, whips, scalding water, burning hair, and body parts that were entirely nightmarish. This worried Xanthe too, and whether so much dwelling was good for her. But Mrs. Fullbarn assured her gently. "Oh no, dear. Tis the best thin' to be sure. For as terrible as what she paints be, she can face it there with the one thin' she always lacked afore. Na'er forget, the one holdin' the brush wields the power."

How well Xanthe knew. There were a host of reasons why she was staying mostly anonymous, the primary being concern that some agent still loyal to Prince Sol's memory might kill her for poisoning him. The second, while unlikely given the Archdeacon's newfound favor, was that she might be accused of witchcraft or sacrilege. Yet the final reason was far more personal. Mrs. Fullbarn's makeover had turned out to be quite permanent, and the power of her brush, and *touch*, was undeniable. Xanthe was keeping to her vow to not care about her looks, but that didn't prevent everyone else from noticing. Her schoolgirl peers especially. They oohed and ahhed over her, wondering how she'd learned the art of makeup so quickly.

There were conspiratorial whispers about it being some touch power, but most concluded "It's Xanthe. Why wouldn't she learn it fast?" Now she was being ambushed and asked questions she really didn't know the answer to. How do you get your lips so red? Do you think that understated blush and shadow, eye highlights would work for my complexion? Where do you get that eyeliner? Can't find it anywhere. At Mrs. Saud's?

No one understood that the color of her lipstick wasn't something that she chose every morning. Rather, her lips made it on their own. Same thing for her eyelashes and eyeliner. Blush and shadow. All changing with her environment. Everyone thought she spent hours in front of a mirror, yet they were wrong. It was a touch power, and not a lesser one either.

They also assumed her sudden interest in makeup had to be because of a boy, and the accusations still, no matter how hard she tried, made her think of Damien, which sent her into a deep guilty blush. Her classmates had no end of amusement to see the perfect clearheaded Scholaress being smitten so dumb, and all agreed that he had to be a super cute bandit, else why was she being so reticent to divulge?

If school was bad, outside was worse. Thanks to the perfect painting of beauty over what she still believed to be her plain face, all the attention she'd so fervently desired less than a season ago was hers, just not nearly as pleasant as she imagined it would be. It wasn't boys' stares she minded, so much as the men's. Some twice her age called after her, yelling crude things, or followed, making her feel harassed. Just yesterday, one in an alley whipped out his privates to wave at her. Xanthe assumed it was to get her to squeak or blush in shock, but all it really did was make her wonder why Celeste was sneaking around dangerous ruins of the ancients to see nearly naked boys, when creepy men did it on the street for free. The thought made her laugh, which turned out to be the perfect response. The perv ran away cursing.

Still, here, now, concealed, Xanthe was not a tourist. Not even to pay her respects. She had a delivery to make, now that she'd received one herself. She weaved through the crowds to the other side of the platform, where the purple and gray banners of Wormwood hung beneath the funeral streamers. Brother Axeman stood there on the platform consoling Nythiea above the corpses of her husband and son – an ominous sign.

The Wormwood widow grieved too. Not by blaming herself, as Tari's mother was doing, but instead, by externalizing it all. She was a ball of rage, doubly incensed at the persistent rumors that Horace had a hand his own father's death. Those questions made it touchy to simply make an accusation and ask for the legal arrest of her son's murderer, as that would require a trial, in which things she'd prefer not to know might be made public. Yet though it was technically against Curate cannon law, hiring an assassin for vengeance was a disturbingly obvious alternative, and Celeste had found out through her father that Brother Axeman had applied to be released from his acolyte training.

The letter she presented to Axeman, therefore, was happily accepted. When he opened it however, his face fell, for it wasn't the written indulgence he'd hoped for, but rather a request for his presence from Celeste. She had no true authority, yet also was not to be ignored. He acceded to the summons.

"I'm sorry," he briefly murmured to Nythiea. "There is some small difficulty. I need to go to the Steeple."

The older woman nodded, granting her permission for him to leave, presumably assuming that this was what it would take to win his release. Xanthe turned then, and walked, knowing that he would follow her, for that is what the letter commanded him to do.

Celeste knelt in the Chamber of Innocents, waiting in the darkness beneath the high bas-reliefs of the Angel Pilot, the Landing, the Banishment of Nightmares, the Great Fall, and the Bastion of blessed Prayerhome, each being shadowed, giving them a sinister rather than comforting look. She faced the sacred chalice, kneeling in a pose of prayer, her back to him, changing not her stillness at his entrance into the arca. Because of the services outside the city, the Steeple was entirely empty, eerie, and quiet. Xanthe moved to leave as a normal Hood would do, but did not exit entirely, instead hiding silently just outside, peering through the entrance's door jamb. Footsteps echoed as Axeman approached the holy daughter to speak.

"There is something here for you, Brother." Celeste's words were soft as he neared. She did not turn.

He spoke respectfully. "I am not a Brother anymore. I've applied to set down my oath. I am unworthy."

"You are both," she declared sternly, then let the silence return. "Accept what is yours in the chalice."

Sighing, the reluctant acolyte approached the dais. "Things are not supposed to be just left there," he told her. "It is meant for prayer, not gifts."

"Do not preach to me, Brother. I did not place anything there."

"Then why am I approaching it?"

"Because it is not empty." She stated flatly. "And what comes returned to you is no gift." Axeman was slightly annoyed and unnerved, which was the point. Xanthe didn't want Royroy to be hunted like an animal. She'd badgered Celeste until she'd finally agreed to make sure it didn't.

The acolyte reached into the chalice and pulled out the chestlet.

"Ginna was her name. I spoke to her in sacred dream, and she forgives you." Celeste told him in a soft devastating voice. "The Creator though, is disappointed."

Brother Axeman gasped. His face twisted in terror.

Celeste went on. "The Sect of Penance misname themselves. They embody arrogance. They hold themselves so high, they think even the Creator needs their aid."

The acolyte shuddered. "How did it even get here?" He fell to his knees.

"The Creator sees all. Horace stole Ginna's pendant from Xanthe when he tried to rape her. Ginna's brother saw him with it and mistook him for his sister's murderer. After killing Horace, he prayed for forgiveness, and received it, for the Creator knew the truth. So, the symbol of your guilt returned here for you to bear. The Creator is willing to forgive, but you must earn it. You owe not only the life you took, but all the lives of Ginna's children that now shall never be."

Axeman broke into a sob. "I will kill myself then. I've been thinking of it."

"No!" Celeste rebuked in a sharp command. "You owe the Creator life, not more death. Not even your own. Do you understand the difference?"

He stared confused. "I... I'm to father children?"

"Do not claim credit for woman's labor, Brother. Your path shall not be so easy. As you slew the innocent, so now you must save the guilty. Many redeemable young witches die with none to speak for them; so too, many old widows telling pixie tales accused of cultism. You are now their champion. Defend them at tribunal, and work to save the souls of the fallen – by which I mean those hellspace bound hypocrites who've placed their own judgment above the Creator's and kill in violation of the sixth decree. The Creator needs no aid. Only mortals do. So, give it. In redeeming them, so shall you be as well."

Xanthe was in awe. They were her own words repeated. Yet Celeste had delivered them so perfectly, weaving in her own ad-libs, that it was hard not to believe that she was a divine instrument, even though Xanthe knew she didn't believe a word of the Holy Manual.

It did have its intended impact on the acolyte. If he could have melted into the floor, he would have.

At length, Celeste rose from her knees. As she turned to leave, Brother Axeman cried out in despair. "Wait! What shall I do about the Wormwoods? I took their coin. I thought I was about to do justice."

Xanthe held her breath. They hadn't planned on this question. But Celeste was unconcerned, or perhaps just a masterful enough actress that it appeared so.

"If you can find Ginna's brother, do so. His name is Royroy. But do not kill him. For the wages of sin need not be earned. Instead, teach him how to hide better. And never, for his sake, confess that you strangled his sister, or the reveal the burden you bear. That shall forever be our secret. Ours and the Creator's. Do you understand?"

He nodded, letting out a small sob.

Celeste turned. "I leave now. Pray until you are at peace."

"That shall be never," he uttered morosely.

"Then pray as you walk and walk far," she commanded in parting. "Creator guide your steps." She left him alone in the dark with his thoughts.

Xanthe walked Celeste back to her room and just had to exult, "Wow, that was amazing!" For another life now was saved. Yet when Celeste only folded her arms, glared, and pronounced "Cir-cus" in two angry syllables, Xanthe knew that she herself remained unforgiven.

"I guess I'll help you run away," she sighed dolefully. "I just... I don't want to lose you as a friend."

Celeste let out a hissing sigh, finally saying, "Not quite yet." She shut the door behind her.

For the rest of the day nothing interesting happened. More deliveries. A make-up for a test she'd missed while running one. Nothing from her father about any 'special' subjects to study. The leaf of her life was once again in an eddy of the stream of fate. Just before bed, she had to heal a kestrel.

Yet in her dreams, in a great floating marble palace of the Creator, Ginna, a transparent white, came and bowed to her in deep respect. "Thank you, your brilliance. For all you have done, and all that you shall. Truly, you are your mother's daughter."

It all was a dream. Still, the world grew bright in Xanthe's smile.

*Fin*

## Glossary

Acolyte
: An apprentice Deacon. They are under special strictures, including not pursuing relationships, and are often sent far afield to find their calling.

Adventurer
: A treasure hunter who find working *Artifacts,* but most wilds *Bandits* call themselves adventurers too. Due to this, few believe there is much of a difference.

Aeterna
: Haven's largest continent is roughly the size and shape of Eurasia. The *Holy Lands* represent about a quarter of the landmass, *outland* nations (including Thule) another quarter, and the rest of Haven is deep wilds.

Amazon
: 1) An independent woman never married by choice. 2) A rare female *adventurer.* 3) A lesbian. These definitions often smear together in the minds of most northerners.

Ancients
: The people of myth. Wielders of holy technology, near perfect and blessed by the *Creator,* they were seduced by evil *demons*, especially the *Five and Eight*, and turned *Earth* into a virtual *Hellspace*. Rescued by the *Holy Pilot* and brought to *Haven,* they once again were seduced by evil and stripped of *Power*. Once redeemed, the people of *Haven* shall all become as the Ancients were. So it is written in the *Manual of the Creator.*

Ancient's Metal
: Far more mysterious than Glasssteel, Ancient's Metal is hard past any normal tool to harm it, and mysteriously self-repairs, leaving traces of green dust as it does. Due to this, it is venerated and usually left alone.

Ancients' War
: An ancient holocaust that many scholars think brought about the *Great Fall*. This belief is controversial. *Curate* doctrine states that the *Great Fall* was a punishment imposed by the *Creator*, and contradictions to those teachings aren't well received.

Angel Pilot
: See *Holy Pilot*. Some use "Angel" instead of "Holy" when referring to the Pilot's moral examples.

Arch-cardinal
: The highest officials in the Curate, responsible for entire nations. They almost exclusively reside in *Prayerhome.*

Archdeacon
: A significant church leader to whom a Deacons report, usually in charge of an entire city. Somewhat equivalent in stature to a Catholic bishop. Reports to a Cardinal.

| | |
|---|---|
| Artifact | A mechanism of the ancients that once did magical things, when it had *power* and/or was not irreparably broken. Most sit on shelves layered in dust |
| Atlatl | Also called whip bows, atlatls on Haven only have passing resemblance to the primitive Earth weapons after which they're named. The arrow-like darts are held by a tiny hook near their point and are snapped toward the intended target with a single overhead motion at the base of a fly-fishing-pole like rod. The largest two-handed versions can hurl darts 250 yards. |
| Balegaunt | For unknown reasons, adult corpses that remain both warm and relatively intact, can reanimate. Roaming balegaunts are fast, uncoordinated, and have a thirst for blood. Yet their most horrific aspect is their familiarity. Being attacked by a dead family member is a terror no one wants to face. They plague the south, but are rare in the northern *wilds*, due to cold and hungry scavenging *monsters*. Unfed balegaunts die. Fed ones become blackwights. Killing them is a job of *proctors*. |
| Bandager | The oldest *Sect* of the *Curate*, Bandagers follow the Book of Life Support. Rare due to their vows of poverty, they are not organized, and have no direct political power, but enjoy much moral authority both within the Curate and secular society. Unlike other *Sects*, they have no *proctors*, never enforce doctrine, and enjoy good relations with everyone, especially *Scholars*. This bond is so close, Bandagers are trained by the Scholars for years without charge. |
| Bandit | Gangs of young *wildsmen* who roam about seeking their fortune. They take anything not nailed down, and sometimes even when it is. They're both disliked and tolerated, as in the rough and tumble *outlands,* banditry is considered a phase of boyish youthful indiscretion, equivalent to girls throwing *witch* sparks. Technically punishable by death, *propriety* keeps most who are caught from that fate. While murdering innocents isn't forgiven, theft and drunken brawls are rarely punished. Nor is bride-kidnapping, the crime for which they're most renowned. Bandits typically settle into less dangerous careers as they age, though some become *Mercenaries* instead. |

| | |
|---|---|
| Beautiful Dark | Evolutionary pressure from lack of UV light (due to Haven's orange sun and much thicker ozone layer), has bleached most of humanity, making this skin tone one of the rarest. Due to that, and its association with sophisticated *Nubians*, it is considered a mark of extreme beauty. |
| Bell | A unit of time, encompassing approximately 72 minutes, with a heavy emphasis on the approximate part. Bells are usually counted in cities by people who ring out when the bell-glass needs turning over. |
| Black blood | Though not spelled out in the *Manual of the Creator*, some *deacons* believe that the black part of blood is a symbol left by the divine to symbolize humanity's mortality. Despite its name, black blood also shows up in breast milk as well. |
| Blackdust | Half-poison, half-disease, blackdust is found in ancient ruins. Contact with it causes delusions and death. The most common delusion is seeing living people as old dead friends and family that one has to greet, and this maniac amiability spreads the poison. Called demon-dust in the east, it is feared, but is reputedly one of the only weapons useful against *Blackwights*. |
| Blackwight | Rarely, a *Balegaunt* feasts on so much blood, it turns into one of these, a black humanoid creature that is stronger, faster, and immune to most physical damage. Aside from its color, it ends up looking exactly like the person it had killed. It also slowly regains its memories, though it must still drink blood to live. The two things known to be deadly them are *Blackdust* and fire. |
| Body Merchant | A slave trader specializing in acquiring virgins to sell as slavewives, an unseemly and, in some regions, outlawed practice. Though feared for kidnappings, most of their stock comes from poor fathers with spare daughters. These they fatten with food and *childboon* so as to increase their value. For the most destitute girls, this is often the best nourishment they've ever had. |
| Breast Sling | A long thin cloth used to bind breasts. Their fit is dependent only on the tier's skill. |
| Chain Monkey | A mechanical engineer specializing in *Torque*. |

| | |
|---|---|
| Chain Tower | These look something like classic clock towers, except with clutches instead of clocks, and cables and chains coming out of them to distribute *Torque*, from some motion source like a water wheel or water screw. Chain towers are most commonly found in *Mechanix* cities. |
| Charon | The second of *Haven's* moons. Absolutely black and barely visible. |
| Chestlet | Lady's jewelry worn along the back, under the arms, and over the breasts, always dangling something between them. It is kept intimate and hidden, as much like lingerie, it is meant to be worn during lovemaking. |
| Childbane | Small heart-shaped seeds of the extinct silphium plant species that the *Ancients* resurrected, these act as a form of birth control. They're considered sinful by the *Curate*, but are traded heavily on the black market. They are rare and expensive, aren't abortifacient (i.e. they don't end an already established pregnancy) but do prevent cramps. |
| Childboon | Small square-shaped black seeds which provide many vital nutrients to help sustain a healthy pregnancy. Childboon is not entirely benign because its natural estrogen makes breasts grow and lactate, and is sometimes given to teen girls to give them a more sexualized body. |
| Chimera | Human animal cross-breeds, the most common being Canisites ("dog peoples"), Felinites ("cat peoples"), and Avarians ("winged peoples"). The Curate's believes their creation helped prompt the *Fall,* making them an unpleasant reminder of *Humanity's* sin. Many take it further, blaming chimera for their own victimization; so most live like gypsies, wandering and despised. |
| Christian | The last known ancient religion of *Earth,* worshipers are reputed to engage in ceremonies where human flesh and blood is infused with the power of their deity and consumed. The Curate naturally is opposed to any and all institutions from the corrupted cradle of man, and hunts down all adherents mercilessly, regardless that they do not fight except in self-defense. |
| Cotburrow | A home in the wilds, doubling as a defensively fortified position. These are often built out of ruins of the ancients spread throughout the wilds. Many are hidden, and most are surrounded by traps. Some |

cotburrows are so large, several families can live in them.

Cradle Lily    A small white garden flower traditionally used in creches and to throw at newlyweds as stand-ins for babies.

Creator    The Curate's name for the ultimate deity, who using the *Holy Pilot* as an instrument, saved humanity despite their sin. The Creator is never referenced using any appellation or pronoun. No "Lord" or "He" or "Him".

Creator's Eye    A strange astrological phenomenon visible in the night sky that looks like a small slash across the heavens, and a second lengthy line perfectly perpendicular to the first. Telescopes pointed at it show that stars twist and writhe when near it.

Christian    The last ancient religion of *Earth* remaining on Haven, the others having been wiped out by the Curate. They're composed of small independent groups of adherents spread across the entire continent. Although doctrine varies vastly by congregation, their common oppression binds them together, making the faith quite similar to its earliest days on Earth. Many Christians convert as a reaction against iniquity done in the name of the Curate.

Common    Common Simple Standard. The trade language of Haven, and universal second language. It is related to the Ancient Tongue found in hardcopy, though pronunciation has drifted. In a few regions, common is the native tongue, including Jagerfeld. Thulian 'farmer' common, is a patois of Common, mixed with Lukomoryen and Norse.

Convocation of Miracles    A *Mechanix* council which awards stipends to people who restore functionality to ancient artifacts, or who perform other technical feats.

Cultist    A worshiper of demons, who supposedly gains powers from them, although never so much as to ever be able to defend themselves against *proctors*. Mostly defenseless old widows, proctors are far more enthusiastic about going after them than Christians and Yamaites, who can (and do) strike back. Still, rumors persist that there are cultists who are real and deadly, but undetected.

| | |
|---|---|
| Curate | The Faith of the *Angel Pilot*, *Haven's* ubiquitous monotheistic religion that worships the *Creator*. It holds a role nearly identical to the medieval Catholic church. An enormous and sprawling entity, it is divided into sects, and its various members' acts range from completely principled to utterly corrupt. A *Bandager* may save your life one day, only for you to be subject to execution by a Dominionist *Tribunal* the next. |
| Days | Though its years are shorter, Haven's days are longer than Earths. Weeks are still seven days, named: Restday, Glumday, Workday, Humpday, Nighday, Freeday, and Churchday |
| Deacon | The most common *Curate* clergy, ranking only above Acolytes. Deacons usually report to Archdeacons, but in many small communities, are the sole authority. |
| Death-hound | A common type of monster in the wilds, resembling wolves with enormous jaws and serrated incisors. Their jaws are muscular, and one can snap a man's forearm in two. Yet they also can be driven off, especially if one is able to hurt them at range. |
| Demibird | All flying species native to Haven. Due to similar evolutionary constraints on aerodynamics, most bear an uncanny resemblance to four winged micro-raptors that lived on Earth 130 million years ago, with the exception that instead of feathers, they have long branching cross-thatched fur that almost perfectly resemble them. |
| Demons | Spirits of evil who possess *artifacts*, oppose the *Creator*, and were the ones who seduced the *ancients* into sin. For *power* to return, holy technology needs to be exorcised of them. This is the doctrine of the *Curate*. Some *scholars* and others take a different view, but these things are rarely spoken of, especially in public. |
| Divulgence | Curate Divulgences act nearly identically to Catholic confessions, except that the topic can be anything, not just sin. The Curate keeps divulgences given in church a secret, but *deacons* sometimes act on what they learn. |
| Dodgy Power | A mild curse phrase, equivalent to "god damned', as the Creator took holy power away. |
| Doormat and Dozen | Phrase for a wife kept servile and busy with children. Akin to "Barefoot and pregnant". Urbane *Mechanix* |

PARTY OF ASSASSINS   437

tend to look down on this as backward. Praetorians
think anything else is sinful.

Dreadwitch
A *witch* who uses her *touch* for evil. Because the *Curate* considers heresy to be "evil", this term is also used for any *Greatwitch* who actively develops and unapologetically uses her powers. Some Dreadwitches become famous before their inevitable demise. As with Christians, clemency is rarely extended to them.

Dzgranti-Root Oil
Juices of the Dzgranti plant, which after concentration, causes LSD-like "trips". It is also highly addictive and illegal in most nations and city states. Dzgranti are destroyed in the south but grows naturally in the wilds. Northerners rarely use it, because keeping your wits about you in the *Outlands* is extremely important.

Earth
The cradle of man. Once a paradise, but later, according to the Curate, corrupted into such evil, that the *Ancients* had to flee to *Haven* by the grace of the *Holy Pilot*. Anything 'of Earth' is by definition evil.

Felinite
A cat-man *chimera*. They look exactly as you imagine. Female Felinites are quite beautiful.

Festival of Favors
A spring Festival unique to Jagerfeld, acting like a cross between Valentine's Day and prom night. It is based on a *Storytelling* in which a beautiful but headstrong daughter of an early royal mayor fled north, rather than be wed to an effete and conniving *Prince*. In a fight with a *Monster* inhabiting the city, she lost her symbol of the *Creator's* favor, without which she could not rule. Soon she was captured by Lord Jager, a masterful and daring *Bandit* chief, who, upon seeing her beauty, instantly reformed. He slew the monster, returned her favor, yet could not help but steal her heart in turn. Knowing that she'd met her true Creator appointed *Keeper*, she gave herself for him to rule. He took her as his *Old-Pledge* bride, *Seeded* her with no less than seven sons, and founded the city. The tale may have grown slightly with the telling (such as Lord Jager killing, by himself, a *Kairn-dragon* with nothing but a spear and his mighty thews) but locals believe every word.

Firesnake
A two-winged and feathered serpent whose plumage are gorgeous colors of mottled red. The animal is not a demibird and may not be a native *Haven* species. It is a relatively rare animal that lives in the wild and its

feathers are rare and pricey. They are said to be exceedingly cunning.

Five and Eight
: The great *Demon* lords of *Earth*, who were responsible for corrupting the *Ancients* from their original divine favor. They are too terrible to be named, lest the naming summon them. Any who worships one as a *Cultist* is put to death by a *Tribunal*.

Flamedraft
: A moderately narcotic orange colored brew distilled from fermented *fungal* sap. It is also extremely slippery and flammable and used for fire-spitting displays.

Free Cities
: The Free Cities of the North are *Outland* settlements in the region of Thule, situated on the edge of the vast trackless northern *Wilds*. They consist of Jagerfeld, Aerie, Northfjord, Warmwell, Antenna, Vaasa, and Großhamar (pronounced grosz-hammer). Sometimes called the *Witchwilds* due to the prevalence of *Wildswives* in them.

Finalizer
: The King of *Nutearea*'s most elite bodyguards, charged with defense of the royal family. The phrase "defense" is interpreted quite liberally and includes proactive elimination of potential threats. As in times of succession, the main threat to the royal family is itself, Finalizers are well versed in assassinating *Princes* as well as protecting them. Each Finalizer takes on a single charge, whose interests they protect above all others.

Fungi
: Not mushrooms, but the native plants of Haven, many which look like overgrown asparagus spears, and/or have tall succulent fronds. Their color tends to be deep purple, as they use a chemical analog of retinal for photosynthesis.

Glasssteel
: A transparent laminate of sapphire glass made by the *Ancients*. Exceedingly durable, but unlike plastic, nearly impossible to work, so can only be incorporated as is.

Great Fall
: As written in the *Manual of the Creator,* the *Ancients* who fled *Earth* in the Great Leap enjoyed many blessings. Yet some still loved the evils that the *Angel Pilot* had delivered them from, and on *Haven* consorted with *Demons* to twist life into abominations. This sin caused the Great Fall, when the *Creator* banished both *Power* and *Demons*. Some brave

scholars note that *Curate* doctrine doesn't even quite agree with itself.

Greatwitch — A *Witch* with extraordinary powers, far beyond spark throwing. Used mostly in the north as a less pejorative term for *Dreadwitch*; few *Sects* distinguish.

Grims — Perhaps the most feared of all *Nightmares,* Grims are horrific shape shifting monstrosities that appear out of nowhere, slaughter indiscriminately, and leave their corpses to rot or turn into *Balegaunts*. Their most fearsome attribute is the supernatural terror they instill in their intended victims; it causes near paralysis.

Hardcopy — Paper printouts of the *Ancients*, as opposed to anything more contemporary. Sometimes, Hardcopy also refers to identical copies of original texts.

Haunches — An ideal of upper crust feminine beauty, especially in the more traditional north, involving thick thighs and birthing hips. Being moderately overweight is considered a sign of having "made it" socially.

Haven — The name of the world. It circles a cooler, orange, K3V "sun" at approximately the orbital distance of Venus. A *Ringed* planet with two moons, Xanthe and Charon, it has a higher concentration of oxygen in its atmosphere, driving evolutionary gigantism among its fauna (*Monsters*), and is in the volcanic separation stage of its super-continent cycle.

Hellspace — The void of absolute loneliness where one goes after death, having disdained the *Creator*. It is also either literally, or figuratively, crossed in the Great Leap. Also used as a curse word.

Highcouncil — 1) Jagerfeld's ruling district, expensive and always guarded. 2) A family who owns property in Highcouncil, meaning they are "old-money" aristocracy because none can buy their way in, unless someone else sells out.

Hi-Lo — A family of related card games in which you are supposed to maximize the number of cards that match rock cards, dealt out of the deck. The unique feature of the game is that you keep discarded cards, and therefore losing early hands can allow you to win later ones.

Holy Lands — Classically the mid-south of *Aeterna*, roughly akin to Europe. Named such since the *Creator* supposedly has forgiven its residents and has abated the curse of *Nightmares*. Still, many *Outlanders* are not impressed with the behavior of those within. In Thule, the Holy Lands are also referred to generally as the South.

Holy Pilot

The savior figure of the Curate, this seraph was sent by the *Creator* to guide *Void Vessels* of the *Ancients* fleeing the evils of *Earth*, through the Great Leap of Hellspace, to *Haven,* and then turned back the Nightmares that followed. After the Holy Pilot, some of the people were once again seduced by the *Five and Eight* and started the *Ancient's War* that began the *Great Fall*. As written in the *Manual of the Creator*.

Honeywort

A flowering green-plant, it has pink perfumed flowers.

Honor Dowry

A payment that men make to women they've *Seeded*, but don't wish to marry. While the sum can be substantial, as it is supposed to be entire payment for the raising of a child, it is quite ignominious to receive in upper classes. *Wildsmen* have nearly the reverse attitude, preferring women who have proved their fertility.

Hood Guild

Named after the long-hoods they wear, the Hood Guild is an anonymous parcel post service. They wrap every package the same, dress the same, and offer quick confidential delivery. Their teenaged runners are small, incurious about what they deliver, and completely unarmed. The guild teaches 'stretching' and 'shortcutting', skills roughly akin to yoga and parkour.

Hospitarium

A shrine for the *Bandager Sect*, usually set inside the churches of other *Sects*. They double as infirmaries. Only in the largest cities, do full-fledged *Bandager* worship halls exist, acting as teaching hospitals and providing apothecarial services.

Humans

Similar to *Ancients,* but with some differences. All have *Black Blood,* most women have the *Touch,* and colorful hair is sometimes passed down through the female line. Due to genetic selection in the womb, humans have more regular features, meaning they're more beautiful. Their "ugly" is our "slightly better than average".

Jagerfeld

One of the free cities of *Thule,* Jagerfeld is a fortified town with 30,000 permanent residents sitting on the demarcation between the *Outlands* and the true *Wilds*. Although there are smaller hamlets to its north and east, it is the last point of the ancient's road, and thus ideally situated for trade of tools and weapons for wild's bounty of fir, meats, and artifacts. The town was founded by Mechanix, and its buildings are plentifully outfitted with *Torque* clockwork, distributing motive power.

| | |
|---|---|
| Juche | Spread across the high Dyanees mountain ranges, this is not so much a country with an army, as an army with a country. The Juche Black Legion has a reputation for unsentimental militarism, laconic humor, and liberal threats of torture to ensure compliance. It famously does not allow proctors within its borders, and *Curate* clergy who displease the high command have a habit of disappearing. It enjoys a constant cold-war with Newmerica that has never come close to threatening its high mountain redoubts. There are persistent rumors that the nation was named after a demon. |
| Kald | A funeral song for fallen warriors in *Talathian* culture. |
| Kairn-dragon | The largest and most dangerous *monster* in the *wilds,* these beasts eat *kranth* like skrags. They're building-sized, exceptionally cunning, and have a taste for human flesh. Their danger is only surpassed by their magnificence, and images of them are often found on royal coats of arms. |
| Keeper | A *slave's* owner. Also used in religious context, e.g. "The Creator is my keeper." Unlike a master, a *proper* keeper cares for their slaves better than any other possession he owns. |
| Kestrel | Not hawks, these are the most common order *demibirds.* Feeds on rodents and roaches. |
| Knights in Shining Armor | Defenders of the Christian faith who assassinate proctors and Curate clergy engaged in attacks against the Christian faithful. Much like the Sect of Penance, their activities are disapproved of by most of their own faith, but without them, Christianity would be wiped out. They are aware of the irony of defending an almost entirely pacifistic religion through assassination. |
| Kranth | A native Haven herbivore, this creature resembles a giant furry iguana, and comes in sizes from "twice the size of the largest horse" to "I think the barn's more likely to fit inside it than the reverse". The smallest breed of this species has been domesticated for farm work and pulling carriages. |

| | |
|---|---|
| Landing Day | The fabled day that the *Holy Pilot* landed the *Void Vessels* on *Haven*, it is the holiest day on the *Curate* calendar. It is set in late-fall, serving double purpose as a harvest Festival. Presents, family, and feasting all combine with religious ceremonies. |
| Lilth | A perfume made from the tiny sex-glands glands of a rare type of *roach*. It is quite expensive. |
| Lodestone | Magnetized male and female gametes of the lodestone *fungi*, whose male and female seeds snap together, completing fertilization. This reproduction is used in lieu of flowering, which hasn't developed in most *fungi*. Lodestone "seeds" are the basis of *torque* and used for frictionless axles on carriages. |
| Lolita-dress | Made in the fashion of *Hardcopy* drawings of young girls with abnormally large eyes, these ruffled baby doll dresses feature lace, bows, collars, and buttons. They rarely reach the knee and are extremely expensive. |
| Manual of the Creator | The great religious tome of the Curate. Divided into the books of Navigation, Life Support, Engine, Security, Personnel, Command, and Power, along with other chapters on the exodus. Many *sects* claim one of the books as their inspiration, most notably the Mechanix Sect focus on the Book of Engine, while Praetorians claim Personnel. |
| Marshal | A proctor commander. Secures an entire city. Reports to a High Marshal. |
| Mechanix | The informal name for the *Sect* of Engineering, one of the most ancient *Sects* of the Curate, named after one of the books in the *Manual of the Creator*. Patron of craftsmen and mechanical engineers, Mechanix also pray to the *Creator* to exorcise demons out of artifacts, thereby removing the *Creator's* curse upon them so power can naturally return. They have a complex relationship with the Scholar's Guild. |
| Mercenary | Hired guards, employed not so much to prosecute wars, but to keep the peace in cities and protect against wilds dangers, mostly monsters and bandits. The line between mercenary and a bandit is sometimes muddy, given that not all employers are themselves benign. |
| Monster | One of the many exceedingly dangerous mega-fauna of Haven, many of which seem almost specifically designed to kill humans. Though *Nightmares* capture |

the public's imagination, it is monsters, due to their ubiquity, that cause the most casualties.

Newmerica — A southern *Holy Lands* nation, and one of the central of the Nutearean empire. "The best of all possible nations" is a phrase they actually believe and others make fun of. It contains Prayerhome.

Nightmare — Supernatural creatures that appear out of nowhere to kill. Little are known about them, but they are said to have followed the *Void Vessels* from *Earth* and were mostly killed by the *Holy Pilot*.

Nightmare Line — An indistinct demarcation between the nightmare lands and the *Holy Lands*. The nightmare lands are further delineated into the *Outlands* and *Wilds*, the former of which have few *Monsters*.

North — The North generally consists of the Thule *Outlands* and the great western wilds, which extends across *Aeterna* something like a vast *Haven* equivalent to Siberia.

Nubian — People of the distant Nubia archipelagos edging the Shimmering Sea, these *humans* still possess a tiny bit of the *Beautiful Dark*. Combined with their education and preservation of *Ancient* knowledge, they enjoy a sterling reputation. The saying goes, "Newmericans think they're better than us; Nubians actually are."

Nutearea — A contraction of 'Nuterranean', the empire claims all known Haven, including the regions Albion, Dixie, Arcadia, Yamato, Nubia, Gaul, Tlaltícpac, Shambhala, Atlantis, Beyul, Lukomorye, Agartha, and Thule. In reality, it controls only Albion, Dixie, and Arcadia directly. More distant regions pay less heed with distance and has no sway over *Outland* regions such as *Thule* at all. It remains the most powerful of nations, and for all its dysfunction, is rarely challenged.

Mayor — A title of nobility indicating dictatorial sovereignty of a city. Equivalent to a Baron, Count, or Duke, depending on the size of the city.

Mouseweevil — A rodent. No one knows if it is native or created by the ancients. Food for kestrels.

Old-Pledge — An archaic form of marriage. Old-Pledge wives can't handle money, work, or craft for any but their own family, speak to men not of their family. Unpopular in the *Holy Lands* due to the strictures on shopping and work, *Prayerhome* declared such vows optional. Yet in the *Wilds*, it remains the only *proper* form of marriage. There, *Wildwives* believe that it's not true love if you marry any other way.

Outlands
Regions just beyond the *Nightmare Line*, but unlike the *Wilds*, not particularly troubled by *Monsters*. Still, full nations cease to exist in Outlands, replaced by smaller city-states like the *Free Cities*. The Nutearean Empire also has little permanent influence, as large-scale army logistics falls apart under threat of *Nightmares*.

Permacrete
A rock building material of the *Ancients* renowned for its hardness and durability.

Pincer
Key Pliers made by Mechanix with unique notches to open a pincer-lock. Their tumblers, set opposite to each other, are quite hard to pick.

Plastic
A mysterious material left behind by the *Ancients*, and extremely valuable. Though more can't be made, an entire profession has risen up around identifying its types and reuse. "Plasticers" melt certain of plastics, forming them into armor and clothes.

Power
More than physical force, a moral one according to the *Curate*. The *Creator* removed power as a punishment for once again adopting the evils of *Earth* on *Haven*. Power can be evil as well. *Demons* are said to have it.

Praetorian
A sect younger than the *Mechanix*, whose interpretation of the *Manual of the Creator* seems to run counter to its surface meaning, especially in regards to women. Their large families give them force of numbers in the *Outlands*, but elsewhere they're thought of nearly like vermin, similar to the way Catholics were viewed in the early 20th century. They claim inspiration from the book of Personnel, although this is still in great dispute.

Prayerhome
1) The seat of the Curate, and its enormous sprawling palace-like churches and religious offices in the metropolitan region of Twinforks. 2) The Curate archcardinals, and their associated bureaucracy, especially their official stances on doctrine.

Pretenders
Circus Carnies/Showies/Clowns/Mummers/Barkers. They're seen as both fun and also as charlatans and/or petty swindlers. They often wear masquerade-like Pretender Masks. Many Chimera are pretenders; it's one of the few jobs they can get.

| | |
|---|---|
| Prioress | A special nun in charge of a priory. The highest rank within the Curate a female can attain. However, they are largely cloistered, not allowed to hold services for the general public, or leave the grounds which they control. |
| Prince | Short for Prince of the Empire of Nutearea. Kings of Nutearea are typically quite profligate, and young princes learn from an early age that they must compete with their half-brothers to attain the throne. Princes are renowned for their charisma and ruthlessness. |
| Princekiller | A girl reputedly so beautiful, she gets *Princes* killed by distracting them. The apocryphal phrase is used even outside of Nutearea, to describe the perfection of female attractiveness. Many *Finalizers* superstitiously think the effect is real. |
| Propriety | Explicitly acknowledged local customs, which often hold more sway than either merchant law or cannon law, though unlike formal laws, they don't have specific enforcers, like guards or proctors. In the *wilds*, even Curate sanctioned killing is considered improper. |
| Proctor | A member of the police and military wing of a *Sect*, responsible for enforcing cannon laws as the Sect interprets them. Proctors report into the priestly hierarchy, but have their own roles, rules, and traditions. They are often cast in a heroic light to the public. The reality is far more mixed, and sometimes proctors of differing sects can come into conflict. They deliver the accused to Tribunals for punishment. |
| Razorthorn | A *fungal* weed with exceedingly sharp, almost invisible, needles, somewhat like a prickly-pear. |
| Ream | 1) A species of *fungi* whose seed pods bear an uncanny resemblance to a human phallus, except that its hard exterior is like a cross between a thistle and a pine cone. 2) The mostly imagined act of forcefully ramming one such pod up someone else's rear, not remotely for their enjoyment. 3) A vulgar swear word, equivalent to "fuck", except without any positive connotation at all. |
| Ream seed | Seeds of *ream* plants, extracted only through meticulous labor. Somewhat equivalent to pine-nuts. |
| Redfruit | Purple on the outside, deep red inside. Easily bruised. Also called 'bloodfruit' in the *Holy Lands*. |

| | |
|---|---|
| Researcher | A scholar who specializes in knowledge of ancient technology, the *Curate*, and *Mechanix* specifically, look to them to guide the focus of prayers to return power. |
| Rings | *Haven* possesses rings in many bands. Their composition is a mystery to *Scholar's* guild astronomers. They're also outside Haven's Roche limit. |
| Ringlight | The light given off by *Haven's* rings. Brighter than its natural moons *Xanthe* and *Charon*. The *Rings* absorb near all orange and red spectra, giving them a dim light blue cast. At night, the edges of the rings glow red with both sunset and dawn light. |
| Roach | Haven's equivalent to insects. They can get quite large, up to a foot in length. They come in hundreds of different shapes, only a few of which look like an Earth roach. They taste like shrimp. |
| Sandskin | The leather of *skrags*, this is a cheap tough ubiquitous material. Only the poor wear it as clothing, except on boots which everyone wears in the north, as sandskin doesn't slip on ice. |
| Scholars Guild | The light of learning in the dark of *Haven's* ignorance, this loose association of academics has complex relations with the *Curate*. *Mechanix* depend on them to understand holy technology. Yet scholars are also viewed with suspicion. Guild schools are routinely patrolled by *proctors* to ensure that no serious contradiction to *Curate* doctrine slips through. |
| Scratch Fight | Any sort of fight between girls. Though it can refer to physical fighting, it's nearly always merely cruel insults, where lifetime wounds to self-esteem are inflicted. |
| Season | A Haven season is about two earth months. |
| Season Born<br><br>(Spring Born)<br>(Summer Born)<br>(Fall Born)<br>(Winter Born) | On Haven, people believe babies adopt the nature of the season in which they were born: Winter Born are supposedly cold and unforgiving, Summer Born warm and kind. It is no accident that the *Festival of Favors* is set exactly so that conceptions during it will be due the following summer. |
| Sect | 1) A branch of the *Curate* (e.g. the *Mechanix*), 2) Any group of organized *Curate* devotees, even if their views are considered schismatic by *Prayerhome* (e.g. *Sect of Penance*). |

| | |
|---|---|
| Sect of Penance | A far-flung group of Curate zealots who believe that humanity can only do proper penance for its sins by killing *Witches*. They are adamantly opposed to less harsh punishments, especially those that let *Witches* bear children, as they think this continues the blood sin. They are officially schismatic, and are sometimes even executed for their assassinations, especially if the *Witch* they kill is a noble's daughter. |
| Seeded | Impregnated, with a strong "having been seduced and taken advantage of" connotation. Knocked up. |
| Sillyroot | A fungal root. Chewing of which gives a moderate high, and nausea. Chewers of sillyroot are called "pukers"; abuse of this drug is only common among the poor. |
| Skrag | A small native armadillo-like creature nearly as numerous as the *Roaches* it eats. They're docile and are sometimes kept as pets, but are also used for their hide, which forms a rough leathery *Sandskin*. Skrags are surprisingly loud when annoyed or in pain. |
| Slats | Thigh-shapers that lift and support a woman's *Haunches*. They're usually uncomfortable, pinch, and are hard to move in, the latter considered a positive attribute, because too much exercise prevents pleasing plumpness expected in upper class women. |
| Slavery | Debt bondage is both widespread and controversial in the *Holy Lands*, and even if not full chattel slavery, is usually abusive. It's rare in the *Wilds*, as involuntarily slavery goes against local *Propriety* and laws. The few slaves in the north are usually voluntary, keeping their word to sell years of service to retire some debt, nearly always with a fixed end date. |
| Slavewife | An enslaved concubine. Being one can be terrible or not, depending on the whims of her *Keeper*. *Mechanix* have strict doctrines about slavewifery, the most crucial being that a keeper cannot part a slavewife from her children and must raise all her children as his own. In the *Wilds*, slavewives are nearly indistinguishable from *Old-Pledge* wives, and in hamlets with too few men, voluntarily becoming one is common practice. In the south they often end up as *Body Sellers*. Slavewives are branded on the buttocks to indicate their status. |
| Slide | 1) A vulgar name for vagina (e.g. "pussy"). 2) A name for women by vulgar men. |

| | |
|---|---|
| Snowcream | Not quite ice-cream, this is more like a frozen pudding |
| South, the | A synonym for the *Holy Lands* that is used in *Thule*. |
| Spongi | A species of *Fungi* which, something like a cactus, stores large amounts of water in its sap. In desert areas this can be filtered for drinking, but in the north, they are usually used for as means of wiping oneself off. |
| Steeltower | High-tech "skyscrapers" of the ancients. Most are in poor condition, having been stripped of materials. |
| Storytelling | Telling tall tales. A common pastime. |
| Straaks | A *Nightmare* that looks like a three-dimensional star-break crack in the windshield of reality. Their bodies are living jagged refractions, and their seeming lack of wit does nothing to decrease their danger. |
| Sweet-lataio | Fermented seeds of a *fungal* bush yield a flavor that tastes somewhat like a cross of lavender and rooibos, though sweeter. |
| Talathian | Even among *wildsmen,* Talathians are known as brutish barbarians. They value force, extreme bravery, and little else. As bandits, they're not friendly, and as mercenaries, they're merciless. They have a passing respect for the Curate's faith, but nothing for the weak and cowardly deacons who proclaim it. |
| Talathis | The language of Talathians. |
| Tigran | Tigers as large as horses, possessing both intelligence and speech. They are not *chimera*, but their own species. There are rumors of Tigran riders, but nothing established. Tigrans have a predatory, cat-like, morality. |
| Toothscraper | A primitive dentist and barber. The best are *Bandagers* with actual medical training. |
| Torque | 1) Clockwork systems used to distribute movement, chains, gears, cable systems, pulleys. Torque is used instead of electricity (viewed with suspicion due to its similarity to witch power), and steam, which is absolutely forbidden by the *Manual of the Creator*: "Burn nothing for power lest the whole world bake". 2) A unit of mechanical force, roughly ½ a horsepower. |
| Touchdown | Capital of the Nutearean empire, this sprawling metropolis is by far the largest on Haven, extending |

deep into both the nations of Dinium and Camelot within the region of Albion.

| | |
|---|---|
| Touch | Short for "the touch of *Earth*" from the *Manual of the Creator*, this is an unnatural ability, by far the most common being throwing sparks. According to Curate doctrine, only girls with impure and licentious natures have such abilities and are *witches* or *dreadwitches*. |
| Tribunal | The court systems that enforce *Curate* cannon law, this is where Proctors being people to be tried. There being no particular concept of Stare Decisis in the Curate, punishments for identical transgressions vary widely by region and sect. Prayerhome has a legal principle of "by their own faith, measured", meaning that the accused should be judged by the standards of their sect. Bandagers are never tried for healing, not even demonists, for they heal all. Still, a Tribunal is a place of fear, subjective judgment, and arbitrary executions. |
| Vask | The most common and least dangerous of Nightmares, these appear like low moving splotches of black, taking on the form of whatever living thing is nearest them. As with many nightmares, little that is physical affects them, but they can be hurt by focused light and/or fire. |
| Vridin | One of the most easily killed of the *Monsters*, this roughly resembles a huge twin horned rhinoceros. Its skin can be made into vellum. |
| Void Vessels | Craft said to have delivered the *Ancients* from *Earth*. Some readings of the *Manual of the Creator* believe these to be spiritual, rather than physical, in nature. |
| Widow's Kiss | A poison that is favored by assassins because it somehow prevents corpses from rising as Balegaunts. |
| Wilds | Most of greater *Aterna* still remains unexplored, with both *Nightmares* and *Monsters* roaming free. In terms of danger, the wilds are to the *Outlands* what the *Outlands* are to the *Holy Lands*. Further yet are the Deep Wilds – trackless wilderness where *Monsters* are enormous and there is no aid whatsoever. Man is not the apex predator, and only the bravest, foolish, and most desperate live there, usually in hiding. |
| Wildsmen | Barbarians of the wilds. Strong, brave, protective, yet conservative and uneducated; almost never literate. Their machismo is legendary. When asked why they |

live in the *Wilds*, the classic laconic answer is "Where else can I live where everything is trying to kill me?"

Wildswives
Capable, tough, she-dragons in defense of their *Cotburrows*. Despite having large families and *Old-Pledge* marriages, in the survival-driven pragmatism of the *Wilds*, they often enjoy surprisingly egalitarian relationships. Also called witch-wives because they'll unabashedly use any touch power they have in defense of their babies, despite their religious piety.

Wipeleaves
A purple *Fungi*, with atypically broad leaves. These are used as a form of toilet or outhouse paper.

Wishing
Praying to the *Creator* for a fortunate outcome for oneself, or against another for a bad one. A mild sin by Curate doctrine, there is a strong superstition in the *Wilds* that wishing brings *Nightmares* or bad lack to balance out.

Witch
A woman with the *Touch*. Considered sinful everywhere, the punishment for witchcraft varies widely by region: death by burning, forcing into slavewifery, a mild penance, to none whatsoever. *Thule* is especially lax, as in the north, it's believed that witch girls are particularly avid in bed, making the showing off of mild *Touch* powers a form of naughty flirtatiousness. Yet even there, tolerance for witchery wanes with age. Once married, it is believed that piety and fidelity remove such abilities.

Witchkiller
See *Sect of Penance*.

Xanthe
Although appearing small due to distance, it is actually the larger of Haven's two moons. Early in its formation it had several sulfur volcanoes. This, combined with reflected sunlight, give it its characteristic yellow color. It is also an uncommon girl's name.

Yard
The unit of measurement is actually just a renamed meter, as the latter sounds vaguely of *Earth* to the *Curate* (even though both terms originate from Earth). A thousand yards, therefore, is a kilometer.

Yamaite
Either a demon cult that act like gangsters, or gangsters pretending to be demon cultists. While demonic favor is doubted, Yamaites use dreadwitches to great effect.

www.ingramcontent.com/pod-product-compliance
Lightning Source LLC
Chambersburg PA
CBHW050021030726
47506CB00001B/48